THE BOOK OF BEBB

BOOKS BY FREDERICK BUECHNER

FICTION

The Wizard's Tide
Brendan
Godric
The Book of Bebb
Treasure Hunt
Love Feast
Open Heart
Lion Country
The Entrance to Porlock
The Final Beast
The Return of Ansel Gibbs
The Seasons' Difference
A Long Day's Dying

NONFICTION

Whistling in the Dark
A Room Called Remember
Now and Then
The Sacred Journey
Peculiar Treasures
Telling the Truth
The Faces of Jesus
Wishful Thinking
The Alphabet of Grace
The Hungering Dark
The Magnificent Defeat

R

FREDERICK BUECHNER

THE BOOK OF BEBB

LION COUNTRY

OPEN HEART

LOVE FEAST

TREASURE HUNT

With an Introduction by the Author

HarperSanFrancisco

A Division of HarperCollinsPublishers

Designed by Harry Ford

FIRST HARPER & ROW PAPERBACK EDITION PUBLISHED IN 1990. REPRINTED BY ARRANGEMENT WITH ATHENEUM PUBLISHERS, AN IMPRINT OF MACMILLAN PUBLISHING COMPANY.

Library of Congress Cataloging-in-Publication Data

Buechner, Frederick
    The book of Bebb / Frederick Buechner.–1st Harper & Row paperback ed.
       p.   cm
    Reprint of works originally published 1971-1977.
    Contents: Lion country—Open heart—Love feast—Treasure hunt.
    ISBN 0-06-061165-0 (pbk.)
    I. Title.
    PS3552.U35B6 1990   90-80330
    813´.54—dc20   CIP

93   94   95   96   97   HCMG   10   9   8   7   6   5   4   3   2   1

This book is printed on acid-free paper that meets the standards of the American National Standards Institute Z39.48 Standard.

To the Leisure Time Arcade

INTRODUCTION

IT BEGAN in a barber shop. I picked up some dog-eared publication with snippets of hair in between the pages, and what it opened to was a news story about a man who was in trouble with the law for running some sort of religious diploma mill and had done time for something else even more baroque in the past. I don't remember any of it very clearly, but I remember some of the pictures—the man himself stuffed into a double-breasted suit, a flat-topped stucco building that he used as a church, an assistant with china teeth and a sick smile. It was all it took.

From wherever it is that dreams come from, a whole world rose up for me more or less on the spot. A seedy little jumping-off place in inland Florida and a Charles Addams manse. A smelly flight of subway stairs. Some mangey lions in an outdoor zoo. And the people rose up more or less on the spot too with faces and in some cases even names already attached. There was a bunch of eccentric Indians and a loose-limbed girl with a bootleg smile. There was an olive-skinned young drifter and introvert who looked a little like the young J.D. Salinger. There was a girl dying in a hospital with tinted windowpanes and a hypochondriac ex-husband with invisible eyebrows and eyelashes. And there was also, of course, Leo Bebb. I believe I had to think a little bit to find his name, but it came soon enough. And then his eye. I didn't have to think up having it flutter shut every once in a while. It did it all by itself while I happened to be watching. It was a wink, a kind of come-on, and it started me off on what was, literarily speaking, the great romance of my life.

"Rages unchecked across the screen!" was the way the previews touted some movie of my youth, and something not unlike that was what happened to me with *Lion Country*. I could hardly wait to get to it in the morning, and I hated to leave it when I had to go home in the afternoon. I skipped lunch, I turned down invitations, and the whole thing was finished in about six to eight weeks.

I haven't looked back to check, but when I started out, I don't think I had any very clear idea where I was going. I know I had some notion of making Bebb a villain, but almost from the beginning I could see that wasn't going to work. Antonio Parr was going to expose him for the charlatan we both thought he was, but then it became apparent that

Antonio Parr himself was the one who was going to get exposed. The loose-limbed girl turned out to be Bebb's adopted daughter, Sharon, but way before I discovered the full story of her origin, I had a strong suspicion that their true relationship was more complex. When Herman Redpath appeared for Bebb to ordain him as a way of restoring his potency, I had no idea who he was or how he was going to behave until, like Antonio, I heard him launch forth into his first non-stop, foul-mouthed soliloquy, just as in *Open Heart* I couldn't guess how he was possibly going to use the things his friends put in the pockets of his corpse—the ten dollar bills, the beads, the Sun Maid raisins—until I saw him actually using them later. It was only when I got to *Love Feast* that I understood about the whistle. And so on. I had heard about single characters running away with the show but never the whole cast—and not just running away with it but refusing to let it end.

When I wrote the last sentence of *Lion Country*, I thought I had finished with them all for good but soon found out that they were not finished with me. And so it was with the succeeding volumes, at the end of each of which I rang the curtain down only to find that, after a brief intermission, they'd rung it up again. What was the secret of Bebb's eye? Why had he done what he did in front of the children in Miami Beach? Was he really from outer space, and, if so, was it outer space as Babe understood it or as Gertrude Conover did? What was to become of Tony Blaine? Step by step Bebb kept me going down that opening flight of subway steps with him until finally he escaped me by turning into Jimmy Bob Luby. Or was that just part of Gertrude Conover's octagenarian dottiness? Has he escaped me? Have I escaped him? I am sure only that, as Gertrude Conover said, he was always good company and that I will always miss him.

So it ended up a tetralogy, and here it is between a single set of covers, one chunky Bebbsian volume at last. It has its faults, Heaven knows—its loose ends and ragged edges, its improbabilities and gaucheries, its barren stretches and lapses of taste. I have done what I could to fix things up. I have revised and edited, taken things out and put things in, polished things off and oiled things up. I could, of course, have rewritten the whole business from scratch, but then it would have become another book, and that was not what I wanted. I wanted it to be essentially the book that I first wrote because what that book seems to me to be, as I look back on it, is a kind of love-letter, and you don't tinker around too much with love-letters without losing more than you gain.

I suppose all such books can be called love-letters of a sort, at least letters addressed to that beloved stranger who right from the first page accepts your once-upon-a-time as his time by an act of faith and lets you lead him by the hand without raising either an awkward question or an eyebrow along the way. Understand me, you say to him. Know me. Know that it is for you that I created the world and set these little almost human beings in motion on it. To the degree that, if you're lucky, they start taking on a life of their own for you apart from the segment of their lives you've chosen to describe, it is a kind of love-letter to them too. Dear Bebb. Dear Brownie. Remember me as I remember you. Forgive me for summoning you up into something like life, for afflicting you with griefs and visiting you with joys, only to kill you off in the end. And maybe there is even more to it than that.

Beneath whatever it is that a love-letter is specifically about—the nouns and verbs of it, the ups and downs, the hopeless silences and hopeful eloquence—there is the love itself which the letter is only a rough translation of, which is there between the unlikeliest lines and glimmering deep within even the paragraph about the trip on the train and the wind-battling gull. And so it is, I think, with the book as love-letter. Apart from who the characters are and the places they go and the things they do, there is the sense of what the old hymn quaveringly addresses as "O love that will not let me go," the sense of an ultimate depth to things that is not finally indifferent as to whether people sink or swim but endlessly if always hiddenly refuses to abandon them. Brownie loses his faith and his teeth. Lucille teeters off to her death on French heels. Open Heart goes up in flames, and the Love Feasts are run out of Alexander Hall. And yet . . . *Here's to Jesus, Here's to you,* proclaims the air-borne streamer high over Nassau Street, and even Antonio Parr wonders at the end if it is maybe more than just a silvery trick of the failing light to which every once in a while the Tonto in him whispers Kemo Sabe, faithful friend. Maybe the reason any book about something like real life is a love-letter is that in the last analysis that is what real life is too.

Only one more thing. *To the Leisure Time Arcade* is the way I have dedicated this plump compendium—not to the nearby teen-age pinball parlor that bears that name but to a handful of very young people and a couple of old-timers who adopted it to describe the foot-loose manner in which they whiled away one early spring and late summer of incomparable beauty. Leo Bebb wouldn't have had either leisure or time enough for it himself—he was always too much in a hurry for that, with too many irons in the fire—but the chances are that he would have approved. As Father Zossima said, "Men are made for happiness, and anyone who is truly happy has a right to say to himself, 'I am doing God's will on earth.' "

Rupert, Vermont

CONTENTS

LION
COUNTRY

For Harry Ford

1

HALFWAY down the subway stairs, he turned. There was a smell of stale urine. It was raining on Lexington Avenue. He said, " 'All things are lawful for me, but all things edify not.' One Corinthians ten."

He had his hand on the stair rail and was looking at me over his shoulder. As he spoke, his right eyelid fluttered part way down, then up again, and I thought he was winking. He was not. It was involuntary, just a lazy eyelid that slid partly shut sometimes.

He said, "We'll be seeing you," and then continued on down the stairs, a fleshy, scrubbed man in a tight black raincoat with a narrow-brimmed hat, dimly Tyrolean, on the top of his head. Happy Hooligan. *We'll be seeing you.* I remember the way he said *we* when there was obviously only one of him there. I remember the urine smell on the subway stairs and the rain and the way he turned and quoted scripture not as an afterthought but as though it was the main thing he had wanted to do all along.

Leo Bebb. He was all by himself, and because I had only that day for the first time met him face to face, I had no way of knowing who his *we* included. But I came to know in some detail later, and when I close my eyes now and try to conjure up again that moment at the subway entrance, I don't exactly see the others on the stairs with him but I sense them waiting for him in the shadows a dozen steps or so farther down. In reality they were all at that time safe, to use the word rather loosely, in Armadillo, Florida, but I nonetheless picture them waiting for Bebb there in the flatulent bowels of the IRT—Sharon, that willowy carnivore, that sleepy-limbed huntress, that hierodule; and Lucille, the mother, with her black glasses and wet, liverish lips; and Brownie with his china teeth smiling his unrelentingly seraphic smile. Bebb descends to them like Orpheus with his lyre, and in the dark they reach out their hands to him while up there at the entrance to the underworld I also reach out my hands. The truth of it is that I probably had my hands in my pockets feeling for taxi money, but I remember waiting to watch him disappear, and that, I suppose, was a kind of reaching out.

He had granted me my interview that afternoon in a lunchroom be-

tween Third and Lexington in the Forties someplace, all tiled walls and
floor like a men's room with fluorescent lights that turned our lips blue. I
had ordered tea, Bebb chocolate milk which he sweetened with sugar. The
man at the counter who took our order had silvery hair and a silvery, age-
less face. "You know what he is, don't you?" Bebb asked when we had
taken seats on either side of a formica slide so narrow that we could not
both drink at the same time without the risk of touching foreheads. "That
one there," he said, nodding back over his shoulder. "He's from outer
space." I had raised the teacup to my lips, and Bebb put one bitten thumb
on the near rim of the saucer, pushing down to make the far rim rise.
"He got here in one of these. *Maybe.*" One finger in the air. "It's when the
hair and face are all one color you can usually tell."

"Silver," I said.

"He's one of the silver ones," Bebb said. "There are gold ones too and
other types. In Scripture they are called angels. There are quite a few of
them around and always have been, but they don't mean us any harm.
Often just the opposite. Ask me any questions you want to. That's what
we're here for."

His mouth snapped shut like something on hinges, a nutcracker man's
mouth or the mouth of one of those wooden bottle-stoppers carved into
faces that they pour whiskey out of sometimes in bars. A workable,
Tweedledum mouth with the lines at the corners, the hinge marks, making an almost perfect H with the tight lips. A face plump but firm, pale
but not sick pale. He was high-polish bald and had hardly a trace of facial
hair, beard or eyebrows even. The eyes were jazzy and wide open and expectant, as if he'd just pulled a rabbit out of a hat or was waiting for me to.

"You ordain people," I said.

Bebb said, "I ordained you."

As indeed he had. I had seen his ad—"*Put yourself on God's payroll—
go to work for Jesus* NOW"—and had answered it, enclosing the suggested
love offering plus a stamped, self-addressed envelope. Ten days later from
the Church of Holy Love, Inc., in Armadillo, Florida, I received an
ordination certificate with my name written on it by Brownie in purple
ink and a mimeographed letter informing me that as a minister I was
now entitled to conduct weddings and funerals and christenings and give
last rites and administer the sacraments. There were also two mimeographed order blanks, one on blue paper, the other on pink. The blue one
was for a pamphlet entitled *Worthy of His Hire*, which was billed as explaining in detail various types of tax exemptions and ecclesiastical discounts and draft deferments available to ministers. The pink one was for
a catalogue of mail-order courses offered by Gospel Faith College and a
description of the degrees that the College was in a position to award,
together with the fees and requirements for each.

"I suppose you must come under a lot of fire," I said. "Ordaining anybody who answers your ad."

"Anybody," Bebb said. "Anybody *male*." That cautionary finger again. "Scripture doesn't say anything about ordaining females. But anybody else, it doesn't matter. When people say I've probably ordained all kinds of crooks and misfits—pimps, sodomites, blackmailers and pickpockets for all I know, you name it—I say judge not that ye be not judged. That's God's business. I am here to save souls. I am here to save your soul, Antonio Parr. What kind of a name do you call that anyway?"

Antonio Parr. An Italian mother, an American father, both long since dead. A World War I romance. That kind of a name, I explained to him. And a face to go with it. An El Greco face, Ellie called it, Ellie the fair, the lily maid of my long bachelorhood. An elongated, olive-skinned (she would not have said sallow) face with eyes that she said she always thought of as rolled heavenward and brimming with whatever the eyes of El Greco faces brim with.

At the time of my first meeting with Bebb I was starting out on my scrap-iron period. Old ratchets, wheels, tongs, strappings, hasps, hinges and nails, whatever I could lay my hands on I would paint with Rustoleum black and then assemble in various interesting and I hoped entertaining ways. I resorted as little as possible to welding but used balance wherever I could or the natural capacity of one odd shape to fit somehow into or on top of or through another—entirely autobiographical, in other words— the idea being to leave the lover of my art (of me?) free to rearrange it with love in any artful way he chose. Permanence, I believed, was the enemy, and no one, least of all poor, unwelded Ellie, could say I failed to live my faith.

I had not long since passed through my teaching period (English instructor and dormitory head at a small coeducational boarding school where with a kind of determined camaraderie teachers and students called each other by their first names), and I had recently moved into the city partly to be near my sister, who was then dying, and partly to set out on my writing period. It was when I was just giving up on my fourth novel— the three earlier ones had never gotten past page 34, an apparently fatal number for me and also my age at the time—that I began edging into scrap-iron. Bebb's ad caught me thus astraddle, and I answered it because I hoped that it would provide me with copy. I would set novels aside, I thought, and try my hand at journalistic exposé. I was ready, in other words, to try out yet another of my periods.

Put yourself on God's payroll: this burning bush tucked in among the hemorrhoid cures and dashboard Virgins and neckties that glowed in the dark. At every level I could have been held accountable on, it struck me as inspired rascality ripe for my exposing—except that I can believe now that in some subterranean way I may have been interested not only in exposing it but also perhaps in, shall we say, sampling it. At least I remember that when I received my ordination certificate and with it license to bury and marry, I found myself almost right away wondering crazily who and where and when. The Reverend Antonio Parr, I thought. The Peculiarly Reverend, the Preposterously Reverend Parr.

I suppose I had been prudent long enough, prudent and earnest and in some miscellaneous sense faithful although welded to nothing: balanced precariously on top—in only the most remote and metaphorical sense, I assure you—of my poor Ellie and our seven-year understanding which promised to lead neither of us quickly anywhere. Ellie and her causes. We marched on Washington in '63 and on the Pentagon in '67 and in between times supported liberal candidates of as many races, colors and creeds as possible and even gave blood together. Ellie's came out in a steady, blue stream whereas mine took hours, and once when they handed me my orange juice afterwards, I fainted. Both orphaned early ourselves, we talked often of starting a school for orphans, an all-year-round school where we would be teachers and parents both, and many an evening during those many years we met in her Manhattan House apartment to lay, if nothing else, our plans.

Sometimes when we tired of planning, I would recline on the floor and she would play the piano—she played very well but was shy about it, played almost exclusively for me—and when I picture her, I am apt to picture her there. A tall, long-necked girl with her hair to her shoulders rather like Tenniel's Alice just after she has bitten into the cake marked *Eat Me,* my poor Ellie sits there at the piano with her fingers on the keys and one foot on the pedal. It is this foot that I see most clearly, a rather generous-sized foot in a heelless brocade slipper working up and down on the soft pedal while I lie there on the floor watching it at eye-level. In answering Bebb's ad, I am sure that I was, among other things, hungry for fortissimo.

Certainly no such thought was in my mind, however, as Bebb and I were sitting there blue-lipped in that dismal eatery and he looked up at me across the formica and said, "I am here to save your soul, Antonio Parr." It was only with effort that I kept my eyes from rolling heavenward at the sudden rush of adrenaline and guilt. After my ordination I had written back that the next time his crusade took him to New York—the Church of Holy Love, Inc., his ad indicated, had many mansions—I would welcome the opportunity to discuss with him various possible directions that I imagined my ministry might take. And here he was talking about saving my soul, and there I was with every secret intention of holding his up to public ridicule and condemnation.

He said, "There are some folks don't care how they abuse a man. They're going to call you a crook, some of them, and say you're using the gospel ministry for sucker bait. Sticks and stones will hurt my bones!" That tidy, fat, nun's face—or was it Fatty Arbuckle's or Juliet's nurse?— those tight little hinges his mouth worked on, snip-snap, those quick and overexcited magician's eyes as he rolled up his sleeve and prepared to grab down into his trick topper. He said, "Bad names aren't ever going to bother me." He lowered his voice. "Sure some of the brethern got itchy fingers, no question about it. Matthew ten sixteen. 'Behold, I send you forth as sheep in the midst of *wolves*,' Antonio. 'Be ye therefore wise as serpents and harmless as doves.' You just bet there are wolves in it strictly for the kill. But I'm in it to bring folks to Jesus. I guess the Almighty can handle the wolves all right." There, did I see? Holding it up by its long pink ears, his face a triumph, a challenge. Could anyone go him one better than that? He lowered a teaspoon delicately into his glass so that a little of the chocolate milk skimmed over into the bowl of the spoon where the sugar was.

"You've got to eat," I said. "How do you make a living out of all this? Is it the love offerings?"

"Love. . . . Listen," he said, laying a finger on my sleeve. "Ninety percent of the answers I get to the ad don't have any love offering. And I ordain them anyway. Now you ask me how do I make a living, and that means how do *you* make one too. There's no reason on earth why you shouldn't ask it. Remember the ox, Antonio. 'Thou shalt not muzzle the ox when it treadeth out the corn.' Deuteronomy twenty-five four. *Maybe*," he said, the finger again, "or twenty-four five. Be wise as a serpent, Antonio Parr. *How* you make a living, that's for later when I know you better and know where your talents lie. Give me time. But what you *do* with your living once you make it, that's for now. You plow it right back into the church, that's what you do with it, and then the I.R.S. can't touch it with a ten-foot pole. Church money is for the church to spend any way it sees fit, and when it comes to your own church, you're the one calls the tune. Set up a discretionary fund, and as long as you're discreet you can dish it out wherever the Spirit guideth. There's plenty of poor families could use a piece of it. Tell me about yourself now, Antonio," he said, his lazy eyelid for the first time in my presence misbehaving. "Do you have a poor family?"

My family was dying, Miriam by name, my twin, and to that extent, I suppose, it could hardly have been poorer—all the family I had or can even well remember having except for her children, two young, pale boys who since the divorce had lived with their father in Westchester because their mother was in no shape to have them live with her. Myeloma was what she was dying of, a complaint that in her case came in like a lamb and went out like a lion. The Merck Manual, a handbook of horrors that no hypochondriac can afford to live either with or without, says of it that "pain may be its only symptom," a phrase that seems to me as curiously noble as anything in Greek tragedy. It is a fatal disorder which has to do with bones, although just what it was going to have to do with and to her bones, ultimately, I am happy to say that neither I nor, I assume, she knew until some time later. As soon as I left Bebb at the subway, watching him until he'd disappeared into the shadows like Orpheus, I took a taxi up to the hospital to see her.

It was November and getting on toward dusk by this time. The picture window in her room was of glass tinted to tinge the most cloudless sky with the illusion of approaching storms. On a table in front of it was a vase of copper-colored chrysanthemums. It couldn't have been later than five or so, but already from the corridors came the rumble and click of tray carts laden with supper, a comforting sound. I felt like Cyrano coming to the convent to bring Roxane the news of the court, his white plume concealing the fatal wound as the autumn leaves fall and he recites, *"Comme elles tombent bien,"* except that in this case the fatal wound was not Cyrano's.

Miriam my sister, my twin, that Mater Dolorosa with her cigarette between her fingers and her black hair spidered out on the pillow. She gave me her left hand to kiss, her name typed out on the plastic bracelet at her wrist. She said, "They can't be expecting it to go on a hell of a lot longer, Tono. They've given up on the cobalt now. I suppose the idea's not to throw good money after bad," and that laid the ghost for that visit, the ghost which always troubled the air in between us, especially the air in between our faces, until one of us named its name. There was a time when she would simply show me where on her back and chest they had marked out with something that looked like iodine the areas for radiation. It was like showing me the map of a journey she was planning to take alone.

"The queerest thing is this feeling I have I'm *going* someplace," she said, "instead of just out, like a match. I should have been a better Catholic. Maybe I'd understand more. All last night I kept dreaming about doors opening."

"Vaginas," I said. "I thought everybody knew that."

She said, "Listen, I'm through with that stuff for good."

Then the nurse came in with her tray, and she became our nurse, mine as well as Miriam's. We were children, and it was suppertime. It seemed to be nearly always suppertime when we were children, suppertime in winter especially, with the lights in the apartment going on at twilight and, fifteen stories down, the muffled baritone of horns as the Park Avenue traffic moved home, an entirely different sound from the morning horns. There was something pastoral about it at the end of day— the lowing herd winding slowly o'er the lea, leaving the world to darkness, and to Miriam and me. And always a nurse coming in, any one of a long dynasty of nurses, and we would have our supper to the accompaniment of the Lone Ranger or Uncle Don or Mr. Keen, Tracer of Lost Persons. If you opened a window, the air smelled gritty-cold and bitter like an iron gate. In the apartment it smelled of lamb chops and fur.

The nurse said, "You eat up now. We want to keep our strength up."

"It's like having a baby," Miriam said. "Only the baby I'm going to have is me."

At school they were always asking us what it was like to be twins. Could we read each other's minds, and if one of us was hurt, did the other one feel the pain? There was some movie about this. If one of us was shot, would the other one die? If one of us had myeloma, would the other one's bones break? The answer, I was to learn, was yes and no.

"You're my baby," the nurse said, taking the cigarette from between my sister's fingers. It had gone out.

The nurse turned on the lamp by the bed and then had Miriam sit up to receive the tray which she rolled up over her lap. A shadow deep in one cheek and down the bridge of her nose, her black hair unbrushed and oddly clumped in back where she had been lying on it, she looked like a young Jewess. I thought of Rachel in Ramah weeping for her children, and I thought of the two small, pale boys living with their pale father in Westchester. Miriam rarely if ever mentioned them, let alone wept for them as far as I know. It was as if she had written off everything except this room and what happened in it, what was going to happen in it. She had herself become her only children.

While she picked at her supper, I told her about the time with Bebb that I had just come from and the secret plans I had for dismembering him. For some reason, I had not mentioned before about answering his ad and receiving the certificate of ordination through the mail, and when I was on the point of explaining it to her here, I found myself thinking better of it. Instead I put it simply that when I read he was in town, I had written for an appointment. Was it out of some fear that if I told her I had been ordained, even by a charlatan, she would look to me for something more than I felt I had in me to give—some deathbed expertise, the "sweet reprieve and ransom" that Father Hopkins describes having tendered to Felix Randall the farrier in a poem my sometime English students invariably loathed? Or was it a deep fear still that she would laugh more definitively at the slapstick of it than somehow I quite could myself at that point, which was of course the real slapstick of it? I don't know. I know only that I moved on quickly to the interview itself with that plump and implausible man in that appallingly plausible joint. The silver-faced visitor from outer space slinging hash at the counter. The sizzle and smell of French fries frying, and just the idea, let alone the act, of putting sugar in chocolate milk, while through the window I could see the rain coming down hard on Lexington Avenue.

Bebb followed his chocolate milk with a wheel of Danish, and it was when he finished that, I told Miriam, that he got down to what I rapidly concluded must have been his chief purpose in being there with me at all.

He said, "Antonio, I'm commencing to get the feel of you a little. You've had me doing most of the talking, but I've been watching your face and your eyes and they've told me many things—*more* things," he had a way of interrupting himself as if taking you down through deeper and deeper levels always nearer to some remarkable truth, "*maybe*," he inter-

rupted again, taking me yet another step nearer, "more things than maybe
you'd ever dream of telling me yourself." Whereupon I had the eerie
sensation for a moment that I who was there to expose him was on the
point of being exposed myself as being there under pretenses so false as
to border on the supernatural.

"You are a sensitive man. You have a tender heart. You've got it upstairs. You are a good listener. What does that add up to? Teaching, Antonio. I see your ministry as first and foremost a teaching ministry."

He had to catch a plane back to West Palm in a couple of hours,
he said, and therefore would come quickly to the point. His proposition
was for me to start a branch of Gospel Faith College on my own. I would
do the canvassing of students myself and would offer the standard Gospel
Faith curriculum, for which I would receive the standard Gospel Faith
tuition fees. If my students passed muster, I would forward their names to
Bebb in Armadillo, and he would send them their diplomas. When my
branch started paying off, I could pass on whatever I thought was fair. He
knew, he said, that when I started cashing in, I would not forget the
Mother Church. This was the first time I had seen him give any sign of
emotion, or at least that is what I took it to be. "The Mother Church,"
he had said, and this was the phrase that seemed to hit him. He glanced
down at his empty plate and with all ten fingers, working out from the
center, divided the crumbs from his Danish into two small piles.

Without looking up, he said, "Foxes have holes, Antonio, and the
birds of the air have nests, but for a while when you first start out, you
may not have any place to lay your head. Only faith. You better believe
that I know whereof I speak." With his face bowed, I was able for the
first time to look at the rest of him—the jacket of his black tropic-weight
suit straining under the arms—the handkerchief in his breast pocket folded
into four neat points so that the monogram B showed.

Partly for information, partly to recall him to a role that I felt better
equipped to cope with, I questioned him about the legality of the operation. Was he accredited to offer degrees? It brought him to life again.

"Inc.," he said. "Inc., Antonio. The Church of Holy Love, *Inc.* Once
you've got yourself incorporated, you can offer any degree you've got a
mind to—almost," he said, breaking in upon himself, "any degree. Almost
any degree to almost anybody—anybody who can meet the fee, that is.
They're not all going to be Harvard graduates, Antonio, but Jesus Christ
wasn't a Harvard graduate either."

Feeling at this point that even if I angered him, he had given me
already rope enough to hang him with, I risked a more direct approach.
I said, "It sounds a little like a diploma mill, doesn't it, Mr. Bebb?"

It was less the substance of his answer that surprised me than the
tone and manner of it. His voice went soft and conciliatory, the hinges
of his mouth working looser, and for the first time I could imagine him
actually working at his trade, asking the blessing in somebody's kitchen or

pronouncing the benediction in a funeral parlor. He said, "It's a mill, all right, but the product isn't diplomas. The product is people who are ready to go all the way with Jesus, hundred-percenters like yourself, Antonio. What comes into the mill is raw cotton. What goes out is something helps keep folks warm and dry when the winter comes."

Rising abruptly and putting his hat on the back of his head as he tried to work his arm into the inside-out sleeve of his raincoat, he said that I was not to rush into such an important decision half-cocked but should take it to the Lord in prayer. In the meanwhile, he would have me sent all the information I might need about the courses themselves and how to administer them. Better still, if there were any chance that I could get down to Armadillo, he woud personally show me the whole process in actual operation from A to Z. He did not press this, just threw it out while I was paying the check—it seemed to me that as Judas it was the least I could do—and he did not refer to it again. I walked him to the subway.

"It smells like half New York dropped by here last night to take a leak," he said when we got there. We shook hands in the rain, and then I watched him go downstairs to where he turned and said that all things were lawful for him but all things edified not—that foolish hat on top of his head and the tight-fitting black raincoat that couldn't give him much protection, I thought, against that chill November. That one lazy and somehow hilarious eyelid with the nether world looming at his back.

"*Lasciate ogni speranza, voi ch'entrate,*" I said to Miriam, bringing an edited rambling version of this account to an end, and only then did I see what had become of her while I was too busy talking to notice.

The shadow in her cheek and the shadow of her nose had met so that one whole side of her face was virtually missing. The remaining eye had gone from oval to parallelogram. It was not looking out any more. It was looking in. Her expression, as nearly as I can describe it, was one of utter disbelief. She was obviously listening not to me but to her own contractions. She was preparing for the time when she would be delivered of herself. It was not the final labor yet, but it was a full dress rehearsal.

2

THREE YEARS BEFORE, for Christmas, Ellie had given me a cat which she delivered to my door with a card around its neck on which, so help me God, she had written, that chaste and comprehensively innocent girl, that she hoped I could use a little pussy. *O tempora, O mores,* shaking my ragged fist in an agony of wild and savage mirth, my El Greco eyes rolled heavenward. The cat was a rather handsomely endowed tom which I could never bring myself to have altered. One of us out of action at a time, I felt, was enough. I named him Tom.

When I got home from my visit to Miriam at the hospital, I discovered that Tom had gotten a fish-hook in his eyelid. There were lots of fish-hooks lying around ready to dip into Rustoleum black for use with my scrap-iron creations, and by some series of gross miscalculations Tom had tangled with one of them. It was a whole day of eyes as I look back on it—first Bebb's, then Miriam's, and now Tom's, although, strictly speaking, in Tom's case as in Bebb's, it was not the eye but the eyelid. It was only when I moved the hook around, trying to extricate it, that the eye itself seemed in danger, and that was why after several unsuccessful attempts with Tom squirming under one arm, I called up the vet. His office was closed by this hour, but he said he thought he could handle it at home if I wanted to bring Tom down. I even brought him down in a taxi. I was that grateful to him in a way for rescuing me with a malaise so circumscribed and manageable from that disheveling afternoon.

When the first shot of anesthetic made no impression on him, the vet gave him a second which in a relatively short time knocked him cold. The vet then pushed the hook through to where he was able to cut off the barb and pulled it back out easily. He rubbed the eye with some ointment, I paid him, and in no time at all I was out on the street again with Tom unconscious in my arms.

It might be some time, the vet had said, before the double shot wore off. In the meantime Tom should be kept warm and in a place where he could do himself no mischief in case he was groggy and irrational when he began to come to. I took him to Ellie's. God knows I had no wish at that moment for political discussion or piano music or orphanage-planning, but Manhattan House was a good deal nearer where we were than home was, and, trying to put myself in Tom's shoes, I decided that Ellie's would be a more reassuring place to come to in with its wall-to-wall carpets and maid service than our own flat, which was all sharp corners and hard surfaces and a great many other fish-hooks which could only stir up painful memories. Ellie seemed delighted to see us. It had been her afternoon at the U.N., she said—she did volunteer work at the information desk—and she had just been wishing that she had somebody around to unwind with.

Ellie unwinding. The imagination runs free. Unwinding like a clock which has been wound so tight that it won't run till you give it a shake? Unwinding like a ball of string which for years has dreamed of just lying around, festooned over sofas and carpets and beds? Somebody to unwind with, she said as I came in with poor, limp Tom in my arms, and I thought of two alarm clocks going off together until the last languid rattle announces that all passion is spent. I thought of two unraveled balls of twine

all messed up together in a tangle on that fuzzy gold rug. And who knows
but what on that particular evening with the small November rain raining
down outside, with Miriam heavy on my heart and the U.N. heavy on
Ellie's, some switch might have been tripped, some tender and little-used
muscle set to twitching somewhere. That Victorian face—those ringlets
almost to her shoulders, those Christmas-bright eyes and orderly little
seed-pearl teeth. She called up and ordered Beef Stroganoff for two. I
poured out two scotch-and-sodas in those narrow highball glasses of hers
with a single tear-drop in the base. We laid Tom near the radiator on a
Turkish towel.

Nothing the vet said had prepared me for the performance that took
place when life began to stir in him again. He was drunk. He was Dionysiac. He staggered around cross-eyed with never more than two legs working at a time. He knocked himself silly against the legs of tables and chairs.
He fell over on his side like a rag to lie there heaving with his eyes rolled
up until the god in him got him started off again. He was entirely indifferent to our attempts, once he had fallen down, to cozen him into staying
down. And he made no noise. If he had yammered and whined, it would
have been better, at least better for us. But he was silent in his mad staggering—silent and relentless and drunk. The life-agony was upon him.

Though usually a model of continence, he had not yet regained control of his functions, and there were damp spots here and there on the
golden rug. Tom himself, with what may have been as much sweat and
tears as anything else, looked half soaked. Except for a few random wisps
that stuck out like pinfeathers, his fur clung flat to his sides, and I realized
for the first time how much of his bristling and impressive bulk was—as
with the rest of us, I suppose—the sheerest fluff. He went weaving around
from pillar to post looking half starved in addition to everything else, and
I must say that Ellie was magnificent throughout. Another woman might
have looked first to the damp spots, but her concern was all for Tom. She
warmed a saucer of milk for him, and when he fell into it whiskers first, his
front legs buckling, she tried to hold him steady so he could drink. He
lapped at it a couple of times and then choked. She put him in her lap,
wet and raving as he was, and tried to stroke peace back into him with
those lovely Tennysonian hands. She helped him back to his feet when
all his own strugglings toward that end failed. And finally she laid him
on her apricot-colored bed, where with pillows from the chaise-longue on
one side and a bolster held in place by an armchair on the other, she at
last consented to leave him—asleep, as nearly as we could tell—convinced
that here at least he could come to no grief. By the time we got back to
our flat scotch-and-sodas, whatever might have been possible between us
before, however remotely, was possible no longer.

It was over the Beef Stroganoff that I told her about seeing Bebb
that afternoon. She had been in on the whole business ever since my
original answer to his ad and had encouraged my plan to expose him in

print. My scrap-iron and my novels had both left her cold—lacking, as she quite accurately saw it, anything much in the way of social relevance—but at the idea of my bringing a crook to justice she was enthusiastic. As it turned out, she had even done some investigating of her own.

After a morning of digging through newspaper files at the Public Library, she had come across a short piece in the old *Journal-American* which she had had photostated and presented to me that evening. The incongruity of it as I look back—Ellie sitting there bright-eyed on her beige couch, so Brearley and Vassar, so *cotillion*, and in her hand, holding it out to me like a dance card, that tawdry relic datelined Miami some eleven years back and, like the subway entrance where I said goodbye to Bebb, smelling of stale piss.

Remembering it, I see the honey-dipped mommas and hash-browned poppas sitting in their rockers like J. P. Morgan on the throne of Minos as they watch the traffic simmer along. I see the window-shopping typists with their hair up in rollers under souvenir bandanas or those mobcaps aflutter with gauzy fish scales. I see fried clams and payaya-juice stands and stuffed baby alligators and vast neo-Babylonian lobbies, see Assyrians hung like bulls in their Jantzens and oiled from their huaraches up to their thundering wings and blue-black beards. And I see Bebb.

Bebb is standing in a side street near the back entrance to a restaurant. There are pails of sweet-and-sour garbage, lobster shells, drifts of wastepaper, all smelling of rancid butter. There is a windowless stucco wall, blinding in the sun. Some children are playing with a tennis ball. Bebb has on a white linen cap with a green-lined visor and little perforated panels at either side to let the air in. He has on a Harry Truman sport shirt with a camera slung around his neck and the kind of sunglasses that look like mirrors from the outside. At this moment they are mirroring the children. He is smiling his climactic magician's smile, his most effulgent and tight-hinged allez-oop of an H, as he reaches down with one hand to pull the rabbit out of the hat. Only it is not a rabbit that he pulls out and not a hat that he pulls it out of. It is a bunch of white grapes. It is a handful of suet. Squab and pale, it nestles like plovers in his treasuring grip, like plovers' eggs.

The first child to notice yells to the others, or maybe just the opposite —stops yelling. They all stop and turn, the tennis ball abandoned among the lobster shells and wastepaper. With the blinding wall at his back and his looking-glass goggles, he stands there for them to see. They run away helter-skelter, skinny and barebacked, like newspaper blowing in the wind. Do they? Or maybe they stand there enthralled with their ribs sucked in. Tattletale-tits. And did they even tell their tattle right, get it straight what that prestidigitator was up to, what that plump and preposterous showman was in his madness trying to show? God only knows. Sebastian full of arrows, Ursula baring her breast, Bebb with his fist full of fire. . . .

Ellie. She read the thing out loud to me and then dropped it into my lap where I sat beside her on the couch. "Little *children*," she said, drawing her shoulders up as though she suddenly felt a cold draft. "Honestly, Tono, whatever you do with this, he's got it coming. Why, the man's a monster," and the air between us turned so dark and heavy with her indignation that for a moment it was as if I was myself Bebb.

At the time, I am almost certain, no such surrealist fancy took me, but now, recollecting it in tranquility, I can't help wondering what extraordinary events would have followed and how both our lives and, for all I know, life itself might have been unimaginably changed if I had at that exact point actually played Bebb there, stolen Bebb's act. By a kind of sympathetic magic his crime had momentarily, in Ellie's eyes, become my crime, and what if in full view of those same eyes I had, like Bebb, committed it, pulled my own rabbit out of my own hat? Hey presto! Now you see it, now you don't, in reverse. The gaudy *what-if*'s of history. What if Eisenhower had taken a black child in each hand and personally led them up the steps of the Little Rock Central High School? What if Barabbas had not been the one to have his execution stayed? But the point, I suppose, is that, given the people we are and the nature of our times, we can't do or be anything other than what we are, at least not anything much. It's as if something in the very nature of chronos almost physically prevents our occasional little stabs at anachronism, and if I had had any impulse at that moment to pull a Bebb on my goggling Ellie, the chances are the very air itself would have somehow stayed my hand. And yet one plays the tantalizing game anyway. . . . What if I had suddenly set my rabbit free, alive and quivering on the couch between us . . . something whose time had not yet come, was perhaps never to come at all, coming? These turning points at which the whole world might have turned. *Comme elles tombent bien*, at least in the memory's convent garden, like golden leaves from a tree that is past leafing.

In any case no such thoughts, I am reasonably certain, crossed my mind at the time. Ellie's moral indignation became my own—indeed, even faded by comparison with mine, because in a moment her face softened into that little frown of hers—half question, half answer—and she said, "The man's sick, of course. He needs help." I felt no such tender concern myself. On the contrary. That Bebb was a charlatan I of course had no doubt, but it must have been that as a charlatan *priest* I expected his charlatanry at least to go decently cassocked. This scabrous new revelation shocked me so deeply that I believe that at some level I must have taken him for a version, at least, of the genuine article, and thus it was now I who suddenly became the molested child. No exposure could have been more indecent than that of my own trusting innocence. By some act of misguided faith, some residual image of even the charlatan priest as somehow priestly, I must have actually believed him when he turned on those malodorous stairs and assured me that everything he did was lawful—not capital L lawful, maybe, but lawful enough. When I discovered from the

Journal-American that the case was indeed quite otherwise, I felt that I, the would-be betrayer, had been betrayed.

And then it was the ludicrousness of the thing that struck me. Bebb the ordainer of thousands, Bebb the bestower of advanced theological degrees, above all Bebb as in his physical presence he had appeared to me that very day all trussed up in his tight black raincoat with his handkerchief in four tidy points, so scrubbed and hairless and in spite of everything somehow so *Protestant*—this same Bebb caught with his pants, in a manner of speaking, down. This picture in my mind supplanted everything else for me, and I burst into laughter which Ellie's earnest incomprehension, I'm afraid, only served to intensify. I can believe that at this moment I might have given up the whole idea of writing an exposé. It is hard to launch a crusade with your funnybone. And there were the unfinished novels, after all, and all that scrap-iron to do something with, maybe try for a one-man show at one of the uptown galleries. I might even have decided to go back to teaching again. Who knows? But then, as twice before that day, Tom fatefully intervened.

Ellie said she thought she heard queer noises coming from the bedroom, and I followed her in to investigate. The noise turned out to be Tom's breathing, as unnerving a sound as I have ever heard. You expect to hear a dog pant as you expect to hear and see and smell almost anything a dog does because dogs wear their hearts on their sleeves, but here was a cat panting—a cat who had never before even let it be known that he breathed, a cat who, like all cats, had always played his cards tight to his chest, who had never to my knowledge—except for this post-operative lapse—made a single undignified gesture.

And here he was apparently fighting for life like any peasant, his mouth ajar, his teeth bared and dry. He was lying on his side on Ellie's apricot spread with his front paws stretched as far as they would stretch forward and his back paws as far as they would stretch backward, as though he were running at a great speed or hung up in a taxidermist's icebox awaiting treatment. He looked very long and very flat, and his ribs were fluttering in and out and his breath coming in hoarse, rapid grunts. He was smiling eerily. There seemed nothing for us to do except stand there and watch—this rare and forbidden sight of a cat struggling with death.

O Miriam, Miriam, my sister, my love . . . I am not and was not then a sentimental man. I do not often, after the fashion of the sentimental, throb more than God does over things. I do not weep at weddings. At the funerals of people I love, I rarely give death more than its due, which is to say I am usually able to stop just this side of where tears for the dead become tears for yourself, for everything and for nothing, those nineteenth-century tears which it is really rather a treat to shed. I take no credit for this. I suspect it comes simply from overexposure at an early age—both my parents were dead by the time I was twelve. Nevertheless, as I stood there in Ellie's bedroom with the clipping about Bebb still in my hand and that same hand around Ellie's shoulder as if we were old war comrades, I suddenly saw the thing that was happening to poor Tom on the bed as Miriam's thing.

From my teaching days I remember De Quincey's essay on the knocking at the gate in *Macbeth,* how he says it is only when the real world floods back in the form of the knocking and the drunken porter's bad jokes about the effects of alcohol on tumescence that you realize the full horror of Duncan's murder. It was only here with Tom that I really *saw* my sister as she had lain there in the hospital with half her face missing, only here that I knew fully and felt in my bones what was happening to her there. It was like walking downstairs in the dark when you think you have one more step to go and take that step only to find that it's not there because you're at the bottom already. The jolt of it is so total that you feel it in your teeth. What I felt in my teeth there in that vestal bedroom of Ellie's was my sister's death.

I tightened my grip on Ellie's shoulders, slipped my hand up into her shampoo-sweet hair and pressed her head in against mine, temple to temple, our two skulls touching hard. I wanted to tell her about Miriam, about her living and her dying and how it was when we were children together in the wintertime with the horns honking homeward and how her hair raying out on the hospital pillow was Medusa's now in my more than memory because it was turning me to stone; but I couldn't. I could never speak easily about one of those women to the other. I could never speak to one about the other without twinges of guilt. And the reason, I suppose, is that with both of them I was more than a little in love.

In love with my twin? Does that mean that I was in love somehow with myself? I do not think so, although I have heard of queer things in my time. At most, I believe, I was only in love with the female part of myself, the part I wouldn't let weep at weddings. Or in love with the childhood we had shared, with the children we had been, those lost persons that it would take Mr. Keen himself to trace. Did I want to go to bed with her?—that oddly touching phrase we use, the one Adam used, surely, of his sister Eve before the unpleasantness over the apple. If so, then only, I think, to that hospital bed perhaps where in no John Donne sense but quite straightforwardly we might die in each other's arms, the gemini, babes in the wood pushing thirty-five, with the dry leaves falling to cover us. *Comme elles tombent bien.*

I didn't speak to Ellie about any of this, didn't so much as mention Miriam's name, as we stood there in bony, cranial embrace watching what I could only believe were poor Tom's last few moments as himself. What I did say was "That sonofabitch Bebb. I'll skin him alive if it's the last thing I do." Skin him alive. As Miriam was fond of saying. there's a lot of Wop in me, and although my customary manner is mostly recitative, I do on occasion burst, at least internally, into aria. I was suddenly

Rigoletto vowing vengeance on Gilda's betrayer—*Maledizione!* with the full orchestra pulsing around me and my fist as well as my eyes raised heavenward. *Maledizione!*—the fool's curse. The jester's revenge. And in my bloodshot and grief-crazed eyes the betrayer, the villain, the one who was somehow responsible for what was happening there on those two sad beds which in my mind had become one, was Bebb. I vowed his destruction. I would skin him alive. "That horny old bastard," I said, not sparing Ellie's blushes, not even aware of them. Wop opera, Miriam would have said. And been right.

Why Bebb? In Hindu iconography, I have read somewhere, the mind of man is portrayed as a monkey swinging from tree to tree, witless, purposeless, grabbing out at whatever new branch happens to come to hand, which I take to mean that it is not we who control our thoughts but circumstances that control them. Let me smell bacon frying, and in spite of myself I am hungry; wave a red flag at me, and I am mad as hell. Or subtler stimuli—a drop in barometric pressure, the look in somebody's eye, the state of my digestion—and willy-nilly I am whatever they make me. Since hearing Ellie read the *Journal-American* piece, my attitude toward Bebb had passed from shocked indignation to horrified amusement and now to Verdian bloodlust. Why? Maybe just because these were the branches that presented themselves. In other words, the flat scotch-and-sodas, the smell of Ellie's hair, the damp spots on the rug—all these may have had as much to do with my feelings about Bebb as Bebb did himself. And yet, although I doubt I could have explained it at the time, I think there was a kind of crazy logic to it too. We are none of us entirely simian.

If Bebb had been a real priest instead of a phony, he might have been able to help. I suppose that would be the briefest statement of it. Help who? Help Miriam and Tom in their dying, or at least help me in my helpless watching. Help how? I don't know how, but if Bebb had been real instead of phony, he would have known. If there had been any priests anywhere who were real, they might have been able to help. I think my unreasonable reasoning may have gone even as far as that, making Bebb personally responsible for the failure of the priesthood in general, blaming Bebb personally for the bankruptcy of God. I would probably not have put it that way at the time, but I suspect this was part of what lay behind my shaking fist and bloodshot glance.

It was a crazy business, of course—looking for holy help in this plucked and perverted fraud with his lazy eye—but it had to do, I think, with my being Catholic. Like Miriam, I was not a good Catholic. I still attended an occasional mass and dropped into St. Patrick's once in a while to light a kind of rabbit's-foot candle to Saint Anthony, who, as both my patron saint and the saint who watches over lost things, seemed worthy of my special attention. But I hadn't made a confession or received the sacrament for years. Yet still from my early training—especially,

I suppose, from my poor mother, who like an old photograph has so faded in my memory that I can hardly tell the light of her from the dark of her any more—I had this notion that once a priest always a priest, that however far Bebb had fallen, he still bore the mark upon him like an old tattoo or an appendix scar. He *should* have been able to help. He *should* have been real. And if he had been real—the more I think about it, the more I believe this may have been the real nub of it—then I would also have been real.

That mimeographed letter I received along with my certificate of ordination informing me that now I was entitled to marry and bury and baptize—and, by extension, certainly to give absolution, to heal even, all these things that my sister and Tom rolled into one so desperately needed—if Bebb had been a real priest, then I whom he had however absurdly ordained would however absurdly have been able to do these things. I would have been a real priest myself. All of which is a round-about way of saying that I think I blamed Bebb for my own inadequacy. I vowed to skin him alive because a hard death was taking place under my nose and there was not a blessed thing I could do about it.

Tom didn't die, as things turned out. It was apparently only the effect of the anesthetic wearing off, after all. Soon his breathing started to return to normal. He closed his mouth, thereby dismantling the unearthly smile and replacing it with what I have always thought of as his Egyptian expression—archaic, enigmatic, and slightly near-sighted. Then he fell asleep.

But I continued to vow revenge anyway, and back in the living room again, where the Beef Stroganoff had gone cold and waxy on our plates, I kept Ellie up way past her bedtime laying my plans. I would not stop at any one-shot assault on Bebb, I told her—the kind of satirical account of my own dealings with him that I had originally planned. I would do a series of articles—a book even, if I had to. I would take him up on his suggestion that I make the trip to Armadillo. I would observe the whole operation from A to Z, as he had put it, and then back to A again as many times as might be necessary to find out all there was to find out. I would dig up the full story of the Miami incident. The *Journal-American* reported only that Bebb had pleaded not guilty and was awaiting trial, and Ellie said that she could find no follow-up in later issues. I would do the follow-up myself.

I would pump his enemies. I would bribe his associates. I would destroy him utterly—and with him every priest everywhere and God and, in some sense, I suppose, myself—for helplessly abandoning my twin sister to her ungodly labor.

My aria turned into a duet then—Ellie answering my vindictive vibrato with little trills of encouragement interspersed with occasional chest tones calling for restraint. I mustn't over-react, she said, and the man was obviously sick besides. It was Tom who transformed us into a trio. He wandered back into the living room in his most urbane manner, looking, except for a slight dampness around the hindquarters, as though nothing untoward had happened. He miaowed several times to indicate not that he *needed* food—he needed nothing—but that if we were to offer it, he would find it not uncongenial.

It was on the way to the kitchen that Ellie found on the dining-room floor a mess that he must have left there earlier when the madness was upon him. He ate Portuguese sardines in the kitchen while Ellie and I cleaned it up—a foul-smelling thing which not even several different types of household cleaner were able to remove entirely. When we finally kissed goodnight at the elevator, it was in a cloud of cat and Mr. Klean.

3

I DECIDED not to let Bebb know in advance that I was coming. Having only just returned from his trip to New York, he would be unlikely yet to have gone off anywhere else, and I would be almost sure to catch him at home. More to the point, I thought, I would be almost sure to catch him by surprise, catch him in the act, whatever exactly I imagined the act might be.

The morning after my supper with Ellie, therefore, I arranged to board Tom at the vet's and got myself a roomette on a train leaving for Florida that very afternoon. There seemed no point in delaying. Anybody else would have taken a plane, but I have always liked trains. Nobody can get at you in a train. You are in the world but not of it as you flash by as free and impermanent as the silver meteor for which my train that day was named.

Before I left, I stopped in at the hospital again to tell Miriam what I was up to. I always dreaded our goodbyes, even as trivial a one as this, fearing that it would be not *a rivederci* but *addio*, and obviously this was often on her mind too—the unimaginable possibility that we were looking at each other for the last time. The doctors admitted to me that they had run through their whole bag of tricks to the point where the only one left was to keep her as comfortable as possible until the end, which might come in a matter of a week or two, they said, or might go on for months. And yet when I saw her that morning of my departure for Armadillo, she couldn't have looked better.

I knew, as I'm sure my sister did too, that these remissions, as in their antiseptic jargon the doctors called them, were only temporary, but they were on the face of it such hopeful times that I always thought maybe, once you got that much hope in a face, it might seep down in to where the cancer was and work a miracle. They were like watching *Romeo and Juliet* allowing yourself for a moment to hope that somehow this time Juliet will wake up from Friar Laurence's potion before Romeo swallows his death.

Miriam was sitting up in bed reading the papers when I came in. She had put on lipstick and a bed-jacket, and her hair was brushed and tied back with a piece of florist's ribbon from one of the plants somebody had sent her. We did not even find it necessary to lay the usual ghost by naming it, and she surprised me by asking if I had brought the martinis. When she was first hospitalized, I had brought them quite often, put the gin and vermouth together at home and then gotten glasses and ice from the nurses. The doctors were all for it. But for weeks now the very thought of gin had made her feel like throwing up—it was the cobalt, she said— and I had long since given the custom up. There was a bar across the street, however, where I had no trouble getting what we needed, and our meeting was in some ways the easiest we had had for a long time.

Without mentioning either Ellie or the *Journal* piece, I told her I was going to Florida for a couple of days to do the article on Bebb, but she didn't seem to remember about him from the day before, and her remission clearly did not involve her being interested enough in the world beyond that room to want me to tell her again. She started talking instead about her children, and that in itself I thought was a hopeful sign.

She said, "Tono, I worry like hell about those kids. The woman he's got taking care of them for him is such a menace with that big bust of hers bouncing around and that voice you could lance a boil with. And Charlie's such a shrinking violet by comparison, besides which he's asleep most of the time anyway. The castrating mother—I mean *her*—and the castrated father. I'm scared to death they're going to turn those boys into fairies. The situation's got all the makings, God knows."

Although I was on perfectly friendly terms with my ex-brother-in-law and knew Miriam would have liked me to see the boys more often, I hadn't been out there for months. Still, it did seem to me that in the original sense of the term at least there was something fairy-like about them—something transparent and insubstantial, a spidery quietness that seemed more than just shyness. They watched you with their mother's dark eyes and didn't smile much. Chris twelve, and Tony, my namesake, ten—they were like old men in their little gray suits, like little businessmen without any business.

I told my sister that I didn't think she had anything to worry about. After all, they had a father who loved them and was around most of the time—he did scripts for some educational TV people out there, working mostly at home—and although the Bouncing Bust wasn't going to win any popularity contests, she was good-hearted and conscientious.

"It's Charlie," Miriam said. "Tono, the man's a bleeding ghost. I'm

not being a bitch—I cut loose, and that's that. But to bring up two boys
. . . Do you know what I *mean* when I say he sleeps most of the time?
I mean he often doesn't get up till noon, and when he naps, he doesn't
just nap when it's raining or something but right in the middle of a
sunny afternoon, for God's sake, with the kids and me roaming around
in bathing suits right under his window. Sleep's his escape from life, Tono.
Someday they'll have to come wake him up and tell him he's dead." And
tell him she was dead, I suppose she also meant, though of course she
didn't say so.

She went on to tell me more about Charlie Blaine than I think she
had ever told me before—Charlie asleep in his underwear; Charlie with his
allergies, taking his kapok pillow with him when he went off on overnight trips; Charlie as a lover, both importunate and oddly passionless, as
though, like sleep, he found her body desirable not in itself but as a way
of escape. Although she never said so, not even indirectly, I felt sure that
I knew why she was going on at such length. She wanted me to see for
myself that her children couldn't be left in their father's hands permanently after she was dead, these children who had my blood in their veins
as well as his and hers. She wanted me to say, if possible without her
having to ask me to, that I would somehow arrange to take them on myself. I felt sure this was in her mind, and for a few moments I came very
close to saying I would do it, or at least making it easy for her to ask me if
I would.

She had to stop talking when the nurse came in to put a thermometer in her mouth, and during that silence it was on the tip of my
tongue to say that maybe Charlie and I could at least work out an arrangement for sharing the children between us. But I didn't. It meant
permanence, for one thing—the pieces no longer balanced one on top
of the other in various interchangeable ways. And it suggested marriage—
if I were to make a home for them, the least I could do would be to
provide them with a mother.

I could marry Ellie, if she would have me, and settle, as the saying
goes, down, settle in, after all my various scrap-iron and teaching and
novelizing periods, settle for, at last, one final period to do me the rest
of my life. But not even for Miriam was I willing or even able to make
such a promise, and I suspect that may be why she didn't ask me to in so
many words, not wanting to give it the terrible sanctity of what would
have amounted to a deathbed request. So, heartlessly, I changed the
subject back to my trip again, and we finished our martinis over that.

When it came time to go home and pack, she said, "For two cents
I'd get the hell out of here and go with you," and for a wild moment I
think we both considered this almost seriously. Why shouldn't she
simply get the hell out of that bed and come with me? For all we knew,
maybe she was no more fatally sick than I was—diagnoses had gone haywire before—or even if she was that sick, why shouldn't she die on the way

to Florida instead of here, if that's what she wanted? The doctors had no right to stop her—she was paying them, after all; they weren't paying her. But then the moment passed, and she reached her arms out toward me.

I leaned down, and she put her hands on my shoulders and kissed me once on each cheek. She said, "*Ciao*, Antonio."

The last glimpse I had of her was reaching over to the bedside table to stub out her cigarette and waving at me with her other hand. It was a rather absent-minded, informal wave, as I think back on it, because she was looking not at me but at the ashtray. And I remember the florist's bright ribbon in her hair.

All this was what lay behind me, and Bebb was of course what lay ahead of me when I got on the train a few hours later, but I thought of neither very much once we pulled out of the old Penn Station and were safely on our way. It is what I like about trains. You are neither here nor there, and you are neither this nor that. You are in between. I mean in between not just in a geographical sense, of course, but like an actor waiting in the wings for his cue to re-enter, or a disembodied spirit drifting between incarnations like an unconfirmed rumor. Who you were last and who you are going to be next hardly matter. The drifting is all. And if you are in a roomette such as mine was, once you have shown the conductor your ticket and told the porter when you want to be woken up in the morning, you can maintain this state of things almost indefinitely. Except for the train people, who don't care, there is no one in the world who knows where you are. You can slide the door shut or zip up the curtain, and there is no one in the world who is likely to bother you.

So I sat there in a kind of trance with my legs stretched out and my feet up on the closed lid of the john, looking through the window at that sad and to me oddly moving wilderness that you pass through when you first come out of the tunnel into Jersey. I felt like Dante being ferried across into limbo with the spirits of the doomed fluttering about him *come d'autunno si levan le foglie*, as he says—those autumn leaves again. And that tundra, those scrubby, colorless flatlands stretching away under the November sky. Those drab and dreamlike cities off in the distance— Jersey City, Hoboken, Secaucus? I know them only by name and have seen them only through the windows of year after year of trains. I do not know one from the other or even that they stand where I think they do. Maybe they are on the other side of some other river. The gray sky with here and there some industrial Stonehenge black as soot against it. Once in a while a tower shooting up jets of fire. One of the few memories I have of my father is of his telling me once that during the Depression the poor people came and lived out there somewhere in shelters made of tin cans and old piano crates, and I thought of them there trying to keep warm on a raw and lonesome afternoon like this. I wondered idly if my father had actually seen them himself through just such a hastening window as mine.

And then as nearly as is ever possible this side of dreamless sleep, I stopped thinking about anything, and the Hindu monkey gave up his pointless swinging and just hung there limp by the tail. Schenectady, Schenectady, Schenectady, went the wheels on the tracks just as Reginald Gardiner used to say they did, and I watched the dusk gather over Newark, was it? or Elizabeth, Rahway, Metuchen, those places that for all I knew existed only in my mind and barely there, so vacant and remote my mind had become, like the landscape we were passing.

When, just as darkness was falling, the buzzer went off over my head, I not only could not guess what it was, I could not for the moment even guess what I was—a man, a disembodied spirit, a pane of dusty glass. I am just under six feet two in my stocking feet with long, cross-country legs, and it took me a moment or two to unfold myself from where I had one knee wedged up underneath the window sill and the other foot braced against the collapsible sink. When I slid open the door, what I found standing there in the otherwise empty corridor was a girl. As nearly as I could tell at first glance, she was naked.

She was not entirely naked, as it turned out. She was wearing a bathing suit of sorts and a pair of those Japanese sandals with a peg that comes up between your toes. She can't have been more than nineteen or twenty but very poised in a sort of semi-professional way. I could imagine her as a Rockette or doing summer stock in some Berkshire resort. Except for a little too much eye make-up for my taste, she was very pretty, with a good tan and what I took to be genuine sun-streaks in her hair. She handed me a leaflet and explained that the train was some sort of tourist special with TV in the club car, a movie for the kiddies, bingo, and fashion models. She was also giving out reservations for supper. There was a choice of two sittings, she told me, and I chose the later one.

Noticing that she had only a few reservation checks left in her hand, I concluded that she must be nearing the end of her run and asked her if this was so. I must have hit what was uppermost in her own mind because she gave me the prettiest and most unprofessional smile in the world—she was a Rockette no longer but coming barefoot off a tennis court in cut-down blue jeans with her shirttail out—and "Thank God, yes," she said. "What I need now is a drink."

The what-if's of history. Though it is a game that is usually played in retrospect, there are occasions when you find yourself playing it on the spot, as, indeed, I did there in that empty corridor. There I was, no longer in the first blush, certainly, but in pretty good shape, all considered—I made it a habit to get laps in around the reservoir at least once a week, and I've always been careful about my diet. And there on that grim November afternoon *she* was, that summer's day of a girl, that Persephone, too old to be my daughter and too young to be my wife, clad only in those two little garlands of lilac and rose and the Japanese sandals with the peg between the toes, saying what she needed most now was a drink. What if I asked her to have one in my roomette with me? Not knowing what I might find in Armadillo, I had packed a fifth of Dewar's in my bag. I could ring for glasses and ice, or we could use paper cups like a picnic in the park. Manet's *Le Déjeuner sur l'Herbe* flashed into my mind—those two *Deuxième Empire* dandies in their frock coats and that marvelous woman looking over her bare shoulder with nothing on but a dim smile.

What if she accepted my invitation? What if it was what she had been waiting for since the beginning? I remember that I got as far as the words "What if" themselves, but how I was planning to finish the sentence I am no longer sure. "What if I asked you to have one with me?" maybe, but maybe just "What if they ask to see your birth certificate?"— something foolish and avuncular like that. Probably I was not sure even at the time what I was going to say, and now I will never know, because a porter appeared in the corridor then with an armful of bed linen and pillows, and thinking, I suppose, that the girl was in a hurry to get through with her duties, he flattened himself out against the wall to give her room to pass. I see him there like a bank teller in a movie stick-up with his hands and cheek pressed tight to the wall. It was a gallantry too strenuous to ignore, and giving me the more professional of her two smiles, the girl squeezed by him, chastely keeping her back to his as she did so, and disappeared through one of those hissing pneumatic doors. What if? What if? Who knows.

I had not thought before this of having a drink at all, but back in the roomette again, I decided I needed one. I had it in one of the paper cups, neat, and it not only tasted of the paper but in some ways, I think, was the loneliest drink of my life. It was dark outside by now, and I watched the lights go by, wondering whether we were in New Jersey still or had crossed into Pennsylvania. I couldn't remember stopping at Trenton, but maybe the tourist specials didn't stop there or I had been too caught up in my reveries to notice. I had not one drink but three before I was done, and what made them loneliest was the thought that except for my ineptitude —or was it fate?—the girl might have been there with me. If the girl had never buzzed at my door, I would have been sitting there with nobody— zero. As it was, I was sitting there with minus one.

I have never been a more than ordinarily sensual man. As a boy away at school I was brought up in the cold-shower and laps-before- breakfast tradition, and growing up with a twin sister took some of the heat off too. I knew what girls *looked* like anyway, and Miriam was never bashful about telling me what it felt like to be one. Later, as a bachelor and virtual celibate, the secret of my success was the obvious one. I kept busy. Girls didn't need sex so much when they had the period, Miriam told me when we were young, and I discovered that this biological mercy held true also for me. The teaching period, the novel period, the scrap- iron period—as long as they were upon me, I was comparatively safe. And, like anything else, of course, continence tends to become a habit.

On the other hand, in the same place probably as where I came across the Hindu idea of the mind of man as a monkey in the trees, I came across a discussion of chastity among holy men. For year after year, I learned, and from incarnation to incarnation, they resist so successfully all the temptations of the flesh to come their way that eventually they reach the point where even the subtlest and most irresistible has almost no power to attract them. In fact, by this time there is almost no element of self left in them to attract. But even among holy men, apparently, *almost* is a key word. As long as they are on their guard, they are safe. As long as they see the shimmering young ranee or fragrant-limbed houri coming from far enough away to give them time to prepare for the encounter, they have nothing to fear. But take them by surprise, let the temptress leap out unexpectedly from behind a piece of temple statuary, and in case after case the game is lost. All the vast quantities of psychic energy that they have accumulated at such enormous cost through life after life of total abstinence are released in an instant to be squandered in one great orgy that may go on for centuries. It is a tale with both its comic and its tragic dimensions.

In my case, too, it was the unexpectedness of the thing that was largely responsible for what happened—being jolted out of my twilight musings by that deafening buzzer and then opening the sliding door to find the girl there in that reverberation of a bathing suit. Add to that the three papery scotches and the loneliness of them. Add to that also the fact, I am told, that one reason truck drivers are reputedly so lascivious is that the constant vibration of the engine works darkly on their prostates as, for all I know, my seat over a wheel of the tourist special was working darkly on mine. Add to that the character of the roomette itself. What had been a hermit's cell, a corner away from time and a window on the world, became suddenly an adolescent's dream. The intense privacy of it—the door could be locked, and no one had any reason to break in on me anyway. The anonymity of it, the almost physical sense of all the others who had sat there with similar stirrings before me. Even the architectural features of it: the mirror on the inside of the door, which turned my legs and thighs into those of a complaisant stranger or, with no more stretch of the imagination than I was then capable of, into Persephone's tanned legs. The collapsible sink, the neat little stack of Pullman towels . . .

I did nothing, of course. I just sat there quietly enough with the scotch in my hand and looked out the window, I suppose, although it was too dark to see much. But in my head I peopled that little room with lurid what-if's from as far back as my childhood. And Persephone! How we dallied with each other there as the train sped southward—the ingenuity, the indefatigability, that little handful of rose and lilac hanging like a bride's bouquet from the electric fan above the door. The ignominy of it, I thought—those adolescent fantasies at my stage of the game. And the sadness of it too, the unutterable sadness of all that aching life caught on a train between periods with no place to go.

I went to bed early after a sandwich in the club car for supper, but sleep gave me little respite. I kept waking up with station lights in my face or the clank and jostle of cars being changed, the shock of coming to a standstill after the cradling jounce of the rails. And in between times I dreamed.

The girl in the bathing suit was in the hospital and I wanted to see her desperately but had a hard time persuading the doctors to let me in. When they finally consented, I found her lying in bed with nothing but a blank where her face should have been. She reached out one hand toward me, but when I took it in mine, it turned out to be not a hand but a fish-hook.

In another dream I was riding in the train with my father, who, it seemed, had never actually died at all. It had been just some complicated misunderstanding that I wasn't able to understand fully. He kept pointing through the window and whispering to me to keep watching because we were about to pass the house where I had been born. But I could see no houses—just the barren Jersey flats with the Pulaski Skyway arching across it in the distance.

But the dream that I remember most vividly and that for obvious reasons disturbed me most took place on a stretch of tropical beach which I recognized somehow as Armadillo. Chris and Tony, my two young nephews, were there. They had very grave expressions on their faces and were sitting in straight-backed chairs with their backs to the sea. They were dressed in dark suits, and I realized they must have come down for their mother's funeral. Charlie, their father, lay asleep at their feet with his face buried in his arms. I was standing in front of them dressed also for a funeral, and their gaze was fixed steadily upon me. Little by little I was undressing. First I took off my tie and jacket, then my shirt, my socks and shoes and trousers, so that finally I had nothing on but my undershorts. There was a cool breeze blowing in off the water, but the sand beneath my bare feet felt warm.

After a while the boys stood up woodenly as though to sing a hymn or at the entrance of the priest, and at that point I dropped my undershorts and stood there completely naked with their solemn dark eyes watching me. Then I lay belly down in the warm sand and started trying to work myself slowly into it like a worm with the early bird hot on its tail. Harder and faster I pushed until suddenly I felt something unspeakable happening to me and cried out to them, "See me! See me!" as though my life depended on it, or perhaps what I cried out was "Semen! Semen!" I do not know which it was, and that's quite all right by me. It was the first dream of its kind that I had had for years, and it woke me up with the sound of that forlorn cry still echoing in my ears.

As I turned on the ghostly blue night-light to look at my watch and so on, I felt sure that I would fit right into things at Armadillo.

4

WHEN I WOKE UP the next morning, it was summer. Just by the way the sunshine flashed off the hoods and roofs of cars you would have known it. The temperature in the train was about the same as when we left New York, but you could feel the difference anyway—something soft in the air, some sense of promise that had not been there before. I could hear Southern voices in the corridor, a man and a woman talking together. They must have gotten on during the night when I was asleep. The unhurried phrases trailing off at the end, the even-toned, bedspread-smoothing, grocery-listing rumble and rise of their courtly morning voices outside my closed door—there is no more reassuring sound in the world as far as I know, and if ever somebody has to tell me that I have only a few more weeks to live or the whole world is about to come to an end, I hope it is a Southerner who does it. It was just the right sound to wake up to after my *Walpurgisnacht*. And breakfast in the dining car was also just right.

The sun almost blinded me, flashing off the white tablecloth and swinging back and forth like a little wafer of fire in the water pitcher, and the parts of me that I could feel it warm on were the parts that I could see reflected in the window as we raced through Georgia—my mouth and chin, the knuckles of one hand and part of my sleeve. Throwing weight-watching to the winds, I ordered both grits and cornbread with my ham and eggs, and the waiter who brought it was the king of an African tribe with a voice like Paul Robeson's in *Othello*. I felt decadent and Mediterranean in his presence and thought how if life were based more on the natural order of things, I would be keeping him cool with a fan made of chicken feathers. I also thought how Ellie would have approved of that feeling.

When we stopped at Jacksonville, I got out on the platform to stretch my legs, and although I had already seen that it was summer through the window, the shock of actually feeling it for myself quite overwhelmed me. I was a child getting out of his last class on the last day of school. I was old Dr. Manette released after all those years from the Bastille. I was the jolly green giant. There was a man selling oranges in net bags, dozens of them heaped up on a luggage cart, and they were so orange, they were so Southern and summery and round, that I couldn't resist buying some although of course I had no possible use for them where I was going. There must have been a good dozen and a half of them in the net bag. I could give them to Bebb as a kind of hostess present, I thought, but, considering the purpose of my visit, that seemed deceitful and Judas-like. Beware of

Wops bearing gifts, my sister Miriam might have said.

It is curious how many changes of heart I was able to have about Bebb when you think that I had seen the man only once and had no reason to believe that he had changed in any way himself during the short time since. But when I got back to my roomette again with the bag of oranges, I found myself feeling almost sorry for him. Here I was, a smart-aleck from the North with a college education and a small private income, and not much to show for either of them. And there he was—a crook certainly, a degenerate apparently, but God only knew with what provocation. The way he had put sugar in his chocolate milk as though to make up for a grim and candyless childhood. That black raincoat that couldn't possibly have been enough to keep him warm. I pictured him growing up in one of the drab towns that now and then the railroad tracks cut through —a filling station, a movie theater, the rows of houses facing the tracks with their jigsaw porches and sagging steps. The wonder of it seemed suddenly not that he had sunk so low but that he had come so far—flying to New York and heaven only knew where-all else to keep tabs on his far-flung if devious interests, the ads that carried his name all over the nation. And when you came right down to it, was there any real harm in what he was doing, or was the disapproval of people like Ellie and me mainly just aesthetic? If he played on the weakness of men, it was at least only on their weakness for . . . what? For the prestige that went with diplomas and ecclesiastical titles; for the easy success and quick approval that are among men's more innocent dreams; in the long run maybe only on their weakness, however slapstick and obscure, for God. Why not? It was hard, suddenly, to blame him.

And yet with Miriam on my mind and my own helplessness to be of any real use to her, it was still not hard for me to blame him for what he was not and for what I was therefore not either. For the first time I found myself wondering why I had answered his crazy ad to begin with. Was it, as I had thought, just to find fuel for my new journalistic period? Or had I answered it more in the way that I lit an occasional candle to Saint Anthony, hoping against all reason that in a world where there was obviously no magic any more, the flickering little wick in its ruby glass cup might still manage to cast a holy spell if only on myself?

In any case, the problem of what to do with the oranges solved itself when we finally pulled into West Palm Beach that afternoon. There, standing prettily on one of the little metal stairs they let down from the cars and leaning out from it with one hand grasping the pull-rail and the other shading her eyes like an old print of a sailor in the rigging, was the bathing-suit girl. She was fully dressed at this point in a powder-blue railroad uniform. My first reaction, I admit, was to run and hide as though I had seduced her in reality instead of just in my florid imaginings, but then I thought better of it. I went up and handed her my bag of oranges, which she took before she realized, I think, what it was or that I was

giving it to her to keep. "These are for you," I said. "They're full of vitamin D, the sunshine vitamin," and then I stepped away quickly before
she had a chance to give them back or protest.

I do not think that she recognized me or that such impulsive gestures
from male passengers were anything new to her, but I treasure the look
that passed between us as the train started to pull out. It was the kind
of look that is possible maybe only for people who feel sure they will never
set eyes on each other again, the kind of look that is sometimes exchanged
between the windows of two trains as they speed in the same direction
along parallel tracks and come for a moment abreast of each other. I like
to think that there may have been even a touch of *what if* in her glance
as well as in mine. She didn't smile or say thank you as the train started
slowly carrying her off with my oranges in her arms, but that may well be
just because she didn't need to. Persephone.

They gave me a choice of cars at the Hertz garage, and the one I
chose was a two-door convertible the color of frozen custard with whitewall tires and upholstery as red as the inside of a mouth. It seemed to fit
my mood, which was a combination of sheer lightheartedness at the
weather and the sense of vacation together with a rather desperate hilarity
as I realized that I no longer had any clear idea what I was on my way to
Armadillo to accomplish or how I would go about accomplishing it once I
got there. But at least I enjoyed driving along the Sunshine State Parkway
with the top down and my hair stinging my forehead in the warm wind.
Once I left the parkway, there was a long stretch of back roads with some
complicated turns, but I had no trouble finding my way and arrived at
Armadillo in something less than an hour after setting off from West
Palm.

O Armadillo, Armadillo . . . thou that killest the prophets and
stonest them that are sent unto thee. . . . What I see in my mind most
clearly as I try to remember is a certain stretch of sidewalk. The main
shopping street comes to an end where some railroad tracks cut across it,
but beyond the tracks the sidewalk continues a quarter of a mile or more
along one side of a pot-holed macadam road that leads south toward Fort
Lauderdale. It is a wide sidewalk made of marble slabs with crab-grass
growing up between them and spider-webbing all over the place. There
are concrete benches every once in a while, the concrete stained with
bird-droppings and the weathered green slats flaked and splintery and in
some cases missing altogether. At regular intervals there are streetlamps,
ornamental streetlamps with fluted shafts once painted the same green as
the benches but with just an occasional flake or two still sticking on them
to suggest the original color. Curlicued wrought-iron brackets jut out
from the tops of the shafts to hold the light globes, but the globes are not
there any more or were perhaps never installed to begin with, just in each
case a few stiff black wires hanging down.

The sidewalk eventually peters out somewhere in the scrubby grass.

It doesn't go anywhere. It doesn't serve any purpose and never did because the town it was originally laid down to serve never got out that far. During the land boom in the twenties, apparently, there were dreams for Armadillo that never materialized, and the building lots that were to have been for millionaire villas and luxury hotels are nothing much now but palmettos and creepers and the kind of junk people throw out of car windows. When I think of Armadillo, it is of this sidewalk I think first—a native American ruin and not entirely without a kind of appeal as it rambles on into the scrub, going nowhere.

Not knowing where to find Bebb, of course, and not even sure that I wanted to find him just yet, I cruised around for a while in my fancy car, trying to get the feel of the place. If it was late June nearer the coast, it was mid-July or August here—not so much that the sun was hotter but that as far as I could see there was no place to escape from it. The main street, where the shops were, was all one- and two-story buildings with false fronts sticking up like garage attendants' pompadours and only an occasional tin awning's worth of skimpy shade. Everything seemed made out of stucco or cinderblock and bleached to about the same shade of oystery white, which caught the sun and reflected it back so dazzlingly from all directions that the only way to escape it was to wait for night or die. I drove around town with my eyes squinted half shut to keep out the hellish glare until finally the perspiration started to make them water and smart so that when I parked in front of a drugstore and went in to buy a pair of dark glasses, the clerk looked at me queerly, as though he thought I was weeping.

The Mother Church I happened on quite by accident. A few miles out of town along the same road that the sidewalk bordered, there was a little complex of buildings dominated by a souvenir shop, a long shed-like affair that displayed coconut husks carved and painted to look like cannibals' faces, rugs with peacocks and sunsets and Red Indians on them, grass skirts, baskets of all kinds, and many novelty items like shrunken heads hung up by their long hair and Florida scenes composed entirely of real seashells. There was also a barber shop with a tankful of miniature turtles in the window—one of them was trying to clamber up the glass with his hind feet braced on a companion's shell, but he fell over backward as I watched him. There was also a 1930's modern building with curved walls painted swimming-pool blue and lots of glass and brick instead of windows. Projecting far enough out from the side of the building to be visible from in front there was an almost life-sized cross made of frosted glass that looked as though it could be lit up from inside. On the vertical member, printed vertically, was the word HOLY and on the crosspiece, printed horizontally and sharing the same o, was the word LOVE with a small red heart preceding the L to make the design symmetrical. It looked not unlike the trademark stamped on Bayer aspirin tablets.

Napoleon gazing on the Sphinx could not have had a keener sense of history than I did sitting there in red-leatherette luxury with the steering wheel hot in my hand and peering up at Bebb's cross through my new dark glasses. What had brought me to this place anyway? There was my discovering Bebb's ad at a peculiarly receptive moment in my life, of course, and then step by step our meeting in the Lexington Avenue lunchroom, Ellie's digging up the *Journal-American* piece, even Tom's getting the fish-hook in his eyelid and the fact that the vet's apartment was not far from Manhattan House—a perfectly plausible train of subtly interlocking circumstances whose consequence had been to land me here between the souvenir store and the fire-insurance building with the Florida sun in my eyes. A simple or not so simple matter of cause and effect—inevitable, impersonal, and automatic. Karma, as those bedeviled holy men would call it. And yet, as Napoleon must surely have felt it there in the sands of Egypt, in addition to the sense of history there was a sense of destiny— a feeling that, no matter what the circumstances, no matter if Tom had not tangled with the fish-hook, or even if I had not seen Bebb's ad, I was bound to end up here anyway. Mysterious powers. The silvery-faced soda-jerk whom Bebb had identified as a visitor from outer space. It was another of my operatic moments. I approached the door to the church like Don Alvaro in *La Forza del Destino*. And it was unlocked.

Inside, the Mother Church seemed to consist of a single low-ceilinged room, empty and smelling dimly of floor wax. About forty folding chairs set up in tidy rows filled it just about to capacity. The sunshine came bright through the glass brick, and thus there was plenty of light in the place even though there was no way to see either in or out. The pink color of the walls reminded me of denture gums. At the far side, opposite the entrance, there was an altar table and lectern. A box marked LOVE OFFER-INGS stood near the door, and above it hung a rug like the ones for sale outside except that instead of a Red Indian or a sunset it bore a picture of Jesus Christ. It was a three-quarters view, head and shoulders, that showed him with a very high forehead and long hair that shone with much brushing and had a wave in it. He looked a little like Charlton Heston and was wearing a simple homespun garment with what I believe is called a *bateau* neckline. There was a faint glow around his head, and his gaze was directed off to the right and a little above the horizontal toward a spot which there in Bebb's church happened to be occupied by a hot-air register.

I sat down in one of the folding chairs in the front row, and because my eyes still smarted from all the open-car wind and sun, I closed them. It was extremely quiet in there, the kind of quiet you are apt to find in empty theaters or restaurants or even empty classrooms, as I remember them from my teaching days, places empty which you usually think of as full, places where the very absence of people becomes a kind of lulling presence. Quite without premeditation—the fact that it was a church, after all, and that my eyes were closed must have tripped some forgotten thermostat—I found myself saying a Hail Mary. "Pray for us now and at the hour of our death," I whispered. And pray for Miriam, I added, at the hour of hers, and I thought of her waving that off-hand wave at me while she was stubbing out her cigarette, and wondered if it was possible that I might never see her again. I had a feeling that it was supposed to be a heresy to pray for the dead, but I decided that this might just be a Protestant idea and prayed for my father and mother anyway. I remembered my father on the train in my dream and how it turned out that he hadn't died at all but that it had just been a complicated misunderstanding. Maybe death itself, I thought . . . just a complicated misunderstanding. I even said a prayer for Tom, which I was almost sure was heretical—Tom penned up in one of those little cages at the vet's. I wondered if his eyelid was sore.

Then I felt a hand on my shoulder and heard a voice say, "Blessed are those who mourn, for they shall be comforted." I thought for an instant that it must be Bebb himself, but as soon as I opened my eyes I saw that it was not. It was a man about Bebb's age, in his fifties somewhere, wearing shorts and a sport shirt. He had the most dazzling set of false teeth I had ever seen and was wearing a pair of glasses that were rimless except across the tops, where the rims were heavy and straight and gave him a very intense and earnest look. He said, "I am Laverne Brown, the assistant pastor. The many friends that the Lord has blessed me with all call me Brownie."

Standing up, I told him my name, and we shook hands.

"Your eyes are red," he said.

"It's this Florida sunshine of yours," I explained, "and I got sweat in them from my eyebrows when I was squinting."

"We were given eyebrows to keep the sweat out, not to put it in," he said. "Never be ashamed of honest tears, dear." And then he smiled.

Two things—first his smile, and then his calling me dear.

Brownie's smile—that low-hung rack of glittering teeth, that fiercely sincere set of horn-rimmed eyebrows, those pale eyes staring out at you. The smile of a man at a joke he has not quite heard the punch-line of? The smile of a man caught cheating in a pay toilet? The smile of a little man who has just been kicked in the crotch by a big man? It was all of these and none of them. The smile was Brownie and as impossible to do justice to in a few words as Brownie himself was. Yet the smile was also the glasses and the teeth, and if Brownie was in the habit of laying them aside when he went to bed at night and if he then had occasion to smile afterwards, I can almost see the teeth trying to clamber out of the water glass like the miniature turtle in the barber shop and I can almost hear the spectacles pulling themselves across the table by their ear-pieces— the way they say French wines corked up in bottles sparkle each year when spring returns to the vineyard of their origin.

And he called me dear—not just then, during the first few seconds of our acquaintance, but a great many times afterward as well. "Never be ashamed of honest tears, dear," he said, and I thought that first time that I had simply heard him wrong or that "dear" was part of "tears" somehow, possibly a repetition of it for effect. The next few times I thought various other things—that he was talking to somebody else perhaps or that it was not a word at all but just a sound, a verbal *tic douleureux* like one that a professor of mine at college had who would throw in the sound "ayeeee," drawn out at considerable length, about every fourth sentence until it got so we hardly noticed it any more. In any event, whatever explanations I arrived at the first dozen times or so, the point of it is that one way or another I got so used to hearing it that by the time I was forced to conclude that it was clearly "dear" he was saying and clearly me he was saying it to, I was so used to it that it seemed quite natural.

I decided against trying to persuade him any further that I had not been weeping. I had been praying, after all, and I suppose that is a kind of tears. I decided also against asking for Bebb or in any other way tipping my hand at this point. I was interested in different churches and religions from a sociological point of view, I told him, and with some time on my hands here in Armadillo, I thought it would be interesting to find out what was going on around here in that line.

He said, "Well you have certainly come to the right place. There is a whole lot going on around Armadillo in the area of your special interest. Right here at Holy Love, to give you an example. We are a church, as anyone can plainly see, but it might interest you to know that we are also a fully accredited educational institution."

"It interests me very much," I said. "Tell me about it."

"You take Holy Scripture," Brownie said. "The Bible is a frequently misunderstood book. I will give you a simple illustration." His accent was Southern, I decided, but with a lot of the nap worn off. His shorts and the plain, sky-blue sport shirt that he wore hanging outside them had nothing sporty about them. It was clear that he wore them purely for comfort the way a man might go around the house in his underwear. He had a laundered look, scrawny-necked, with arms that were as surprisingly hairy as his bare legs were surprisingly hairless. I caught a whiff of aftershave as he crossed in front of me on his way to the lectern. He opened the Bible that lay upon it.

He said, "I will read from the Apostle Paul to give you a simple illustration. The Epistle to the Romans, chapter twelve, verses nineteen to twenty-one inclusive. 'Dearly beloved, avenge not yourselves, but rather give place unto wrath, because it is written, "Vengeance is mine. I will repay, saith the Lord." ' "

The words came out in a kind of hushabye sing-song that seemed oddly at variance with what I thought was the Apostle's rather forceful tone, and when he reached "saith the Lord," Brownie paused and smiled as though the Lord had just promised a major tax cut. He held up one

hand with what looked like several fraternity rings on the fingers and a
gold spring-band around his hairy wrist.

"But this is the part I want you to pay special attention to. Verses
twenty and twenty-one. 'Therefore if thine enemy hungers, feed him; if he
thirsts, give him drink; for in so doing thou shalt heap coals of fire on his
head.' 'Thou shalt heap coals of fire on his head,'" he repeated. "Dear,
would you be interested in knowing what the Apostle means about heap-
ing coals of fire on your enemy's head?"

I said, "It sounds like one-upmanship to me. Your enemy craps on
you, and in return you do all sorts of nice things for him. That makes him
feel like a heel." I came within an inch of saying "like a shit" but substituted heel at the last minute. Crap, shit—what was there about Brownie
that made me want to use such language? But I do not think he heard it,
because all the time I was giving my explanation he was slowly shaking
his head back and forth as though he knew in advance that I would
explain it wrong and didn't particularly want to listen to me do it.

"That is a very common misinterpretation of this Scripture," he said,
"and I'm not surprised to see you fall into it. You say you are interested
in religion, so you might be interested in hearing what the Apostle really
meant. How can a person know what he really meant? By studying the
background and by familiarizing himself with the customs of the times."

Brownie was looking toward me in one direction and the picture of
Jesus was looking toward the hot-air register in the other direction, but
Brownie turned at this juncture and pointed at the picture. "Treating
your enemy nice to make him feel bad. Does that sound like the kind of
thing any apostle of *his* would say? I will tell you a little-known fact about
the Holy Land back in Saint Paul's time. When winter came and it got
cold, not everybody had his own fire. Fuel was sometimes scarce, for one
thing, but that wasn't the only problem, because even if you had the fuel,
what were you going to light it with? They didn't have matches then,
dear. So the custom was this. The baker was the one who had the fire,
and he got it started real early in the morning so as to get his ovens hot
for baking. Then when folks wanted to start their own fires, all they had
to do was go down to the baker's. They would take with them an inex-
pensive pottery vessel, and for a small consideration the baker would let
them have several of his burning coals. They would place these coals in
their vessels to take them home, and maybe by now you can guess how
they carried them. Yes. They carried them just the way some of our black
sisters still carry their washbaskets. On their heads. You can well imagine
what a good feeling it was—the warmth from the baker's hot coals
traveling down their neck and shoulders on a frosty morning. And when
they got home, they used them to start a fire of their own with, as easy
as rolling off a log. That clears up a lot of things, doesn't it?" Brownie
was smiling—those teeth, those glasses—and looking intently at me.

"The Apostle says, 'If thine enemy hungers, feed him; if thine enemy thirsts, give him drink' because that will give your enemy a nice warm feeling, and he will repent and do likewise unto others. He will take the coals of fire you heaped on his head like the baker and start a fire of his own. If you used this as a sermon text, you could title it like the popular song—'I've got my love to keep me warm.' "

"It certainly puts the passage in a new light," I said. I had sat down again when Brownie started speaking, but now that he was finished, I felt it put me at a psychological disadvantage. I started to get up, but he motioned me to stay where I was.

He said, "You've got to know the background and the customs."

"You spoke of running an educational institution in connection with this church," I said. "Am I right in thinking this is part of a course maybe?"

"It is part of two courses," Brownie said. "Exegesis and New Testament Background. It comes up in both."

I said, "Would I be right also in thinking these are correspondence courses, or do you have students actually in residence here in Armadillo?"

"Gospel Faith College," Brownie said in a rather absent-minded way, looking down as he spoke. "Full accreditation from the State Board of Education." He had not answered my question, and at first I thought that it was because he chose not to, but then I saw that he was running his finger down a page of the Bible, evidently looking for something. I don't think he had heard my question.

"Mark, chapter seven reading from verse twenty-four down here to verse thirty. The Syrophenecian woman. This is another case in point, only here the true explanation comes from a knowledge of the original tongue and not from a knowledge of ancient customs. And this time it's not the Apostle Paul. It's Jesus." The way he said Jesus, drawing it out into two distinct syllables, I saw the name G. Zuss in my mind.

Brownie said, "This Syrophenecian woman came to G. Zuss and besought him would he cast forth the devil out of her daughter, she had an unclean spirit in her. . . . This Syrophenecian woman's daughter, she was unclean, dear, and the Syrophenecian woman went and fell at the Master's feet. . . ." He seemed to have been reading ahead of the part he was paraphrasing, but looked back up at me here with his finger marking the place. "Here it is. Listen to what G. Zuss said when the mother finished begging him to heal her girl. He said, 'It is not meet to take the children's bread and cast it to the dogs.' How do you like that?"

"Maybe he had a headache," I said, "or she interrupted him in the middle of something and he felt cross. He was human, after all, whatever else he was."

Brownie said, "He was the Lamb of God, dear. He was the Rose of Sharon," and he spoke the curious old titles in a dreamy way as though they had come drifting into his memory from far away. "He didn't have headaches. And he didn't go around using language like that either.

It sounds pretty bad in English, doesn't it?—referring to all the Syro-phenecian people as dogs. But that's just the translation. In the original tongue the word isn't 'dog' at all. It's more like a pet name for dogs—like pup or pooch. Poochie," he said, "would be closer to the original meaning of G. Zuss."

"Poochie," I said. "That would take a lot of the sting out."

Brownie said, "There wouldn't be any sting then at all. It was just his little joke—using a pet name like that. And this is supported by the fact he went ahead and cast the unclean spirit out of the girl anyway. In John two four, when G. Zuss and his mother are attending the wedding service in Cana and his mother asks him to do something about the wine running out, G. Zuss says to her, 'Woman, what have I to do with thee!' Now you take the word 'woman' that sounds so spiteful and mean in English . . ."

It was obviously not in my interests to antagonize the man, and de-tails like these of the Gospel Faith curriculum might prove very useful to me later on, but something came to my mind that I couldn't resist throwing at him. It must have been the phrase "original tongue" that did it, because I found myself thinking of the one place in the Gospels, as far as I know, where the words of Jesus are given in the language he's supposed to have actually used. Ellie and I joined the Canterbury Choir group one winter and I remembered them from Schütz's *The Seven Last Words of Christ*, which we did—she in the alto section and I a marginal baritone.

"'*Eli, Eli, lama sabachthani?*'" I said, interrupting him. "You can't get more original than that, and it seems to mean he's calling God a sonofabitch for running out on him. Or was it just an old Jewish custom to ask the Deity theological questions when you were being crucified?"

Brownie said, "'My God, my God, why hast thou forsaken me?'" He was not smiling. He had taken off his glasses to wipe them, and without them he looked old and confused in his Youngstown haircut and the over-sized sport shirt that hung down over his shoulders. "No, dear," he said, putting back his glasses. "Those terrible words mean just what they say. They mark the moment when he knew that before the resurrection he was going to have to descend into Hell."

"Maybe he was there already," I said.

We were silent for a few moments. Jesus descending into Hell, I thought. Maybe the reason he was so intent on the hot-air register was that it awakened old memories of that trip—the long downward chute, the belching heat. I remembered dimly from catechism class that the reason he had gone down was to save the souls of the good people who had lived too early to be saved by him through the normal earthly channels. Maybe he had found time to save a few of the bad ones too. I hoped that was so and wondered if Brownie might be engaged in similar theological specula-tions. He had closed the Bible and was standing there with both hands on the cover, staring vacantly at one of the glass-brick windows. Out of nowhere and without looking at me, he said, "You said your name was Antonio Parr, didn't you?"

I said that I had.

"Mr. Bebb's in Texas on the Lord's work. He'll be coming back in a day or two probably. But he left instructions about you before he went."

"Bebb knew I was coming?" I couldn't keep the surprise out of my voice.

Brownie said, "He said if you came while he was gone, to tell you you would be welcome to stay at the Manse."

It is hard to describe the combination of uneasiness and grudging admiration I felt at the thought that Bebb had known I might be coming to Armadillo before I had the faintest idea of coming myself. He had undoubtedly based his assumption on the premise that I was genuinely interested in cashing in on my ordination by starting a diploma mill of my own even if it meant going to Florida to learn how, but though his premise was wrong, the assumption itself had proved right. I was there. Bebb had known something about me that I had not known.

Brownie was smiling at me from the lectern, his eyes pale and watery through his glasses, and I found myself uneasier still at the thought that he too had known something about me that I had not known he knew. From the moment I gave him my name, he knew who I was and what I was ostensibly there for—to learn the ropes and join Bebb's sordid little team. At least part of his smile must have had to do with my story of being interested in different churches and religions from a sociological point of view. But Brownie gave no sign of holding my duplicity against me. Specialist as he was in making the rough places of Scripture smooth, he had probably explained it away already on the basis of my background and customs or the tongue I spoke.

And of course there was my true reason for being in Armadillo—the deeper duplicity that I devoutly believed Brownie could not know nor, heaven help me, Bebb—which was to skin Bebb alive, as I had put it to Ellie that fateful Beef Stroganoff evening. And who could say? Beneath that, perhaps, there was a truer reason still for my being in Armadillo which even I did not know any more than Napoleon can have known what inexorable power had drawn him at last to the sandy lion-paws of the Sphinx. In any case, it was such a tricky game I played that I decided against accepting Bebb's invitation to stay at the Manse, useful as it might have been for my private purposes. I might talk in my sleep. So I lied again and said I had made arrangements to stay at the motel I had noticed on my way into town. I even remembered its name—the Salamander—in case Brownie should ask me, so wily had I become.

But he didn't ask me. He put his arm around my shoulder and walked me to the door, where we made our farewells under the frosted-glass cross. "Lights up," he said and pushed a switch just inside the entrance. It did.

HOLY LOVE with the light shining out from it and the small red heart to make things symmetrical. He turned it off again.

It was late afternoon by now, and the sunlight had gone mellower, more golden, so that I no longer needed my dark glasses. At the souvenir shop a man was gathering in the peacock rugs and shrunken heads for the night. Brownie closed the door of my car for me and then leaned on it with his hairy arms. I was aware of his after-shave again. Those battered eyes under the horn-rimmed eyebrows. Those seraphic choppers.

He said, "Here's what you do. You go on back and get settled at the Salamander Motel. Take your time and wash up, and then when you're ready, you come over to the Manse. Mrs. Bebb will give us supper, and I will show you around myself." We shook hands on it.

Fortunately for my lie to Brownie, there was room for me at the Salamander. I gave them my license number and the address of the apartment Tom and I shared in New York, and then, just as I was about to sign my name on the register, I stopped. Should I or shouldn't I? Was I or wasn't I? I decided then that if I was going to play the game, I might as well play it, and with a ball-point pen that didn't do well over the place where my sweaty hand had hesitated for a moment, I wrote *The Reverend Antonio Parr*. For all I knew, Bebb or Brownie might check it someday. They would have thought it queer if I'd signed myself any other way.

IT HAD NEVER occurred to me that Bebb might be married. Perhaps it was because of some lingering childhood image of the priesthood that had come loose in my subconscious and attached itself to him—the priest as celibate with the Church his only bride and all men his children. Or perhaps it was because the one time I had seen him in the city he had seemed so much on his own, so sure of himself and in charge, that it never crossed my mind he might have a wife who knew all his tricks by heart, somebody he went away from and came back to and maybe even depended on, if only to fold his pocket handkerchief into those four points and keep buttons on his raincoat. I was not prepared even for the idea of a Mrs. Bebb, let alone for its incarnation in Lucille.

Brownie took me in to her. He must have seen me coming, because he was standing on the porch waiting when I pulled up to the curb in my rented convertible. It was one of the older streets in Armadillo, with a few trees big enough to cast some shade, I imagined—the sun was setting as I arrived. Instead of the stucco bungalows and flat-roofed split-levels that I had seen virtually everywhere else, there was a row of good-sized frame houses that must have made it one of the more fashionable parts of town in its day. The Manse itself was a modified Charles Addams with too many windows and a fair amount of scrollwork around the eaves and porch. One corner was rounded off in the suggestion of a turret, and there were dormers and bays in unexpected places. Off to one side but visible from the street was one of those children's gym sets, a rather rusty-looking slide attached to a swing and seesaw. There was also a sandbox with a broken chair in the middle of it, and I found myself wondering whether, having only recently adjusted myself to the fact of Bebb's having a wife, I was going to have to prepare myself now for the possibility of children —roly-poly little replicas of Bebb running around in small black raincoats of their own.

Unfamiliar with the amenities of dining out in Armadillo, I came dressed much as I had been on the train, in a shirt and tie with a seersucker jacket to replace the heavier one I had traveled in. Brownie, on the other hand, had not changed out of his shorts and sport shirt, and the disadvantage was clearly mine. I was the carpetbagger, the fast talker from the North. Brownie was all palm-leaf fans and hot verandas and flies in the honeysuckle. He looked as though he had been working at something— there were two wet stains at his sky-blue armpits, and I thought his glasses were slightly fogged up—but he greeted me cordially, expressing the hope that I had found everything to my liking at the Salamander, and held the screen door for me as we entered the Manse.

As we walked down the dim hall toward what turned out to be Mrs. Bebb's private sitting room at the back of the house, my eye was caught by a doorway standing ajar under the staircase. It was a bathroom, as I had guessed, and glancing in as we passed, I got a glimpse of the toilet. It was the old-fashioned kind with an overhead tank and a pull chain, altogether what I would have expected to find in a house of that vintage, but what I didn't expect to find only because I had forgotten they existed was the toilet seat, which was not form-fitting and white and shaped like the victory wreaths they hang around the necks of racehorses but a little flat ring of varnished brown wood. How it carried me back, that brown toilet seat—carried me back to my childhood and beyond to some Victorian incarnation perhaps—and just as you think of the Capitol by its dome and Saint Patrick's perhaps by its great bronze doors, so it is by that toilet seat that I will always think of the Manse—shiny and brown and out of another world entirely.

Mrs. Bebb's sitting room was at the end of the hall, and Brownie opened the door without knocking. There was the smell of a hot TV set in the air and the unmistakable intonations of a sports commentator. It was a color set, I discovered when I finally located it, and Mrs. Bebb was sitting in a high-backed wicker armchair at an angle that put her back both to it and to me, so that the first part of her I saw was a thin bare arm slanting down straight toward the floor. Just an inch or so above the floor she was holding a tall glass of what looked like Florida orange juice. Speaking louder than usual in order to be heard above the TV—it was a football game, with the color tuned wrong, because the faces of the players looked green and the reds seethed like burning embers—Brownie said, "This is the Reverend Parr. The one I told you about." And then the bare arm rose slowly and retracted, and Lucille Bebb craned around the armchair back to take her first good look at me.

She was wearing dark glasses, and partly because the light in the room was not good—just the remains of a sunset through the window and a single bridge lamp near her chair—her face, like the TV set, looked as if the color had been tuned wrong. The lips I can only describe as liverish, by which I mean not only the maroon color of raw calves' liver but the wet sheen as well. Her complexion, consistent with this butcher-shop image, reminded me of a certain kind of bologna Tom and I were both partial to, which is coarse-grained in texture and somewhere between pink and gray in hue. She had thin, arched eyebrows that showed above her dark glasses, and she had dropped her lower jaw in what, as with newborn babies, could have been either a smile, I thought, or gas. Because of the glasses I could not be sure which of us she was looking at, but it was to Brownie that her first words were addressed. She said, "Brownie, go get the man a Tropicana. And on the way out, fix that pukey color. It's making me sick."

I do not remember in any detail what Lucille and I talked about those first few moments of our acquaintance when Brownie left us alone together to do what he was told, but I remember that most of it was done by me. I have always found it disconcerting to speak to someone who is wearing dark glasses, and make it a point if I am wearing them myself either to take them off or at least to lower them when someone comes up to speak to me. Little as we actually make use of it, we ought to have at least the option of looking each other straight in the eye. But Lucille obviously felt no such compunction, and I remember thinking that if I had brought along the sunglasses that I had purchased in Armadillo that afternoon, I would have been tempted to put them on as a counter-measure. Instead, I rattled on about such matters as my trip down and the weather, and such replies as Lucille made were rather brief as I remember, and always had, no matter how straightforward in content, an air of the arch or cryptic about them by virtue of her habit of dropping that lower jaw.

When Brownie returned with my Tropicana, I discovered to my surprise that although part of it was orange juice as I had surmised, another part of it was gin. Brownie did not bring one for himself and took a seat a little apart from Lucille and me so that he was neither quite in the group nor quite out of it, as though, having brought the two of us together, he was not sure what Bebb would want of him next. He joined in the conversation once in a while, but at nothing like the length he had permitted himself in the church that afternoon, and much of the time, I think, he was watching the football game. Lucille sent him out of the room twice to replenish her Tropicana, but he took several other unexplained trips on his own which made me wonder whether by any chance he was fixing supper.

Lucille seemed rather vague about Bebb when I finally maneuvered the conversation around to him. "Long enough to know better" was her answer when I asked how long they had lived in Armadillo. I asked her if she found that her duties as pastor's wife took up a lot of her time, and she said, "Bebb doesn't need a wife. He's got Brownie." Not wanting to seem suspiciously inquisitive, I told her a little about how Bebb and I had met in New York and how he had generously invited me down to observe his entire operation at first hand.

"He's an operator, that's for sure," she said. "I've lost count how many operations he's pulled off in his time, and once or twice he's got operated on himself, hasn't he, Brownie?"

Brownie smiled somewhat wanly, I thought, looking back at her from the football game. "Spiritual operations," he said. " 'If thy right eye offend thee, pluck it out. For it is profitable for thee that one of thy members should perish and not that thy whole body should be cast into hell.' "

Lucille said, "Brownie, turn that lousy set down. I can't even hear myself think, let alone Scripture."

Going back to the subject of our meeting in the lunchroom, I found myself telling her how interested I had been in Bebb's theory that the soda jerk was a visitor from outer space. It was the first time she showed any real interest in what I was saying.

"A gold or a silver?" she asked.

I said a silver.

"Hear that, Brownie?" she said. "Bebb racked up another silver in New York."

I could not make out whether Brownie's smile was in response to her or to the commercial he was watching, which showed the vapors rising from an acid stomach into the esophagus and causing heartburn.

Lucille said, "He runs into those outer-space people all over the place. They are silvers mostly, but once in a while he finds a gold. The golds are scarce as hens' teeth. He says they are here on this planet to keep an eye on things."

"Has he ever talked to one?" I asked. "Does he have any idea whereabouts in outer space they're from?"

Lucille said, "How should I know?" She took a swallow of her Tropicana, looking at me over the rim of her glass.

"Do you believe they're from outer space yourself?" I asked her.

She took her time about answering. She dropped her lower jaw at me and set her Tropicana down on the straw rug. Her last swallow had left her with a little wet mustache. "Do you know what I believe?" she said finally. "I believe it takes one to know one. Sometimes I believe Bebb is from outer space himself."

Brownie, who had gone out of the room on one of his short trips, returned at this point. Lucille said, "How about it, Brownie? What do you believe?"

Brownie looked understandably puzzled. The sweat stains under his arms had spread, and what with the gin and the fact that the windows in the room were all closed, I felt quite warm myself. Brownie said, "What do I believe about what?"

Lucille said, "Ever stop to think maybe Bebb was from outer space?"

It was a difficult question. I admired Brownie for simply not answering it. He stood there sweating in the doorway with the TV screen reflected in his glasses and his hairy arms hanging straight at his sides. "Supper is ready" was all he said.

We ate in a high-ceilinged dining room which looked out on the street, where, although it was barely dusk, the lights had come on. Across the street a man in a bathing suit and a golf cap was watering his lawn. I could see my car where I had parked it at the curb, and although it had come into my temporary possession only a few hours before, it seemed a link somehow with the whole world I'd left behind me in New York, and I found the sight of it oddly touching and reassuring.

"When did you say your husband was coming home?" I asked Lucille.

She said, "You tell me."

"Probably tomorrow," Brownie said.

"He's got a big Texas rancher on tap down there," Lucille said.

"Oil, dear," Brownie said.

"Anyway," Lucille said, "sure as God made little green apples, he's not going to rush that one."

I decided that I had been right in my guess about Brownie's making supper; at least, there was no sign of anyone else who could have done it, and Lucille hadn't lifted a hand since my arrival except to raise the Tropicanas to her lips. We had corned beef and turnip greens and corn sticks. If Brownie had done the cooking, he also did the waiting on table—brought the plates in and kept our glasses filled with ice water. Lucille sent him out twice for extra butter for the corn sticks.

We had little conversation during the meal. Still wearing her dark glasses, Lucille seemed intent on what she was eating although once or twice I thought I caught her looking at me. Brownie was up and down a good deal. At one point, however, remembering the gym set in the yard, I asked if the Bebbs had any children. Lucille and Brownie both stopped eating, and Brownie raised his napkin to his chin, I remember, and kept it hanging there as though he had forgotten he was holding it.

Lucille said, "We had a little baby once, but it died." Her forkful of turnip greens was poised halfway to her mouth, and her arm looked so thin that I thought I could probably get my thumb and forefinger around it. She said, "It was a long time ago."

Brownie said, "There's Sharon. Don't forget about Sharon."

"Sharon!" Lucille said, and this time it was unquestionably a smile that had disarranged the lower part of her face. "The man said *children*."

Did she mean that Sharon was not a child, or that she was not *her* child, or that, though perhaps both a child and hers, the term *children* seemed somehow misapplied in Sharon's case? It was hard to tell what Lucille meant in general, with those impenetrable glasses and the eyebrows arched above them. For the moment I decided against pursuing the subject further, but Brownie would not let it go.

He said, "Mr. Bebb is like Jesus. He has a very warm spot in his heart for children. He loves having them around. You take a pretty little child, black *or* white, he can get almost anything he wants out of Mr. Bebb anytime."

"Anytime," Lucille said. "Day or night."

Brownie said, "I think it is their innocence and their sense of wonder. He loves taking them around and showing them things. The lions, to give you an example. Only last week he took a pack of them out and showed them the lions."

Lucille said, "Soon there won't be anything left in Florida he hasn't shown them."

Just for a moment I had the insane suspicion that they were working the truth nearer and nearer to the open air until at any moment, with shrieks of laughter, they would pull it out in all its throbbing nakedness. Bebb himself would come crawling out from under the table in his Happy Hooligan hat, and the three of them would dance around me committing indecencies. Or was the truth working its own way to the open air through the very vigor of their effort to conceal it, like the harassed lady asking J. P. Morgan if he wanted cream or lemon in his nose? Or was there any truth at all except that, like Jesus, Bebb had a warm spot in his heart for children?

Then Lucille said, "Brownie, get me some more of that ice water. Those Tropicanas always leave me spitting cotton," and Brownie—no wonder the wet spots under his arms, I thought—got up again to do her bidding.

As soon as she had finished her meal, Lucille got up. She said she was pleased to meet me, and it occurred to me that maybe she really was pleased, what with just Brownie there to keep her company and the color TV acting up. "Now Brownie will show you around if you want," she said, "but don't expect much. Maybe Bebb will be back tomorrow. I wonder if he's seen any silvers in Texas." Then we said goodnight, and I could hear her all the way up the stairs, shiny and brown like the toilet seat.

It interested me how neither of them called Bebb by his first name.

I wondered if Mr. Bebb was what Brownie called him to his face or just the way he referred to him to outsiders. I wondered if there was anyone anywhere who called him Leo.

The College, as it turned out, was in the garage out back. It was the same vintage as the house but, as Brownie explained, had been converted to this use several years back when the work had grown beyond what could be handled in the Manse. There was an uncompleted sign over the entrance—a white board with all the letters of Gospel Faith blocked out in pencil but only the first two painted in with black, so that from any distance at all the sign seemed to read just GO, whether in evangelical exhortation or dire warning who could say?

Inside, it reminded me of a World War II induction center with its air of impermanence and disheveled urgency. There was a large central room with a couple of desks in it and a number of folding chairs stacked against the wall, and then there were several smaller rooms blocked off with partitions that didn't come even close to reaching the high ceiling. One of these was Brownie's office. There was a desk in it with a sign saying *The Rev. Laverne Brown B.D., S.T.M., Th.D., D.D., Dean,* and a mimeograph machine. On a table there were several piles each of the pink and blue order blanks that I remembered receiving with my ordination certificate, one for the pamphlet on ecclesiastical discounts, tax exemptions and military deferments, and the other for a complete prospectus of Gospel Faith courses. Framed on the wall were a number of Brownie's personal credentials—his Bachelor of Divinity, his Master of Sacred Theology, his Doctor of Divinity, and other certificates, licenses, and testimonials whose exact nature I didn't have time to determine, but all of them, as nearly as I could tell, issued under the seal of Gospel Faith College and signed by Bebb.

Bebb's office, which Brownie took me to next, was slightly smaller, and there were no diplomas of any kind in evidence on the walls. Compared with Brownie's, the sign on his desk also had a kind of stark simplicity about it—just *The Rev. Leo Bebb, International President.* There were some photographs on the walls: Bebb shaking hands with an Indian chief in full regalia; Bebb in a white robe standing in front of what I recognized as the altar table in his church with his hand raised in benediction; Bebb with a visored cap sitting at the center of a semicircle of children on what seemed to be a playing field of some kind. There was one which by the look of the clothes and the sepia cast of the print I recognized as considerably older than the others. Bebb was sitting on the front stoop of a house, squinting into the sun. He was wearing knickerbockers and holding in his lap what I took to be a baby, although with the glare of the sun and the fading of the print it was quite faceless. Beside Bebb, with one hand on his shoulder, was a young woman in a long, filmy-looking dress. She had an unmistakable look of the 1920's about her, with a

Mary Pickford mouth and her dark hair shingled, but there was also something soft and timeless in her expression as she gazed down at the white bundle in Bebb's lap. Bebb himself, I noticed, looked remarkably the way he still did—a few pounds lighter, perhaps, but the same firm, round face and tightly hinged mouth. *This baby . . . this woman . . . ,* I could almost hear him say. *All things are lawful for me.*

"Lucille?" I asked Brownie, indicating the young woman in the filmy dress. Brownie nodded. "The years have taken their toll," he said. And thus it must also have been the baby that had died, I assumed. It could almost have been dead when the picture was taken—so small and white and faceless in Bebb's lap. Perhaps it was all the hot sun that day that had killed it.

In a room adjoining Bebb's office there were several tall filing cabinets, and Brownie showed them to me with particular pride. Every ordination that had ever been issued, every degree that had ever been conferred, every course that had ever been taken, it was all on file here, he explained, complete with names and dates and whatever other information seemed useful. Brownie pulled open one of the drawers and removed a manila folder apparently at random. It belonged to somebody named Arthur Krebs, and inside there was a single sheet of paper. It read: "KREBS, Arthur (white). Ordained to Gospel Ministry June 1, 1958. San Quentin. 15 years. Love off. $5.00. N.D."

"San Quentin Prison?" I asked.

Brownie said, "Dear, the Spirit bloweth where it listeth. When a man is behind bars, he has time for reflection. Many things that seemed important to him on the outside do not seem so any more, and vice versa. We do a lot of business with the prisons. Remember the good thief."

"Fifteen years is what he got sent up for, and he coughed up five bucks for the Mother Church, but what about N.D.?" I asked. All the other information was typewritten but N.D. had been added in pencil.

Brownie said, "It is a code that Mr. Bebb uses, and he wrote it in there himself, as you can see. I don't know what all his symbols mean, and I am not at liberty to divulge all I do know, but in this case I don't see any harm can come of it. N.D. stands for No Dice. It means that when Mr. Bebb took the name of Arthur Krebs to the Lord in prayer as he does for everybody he ordains, he received negative vibrations concerning Krebs' future in the Gospel ministry."

"But he ordained him anyway," I said.

Brownie said, "Mr. Bebb ordains everybody who applies as long as they are of the male sex and over eighteen years of age. He may have negative vibrations about a certain individual himself, but he knows that the Lord moves in mysterious ways, dear, and that judgment is his. Mr. Bebb says there is a priest in every man. All you have to do is lay your hands on it, and the Lord will do the rest."

As Brownie replaced Arthur Krebs in the file, it occurred to me that in one of those drawers somewhere there must be a folder on me. Presumably Bebb had taken my name to the Lord in prayer too, and I wondered what that involved. I imagined him taking something like the baby in his arms, something faceless and white, and lifting it up into the hot glare of the sun. Or something like Tom the way he was when I carried him back limp and unconscious from the vet's. And after that, what vibrations had Bebb felt and what symbol had he written next to my name? Would Brownie be able to translate it for me, and would he if he could? It would have been easy enough to ask him, but I didn't, finally—not that I lacked interest so much as that I lacked courage.

Brownie said, "When Mr. Bebb was away those years, I kept these files up single-handed, and I can tell you it was no easy task."

I said, "Where did he go? Outer space?"

Brownie had walked ahead of me into the last of the partitioned rooms, which was presumably the College library. Bookshelves lined three walls, and there was a small hand press and a tray of type on a table against the other. Stretching out one arm toward the books as though about to continue his guided tour, Brownie seemed not to have heard my question, so I repeated it. "Those years he was away," I said. "What was he up to?"

Brownie kept on pointing toward the books, but at the sound of my voice he turned and looked at me over his sloping shoulder with a smile in some way unlike his usual one, as if it was the smile itself he was smiling at. He said, "The Lord's work, dear," and then went on to ask me if I would like to pick out a book to take back to the Salamander with me. The one that caught my eye caught it because among all the gaudy paperbacks and flashy jackets and compelling titles that seemed to be vying for my attention, it was the only one that looked reserved and scholarly and as if it couldn't have cared less whether I gave it my attention or not. It was an Oxford University Press book entitled *The Apocryphal New Testament* and edited by someone named Montague Rhodes James. "A trustworthy collection of rare writings," the jacket flap announced in moderate tones.

Running my eye down the table of contents, I was struck by at least the rarity of it—Fragments of Early Gospels, Lost Heretical Books, a Coptic Passion Narrative entitled "The Book of the Cock," a miracle story from the Gospel of Thomas entitled "The Children in the Oven," but what made me decide to take it back and read myself to sleep with it at the Salamander Motel that night was less these baroque and provocative titles than a sober biographical note about Montague Rhodes James himself which was also quoted on the jacket from *The Times Literary Supplement*. A competent scholar, an exceptionally learned student, an eminent medievalist, Dr. James was, *The Times* maintained, "pre-eminently fitted to handle this vast and chaotic mass of material." If this was indeed true of him, I thought, then it was Dr. James whom I wanted to go to bed with that night. It was to his sane and orderly scrutiny that I wanted to submit the chaotic mass of impressions that I had gathered from my first day in Armadillo. Brownie said by all means to take him along, and this compact seemed to signal the end of my tour.

When we stepped outside, the moon was nearly full. There was a sweet fragrance in the air—magnolia, bougainvillea, oleander? Unlike Ellie, I know nothing about trees and shrubs, but just the names themselves sound fragrant. There were some lights on in the Manse and a few of the other houses along the old street, but otherwise no sign of life. Brownie was silent at my side. It was a singularly tranquil moment, as though the spirit of Montague Rhodes James had already begun its work, and thus I was as unprepared for what happened next as I had been for the sound of the buzzer in my roomette.

I heard the sound of a window being raised and then a girl's voice calling through the dark, a cool, silky voice with a certain laziness in it that seemed to belie the vigor of the words. "Hey, peckerhead," she called. "Shut the door out there this time. You left it open last night, and the place was full of batshit." Then the sound of the window again and a glimpse through the wavy panes of a pair of bare shoulders and a white slip.

"That Sharon," Brownie said. He closed the door to the College behind him and then pulled at the handle until he heard a click.

"Bebb's daughter?" I asked.

"Adopted, dear," Brownie said, and then, after a little pause, "I've never seen a bat in Armadillo."

Poor Brownie. I kept thinking about him as I drove back to the motel. Maybe peckerhead was only a misleading translation and in the original tongue meant something like Honey or Gramps. Maybe he didn't always have to fix supper. It could have been the cook's night out or just that corned beef and turnip greens were his particular specialty. Maybe Bebb and Sharon were usually on hand to help him keep Lucille supplied with Tropicanas. In any case, his smile took on a new dimension for me— the smile not so much of a man who hasn't quite gotten the joke but of a man who after years has finally gotten it.

The main street of Armadillo was empty as I drove slowly through with the top down. I had taken off my seersucker jacket and was perfectly comfortable in my shirt sleeves. It was South, it was midsummer night's dream. But the stucco and cinderblock buildings, the tin awnings and deserted sidewalks, glittered white in the moonlight like new-fallen snow. It was a town of ice I was passing through, and I thought of Dante's ninth circle with Brutus and Cassius and Judas Iscariot stuck fast in their frozen lake.

6

MY ROOM at the Salamander Motel reminded me of my roomette on the train. It was considerably larger, of course, but, like the roomette, came fitted out with almost everything a man needs to keep himself going—a bed, a sink, a toilet, an electric fan and, in the case of the Salamander, a TV. It was a room to stand siege in, a fallout shelter, an isolation ward for one. It was a solitary-confinement cell in one of our more progressive prisons, and I thought about Arthur Krebs in his cell at San Quentin and how Brownie had said that being behind bars gave a man time for reflection. I thought of my own overheated reflections on the train coming down and of my dream about the sandy beach. And I thought of Tom in his cramped cage in New York and wondered what imponderables were crossing his mind as he crouched there with his feet and tail tucked under him, outstaring the universe. I took my shower, got into bed, and was on the point of turning to my book when I was distracted by a device on the bedside table that I had not noticed before.

It was a black metal box about the size of a small radio attached to my bed by several stout electric cords. There was a card taped to it which described its nature and purpose. It was called Magic Fingers, and if you dropped a quarter into the slot on top of the box and then lay down on the bed, for the next ten minutes approximately you would receive through the mattress a steady, deep vibration which did wonders for the sore muscles and frayed nerves of travelers like myself. I resolved then and there to put it to the test, but, not being sleepy yet and feeling under some obligation to Dr. James, who, even unread, seemed already to have had a soothing effect on me, I decided to have a look at *The Apocryphal New Testament* first.

I looked first at the miracle of "The Children in the Oven." It told how for unspecified reasons some children ran away from Jesus one day and went and hid themselves in an oven. Jesus chased after them and stumbled on some women who had seen the children go into the house and knew perfectly well where they were hiding but weren't about to give them away. There were nothing but goats in the house, the women said, whereupon Jesus commanded the goats to come out, and when they did, they were goats indeed. Jesus then delivered himself of a rather obscure homily having to do with black sheep and the house of Israel, after which the women asked him if he'd mind changing the goats back into children again. He granted their request, saying, "Come ye children, my playfellows, and let us play together."

I liked the idea of the children running away from Jesus in the first place—"suffer little children" and so on to the contrary notwithstanding, I had always suspected he wasn't Captain Kangaroo—and I liked him for chasing after them and turning them into goats. It threw a scare into them they probably needed. I had a feeling they then played with him only till the first chance they got to give him the slip again, and I had a feeling he was probably just as glad.

I was drawn next to "The Book of the Cock," which, whatever the title had led me to expect, turned out to be a tale which, according to Dr. James, is read in the Abyssinian Church on Maundy Thursdays. At supper one evening Jesus is served a cock that has been cut up in pieces and set before him on a magnificent dish. He is just about to start eating when he notices Judas slipping stealthily out of the room, and as soon as he has gone, Jesus brings the cock back to life with a touch and tells him to tail Judas and find out what's going on. The cock overhears Judas' whole sordid scheme, and then, translating from the Ethiopic, "the cock returned to Bethany and sat down before Jesus and wept bitterly and told all the story."

Lying there in my bed at the Salamander Motel, I could imagine him in the center of the table giving his report to Jesus with his wings outstretched and his comb and wattles askew after the long chase. I could imagine the bitter tears trickling off the end of his beak. The disciples also wept, the text continued, and maybe as much for the cock himself, I thought, as for Jesus. It couldn't have been the easiest tale in the world to tattle. But tears were not the end of it because as soon as the truth about Judas was out, Jesus thanked the cock and placed him in the sky for a thousand years. It was nice to think of the cock, like Romeo, cut out in little stars so all the world, including the world of the henyard, could be in love with night; and it was nice too to think of the Abyssinians remembering him so faithfully for so many centuries, Haile Selassie and all of them. It was a pleasant vision to go to sleep on, and I was on the point of slipping my quarter into the Magic Fingers and turning off the light when my eye was caught by a subtitle listed under "The Gospel of Nicodemus" as "Part II. The Descent into Hell."

I thought immediately of Brownie's reference to this event in church that afternoon, how it was at the moment Jesus knew he was going to have to descend into Hell that he gave out that terrible cry in his original tongue: *Eli, Eli,* as Ellie and I had so blithely sung it several millennia later with the Canterbury Choir, *lama sabachthani?* And I thought too of the Charlton Heston portrait of Jesus staring grimly at the hot-air register there in the Church of Holy Love while, outside, the miniature turtles and shrunken heads went on with business as usual. Dr. James presented the text in three versions, which he printed one above the other as Latin text A, Latin text B, and Greek. I chose Latin text A because it was printed at the top of the page and looked somewhat fuller than the others.

Like *Don Giovanni*, it begins in the dark, and, like *Don Giovanni*, it is opera. In fact, I remember thinking as I read a little further along that in some ways Dr. James might have presented it as a kind of sequel to *Don Giovanni* with the Don, that *galantuomo*, turned Mr. Keen, Tracer of Lost Persons, as he is led down, down, down in the Commendatore's stony grip.

The story begins in the dark with three hysterical rabbis who come rushing in and in breathless *recitativo* try to tell a solemn assembly of priests and Levites about a miracle they have just witnessed. One of the priests rises, a basso in robes reminiscent of *Aïda*, and in a brief passage, with French horns pulsing in the background, asks the rabbis to try to express themselves more clearly. It is here that Rabbi Addas, a baritone, has his first and only aria, since he does not appear again after this opening scene or prologue. With a hand on his heart and his other arm outstretched, he tells how he and his companions were on their way from Galilee into Jordan when they ran into a crowd of men wearing white garments whom they recognized immediately as spirits of the dead. What was their errand here in the land of the living, the rabbis asked them, and the spirits' answer was, "We arose with Christ out of Hell and thereby may ye know that the gates of death and darkness are destroyed."

The assembly of priests and Levites is thrown into an uproar by this news, and in the manner of opera choruses they turn to each other with their beards wagging and their hands gesticulating and murmur fiercely back and forth *rhubarb, rhubarb, rhubarb* perhaps, or whatever syllables sound most like a mob murmuring fiercely in Hebrew. Then the basso priest steps forward again and tells the rabbis to produce the ghosts themselves so that they may verify this extraordinary report and fill in the details. The rabbis are quick to obey and in a moment return with two white-robed figures. Again there is the same kind of horrified stir among the priests and Levites that I associate with such early Gluyas Williams cartoons as "The Day a Cake of Soap Sank at Procter & Gamble's." The basso restores order, however, and the two ghosts are sent off into two different cells, each to write down his own account of what happened in Hell. There is a good deal of pizzicato from the orchestra to suggest the scratching of their quills, followed by a lyric passage from the strings and harp to represent divine inspiration, and finally there bursts forth simultaneously from each of the two cells a triumphantly sustained Amen. The ghosts have finished at precisely the same instant and emerge bearing their scrolls. Taking a scroll in each hand, the basso raises them heavenward with a ghost at each elbow, and the ensuing trio marks the finale of the prologue. Miraculously, the two accounts have turned out to be identical, and "The Truth is One!" the basso priest sings while the ghosts, both tenors, continue their triumphant Amens.

At about this point in my reading, I remember, a fly appeared inside the shade of my bedside lamp. Since a fatal swat is virtually impossible under those circumstances, I flushed him out of the shade and waited for him to land on some more substantial surface. Still crazed by the scorching splendor of the light-bulb, he swooped around the room in braggadocio parabolas until at last he lighted squarely on my bed at about the level of my knees so that I could have swatted him easily without even having to change my position. Maybe it was because the shot was too easy, or maybe it was because the only weapon I had at hand was *The Apocryphal New Testament,* or conceivably, like Uncle Toby Shandy, I simply thought, "This world surely is wide enough to hold both thee and me," but, whatever the reason, I decided to spare him. It may have been that the shock of finding himself still alive was as fatal as the swat would have been or just that I got too absorbed in my reading to notice, but I do not remember being disturbed by him again.

"On a sudden there came a golden heat of the sun and a purple and royal light shining upon us" is the way Latin A describes it. A purple light is hard for me to picture, but red lights and blue lights I have seen on the stage often enough, and I suppose there is no reason why they couldn't be mixed. In any case, the opera proper—a dramatization of the accounts the two ghosts wrote on their scrolls—opens in Hell. Like the gypsies at their campfire in the second act of *Trovatore,* the dead are gathered around in the purple and royal light, and as the curtain rises, you can hear them humming a quiet, somber theme in the key of B minor. They are dead, and the light is dim, and there is nothing much to shout about. Besides, after all, it is Hell. Everything is dark and quiet, including the audience. Only an occasional muffled cough breaks it and a firefly flicker as here and there people bow forward to consult their programs. Ushers lean against the gilt pilasters with their white-gloved hands crossed in front of them. It's the old Met, of course—the great golden curtain, the Diamond Horseshoe with its plush-covered rails. Miriam and I were sent to hear *Hansel and Gretel* there once as children. I remember she wore a velvet dress and a velvet band to hold back her long hair.

As the light grows brighter, the tempo of the humming quickens somewhat, and it becomes possible to identify certain people. Adam is there and the patriarchs Abraham, Isaac, and Jacob with silver beards. There are prophets too, Isaiah and Micah. Habakkuk also is there, whoever Habakkuk was. There is no mistaking King David with a crown on his head and golden hair that curls down to his shoulders. The humming opens out into words, and "The people that walked in darkness have seen a great light," the chorus of shades sings softly, "and now hath it come and shone upon us that sit in death."

We sit there in the dark, my twin sister and I, and I wonder if at twelve or thirteen or whatever we were then, death was already in her like an ovary only waiting for God knows what or who to come fertilize it. Like the witch in the gingerbread house. *Ciao,* Antonio.

Simeon is there, the old Jew who was on hand when Joseph in

knickerbockers and Mary in something filmy brought their child to present him at the Temple. John the Baptist is there, looking a little like Basil Rathbone. He seems uncomfortable and out of place in his leopard skin. Simeon and John come downstage and sing about how they both knew Jesus back when, and how much they are looking forward to seeing him again now that he has finally made it.

Adam is dressed in flesh-colored tights like an acrobat. He seems too old for the part. His neck is stringy, and his legs have no calves. There is something soft and a little peculiar in his manner as he comes and stands so close to the footlights that his make-up shows. One expects a voice on the order of Richard Dyer Bennett's, but he turns out to be a baritone. In his aria he tells a story within a story within a story. And again within a story if you consider it as all part of my account of what happened that evening at the Salamander Motel in Armadillo.

Adam starts out very soft and *andante*, all head tones with his teeth showing, and you can see the conductor with his puckered lips and cautionary left palm trying to quiet down the strings. "*Mio figlio,*" Adam begins, sustaining the phrase in a rather lovely, vibrant way but with something in his powdered face and the way he holds his hands that suggests it is really not a son he is talking about. There is some restive stirring among the patriarchs. Abraham is scowling down at his feet, and Isaac is twisting and untwisting a strand of his beard. Son or whatever, the name is Seth, and Adam tells about an errand he sent him on to the Archangel Michael at the gates of Paradise. "Entreat Michael to give thee of the oil of the tree of mercy that thou mayest anoint thy father Adam for the pain of his body," he sings, and you can see them there, Adam and Seth, on the beach together at Fire Island.

Spreadeagled in the full sun, Seth is moist and brown as a young pearl diver in his tight black trunks, but even under the striped umbrella Adam has started to peel. He reaches out and gives Seth's foot a little shove with his. "Now you just go *on* up there and get me some Coppertone," he says. *Mio figlio . . . Mio figlio . . .*

At first the Archangel is not encouraging. Five thousand and five hundred years must be accomplished before Adam can have oil from the tree of mercy for the pain of his body, but then, he tells Seth to go back and say, ah then . . . Adam sings it with his eyes half closed at the memory of how Seth brought back the message from the gates of Paradise: "Then the Son of God shall come down even unto Hell and will bring our father Adam into Paradise unto the tree of mercy." Not even the patriarchs remain entirely unmoved, and when Adam finishes and stands there with one knee slightly bent and his chin on his shoulder like a Picasso clown, the whole chorus of the dead rises and, joined now by the full orchestra, sings out fortissimo in praise and rejoicing.

During the intermission Miriam has to go to the bathroom, not because she has to *do* anything, she says, but because in theaters, restaurants, gas stations, even department stores and churches, she always goes to the bathroom just to have a look around. I remain in my plush seat, putting my overcoat and hat in my lap and drawing up my knees to let people squeeze out past me into the aisle. I wish that I hadn't been made to wear the hat. It is a gray fedora from John Ryan's, and because I haven't begun to get my growth yet, I am afraid it makes me look like a dwarf. The house lights have already started to dim by the time Miriam gets back. It is the fanciest Ladies' Room she has ever seen, with a dressing room full of tables and mirrors and a round, tufted sofa in the middle just like a whorehouse. Her breath smells of peppermint as she whispers this in my ear, and she has brought a Mound's back with her, half of which she gives to me. Even at the time, it occurs to me to wonder how she knows about whorehouses and the kind of sofas they have in them.

Hell is not only a place in Latin A, it is also a person. Hell and Satan are alone on the stage when the curtain goes up. Satan is dressed traditionally, like Mephistopheles in *Faust*—scarlet doublet and tights and a hat that comes down in a widow's peak in front and has several long feathers sweeping back. Hell cuts a very different figure. Short and on the flabby side, he is dressed in black leotards that are perhaps supposed to suggest a medieval torture chamber and is naked from the waist up. He is smudged here and there with soot and has those rolls of fat above the hips that Miriam calls love handles. He has a skin-tight helmet of black cloth which comes down low on his forehead and has loops cut out for his ears. His face has a worried, sweaty look which reminds me of the late Lou Costello. He and Satan converse in recitative with a single piano providing punctuation marks and stage directions in between.

Satan makes his point with his arms crossed at his chest and his feet planted wide apart. Jesus is on his way to Hell—there is no doubt about that—but they will make mincemeat of him once he gets there. But how can they be sure of that, Hell asks. That is easy, Satan says. He is afraid of death. Didn't he sweat blood in the garden and ask that the cup be taken from him? Besides, Satan says, he was able to tempt him just like other men. But he resisted, says Hell. Luck, says Satan. Three or four sharp, crisp chords on the piano, and then the entire string section introduces Hell's bass aria, "Remember Lazarus."

It is short, only twenty measures or so, and Hell sings it with his hands clasped over his sooty navel. It is more plaintive than anything else, like a man not given to making scenes but forced at least to register protest. There was a man named Lazarus who died and was buried and Hell swallowed him down into his entrails as from the beginning he had swallowed down everybody. Then his belly pained him and he knew that all was not well, whereupon with not even the by-your-leave of a prayer but with just a word or two, somebody from the land of the living snatched Lazarus up out of Hell's entrails, and "he flew away from me not like to a dead man but to an eagle, so instantly did the earth cast him out."

Hell draws his aria to a close by saying that he has every reason to believe that the one who did the snatching is the same one who is on his way down to make trouble now. In which case, who is going to make mince-meat of whom? Satan recoils with his caped arm crooked out in front of his widow's peak, and from offstage can be heard the chorus of the dead singing. "Remove, O princes, your gates, and be ye lift up, ye everlasting doors."

The longest scene follows then, and in many ways it is the least interesting. Everybody has to have his say as they stand around waiting. David the King and Isaiah the prophet come in and make the point that since they both predicted Jesus' triumph untold generations before, he is certain to be entirely triumphant here as everywhere else. Various saints echo these sentiments. Then King David and Hell have a rather florid duet where David echoes the earlier words of the chorus—"Be ye lift up, ye doors of Hell, that the King of Glory shall come in"—and Hell asks, by no means rhetorically but with the closest he can come to a sneer on his hopelessly sincere and anxious face, "Who is this King of Glory?" The duet ends with Hell repeating his taunting question three times and David replying to each, "The Lord strong and mighty, the Lord mighty in Battle, he is the King of Glory."

It is at this point that the lights, which have been growing steadily brighter, reach an almost blinding intensity, and at the last of David's three *glory*'s, amid a blast of trumpets, horns, tympany, Jesus enters from the wings, and even Montague Rhodes James, you feel, must have had to sit on his hands to keep from putting in a footnote to the effect that at this moment all Hell breaks loose.

The Jesus I see looks less like the picture above Bebb's altar table than like Don Giovanni, the great lover himself. I see him all in white, but instead of that homespun garment with the *bateau* neckline, he is magnificently dressed in the height of eighteenth-century fashion with a cloak that flares out at his heels as he strides in and a plume in his hat and silver buckles on his shoes. He wears a grandee's little earring in one ear and carries a rapier in his hand. "Who art thou that didst lie dead in the sepulcher? Who art thou that settest free the prisoners? Who art thou that sheddest thy divine light upon them that were blinded by darkness?" Hell and Satan and the whole chorus of demons cry it out, and Jesus' response is a model of directness. He simply takes his rapier and runs Satan through the shoulder with it, not to kill him but to render him helpless. Then he signals to Hell, who comes up from behind and pinions Satan's arms to his sides as Satan's head drops to his chest in defeat.

Hell then sings his final aria, which goes on rather too long and during which everybody on stage including Jesus freezes in place as though it is somehow the least they can do for Hell because he is so much shorter and stouter than Satan and looks so much less able to cope that you wonder if he will be able to pull things off after all. Satan should never have hanged the King of Glory on the cruel tree in the first place, Hell says, and now he will have the rest of eternity to learn what torments he must suffer in place of Adam and his children. Hell, Satan and the whole hellish multitude then depart.

Here, for the first time, Jesus speaks. He sweeps off his plumed hat, stretches both arms out as far as they will go to either side so that his white doublet glitters between the outspread wings of his white cloak, smiles a smile that would put Errol Flynn and Douglas Fairbanks, Jr., both to shame, not to mention Cesare Siepi, and says, "Come unto me, all ye my saints which bear mine image and likeness!"

Adam comes first. He walks perhaps a little too straight, a little too steady-hipped, but when he reaches the hand that Jesus is holding out to him, he falls to his knees at Jesus' feet with tears that are at least real enough to start some mascara running down one cheek and says, "O Lord, my God, I cried unto thee, and thou hast healed me, thou hast brought my soul out of Hell." Then David and Isaiah follow and behind them Abraham, Isaac and Jacob and all the patriarchs and prophets and saints until finally Jesus is completely hidden in their midst. "Sing unto the Lord a new song," David cries out, "for he hath done marvelous things." And the entire company replies with "Amen! Alleluia!" as the curtain comes down.

That is the end of it, really. There is a short last scene or epilogue at the gates of Paradise not unlike the one in *Don Giovanni*, where Donna Anna, Donna Elvira and Don Ottavio come rushing in after the Don has descended into the flames and smoke. But, as in the case of the one in *Don Giovanni*, it is rather heavily moralistic and doesn't add much. So I skimmed it at the time there in Armadillo and do no more than mention it in passing here.

I preferred to go to sleep with the echo of David's last cry and that final rousing chorus still ringing in my ears, so, first depositing my quarter, I turned off the light and gave my sore muscles and frayed traveler's nerves over to the vibrating solicitude of the Magic Fingers.

I WAS AWAKENED the next morning by Bebb himself. He didn't shake me or say anything, but even asleep I must have sensed a presence, and when I opened my eyes, there he was standing at the foot of my bed. He said, "Antonio, you'll have to excuse me for busting in on you like this, but it's after eleven. I was afraid you might be dead."

It took me a moment or two to put it all together. I had the sense of having slept too hard and deep for dreams, and for a few seconds it was such a shock to see the world again that it was as if I had been dead indeed. The sunlight was flooding in between the slats of the Venetian blinds, covering everything including Bebb with horizontal golden stripes. And there was Bebb himself, my victim, my San Graal, the Dr. Livingston to my Mr. Stanley, and the strangest thing about finding him there at the foot of my bed, of all places, was that it really wasn't so strange—as if I had been expecting him almost, or as if he had been waking me that way every morning for years. He looked slightly larger than I remembered him, both taller and stouter, or squarer anyway with his short neck and heavy shoulders and that rather massive bald head that reminded me a little of Daddy Warbucks. He was dressed much as I had seen him in New York in a nondescript dark suit with his four-pointed handkerchief and mono-grammed B showing, but here in Armadillo it seemed to hang easier on him and looked less like a uniform he wasn't used to wearing.

"I took you up on your invitation," I said and realized that I didn't know what to call him. I thought of him as just Bebb, but that was pretty clearly out, and if Mr. Bebb seemed a little too much at this point, Leo seemed a little too little even though he did call me Antonio. So I called him nothing.

He said, "I had a feeling you would," and extended his right hand, which I had to crawl out of the covers to shake. Because of my disturbingly realistic dream on the train, I had rinsed out my pajamas in the shower the night before and gone to bed without them, so that when I look back on our second historic meeting as it took place in Armadillo, what I see is Bebb, the International President, standing there in his sober Mother Church suit and myself half crouching on the bed as naked as the day my poor mother bore me. We are reaching out over the covers toward each other, and our two hands are just touching. It is a picture which belongs in the Sistine Chapel.

Bebb said, "I had a feeling you might come, and I'm pleased as punch you did. I've got a lot to show you, Antonio, and I've got a lot to tell you about, so you just throw on your clothes and we'll grab you some coffee and be on our way."

My clothes were all of them right there in the bedroom, but finding myself reluctant to get dressed with those Open Sesame eyes upon me, I muttered some vague explanation and carried them into the bathroom. I left the door ajar, and the mirror on the inside of the door allowed me to see Bebb without being seen myself. He sat down on the foot of my bed and talked to me while I got dressed.

"Antonio," he said, "I think that maybe the Kingdom has come at last. It is possible that Gabriel is finally getting ready to blow his horn. I've been to Texas. I just got back from Houston a couple of hours ago while you were fast asleep here in the Salamander Motel, and, Antonio, let me tell you Texas is not only a big state but Texas has got some big men in it. Ever heard of Herman Redpath? Red as in red and path as in path. Redpath. He says it's an Indian name, and he's got lots of Indian blood in him. You can see it right off. You could put his face on the head of a nickel and nobody'd hardly know the difference. Herman Redpath is a big man from a big state. And you talk about your Christians, why, he's —" I had forgotten about his habit of interrupting himself as he did here, looking out pop-eyed and intent into the empty room as if I'd been sitting right there on the bed beside him. "Antonio, that Herman Redpath is what I call a *Christian*. The Lord doesn't make them much like that any more. Why, all that man thinks about is giving. I doubt he even gets out of bed in the morning without he gives somebody something first just to get warmed up. I don't see how he's got anything left to call his own, except the more he gives away, the more he gets. That Herman Redpath," Bebb said, holding up one finger, and that eye, that marvelous, lazy eye, flickering shut for a moment and then opening again, "he is the givingest Christian it has ever been my privilege to meet. He is a blessing, that man. He is a light unto the gentiles."

"You've ordained him, have you?" I asked. I was standing in front of the shaving mirror, wondering whether Bebb would expect me to put on a tie or not. It was Florida and it was summer, but he was wearing a tie himself, and I had no idea what paces he might be planning to put me through. I had just about decided not to wear one anyway when I heard Bebb say, "Don't you go getting all dolled up now, Antonio, this isn't New York City. Just any old thing that's comfortable," and for a moment I thought he must have been able to see me in the door mirror standing there with the tie in my hand, but the angle of the door was all wrong. He couldn't possibly have seen me. "This Mr. Redpath," I said. "You've ordained him, you say?"

Bebb said, "That's what I'm getting at, Antonio. That is exactly the point. That is what I've just been to Texas about, and let me tell you all these airplane fares are setting the Mother Church back plenty. Herman Redpath has heard the call—just like you heard it yourself, just like thousands of others have heard it. But there's one big difference. I say unto you—Matthew nineteen—it is easier for a camel to go through the eye of a needle, Antonio, than for a rich man to enter the Kingdom of God. But for Herman Redpath it is as easy as taking candy from a baby. It's like he's a thread was made on *purpose* for that needle. It's what I've been down there in Texas talking to him about. You should see this place he's got. You could put Holy Love in one of his swimming pools and still have plenty of room left over for a boat race. Just the room where he keeps his hi-fi and his victrola records makes Holy Love look like a gym locker."

I had finished dressing by this time and stepped out of the bathroom in khaki slacks and a navy-blue polo shirt Ellie gave me once with an alligator on the pocket. It made me look like a Latin lover, she said. I had my camera slung over one shoulder—it had occurred to me that there ought to be some pictures to go with my article, and if I got anybody else to take them, Bebb was bound to get suspicious—and I had also put on the dark glasses I had bought in Armadillo the day before, so I looked like something right off the tourist special. I wondered if even at that moment Persephone was making her way down the Pullman corridors in her bathing suit, passing out reservation checks for lunch. I wondered what she had done with my oranges.

There was no restaurant in the Salamander, but Bebb took me across the street to a big gas station that had food in slot machines, and I drank a quick cup of coffee and ate an egg-salad sandwich which was so cold inside that the first bite made my teeth ache. Then he said we would stop by first at the Manse. He insisted we take his car, and I found to my surprise that, like mine, it was a convertible. I had expected something more in keeping with the tight black raincoat and Tyrolean hat. It was a large convertible with fins, a plastic Jesus on the dashboard, and the initials L.B. on the door—was the L for Lucille or for Leo, I wondered. Bebb had the top down. As we drove to the Manse, Bebb continued to tell me about Herman Redpath.

Bebb said, "Herman Redpath is not ordained—he's not ordained *yet*. That's what I flew down to plan with him about. It was a planning trip, you see, so it's perfectly legal to write it off. You'll never get into trouble that way. He wants to be ordained bad, Antonio. Why? It is not given to us to know why. Thy ways are not my ways, saith the Lord. And when you get right down to it, why does anybody want to be ordained? Why did you want to be ordained yourself, Antonio? Have you ever asked yourself that?" This was while we were at the gas station, and he caught me with my mouth full of egg salad, so that all I could do was nod yes, I had asked myself that.

Bebb said, "Herman Redpath has got everything a man could want, but he wants this too—*more*," he said, raising his finger. "He wants this more than anything else he's got. Think what that means. A man with his wealth—he drives a car makes this one look sick—and his influence. . . . Antonio, I'm telling you this makes everything I've ever done before look like small potatoes. Meaning no slur on yourself," he added, "or any of the other Christians I've been privileged to draw into the Gospel Ministry. In the eyes of the Lord we're all pretty small potatoes, Herman Redpath included. But speaking not in the language of Zion, Antonio, this is no jackrabbit. This is no red squirrel or gopher. This is a bull moose. This is a twelve-point buck, Antonio."

When we reached the Manse he pulled up at the curb just about where I had the evening before, but he held me there a few moments longer. With some difficulty because of the way the wheel was digging into his stomach, he turned in his seat to face me and placed one hand on my shoulder. He said, "Manna, Antonio. Riches. The green stuff," and he held his other hand in the air between us and rubbed his fingers together in the ancient gesture of avarice. "What is a man profited if he shall gain the whole world and lose his soul? And consider the lilies of the field, Antonio. Consider just that chickweed over by the sandbox. Even Herman Redpath in all his glory was not arrayed like one of these. Nobody knows that better than me. Horse shit." I was startled at first, but realized then that for Bebb the term was purely descriptive, like "bitch" for a dog breeder. "In itself, money's horse shit. But in terms of what it—put it to *work*, Antonio, and the sky's the limit. All a man's wildest dreams. . . ." He took the handkerchief from his breast pocket and, without unfolding it, wiped the top of his head. Before he replaced it, I could see that on the inside, where it didn't show, it was grimy from what I presumed were many similar wipings. "What I mean is put it to work for *Christ*, Antonio," and this time there could be no doubt about it. The eye drowsed off and then came slowly awake again as if with a life or a death all its own.

Bebb gave three honks on his horn. My glance followed his toward the Manse, curious to see who would come out. Over at the gym set, one swing was stirring slightly in the breeze, and I wondered if it could have been for his baby that Bebb had originally bought it. If so, I gathered from what Lucille had said that the baby probably never got big enough to use it, and I thought of something I had bought to give Miriam the next month for Christmas—a long pair of wooden tongs with magnets on the tips for picking things up when you dropped them. She was always letting things fall off her hospital bed like cigarettes or Kleenex or the paper, and she said the nurses chilled her bedpan if she rang for them too often. Like the swing, it was possible that years might go by, I thought, and those tongs would still be sitting in the closet or wherever I'd put them, ungiven. I could always paint them with Rustoleum black, I supposed, and use them that way.

When no one answered his horn, Bebb blew it again—not just three snappy honks this time but six or seven long blasts without rhythm or pacing, like what you hear in a traffic jam on a crowded summer afternoon. In a moment or two the screen door opened and Brownie stepped out on the porch. He was wearing the same shorts and shirt he had had on the day before, but I was glad to see that as yet there were no stains at the armpits. Lucille probably didn't start sending for Tropicanas until later in the day. Even with my dark glasses on, he seemed to recognize me and gave a restrained little wave. I had not had time to wave back when Bebb cupped one hand to his mouth and yelled at him.

"Not you," he said. "The girl. Go tell that girl to get her tail down here in five seconds or we'll leave without her."

It's surprising what subtleties you can inject even into a shout. I could tell perfectly well that when Bebb said "not you" to Brownie, he meant it, but when he said "five seconds" he meant thirty minutes or an hour or whatever it took. He might keep on honking the horn, but he'd wait. He could only mean Sharon, I decided. It was conceivable that he might speak of Lucille as a girl, but his referring to her tail was inconceivable. Brownie turned and went into the house again, and Bebb switched on the radio.

It would have seemed to me a reasonable time for him to explain where he was planning to take me and what he had in mind to show me once we got there. He might have dropped some hint about why Sharon, if it was indeed Sharon he meant, was going with us—whether she was to be just supercargo or part of the act. From his first appearance at the foot of my bed that morning, I had been waiting for him to open discussions about what had presumably brought me all the way down from New York in the first place, which was the matter of his proposal that I start an affiliate Gospel Faith in the metropolitan area for our mutual gain. This would have been a plausible time for him to open that up, and if he didn't, I was prepared to open it up myself, partly for the sake of making my disguise all the more secure but partly also because I found myself offended that he considered me so much less interesting a subject than Herman Redpath. But for the moment Bebb did not seem interested in further discussions of any kind. After the blast at Brownie, his mouth had snapped tight shut on its hinges, and one after the other he was punching the automatic selector buttons of the radio with his finger. He was through with words for a while. He wanted music.

The music he found I can still hear in my mind's ear, and if when I think of Armadillo what I see is that useless stretch of sidewalk petering out in the scrub, what I hear when I remember Armadillo is the song that Bebb and I listened to as we sat in his open car in the sun waiting for the girl, whoever she might turn out to be, to get her tail down there. It was played on a honky-tonk piano, and you got the impression of a good deal of activity going on in the background, like glasses clinking and the hiss of draft beer being drawn and the sound of the saloonkeeper sliding the free-lunch platter down the mahogany bar to an old customer at the far end. It was the Yukon, it was *My Little Chickadee*, it was a Victorian whorehouse in Natchez, Mississippi, and if you'd listened hard, you could probably have heard the customers shifting around on one of those round, tufted sofas like the one Miriam had seen in the Ladies' Room at the Met the day we were sent to hear *Hansel and Gretel*. It was a bouncy little boilermaker of a tune, and just about the time I was getting to where I could have whistled it, somebody started singing the words. A man started singing them, a kind of shiftless, raspy bass, and I could see him in my mind as clearly as if he had been standing there on the lawn in front of the Manse. He was a big Victorian stud with a deep Southern twang and a handlebar mustache and a flashy stickpin made of paste and egg stains on his fancy vest. In between singing, he kept calling out in a loud, pleading voice, "Come on, Honey, you *know* what I like!" and you could all but smell his hairy, beery smile as he said it with the gaps between his teeth. I was unable to get many of the words at the time, and though I had occasion to hear it more than once afterwards, I have never been sure of all of them, but the chorus begins,

> *Chantilly lace*
> *And a pretty face*

and then there's something about

> *And a wiggle in her walk*
> *And a giggle in her talk*

and then maybe a few more "Come *on*, Honey"s and

> *Makes you feel all loose*
> *Like a long-necked goose.*

You could just see that big sweet-talking traveling man with his flat feet and his goose-greased lovelock and that twitching little butt in Chantilly lace he was salivating over. And then just as I was hoping I could get more of the words the next time round, I felt a touch on my shoulder and heard a girl's voice say quite close to my ear, "Big Bopper."

"Me?" I said.

"The man who's singing the song," she said.

"What's the name of the song?" I asked. "It's great."

"*Chantilly Lace*," she said, "but don't let it throw you."

Bebb said, "Move it over, Antonio. There's room for us all up front. This is my daughter Sharon. The Reverend Antonio Parr from New York City."

If Bebb had chanced on some other tune when he was punching those radio buttons, would it have made a difference? If he had happened to hit on *Laura*, say, or *My Alice Blue Gown*, so that it was to those more subdued strains that I first came face to face with Sharon, would it have started our relationship out on such a different footing that everything from there on would have proceeded differently? I know only that from the very start my view of her, and perhaps in some way her view of me, was colored by that foolish novelty song played on the tinny piano as she squeezed into the front seat beside Bebb and me. She was wearing a pair of white sailor pants that she must have used a shoehorn to get into and a loose-fitting shirt the color of raspberry ice which hung outside. She wore rope sandals on her bare feet and carried a straw hat with a big, floppy brim. I haven't the faintest idea what Chantilly lace looks like, but as far as I'm concerned, that's what Sharon had on that first day I met her.

Chantilly lace and a pretty face. The face of Sharon Bebb. How do you describe a face like that, or any face, for that matter? In fact, the better you know it, the harder it is to describe. I have discovered that if I shut my eyes and try to see in my mind the faces of people I know, it is

quite easy to summon up the fair-weather friends and casual acquaintances, the students I've taught, the vet who took care of Tom, but when
it comes to somebody like Miriam whom I've known all my life, the best
I can usually manage is a photograph of the face. I can't see it moving
and changing the way faces do. And so it is with Sharon.

In her case the photograph I see is one I must have taken later on that
same day with my spy camera. She is sitting on a railing somewhere in the
slightly round-shouldered way taller girls tend to. Her long hair looks as if
it could stand a good brushing, and it has divided above one ear so that
you can just see the earlobe through it. She is gazing down at something
in a rather moody way—that straight nose, that almost somber tilt to the
corners of her mouth, that curve of chin and throat arching down into the
unbuttoned collar of her raspberry-ice shirt. I suppose that maybe, like
mine, it is essentially an Italian face—a little sullen, a little self-indulgent,
a little untrustworthy. A Florentine page boy caught peering through the
keyhole at his mistress' bath. Some daughter of the lesser Medici given
to lurking around the Colosseum by moonlight. Maybe there was something Italian too about the surprise of the face, which was the smile, that
smile which is the only part of her face that I can sometimes make happen in my mind when I think of her. It was a surprise just because I
would not have expected anything so unguarded and unabashed from that
moody, downward glance. Whatever the secret of Sharon's face was,
when she smiled the secret was out. Those wet white teeth. Those startling, minstrel-show eyes. There wasn't a wiggle in her walk exactly, but
when she moved along in her lazy, loose-limbed way with that floppy hat
in her hand and those white sailor pants, you knew there was a lot more
going on than just somebody traveling from one place to another.

I shoved over into the middle of the seat as Bebb had told me to, and
with Bebb on one side of me and Sharon on the other and that plastic
Jesus on the dashboard getting in the way of my view, we set off for I had
no idea where.

It was Sharon who got this information out of him almost immediately. She said, "Hey, Bip, where are you taking us to anyway?" and Bebb
said, "I'm taking you to the lions. Your old Bip's all wound up from his
trip, and Antonio here is one of those city boys are tied up in knots most
of the time anyway, so we're just going to find us some sunshine here in
the Sunshine State and unwind. The lions are the unwindingest place I
know."

It was the most expansive I have ever seen him, and I assumed it was
Sharon's presence that had brought the change about. The raincoat tightness, the air he had even when glorifying Herman Redpath of keeping
some vital part of himself buttoned up, the watchfulness that made that
one drowsy eye such an anomaly in his face—all of this seemed to disappear as he drove along at seventy or seventy-five miles an hour back up
some of the same pot-holed roads I had taken down from West Palm the

day before. He kept the radio going and loosened his tie, and with his mouth snapped tight not so much now to keep something possibly incriminating from escaping, I thought, as to keep something particularly flavorsome from getting lost, he seemed for the time being quite oblivious to both Sharon and me. I tried at several points to make some kind of conversation with Sharon myself, but what with the roaring of the wind in our ears and the fact that we were squeezed in so tight that to turn toward each other to make ourselves heard was almost to touch noses, I finally gave up so that the only communication between us was the soft collision of our flesh which Bebb in a sense forced upon us by taking up with his sizable bulk a good deal more than his third of the seat. It was only when we got out on the parkway and Bebb turned the radio off when the news came on that talk was possible again.

"Tell me about those lions," I said. "I never thought they were something Christians went out of their way to throw themselves to," but before Bebb had a chance to answer this rather pallid witticism, Sharon turned and said, "First tell me about that rich little Indian jerk. Luce says you've asked him home."

As she turned to speak, some of her hair blew into my face. It was the first time this had ever happened to me, and I remember it still. Such as it was, I had had my own hair blow into my face before, but never anybody else's. Unlike Ellie's hair, which smelled of shampoo, Sharon's smelled somehow of sleep is all I can say, smelled faintly musty and sweet anyhow, and before I had a chance to brush it away or whatever I would have done—a strand of it, I think, had even gotten into my mouth— Sharon reached up and did it herself. She did it by drawing her hand down from the top of her head to her cheek so that the hair came away by itself, and then she held it there close to her throat so it wouldn't blow again and looked past me at Bebb. This is another picture I can sometimes get of her in place of the one where she is sitting on the railing looking down.

Bebb said, "Herman Redpath is coming to Armadillo, yes. Your mother was right. He's flying up from Texas in his private plane sometime —he'll be phoning to let me know just when—and I am going to ordain him to the Gospel Ministry personally right there in the church. It will be a great day for Holy Love. It will be a great day for all of us, Sharon, and don't you go around referring to him as a little Indian jerk."

Sharon said, "I referred to him as a *rich* little Indian jerk."

"I wish you'd take her in hand for me, Antonio," Bebb said.

Sharon looked at me and gave a little shrug.

"Sharper than a serpent's tooth," I said.

"Talk about your teeth," Bebb said. "How'd you like to try a set of those on for size? Puts even Brownie's to shame."

He was pointing toward a billboard that we were approaching. It showed the head of a lion with his mouth open in a great MGM roar and his upper fangs hanging down like stalactites.

Sharon said, "The last time we were here, one of them took a leak on the car. It was the high point of the day."

Bebb said, "Antonio, I wish you'd get to work on her language for me. It's the first thing needs to be cleaned up. But you know," he said, "the girl's right. It was the high point of the day, at least it was for me. Think of it, Antonio. There's no bars in this place. None of your little zoo cages with the poor jungle creatures wasting their lives away pacing back and forth, back and forth, on that cement floor until their claws are all wore off nearly—people throwing them peanuts and making crazy faces and poking at them with balloon sticks. They're free as the breeze in this place, Antonio. Go anywhere. Do anything. If they get a notion they want to take a leak on somebody's car, they just go straight ahead and take it."

"You're going to have me in tears in a minute," I said. "I have a cat I live with in New York, and when I knew I was coming down here, I took him to the vet's to board. I hate to think of the size cage they've got him in right this minute. Probably even worse than a roomette."

Bebb said, "Well, but a cat's a cat. A cage gives a cat time for reflection. Keep a cat fed, and he'll make out just about anyplace. But a lion," he said, turning off at the next exit with so little reduction in speed that we were all tossed even more tightly against each other. "A lion feels a cage just like a man would—more," he said, reaching up to adjust the rear-view mirror as though he thought someone might be following us, "a lion feels it more than your average man would because he's king of the jungle. Five years, ten years, fifteen years. Think of it, Antonio. A king in a cage all that time, just wearing his claws off."

Because Bebb's was a convertible, he had to exchange it for another car. He left his in the parking lot and rented another from a man in a concrete pillbox who explained the rules. You kept your windows closed tight and your doors locked. Under no circumstances did you get out of your car after you passed through the gates. If you needed help, you just stayed where you were and honked your horn until a hunter came—hunters were easy to spot because their cars were painted with black and white zebra stripes. Bebb had Sharon and me sit in the back seat because he said you could see more there, and he did the driving again although I had offered to.

Lion Country. I have never seen Africa, but the flat, mangy, zoo-colored acres we were driving toward with a palm tree sticking up here and there or a clump of brush by a water hole looked about as much like it, I thought, as anything I'd ever run across. At a gate in what must have been a twenty-foot-high fence of heavy wire mesh, a man with a rifle checked our ticket and let us through, and then in another few yards we had to go through a second fence just like it. Although, as the man in the pillbox had told us, the area extended over several square miles, we were, in effect, in the lions' cage, and I said as much to Sharon, who was gazing out of her window rather drowsily, I thought, with her chin in her hand.

"Don't panic," she said. "This kind of a hot day, they're probably all at the movies."

For a while I decided she must be right. Bebb was cruising about ten miles an hour along the narrow, twisty road, apparently too intent on his own unwinding to pay any attention to his passengers in back, and there wasn't much to see except for an occasional snow-white cattle egret and in one scummy pond what I thought might be the snout of an alligator. There was another car parked around on the far side of the pond, but I couldn't see that they had anything more to look at than we did. A hawk or buzzard of some kind was spiraling slowly way up in the faded sky, and I was going to try out some quip about vultures on Sharon but thought better of it. She had leaned her forehead against the window, and I could see a triangle of cheek and one eyelid where the sun touched them reflected in the glass. I wondered if she could be asleep.

And then we began to see lions. Rather like Brownie calling me dear, it happened so gradually that it took a while before I realized it. There was a female lying in the rose-colored dust not more than a few feet back from the road. She was yellower than I remembered lions being except for her underbelly, which looked feathery and white, and she was licking her paw with her head tipped way over to the side and the paw more or less straight up, the way I have seen children trying to lick the drips off an ice-cream cone without dumping it. She gave no sign of noticing us as we drove past. I had seen Tom do his paw that same way, and the lion didn't seem much more than a somewhat larger version. A bit farther along we came across two males. One of them was rubbing his shoulder back and forth against a dead tree. He had a pained expression on his face as though it wasn't getting at what was really itching him. The other was standing utterly still with his hind legs stretched back the way they make dogs stand at shows, and his tail, which had a slight S-shaped kink in it, bent almost straight up in the air.

Sharon leaned forward and touched Bebb's fat neck with one finger. She said, "Hey, Bip, eyes right," and it was only then that I saw the lion was pissing. Bebb didn't say anything, but glanced over where he had been told and smiled, I assumed—from behind I could see one cheek expand and the tip of his nose move. Without turning, he reached over his shoulder to touch the hand Sharon had touched him with, but by then she had withdrawn it and was using it to support her chin again.

At first it was like a zoo. We were here and the lions were there, and if you'd seen one lion, I thought, you'd seen them all, and the lions looked as though they had exactly the same feeling about people. But little by little this changed, although I couldn't say why. Little by little it began to get to me that they were lions and that they were here and that we were here too, Bebb and Sharon and I, not there but here with the scraggly palms and the water holes. It got to the point where lions' faces didn't even look like just lions' faces any more but like this lion's face and that lion's face. There was one lounging by a rock who looked a lot the way I imagined Herman Redpath did—all nose and mane and a rather undershot jaw. Another, if there is such a thing as a witty lion, looked witty to me—he was lying on his back with his belly in the sun, and as Bebb drove us by, he seemed to cover his eyes with his paws as though in some kind of arch reference to his comprehensively exposed parts. When we rounded the next bend, we came upon a large pond where there must have been at least twenty lions all more or less together—a whole pride, I imagined, although I had no idea how big a regulation pride is supposed to be. Some were strolling near the water, others were squatting on their haunches in the dust. I saw no evidence of cubs anywhere and wondered if even such humane captivity as this inhibited their breeding. There were several padding toward us down the middle of the road, and Bebb pulled the car over to the ditch and stopped.

He said, "If you want to get some photos with that camera of yours, Antonio, here's your chance." Even as he spoke, one of the males who had been walking down the road reached the car and came abreast of Sharon on her side. Through the window you could just see his eyes and mane and the hairy tip of his tail. I took the camera off my shoulder and got a shot of him, aiming a little to the side in order to get a bit of Sharon's profile in too, I hoped—the nose and chin anyway and a little of the hair.

Bebb said, "You won't take any prizes that way, Antonio. The light's no good in the car. Go on outside where the sunshine is. Those lions are so used to people they won't hardly notice you. I've done it myself lots of times."

I thought at first that he was joking, but it became obvious right away that he wasn't. He turned around in his seat, laying his arm out along the back, and explained how if I took a picture from a shadowy car of a lion in the bright sun, it was bound to come out wrong. I could leave the door open if I wanted to so I could get back in in a hurry if the occasion arose. And I could keep the car between the lions and me. There was no need to worry about the hunters. People did it all the time, Bebb said, and he knew quite a few of the hunters anyway. Then his mouth swung tight shut, and he lowered his chin to the back of his hand and waited for me to pull something out of my hat. The thought suddenly occurred to me that maybe this was some kind of initiation or ritual test. I remembered reading somewhere that before you got to be a full Druid, you had to lie naked in a frozen stream for a night or two. Would I or wouldn't I? Was I or wasn't I? Perhaps this was what Bebb was waiting to find out, I thought.

And Sharon was waiting. All I could see of her out of the corner of my eye was those white pants and a tan arm, but I felt her eyes upon me. If my Druidship was at stake, I felt sure, so was my manhood.

I said, "Look now, I'm sorry. I don't want to lose any more points than I have to, and I've got my pride just like everybody else. But I'm a city boy and an ex-schoolteacher. I do laps around the reservoir, and I don't smoke cigarettes. I watch my calories. So all in all I'm in pretty good shape for somebody my age. But I don't feel like tangling with a lion even if you leave the door open, and I'll bet I can buy better pictures back there at the gate than I'd get with my arm clawed off anyway."

Almost before I had finished speaking, Bebb had his hand out toward me. He said, "Antonio, I don't want you to think for one second I'm putting you on the spot or want to embarrass you in any way. Some folks are allergic to things other folks don't even notice. Me, I'm scared to death of heights. I'd rather have a tooth drawn than go up in an airplane. But wild animals I've never minded any more than bugs. You let me have that camera now, and I'll get you a picture that's a picture," and before I knew it, he was out of the car with my camera in his hand.

He didn't leave the door open, and he didn't make any effort to keep the car between him and the lions, and he couldn't have anyway because there were lions all around him, none so close that he couldn't have made a run for it if he'd had to, I suppose, but a lot closer than I'd ever seen a man and a lion before without so much as a ditch between them.

He stood there in his dark suit with the Florida sun glancing off his bald head and my own spy camera pressed up against his eye, and no more than a car's length away those lions padded around in the dust with their great, soft feet and tawny velvet flanks and wild, Old Testament manes. Androcles in the Colosseum? Jerome in the desert? Happy Hooligan meets Simba? All I know is that no picture he took was a match for the picture he made as I crouched forward there with my elbow on the front seat touching Sharon's elbow and watched him through the windshield of the rented car.

With an almost mystical smile, I thought, as though answering voices from on high, the most majestic of the male lions sauntered over to one of the females and mounted her. There didn't seem to be any passion about it as far as I could tell, but on the other hand it didn't seem perfunctory either—rather like two old friends seeking refreshment in each other's company toward the middle of a hot afternoon. Bebb swung my camera around and, as nearly as I could tell, got his shot in before they uncoupled.

"That Bip," Sharon said. "You've got to hand it to him." It was the first indication I'd had that, despite my failing the lion test, I still belonged to the human race in her eyes.

Another confirmation of this, I thought, came later. Once our safari was over and we were back out on the safe side of the two wire-mesh fences again, we had a late lunch at a combination hot-dog and souvenir stand near the entrance. There were a couple of round tables with umbrellas, and we sat down at one of them with our paper plates and bottles of

soda pop. Neither Bebb nor Sharon had so far expressed any particular
interest in knowing more about who I was or what I did with my life
when I wasn't down in Florida going to zoos, but I had the impulse to tell
them a little about myself anyway. There under false pretenses as I was, I
wanted, at least within limits, to have some of the truth of me known.
So with Bebb not really paying much attention as far as I could see and
Sharon looking at me with a slightly puzzled frown—she seemed less
puzzled at what I was saying, I thought, than at the fact I bothered to say
anything at all—I told them about having taught English at a coed boarding school for a while and about the things I made with scrap iron. I even
found myself telling them about Ellie. I don't know why I felt like telling
them about Ellie. In part it may have been a kind of substitute for telling
them about Miriam because I didn't feel like thinking about Miriam just
then. But in any case I mentioned our orphan-asylum plans vaguely and
how she worked at the U.N., and even as I was speaking I thought to myself how incongruous just the sound of her name seemed here among the
three of us under our umbrella.

I tried to imagine Ellie and Lucille meeting, or Ellie and Brownie—
it would be like the encounter of matter and anti-matter, I decided, one
simply canceling the other quite out of existence—and I wondered what
Ellie would have thought of Lion Country. I could imagine her little
murmurs of wonder and surprise and how she would have pretended not to
notice when the lion with the kink in his tail took a leak. And then I
thought of the picture Bebb had snapped with my camera of the lions
coupling, and how, if it turned out, I might bring it up to Manhattan
House when I got back and Ellie could build a whole evening around it,
maybe invite in some of her U.N. friends. I had paused to take a bite of
hamburger and at this thought I choked on it, and that was when I received what I took to be confirmation that, despite my failure at the lion
test, Sharon accepted me as a member of the human race anyway. I choked
on my hamburger, and the result was that a half-chewed crumb of it went
shooting out of my mouth and hit Sharon somewhere in the neighborhood
of the eye.

It is a nearly universal experience, I think, that when anything like
that happens between people—you touch somebody's foot by accident
under the table, say, or open the door when they're sitting on the can—
the result is instantaneous apology on one side and embarrassment and
confusion on the other. I apologized, all right, but Sharon—how can I say
it? She didn't make much of it, didn't laugh or exclaim or anything like
that, but the puzzled frown was shattered by that always surprising smile
of hers—the smile of a gondolier who knows he has overcharged you and
knows that you know—and what I understood her to be saying as she
wiped at her cheek with the back of her hand was that something half-
chewed had flown out of my mouth and hit her in the eye, and all in all,
like Bebb's lions taking their pleasure by the water hole, it wasn't a bad

idea for a hot afternoon with nothing much else to do. It livened things up a little. That crumb, you might say, was the first real bond between us.

Two more things. At the souvenir stand she bought Bebb an absurd hat. It was a black beanie with *Lion Country* written across the front in yellow, and at each side, so they stuck out over your ears when you wore it, a little propeller. She made the poor man wear it on the trip back to Armadillo, and of course the rush of air as we sped along the parkway made the propellers spin crazily. As I looked at him there with his fat, pale face zipped up against the wind and the glare, and the propellers sticking out of his head, I couldn't help remembering Lucille's words to me at the Manse the evening before. "Sometimes I believe Bebb is from outer space himself," she said, and for a moment I took the idea almost seriously.

When we got back to Armadillo toward the end of the afternoon, Bebb drove straight to the Manse instead of dropping me off first at the Salamander Motel. He opened his door and got out, at the same time indicating that Sharon and I were to stay in. Bebb said, "I'm expecting the call from Herman Redpath about now, so I want to get right on in to be there when it comes. Sharon, be a good girl and take Antonio back to the motel. Antonio, you and I've still got a lot of business to do, but I expect I'll be tied up with Texas most of this evening, and yours and mine isn't anything won't keep till tomorrow anyway. There's plenty to see in Armadillo. Get Sharon to show you the sights. I'll tell you what." He remembered here that he was still wearing the beanie and took it off. He then reached into his trouser pocket and drew out a little snap purse such as women use for change in their pocketbooks. There was a small roll of bills in it, one of which he peeled off and handed to me before I had time to protest.

He said, "Antonio, how about you keeping Sharon out for supper for me? I'll get a whole lot more done with her out of the house. No, no." He pushed my hand away as I reached out to return the bill. "We've got a special entertainment account down at Holy Love. I write it right off, and it's a hundred percent legal. Now, you two young people have some fun together and get something to eat when you're hungry, and that'll be just fine."

It was the first time I'd seen Sharon show anything like embarrassment, and for the first time too it made me stop to wonder how old she was. Not more than nineteen or twenty, I decided, twenty-one at the outside. She said, "My God, Bip, you're one for the books all right. What can the man say?"

I said, "Yes, Bip, and what can the child say either?" and that was the second thing. It was the first time I'd called him anything, and I called him Bip. I have never particularly liked to hear adults calling each other by the names that children call them. I have known grey-haired men who called their blue-haired mothers-in-law things like Nana and Googoo because those were the grandmother names their children used. And now

I heard myself doing the same thing because Sharon had done it and the name seemed to fit him somehow. Bip. I said, "Bip, for you we are prepared to say anything or do anything. If it's O.K. with you," I added to Sharon.

"If it's O.K. with you," she said, "then I guess it's O.K. with me."

Chantilly lace, I thought. That slightly corrupt gondolier's smile.

8

I HADN'T REALIZED how hot it was till we got back to the Salamander Motel. I wanted to pick up my own car, and if I was to take Sharon out to supper later on, I thought I'd better change my shirt, so that's where we headed for first. There was no breeze, and there was no shade, just the little bits of eave projecting over the two rows of rooms which stuck out not unlike Bebb's propellers from each side of the small white stucco office. The immediate problem was what to do with Sharon while I changed my shirt. It didn't seem humane to ask her to wait for me in the hot sun or in the office, which as far as I could remember had nothing much in it but a desk and cigarette machine, and it didn't seem decorous to invite her into my room. Sharon, as it turned out, solved the problem herself. She said, "I feel like I've got lion all over me. How's about if I come on in and wash up?"

No one had touched the room since I left, and it was a mess. The bed lay unmade with the top sheet pulled down to the foot and half coming off onto the floor where I'd crawled out to shake hands with Bebb. Despite my effort to hide it behind the curtain, the Dewar's bottle was clearly in sight on the windowsill. The pajamas I'd rinsed out the night before in the shower were over the back of the one comfortable chair. The only compensation was that no one had turned the fan off, and that, together with the fact that the Venetian blinds had also been drawn all day, made it somewhat cooler than it was outside.

"It feels like a movie theater in here," Sharon said, "or a cave." Her white sailor pants and her raspberry-ice shirt looked brighter in the artificial dusk of the Venetian blinds than they had in the sun, like flowers on a rainy day. I apologized for the mess and offered her the bathroom if she wanted to wash the lion off right away, but she seemed in no hurry about that and sat down in the chair with my pajamas on the back in such a settled sort of way that I found myself more or less obliged as the host to sit down myself on about the only place that was left, which was the foot of the unmade bed.

If my purpose in Armadillo was to find out as much as I could about Bebb, it occurred to me, this was about as rich an opportunity as I'd yet had—a daughter who would probably know most of the story from the inside and yet an adopted daughter who mightn't have the same hesitation about telling it. I felt no special remorse at the thought of pumping her because at this point the idea of getting back to New York and writing my article seemed so remote that I wanted to hear the story mainly just for the story's sake, particularly the story of Sharon herself. She sat there looking as if she'd been called into the principal's office for copying somebody's homework, and yet I felt oddly that she was the one who was the principal.

"I feel all loose," I said, "like a long-necked goose."

"Like the Big Bopper," she said.

Come on, honey, you know what I want is what I might have said then, but I didn't. What I wanted, I might have said—and she almost looked as if she knew that I did—were the facts, the facts maybe most of all at that point about her, but the facts about Lucille too and Brownie and Herman Redpath and especially, of course, about Bebb. Not so much so that I could skin him alive just then, but so I could understand something about what went on inside that tight skin of his, that plump, pale sausage of a man with his rebellious eye and his heroism among lions. Rather have a tooth pulled, he had said, than go up in an airplane, and I thought of his flight to New York, to Texas, to God only knew what other places Holy Love took him to, and I wondered if he sat there every time with his coat buttoned tight as his safety belt and his mouth snapped shut to keep the terrible fear from showing. How much of a crook was he, and just how full was the accreditation of Gospel Faith? What was the truth about what had happened at Miami, and how had the trial come out? How about the five lost years when Brownie kept the files? And what about Lucille and the Tropicanas and the dead baby and the silvers and golds from outer space? *Come on, honey, you know what I want,* I thought. What I said was, "Tell me about yourself," and I leaned back on my elbow in the twisted sheets and tried to look both casual and interested, whereas the truth of it, needless to say, was that I was not at all casual and a great deal more than interested.

It is the perfect sentence to stop conversations with, of course. I have been asked the same thing myself—Tell me about yourself—and my instinct has always been to flick my lower lip with my thumb, blub blub blub.

Sharon looked blank enough for a while. She had turned around in her chair and swung her sailor legs over the arm so she sat there sideways gazing out toward one of the drawn blinds with her hair dividing over her ear again. "I am adopted," she said after a while. "Bip adopted me when I was two, and I don't know a thing about my real parents, and if anybody else does, they've never told me. I don't know when my real birthday is, but we always celebrate it on Luce's because I was Bip's birthday present to her."

"They had their own baby once," I said. "I saw it in a photograph."

Sharon said, "It died." She looked back from the window to me at this and drew her hand down flat over her hair the way she had in the car when it blew into my face. "It was some kind of freak accident, and they don't either of them talk about it. Killed Luce, I guess."

"The Tropicanas?" I said.

Unexpectedly, she laughed. "That fruitcake Brownie," she said. "He told Luce she shouldn't offer you a Tropicana, being Holy Love and everything, and Luce told him you were from New York and go shove it. You should have seen your face the first time you tasted it wasn't just orange juice."

"You mean you saw my face?" I said.

"I was in the hall," she said, "and half the time Brownie didn't shut the door after him."

I said, "Spies get shot."

"We're all spying on each other," Sharon said. "Bip spies on the lions. And you spy on Bip. I can see you watching him just like the rest of them."

"Who are the rest of them?" I asked.

"All the Holy Lovers," she said. "The ones like you who come around, anyway. They're all trying to see if they can figure out how he does it."

"Learn his tricks," I said.

"You might say. Whatever you call it what he does."

"He loves you, doesn't he, Bip?" I said. "Just the way he says your name."

"He says it's a dime-store name. Luce gave it to me. He wanted something else," she said.

"Brownie said he went away for five years," I said. "By the way, Brownie shut that door on the bats last night. He pulled it till it clicked."

"You know what that Brownie drinks?" she said. "He won't touch Tropicanas or anything else hard, but he drinks after-shave. I caught him doing it once. I guess he figures if people smell it on his breath, they won't think it's his breath."

"Maybe it's what gives him such a sweet smile," I said. I didn't mean to be unkind about Brownie. "You come down pretty hard on Brownie," I said. "All of you."

Sharon said, "He's so soft. Maybe he needs something hard."

"Brownie said the five years Bip was away he was doing the Lord's work," I said.

Sharon said, "He was in jail."

It was like reaching out in the dark for your watch or a glass of water and finding that instead of having to grope all over the place for it, you've put your hand on it first thing. I had expected to have to knock over a lot of things in my clumsiness and now that I'd come on it so easily I wanted to move away from it. I needed no one to help me imagine Bebb pacing back and forth in his cell wearing his claws off. I had seen the way he looked there in my room that very morning with the stripes of light from the blinds cutting across him like bars. "That's tough," I said. "I'm sorry."

Sharon said, "A lot of people have it in for Bip. They got some kids to frame him, and the judge was in on it too, so they gave him five years. There wasn't a thing Bip could do about it."

"It must have been tough on you and Lucille," I said.

Sharon yawned and stretched her arms up in the air till there was a bare strip between her white pants and her shirt like a dancer. One of her sandals fell off. "I hate to admit it," she said, "but Brownie looked after us pretty well. And there were always some Herman what's-his-names around too, only maybe not quite so loaded. Bip's got enemies, but he's got friends too." She reached down for the sandal. "Hey, is your name really Antonio?" she said.

I explained about my father's World War I romance and my Italian mother. I told her that, except for Bebb, most people called me Tono. Miriam said it made me sound less like an organ-grinder.

Sharon said, "Antonio, would you be shocked if I asked you something?"

If I was a spy, I thought? If I was still a virgin at thirty-four? Was I really in love with my twin sister? Did I believe in God? Did I masturbate? "I don't know," I said. "Maybe I would be."

She said, "Would you be shocked if I asked could I wash the lion off here in your shower bath?" She sat there with the sandal in her hand and the one bare foot up on the arm of the chair. "I haven't gotten to have one since the last time Bip took me with him to Atlanta. All we've got home is tubs."

Looking back on it, I suspect we both knew what hung on my answer—not that I could have really answered anything other than of course the shower was all hers if she wanted it, but on how I answered it anyway, the look on my face, the way the air felt between our faces. She waited there in that one comfortable chair with her ear showing through where the hair divided over it and her cheek resting against the back where my pajamas were, and I waited. I was still sitting on the foot of the unmade bed, leaning sideways on one elbow. I glanced downward to rest from her eyes for a moment and noticed the little alligator on the pocket of the shirt Ellie had given me. Ellie.

I could offer to get out of the room till she was through, I thought. I could do a couple of laps around the motel while I was waiting. I could find another room somewhere and take an ice-cold shower. In my mind, at least, I could light a candle to good Saint Anthony and ask that all not be lost forever, for me or for Sharon either. I crossed one leg over the other and, looking back up at her again with the steadiest glance I could manage, I said in a cool, Madison Avenue voice, "Help yourself. I think there's a clean towel in there, and I haven't touched the washcloth." Who ever heard of taking a shower with a washcloth? But I was grateful for whatever words came to my mind. It made no difference what they meant.

I remember the sound of the water splashing. Hot water splashing makes a different sound from cold water splashing—a finer-grained sound —and I could tell it was hot water she was using. I didn't try to picture anything, tried not to, in fact. I lay back on the crumpled sheets with my feet still on the floor, and with the toe of one and the heel of the other I worked off first one loafer and then the other. I looked up at the ceiling and thought of a line from *Madeline* that Miriam and I had liked as children about how on the ceiling of the hospital there was a crack "that had a habit/Of sometimes looking like a rabbit." There was no crack on this ceiling, just a light fixture which looked something like a pinwheel.

I suppose if I tried I could remember everything, the whole sequence of what followed from the time of Sharon's question and my answer up to the time we finally left that room a good while later. How one thing led to another, as the saying goes. Bebb's ad, Tom's eye, the dream on the train, "The Book of the Cock," the lion trying to get rid of its itch against the dead tree, and now me on my unmade bed with the Dewar's on the windowsill and the sound of the water splashing and all that came after. There can be no doubt about it. One thing does lead to another very much as the Hindu monkey swings from branch to branch and sometimes, I am tempted to think, without much more in the way of rhyme or reason.

I remember how after a while she was standing there by the bed with the towel wrapped around her like a sarong and holding her damp hair in a pile on top of her head and asking me if I knew where something was, though I haven't the faintest idea what it was she was asking for and hadn't the faintest idea then. I remember her face was wet still, and there were drops of water caught in her eyelashes. And I remember how far away and almost detached I felt as I reached up with one hand and touched the place just below her shoulder where she had the towel tucked in on itself and how at my touch the towel didn't fall straight to the floor as you might suppose but sideways instead and quite slowly, catching for a moment on the way down.

If I forget thee, let my right hand forget her cunning. If I do not remember thee, let my tongue cleave to the roof of my mouth. I remember that Sharon—that dime-store name—frowned, did she? or smiled her young thief's smile as she raised one hand to her shoulder where my hand had touched, and stepped free from the towel at her feet.

If I tried, I suppose I could remember how it all went, one thing leading to another thing, and when it comes my time to die and my whole life passes before me as they say a life does, I suppose I will see it all again and remember how it was with us there and what we did and what we said, which was not much, and how all the time the electric fan was going and if we had stopped to notice, we would have seen whatever there is to see of a sunset when the Venetian blinds are down. But "O my America! My new-found land," Donne wrote to his mistress on going to bed, that strange man, part priest and part satyr, who all his life was half in love with death. "My Myne of precious stones, My Emperie." And then "How blest am I in this discovering thee! To enter in these bonds is to be free. Full nakedness! All joyes are due to thee." Anything I might add to that would have to be on the order of footnotes.

But as Montague Rhodes James would be almost certain to agree, a few footnotes are probably in order. The time finally came when I decided to take a shower myself, which I did, a rather brief one that was neither hot nor cold but pounded down hard on my neck and chest, and when I came back into the bedroom again, dripping water all over the rug, I caught sight of myself in the dresser mirror and paused for a moment, God knows why, to get a better look. I was still soaking wet mostly, and my hair was in my eyes, and there were beads of perspiration on my upper lip and running down my sideburns. In the words of the Big Bopper, I looked all loose like a long-necked goose, and there was that about me which looked so particularly loose, looked such a limp and wretched souvenir of the thing it had been when we started, that with something like real indignation in my voice I said to Sharon, "Just see me. *See* what you've gone and done," and Sharon answered with something I can't remember except that it made me remind her that Bebb had said the first thing I was to clean up was her language, and Sharon said, "You better make that the second thing."

And I remember how later my strength returned and kept on returning so many more times than I would have thought possible that I told Sharon about the Hindu holy men who sometimes lavish all the vast accumulations of their abstinence on a single night that may last for centuries, and she seemed quite interested. I remember also how at some point I asked her if this was her first time. It was nearly dark by then except for a pearly greyness at the windows and the bluish-white sheen, almost like moonlight, of the sheets. She was lying on her side with her hands tucked under her cheek, palm to palm, like pictures of children asleep, and she said it wasn't her first time and it wasn't her last time either, and I wondered whether she meant that it wasn't her last time with me or just wasn't her last time. I wondered what difference it would make to me to know and what difference if any it made to her.

There in the Salamander Motel we went to bed together, Sharon and I, and I thought to myself that in the highly unlikely event that I was ever to tell Ellie about it, or even if I was to tell Miriam, that was the way I would probably put it—that we went to bed together. It seemed such an impoverished expression, but then as we lay there side by side in the semi-dark, I decided that maybe there was more to it than first met the eye. For the second time that day, I had some of her hair in my face, but I let it stay there now, not smelling so much of sleep any more as of the shower. For quite a while we hardly said anything, and when we touched each other, it was as much like friends almost as like lovers. We'd gone to bed together, my new-found land and I, and maybe just that was what had been at the heart of my desire all along.

Then after a while we talked, or at least Sharon did. She'd told me three lies, she said, and since I'd been decent enough to let her wash the lion off in my shower bath, she thought maybe she ought to come clean about them. The first lie was about Brownie. She had never really caught him drinking after-shave, she said. She believed that he drank it and Luce believed it too, but neither of them had any real proof. Maybe the only reason he smelled of it so was that he dowsed himself with it. The second lie was about Bip, and since I could not see her face very well—it was too close to see and there wasn't much light—I was not quite sure in what spirit she told about it. She was talking quite softly, half into the pillow, and there was an oddly deadpan quality to her voice.

About Bebb's being in jail, she said, she wasn't really sure that he had been framed. Some said he was, and some said he wasn't. There were witnesses who claimed that they had seen the thing happen, and Sharon told me exactly what they had said they saw. It was of course possible that they were lying because there was no question there were people out to get Bip for one reason or another. Bip himself had pleaded not guilty at the trial, but she had no idea what he had said in private because she had never heard him talk about it in private or anywhere else for that matter. Lucille talked about it sometimes when Bip wasn't around, but it was usually after a good many Tropicanas and you couldn't be sure what Lucille thought about it. The last time, Sharon remembered, Lucille said that people from outer space were queer as Hell. But you couldn't be sure what Lucille meant by queer.

The last lie was about Bip's baby, she said. She put both her hands flat on my chest as she started to tell about it and pushed herself a little bit away from me. Her hands felt cool against my sweatiness, and I reached for them in the dark and put one of them back on my chest and the other on my whiskers. It was true that the baby had died, she said, but it was not a freak accident as she had told me. Lucille had killed it, she said. A lot of people thought, as of course I had myself, that it was the baby's death that had led Lucille to Tropicanas, but actually it was the other way around. Bebb was away somewhere at the time, and Lucille was drowning her sorrows all by herself one evening when the baby, who was colicky and had given them lots of trouble from the start, started screaming its head off. Lucille went into the large, old-fashioned bathroom where they kept the crib and went after it with a toilet brush. When Bebb got back the next morning, he found the baby dead and Lucille very nearly dead herself. She had tried to cut her wrists with a razor blade but had made such a bad job of it that they were able to save her. The coroner was a friend of Bip's, and between them they were able to fix it up somehow to look like an accident, but a lot of people had their suspicions, and it was not long afterwards that Bip moved to Armadillo. They had been living in Tennessee when the thing happened. In those days Bip had been a Bible salesman.

Bip himself, Sharon said, had told her this story. It was on her sixteenth birthday, thus also Lucille's birthday, and Bip had planned to take them both up to West Palm for a lobster dinner and the movies. But Lucille hadn't felt well, so Sharon and Bip had gone alone. After the lobster dinner, there turned out to be no movie they wanted to see, so they went to some professional *jai alai* matches instead. Bebb drank two bottles of beer, which was unusual for him, and it was on the drive home in the dark that he told her. She wasn't to think too hard of Lucille, he said. She hadn't been in her right mind when she did it. She had loved the baby more than her life, as proved by her attempt at suicide afterwards. He was telling Sharon, he said, because she had a right to know and because he needed to tell someone, but she was never to let Lucille know she knew.

When he finished, Sharon said, she told him she could not understand how in spite of all this he had ever been able to forgive her. And at this, Sharon said, Bebb had pulled the car off the road and stopped and then opened the door enough so that the light inside went on. He had looked at himself in the rear-view mirror and then turned to Sharon as if wanting to make sure that she could see his face as he spoke. "How do I know that I have ever forgiven her?" he said. And then, after a while, "How do I know that I have ever forgiven myself?"

It was not until almost eleven that Sharon and I left the Salamander Motel. There was no place left open for supper in Armadillo, and we decided we weren't hungry anyway, even though our only lunch had been the hot dogs at Lion Country. So I drove her home in Bebb's car in case he needed it the next morning, and I planned to get back to the motel on foot. It wasn't that far. There were no lights showing in the front of the Manse, and we kissed quite chastely in the shadows of the porch. Sharon had left her hat in my room, she said, and would I bring it around if I came the next morning. Would she be there if I did, I asked her, and as I waited for her to answer, I realized that in some way I had placed my life in her hands with the question. It was a feeling in the pit of the stomach like suddenly being afraid that you're lost as a child.

"This wasn't the first time," Sharon said, "and it wasn't the last time either," and then "Good night, Big Bopper," she said and had started for the door when I remembered the money Bebb had taken out of his snap purse and given to me for our supper when we left. I took it out of my pocket and handed it to her. Sharon tilted it into the moonlight to see what it was. "Five bucks," she said. "I guess he didn't expect us to eat much."

9

AS IT TURNED OUT, I didn't see Sharon the next day, not because she wasn't there when I arrived but because I never arrived. There was no phone in my room, but I had noticed a booth in front of the motel office and stopped there on my way back to have a slot-machine breakfast at the gas station across the street. It was the second day since I'd last seen Miriam, and the way things were, I thought I'd better check in with her. She had her own phone, and it wasn't a bad time to call her because she would have already had her breakfast by then and the doctors didn't make their rounds until later.

Vast as the distance seemed in every way between the Salamander Motel booth and that hospital room of hers with the storm-tinted window, I got through to her with no trouble at all, paying for three minutes with a whole fistful of change that I had picked up at the office. It rang out like the Bells of Saint Mary's as I deposited it coin by coin, and at the last peal of the last bell I could hear Miriam's voice at the other end. She made no introductory remarks, asked me nothing about how the trip was going or where I was calling from, but started right in with what was most on her mind.

She said, "Oh Tono, thank God it's you. Listen. Charlie phoned me yesterday. He's bringing Chris and Tony into the city today. They've got dentist appointments this afternoon and he's taking them to Radio City Music Hall afterwards, and in between times, around four or five, he asked if I'd like him to bring them up here to see me. I'm sure he had to take about six phenobarbitals to steel himself for the call, and it was sweet of him to do it, but I told him no. At least I told him I didn't want *him* to come. I think I could take it all right, but I knew he couldn't. So what I suggested, Tono, was if I could get hold of you, maybe you could meet them somewhere and bring the boys up yourself, and he said if this was the way I wanted it, it was O.K. by him. Frankly, I think it was a huge load off his chest not to have to come himself. So, Tono, will you get hold of him this morning please—before they leave? That head doctor, the Groucho Marx one, says I seem to be holding my own, and I'd like to see the kids again while that lasts, before the fireworks start anyway. So I'm counting on you, Tono. Call Charlie and fix a place where he can hand the kids over to you."

While she was talking, I had been watching a Negro woman carrying a vacuum cleaner down the row of rooms where mine was, and I wondered if she would get to mine this time and if there would be anything there to tell her about Sharon and me and what she would think about it if she thought about it at all. The whole time Miriam was talking, I had been waiting for pause enough to tell her that what she was asking was totally impossible. Here I was fifteen hundred miles away or whatever it was on a summer's day with a floppy straw hat in my hand that belonged to a girl I had gone to bed with the night before and a queer floppy feeling in the pit of my stomach at the thought that when I got to the Manse maybe she would not be there or maybe she would. What Miriam was asking was a complete impossibility, as she herself would surely realize if I just reminded her of the geography of the thing, and as soon as she stopped talking I would remind her. Then it occurred to me that of course Miriam had no idea I was in Florida at all.

Her only world was the world of that hospital room, and if she had even been listening the day I told her I was planning to take the train down, she must have put it out of her mind long since or assumed vaguely that I must be back. In any case, I was not in Florida because basically, for her, there was no such place as Florida. I was only twenty or thirty blocks away at my apartment with Tom, and thus when she said she was counting on me, she was really counting on me, and what she was asking me was not an impossibility that I could make her understand in a minute but an urgency that I could not refuse. What she was asking me was to make it possible for her to see her two sons once more while she still had eyes to see them with, and when you came right down to it, there was no reason I couldn't do it. Though I was no more of a flier than Bebb, there were planes, after all. I could be at the airport in West Palm in an hour, three or four more to Kennedy, say another hour into the city. It was only about eight thirty now. The Negro woman had just set her vacuum cleaner down two doors from mine and was fumbling with a ring of keys when Miriam stopped and I heard myself saying, "I'll get Charlie on the phone as soon as we hang up, and I'll bring Chris and Tony up around four."

Miriam said, "Thank God it was you, Tono. I don't know what I'd have done. Don't you forget, now," and I told her I wouldn't forget.

I had to go back to the office for some more change and then called Charlie. He sounded sleepy and confused but finally understood what I was getting at and confirmed all that Miriam had told me. The dentist's office was across Forty-second Street from Grand Central, so why didn't I plan to look for him and the boys under the clock at the Biltmore a little before four. The dentist was just for prophylaxis this time, so they should be no later than that. The boys and I should be able to have a good hour with Miriam afterwards because the Rockettes didn't go on until seven and that would still leave him and the boys plenty of time for supper. The dentist, the last meeting with their mother, supper, the Rockettes—we plotted the boys' day out, Charlie and I, and I could see him sitting there in his pajamas on the edge of the bed, his face still blurred with sleep. I was going to tell him where I was so in case I didn't make it on time he would understand and wait, but then I thought better of it. If Miriam didn't know, I didn't want Charlie to know either.

My third and last call was to Bebb to tell him that I wouldn't be able to keep our appointment that morning. Brownie answered. Bebb hadn't come down yet, he said. He had been on the phone most of the evening and hadn't gotten to bed until late. I asked for Sharon, and Brownie said, "Dear, you don't see Sharon up and around much before ten unless it's for something special," and I wondered whether, if I had come over as I'd said, the sound of my voice in the hall would have counted as special enough. I thought of her asleep with her two hands tucked under her cheek. I asked Brownie to tell Bebb that I had been called back to New York unexpectedly but hoped to return to Armadillo the next day and would call when I did. I thought of adding something about Miriam and why I was going, thought for a moment even of asking if Bebb would hold up my name in prayer for the plane trip, and Miriam's name too, but Brownie said, "I'll have to go now, dear. The bacon's burning," and hung up.

I left all my luggage at the Salamander, thinking to be back so soon, and took only my overcoat for when we got to New York and it would be November again. The weather at the airport was perfect, warm and bright and without a cloud in the sky, and I felt eccentric and valetudinarian with the coat over my arm and wondered if that explained Bebb's inadequate black raincoat the day I had met him in the city—not that he didn't have something heavier but simply hadn't felt like getting on the plane with it. I thought also of how Bebb said he was scared to death of planes and wondered if he really was or had just said it to make me feel better about not wanting to get out of the car in Lion Country. As for me, I wasn't so much scared of planes as I was irritated by them. I was irritated by their misleading look of sleek invulnerability and by the hostess who came down the aisle as we were about to take off from West Palm taking drink orders. What a far cry from my Persephone of the trip down, I thought. She looked like the editor of the yearbook at a Baptist college, and for all her professional solicitude to the contrary, I had the feeling that anybody who ordered a drink at ten thirty in the morning would find a rather unpleasant quotation beneath his senior photograph in June. I ordered a double martini, therefore, following it shortly with a second, and slept most of the way to New York.

"With the first dream that comes with the first sleep," Alice Meynell wrote, "I run, I run, I am gathered to thy heart," and as soon as I closed my eyes there some thousands of feet above the earth, I found myself starting to dream about Sharon. I thought of the way she had looked as she stood there holding her wet hair in a pile on top of her head and how she had said she didn't know when her real birthday was. I thought of how Bebb had made her look at him when he answered her question about how he had ever been able to forgive Lucille for the baby. But I did not want to think about Sharon until I found a time and place for thinking about her properly, and made myself look elsewhere for something to fall asleep on.

I decided to think about my article on Bebb. How would I begin it, I wondered, and what would my approach be? In one sense I didn't know enough yet for a real exposé, and in another sense I knew too much. It was one thing to expose the fat stranger who had put sugar in his chocolate milk and talked about making checks out to cash to keep the Internal Revenue Service out of your hair, but Bebb in knickerbockers with the faceless baby in his lap, Bebb standing unarmed among the lions, even Bebb doing whatever he had done and for whatever reasons in front of those children in Miami. And was it possible for me any longer to expose Bebb without at the same time exposing myself, I who had drunk Tropicanas with his wife, who had let him risk his life to get a photograph for me of lions copulating, who had accepted money from him to take his only child out for supper and had then taken her back to my unmade bed at the Salamander Motel instead? And photographs—how could I get a photograph of Bebb's eye lazing shut, what kind of Cartier-Bresson or Karsh would I have to be in order to capture the expression I had seen in his face when he was looking at Sharon as she put the beanie with the propellers on it upon his bald head? Despite all my efforts, Sharon kept drifting back into my mind, and, groggily poised as I was on the very sill of sleep, the thought of her and the thought of Bebb became all confused with one another, even their faces, and I could not think clearly which of the two of them my article was to expose or whether it was they who were exposing me or I who was exposing myself and whether it was a good thing or a bad thing. I remembered how I had stood there in front of the dresser mirror shouting to Sharon, "See me. See what you've done," and then gradually the two double martinis and the hum of the engines pushed me over the sill, and I slept until we reached New York.

It was typical somehow of Charlie Blaine to pick under the clock at the Biltmore for the place where he and the boys were to meet me. Juniors up from Princeton and sophomores down from Smith, young ensigns on leave from the Pacific and girls who wept at *Mrs. Miniver* and did their turn at the USO, attractive young people all the way back from himself and Miriam, I suppose, to Zelda and Scott—this was undoubtedly the way Charlie thought of the Biltmore, and of course he was dead wrong on two counts. Number one, if it was still the kind of place he remembered its having been, it was the wrong place to meet the brother of your ex-wife when she was dying of myeloma. Number two, it was no longer the kind of place he remembered and hadn't been for years. When I got there the only people sitting on the curved banquette under the clock were an elevator man picking his nose and a fat woman with an orchid corsage pinned to her coat who was reading the *Daily News*. In a moment, around the corner from the newsstand where they must have seen me walk in, came Charlie with my two nephews.

Tony, the ten-year-old, was dark and had something of Miriam around his eyes and nose. He was a lot fatter than I had remembered him and looked sleepy. Chris, who was twelve, was a shadow of the shadow who was his father—his face and hair were both about the same color, which was dimly blond. I could see right away that Chris had been weeping, and since he had always been the closer of the two to Miriam I was not surprised. His eyes were pink, and there was a damp smear on his cheek. The boys were both wearing grey flannel suits with long pants, and Chris had on a hooded jacket that was approximately the same color as his hair and face. Charlie stepped forward to greet me with a warmth that made me remember Miriam's speaking of his love-making as importunate but strangely passionless. He was glad to see me, I think, not because of who I was but because of what I was about to relieve him of. Tony and Chris both shook hands and called me Uncle Tono.

I said, "Hey, Chris, I can't take you up to see your mother looking like that. We've all got to put on a good show for her this afternoon."

Charlie said, "That's all right. It's not about Miriam. The nurse found a bad cavity, and the dentist decided he'd better fix it then and there. Chris says it still hurts from the drilling."

"The Novocain's all worn off," Chris said, "and it feels like he must have left something in there under the filling by mistake. I think we better go back and have him look at it." Even as he spoke, I could see the tears well up in his eyes again.

Charlie said, "It's just the reaction to the drill. It will go away. Besides, you've got to go up to see your mother with Uncle Tono. You know how sick she is, and she's been expecting you all day."

Tony yawned. "Maybe if he could suck on a piece of ice, that would help," he said, and I said that sounded like a good idea to me and gave them a dollar to go downstairs to the grill and get something in paper cups with ice in it and then Chris could suck it. I did this partly because it seemed to me it might help and partly, I think, because, although we were all there well ahead of time, Charlie was obviously eager to get rid of us and I saw no reason why he should be let off as easily as all that. If Miriam was right that he couldn't take going up to the hospital, he could at least take this. As soon as Tony and Chris had gone, I said, "Charlie, have you told them how sick she is? Do they have any idea they may be seeing her for the last time?"

"I don't know why you say that," Charlie said. There was a faint smile on his face, but I thought I could see that he was irritated. "I understand the doctors say she may go on a lot longer, which means this probably won't be the last time at all."

I said, "Even if she does go on for a lot longer, this may be the last time she'll be able to see them in any sense that means much. So I think she's going to make it her business to have it be the last time."

Charlie said, "Well, I don't think the boys have any idea of that. At least, I'm sure Tony doesn't. He was up so late watching TV last night, he's half asleep anyway. Chris maybe. He's the sensitive one, and I think his tooth really hurts him. Do you suppose I ought to take him back to the dentist?"

I said, "That's up to you, Charlie. You know him better than I do."

Charlie seemed to give the matter serious thought. "No," he said at last. "On second thought, I think definitely not. If this really turns out to be the last time, it would hurt him more later to know he didn't go than his tooth hurts him now."

"How about you, Charlie?" I said. What I think I meant was how about him in a general sort of way—how was he getting on, how did it feel to be losing a wife he had already lost—but he took me to mean how did he himself feel about not going up there to see Miriam this afternoon now that he had firmly committed his sons to it.

He said, "I'll tell you how it is with me, Tono," and his faded blue eyes took on a faraway look as though he was remembering some old script he had worked on for educational TV. "I'd like to go up there with you in many ways, but in another way I'd rather not. You see, I prefer to remember her the way she was."

I said, "That's great for you, Charlie. You'll be able to keep your happy memories intact that way. But suppose everybody decided the same thing? Then everybody would stay away so they could remember her the way she was, and she would die all alone there the way she is."

Charlie said, "You're her brother, Tono. You belong there with her, no question about it. And Chris and Tony too. They're her flesh and blood. But, to tell you the truth, I don't think Miriam wants to see me. She told me she didn't think she could take it if I came."

I said, "What she told me was she thought she could take it all right, but she didn't think you could." As soon as I said it, I regretted it. I regretted it because Miriam wouldn't have wanted me to say it and because I could see that it had left its mark on Charlie. It was the first time since we had started talking that he looked fully awake.

"Oh God," he said. "Did she say that?" I nodded, and he sat down there under the famous clock not far from the fat woman with the corsage, the skirts of his overcoat touching the carpet and his fedora on his knee. "The truth of it is she's right, Tono. I'd be scared to death to go."

I felt suddenly so sorry for him that I reached out and put my hand on his shoulder. I said, "Well, Charlie, don't take it too hard. I didn't mean to put you on the spot. Everybody's scared to death of something, and you just happen to be scared to death of death. For me it's life."

"Thanks," he said, although I was not sure what he was thanking me for, and then the boys came back up the stairs, and Tony said, "The man told us there hadn't been a grill down there for years. It's a florist shop."

"We'll get Chris some ice at the hospital, then," I said, and then added to Charlie, "You and I, Charlie. We belong to another age."

When we got to Miriam's room, we found her sitting up straighter than I had seen her for some time. They had cranked the bed up higher and put an extra pillow behind her, and there was something about the way she was propped there with her shoulders slightly hunched and one hand lying palm up at her side that made me think of a large doll. Her other arm was in a plaster cast from the wrist to above the elbow, and this was the first thing the boys asked her about once they had kissed her and taken off their coats and sat down side by side on the broad windowsill where she directed them.

Miriam said, "Isn't that the last straw? I tripped and fell on my way to the john the other day and broke the damned thing," and then she started right in asking them about themselves, how the dentist had been and how school was and if they had been taking their vitamins as though lining up in advance enough questions to keep them going the whole hour. It was at this point that I gestured to her that I would leave the three of them alone together for a while and had just started for the door when she interrupted herself in the middle of a sentence and said, "For Christ's sake, don't leave me, Tono," which was the only time that afternoon that I saw anything like terror in her eyes.

Chris had started telling her about his tooth, and she was asking him about it, and then she stopped so utterly dead in her tracks at the sight of me heading for the door that it was apparent even to Chris, I think, that the words we were all using seemed to count for a good deal less than words usually did, or at least to count for something quite different. It took a moment or two to get conversation started again, and this was the only difficult part of the whole time, those few moments when we sat there with nothing but silence to hide our nakedness behind. It was Chris who saved the day by asking if he could get some ice for his tooth. There turned out to be some in the water pitcher, and in trying to crack it on the radiator he smattered some on the floor, so that Miriam had to tell him to get a Kleenex to wipe it up, and suddenly we found that we all had words to wear again and familiar parts to play in their familiar garb.

Tony got started on the movie he had sat up so late the night before watching on television, and before he was through he gave a fairly complete outline of it. It was an old Abbott and Costello film called *Abbott and Costello Meet Frankenstein and the Wolf Man*, he thought, or something like that, and as I sat listening to him tell it—he was perched there on the windowsill in his long grey pants with the fly half unzipped because of his paunch and waving his hands around and rolling his dark eyes—I thought to myself that the operatic Italian strain from my mother had survived another generation. There was one part of the story that had particularly appealed to him, and his account of it went into particular detail and became at times particularly operatic.

Abbott and Costello were on this island, he said, and Frankenstein and the Wolf Man were there, and Dracula was there too. Dracula was the worst of them all, he said, because he kept trying to sneak up on Costello because Costello was so fat and juicy he wanted to drink his blood more than anybody else's. And then Costello finally made a break for it and tried to get away in a motor boat, he said—all of this in one soprano stream broken only by an occasional heavenward rolling of his eyes and short, rapid intakes of breath. But when he reached the getaway scene, he slowed down and really gave it all he had.

He was Costello fiddling with the outboard motor in a panic to get it started before the monsters showed up. He was the outboard starting, coughing, stalling. He was Dracula. Dracula appeared in the mouth of a shoreline cave in his opera cape with one arm crooked out in front of his face so that just his tortured, piercing eyes showed above it, and Tony made his eyes tortured and piercing. He furrowed his brows. He made hypnotic gestures at the back of fat little Costello trying to escape, made them at his mother propped up there in her bed.

"You should have seen it, Mum," he said. "All they show is Costello's face. The whole screen. Dracula's up there in the cave zapping him from behind, and you can tell on his face how it's getting to him. He starts to sweat and go duh-duh-duh, and you can tell he can't resist because Dracula's too powerful for him the way he's zapping him from behind. He's pulling him like a magnet, and Costello gets out of the boat and starts walking back to the black cave. He goes real slow at first because he doesn't want to, but he can't help himself. And then the best part, Mum. The best part's when little by little he gets going faster and faster till finally he picks up his coattails like a girl and starts *skipping* back to old Dracula. You should have seen it, Mum," he said. "It would have killed you."

Skipping back. The black cave. It was Tony's one aria that afternoon, and he got through it well, and only when it was over, as though the strain of it together with his late hours the night before were too much for him, lapsed back almost immediately into drowsiness.

Miriam also seemed drowsy for a moment, I thought. She had been listening to Tony more attentively than I felt she'd listened to anybody else up to then, and when he finished, she kept on looking at him as though he were still talking. Then both her eyes did a very Bebbsian thing—they fluttered lazily shut for a moment and then came open again. Her hair was pinned back behind her ears with too many bobby pins, and I wanted to take the bobby pins out and let the hair fall down over her shoulders the way I was used to seeing it. I wanted to open the louvers on either side of the picture window and let some fresh air in and the smell of the hospital out. I wanted to tell her about Sharon and about the lions screwing and the fat lady with the orchid corsage. And that broken arm—the only good thing about it was that she said she'd fallen on her way to the john. I hadn't thought she could even get to the john any more.

A little incoherently, because of the ice in his mouth, Chris was telling her about school—how he hated science and math and loved English, and I saw a whole life flowing out from there. That great watershed of the young: do you like science and math, or do you like English and possibly history? If it's the first, then your life goes one way, and if it's the second, then your life goes the other way, and the whole thing's usually settled before you even get to high school. Chris had a poem in the magazine, he told his mother, and he hoped to get a part in the play, and maybe he would end up in educational TV like his father, I thought, or writing novels up to page thirty-four like his uncle, who could say? But at least in a general and rather depressing way, I felt sure, you could say plenty, and I wondered what Miriam was thinking as she lay there watching him too and possibly even listening—his face and hair that were nearly the same color or absence of color, his wiry hair itself that curled flat to the scalp, the faded eyes of his father. I remembered Miriam's saying she was afraid Charlie and his housekeeper might turn her sons into fairies if they weren't careful, and in Chris's case I could picture it easily enough. Not that there was anything particularly feminine in his manner any more than there was anything particularly masculine in it—at twelve he stood just on the fringes of that great, sweaty free-for-all and hadn't chosen his side yet—but I could imagine its happening the way his mother feared. Chris in his forties teaching English at Choate, say, or Hotchkiss, taking his pets out to dinner in town, telling risqué stories in class, keeping photographs of former students tucked into his dresser mirror and inscribed to him by his first name.

Miriam said, "There's a color TV down at the end of the corridor in the sun room. Why don't you kids run take a look while I talk to Tono about a couple of things? We'll call you back," and when they had gone, she let her head sink into the pillows in a way that made me realize for the first time that she had been working at holding it up. "Jesus Christ, Tono," she said, and when I came over and offered her a cigarette from the pack on her bedside table, she waved them away with her good hand. "I've given them up for keeps," she said. "They're bad for my health."

She lay there looking off toward the window. It was getting quite dark outside, and I thought I saw signs of a little snow flurry in the air. Her good arm was still lying at her side much as it had been when we first came in, and I had the impulse, which I resisted, to reach down and touch the upturned palm.

"I lied to the kids," she said, and remembering Sharon's three lies, I wondered what there was about me that made people keep confessing their sins. "I didn't have any fall going to the bathroom. I've been using that damned bedpan for weeks. You'll never believe it, Tono, but you want to know how I broke my arm?"

I nodded, I guess, standing there at the side of her bed looking down at the pack of cigarettes she'd given up.

"Night before last I woke up and reached out to get a glass of water from the table, and it just broke. I could hear it, Tono. It sounded like when you step on a stick in the woods."

I have never been a cigarette smoker, but I took one out of the pack, and with the matches that had been tucked in under the cellophane, I lit it. It tasted like dust.

"Do you think anything happens?" Miriam said. "After you're dead, I mean. I'm not being morbid, I'm just damned curious."

Three or four times in my life it has been given to me, as Brownie might have put it, to say the right thing, and this was one of them. I take no credit for it anyway. The Hindu monkey just happened to reach out for the right branch at the right time, that's all, and was lucky enough to catch hold of it. I remembered Montague Rhodes James and Latin text A and the part where Christ enters at the end in a blaze of light as Don Giovanni, and I started to tell Miriam about it. I described his glittering white cloak and doublet and the silver buckles on his shoes, and I pictured his smile to her, the flashing white teeth and pointed beard like Errol Flynn or a young Ronald Colman. I told her about the little earring in one ear and how he drove his rapier through Satan's shoulder and signaled Hell to pin his arms to his sides. I told her how he stretched his arms out wide and said, "Come unto me, all ye my playfellows who bear my image and likeness." And I told her how Adam had come up, and then King David and all the patriarchs and prophets.

She really listened to the whole thing, I could tell, and when I finished, she reached out for my cigarette, which I gave to her. She took a puff on it and said, "*Bene, bene*, Antonio," then after another puff handed it back to me, and I stubbed it out in the ashtray for her. "Go tell the kids to come back in," she said, "and then you better get them back to Charlie."

There was a button hanging by a thread on Chris's hooded jacket, and she told him to get somebody to sew it on for him before he lost it. She asked him how his tooth was, and he said it was some better. Tony, she said, shouldn't watch television so much. It ruined the eyes. He was to tell Charlie that for her. Charlie was going to take them to see the Rockettes, they told her, and she said she'd never been crazy about the Rockettes herself but everybody ought to see them at least once.

After she had kissed them goodbye and we were about to leave, Tony gave an enormous yawn, stretching one fat arm up into the air and knuckling his eyes with the other, and it seemed to rub her the wrong way because she sounded quite angry when she spoke to him and in some ways more like herself than I'd heard her for a long time. "Now you stay awake, Tony," she said. "You just keep your eyes open and stay *awake*."

There was a lot of life in her voice, a lot of Wop, and I can hear her saying it still. *Stay awake*, she told him as we left, and part of what she had in the back of her mind, I suppose, was poor Charlie with his naps and his kapok pillows sleeping his life away. *Stay awake* were the last words she spoke to my younger nephew and namesake, and looking back on it, not just the words but the fire inside them, what I think she meant was stay alive. "You just stay alive" was what she told that fat little boy with his zipper half unzipped, or there would be Hell to pay. And then we were gone.

After I delivered the boys back to Charlie at Reuben's on Fifty-eighth Street, I thought of spending the night in New York. As much as I'd had a plan, that had been it. I could ring up Ellie, I'd thought. I might even drop in at the vet's the next morning and see how Tom was getting along. But at the last minute I decided against it. Instead, I caught a night flight out of Kennedy and was back in West Palm by about midnight, where I picked up my cream-colored convertible. I had not realized when I left how homesick I would be for Armadillo.

10

I DREAMT that night about Sharon. We were walking through the grass somewhere, and the wind was in her hair, blowing it against my face again, and when I reached up to brush it aside, she wouldn't let me. "Don't touch me," I thought she said, and it made me feel sick and lost until I realized that she had her hands on my cheeks and was gently nodding my head from side to side. "Rise and Shine, Big Bopper," she was saying, "rise and shine," and her hands felt cool on my face, and I felt that something was rising somewhere and for all I knew shining too, and when I opened my eyes, I found that Sharon herself, no dream of Sharon, was there beside me. "You're the one," she said. She was holding my face in her hands as though it was something that interested her.

You can never step into the same river twice, as whichever Greek said who said also that the only permanent thing about life is change. It was different with Sharon and me that morning from what it had been two evenings before, in no sense less than it had been then and in some ways possibly even more, but different anyway. She was not my new-found land now but a land that I had touched on before and where I had left a flag against my returning, a land that as soon as I touched it again I knew I had never stopped being homesick for and that I returned to now like a king returning from exile who stoops to kiss the earth beneath his feet. It was not Venetian-blind dusk in the room as it had been the first time but Venetian-blind morning with the sun streaking in through the slats and fanning out across the wall above our heads; and from what must have been from the room next door to mine, to ours, we could hear the sound of a vacuum cleaner as the Negro woman whom I had observed from the telephone booth the day before drew every day closer like Fate itself.

Sharon's dress was a circle of green and yellow on the rug where she must have stepped out of it while I was still asleep, and one of her sandals was poking out from underneath. I drew her eyelids sideways with my thumbs, and she became the shimmering young ranee or fragrant-limbed houri and I the fallen holy man with his hair every whichway, bleary-eyed, unshaven, and unwashed. We were not together for anything like as long as the first time, but we were together long enough to be quiet and still for a little while too, and then Sharon said, "I came to pick up my hat. Bip saw your car outside and told me to come get you. When you've had your breakfast, he wants to see you down at the church."

I said, "It was nice of you to come, and I hope you'll feel free to come again any time you take a notion to. I've been keeping your hat in the closet for you."

"It's nice to come together this way," she said, and then, "Come," again, standing there by the side of the bed now and reaching out to take my hand. "You better get up and get dressed now. Bip needs you. He's in a real sweat, you should see him."

And he was, figuratively and otherwise. I dropped Sharon off at the Manse after a slot-machine breakfast which I ate with her floppy straw on my head where she had put it—made me look like a half-breed, she said—and then I drove on to Holy Love. I stopped in for a moment at the souvenir stand first and bought a shrunken head for Tony, a wickerwork monkey for Chris, and a small rug with a Red Indian on it for Ellie. I considered one with a sunset on it for a while, but then decided that the Red Indian might do more to liven things up at Manhattan House. I wanted to get something for Miriam too, but I couldn't find anything that I thought she'd like. Maybe on the way home on the train I could get her a bag of oranges, I thought, but I wasn't even sure they'd let her eat oranges. When I entered the church, I found both Bebb and Brownie there.

Brownie was up on a chair washing the glass-brick windows. He had shorts on again and sneakers with bobby socks, and he smiled as he greeted me, his glasses fogged up and the stains under his arms bigger and darker than I had seen them before. Bebb was dressed in what I began to think must be his only suit, but this time he had laid the jacket over the top of the lectern and was standing there with his shirtsleeves rolled up and his face damp and shiny. He was vacuuming the carpet, and the folding chairs were all folded up and stacked against the walls. He switched off the vacuum as soon as he saw me come in, and "Herman Redpath," he said, wiping his handkerchief over the top of his head. "Herman Redpath is flying up in his private plane first thing tomorrow morning, and I am going to ordain him personally right here at Holy Love. Thank the Lord you've come, Antonio. I need somebody to talk to. Brownie, you pismire, watch what you're doing. You're dribbling dirty water all over the floor."

I would never have thought Bebb capable of looking so overwrought. Whatever might be stirring down underneath somewhere, I had always thought of him as keeping it pretty well tucked in with only that occasionally giveaway eye to hint at its hidden presence. A parlor magician keeps himself buttoned up pretty close against the possibility of exposing his trick, and just the look of Bebb suggested as much—the skin stretched tight almost to splitting over the plump flesh, the nutcracker mouth snapped shut, that skimpy black raincoat I had first seen him in which bound him under the arms and across the rump. But on this occasion his jacket was off, his shirt undone at the collar, his tie pulled loose, and he seemed prepared to express himself without constraint. He unfolded two of the chairs and set them up for us in front of the altar table and proceeded to range over a number of different topics, all the while playing with the vacuum-cleaner hose, which he would double up in his fist or snake along his knee or shake back and forth like a rattle, while off to one side Brownie got on with his glass-brick windows.

On Herman Redpath: "Antonio," Bebb said, "twenty-four hours from now I will be—twenty-*three* hours from this moment almost to the dot— I will be laying my hands on the head of Herman Redpath. The wealth of that man is beyond the dreams of avarice, and he made every nickel of it himself. He is a fine Indian Christian and one of nature's gentlemen, and he will be flying here to Armadillo with a whole planeload of close friends and kinfolk to be present at the ceremony tomorrow. Brownie, unless you put some elbow grease into it, you're wasting your time. You're so flabby and hopeless. Brownie and me, we've got to lick this place into shape so when Herman Redpath and his party get here I won't have anything I've got to be ashamed of. Herman Redpath will stand just about where you're sitting now, and I will stand up there behind the altar table. Then at the proper moment Herman Redpath will kneel down, and I will move down to in front of the table and lay my two hands, like this, on top of his head—if there's any other clergy present, it's etiquette to invite them to step up and lay their hands on his head too—and then I will call upon the Almighty to send down upon him the gift of charity—charity is the most important gift of them all, Antonio—and the gift of faith, and the gift of the word of wisdom. Those three are absolute musts. Without them you're licked before you start. And for Herman Redpath I may also request the special gift of healing because as a direct descendant of the American Indians he probably has a gift for healing already. Herbs, Antonio. Herbs and roots and an understanding of many growing things that the white man knows not of."

On his dreams: "Scripture tells us how the devil took Jesus up unto an exceeding high mountain and showed him all the kingdoms of the world and the glory of them, and then the devil saith unto him, 'All these things will I give thee if thou wilt fall down and worship me.' The kingdoms of the world, Antonio, and the glory of them. Who hasn't seen these things, if only in his dreams? Show me the man who says he hasn't been tempted to bow down and worship Mammon for these things, and I will show you a liar. I have dreamed, Antonio, and God knows I am not beyond tempta- tion. I am chief among sinners. And the wealth of Herman Redpath . . . the cash-on-hand, the blue-chip securities, the oil leases, the cattle lands. . . . He has put nothing down on the dotted line yet, but hints have been dropped, promises have been made. Herman Redpath has extended to me the right hand of fellowship, Antonio, and I would not be human if I had not given some thought to what that—to what it all *might* mean. The things of this world and the glory thereof. A fine new car with air- conditioning for this infernal heat. A bungalow along the coast some- place where Sharon could go for a week-end with her young friends, where I could send Lucille for July and August when she gets her rash. A new color TV—the one we've got gives us nothing but trouble. Cameras, clothes, transistor radios, money in the bank, not to mention power and influence and a voice that when you say something, people listen to you the way they listen to Herman Redpath. I believe I would be able to resist these things, Antonio, although in my dreaming I have not always chosen to resist them. I believe that when Herman Redpath and I have joined forces, together we will take the great riches that he has earned by the sweat of his brow and put them to work for Jesus, Antonio. I see Holy Love swelling like a mighty stream. I see Gospel Faith expanding its activities. I see more and better ads, Antonio, and more personalized attention to each one of them, more follow-up. And at the end of it all, I see an old man named Bebb living out his declining years in peace. There have been deep hurts and bitter memories for me, Antonio. There have been fierce battles where blood has been shed. But I dream of a time when the lion shall lie down with the lamb right here in Armadillo, Antonio, and in my heart. And no longer shall they hurt or destroy in all my holy mountain, saith the Lord."

On Sharon: "When King David was an old man, Antonio, they brought him a maiden named Abishag to warm his heart and give him strength again. I am no King David, and I am not what you would call exactly an old man either, but from the moment she first entered our house—a poor, wizened little thing didn't anybody want, with no daddy

to give her his name and a mother couldn't keep her—from that moment
I began to see what the love of God was all about. The love of God is a
wizened little thing doesn't anybody want, Antonio, but once you receive
it into your heart, it gives you your strength again. We had a little bit of a
baby of our own once that didn't live, Lucille and me, and Sharon brought
us healing and forgiveness for our grief. And trouble, Antonio. I won't let
on for one moment she didn't bring us plenty of trouble too. A child that's
not your own flesh and blood, you try to make up to it for what you aren't.
You lay your heart open before it. You expose your tenderest part to it to
love or to hurt or to run away scared from, however it happens to feel.
When you love a child, you put yourself at that child's mercy, Antonio,
and there has never been a child, but one, was always merciful. Sharon
more than most maybe. We have been fortunate. You have seen her for
yourself now, Antonio, 'Who is she that looketh forth as the morning, fair
as the moon, clear as the sun, and terrible as an army with banners?' She
is the warmth of my heart and my strength, Antonio, and I want her to
be happy more than I want anything else. I want her to settle down with
a good man—not one of your world-beaters or a millionaire or a Rudolph
Valentino—but a man with a patient heart who will see to the good in
her even when she is sometimes crazy and spiteful and who will treat her
with courtesy and use her kindly. I would fly from here to Timbuktu to
find such a man for her, Antonio, and I've told you I would rather have
a tooth drawn than go up in a plane."

   On Antonio Parr: "You and me, Antonio, we have business together.
The first time I set eyes on you in that greasy spoon in New York City, I
said there's a man I respect. He is a smart man who doesn't hardly ever
say more than he means and who may sometimes say less than he means
but probably only if he thinks it's easier on you that way. I won't say I
trusted you right off, Antonio. That would be an exaggeration. On account
of my ads and Gospel Faith and all of it, I have had my run-ins with the
authorities. The IRS goes without saying and I have already mentioned it
to you, but the Better Business Bureau, the U.S. Post Office, the Federal
Trade Commission, and the U.S. Department of Education—at one time
or another they have all been on my tail, trying to prove what I do is
illegal. Everything I do is legal, Antonio. I have seen to that. I am vigilant
because I have to be vigilant, and when a young fellow writes a letter like
you did and expresses an interest in talking with me, I am suspicious. It
would not be the only time that even high-up officials have stooped to that
kind of stunt with me. When I first saw you, Antonio, I wasn't sure what
you were up to, but whatever you were up to, I could tell you had a kind
heart and wouldn't ever do anything on purpose to hurt a person. So I
trusted you up to that point, and I would trust you farther than that
point now. If you are really interested in starting a branch of Gospel Faith
up North, you just stay around a few days more and we'll talk about it. I
want you to do this very much, Antonio. Don't go away until after the

ordination anyway, because if I am talking inches now, after Herman Redpath joins us I will be talking miles. I like you, Antonio. Lucille likes you. She says you have fine manners and are a gentleman. And Sharon likes you. To be frank with you, she has never said she does, but she doesn't have to. If she said she liked you, chances are it would be one of her jokes. So you hang around a couple of days longer, Antonio, and we'll have a chance to do some business together."

On Brownie: (Bebb did not make this whole speech at once. It came out at various points during our conversation as Brownie did various things to prompt it, like dribbling the water or not rubbing hard enough and sometimes things that I did not notice myself like just the expression on his face, I suppose, or the way the back of his neck looked.) "Brownie, you wash those windows like you teach Scripture. You just skim the surface. You just smear around a little soft soap and water, and it may look good while it's still wet, but when it dries, any fool can see what a mess you've made. You've got to get in there and sweat and rub till your arms ache so the light can come through. Same way with Scripture. Sweat and grunt and maybe the light that comes through blinds you almost, but at least it's the light. It's the light that shineth in darkness even if the darkness comprehendeth it not. There's a sermon in that, Antonio. Brownie, the way you pour on that after-shave, you've got this church smelling like a whorehouse. Now, you take a man like Brownie, Antonio, and you ask yourself where the Almighty went wrong. Well, I tell you it's not the Almighty went wrong, it's Brownie went wrong. The Almighty gave Brownie life, and Brownie never lived it. He just shoved it up his ass. But it's not too late for him, Antonio. Even for Brownie there's hope. There's got to be. Because if there's no hope for just a single one of us, then there's no hope for any of us. Brownie, he does most of the work on the courses. That's why he's Dean and why his signature's on the diplomas. The way it runs is you pick out of the catalogue which course you want to have and just send in a check or money order made out payable to Gospel Faith for the tuition fee. Then Brownie sends you back the required reading. Good paperback books, Antonio, none of your cheap stuff. You write out full outlines of all those books and mail them off on eight-by-eleven paper to show you've done the work. If they meet our standards, Brownie mails back your diploma. Services rendered for cash received. Is there anybody would like to explain to me what's illegal about that? I don't hold a man's past against him any more than Jesus did. Remember the good thief, Antonio. Remember the woman taken in adultery. But there's people like Brownie that hold their own past against themselves till it gets where they can't break loose out of it any more. Brownie did a little time here something like twenty-five or thirty years back. Cashing bad checks. You ever noticed his smile, Antonio? That's a smile you turn on the warden or the judge. It's a smile to use on cops. It's a smile says *Who, me?* It's a smile says *Kick my ass, and I'll still kiss yours.* What have you got against getting married, Brownie? The trouble with you is the only sex you get is in the bathtub. I don't mean to take off on you like this all the time. It's just something about the way you are and the way I am. I'm sorry. Forgive me, Brownie."

There was more which I do not remember, and although I listened to it carefully, all the time Bebb was talking I kept thinking in the back of my head that not an hour earlier I had been in bed with his daughter, and not for the first time and probably not for the last time either. Bebb sat there in his folding chair, tipping back in it sometimes and playing with the vacuum-cleaner hose and mopping the top of his head as the morning wore on. I didn't do much talking myself, and Bebb obviously didn't expect me to. It was his time to let things out, and I had a feeling there might be still more to come when he looked at his watch and rose quickly. He said, "Herman Redpath. He's supposed to be calling me at noon to finalize things. If you would stay here and help Brownie get things set for tomorrow, I would be much obliged, Antonio."

As soon as he had gone, I said to Brownie, "Brownie, how can you just sit there and take it from him like that?"

Brownie had moved his chair over to the next window and was standing on it with a wet rag in his hand and several dry ones hanging out of the rear pocket of his shorts. He turned as I spoke and, removing his glasses, wiped each eye with the back of his wrist. He did not put his glasses back on right away, and looking at him without them, I felt I had caught him off-duty and out of uniform. Seeing Brownie without his glasses was like seeing Mary Baker Eddy on the can, and I was prepared for anything.

Brownie said, "I've taken a lot from him, it's true. But I have been given a lot by him too, dear."

I said, "What have you been given, if you don't mind my asking?" Tropicanas to serve, I thought, and suppers to make, and windows to wash. Eight-by-eleven outlines to read and diplomas to sign. For the first time in a long while I found myself wanting to skin Bebb alive again, and although I thought then that it was for Brownie's sake, I have thought since that it was probably because of Sharon. I had made clandestine and illicit love to the warmth of Bebb's heart, and it made me hate him. "What has Bebb ever given you that entitles him to treat you like shit?" I asked Brownie. Saying *shit* in Bebb's church, I suspect, was another way of getting back at him.

Brownie said, "He has given me my life, dear. Leo Bebb raised me from the dead."

"Come again," I said.

Brownie smiled at me, and without his horn-rimmed eyebrows his smile was much vaguer and more random. He said, "I mean like Lazarus. Dear, I was laid out dead in Knoxville, Tennessee, and Leo Bebb came in and raised me up."

Brownie told me the story standing in the chair with his glasses dangling from his hand. I had crouched down to change the head around on the vacuum cleaner and remained there—Bebb had been using the brushy side on the rug rather than the plain one, I discovered. As Brownie talked, I was looking up at him from below and Jesus was looking as usual toward the hot-air register. Behind Brownie I could see the glass brick drying in cloudy streaks just as Bebb had predicted it would.

It was back in the days when Bebb had been a Bible salesman, Brownie said, and just after Lucille's baby was born. Brownie himself was a salesman working on commission in a used-car lot and came to know Bebb through doing business with him. Bebb had a large territory to cover with his Bibles, and over the course of a few years he bought and traded in several times. They were not close friends, Brownie said, but they were more than just acquaintances because he remembered that when the baby was born, Bebb came by the car lot on purpose to hand him a cigar and tell him it was a boy and they had named him Herman, which, as soon as Brownie said it, made me wonder if this might be part of the reason Bebb had such a warm spot in his heart for Herman Redpath. Within a day or so after this, Brownie said, he, Brownie, died.

It was a freak accident. There had been a heavy rainstorm with high winds the night before, and a power line had blown down along the street that Brownie walked every morning to work. Brownie noticed that it was down, but didn't realize the danger, and about a block away from the car lot he stepped into a puddle where the line had broken in two and received such a jolt of electricity that it stopped his heart and killed him. There was no doubt about its killing him, he said. His boss from the car lot saw it happen and got help, dragging Brownie out of the puddle by a rope he'd managed somehow to loop around Brownie's foot without getting electrocuted himself. They tried to administer artificial respiration and sent for a doctor, but their efforts were unsuccessful, and when the doctor finally arrived, he pronounced Brownie dead.

Brownie said, "At that time I was sharing a couple of rooms with a friend of mine who was a barber, and since I had no wife or family—I've never been married, dear—they got hold of my friend first thing, and he came right down in his white tunic, leaving a customer in the chair, they say, with only half his face shaved. All of them except Billy—that was the barber—were in favor of taking me straight to the undertaker, but Billy was very devoted and he wanted me brought back home first. I was quite a mess to look at, as you can imagine, and he felt it wasn't right to let a stranger handle me, at least not until he cleaned me up and got a chance to say goodbye first. It was a touching gesture and also a very fortunate one, as it turned out, because if they had taken me straight to the undertaker, the chances are he would have slit me up under the arms the way they do and started draining me and in that case it is doubtful I would be here telling you the tale now.

"Well, news travels fast in a town the size Knoxville was then, especially bad news, and it wasn't more than an hour or two before Mr. Bebb heard it, and as soon as he heard it, he came right down to where Billy and I lived to see was there anything he could do. Being friends, I had also made him a very good price on a Chevy wagon he was considering at the time, and I believe he wanted to find out if I had left anything in writing on it, knowing I was in the habit of setting such things down in a notebook I carried around in my pocket. When he came into our room, there was nobody there except just Billy and I, and Billy is the one who gave me a full description later on of what happened. But there is no need to go into the details. We've got our work to get on with.''

"Please," I said. "Go into the details."

"Billy had me lying on the bed in my underclothes," Brownie said. "He had scrubbed me up and trimmed my hair around the ears and combed it. He had laid out a clean shirt and tie and the suit I wore to church Sundays, and he was just fixing to get me dressed when all of a sudden Mr. Bebb came in. He didn't even knock, Billy said—just walked right in and stood there at the foot of the bed and looked down at me lying there dead. 'Billy,' he said, 'tell me exactly what happened,' and Billy told him.

"When Billy was done, Mr. Bebb looked at me awhile longer and then finally he said, 'Billy, do you believe in the Holy Ghost, the lord and giver of life?' Poor Billy, he was not what you would call a religious man. He was of French Canadian extraction and had been raised a Roman Catholic, but he ran away from home when he was only thirteen and hadn't been to church since. So when Mr. Bebb asked him the question point blank like that, Billy told me he didn't know what to say. But we had been very close for several years by then—I was thirty-three at the time and he was still in his twenties—and the sight of me laid out there cold and still on the bed that way made him feel like he had to believe in something, he said, so he told Mr. Bebb yes, he believed in the lord and giver of life, and Mr. Bebb said, 'Well, Billy, that makes two of us, not counting Brownie. And counting Brownie makes three because Brownie was a believer too.'

"Being in the business of selling Bibles, Mr. Bebb knew his Scripture even back then, and going by what Billy told me later, I think he must have had John eleven in the back of his mind the whole time. He said, 'Billy, our friend Brownie sleepeth, but I go that I may awake him out of sleep.' Then he walked up to the head of the bed and laid both his hands down on top of me where Billy had my hair all fixed up and combed. He raised his eyes and seemed to be praying, Billy said—I am the resurrection and the life, he said, he that believeth in me, though he were dead, yet shall he live—and then, after a few moments of silence when Billy said his face got as red as though he was holding his breath, Mr. Bebb called out in a loud voice almost like he was mad, '*Brownie, you stand up!*'

"Billy said at first he didn't think anything was going to happen. I just kept on laying there with my face about the same color as the pillow, but then Billy thought he saw something move. Now, because I am not telling this in mixed company, dear, but just to another member of the male sex, I do not mind telling you that what Billy said he first thought he saw move was my private parts—just a very faint movement down there the way it can happen sometimes for no reason and you don't even notice it, but I was wearing only my underdrawers at the time so Billy noticed. Then he thought he saw some color returning to my face, and Mr. Bebb held his arm out, crooked at the elbow, and after a while I reached out and grabbed hold of it and pulled myself up to a sitting position. Billy said he did not know if what he saw running down off Mr. Bebb's face was tears or sweat.

"From then on I can tell the story myself, and there is very little left of it to tell. The first thing I remember was, it was like if I was lying at the bottom of a deep pit and way up at the top I could see this arm, and I knew if I could only manage to reach it, I would be all right. I did not know or care whose arm it was. I just knew I had to reach it or perish, and fortunately I reached it. When I opened my eyes, it wasn't Mr. Bebb I saw first, it was Billy. The light seemed so bright it made my eyes ache, and for a moment I thought he was on fire."

Brownie had been standing on the chair all this time, and when he finished his story and kept on standing there without his glasses looking so pale and unsteady I got up to my feet in case it proved necessary to catch him. But then he hooked his glasses back over his ears again, and his whole face seemed to come back to life—the smile I had grown accustomed to, the heavy, plastic eyebrows. I said, "Brownie, are you sure you were really dead?"

He said, "Dear, I would not tell such a story if I was not sure."

"Do you remember what it was like to be dead?" I said.

He said, "There is nothing to remember about that because there was nothing there to remember, and there was nothing left of me to do the remembering with even if there had been something there. Death is zero, dear. It is zero minus."

I said, "Well, it was a miracle then. It was one of the miracles of the age, and I don't see why it didn't put Knoxville, Tennessee, on the map. There should be a shrine there with little girls in white dresses marching around with candles and piles of crutches stacked up. Bebb should be riding around in a white Cadillac with people scattering rose petals every place he goes."

Brownie said, "Yes. Only that wasn't the way Mr. Bebb wanted it. First thing he said when he had me sitting up again was for me and Billy not to go around shooting our mouths off because there would be an awful fuss if we did, and it would probably lose him his job with the Bible company because they wouldn't want the publicity. He said that losing his job would probably kill Lucille, who had just had the baby and was feel-

ing blue enough anyway and wasn't getting much sleep nights. But of
course it was bound to get out, whether we shot our mouths off or not,
because there were plenty who had heard about the accident, and then
the next thing they knew, there I was back at work again as good as new."

"Exactly," I said. "So how come there's no shrine and piles of
crutches? How come Bebb's still driving a Dodge with fifty thousand miles
on it that doesn't even have air-conditioning?"

Brownie said, "There is a very simple explanation for that, and with
your interest in religion, I am surprised you have not thought of it for
yourself. When you come right down to it, dear, you see, people don't
want miracles."

"But that's just what they do want," I said. "Get the rumor started
that a statue of the Virgin's nose has started to run, and within twenty-
four hours people will be lined up six deep."

Brownie said, "Little miracles, yes. People will flock to little ones like
that the way they would flock to a magic show. But you take a real miracle,
like resurrection—nobody wants those kind, dear, because they make it so
you've got to believe whether you want to or not."

"You're crazy," I said. "That's just the kind people do want." People
like Miriam, I thought. People like the fat lady with her corsage under
the clock, like Charlie Blaine even, sleeping his life away on his kapok
pillow. "They'd give their right arm for a miracle big enough to believe by."

"They'd just explain it away like Easter, dear, and say it never really
happened," Brownie said. "Take the miracle of life, for instance. People
say it's all just acids."

"How did they explain away what Bebb did for you in Knoxville?"
I said. "How do you explain away a thing like that?"

Brownie said, "Oh, that wasn't very hard, dear. They made out that
the power in that broken line had been turned off before I stepped my
foot into the puddle and I just blacked out for some reason. I took a little
something every now and then back in those days, and people said I was
probably under the influence that morning. It is true that the night before
happened to be Billy's birthday."

"But how about the doctor?" I said. "The one they sent for who pronounced you dead."

"Clyde Binney," Brownie said. "A clean, nice-spoken young fellow
who got to be a friend of Billy's later on. It's strange how our lives cross
and crisscross each other, almost like there was a kind of pattern to it.
Clyde wasn't exactly a doctor, dear, although he'd spent a couple of years
in medical school before circumstances forced him to leave. He was more
what you would call a chiropractor. He said he could have been mistaken
when they asked him about it later. It might have been just a very weak
pulse rate and in all the confusion and everything . . . he could have
jumped to conclusions."

"But what does Bebb think about it himself?" I said. "Does he really believe himself he raised you from the dead?"

Brownie had started to work on the window again, rubbing hard at the cloudy streaks with one of his dry rags, but he turned here and looked at me over his shoulder. He said, "We almost never discuss it any more—this happened twenty years ago, dear—but I hardly see how he could believe anything else. Billy said that when he touched my body, it was cold as ice and had already started to go stiff. There was no color in my face. I do not think there is a single doubt in Leo Bebb's mind but that he raised me from the dead in Knoxville, Tennessee. And I think it is also a clue to why he sometimes treats me the way he does. Sometimes I think Leo Bebb thinks he didn't quite get the job done that first time. I think that sometimes with his cruelest words he's just trying to bring me back from the dead again, only this time all the way back."

I started the vacuum cleaner. I did not mean to start it, but I was standing there with one foot on its torpedo-like back, and by accident my foot slipped and turned on the switch. That droning, whining roar, that sudden flooding back of reality. I think Brownie was grateful for the interruption because he immediately went back to the glass brick with fresh vigor, and I was grateful for it myself. I picked up the vacuum gratefully and started cleaning hell out of Holy Love. I wondered if the Negro lady at the Salamander had hit my room yet.

Bebb returned after a while, carrying several long florist boxes full of green tissue paper and cut flowers and bringing Lucille with him to arrange them. Lucille had her black glasses on again with her eyebrows arched above them, and she moved around through that sunlit church in a rather abandoned way at first, I thought, like a groundhog on Groundhog Day hoping to see his shadow so he can return to his dark burrow for six more weeks of winter. But she settled down to the flowers eventually, and while Bebb and Brownie started to set the folding chairs back up in their neat rows again, I tried to help her with them.

I remembered the photograph I had seen on the wall of Bebb's office and tried to read back from what I could see of her face now to the face of the young woman in the filmy dress and shingled hair gazing down at the baby in her husband's lap. After a while I thought I could almost do it—something about the angle of her cheek as she laid the flowers down on the altar table, something about the way her hair was combed out from the temples. It is easier, of course, to read back to a face that used to be than to try to read ahead to a face that will be someday, as, sitting in Miriam's hospital room, I had looked at my nephew Chris and tried to read ahead to his face at forty. And I thought of the curious prescience of the photographer who had caught Lucille's baby in a way that showed no face at all.

Lucille did not talk to me much, and at first I did not think she knew who I was or could see me clearly enough through those black glasses to

be sure, but at one point she dropped her lower jaw in what I felt certain
was a smile and said she heard Bebb had already taken me to see the lions.
"That Bebb," she said, "he's just like a kid. He's never learned to keep his
shirt on. He gets so excited he wants to show everybody everything the first
day and have them be crazy about it like he is, be crazy about him."

"These people from outer space," I said, "they're different from the
rest of us."

Lucille said, "You're telling me?" standing there cradling a skinny
armful of gladiolas. I wondered how much she knew and how much she
would tell, or even how much she had told me already. Had she had to
bite her tongue not to say that Bebb had never learned to keep his pants
on, not his shirt? But then Bebb himself interrupted us.

He took me by the elbow and led me to where he had the entrance
door propped open to let the dust out and the fresh air in. We stood there
under the frosted-glass cross, and he looked me straight in the eye and
said, "Antonio, she'd spit right in my eye if she knew I was saying this and
don't you ever let on I put you up to it, but I happen to know Sharon is
itching to go to the beach this afternoon. She's laying around the back yard
in her bathing suit right now with the sprinkler on, and I just know if you
dropped the word, she'd jump at it."

Whereby he added a few more questions to my already growing list.
Did he know as he stood there under the cross mopping sweat that we
had already made holy love together, the warmth of his heart and I? Was
that why he'd invited me down to Armadillo in the first place? "I am
here to save your soul, Antonio Parr," he had said back there on Lexington
Avenue in the rain. Or Sharon's soul? Or both?

"I'd take her myself or send Brownie," he said, "but we've got our
hands full right here."

11

MY TRIP to the beach with Sharon turned out to be less than a success. I
found her behind the Manse stretched out in the sun in her bathing suit
with the sprinkler adjusted so that it kept up a steady patter on her bare
feet, and, as Bebb had predicted, she seemed glad enough to go once I
suggested it. She was ready to leave in minutes, just slipping on what I
believe is called a muu-muu over her bathing suit and tying a yellow scarf
under her chin to keep her hair from blowing, but almost as soon as we
were on our way she began to seem moody and withdrawn. It must have
taken the better part of an hour to reach the stretch of public beach she

knew about at Hobe Sound, and I don't suppose we talked more than three or four times the whole way.

We stopped along the road somewhere for ice-cream cones, and the one bright spot of the trip that I can remember happened in that connection. I was eating my cone as I drove, a double-dip chocolate, and at some point a bit of the overhang dropped off and fell half into and half on top of the open neck of the navy-blue polo shirt that Ellie had given me. We had some paper napkins, and with one of them Sharon got what she could off my shirt for me. She then reached down inside the neck and wiped off my bare chest, and I remember still the touch of her hand there as we drove along with the sun bright in our faces and the warm air roaring in our ears. But this didn't last long, and the rest of the drive was, at best, uneventful.

When we finally got there, the beach was dotted with Portuguese men-of-war, those creatures from outer space with their transparent bladders of turquoise shading up into purple and those long, wispy stingers that I am told burn like fire if you touch them. They looked quite beautiful floating here and there in the water, especially when a wave picked one up so that you could see it tipped for a moment against the glassy wall, but they pretty well eliminated the possibility of swimming. We kept on walking until we left the public part of the beach behind and started passing the houses of the rich people, houses so rich and elegant that they didn't have to look it but sat back almost inconspicuously there among the palms and sea grape, each with its own little flight of steps leading up from the sand to the green lawn, each with its low cement groin projecting out into the sea to keep the beach from washing away.

Ellie, I knew, had visited here several times, and she had described to me with a curious mixture of disapproval and fascination the extraordinary lavishness of the place that seemed all the more lavish for being so pastel and hushed, like the sound of whitewall tires on an oyster-shell drive. She described the rich people themselves, her parents' generation for the most part but dressed in the cockatoo colors of childhood, the starched nannies wheeling the great-grandchildren of Presidents down to the sandbox and swings near where the yachts were moored, the little fringed golf carts, the masseuse arriving at the door with her collapsible table. I remembered particularly her telling me how when she asked some retired tycoon in canary slacks and an avocado blazer how he liked retirement, he replied that all in all he liked it well enough except that he missed the vacations.

I was haunted by my memory of all this as I walked along the beach with Sharon Bebb of Armadillo. I thought of Ellie going out to dinner in one of these very houses perhaps and conscientiously trying to talk civil rights to the Goldwater Republicans or, out of consideration for her hostess, tactfully trying not to. I thought of the old Yales and Harvards with their prostates and hearing-aids padding over to the edge of the heated pool for one quick dip before the pre-lunch martinis. I thought of how I myself belonged neither to their world nor to Ellie's nor to Sharon's either but how, like my scrap-iron sculpture, I could be arranged in different ways to suit different worlds, and before long I found that I was becoming as depressed and withdrawn as Sharon seemed.

We got back to Armadillo toward sunset. We were sticky from the salt air, with sand in our hair and tar on our feet, and when I asked Sharon if she'd like to come back to the Salamander with me for a shower, I think she considered it for a minute. She had drawn her hair into a long, loose braid and somehow looped the yellow scarf in and out of it. Her eyes looked more green than brown as she squinted into the sun at me, frowning, and then finally shook her head, no. She said, "Bip put you up to taking me, didn't he?"

"Is that what's been the trouble?" I said.

"Didn't he?" she said.

I nodded.

"Oh well," she said. "It was better than Brownie."

It was the kindest thing that I think she'd said to me up to that point, and after dropping her off back at the Manse, I lay down on my bed at the Salamander, slipped a quarter into the Magic Fingers, and fell asleep on the memory of it. There would be other times, I thought, and I found myself not only looking forward to those times whenever they should come and whatever they should bring but also enjoying this time to myself before they came. You don't lose the habits of a lifetime all in a minute, and for the space at least of that long nap—I woke up a few hours later just long enough to phone Bebb that I would be at the Manse first thing in the morning to help get things ready for the big show—I returned to my celibacy and my bachelor solitude with a zest no less keen for knowing that they would not last forever. Although I did not know it then, it was the last peaceful moment I was to have for some time to come.

When I arrived at the Manse the next morning, it looked like an Italian wedding. There must have been four or five limousines parked along the street with their uniformed drivers lounging around in various attitudes, one of them apparently asleep in the back seat with his visored cap pulled down over his eyes, another with his cap pushed back, idly buffing a piece of chrome with his handkerchief. There seemed to be children everywhere, dark-haired, dark-eyed children from kindergarten on up and all of them dressed as if for a wedding or a first communion in white dresses and uncomfortable, boxy-looking little white suits with their hair slicked back or frizzed up with white flowers in it and here and there a lopsided veil pinned on. Some of them were at the sandbox and swings, others climbing around the porch and in the palmettos, and as I got out of the car, a couple of them came tearing around from behind the house with what I recognized as the hose and sprinkler Sharon had been using to keep her feet cool the morning before. By the porch steps, filled with white glads, there were several tall baskets with high, arched handles such as are sent to funerals or *bon voyage* parties on ocean liners, and there was one elaborate arrangement of white carnations laid out on an easel-like frame in the shape of a cross. Sitting near the front door there was a bulky object about the size and shape of a garbage can which on closer inspection turned out to be a rolled-up length of red carpet. When I knocked at the door, it was Brownie who came.

It was the first time that I had seen him in anything but shorts, and the change it made in his whole appearance was quite startling. He had on a double-breasted powder-blue suit with a silvery clip-on bow tie and a sprig of lily of the valley pinned to his lapel. He could have been the owner of a successful haberdashery store or the president of Armadillo Fire Insurance, and the fragrance of his after-shave was even more powerful than usual. His forehead was wet with perspiration, and the smile he gave me seemed so much the product of his dentures alone that I felt Brownie himself could hardly be held responsible for its almost total failure. He said, "Herman Redpath and his party arrived earlier than expected, and the Bebbs are entertaining them till it's time to go to the church. I know they'll be glad to see you, dear. They were about to send me to the motel." Then he led me down the hall, past the bathroom under the stairs with the brown toilet seat, and all the way back to the sitting room where Lucille had received me that first night in Armadillo, which seemed to me already to have taken place as many months earlier as it had actually been days.

The room was crowded with people. Lucille in dark glasses was seated in her high-backed wicker armchair in a dress much like the filmy one from the photograph, and she was holding, clamped between her knees, a glass which I took from its color and height to be a Tropicana. On the arm of her chair sat Bebb speaking with great animation to someone with his magician's eyes open-sesame wide and his bald head buffed to a high polish. He did not stop talking when I came in, but I could tell that he had seen me. At his elbow the color TV was on. A man with a green face and a reddish-purple aura around one ear and under his chin seemed, like Bebb, to be making a speech of some kind, but it was impossible to know what he was saying because the volume was turned off. All around the room, particularly on one sofa, there were Indians.

Perhaps if I had not already known from Bebb about Herman Redpath's ancestry, I would not have recognized them as Indians, but as it was, there could be no doubt of it. Their clothes, which, like the children's, were predominantly white, only served to emphasize the fact by making their skin look even swarthier than it was and their hair look even blacker. There must have been between fifteen and twenty of them all told, fat ones and thin ones, old ones and young ones, more women than men. There was a plump one who looked like Jack Oakie sitting on the floor with his arms around his knees and an old woman with a face like

a relief map of the Rockies wearing a peekaboo blouse. Sharing an ottoman there were three young women with so nearly the same face—a high-
cheekboned, flat-nosed face suitable for patching teepees with or trapping
small game—that it would have taken their mother to tell them apart. And
their mother, I felt sure, was also there. She was one of a number of squaws
on the sofa and by far the largest. She had her daughters' features but so
lost in the great expanse of her face that you had to look sharp to see the
resemblance. She was sitting side-saddle with one leg thrust out into the
room, and at first glance I took the sofa to be laden with nothing but the
white finery and piled black hair and corsages of the other squaws until
suddenly, toward the center, I noticed the thin figure of a man who
seemed to be made entirely of chocolate. It turned out to be Herman
Redpath.

Herman Redpath was wearing a brown suit with a brown shirt and,
in place of a tie, a medallion of horn with two strings hanging down. He
had on a brown, broad-brimmed felt hat of a kind that I associate less
with the Wild West than with Methodist circuit riders, and the brown
face of an ancient Pharaoh. It was a narrow, wedge-shaped face with a
large, high-bridged nose and the skin pulled so tight that it seemed to keep
his thin lips from quite closing over his teeth and his eyes from opening
much wider than a horizon-scanning squint. I could not make out whom
he was talking to, and everybody else seemed to be talking at the same
time, but his voice was the one I heard through all the others and recognized immediately as his. What he was saying was, "I bet you can't guess
what it cost me to fly all these sonsofbitches out here not even counting
the limousines and the drivers at the airport cost me somewhere in the
neighborhood of three four thousand dollars but I don't give a fart how
much it cost because it's worth it to me and it's worth it to Leo hey Leo,"
he called out, pushing a white elbow aside in order to catch Bebb's eye,
"who the hell's that?" and I realized he was referring to me.

Herman Redpath took an immediate liking to me, and as soon as I
saw him, I could have predicted that he would. All my life it has been
that way. The boy with the worst breath in school, the aunt who has made
ouijaboard contact with Lillian Russell, the person who has recently had
his gallstones removed and is carrying them around in an envelope—I have
inevitably been the one they felt drawn to. Ellie always said that it was
my sympathetic El Greco eyes and Miriam that they recognized me as a
brother, but whatever the explanation, it was not Bebb or Brownie, not
Sharon or Lucille or anybody else in Armadillo that Herman Redpath took
a shine to. It was me.

He cleared several Indians off the sofa and made me sit down beside
him and then talked to me for a long time without interruption, by which
I mean not just that he did not pause long enough between sentences for
me to interrupt with some comment of my own but that he did not pause
long enough between sentences for me to know where one sentence ended

and another began. As nearly as I could tell, he was talking about God, although his approach was untraditional and his images were drawn from unexpected places.

He said, "You take your Ezekiels and your Jeremiahs and your Saint Paul the Apostles all your kiss-my-ass holy joes Leo he says they were always seeing God places he was always popping out at them got up like a wheel with eyes for spokes or some damn thing a blinding light far as I can see they must have spent their whole life shitting in their pants I know I would just the sound of a buzztail when I don't see it coming knocks the shit right out of me I steer clear of God and him me hell I don't blame him but there's plenty other things I've seen you bet your ass I'm Indian clear through what the hell you think I'm a goddamn Eskimo an Indian he sees things you boys wouldn't in a million years you think it's all dried up and dead out there the desert's dead the dead scrub seed dried up and dead in the ground the hell you say listen come sundown and the wind near to freezes your balls off some old squaw itching herself side of the fire there's times I've seen how there's nothing is is dead no matter what they say rocks and sticks clouds air I've seen things move that's got no way of moving in them things wink their eye at me and sometimes holler out you got to be quick and sharp to see the life in things how it shoots out like fire once I saw a cactus rear up and squirt it looked like milk two dead stumps humping there's nothing so dried up and dead by God but it's still got the seed of life in it someplace like an old man's got it in his belly clear to the end got spunk in him enough to raise more family with a man can't leave too many behind that's got his brand on them hell no it's not like when you're eighteen nineteen doing it like a jackrabbit and never running dry who gives a fart long as it's enough to hit the bullseye the trick's to keep it up long enough to plant with that's where Leo here says it's God does it the holy damn spirit who gives a fart what he calls it I like him he doesn't kiss my ass like the rest of them do they say he's done time so what if he's done time when he lays his hands on you you get it up he says the life comes through his hands the God you name it that's what I'm here for cost me an arm and a leg the life the life I don't care whose hands time's running out the seed's no goddam use if you don't have what it takes to plant it who the hell cares what it cost time was I'd keep one on all night ready for action they say an Indian's born with one on and busts through the western gate the same way if the luck's with him and the old keeper lets him through let Leo Bebb see can he give me the life back and I'll build him a church makes this one look like a hencoop take a look at that daughter he's got with the pretty little ass on her like a pair of sweet melons who the hell are you anyway looks like you got Indian blood in you too I spotted it soon as you poked your head in the goddam door."

That Tutankhamen face, those delicate brown hands on the chocolate pants, that sofa full of squaws in white dresses with gardenias and lilies of the valley in their hair. I could see Bebb trying to signal me from the door, and as soon as Herman Redpath drew a brown silk handkerchief out of his breast pocket and pressed it against his mouth for a minute as if to spit something out, I made a break for it. Looking back over my shoulder, I saw that he was talking again to someone else or to no one else or to everyone, and I do not think he even noticed that I had gone. He had his hand on the huge white knee of the fat woman sitting sidesaddle next to him, and it lay there fragile and sere like a dead leaf.

Bebb drew me out into the hall. He said, "Antonio, the hour is at hand. I'm going to take Herman Redpath and his party down to the church. I want you to stay here so if anybody comes to the house you can direct them. Herman Redpath is an important man, and there may be reporters. Sharon's going to stay too case there's any ladies come who need the facilities. When the time comes, you bring her down to Holy Love with you."

Sharon and I stayed, but nobody came. We stood on the front porch watching the withdrawal of the Indians. The children were rounded up, some of their white clothes the worse for wear after their rout in the sandbox and among the palmettos. The tall baskets of flowers were somehow loaded into the limousines, and it was Brownie who staggered down the steps under the weight of the rolled-up red carpet. The fat mother of the three daughters got in beside one of the uniformed drivers by sitting down first and then having the Jack Oakie man pick up her legs and swing them in after her. The old lady in the peekaboo blouse ended up sitting on somebody's lap. I could see her through a window perched there like a medicine man's poppet.

The last ones to leave the house were Bebb and Lucille themselves with Herman Redpath following behind them. It was like the royal family coming out on the balcony at Buckingham Palace. They stood there at the top of the porch steps for a few moments while an Indian with a Graflex took pictures—Bebb on one side, plump and glittering, Lucille on the other with her lower jaw dropped and one skinny arm on the railing, and between them Herman Redpath, who stood little higher than a child. He had removed his hat, and his brown scalp was almost completely bare except for a few wisps of black hair, one of which the air stirred so that it stood up like a feather. When the photographer finished, Herman Redpath raised his arm and waved at the waiting limousines. There were several answering honks, arms reaching out of windows, handkerchiefs and flowers waving, and then the party descended the stairs, got into Bebb's car—Bebb and Lucille in the front seat, Herman Redpath by himself in the back—and drove off with the limousines following behind.

Sharon and I waited around on the porch for a few minutes, but when nobody seemed to be coming, we went back inside. We still had a quarter of an hour or so before the ceremony was to begin, and it was cooler out of the sun. We stood there in the hall in that trance-like way people have when there is nothing to do but wait, and all by ourselves in that old house as we were, and both dressed up for Herman Redpath's ordination, for a few moments it was if we were strangers. For the first time Sharon's hair looked properly brushed to me, sleek with a glint to it and not divided above the ears, and she was wearing gold hoop earrings as big around as silver dollars. After our day on the beach, she was almost as brown as one of the fairer Indians, and stepping out of her sandals, she stood there barefoot. I could think of nothing either to say or to do, and neither apparently could she, so I stuck out my hand finally and said in my Madison Avenue voice, "I'm Antonio Parr. I'm pleased to meet you," and she said nothing at first, just stood there with her hand in mine, looking rather somber and illegal. Then she gave my hand a little jerk and said, "Come on up while I wash the Indian off."

I am no fool. Even at that instant I knew perfectly well what would happen if I followed her. She had already started up the stairs, but paused for a moment and half turned with one hand on the banister and the toes of one bare foot resting on the instep of the other. I knew that if I followed her up, there would be no one to direct the reporters if they came. I knew that any ladies who might appear would have to find their own way to the Victorian facility under the stairs. I knew, or thought I knew and perhaps actually did know, that Bebb had left me there believing that I would carry out my charge and then get both Sharon and myself to the church on time because in different ways he needed us both there as much as he ever could be said to need anybody. All this and more I knew, but I am no hero. I followed her up two steps at a time once I got started, and that is how it happened that we missed the ordination of Herman Redpath as I knew we would from the moment my foot touched the first stair and as Sharon, I suppose, must have known even sooner.

We missed the ordination of Herman Redpath, and how, if at all, it would have proceeded differently had we not missed it, and how a number of lives including our own might have been changed either for better or worse thereby, must remain forever among the other what-ifs of history. We missed it, and we knew that we were missing it, and we didn't even stop to mark the moment's passing if it could even be said to have passed, because there are times beyond time or this side of time when moments do not pass so much as they accumulate like different colored filters on a camera lens, bringing the clouds out and making the shadows look deep and rich. The curtains moved, I remember, muslin curtains as soft as cobweb from years of washing. They floated in and out of the open window to the smell, I think, of honeysuckle—or could it have been some lingering trace of Brownie's after-shave?—and there was a soft rattle way off in the distance of somebody's lawnmower. George Hamilton and Ringo Starr were there on the wall together with several nameless young men, one in an airforce uniform who looked like an advertisement for Bryl-Cream and another crouched on a beach with his mouth open and holding what looked like either a football helmet or a horseshoe crab between his thighs. Bebb was there shaking the hand of somebody who might have been Oral Roberts, and there was a Florida State pennant, a water-color sketch of a palm tree with a sailboat way off in the water behind it. We didn't have all the time in the world and we knew it, but we took our time anyway, and if a reporter had wandered in on us to ask the way to Holy Love or if Lucille had come back for her dark glasses or Brownie for his teeth, I suppose we would have noticed them, but I do not think it would have mattered much any more than the curtains mattered or the sound of the mower.

And then all hell broke loose. The door slammed shut downstairs so that you could feel the whole house vibrate from it, then the sound of Brownie's voice calling something I couldn't make out, footsteps hurrying noisily down the hall, another door closing or opening, and the sudden, hard splash of water in a sink. They were the unmistakable sounds of catastrophe, and we both knew it, and yet we stayed there for a moment or two longer as if we didn't know it, and I remember thinking for no reason of Robert Frost's "two roads diverged in a yellow wood" and deciding that Sharon was both the two roads diverging and the yellow wood too. And then, as soon as we could, we went down.

We found Brownie and Lucille in the kitchen, and I have wondered since why it is that at times of crisis it is so often the kitchen that people repair to as if there among the pots and pans the bitterest pill or craziest salad can be somehow swallowed down and cleared away like a meal. Lucille was sitting bolt upright at the kitchen table with one arm hanging straight at her side and the other stretched out on the table in front of her as though she was about to give blood. Brownie was standing bent over at the sink, where the water was running. He was holding a wet dishrag to his face, and his nose was bleeding. I do not know to this day what caused Brownie's nosebleed, but I assume that it was either just nerves or possibly something to do with the slamming of the door.

Under different circumstances they might well have asked us how we happened to be there then, I in my shirtsleeves and Sharon barefoot and without her gold hoop earrings. They might have asked us why it was that we hadn't shown up at the church an hour before as we had been told to, but there was obviously no place in their minds for such questions as those, and if there had been, I do not know how we would have answered. Their story, as it gradually emerged, came partly from Brownie and partly from Lucille, sometimes in sequence and sometimes simultaneously, but I can no longer disentangle the strands of one from those of the other, and where their two accounts differed, sometimes quite radically, I can no longer be sure on what grounds I made my choice between them. I have since listened carefully to one or two other people tell about what happened at Holy Love that day when Sharon and I were not there, and even certain photographs were at one point made available to me, but I am under no delusion that mine is the definitive account. It is just a version like everybody else's, and I suppose it is no less flavored than all the others by the cask that it was aged in.

At the beginning, apparently, everything went along much as might have been expected. Bebb noticed that Sharon and I had not yet arrived by the time things were supposed to start, so he tried to stall for a while, but then some of the younger children began to get restless and there seemed to be some danger that the old lady with the blouse might be overcome by the heat if she had to wait much longer, so finally Bebb had to set things in motion without us. He and Herman Redpath sat alone together in the front row and behind them Lucille and Brownie with the Indians, a reporter from Fort Lauderdale, some hard-shell Baptists who were there primarily for the music, and a handful of passers-by who had simply wandered in, attracted by the crowd.

The Baptists had lent their junior choir for the occasion, and the service began with a half-dozen hymns or so, including "Throw out the life-line" and "When the roll is called up yonder," after which some of the Baptist parents of the choristers pointedly withdrew. Then there were some free prayers offered by Brownie, after which Brownie gave a kind of charge to Herman Redpath, reminding him of his sacred obligation to propagate the Gospel faithfully and above all accurately, and taking for his text Matthew eighteen six, where Jesus gathers some children about him and warns the disciples that rather than cause one of those little ones to sin, "it were better for him that a millstone were hanged about his neck and that he were drowned in the depth of the sea."

In explicating the passage, Brownie drew attention, as might have been expected, to some facts about the ancient world that illuminated the meaning and prevented the possibility of certain obvious misunderstandings. In the time of Jesus, he pointed out, G. Zuss, the grain was of such poor quality and so easily pulverized that millstones were often made of a very light, porous stone resembling pumice. This stone was, indeed, so unusually aerated almost in the manner of styrofoam that, combined with the fact that the salt content of the Dead Sea was so notoriously high that even fat men could float in it like corks, a millstone around the neck might under certain circumstances serve the function of a life-preserver. And this was clearly what the passage intended, Brownie argued: it was better not to cause one of the little ones to sin—there could be no question about that—but if you slipped up, then out went the life-line with a floating millstone tied to the working end, and very few people ever drowned in the Dead Sea anyway. Then there were some more hymns, some more prayers, and finally Bebb rose for the ordination itself.

Bebb was dressed in his white robe, and what with the heat and the fatigue of the day, his face was apparently more drained of color than usual, so that when I try to picture him standing there behind the altar table, I see a palely shimmering Moby Dick or Taj Mahal of a man, and in front of him, with his back to the congregation and facing Bebb, that little chocolate-colored Choctaw, that Mohawk midget, who was Herman Redpath.

Bebb prayed some general prayers first. He prayed for rain to come so the citrus crop wouldn't be ruined, but not too much rain for the visitors from the North. He prayed for the sick and the dying and asked the Almighty to provide them with healing where he could and with courage and comfort where he could not. He prayed for the President and the Congress and for all judges everywhere that they might perform their duties faithfully but always remember that Jesus was a friend of sinners and temper justice with mercy. He prayed for all prisoners. He prayed for old people in nursing homes and for little children. He prayed for the Armed Forces and for all men who did battle everywhere, especially, he said, for those whose battle was a secret one that went on inside their skins. And then he stepped around in front of the table and placed his hands on Herman Redpath's nearly naked scalp.

Except for Brownie's address about the millstone, the prayer that Bebb delivered at this point was the only part of the service, as far I know, that was written down, and I record it here as I have myself read it.

"O God mighty in battle and the sinners' friend, thou who hast counted up the very hairs on our heads and callest forth also the stars and the planets of outer space by name, send down the snow-white dove of thy holy spirit to roost upon thy servant Herman Redpath. He is here to feel thy life throbbing through his veins, so bestow life upon him. He is here that he may mount up in thy service like an eagle, so grant him the strength of a young man to mount with. Herman Redpath is here to receive from thy hands the holy power to love, so of thy love-power give him good measure, pressed down and shaken together and running over so that he may receive it into his lap and scatter it abroad like seed. Grant him the gift of charity so that he may be very charitable. Grant him the gift of faith so that he may always keep faith with us who are his faithful friends and with thee. Grant him the word of wisdom so that his word may be his bond and as sound as a dollar. And finally grant him the special gift of healing so that whomsoever he lays his hands upon in love may respond yea even beyond his fondest dreams. Amen."

At this point Bebb stepped back a few steps from Herman Redpath and, raising first his face, pale and moist as cheese, he started slowly to raise his arms also until like great white wings they were stretched up on either side as far as they would go. Some say that he called out something unintelligible here—some final glossolalia or paean perhaps, like a Druid at the moment when the first ray of the midsummer sun shoots in across the great lintel stone—but some say that he made no sound at all and just stood there with his arms spread and his head thrown back. In any case, virtually everybody agrees that it was at this moment rather than earlier that it first became apparent that during all the time he had been raising his arms, his white robe had been coming farther and farther apart up the middle until here, as his arms reached their zenith, it could be clearly seen that the veil of the Temple had been rent asunder and the Holy of Holies exposed. It was here that the terrible mystery was made manifest, the rabbit pulled white and squirming out of the magician's darkness.

You see in this world mainly what you expect to see, and what you do not expect to see you are usually blind to, and this was apparently the case for a few moments there at Holy Love while the Indians and the Baptists and the passers-by and the reporter from Fort Lauderdale no less than Brownie and Lucille themselves sat there not simply not believing their eyes but not even believing that something had happened for their eyes to try not to believe. When finally they did see, I suspect they were all struck blind in some measure, or at least this is suggested by the fact that each of the various accounts I have heard has differed substantially from the others as to exactly what there was to see and in what state and with what apparent motive and to what supposed end. Of the six or seven flashbulb shots that the Fort Lauderdale reporter somehow mustered the presence of mind to take, all but one either failed to turn out or showed only a blaze of white robe, white face, white wall, with the shadowy figure of Herman Redpath standing in just the wrong place, or right place, depending on the side you took. A copy of the one picture that is said to have turned out reasonably clearly came into my possession much later on, but after giving the matter a great deal of thought, I decided finally to destroy it without looking at it. When it comes to the truth of the matter, the real truth, a camera is no more to be trusted than any of the rest of us.

So what exactly happened there no one will ever know, I suppose, but that something seismic happened there can be no doubt, because within a matter of minutes there was neither a Baptist nor an Indian nor a passer-by left in the place, and within minutes of that, Brownie was back at the Manse with his nose bleeding into the sink and Lucille was sitting there reaching out with an unsteady hand for the Tropicana that Sharon had made for her.

Once Brownie had gotten his nose under control and Sharon had taken Lucille upstairs to lie down, Sharon and I drove down to the church to see if we could locate Bebb. Neither of us, I think, expected to find him. Brownie said that he had seen two state troopers leading him out the back way through the fire-insurance office, and he feared the worst. It was Mr. Bebb's second time, he said—the only reference I ever heard him make to Bebb's five missing years except that time he spoke of it as having been spent on the Lord's work—and to make matters worse, Brownie added, there had been a number of children in the congregation. Lucille said that she had not noticed any troopers but had seen Bebb jump into his car and start south, which meant that he was heading for the Keys very likely and then on to Cuba. This well exemplifies the difficulty of putting together a story from such witnesses because both Brownie and Lucille seemed quite sure of their conflicting reports, and yet, as it turned out, neither report was true. When we got to the church, Bebb was sitting there on the stoop under the frosted-glass cross.

It was just a little past noon with the sun almost directly overhead and no shadows. The souvenir-stand people must have gone off to lunch leaving their shrunken heads behind them because there was a sign with a clock-face on it hanging from the knob of the screen door. There seemed to be nothing going on at the barber shop unless perhaps among the minia-ture turtles in the front window. It seemed a deeply yet precariously quiet moment like the lull between breakers at the seashore when one wave has just been sucked back hissing down the sand and the next one has not yet broken.

Bebb sat there in his shirtsleeves with the jacket to his suit folded neatly beside him so that the four-pointed handkerchief in his breast pocket faced up. He had his chin in his hands and seemed so lost in thought as he gazed down at his feet that at first I assumed he hadn't seen us. Then Sharon said, "Bip," and at the sound of his name, without look-ing up but as if he had been talking to us for some time and was simply resuming where he had left off a few moments before, he said, "Herman Redpath was all shook up, you could see that, but I don't doubt for a sec-ond that when he gets back to Texas he will feel like himself again. That man is generous to a fault, Antonio, and no power on earth is going to make him withdraw the right hand of fellowship or go back on his word. I could see it written on his face when he left as clear as day. That place is as full of flowers in there as a funeral parlor, glads lying around every-where. Sharon, you see somebody gets them to the hospital or the old folks' home."

Sharon said, "How come you did it, Bip?"

He said nothing for a while. Sharon had dropped down to the stone step beside him, and he reached down and laid his hand on top of hers, carefully, as if to leave nothing of hers showing beneath his. He said, "Sharon honey, it was one of those things that happens, that's all it was. A accident." He said, "It was," then interrupting himself with one finger raised, "it wasn't a accident exactly. How you want to say? You might call it something on the order of—" and as he kept breaking in on himself, I thought, it was as if he was taking Sharon and himself too always down, down, to some deeper sub-cellar still of whatever might be the truth of it, some lower, urine-smelling level of the IRT.

He said, "Time comes a man wants to be known for what he is, the bad with the good of him, the weakness with the strength. He wants to lay the whole shebang out in the light of day where the sun can get at it and folks can see all the shameful, hurtful parts of him same as the other parts that's decent and straight."

He said, "You say how come Bip went and did a thing like that.

Honey, some things you don't plan out ahead of time so you can explain it out afterwards how this was why or that was why. It's like one day you just all of a sudden get wore out playing it safe all your whole life and you take a crazy chance. You go and do something they'll see all there is to see and understand it all and wipe all the tears away out of your eyes and out of your life which maybe they will and maybe they won't, but if you play it safe all your life through, you end up like Brownie that's mostly dead, poor soul, safe and dead both. Honey, I expect you left Brownie home to be a comfort to your ma."

Sharon nodded. Beside her, Bebb looked bigger and whiter than ever, but with some of the bounce gone, like a New Year's Eve balloon the next morning.

I said, "Bip, what are you going to do next?"

He said, "Antonio, I'm not kidding myself. What I do next may be in my hands or then it may not be, and that's what I'm waiting here to find out. They're always locking people up for the wrong reasons—the right people maybe, but the wrong reasons and the wrong times. Think of it, Antonio—this thing I've been dreaming about come true at last. I threw out the life-line, and the one caught it was Herman Redpath in all his wealth and power. And now the lock-up. But my ways are not thy ways, saith the Lord. Antonio, you take a man's been in prison a couple years, and he's ready for Jesus like he's never been ready any place else. He's ready for anything has got some hope and life in it. Life, Antonio, is what a prisoner's ready for. Freedom. Lion Country. It's worth breaking the law just so you can get put in the lock-up, where the grapes are ripe for the harvest and the Lord needs all the hands he can get for the vineyard. You should hear the way they sing hymns behind bars, Antonio. Makes you go all over gooseflesh."

"Give us one, Bip," Sharon said. She drew her hand out from under his and let her head come down to rest on his shoulder.

The noon sun was almost blinding, but Bebb looked straight out ahead of him without so much as blinking and, with his mouth snapped shut even tighter than usual and his nostrils swelling, started to hum a few tentative, uncertain things that could have ended up being almost any hymn in the book. The one he finally settled on was "Rock of Ages," and although Sharon's head was on his shoulder as he sang it, he did not sing it to her or to me or to Jesus or anybody else as far as I could tell, but more to himself or possibly even to Herman Redpath up in the sky there somewhere on his way to Texas.

"Rock of ages, cleft for me," Bebb sang in a kind of 1930's radio voice. "Let me hide myself in thee. . . . Nothing in my hand I bring, Simply to thy cross I cling," and over his head, I noticed, almost too good to be true, some Indian I suppose had flicked on the light in the frosted-glass sign so that even in the daylight it shone out a little with HOLY LOVE written up and down it like the cross on a Bayer aspirin tablet.

12

DURING MY YEARS as an English teacher, students were always handing in stories that ended up with a sentence or two to the effect that the next morning they woke up and found out the whole thing had been just a dream. It is one of the easier ways, certainly, to bring a story to a close—it saves you from having to draw all the loose ends together, for one thing, and excuses you for any improbabilities you may have committed along the way, for another—and for reasons like that most of my colleagues regarded the practice with considerable disfavor and docked the grade accordingly. I, on the other hand, always tended to like such stories. In life as in fiction, it seems to me, the richer and more memorable moments inevitably do take on a dreamlike quality once you emerge from them. The birthday party, the walk through the park in the snow, seeing the old man with the umbrella knocked down by the taxi—did they happen really, or did you just dream that they happened? It is De Quincey's essay on *Macbeth* all over again—the knocking on the gate, the drunken porter's bad jokes about liquor and sex, the *realia* of life, in other words, and by contrast the bloody end of the old king takes on the quality of nightmare.

In the case of this story about my days in Armadillo, on the other hand, just the reverse is the case. When I got back to New York and to the routine again of my life there, I had the feeling that it was they that were dreamlike and that it was in Armadillo that I had left reality behind. Just the difference of season was part of it, I suppose: the grey and ghostlike city winter with the lights going on early down the center of Park Avenue and the tops of the buildings lost in dusk, whereas in Armadillo the blaze of summer was almost too bright to see by and either no shadows at all or shadows as clear-cut as life and death themselves. I moved a little like a dream or a ghost myself those first days especially of being home, and it was only when I thought back on how it had been for me in Florida that I could feel something like a real heart beating against my ribs.

I flew back to New York the same day as the climactic events surrounding the ordination of Herman Redpath, and the reason was Miriam. I called the hospital to check in with her, and they gave me a doctor who said they had been trying to locate me for over a day to say that she had taken a decided turn for the worse and I had better be prepared to stand by. No one had known where I was, of course. Miriam, who probably wouldn't have remembered anyway, was past remembering, I had never told Charlie Blaine, and no one thought about Ellie, who would have been able to put them on the right track. So, with Miriam so much on my mind that I had a hard time focusing on anything else, I left the Bebbs and

Brownie in the hour of their need without any clear notion of what I was leaving and said goodbye to Sharon as though goodbye was only a poor translation of some word which in the original tongue meant something quite innocuous.

Miriam lived for several weeks after my return, and I saw her again a number of times, but although there may have been moments when she was trying to respond, I am not certain that she ever again really saw me. Other bones broke, broke like her arms for no cause other than that she moved them the wrong way or simply tried to shift her position in bed, and in the end there was apparently not a major bone in her body that remained intact. The last time I saw her, they had her in a giant cast that resembled the letter A with both her legs sheathed all the way down to her ankles in plaster and in between a crosspiece to keep them from moving. The nurses advised me to go home and get some sleep because she was under such heavy sedation that she couldn't possibly know or care whether anyone was there or not, but I stuck around on the off-chance that she might come to if only for a moment and I didn't want her to find herself alone in that room that for so many weeks had been her only world.

Part of the time her eyes were open—there was never anything broken-looking or sick about her eyes, which to the last seemed to have more anger in them than anything else—and during those times I talked to her, even though there was no indication that she could hear a word I was saying. In that sense it was a little like praying, and like it also because it was more for my own sake, I think, than for hers, just as I have always suspected prayer is more for man's sake than for God's—it is not God who needs to be praised but we who need to praise him, whether we believe in him or not. On the other hand, there was nothing especially prayerful in what I talked to her about. I talked to her a lot about how it had been when we were children, and I went on at some length about the radio programs we used to listen to—*Mr. Keen, Tracer of Lost Persons* and *Uncle Don, Easy Aces,* where we always got a kick out of Jane Ace's saying "You could have knocked me down with a fender," and one called *Omar the Mystic,* which nobody but me seems to remember, where at the end of each episode they used to tap out a secret message on bells which you could decode for yourself if you sent in a boxtop of something for one of their secret decoders. I reminded her of the time we were sent to the Met to hear *Hansel and Gretel* by Humperdinck—or was it *The Harrowing of Hell* by Montague Rhodes James?—and I talked about the smell of our apartment on winter evenings and the sounds of the horns heading home up Park Avenue.

At one point I even tried to give her a picture of some of the things that had happened while I was in Armadillo. I tried to describe Brownie and his smile, for instance, and Lion Country and the way Bip had looked driving home in his beanie with the propellers on it. What I wanted to describe most to her, of course, was Sharon—my sister might have liked Sharon, I suspect, in a way that I'm afraid she would never have liked poor Ellie—but partly because the nurse kept coming in and out, and partly because for reasons that I suppose Dr. Freud would have found interesting I never was much good at telling Miriam about the women in my life, I stayed away from Sharon and told a little about my meeting with the girl in the bathing suit instead.

When I finally left—whatever they try to say, even the bonds between twins can hold only so long and I reached the point where I was literally unable to keep my eyes open any longer—I knew without any doubt for once that I was seeing her for the last time. There was something oddly anti-climactic about it. The real last times, I think—the last times I had really seen *her*—were when she had tossed that vague little wave to me as she was stubbing her cigarette out in the ashtray and when with such ferocity in her voice she told her younger son, Tony, to stay awake. My actual last sight of Miriam was last only in a chronological sense, because it seemed not so much Miriam I was seeing but rather the first letter of the alphabet. It was a giant A—*so* meaningless by itself, though so rich in combination—lying there, white on white, on that hospital bed. I made no attempt to say goodbye and neither shed any tears nor felt like shedding any but just left when the time came and closed the door behind me. If A stood for anything, I thought, it stood for *andiamo* or *avanti*, meaning *Let's get the Hell out of here.* I could imagine Miriam thinking that somewhere deep inside all her sedation and plaster, and I thought it also myself.

She was buried on Christmas Eve day in an enormous cemetery in Brooklyn because our father had had Brooklyn connections and both he and his Italian bride were buried there. No one came except Charlie with his two boys and me, and the service, such as it was, was conducted by a young Episcopal priest, an acquaintance of Charlie's, who looked about as pale and helpless to me as Charlie himself did. Because of the divorce, it was really up to me to make the arrangements, but Charlie seemed so eager to handle them himself—perhaps, I thought, to make it up to Miriam for not having gone to see her that day he took the boys to the Rockettes— that I let him do it. He decided against having any funeral, just the brief Episcopal business there by the graveside, and the reason he gave was that Miriam wouldn't have wanted any fuss, by which I understood him to mean that he himself didn't want any. Miriam, I suspect, might have enjoyed a real Wop affair with everybody sobbing noisily and a lot to drink afterwards, but Charlie Blaine didn't want to make any fuss about death any more than he wanted to make any fuss about life. His idea was to get through both as quietly and painlessly as possible, with plenty of long naps along the way.

Everything the priest read was familiar to me until he got to a passage which included the words "make me to hear joy and gladness that the bones which thou hast broken may rejoice." It is the Fifty-first Psalm, I discovered later, and maybe Episcopalians always use it, but if so, I had never happened to notice it before. The peculiar aptness of it struck me first as grisly and depressing and then almost immediately as just right. I didn't like the thought of God's being the one who had broken Miriam's bones, but, remembering Don Giovanni with his rapier in Dr. James's Hell, I decided that he had always been one to play rough, and if the last word was really going to be one of rejoicing, I could forgive him almost anything—like Adam when he finally got that oil from the tree of mercy for the pain of his body. Charlie stood there with a Vicks inhaler— his sinuses always kicked up in damp weather, he said—and the boys got through it all right. Chris got through it almost too well, I thought— maybe he was thinking about the poem he would write about it afterwards, or maybe his tooth was hurting him again—but Tony pleased me by looking as though at any moment he might burst into great, fat cadenzas of Italian grief. He didn't, I'm happy to say, but I think his mother would have been pleased to note that he almost did. It proved, among other things, that he had stayed awake.

The dreamlike quality of those first weeks after my return from Armadillo, or maybe just the dreamlike quality of myself, was increased by the unexpected behavior of both Ellie and Tom. Given the undemonstrativeness of cats generally, I didn't expect Tom to burst into the Halleluiah Chorus when I went down to get him at the vet's, but I expected more than I got. The vet opened the door of the cage where Tom was sitting on his haunches with his tail curled around in front of him in one of his Egyptian moods, and without so much as a sidelong glance at me, he went stalking straight across the linoleum to the radiator where he sat down and with determined upward sweeps of his tongue started cleaning one of his wrists. Perhaps he was just showing me how deeply offended he still was by my having abandoned him all that time to a prisoner's cell, but I remember wondering at the time if I had become so ghostlike and transparent that he simply hadn't noticed I was there.

Ellie's reaction struck me as essentially the same thing transcribed for piano and strings. We kissed when I met her out on the plaza in front of the U.N.—there were snowflakes in the air, with the flags of the nations hanging spent and limp from their staffs—and she asked me all the proper questions about Miriam and Florida and Tom, but I could see that her heart wasn't in it. I think she may even have forgotten why I went down in the first place. She made some vague reference to my writing, but I do not believe she could have told me, if I'd asked her, exactly what I had gone down there to write about. And I was in no hurry to put her to the test.

The only writing I ever actually did on the Bebb article was in the form of a few notes I jotted down on the back of a receipted Salamander Motel bill on my late flight back to West Palm the same day I'd flown

up to take the boys to see Miriam—the management had said they'd hold
the room till my return, but asked me to pay for the two nights I'd already
spent there. All I'd written on the back of the bill were a few incomplete
and in most cases inaccurate sentences. "Nobody calls him Leo," I wrote.
Herman Redpath called him Leo, but I didn't learn this until later. "Tropicanas two orange to one gin." Though only a guess, I eventually discovered from Sharon that in this case I was one hundred percent accurate. I
wrote, "Brownie must hate his guts—B. treats him like shit." Nothing
could have been more inaccurate than the first part—if Bebb died first,
Brownie would probably see to it that his guts were enshrined somewhere
like the Buddha's tooth—and as for the second part, though forced to
agree that Bebb treated him like shit, Brownie would probably say that
Bebb did it the same way the Lord did when he picked up that handful
of shit in Eden and formed it into the shape of a man, breathing into its
nostrils the breath of life so that it might become a living soul. "Toilet
brush," I wrote down, and "Framed or not framed?" and that was about
the sum of it. I realized by now that I hadn't the faintest intention of
writing any article and was grateful to Ellie for not bringing the matter up.

Like Tom, Ellie seemed to regard me as the Ghost of Christmas
Past, and since, chronologically speaking, little more than a week or ten
days had gone by since our Beef Stroganoff supper when Tom had so
nearly succumbed to the vet's anesthesia, I can explain her attitude only on
the grounds that, like me, she sensed that on the eve of my departure for
Armadillo we had approached what might have been the point of no
return in our relationship and then, unaccountably, returned. I remembered how we had sat there in Manhattan House over our scotch-and-
sodas with the rain coming down outside and how I had thought that
things might possibly take place between us then that had never taken
place between us before. The time had been right, and we were both
lonely, and her hair smelled sweetly of shampoo, and then Tom had gone
eerily into his dance of life-in-death or death-in-life, and the golden rug
became damply stained, and as quietly and inexorably as a man's last
breath, the golden moment passed.

At some level of her cautious and sensitive being, Ellie too must have
marked its passing, I think, because though only a week or ten days went
by before we met again there in front of the U.N., it had been time
enough for her to immerse herself even more passionately than before in
a world where passion was not a private possibility but a public cause. I
took her to supper at Giovanni's that evening, and her talk was all of Red
China and low-income housing and the Job Corps, and although she
pressed my hand and gave me her loveliest pre-Raphaelite smile as we
kissed goodnight at her apartment door, I felt that it was a parting of
phantoms. It was bad in its way but, like Miriam's death, not quite as bad
as I might have thought. The one advantage I know to living in a dream
is that in dreams you may never get more than a shadow of the things you

really want, but you also never really get hurt either. You can fall out of a window or sleep with your sister or preside stark naked over the Security Council, but in the end you always walk away more or less intact on your shadowy feet.

I wouldn't want to live there, but dreams are not a bad place to visit, especially after an overdose of reality, and that is probably why I delayed as long as I did before trying to reestablish communication with Armadillo. Miriam was buried on the day of Christmas Eve, I spent a cheerless Christmas watching TV with Charlie and the boys in Westchester, and it was not until the day after Christmas, that low ebb of the year, when I was back in my apartment again with Tom, that I tried putting in a call to Bebb. I put it in person-to-person, although I do not know why since there was no one in that house I wouldn't have been glad to talk to, even Lucille. Maybe it was just that I wanted to talk to Bebb first so that there would be no suspicion, especially not in my own mind, that I was doing things behind his back. The article having long since been abandoned, my concern by that time was in no sense conspiratorial. Somewhere along the telephonic process my Northern operator in her impersonal efficiency exchanged words with a Southern operator whose voice sounded rich and slow with compassion, and the next thing I heard was Brownie fifteen hundred miles away explaining to one or the other of them that Mr. Bebb was no longer in Armadillo, he had left no number where he could be reached, and there was no telling when if ever he might come back. I told the operator that I would talk to Brownie instead. Even across all those miles then I could almost hear his smile as he recognized me by my voice, and by way of demonstrating the uncanny sharpness of human perceptions, especially when fresh from a long sleep, I even thought I could detect a whiff of after-shave.

Brownie said, "I can't talk over the phone, dear. They left just a day after you did, all three of them. I would have left too, but Mr. Bebb asked me to stay and straighten things up here. I've got all their belongings to pack and the house to close, and you wouldn't believe the heat we're having."

"Where did they go, Brownie?" I said. "Was there any trouble, or did everything just blow over?"

Brownie said, "Dear, you never know who's listening. I can tell you this, though. Before they left, they asked me to give you a message."

"Sharon did?" I said.

Brownie said, "No, it wasn't Sharon. It was Mr. Bebb. He said if you called, to tell you to remember how when Moses led his people out of bondage in Egypt, the Lord opened up a path for them right through the Red Sea."

"How could I forget?" I said.

Brownie said, "There are many treasures hidden in Scripture, dear, and many things written that he who runs may read."

"He who runs where?" I said.

Brownie said, "There's never any telling where a man may run to except that even if he takes the wings of the morning and flies to the outermost parts of the sea, he can never run away from the Lord."

"Not even in Texas, I suppose," I said.

Brownie said, "I certainly wouldn't think so, dear."

"Not even in Dallas," I said.

"Not in Dallas and not in Houston either," Brownie said.

I said, "Brownie, I miss you. I miss you all, and I even miss the Salamander Motel. By the way, by mistake I took *The Apocryphal New Testament* edited by M. R. James home with me in my suitcase. How can I get it back to you?"

Brownie said, "Don't you worry about that. Just keep it until we meet again someday, and that will be time enough."

I said, "I hope we do meet again someday, Brownie. All of us."

Brownie said, "If not in this world, dear, then in a better world to come," and when he hung up, I could see him there with the smile already fading and the sweat stains dark on his shirt as he turned back to the debris of Gospel Faith—the half-filled suitcases, the bulging cartons, and, for all I knew, even the rugs rolled up in the downstairs hall and Lucille's color TV in a crate. Had Brownie, that disentangler of meaning and lover of clarity, resorted to the veiled language of espionage as an act of midsummer madness, I wondered, or did the walls really have ears listening for just the faintest echo of Bebb's footsteps so that the pursuit could begin? I did not know, but, deciding that even the most ingenious pursuer would be unlikely to overhear me at so great a distance, I got Herman Redpath's number in Houston from information and put in a second person-to-person call to Bebb. The phone was answered by what I took to be the voice of some Indian, and in minutes I found myself talking to Bebb himself.

He said, "Antonio, this is the day that the Lord hath made, let us rejoice and be glad in it," and I could tell right away that it was the old Bebb still. I could tell that nothing he had let loose or that had been let loose upon him had taken the bounce out of him permanently, and I suppose the fear that it might have been otherwise was part of the reason I had delayed so long in calling. Though obviously glad to hear from me at last, and eager, I thought, to tell me many things, Bebb was almost as guarded over the phone as Brownie had been, and I was able to get virtually nothing out of him about what had happened in Armadillo after my departure or what he was doing in Houston or what he was planning to go on to next. Even on the subject of Herman Redpath he was unusually reticent except to say that although they were guests in his house and beneficiaries of his fathomless generosity, they had not seen a great deal of Herman Redpath himself because he was much occupied elsewhere. It was when I inquired for Sharon in as restrained and casual a manner as I could manage that Bebb came out with what must have been on his mind from the beginning. He said, "Antonio, maybe you better hop on a plane and see for yourself. In Herman Redpath's house there are many mansions, and there isn't anybody here wouldn't welcome the sight of you with open arms."

The apartment that Tom and I shared was on the third floor of a brownstone on upper Madison Avenue, and I remember that as Bebb made his suggestion, I was sitting in the front room with my feet up on the radiator. It was the room I used as a studio, and it was littered all over with cans of Rustoleum black and newspaper spread around to catch the drippings and a great many pieces of scrap iron both assembled and unassembled. I remember the greyness of the day and the look of the apartment building across the street with its narrow concrete balconies and its picture windows that pictured nothing but other people's windows on my side of the street. I remember the sound of a Madison Avenue bus starting up from the bus-stop at the corner—that pneumatic hiss followed by the world-weary groan of the gears. "Maybe you better hop on a plane and come see for yourself," Bebb had said, and in response to his words certainly, and to the sense of great promise that seemed somehow implicit in them, but in response also to the bus and the scrap iron and the grey New York day generally, I heard myself saying that it didn't sound like a bad idea at that, and if I could get things in order in time, I'd fly down the next day and call him from the airport.

On such slender threads hang the destinies of men and nations. For want of a nail the kingdom was lost, the old poem says, and I have thought since that if any one of a great number of factors had been missing at that particular moment on the day after Christmas—if it had been the day after the day after, say, or if the Madison Avenue bus hadn't chanced to start up just then with those ghostly sighs of weariness and despair as it shifted from low gear into high—there is no telling how differently I might have responded to Bebb's invitation or what kingdom, what mine of precious stones, might have been forever lost to me. But whether by chance or by providence, things happened precisely and encyclopedically as they did happen, and I told Bebb I would go, and I went. With a sense of guilt so acute that I could hardly bring myself to meet his eye on the taxi ride down, I left Tom once again at the vet's and arrived at Houston the next afternoon.

I will make no attempt to give a full account of all that happened there. It would take too long, for one thing, and it would be misleading, for another, because the Cecil B. DeMille quality of it, the cast of thousands, the pageantry, the drama, would tend to give it more significance than it really had. With time as with everything else, needless to say, it is not the quantity that counts, it is the quality, and under certain circumstances a sunset glimpsed through a Venetian blind or even not glimpsed can count for more than two weeks in Venice with your eyes open the whole time. Let a single scene out of the whole Texas extravaganza, then, represent all the others.

Bebb himself met me at the airport and drove me out to the Red Path Ranch, and that same evening there was a big barbecue. Up to that point I had seen nobody, not even Sharon, who had been supposed to come with him to meet me, Bebb said, but had gone out on horseback earlier and hadn't returned in time. Bebb told me little I wanted to know —he seemed much more interested in pointing out to me the splendors of the ranch as we drove through—and almost as soon as we arrived at the building where I was to stay, he left me, saying that he was already late for an appointment with our host and would see me at the barbecue that evening. My building was a one-story stucco affair with a tiled roof and built around a quadrangle with a swimming pool at the center. I took a dip in the pool to wash the city off and then clocked about three miles on an exercycle which I found under the pillared roof of the walk that ran around the quadrangle on all four sides.

Lying there in the sun afterwards, I kept thinking that maybe Sharon would return from her ride and come looking for me, but she did not come, and after a while I fell asleep and had a dream. It was a very short dream, and it was about Miriam. I cannot remember how she looked or where we were, but I remember the sound of her voice and the sense of calm after storm, the sense of walking out into the fresh air again after a bad movie, as she said, "My God, it's good to get that cast off, Tono." That was all there was to it, but it was worth going to Texas to hear.

When I woke up I couldn't stop thinking about that giant A—how they must have taken it off before they let the undertakers have her and how some remnant of it was still probably lying around somewhere at the bottom of an incinerator or in the city dump just as, for all I know, there are old books or old coins lying aound that Shakespeare must have held in his hands once or at the bottom of the Jordan maybe a piece of rock Jesus threw out at some moment of frustration or somewhere else a boulder that he stepped behind to take a leak. The world must be full of such lost souvenirs, and I suppose no one has ever lived without leaving many of them behind. But of course what I was gladdest to take back with me out of that dream was the idea that wherever my sister was, if only in her Brooklyn grave, she at least didn't have that A to contend with any more. "That the bones which thou hast broken may rejoice," the pale priest read, and if I could not think of it yet as A for *alleluiah* or *amen*, I could at least hear it as a long-drawn *ah-h-h* of relief and astonishment as somebody's scissors, or possibly even rapier, cut the damned thing away.

And then, that night, the barbecue. It reminds me of a book Miriam and I had as children called *Great Characters out of Dickens*, I think, where many people from many of the different novels are brought together between the same covers—Mr. Micawber and Sarah Gamp, old Magwitch and Pickwick and Tom the copper's nark. Bebb was there, and Lucille,

and Herman Redpath, and eventually Sharon, not to mention a number
of Indians that I recognized from the ordination—Jack Oakie, for instance,
and the old lady who some said was Herman Redpath's wife and others
his sister and Sharon said both—and a number that I had never seen before. Just about everybody was there except for Brownie, who was still
back at Armadillo packing things up. A whole steer was roasting on a huge
spit, and there were accordions and a marimba band and Japanese lan-
terns. There was beer and champagne and even Tropicanas, for all I know,
plus a portable outhouse with the Red Path brand painted on the door in
case anybody needed that out there under the Texas stars. There was a pit
full of red-hot coals, and it was there, squatting beside it, that I found
Herman Redpath again. He was wearing the same brown suit, brown shirt,
brown hat, and he reached out and grabbed me as I passed by.

He said, "That sonofabitch Bebb I don't give a fart what he is or
what he did time for all I know is soon as we got back here that same day
after he pulled Jesus knows what-all kind of a crazy trick damn if the
thing didn't start working right off the life the Jesus life any name you want
to call it why I'll kiss your ass if that same night we got back I didn't get
one on stiff as a poker must have lasted better part of twenty minutes
maybe more if I haven't planted me a pack of seed around here since then
you can bet your balls it wasn't the want of seed or there was anything
wrong on that end it was something wrong with the hole I planted it in
I got the life in me again thanks to that bastard you seen the little brown
tits on that daughter of his what I wouldn't give for a handful like that
the life I got back I'm not tear-assing around spending it just any place
I'm saving up and spending it where you bet your sweet ass it counts don't
do much days any more stick pretty close to home I wouldn't be out here
now spending the life in me on all these sonsofbitches weren't it for Leo
asking me to he wanted something special for you your first night I took
a shine to you myself soon as you poked your tail in the door looks to me
like you got Indian blood in you it's nights not days I spend the life I got
you take that Leo Bebb I don't give a fart what he done time for he gives
me back the life again every week he lays his hands on me another time I
got me a six-shooter now like the old days I can keep it in firing position
twenty twenty-five minutes maybe that's his daughter over there now take
a look at the pretty little ass she's got on her," and with a wrench no less
than the one John Glenn must have experienced when he blasted off
from his thundering pad into the silences of outer space, and making an
ascent no less great, I turned from the firelit face of that old sachem just
in time to see Sharon coming through the place between the marimba
band and the roasting steer in a dress the color of moonlight with a glint
in her hair and her arm in a silk scarf tied into a sling.

"Terrible as an army with banners" were among the words Bebb had
quoted from the Song of Solomon in an effort to describe her to me once,
and for the first time I realized that what Solomon if not Bebb must have

meant by such a curious image was that one way mortal man has always reacted to beauty like hers is with terror in his very bowels. I was scared stiff as I saw her picking her way toward me through all the Indians, and as nearly as I can tell, I was scared not so much because of the terrible power her beauty gave her over me as because of my own terrible inability to respond to it in anything remotely like the way the stars themselves cried out for me to. In face of such a sight and mystery as a girl can present when she walks toward you through the firelight in a moon-colored dress, it is possible for any one of us to be like whichever prophet it was who, when he beheld the Lord himself sitting high and lifted up among his angels, could only cry out, "Woe is me, for I am undone . . . I am a man of unclean lips. . . ." Nor, Brownie would be pleased to note, is that the only reference to Scripture that this moment of seeing Sharon again at the barbecue recalls, because Bebb had come up behind me by this time and said softly into my ear as she approached, "Behold, I saw the holy city, new Jerusalem, coming down out of heaven like a bride adorned for her husband," and the next moment she was there holding out her good hand toward me and saying, "Take it easy, Bopper. Herman's mare threw me, and it's taken till now to wash the horse shit off"—*horse shit* not as an obscenity but the way Bebb had used it once as a technical term for something that smells of grain and musk and sun and makes the vegetables grow.

It was later that same night that I asked her to marry me. It wasn't much, I realized even at the time, but it was the best I could find to do.

She said, "Bip put you up to it, didn't he?"

I said, "Bip certainly had his hand in things right from the beginning. There's no getting around that."

"Didn't he?" Sharon said.

"Not in so many words," I said.

Then she said, "Well, at least you're better than Brownie," and I interpreted that, correctly for once, to be an acceptance.

Ellie was wonderful all the way through. There was no need to be wonderful about letting me go because that had already happened—like people shaking hands through a car window, we had come apart finally not because either of us especially chose to but because life moves, that's all— but she was wonderful in her way about Sharon when I brought her back to New York as my bride. We were married in Texas early in the new year, not by Bebb as it turned out—there was some question as to whether Texas law would recognize his ordination—but by an Episcopal priest in a mission church packed full of Indians on the fringes of the Red Path Ranch. Bebb gave his adopted daughter away and pronounced the benediction afterwards, Lucille held the bride's bouquet while we exchanged our vows, and Brownie arrived from Armadillo in time to stand up in a cloud of after-shave as my best man. It seemed fitting that we should go back to the Salamander Motel for our honeymoon, but, fearing our presence in Armadillo might stir up trouble for Bebb, we flew to Nassau instead. It was when we returned from there that Ellie went out of her way to be nice to Sharon and showed her around the shops, talked to her about clothes, and took her on a tour of the U.N., where Sharon sat in the visitors' gallery in the General Assembly with a set of those instantaneous translation earphones on her head and looking, I'm sure, as much like something from outer space as Bebb ever had. Matter and anti-matter, they met without mutual annihilation, my young bride and my old comrade, and like one of those human-interest photographs at the back of *Life* that shows a cat and a mouse, say, sharing the same bowl of milk, I think they even took a rather eccentric fancy to each other.

Not least among Ellie's kindnesses was that she took Tom off my hands. The first moment she saw him, Sharon took a dislike to that cat—among other things, he made her itch, she said—and Tom seemed approximately as enthusiastic about her as he had been about me when I went to get him out of his cage at the vet's. So he moved into Manhattan House, and I saw him there occasionally when Ellie asked us in for an evening with some of her U.N. friends. He made a place for himself on the golden rug under the piano and spent most of his time either there or in the corner where the hot air came through.

For the first three months we lived on in the Madison Avenue apartment, Sharon and I, but it was not a happy arrangement. The apartment seemed cramped and airless after the Manse in Armadillo, and as for the city in general, every time she came back from wandering around in it, she said that she had the feeling she'd been mixed up in a fight she'd somehow lost. So when spring came, we rented a house in Connecticut not far from the Sound, and in the fall I went back to teaching—four classes of English and coaching track at the local high school. It was not a bad place to live, and although the beach was a far cry from the one at Hobe Sound we drove to once, Sharon enjoyed it in the summers, and at least there were no Portuguese men-of-war.

Miriam's two boys came to live with us eventually. There was never any one decisive moment when the move was made, and I cannot say that I ever consciously reached the point even in my own mind when I decided that the time had come to grant the last request that my sister had charitably never quite brought herself to make of me. Charlie's house was only a few hours away, and gradually my nephews just took to spending more and more time with us—only week-ends and vacations at first, but eventually through his educational TV connections Charlie decided the school where I taught was better than theirs so they ended up moving in with us on a more or less year-round basis. Charlie fretted about them and missed them and in many ways was a good father, but in the long run I think he was just as glad to be rid of them. Boys are a good deal of fuss when you come right down to it, and it was fuss that he spent a lot of his waking hours and all of his sleeping ones trying to avoid.

It was a good move for Charlie and by and large also a good move for Sharon and me, but whether it was a good move for Chris and Tony themselves, who can ever say. During those early years of our marriage when we had no children of our own and lived in a town where neither of us had any roots or knew anybody very well, we needed people besides just each other to bounce our lives off of. In fact, we needed not just people in general but people more or less like the people we had had before, so that without realizing it we tended to assign those two boys roles they could hardly have been aware of but were always in some danger, I suppose, of taking up on their own. Chris in many ways became Tom for me—the silent awareness by the fire as I corrected themes in the evening, the all-knowing gaze that I would talk to myself to when nobody else was around, the dignified presence whose eccentricities I tended to publicize as a kind of joke on us both. And Tony, I think, filled part of the place in Sharon's life that Bebb had occupied. He was fat and she loved deviling him, and at one level of their being or another they were always catching each other by surprise—being or doing unexpected things to each other at unexpected times—and thus bringing out both the saddest and the gayest in each other. On the whole, however, I think Miriam would have been pleased. In addition to everything else, especially after Sharon took up the guitar and I put a ping-pong table in the cellar for the boys, we tended to get too little sleep in our house rather than too much. And with the aerial we had, we could get only two channels on the TV and those not very well.

Bebb stayed on at the ranch in Texas, Lucille and Brownie with him of course. Evidently no one ever pressed charges for whatever had gone on at Herman Redpath's ordination—perhaps because it was his own church where it happened and most of the Baptists had already left with their children—so conceivably he might have returned to Armadillo. But he never did. He continued to serve as Herman Redpath's beadsman or medicine man, and the weekly laying-on of hands apparently never entirely lost its magic, or, if it did, Herman Redpath kept Bebb on anyway as a souvenir of splendors past and in hope perhaps of others still to come, or maybe just as a charm against the evil eye. But Bebb's labors in the vineyard didn't end there. Good to his word, Herman Redpath built him another Holy Love much larger and finer to replace the one that he had to abandon in Armadillo. It was built on the ranch property to resemble the Alamo, and on Sundays he held services of some kind there which were attended faithfully by Herman Redpath and the Indians. The *Put Yourself on God's Payroll* ads continued to appear among the glow-in-the-dark Virgins and hemorrhoid cures, and the files of Gospel Faith kept on growing.

I pulled my own folder out once when Sharon and I were down there on a visit and nobody was around, and the code letter that Bebb had written on it long before in his own hand was, curiously enough, an A. Average? Appalling? Article-writer? Or possibly an eerie foreshadowing of Miriam's last days? I do not know. I never asked either Bebb or Brownie about it and never shall. Like most oracles, I suppose, it was destined to mean whatever I chose to make it mean, maybe that in the end I would become just Antonio again or in a way, you might say, Antonio for the first time, since for years almost everybody except Bebb had called me Tono. Sharon didn't like Tono—she said it came too close for comfort to her baby word for number two, which had been nono—so Antonio I became, except once in a while Bopper or Bop. Bip and Bop. I told her once that she should have us framed on either side of the mantel clock like Mike and Ike or the Gold Dust twins.

Down and then up again, south and then north again. If these events in my life had a pattern, it was something like that. If a shape, then a V, or even, by stretching it somewhat, an upside-down A, I suppose, with the little bar in between representing the bridge that always connects the present with both the past and the future. Because when I was on my way down in my roomette as Tono, I had in me already seeds of the Antonio I was to become; and when I finally went up again with Sharon as my bride, I carried as part of my baggage and will carry always the celibate dabbler in unwelded scrap iron that I had been on the way down. All of which goes to show, as if that were necessary, that you cannot escape the past or the future either, and at my best and bravest I do not even want to escape them. Miriam's death, the faceless baby, Lucille's Tropicanas and in a way also Brownie's smile and that slightly mad and rebellious eye of Bebb's—all the sad and hurtful things of the past I would prevent having happened if I could, but, failing that, I would not wish the hurt of them away even if that were possible.

When Miriam's bones were breaking, for instance, if I could have pushed a button that would have stopped not her pain but the pain of her pain in me, I would not have pushed the button because, to put it quite simply, my pain was because I loved her, and to have wished my pain away would have been somehow to wish my love away as well. And at my best and bravest I do not want to escape the future either, even though I know that it contains what will someday be my own great and final pain. Because a distaste for dying is twin to a taste for living, and again I don't think you can tamper with one without somehow doing mischief to the other. But this is at my best and bravest. The rest of the time I am a fool and a coward just like most of the other lost persons that in the end it will take no less than Mr. Keen himself to trace.

OPEN HEART

For Jamie and Jackie

1

"GET UP, Herman Redpath," my father-in-law Leo Bebb said. His fat face was slippery with sweat and his eyes tight shut as though he'd gotten soap in them. The box had not been lowered into the ground yet but still hung cradled in canvas straps. Inside the box, Herman Redpath was laid out in his brown silk shirt and chocolate-brown suit with a Navajo blanket tucked around him at the waist. Possibly there were damp spots on the blanket. My father-in-law crowded him with his prayer as though if he didn't, the old man might dawdle there indefinitely.

"It's time to move out," Leo Bebb said. "So get going, Herman Redpath. Go forth now from strength unto strength. Rise up now from glory unto glory." Bebb made it sound uphill all the way. If I had been Herman Redpath, I would have pretended not to hear. It was a muggy spring day with thunder in the air.

Herman Redpath, that comic-strip Indian and Cherokee Croesus. I was informed later that he did hear. He set forth across impossible prairies. He clambered up mountains that only seemed to be mountains. He padded down canyons that he must have known weren't really canyons. He came at last to a place that was not a place, and he was challenged there by a stranger who was not a stranger. So I was told anyway, although on authority that I must admit was not unimpeachable. Who knows? Maybe it was so. Maybe a lot more began for Herman Redpath with his death than ended for him. And for the rest of us too.

Certainly for me his passing opened more doors than it closed. And even for Bebb it did although no one would have guessed it at the time since Bebb worked for the old man after all, was his beadsman, his medicine man, his charm against the evil eye. When the old man went, Bebb's job went with him. But if a chapter was ending for Leo Bebb as he stood there in his maroon Holy Love robe nagging at Herman Redpath, at the same time, in ways we were unaware of, a brand new chapter was just getting started. And for Sharon too, my young wife, who should have been there with her father and me but wasn't—because of the baby, she said in a wild flight of fancy. It was Chris, our eighteen-year-old nephew, who worried about the baby.

Bebb wired me as soon as he saw that Herman Redpath was dying, and I caught a plane out of Kennedy that got me there while he was still alive, after a manner of speaking. In the Red Path Ranch there were many mansions—stucco, mostly, with patios and tiled rooms—and the one in which Herman Redpath drew his last breath was built like an L lying on its back with its foot sticking up in the air. This foot was the living room which was two stories high to accommodate the pipes of the organ that Herman Redpath had had installed there. He did not play the organ himself and neither did any of his Indians as far as I know, but every once in a while somebody would turn up who did. Sometimes of an evening he would get Bebb to bluff his way through a hymn or two. With some slow, fuzzy chords in the background, Bebb used his scratchy tenor to carry most of what there was in the way of a tune. *When the Roll Is Called Up Yonder,* Bebb would sing, or *The Old Rugged Cross,* or *Rock of Ages,* and Herman Redpath would sit listening in the dead center of the settee with his hand on Mrs. Trionka's enormous thigh. He died without much in the way of organ accompaniment, but it was in this large, high-ceilinged room that he did it.

I arrived there about the same time he did. A tall brave in a gag T-shirt with *Alcatraz* 12230015 stenciled on it came in carrying him in his arms and propped him up like the Infant Jesus of Prague in an overstuffed armchair. He had had them dress him in the same chocolate-brown clothes they later buried him in, and he wore a string tie with a Mexican silver medallion which moved when he swallowed, the Adam's apple bobbling and the silver glittering each time he tried to choke down what little spit he must have had left by then. His skin was stretched so tight he could hardly close his lips over his teeth, and long after the brave who carried him in had left, he kept his gaze directed up to the empty place where the brave's face had been. Someone set a bench in front of him to prop his bare feet against so that he wouldn't slip down. His feet were too swollen to get his shoes on.

The place was crowded with Indians, and when Bebb brought me up to pay my respects, I wasn't sure that Herman Redpath knew that I wasn't just another of them. I said, "I'm the one that married Bebb's daughter. You remember me. Antonio Parr."

He didn't look as if he even remembered what it meant to remember. I said, "Armadillo. We met in Armadillo, Florida, five years ago. We were both there to see Bebb."

I said, "I'm teaching school in Connecticut these days," as if the poor old Cherokee gave a damn. Eyebrows raised, eyes goggling, dry teeth parted, he looked as though I'd made some unprecedented disclosure: that for years before she died I'd been half in love with my twin sister, Miriam; that even in the sack there lay some queer sadness between my young wife and me.

I said, "Sharon. You remember Sharon Bebb. I'm the one that married her." It was to be my last stab at self-identification, the single most substantial piece of evidence I could think to offer either him or myself that I truly existed, and this time it seemed to work.

He raised one hand a little off the arm of his chair and said something. What I thought he said was something like "sweet little *butt* on her," a reference I had heard him make in happier days to that aspect of Sharon's charm that he found especially congenial. But Bebb said he was either clearing his throat or possibly asking somebody to undo some *button* somewhere. In either case, he didn't seem inclined to pursue the conversation with me any further.

Bebb said, "Herman Redpath, they're all here, and now Antonio is here too. But if you added up the total number, you'd come out one short. The reason is there's one other one that's here too only there's not anybody can see him because he's invisible. But he faileth not. He's on deck with the rest of us."

Herman Redpath had not tried to close his mouth since whatever it was he may have tried to say to me. His tongue looked humped and dry like a parrot's. His next words, however, came through with surprising clarity. "Harry Hocktaw," he said. It was only the last name I wasn't sure of—Hoptoad, Hotstraw—but Bebb recognized it immediately.

"Harry," Bebb said, looking back over his shoulder. "Harry Hocktaw," he said. He snapped his fingers like a maître d'hôtel.

Harry Hocktaw turned out to be one of the Indians I remembered from earlier visits. He looked less Indian to me than he did Eskimo. He reminded me of Jack Oakie. He was wearing a Hawaiian shirt and squatting not far from Herman Redpath's chair with his back to a circle of children who had some comic books spread out among them on the floor. When Bebb snapped his fingers, Harry Hocktaw started to get up, but Herman Redpath stopped him by suddenly raising one arm. "Harry Hocktaw," he said in the same parrot accent. Harry Hocktaw sank back to his heels and waited.

Herman Redpath curled the fingers of his raised hand carefully down into a fist as though he was picking something dangerous out of the air and then drew the thumb in tight over the knuckles like a latch. For a few moments he held the fist motionless. Then he gave it a few small, rapid shakes. Then he stopped. Harry Hocktaw was watching, and so were Bebb and I. A lot of the Indians were watching too but trying to look as if they weren't. Then Herman Redpath shook his fist again. He shook it more fiercely than the first time but delicately too. He was looking straight at Harry Hocktaw now instead of at the empty place in the air, and this time Harry Hocktaw caught the old man's meaning. Like the squirt of a water pistol, he caught it full in the face, and a tabby smile swelled his cheeks. His eyes came alive with a look of hilarious recognition, and he reached into the pocket of his green and yellow pineapple shirt and pulled out a rattle. It was one of those rattles you find in Latin American dance bands made out of a dried gourd filled with seeds. I knew there was a special name for it, but I couldn't remember what the name was, and off and on the whole afternoon of Herman Redpath's dying I kept trying to remember it. In any case, Harry Hocktaw held his rattle up and gave it a few rapid shakes just the way Herman Redpath had shaken his fist. You could tell from the way the old man let his hand fall back to the arm of his chair that this was what he had wanted right along.

The sound the gourd made was less of a rattle the way Harry Hocktaw shook it than a kind of hiss. Sometimes he made it sound like footsteps on a gravel drive, sometimes like the dithering of crickets before rain, sometimes like dice in a cup. After he'd shaken it, he would stop for a while before shaking it some more. Sometimes he stopped so long between shakes that you'd think he'd stopped for good, but then he would shake it again, his arm crooked out in front of him and all the movement limited to his hairless, brown wrist. I assumed at first that there was no pattern to his rattling, but as the afternoon wore on, I began to wonder. It was like the stars at night. Either there is no pattern at all or a pattern so vast and simple nobody can figure it out.

I also couldn't figure out the purpose of the rattle. Was it a sound to scare death off with—Herman Redpath sitting there barefoot in the big chair while death waited under the comic book or in the organ pipes for a silence just the right size and shape to slip in through? Or was it to give death a beat to enter by—a noise to bump and grind to as it postured its way in through the Indians? Maybe the rattle was death itself. Maybe Harry Hocktaw had smuggled death in with him in the pocket of his Hawaiian shirt and had kept it hidden there till Herman Redpath gave him the signal. Crowded between the great, round cheeks, Harry Hocktaw's nose and upper lip looked stitched together like a cat's with several stray black whiskers at the seam. The bare feet of Herman Redpath angled out from the heels like halves of a broken ivory fan.

The big room was full of Indians who were there to be with him when he died presumably, but none of them seemed to be paying him any particular attention. The three flat-faced Trionka sisters were watching a quiz show on TV, and their huge mother sat dozing over a copy of *Life* spread out on her knees. There was a poker game going on between four Indians, one of them the man in the Alcatraz T-shirt and another wearing a cap made of a handkerchief knotted at the corners. An old woman in a peekaboo blouse was sitting at the organ. She was mending something flesh-colored, using the keyboard to hold her sewing equipment, and every so often in reaching for something she would strike a note by accident, usually one of the higher, shriller ones, which made a more inscrutable music still out of the inscrutable rhythms of Harry Hocktaw. One small boy, naked except for an orange life jacket, came up behind Herman Redpath, who had his mouth wide open now as if he was trying to sing something, and started to urinate on the back of the chair before a woman in a bathing suit snatched him away. There were children of all ages milling in and out, brown-faced, dark-eyed children, and many of them, I knew Herman Redpath would have said, had been begotten by him on one kinswoman or another.

Children maybe and grandchildren certainly, great-grandchildren, they were all there that afternoon with the nephews and nieces, the wives and cousins and hangers-on, none of them paying much attention to the small chocolate figure melting slowly away in the armchair although from time to time one of them would come up and stand near him for a moment or two. Once I saw a woman with a braid down her back offer him her naked breast the way a nurse might or a mother whereupon with one hand the old man covered his mouth and with the other seemed to be trying to push her away. I suppose he thought they were just trying to force down his throat some final bitterness. And then suddenly the hiss of the snake again, the clatter of dice in a cup, and *marimba, cucaracha, hacienda* . . . ? For the life of me I couldn't remember the name for a dried gourd filled with seeds.

A middle-aged Indian in jeans that smelled of horse came up to me where I was standing not far from the trio of Trionka sisters. His upper front teeth all had their own little frames of gold, like cufflinks. He said, "Your wife. How she doing these days?"

I said she was doing well. Home taking care of the baby.

He said, "How many babies you got now anyway?"

"Just the one baby," I said. To take some of the curse off, I said it was a boy.

"Just one baby?" he said. He pushed a finger into his cheek. "Who's going to believe that, a big boy like you?"

I said, "What's with that thing Harry Hocktaw keeps rattling?"

He said, "Hocktaw? I don't hear him rattling nothing."

"He's got it in his hand," I said. "In a second he'll hold it up and start rattling it again."

"I don't see Hocktaw's got anything in his hand," the Indian said. Almost as soon as he said it, Harry started in again, a barely punctuated trembling of sound this time, not unlike the sizzle of rain on a sidewalk. I kept my eyes on the Indian's face the whole time it lasted. When it was over, he smiled at me handsomely.

Through his golden teeth he clucked out the syllables rapidly, "Chicka-chicka, chicka-chicka, chicka-chicka." He said, "The cicadas they sing sometime. Could be that's what you think was Hocktaw. Just one baby." He sucked in his breath through puckered lips, a backward whistle. "Better get going, boy." He went over and sank down in front of the quiz show at the feet of one of the Trionkas.

I had the feeling death himself was there in that room like a celebrity. All of them except me had spotted him, and out of the corners of their eyes they were watching every move he made. Like a movie star he was there in some transparent disguise which they were all tactfully pretending not to see through. The poker players, the old woman at the organ, fat Mrs. Trionka dozing over *Life*—it was their air of utter unconcern that was the dead giveaway. You couldn't look that unconcerned without working at it. Harry Hocktaw shaking his rattle at odd moments as though nothing could matter less than whether he shook it or not. My friend saying it was cicadas. Everybody in that room except me knew that one of those Indians wasn't an Indian.

I found a telephone and called Sharon. Herman Redpath was melting fast. One arm had already started to run down the side of his chair, and some parts of his face were starting to go. One of those Indians was death warmed up, and I was homesick for life. I called Sharon up because for better or for worse she was the alivest thing I knew.

"That sonofabitch Tony," she said, referring to the younger of my two nephews, Miriam's boys, who lived with us. "When he got home from practice this afternoon, he put the African violets in his jockstrap and hung it on the hall light so when Anita came in with my guitar, it practically totaled her. You should have heard him knocking himself out over it in the can upstairs. He gives me a pain in the butt."

"Butt reminds me," I said. "Herman Redpath asked after you first thing."

"Old Herman," she said. "Has he made it to the happy hunting ground yet?"

I said, "Not yet, but he's struck his wigwam. One of the papooses tried to take a leak on him."

"I bet he got a bang out of that," Sharon said.

"What are you up to?" I asked her.

"Not much," she said. "I think there's going to be a thunderstorm. Chris has got the baby's bottle heating, and two-ton Tony's out lifting weights to keep from doing his homework. I was just about to wash my hair. I left the water running."

She was upstairs then. I could see her sitting on our bed long-legged, barefoot, with one foot up on the bed beside her so she could pick at a toenail. She was looking down at her foot so all you could see of her profile was a patch of forehead and the bridge of her nose.

I said, "I'm sorry about yesterday. We can't let a swami come between us."

"He's not a swami," she said. "He just teaches yoga. He comes from Beloit, Michigan."

"Wisconsin," I said.

"Have it your way," Sharon said.

I said, "How's the baby?"

"Chris thinks he's going to start walking soon," she said. "I wish to God he'd start getting some hair first. Tell Bip he looks more like him every day, I'm afraid. What's Bip think he's going to do anyway? After Herman croaks."

"I haven't asked him," I said.

She said, "Tell him for me he better start taking it to the Lord in prayer."

"Listen," I said. "Everybody's hanging around to see old Herman off, and there's this Eskimo with a rattle and a lot of kids and old squaws all playing it real cool except I've got an idea the whole bunch of them is doing something basic and subtle to help something happen or not happen and I'm the only one who isn't in on it. I've got a strong hunch every Indian in there knows something I ought to know too only I don't. When they think nobody's watching, they've all got their eyes on something I can't see. Maybe it's just as well."

"Have you checked your zipper lately?" Sharon said.

"How old are you anyway?" I asked her.

"Going on twenty-seven," Sharon said.

"Well don't go on," I said. "Just stay where you are, kid, and don't go on."

"Lucille's been dosing you with Tropicanas," she said.

"No such luck," I said. "I haven't laid eyes on Lucille yet."

She said, "It must be Herman then. Is it pretty bad for him?"

I said, "It's not bad at all. That's what's bad about it. A child could do it without half trying. You go back and wash your hair now and leave a lamp in the window. Tell Tony he's sixteen now. It's time to stop acting like a sixteen year old."

Sharon said, "You should have seen Anita's face when she figured out what the damned thing was. I think it's the closest to the real McCoy she's ever been." She said, "Tell Herman hello for me. Tell him something for me anyway. Tell him happy hunting. Say happy hunting to old Herman Redpath for me, will you, Antonio?" And when she hung up, I could see her sitting there barefoot a few moments more before getting up and moving across that messy room to the bathroom. I could see the way her hair divided over her ears and the lazy, loose-limbed way she had of walking, and I decided that if it was true that it was only "Button" that Herman Redpath had said when I mentioned her to him, he had already slipped farther than I thought.

I might still have made it back to him in time if at that point I had not heard the sudden scraping back of a chair and the sound of breaking glass. The phone I had been using was in the kitchen, and the noise came from a dining alcove around the corner. There was a bay window filled with potted plants that were glowing gold and green in the afternoon sun. There was a table and some chairs, and in one of them, sitting up straight as a stick with her eyebrows arched into a question above her black glasses sat Lucille Bebb, my mother-in-law. She said, "Find me a Handiwipe, will you? I was going to come tell Sharon hey, and then I spilled my

Tropicana all over Herman Redpath's linoleum."

I said, "You wouldn't happen to have another one on hand, would you?"

"Are you kidding?" she said. "These days Bebb makes Tropicanas for me one at a time."

The sun through the leaves gave a soft, greenish light as if we were meeting at the bottom of the sea. I sponged up what I could of the Tropicana and broken glass and sat down across from her at the table. She was even skinnier than when I'd seen her last, and instead of limiting herself to her usual cropped utterances thrown out take-it-or-leave-it, she seemed almost talkative.

She said, "I heard what you were saying to Sharon, and there's one thing I can tell you. You hit the nail on the head about those Indians. They know plenty, and they're not talking. They're born knowing plenty that folks with white skin don't know and won't ever know. Except Bebb. I think Bebb knows just about everything Indians know and then some. I'll tell you something else. When it comes to Indians, I'm fed. I haven't anything to say against Herman Redpath, especially now. He has always behaved like a gentleman in front of me. So I've got nothing but good to say about Herman Redpath, and I would never have wished on him what's happening to him in there right this minute. But as long as it's got to happen and there's not a thing in this world anybody can do about it, I don't mind saying it suits me just fine because I know as soon as it's happened we'll be getting the hell out. I'm up to here with Indians. They've got a rancid odor to them, and like you say, they know too much. Sharon says the way they look at you sometimes, it's like they knew the last time you had the period."

It may have been the longest speech I ever heard her make. She must have cut her finger trying to pick up the broken glass because she was holding a wad of Kleenex pressed against it, and I thought to myself she didn't look as if she had any extra blood to throw around.

"What else do those Indians know that we don't?" I asked her.

She said, "You tell me." She was back to her usual conversational style. "Ask Bebb," she said.

I said, "You think he knows?"

"Look," she said. "I don't think. I live with the man. He's from outer space." A huge elephant's ear turned into green fire behind her.

I said, "Maybe you're from outer space yourself. It takes one to know one."

"Listen," Lucille said, straightening her black glasses. "I could tell you plenty."

If you get to gazing out the window for a certain length of time with other things on your mind, you can look at something for quite a while before you actually see it, and in the same way, I suppose, you can listen to something quite a while before you actually hear it. Off and on the whole time I'd been out there in the kitchen with my mother-in-law, the sound of Harry Hocktaw's rattle must have been perfectly audible—there was only a hall between us and both doors were open—but it was not until this point that I became conscious of it again. It had speeded up considerably—*chicka-chicka chicka-chicka chicka-chicka chicka-chicka*—with hardly so much as a breath in between chickas, and it was also louder. If, before, it had been someone walking on gravel, now it was someone running, or something running—something heavy-footed and in a terrible hurry. That was not all. There was a hollow tock-tock of wood against wood such as you might hear in a kabuki theater, about four of these, very sharp and forceful with shuddering pauses of silent air in between them. Then, so help me, there was a desperate, flapping sound like a flushed partridge. The tocking had plainly come from the big room, but the wings could have been anywhere—wings in the big room, wings in the hallway, wings even in the kitchen with Lucille and me and the plants.

Some windowshade fluttering in a freak gust of wind? Some echo of Mrs. Trionka waving her copy of *Life* around her head in a sudden assault of grief? Or could it really have been, as I'm sure at the time I wanted it to be, the soul of Herman Redpath mounting up like an eagle, that chocolate-clad Cherokee flip-flapping his way through the house to be gathered to his fathers at last? I see him swooping out of the window all hung with sharks teeth and wampum with his hands together like a diver's to cleave the humid Texas dusk. There was an electric fan in the bathroom, and Lucille told me later that what I heard was the sound an electric fan makes if it gets blowing toward a shower curtain.

The third noise was the last. As children my sister Miriam and I were taken to see an early movie version of Rider Haggard's *She*, I think it was, and there was a scene in Aisha's underground jungle palace where Aisha herself came rising up out of a flaming crater, and all around it writhing savage women in grass skirts and Theda Bara headdresses joined together in a foreboding, choral wail. This was the sound I heard again in the kitchen with Lucille except that it flickered off and on a few times like a phonograph when you pick up the needle. A foreboding, choral wail. Then we heard footsteps running down the hall, and in a moment Bebb stuck his head in.

His plump, white face was closed tight, his mouth sprung shut, but his eyes were round and quick as a bird's.

He said, "Antonio, tell it not in Gath, publish it not in Askelon lest the daughters of the uncircumcised triumph. Herman Redpath now rests in the bosom of Abraham."

"Believe me," Lucille said, wiping some Tropicana off the table with her bloody Kleenex, "I could tell you plenty."

2

LEO BEBB sits halfway down the porch steps watching the sun set over the Red Path Ranch. Between his socks and his trouser cuffs, his hairless calves are the color of skimmed milk. The color of the sky is orange with a few long, flat clouds. There is no sound. He says, "Antonio, it is easier for a camel to go through the eye of a needle than for a rich man to enter the Kingdom of Heaven. That miserable Brownie, he claims the true translation is that it's as easy as a needle going through the eye of a camel." In his lapel he wears a little gold cross made up of LOVE going across and HOLY going down. Identical crosses are available at the gift shop attached to the church that Herman Redpath built for him. Also available are postcards including one of Bebb in his maroon robe with his right hand raised in benediction and another one of Herman Redpath in a feathered headdress and business suit presenting a pipe of peace to Lyndon B. Johnson.

Leo Bebb is washing his hands in a men's room in a Houston gas station. His nostrils are swelled out and his lips pressed together. He is humming a tune. Looking at himself in the mirror, he turns his head a little to the right and then a little to the left. He pulls his handkerchief up by the points just enough for the monogram B to show. He starts to leave but then comes back and swings open the door of the cubicle where the toilet is. On the inside of the door there is a heart with an arrow through it drawn with a ball-point pen.

The sun is setting, and in the two-story room the old woman in the peekaboo blouse is taking her turn keeping the flies off Herman Redpath. Outside, on the porch steps, the only thing that is moving is the trick eyelid of Leo Bebb.

Leo Bebb stands at the bedroom door and knocks. In his right hand he is carrying Lucille's Tropicana with half as much gin as usual and twice as much orange juice.

Bebb hates to fly, but he flies anyway. When he is flying, if you took away the plane, the crew and all the other passengers, what you would have left in the sky would be just Bebb. He is sitting there above the clouds with his knees pressed together and his eyes shut. His chicken sandwich is untouched. Depths have never bothered him, but he is scared stiff of heights.

* * *

"Dear Bip," I wrote him once from the top of a Green Line bus between London and Hampton Court. "Did you really raise Brownie from the dead in Knoxville, Tennessee? What was it, if anything, that really *happened* that day with the children in Miami Beach? Have you ever forgiven Lucille about the baby? I don't care so much how you answer. Just answer." Bebb was sitting in the front seat of the bus peering down at the traffic so he could get the feel of driving on the left, he said, in case Gertrude Conover should ask him someday to take the wheel of her rented Daimler. I never gave him the letter.

The sun had almost set when Mrs. Trionka came out of the house and joined Bebb and me on the porch steps. She was wearing a white terry-cloth bathrobe and had rollers in her hair. She was carrying a glass of root-beer with a scoop of vanilla ice cream in it. It was her favorite warm-weather drink, she said. She called it a brown cow. She was a brown cow herself, but in the gathering twilight her robe made her look more like Pope John XXIII.

She said, "Things aren't going to be the same around here without Herman." The brown cow had left her with a white mustache.

Bebb said, "In a way that is true, but in another way it is not true. When the right time comes—later," he said, interrupting himself, "later on I'm going to explain what that means."

Mrs. Trionka said, "Watching the sun go down always makes a person think. It makes a person wonder what's it all about anyway."

Bebb said, "Antonio, you've had a college education, and you're a deep thinker. In there they've got Herman Redpath laid out in his brown suit, a fine Christian gentleman snatched away when there was still plenty of mileage left in him. Out here the Almighty is washing the underside of those clouds with gold same as if today was no different from yesterday or tomorrow. You tell Mrs. Trionka and I what it's all about."

He wasn't trying to put me on. I don't think he believed I could tell him but thought it might be worth a try. The horizon was the color of smoked salmon as he turned away from it to see what I was going to say. I was sitting behind him on the top step. Mrs. Trionka was standing by the door of the house with her white robe almost touching the ground at her heels but hiked up to her shins in front.

Without being sure why, I found myself answering this metaphysical question by giving him and Mrs. Trionka a detailed description of something I had been making in a shed off the garage. Before marrying Sharon, I had tried making things out of odd pieces of scrap-iron dipped in Rust-oleum black. Since then I had turned to making things out of wood.

The thing I described to them was a six foot high triangle of raw pine planking. From the apex hung down thin tongues of wood of different lengths, some spear-shaped at the end, some spatulate, some notched or rounded. The three vertical planks that side by side made each leg of the triangle had spaces between them, and fastened into those spaces were wooden balls and cubes and discs that could be turned on their axes. The planks of one leg were not always pierced to match the planks of the opposite leg—a square hole on one side might face a circular hole on the other, a star a diamond, an X an O—but wherever there was a triangle cut out of one leg, there was an identical triangle cut out in a comparable position across from it. I have no idea why. Between the two legs and somewhat nearer the top than the bottom there was a bridge made of three strips of wood each a few inches above, and thus a few inches shorter than, the other. These strips had been slotted so that the tongues from the top could pass through without touching the slots. The base of the triangle was an open wooden grille at the center of which I thought someday I might put a smaller triangle which would duplicate the large triangle and inside that maybe a smaller triangle still. The whole construction was suspended by a chain from the roof of the shed and hung about eighteen inches off the floor. The shed was not air-tight, and sometimes when I was out there after dark with the light on, the thing swayed a little from its chain and made complicated shadows on the floor and walls.

To Bebb and Mrs. Trionka I said, "It's made of wood, and it's got a woody smell. It holds together. The air moves around inside it. But if you asked me what it was all about, I couldn't tell you. I don't know what it's all about. So when it comes to what Herman Redpath is all about and the sun setting, I can't tell you that either. That's your department," I added to my father-in-law.

Bebb said, "It's good for a man to have work for his hands, Antonio." He sat there on the steps gazing west.

Mrs. Trionka said, "When it comes time for us to go, we all of us got to go, and it don't make a bit of difference if we know what it's all about or not." She sloshed her glass back and forth a few times and then tipped her head back like a sword-swallower to drain it. The scoop of ice cream must have rolled down against her lips. I could hear the sounds she made dealing with it inside the glass.

It wasn't until she had left that Bebb spoke again. By this time it was nearly dark. At Holy Love they had switched on the recorded chimes, and *Abide with Me* went trembling out over the fading grassland. Bebb said, "I didn't want to talk about it in front of Beatrice Trionka, but I'll tell you one thing about what it's all about, and that is that it's hard, Antonio. It's all of it hard. Right down to the end. Even the things are supposed to be easy, they're hard too. You take what Herman Redpath's up against now. 'In the twinkling of an eye we shall all be changed,' Scripture says. *In the twinkling of an eye*, Antonio, like it was the easiest thing in the world. It is not easy. Out there somewhere now Herman Redpath and his Maker are sweating like horses. You ever seen anything getting born looked easy, Antonio, let alone anything getting born again?"

From behind, Bebb had no neck to speak of, just a coil of fat above his collar. He looked diminished against the huge sky.

I said, "At least it's nice you believe there's something left of Herman Redpath to sweat with."

"Listen," Bebb said. "That's not even a half of what I believe."

"What else do you believe?" I said.

"Antonio," Bebb said. "I believe everything."

It was a remark of such classic grandeur that for a few moments I sat there in the twilight silent before the sheer magnitude of it.

"You make it sound almost easy," I said finally.

"Don't kid yourself," Bebb said, turning slowly to where he could look at me. "It's hard as hell."

The building where Bebb and Lucille lived was near Herman Redpath's and much like it except that the living-room ceiling was of normal height. I stayed with them the two days I was down there, and the second night—Herman Redpath had died the day before, and the funeral was to take place the day after—I had a hard time getting to sleep. I was almost there—drifting toward it like leaves, like smoke—when, at the very threshold, I tripped over something. I could feel the bed springs bounce under me as I came down on them, and the next moment I was more awake than awake, which is to say afflicted with that awesome clairvoyance of insomnia where even through closed eyelids you can't help seeing, and past, present, and future are all there to see at once.

I thought about home. I thought about my unfinished masterpiece hanging forgotten in the shed month after month while daylight came and went and the seasons changed and weather happened. I pictured it turning pink at daybreak or with snow falling past the window. I pictured a spider using it for something, or a mouse. I thought of the soft and steady downward pull of its suspended weight, the cumbersome woodenness of it with dusty shafts of sunlight sometimes lighting up random surfaces and quirks of it. I thought about the imponderable innocence and gravity of inanimate things, and how even with nobody to watch it, it must sometimes move on its chain.

And I thought about Sharon, of course. The swami from Beloit gave his yoga lessons in the Masonic hall over the bank, and she would drive home from them in her Volkswagen wearing her black leotards with maybe a raincoat thrown over them. Almost as soon as she stepped into the house she would start practicing. She would lie there with her hair spread out on the living-room rug or squatting in the lotus posture with her hands palms up in her lap.

Earlier on the same day that I flew down to Herman Redpath's deathbed, I had come home for lunch to find there was no lunch ready. Chris and the baby were upstairs and Sharon was on her back with her legs so far over her head that her toes were touching the floor behind it. Then Chris came down and said in his muted way that the diaper had slipped out of his hand while he was flushing it out in the toilet and now the toilet was plugged and overflowing onto the bathroom floor. There in the warm Texas night with the sound of either Bebb or Lucille snoring down at the other end of the hall, I relived the low comedy of what had followed—my elephantine sarcasms, the banging doors, the bitter silence as I made my own sandwich in the kitchen. Through closed eyelids I saw Sharon the way she had stood there in her black tights. She told me I was a shit and for God's sake not to hurry home.

No man is ever quite sane in the night, Mark Twain said, and in the dark I reached out for her as if she was actually there only to feel hurt and betrayed all over again when I found my fingers coming down on emptiness. I threw the top sheet off and lay on my stomach with the knuckles of one hand touching the bare floor.

It wasn't the yoga lessons that I held against her. It was the speed reading too. She would sit on the lawn with the sun on her bare back as she drew her fingers in sinuous zigzags down the pages, flipping them over one after the other at a rate sufficient to get her through most of the Sunday *Times* in an hour. Yoga to control her mind and Evelyn Wood to pack it full at increasing speeds—it was like going to the Tour d'Argent with your belt tightened, I told her. Her answer was, "Everybody in this whole damned house can *do* something except me."

It was the closest she ever came to an explanation, and it never seemed to me to explain much. Tony was a raging jock who probably couldn't have gotten through the Sunday *Times* in a month. At eighteen Chris had read all of Virginia Woolf and a good deal of Henry James, got an occasional poem in the senior literary sheet, and was Cinna the poet in the winter production of *Julius Caesar;* but he was bookish as distinct from bright, I'm afraid, got mediocre grades in History and English and flunked math two marking periods in a row. As for me, I taught sixteen year olds *Cry the Beloved Country* and how to identify iambic pentameter and what was wrong with "like a cigarette should." I coached track. I had my six foot mobile casting complicated shadows in a shed off the garage. That was all we could *do*, the rest of us, but maybe it was enough to have precipitated Sharon's remark. I don't know. But whatever the motive, she studied the guitar too, took it up, in fact, before she'd even heard of Evelyn Wood or the swami.

She bought a secondhand Goya when she was seven months pregnant and found a woman named Anita with a grey crew-cut and a face like an unshelled walnut to teach her to play it. She bought a shoulder strap and for weeks carried it all over the house with her playing "I've got a little gal in Kingston town" until I feared for the sanity of our unborn child. Under Anita's supervision, however, her repertoire grew considerably, and it became the only one of her extracurricular interests that I did not begrudge her. Leonard Cohen's *Suzanne* was one of her best. "Jesus was a sailor when he walked upon the water" she would sing with her head to one side so that her hair touched her bare forearm.

And I thought of our unborn child who in spite of everything managed to be born. When they told Sharon it was a boy, she said, "That house of ours is so full of balls it's turning into a goddamn bowling alley." It was the first time I ever saw her cry. Just her eyes cried—none of the rest of her face seemed to have anything to do with it. Under the fluorescent hospital lights the tears turned her cheeks silver. I don't know why she cried. I'm sure it had nothing to do with the baby's being a boy. Maybe it was just that for the first time she felt the walls closing in around her and hadn't yet found Evelyn Wood and the swami to come to her rescue. If that was what she found them for. Anyway, we called the baby William because she thought just plain Bill would be a good antidote for Sharon on one side and Antonio on the other. Right from the beginning he was a good baby. He slept nights. He took his bottle without a fuss. He didn't seem to mind that his mother turned most of the care of him over to a soft-spoken, introspective eighteen year old who had played Cinna the poet in *Julius Caesar*.

My son lies on his stomach in his play-pen. It is a warm spring day, and he has nothing on but his diapers and a pair of rubber pants. He has rings of fat around his arms and legs and looks like the Michelin tire man. Near him on the grass is my nephew Chris. Narrow chested and white, he looks out of place in a bathing suit. He is reading *The Prophet* and every once in a while, without having to look up, he moves the wooden beads of the play-pen abacus with his bare foot to keep the baby entertained.

That is the scene I finally went to sleep on. There was no luxurious moment of knowing that at last sleep was on its way, of feeling it lap around the edges of me like a warm tide. It fell sudden and heavy like a headsman's ax. When I woke up, my father-in-law was standing by my bed in a saucer-shape of sunlight softly tapping me on the shoulder with a copy of the last will and testament of Herman Redpath.

THERE WERE times when I wondered whether Bebb ever went to bed. He was always fully dressed when I went to bed myself, and he was always fully dressed when I got up the next morning. If he slept in between times, I never saw any evidence of it. I can't imagine him asleep. I can't picture him abandoning that overcrowded face even temporarily, can't imagine those busybody eyes turned inward on the puzzle of some dream. The most I can picture is Bebb tucked in like a tin soldier. He's got on his Palm Beach suit, and his arms are stiff at his sides. He is staring up into the dark.

He said, "Antonio, wake up and take a look at a wealthy man. This is the third day for Herman Redpath, and with Herman Redpath I will arise from the dead and shine too. How beautiful upon the mountain, Antonio, are the feet of him that bringeth good tidings. You can read it for yourself when you've had your coffee. One hundred thousand dollars is what it says. One hundred thousand dollars to my loyal friend and pastor Leo Bebb."

I had never seen him more excited. I was still half asleep, and the whole room seemed to be turning to gold, the shallow pool of sunshine where he was standing, sun on the wall, sun drenching the curtains, sun on my pillow and in my eyes.

He said, "Think what a man could do with a sum like that, Antonio."

"I do hereby devise and bequeath," I read out loud with my hair in my eyes. "To my loyal friend and pastor."

Bebb said, "There is absolutely nothing in the—hardly anything in this world a man would not do with wealth like that."

He stood there by my bedside dressed for Herman Redpath's funeral in his gents'-furnishings suit with his shoulders too square and his ribbed silk tie and his pointed black shoes, and "Expensive clothes," I said, "and expensive women and an air-conditioned Cadillac automobile and color TV in every room. For openers."

Bebb was not listening. He was dreaming. He was glittering in the morning sunshine, his face powdery pale. He said, "Yes, that is so, Antonio. All the kingdoms of the earth spread out at my feet like a wall-to-wall rug. My father was a house painter. He took a bad fall when I was small and spent most of the rest of his life in bed. His fingernails were always dirty. I never did see how a man could get his fingernails dirty just laying around in bed all the time, but he did. Someday I will tell you more about him. My mother was a hard-working woman, a good woman, but she didn't have a particle of charity, Antonio, and without charity her goodness didn't profit anybody anything, herself included. Makes you wonder what a pair like that would have done with a hundred thousand dollars in cash money. They wouldn't have even believed it, most likely."

I had never thought of his having had a mother and father. I said, "Tell me more, Bip."

The one lazy eyelid flickered down for a moment, and I was afraid I had put him on his guard. He said, "Antonio, I will tell you this much for now. I was born and raised outside of Spartanburg, South Carolina, and that is where I got acquainted with sin and death for the first time, and many other things besides. The first time I got acquainted with death was in the railway depot. I don't suppose I was more than six. There was a big, long box sitting out on a hand car waiting to be loaded on to the Atlanta train, and I asked my mother what was inside it. Well, she didn't want to say, naturally, what was in it, but I wormed it out of her. She said it was a dead man was in it being shipped to the crematory with his name written out on the shipping labels just like there was horse feed in there or dry goods. The peculiar thing, Antonio, is I knew it wasn't a dead man. I knew it was a dead woman. It was an old woman, and I could see her in there plain as if I had x-ray eyes. Now you explain that any way you want. She had got on a pair of pink bloomers and a summer dress, and they'd put sticking plaster over her mouth, don't ask me why. It was the first meeting between me and death, Antonio. I have never forgotten it."

He was sitting on the edge of my bed with his hands on his knees looking down at the sun on the floor. I had a momentary impulse to run my finger down his stubby profile the way you might with a statue or a child. Instead, I said, "How about the first meeting between you and sin, Bip?"

Bebb said, "Around Spartanburg it's a lot of good peach country. You wouldn't think so maybe to look at all the red clay, but it is. One summer they commenced dumping peaches to keep the price up. There was piles of peaches heaped up all along the sides of the roads and in the orchards. Antonio, there was peaches every place you looked nearly— big, pinky-yellow, juicy peaches enough to make your mouth water—and there they were, going brown and rotten in the sun. It made you sick the same way as sin makes you sick." His jaw snapped shut as though on a spring.

Bebb said, "Sin is waste, Antonio. Sin is life wasted. Now you take this," he added. Reaching forward he took the last will and testament of Herman Redpath out of my hand. He said, "Everything is accounted for here, and that means nothing is wasted. Everybody has come in for his share, Antonio. I'm fixing to explain it all out later at the funeral." Someone was knocking at my bedroom door, but Bebb took no notice of it. "Jesus has come in for his share too," he said. "A trust has been created to take care of the operating expenses of Gospel Faith College, and there won't have to be any 'Closing Out' sign hung up on the door of Holy Love either. I wanted you to be among the first to know, Antonio. Nobody has been left out in the cold, not even Jesus."

I said, "Maybe that's Jesus now. The knocking."

It was Brownie. He had been off on some errand for Bebb when I had arrived the day before, and I got out of bed now to greet him. He said, "I'm sorry for the sad occasion that's brought us together, dear," and when he smiled, I decided that the way to do Brownie's smile properly would be first to form the expression of a man who has just been kicked in the crotch and then to say "cheese."

Brownie turned to Bebb and said, "I was just over to the church checking on the flowers, and I thought I ought to let you know that I noticed a certain person hanging around outside again. Mrs. Bebb said she found him in the gift shop when she got over and he bought five postcards of you. She said afterwards when she come to look at the money he'd given her, she found this."

Bebb took the object that Brownie handed him and examined it carefully. It had apparently come from one of those machines they used to have in the waiting rooms of big railway stations where you put a quarter in a slot and, by turning a wheel with the alphabet on it, could stamp out your name on a perforated aluminum disc about the size of a fifty cent piece. The one that Brownie handed Bebb had no name on it, however, but just the word SWEETHEART. On the upper rim were printed the words GOOD LUCK.

"Good luck, Sweetheart," Brownie said.

Bebb put the piece in his pocket and said, "Brownie, did he say anything to you when you saw him?"

"He was standing out there in the wet grass like he was reading the bulletin board," Brownie said, "I told him the church was going to be closed to the public today because we were conducting a private funeral."

Bebb said, "What did he say when you told him that?" They were standing together in the morning sunlight: Bebb had the knob of his chin thrust forward a little, the flesh beneath it slightly in motion.

Brownie said, "He didn't say a word. He just gave me a real friendly smile and started walking away. The bottoms of his trousers were all wet from the grass. That man must weigh a good two hundred and seventy-five stripped."

Bebb said, "You strip him, Brownie." He stood there at the window looking out with his thumbs linked behind him. Without turning around, he said, "Antonio, some of those big government agencies won't stop at anything. The Federal Trade Commission, the U.S. Post Office Department, the Better Business Bureau, you name it. I've had my set-to's with all of them on account of Gospel Faith, and one time or another they've all sent plainclothesmen down here to snoop around. He's one of them probably."

"Why don't you ask him?" I said.

Brownie said, "Dear, that is just the trouble. Up till today he never came close enough to talk to. Before, you might catch sight of him looking out at you through the dime-store window or hanging around by the swimming pool the day Herman Redpath had open house for Rotary, but he never came near enough so as you could get a chance to have a conversation with him."

I said, "Maybe he's bashful."

Brownie said, "Maybe he is, dear." Like Bebb, he had on a dark suit for Herman Redpath's service.

Bebb said, "Good luck, Sweetheart. You don't generally wish a man good luck unless you think he's going to need it."

"What's he look like?" I asked.

Bebb said, "He looks flat. He looks like he was cut out with a cookie-cutter."

"Flat," Brownie said, "but wide. Very wide, dear."

When Bebb picked Herman Redpath's will off the bed to put it back in his pocket, the reflection of it flickered in the window like a white bird. He said, "If you stick around for a while you may get a look at him yourself, Antonio."

I did stick around, of course—for the funeral that morning and for the burial afterwards—and before I caught the plane back north, I did get a look at him as Bebb had predicted, but not before getting a look at a variety of other things first. There were times during the funeral when I couldn't believe what I was looking at and these are the times I remember best.

There were no special pews reserved for the family because one way or another they were all family. I took a place near Mrs. Trionka toward the back because it gave me a good view of the whole church, and when I was settled down I said a kind of prayer for Herman Redpath. I tried to picture him and his maker sweating it out together the way Bebb had described it and wished them both a happy issue out of their labors. When that was finished, I passed the time until the service was to begin by seeing how many of the Indians I could identify. The Trionka sisters were easy, the three of them drifted together like snow in their flowing white dresses, several rows in front of their mother and me, and I had no trouble with Harry Hocktaw or the small boy who had urinated on Herman Redpath's chair. I recognized the woman who had offered Herman Redpath her breast and the old woman who for the first time in my experience was wearing not a peekaboo blouse but something high-collared and Victorian that buttoned up the back. I looked a long time for Lucille before I discovered her sitting by herself in the choir loft with her dark glasses in place. There were also a few children whose faces I remembered from one visit or another, and of course there was Herman Redpath himself. The coffin was open, and by raising myself slightly in my pew I could just see his nose jutting up out of the white satin like the fin of a shark.

It wasn't until everybody stood up for the opening hymn that I discovered that several members of the congregation were as far as I could see naked. There were just a few of them scattered here and there among the fully clothed ones, and apart from their nakedness they didn't seem to have anything else in common, some male and some female, some old and some young. They did not turn out to have any special role to play in the service either but just stood up and sat down with the rest of us. I convinced myself at one point that they were possibly a little taller and handsomer than the others and wondered if they could have been special favorites of Herman Redpath's who were using this device to say so. Or was it conceivably their way of dramatizing that they had been dealt with inadequately in the will and thus sadly reduced? Or could it just be an overreaction to the Texas heat that day? I don't know. When I asked Bebb later, he said he didn't know either. In any case, nobody seemed to pay them any particular attention, and I am surprised how quickly I reached the point myself where a bare brown shoulder or buttock or breast seemed no more out of place than a straw hat or a hymn book.

After the funeral was over, Bebb was able to explain to me at least something about the eccentric behavior of John Turtle, but at the time I was unprepared for it. Bebb said, "Seems like every one of your big family groups has got what they call a Joking Cousin, and for Herman Redpath's family group it's John Turtle. A Joking Cousin's main job is to make jokes, but he doesn't make your run-of-the-mill jokes, and he doesn't make them at run-of-the-mill times either. Say there's a marriage being arranged and the heads of both families are there all dressed up to make terms. Or say a man's dying or just died and the women have come over to pay their last respects. Maybe a girl gets herself in trouble, and there's a pow-wow what to do about finding her a husband. They're the times when the Joking Cousin does his stuff. Seems as if the Joking Cousin is the Indians themselves mocking and blaspheming their own holiest times so as nobody else will. Seems to me like an Indian thinks if he mocks the holiest times he's got, maybe then the evil spirits will be fooled into letting the holy times alone. Maybe even God will let them alone then, Antonio."

I don't know about Bebb's explanation. I know only that at the funeral of Herman Redpath at Holy Love, John Turtle played the part of the Joking Cousin. John Turtle turned out to be the one who had teeth like cufflinks and had told me he couldn't hear or see Harry Hocktaw's rattle.

"I am the resurrection and the life," Bebb said from the pulpit pale as death, and John Turtle stood behind him holding two fingers up over Bebb's head like rabbit ears. When Bebb was winding up his eulogy of Herman Redpath by giving out the details of the will—explaining how even from the grave Herman Redpath would continue to finance the ranch indefinitely and everyone was going to have his share including Jesus—John Turtle picked his nose on the chancel steps. At several points in the service, he even tried to get Bebb to enter into dialogue with him.

"The Lord is my shepherd, I shall not want," Bebb read from the lectern, his face glistening with perspiration, and "I know what *you* want right enough," John Turtle said from the foot of the casket.

Bebb said, "He maketh me to lie down in green pastures, He leadeth me beside the still waters," and John Turtle said, "I know a girl what lives on a hill. If she won't do it, her sister will." You have to hand it to Bebb. He never batted an eye.

"Chicka-chicka boom, chicka-boom, chicka-boom," went the Joking Cousin not unlike the sound of Harry Hocktaw's rattle all through the

Lord's Prayer. And during one of the hymns he ate a slice of watermelon. When he finished it, he made the motions of turning a crank in his neck and made his head tilt slowly backward like an anti-aircraft gun. When he reached maximum elevation, he turned another crank to make his head swivel around to face the congregation. With his lips puckered out to a point and his cheeks puffed he waited until the Amen came and then pulled one ear to fire. Watermelon seeds flew out toward the front pews like shrapnel.

Unlike the small boy in the orange life preserver, nobody came up to snatch the Joking Cousin away when just after the benediction he walked over and either took or pretended to take a leak into Herman Redpath's open coffin.

Oddly enough, the most vivid memory I have of Herman Redpath's obsequies involves none of these extraordinary events but one which was comparatively speaking rather ordinary. The whole congregation was standing up for a hymn, and when it was over, Bebb patted the air with one hand to indicate that everybody was to sit down and said in his pulpit voice, "Brothers and sisters, let us bow our heads in prayer." As far as I could tell, everybody obeyed and sat down and bowed their heads. I bowed my head too but not so far as to keep me from seeing what was going on.

At first I thought that for once there was nothing going on. Bebb was praying his prayer, getting more and more vehement with God about something. Even John Turtle was for the moment quiet. The Indians had arranged themselves in varying attitudes of worship and inattention —some with their faces in their hands or their foreheads resting on the pew in front of them, some half-sitting and half-kneeling, several with their heads down almost in their laps as if they were trying to keep themselves from being sick. A few pews in front of me I noticed that the shoulders of one of the Trionka girls were heaving and wondered if it was from grief or some dark spasm of mirth. A naked boy was leaning forward with his head cradled in his arms on the pew in front of him, and under one arm I could see the hair dark and luxuriant as fur. It wasn't for some moments that I glanced in the other direction and discovered that one member of the congregation had remained on his feet. He was standing there with his hands in his pockets, and as soon as I saw him, I knew that he was the stranger Bebb and Brownie had been discussing that morning.

From shoulder to shoulder, hip to hip, he was a very wide man, and anybody meeting him head-on would have thought he was enormous. Seeing him from the side, however, I appreciated the accuracy of Bebb's remark about the cookie-cutter. From back to front he was not enormous, and the only place where his thickness came near to matching his width was below the waist. It was not a paunch because it was too low for that and too spread out laterally. It was as if he was wearing some kind of inner tube or bolster which had slipped down over his loins, a massive eave of flesh swelling out over his crotch. His face was sallow and wrinkled, but when for no apparent reason he smiled at one point, his teeth showed strong and white and young. It was the smile of a pretty girl.

There he stood in the midst of Holy Love, cumbersome, relaxed, while all around him everybody else including myself were sitting or kneeling with our heads bowed. What made the moment so peculiarly vivid, I suppose, was the sense I had that he was the one we were bowing to. Bebb went on praying with his eyes screwed tight shut, and when the stranger smiled that oddly gay and youthful smile, it seemed a kind of graceful acknowledgment that even the prayer was addressed to him.

After the service was over, I hoped that I could get close enough to hear what his voice sounded like, perhaps even to speak to him, but I lost him in the crowd while I was waiting to shake hands with Bebb on the way out and caught only one more glimpse of him later. He was way off beyond the parking lot by then, drifting along through the high grass like an oddly shaped swarm of bees.

Later that afternoon when we had come back from the cemetery, Bebb and Lucille drove me to the airport to catch my plane home. Brownie came along for the ride, and when it turned out that the plane was going to be more than an hour late, Lucille insisted we all go into the lounge for some refreshment. Through the picture window you could see planes landing and taking off into the hot, pearly sky. Bebb and Brownie both had iced tea, and I joined Lucille in an airport lounge version of a Tropicana.

After a while Lucille said, "Golden, Brownie. When he bought those postcards, I asked him what his name was, and he said his name was Golden." It was a statement, but she left it hanging like a question. Bebb seemed remote and preoccupied, watching a big airliner go taxiing down the runway. Lucille and Brownie sat looking at each other in silence, Lucille behind her black glasses and Brownie behind his horn rims. "That's one for the books," Lucille said.

Brownie smiled dimly. He said, "I've heard stranger names than that in my time. I knew a boy once named ToeWater. Fred ToeWater."

There was another long, interrogatory silence during which Lucille lifted her glass to her lips and stared at Brownie over the rim of it, her eyebrows raised. She said finally, "Golden's a Jewish name."

Brownie said, "Some of my very dear friends are Jewish."

Lucille said, "If that man's Jewish, I'm a nigger."

Bebb turned slightly more toward the window like a man stirring in his sleep. Over the loudspeaker a voice read a long list of flight numbers. Brownie placed his hands palms down on the table in front of him. He wore three rings which looked like fraternity rings and a gold spring-band watch around one hairy wrist. Without looking up from his hands, he said, "What are you getting at, dear?"

Lucille dropped her lower jaw slightly. She said, "You tell me."

Brownie shrugged his shoulders and laid one hand on top of the other.

Lucille said, "He's no more Jewish than Bebb is, but when I asked him what his name was, he said it was Golden. That's Jewish."

"Are you inferring that Golden is an alias, dear?" Brownie said.

Lucille said, "The only thing I'm inferring is suppose he hadn't said his name was Golden. Suppose he said it was Silver."

Bebb's face looked vigorous and fresh as he interrupted them. He said, "Brownie, how'd you like to start being number one man at Holy Love?"

It had been a long, hot day. I was starting to feel a little drowsy from the Tropicana, and didn't listen as carefully as I might have otherwise to the conversation that followed. When I got home late that evening, Sharon was irritated by my incomplete and garbled account of it. She said, "My God, all our lives are at stake and you weren't even listening. What kind of a peckerhead are you anyway?" And of course she was right. One way or another our lives were at stake.

All the time Bebb had been praying in his maroon robe with the sweat running down, all the time John Turtle had been trying to distract the evil spirits or God or whoever it was, all the time we had stood there under the low clouds waiting until Herman Redpath's urine-stained coffin was finally lowered into the Texas soil, Bebb had apparently been making plans. There in the airport against a backdrop of silver wings and pewter clouds he had revealed them rapidly, one after another, like a magician pulling silk scarves out of somebody's ear.

What I remembered best was how he talked about the money Herman Redpath had left him. "One hundred thousand in cash, Antonio, with no strings attached," and he made it dance there, stringless, on the Formica before us. The money was power, it was promise, it was all the benevolence of Herman Redpath rolled into one. The money was freedom and adventure and fun, and as he stacked his words higher and higher, I wondered if he was thinking of his bed-ridden father again with the dirty fingernails in Spartanburg, South Carolina, and the piles of golden peaches abandoned along the roads to keep the price up. "The sky is the limit," he said—the sky behind his bald head looking electric and dangerous—and he stuck his finger into his tea and stirred the ice around until it rattled.

Herman Redpath had endowed both Holy Love and Gospel Faith in perpetuity, *saecula saeculorum*, so he, Bebb, was no longer needed there, he said. He had planted the seed and watered it with the sweat of his brow and tended the young shoots, and now he would leave it to Brownie to supervise the harvesting. Even Brownie should be able to handle things from here on out, Bebb said, and Brownie sat there in his short sleeves listening to him.

Bebb said, "Antonio, I have heard the voice of the Lord saying, 'Whom shall I send?' and I have said, 'Here am I. Leo Bebb. Send me.' I have labored in these Texas vineyards long enough. I may not be the man I once was, but I am not an old man yet either. There are souls to be saved same as there always was and always will be, and one hundred thousand dollars will take me a long piece down the road toward saving them. Indians aren't the only lost sheep of the House of Israel."

Lucille said, "I've got your Indians up to here," and drew one horizontal hand across her face at nose level, knocking her glasses crooked along the way. "That Turtle wasn't just pretending to piss on Herman Redpath. I was sitting upstairs by myself, and I could look right down and see it soaking into the Navajo blanket. Show me an Indian," she said, "and I'll show you a slob. I'm getting out of here if I have to push a peanut with my nose clear to Savannah."

Bebb talked about the North, I remember, with such poetry and zeal that it took me a while before I was sure what he was talking about. "The pilgrim's pride," he said. "The place they landed at in their old-time hats with buckles on their shoes and kneeled right down on that rock-bound coast with the waves pounding in their ears to return thanks to the Almighty. I am proud to be a Southerner born and bred, Antonio, but North is where the history was made and where the history is still being made to this very day. North is where the money is. North is where the power is. And the great whore is in the North too, Antonio, holding a golden cup in her hand full of the abominations and filthiness of her fornications. We have not been called to sit on our tails by the swimming pool forever and break bread with multi-millionaires of Indian descent. We are called to the North where the fighting is thickest. That's where we must work and fight while we can, for the night is coming. At any moment the end may come, Antonio. Like a thief in the night."

It was on this part of my report that Sharon questioned me most closely later. Did Bip mean that he was coming north to *us?* Could he possibly mean that he and Lucille were going to live in our house? Did he plan to create a new Holy Love right there with Tony going around hanging up African violets in his jock strap and me having a hemorrhage every time my lunch wasn't ready on the dot? Did he say *when* he was coming—like next year or next month or next week?

I failed miserably to give her the information she wanted. It was the rhetoric I remembered, not the facts. I wasn't even sure whether Bebb himself had given facts. I was sure that there was no need to start emptying bureau drawers that night, I told her, but that was all I was sure of.

The boys had both gone to bed before I got home, and the baby was asleep. The house was stuffy and still smelled of hamburger and onions so we were sitting outside under the spring stars. Even outside it was very warm, but, unlike Houston, there was at least a little movement in the air. When I finished my lame recital, Sharon did something she had learned in yoga maybe. I was lying face down in the damp grass, and she got up and stood on my back in her bare feet. She stood on the small of my back. She stood with one foot on my neck and the other between my shoulder blades. I could feel the cool soles of her feet through my shirt, and sometimes when she changed position the weight of her pressed the breath right out of me, but I could also feel it ironing out all the soreness and snarls left by my hours of sleeplessness the night before and by the long flight north and by my memories of how Herman Redpath's nose had looked jutting up out of the white satin.

Being stepped on almost put me to sleep before she was through, but she didn't let it. I was lying on my stomach, and she slipped one bare foot underneath me and did something unexpected and just painful enough down there to remind me that where her foot had touched was also part of who I was and that the three whole days and nights I had been away, that part too had been living, however obscure and neglected, a life of its own which she restored now, that accomplished young acrobat, that speedy reader, that guitarist, on whose charms Herman Redpath may or may not have expended the last words I ever heard him speak.

4

I SUPPOSE it is from my days as a schoolteacher and from my own school days that I have inherited the feeling that the year really starts in the fall. Fall is the time when the long dream of summer comes to an end and you settle down to the true business of your life. Spring, on the other hand, is the time of ending, and it is the season when I feel most vulnerable and anxious and haunted. Something more than just school is coming to a close, and all the poignant and beautiful things that are happening in nature only serve to heighten by contrast all the dim and disturbing things that are happening in me.

For the first few days after I got back from Texas, much of this vague, floating malaise tended to attach itself to my uncertainty about what Bebb's next move was going to be and Sharon's growing horror that he and Lucille were probably about to arrive on our doorstep as permanent guests. She didn't want to call or write to find out his plans for fear of pushing him into something he might not yet quite have decided on so she just moved around from lesson to lesson in a somber, inflammable state waiting for our doom to be announced. The boys stayed out of her way as much as they could, Chris drifting around the second floor like a ghost and even Tony making a visible effort to use up less oxygen than usual. As for me, I found sanctuary in the classroom. To teach a class, whether you do it well or badly, is to achieve fifty minutes worth of self-forgetfulness. More even than the long summer vacations, it is the principal side-benefit that the profession offers.

Commencement was only a few weeks away. The seniors in my English class were still willing to go through the motions, but obviously they felt that the battle had already been either won or lost by then and in either case they were through battling. It was folly to try starting anything new with them at this point, but I had committed myself to it during an assault of winter energy and the books had arrived and been paid for. It was *King Lear*, and the only bright side of our ill-timed study was that it is the one Shakespearean tragedy I've never been able to read without a lump in my throat.

For various obscure scheduling reasons, the class met during one of the two lunch-time periods those last few weeks, and about half the students would come in with their trays and sit there eating Spanish rice and fruit jello while I tried to engage them in literary discussion. The day we started out on *Lear* there was gingerbread for dessert, and I can still remember the rosettes of ersatz whipped cream and the sound of the big electric mower working out on the playing field, the classroom smell of pencil shavings, floor cleaner and flatulence. Almost a week had gone by since Herman Redpath's funeral, and although there was still no word from Bebb and no lightening either of Sharon's dark mood or my spring-time melancholia, I was able to forget all of this in my effort to interest twenty adolescents in what one of them launched our discussion of Act I, Scene 1, by describing as a boring fairy-tale. The one who made the crushing remark was Laura Fleischman, a girl as golden as one of Bebb's South Carolina peaches but still attached to the tree untouched, untasted, and to all appearances totally unaware that there was any danger of ending up by the roadside someday to go spoiled in the sun.

But later that afternoon, by way of compensation, there was a good turn-out for track practice. As coach I was there in my usual baggy sweat suit with grass stains at the knees and a whistle around my neck, and I got the names down on my clipboard as one by one they straggled out, my hurdlers and sprinters and broad jumpers, my shot-putters and javelin throwers. They were a pretty seedy looking crowd with nothing much in the way of ability, but they worked hard that spring and had done quite well in competition. The only real star among them was my sixteen-year-old nephew, Tony Blaine, and everybody knew it including Tony himself. The pole vault was his specialty, but he had versatility and endurance enough to do well in almost any event. I had to put him in as a miler once, and he broke the school record. He was a natural athlete and took it seriously. He took his body seriously—watching his diet, lifting his weights, getting enough sleep—but there was nothing grim in the way he went about it. He kept himself in shape the way a great lover might, as if he knew that the end he kept himself in shape for was in the last analysis not the most serious end a man could pursue or else so serious that, like the Joking Cousin, you didn't want to let on to the gods it was. He horsed around a lot. He was also very emotional—one of his bonds with Sharon was that they both cried at movies, even TV movies. He was also quick-tempered and in that way reminded me of his mother.

As I watched him jogging around the cinder track naked to the waist and barefoot like something straight off the Parthenon, I thought of the mystery of human generation. My sister Miriam with her poor broken bones already turning to dust in a Brooklyn grave; my ex-brother-in-law Charlie Blaine, that nap-taking valetudinarian trying to get through his life making as few waves as possible; and out of their almost unthinkable passion this boy who was both of them and neither of them, this cocky godling and larky shambles of a boy who himself at this moment carried in his belly the seed of unimaginable progeny. He came running over to me with his dark hair in his eyes and that panicky, inward-looking frown that comes with being out of breath and panted out, "I wish to God you'd tell Sharon not to hang around here in that get-up." I hadn't even seen her arrive.

She must have driven over straight from the swami's because she had on her black leotards as she lay there on one elbow in the grass. She had her hair tied back with a yellow scarf and was wearing hoop earrings. If she was aware of the stir she was causing among my sweaty charges, she gave no evidence of it. Shielding her eyes with one hand, she was squinting out to where beyond the track a solitary boy was practicing. He was running with a javelin at shoulder level, and the sun had turned the shaft of it to gold. She looked as though if she turned her thumb down, the boy would be thrown to the crocodiles, and as though she was thinking seriously about turning her thumb down.

Tony, his bare chest heaving. The smell of the freshly mowed field in the sun. The boy with the golden spear. Sharon reclining there like Sheba herself or some Coptic call-girl with every lazy hill and valley of her young flesh exposed to the gaze of the circumcised and uncircumcised both. To my steaming nephew I said, "She is black but comely, O ye daughters of Jerusalem. There's not an awful lot I can do about it," and after looking as though he might bite his thumb at me and spit on the ground, he tossed the hair out of his eyes and went on back to his laps.

That evening couldn't have started out more auspiciously. Sharon and I had a drink before supper, and she took out her guitar and played a few songs. She tried a setting Anita had taught her to "As ye came from the holy land of Walsingham" and "I know where I'm going" and Donovan's "Jennifer Juniper," and after a while Chris came paddling downstairs to listen, and it wasn't long before Tony was there too. He had forgotten all about his earlier irritation and sat on the arm of her chair reading the words over her shoulder. Except for the way we were dressed, we presented a family scene of almost Victorian felicity with Sharon and Tony the brother and sister or young newlyweds and me the benign avuncular presence. Tony and I were in khakis and shirtsleeves and Sharon in blue jeans, but Chris, though he had taken off his jacket, sat there with his necktie on, his loafers polished, and a crease in his pants. He could have been some resident cousin or visiting parson. All we lacked was Bill clapping dimpled hands at the sunset through the bay window, but he was still in his crib upstairs napping. From the kitchen came the smell of supper, and every once in a while when there was quiet enough you could hear the peepers from the vacant lot across the street. We moved into the kitchen to eat.

It would be interesting to know how it happened. I suppose that when any group comes together, it is like a comic strip where in addition to the balloons where the words are, there are the clouds where the light bulbs and exclamation points and naked women are, and sometimes the clouds collide without anybody's being aware of it until all of a sudden there is a roll of thunder or in one corner of the room it starts to rain. At the level of the balloons nothing seemed to go wrong. I repeated some of what Bebb had told me about Joking Cousins. Chris got to laughing in his own curious style which involved not laughing *out* ha-ha but laughing *in* in an asthmatic way with his head tossing back and forth and his steel-rimmed glasses fogging up. Tony repeated some crude gossip about Laura Fleischman which was completely at odds with the impression she had given me that afternoon during the *Lear* class. I don't remember Sharon's saying anything in particular, but she gave no sign of taking offense at anything and seemed to join in whenever she felt like it. Then suddenly the first drops were starting to fall, heavy and cold. May had turned without warning into November.

It is Chris I see, his colorless face and his wiry, colorless hair that grew flat on his scalp like a cap. I see his father's pale, noncommittal eyes looking out through his glasses. He has tied his bow tie himself but it looks like the kind you clip on. There is a tendency to pinkness around the underside of his nostrils that makes you think he has a slight cold. It is the face that he uses for doing his personal business behind. It is impossible to tell what kind of personal business he is doing behind it as he sits there twisting his senior class ring around and around his finger and listens to Tony tell Sharon that she ought to start taking care of her own baby herself. Tony is very Italian, very like his mother, and keeps cutting backward with one hand while he speaks, as though there is a hornet trying to get at him from behind. His voice is rapid and rising in pitch like a sports announcer's.

She should wash the crap out of the baby's diapers herself, he says, and get up in the night when it cries. She should be the one to give it its bottle for Christ's sake. She should stop turning his brother into a god-damned nursemaid fairy.

A mist or ragged lower edge of cloud has come drifting down until all there is left to see of Chris's face is the lower part, the tiny pimples around the chin, the dry lips with the little film that seals them at the corners and then breaks as he parts them slightly to moisten them. The pussy-cat tie moves with his Adam's apple. Tony's football-huddle arm is suddenly around his shoulder, and Chris's neck does an odd little side-ways movement like a temple dancer's.

The rain, coming down heavier now, has for the moment washed all expression out of Sharon's face. Tony has caught her by surprise as for better or worse she and my namesake Tony are always catching each other by surprise. Her face is as perfect a blank as Eve's must have been at the moment of her creation. Anything can happen in that face. What happens is she picks up her glass and flips the water at Tony. The water hangs unfurled in the air for a moment like a split-second photograph. It misses Tony and soaks the front of Chris's white shirt. His flesh shows through.

Tony's chair-legs stutter noisily against the linoleum as he thrusts back hard. I bring the flat of my palm down slam on the table. We make a rain-dance beat. The wet wind has blown Sharon's hair across one cheek. She says, "You goddamn muscle-bound jock."

He says, "The way you come swinging your cock-tease tail around at practice every afternoon."

She says, "If I ever dreamed I'd have some little prick like you on my hands the rest of my life . . ."

Jock, cock, prick—the invective is exclusively phallic, a ritual copula-tion so that in the sky the gods will also copulate and the wet come streaming down to fertilize that kitchen where I stand up to defend my wife. I say it's a fine way to repay her for her friendship and interest. Month after month she comes, huddled in the empty bleachers at foot-ball time, standing in the cold mud for soccer, in the humid jungle haze of the swimming pool where wet boy voices echo like parrot cries from the tiled walls. I think of her leaning forward there with her chin in her hand.

A banana of all things is what she is shaking at him there by the red-topped counter where a bowl of them sits, our dessert, and where the hell does he think she can find time to take care of a baby or anything else when she has to spend the whole damn day picking up after him—his cruddy socks and underpants and that wreck of a room where she hates to open the door for fear of what she . . . For fear . . . opening the door.

At *fear* she stops and everything stops including the rain which be-comes suddenly a slow, cold drizzle. We are all standing up now except for Chris, who is still sitting down at the table in silence. In the overhead light he is as white as his wet, white shirt. You can see one nipple through it. The corned beef hash has gone cold on his plate. Everything around him in the circle of light glistens from the drizzle, the rest of us shadowed. His eyes are pink. His voice comes cracked, plaintive through our silence which is soggy and soft as wet leaves.

He says, "Who says I'm a goddamned nursemaid fairy?"

For a moment or two we are all caught unfurled in the air like the water from Sharon's glass. Upstairs Bill has woken up from his nap and is crying.

After dark I went out to commune with my Thing. It looked bigger than I remembered it, hanging there in the light of the one bulb. Just a touch from my finger was enough to set it stirring on its chain. It felt very heavy. Shadows rose and fell and crisscrossed. The air smelled woody. I sat on the workbench and watched it a while. Raw pine. The parts where I'd sanded it were soft as skin. I noticed a part I'd missed inside the upper arc of one of the round holes cut out through a leg plank. Through the hole, I could see a piece on the other side begin to appear as the whole thing ponderously, almost imperceptibly, turned. As it turned, the piece seemed to come down across the hole like a wooden eyelid. Nothing is as fascinating as something you've made yourself. Just your own handwriting on an envelope, or a shelf you've put up, even a crap you've taken—they give you the feeling, if you look in a certain way, that they contain a secret and that if you could only get at the secret you'd find out that maybe it was the secret of your life. I must have sat out there a good half hour or more watching the thing before I was interrupted by Sharon.

She didn't come in but called to me through the window. She had a flashlight, and in order not to shine it in my eyes, she shone it upwards so that all the shadows on her face went the wrong way and made her look like somebody else.

"Bip phoned," she said. "He's got his plans all made. He wants us to get moving and find a house for him and Luce. He doesn't care what kind of a house it is, but he wants it to have a barn or a garage that's big enough to start preaching Holy Love in. He talked a lot about the great whore and her abominations and fornications."

I said, "You've got to hand it to him."

Sharon said, "It could have been a whole lot worse. He could have said they were coming to stay with us."

On the way back to the house, I asked her if everything was all right with her and the boys. I hadn't gone out to the shed until I'd thought it was, nobody shaking hands and making up or anything but Sharon being the one to go upstairs to see to the baby and Tony doing the dishes single-handed while she was gone. With November turning to May again, Chris and I had just wandered off like the swallows going back

to Capistrano. I thought everything was probably all right, but I wanted
to hear her say it.

"Poor old Chris," she said. "I felt so sorry for him I could have
kissed him right there in the kitchen."

I said, "If you ever kiss one of them you better kiss the other one too."

She stopped right there in the dark. She said, "Hey *Antonio*. Are
you kidding, Antonio?"

She didn't call people by their names very often and didn't have to.
You could usually tell from the way she said a thing whom she was saying it to. It was more intimate than using names. But this time she used
my name twice. It was as if I had slept through the alarm and she was
trying to get me to wake up.

5

WORDS WERE the least important part of what Lucille Bebb used when
she was telling a story. She used long pauses. She used her lower jaw. She
used her dark glasses and her eyebrows. But lots of clouds came dot, dot,
dot out of her head with thoughts in them. Lucille's genius was to make
these clouds somehow visible to her listener. You left her with the sense
that she had described in detail events which as far as her words were
concerned she had barely suggested.

Since Bebb had insisted that expense was no object, within a few
days I was able to rent him a farmhouse about halfway between Sutton,
where Sharon and I lived, and Stamford. The house belonged to a university couple who were away on a year's sabbatical and it came completely furnished so that Bebb was able to fly up from Houston with
Lucille, sign the lease, and move in all within little more than a week of
his original phone call. As Bebb had specified, the house came with a
barn, and it was in the barn that Lucille gave me what turned out to be
the first installment of an epic. Bebb had gone off to New York to see
about having a sign made for his new church, and Lucille and I had
our conversation alone. In setting down what she told me, I am giving
perhaps ten times more than what she actually gave me, but this does not
mean that I have taken liberty with the facts or embellished them un-
duly. It means simply that I have included the contents of the clouds.

She started off by telling me about elevators. She said there were elevators and elevators. There were the regular everyday elevators that you got
into on the fifth floor or the sixth floor, say, and could ride on down to
the ground floor. If you had business there, you could ride them down
to the basement. There were some places where you could ride them

clear on down to the sub-basement or whatever the bottom-most floor was called. But then there were also some other elevators, she told me, that you could ride farther down than that. There were elevators that went deeper than the bottom. Farther down than down. If I knew what she meant, she said, raising her eyebrows. I asked her where these elevators were supposed to take you. She paused for a while, then said, "Ask Bebb."

After a while she said there weren't too many elevators of this second kind. To your average person, they would look just like your average elevators. You had to be special yourself to know they were special, to know how to work them and where they went and why they went there. She happened to know there was one in Houston. She wasn't sure just where in Houston exactly, but she had an idea it was in one of the big department stores. And scattered over the country there were maybe ten or a dozen like it, mostly in big cities. There was one in Chicago, one in L.A., one in Seattle. There were more of them in the West than in the East for some reason. But there were supposed to be two of them in New York City.

She did not say anything for a while then, and part of what she did not say was that at that very moment, as we both knew, Bebb was in New York City himself. She just said there were two of these special elevators in New York City and let it go at that, let it go but on a rather long leash and for a rather long time. During this time one of the clouds rose up out of her head puff-puff like a child's picture of steam coming out of a steam engine.

In the cloud I saw Bebb. Bebb was standing alone in an elevator. He was wearing a raincoat buttoned up to his chin and his little Happy Hooligan hat planted squarely on top of his head. He had a very determined expression and was keeping track of the floors by watching the window in the elevator door. Down, down, the elevator went, and at each new floor a light flashed in through the window and lit up Bebb's face. The elevator went down to the ground floor, the basement, the sub-basement, and kept on going. Bebb's face was light and then dark again, light and then dark again. His arms hung stiff at his sides.

Lucille said, "They have their meetings down there."

I said, "Who have their meetings?"

The barn where we were standing was more or less empty. Hanging from one of the beams there was a knotted rope for climbing and from another a child's swing. There was a *Make Love Not War* poster on one of the walls. On the floor Bebb had marked in chalk where he wanted the altar table to go and the pulpit. He had ordered them already and expected them any day. Lucille was standing near another poster. It showed W. C. Fields in a beaver hat looking up furtively from a poker hand. I had not noticed before the resemblance to Bebb. Maybe it was just that they were both poker-faced.

Lucille said, "They come from way up, but they have their meetings way down."

It was only about eleven o'clock on a Saturday morning, but I said anyway, "You've been hitting the Tropicanas a little earlier than usual, haven't you?"

Lucille said, "You blame me?"

She had moved and was standing in front of one of the windows. With the light coming from behind, you could see how thin her hair was. You could see the curve of her scalp through it. She said, "You remember Mr. Golden, don't you?"

It took me a moment or two, but then I remembered. I said, "What about Mr. Golden, Luce?"

She dropped her lower jaw slightly. She said, "What about Mr. Golden yourself?" After a while she said, "Bebb told me once that to every one Golden there's maybe half a dozen Silvers."

I said, "Bebb talks to you about this kind of stuff?"

Lucille said, "Sometimes I can't worm a thing out of Bebb. Other times I can't hardly shut him off."

I said, "All he ever told me was he believed there were people around off of flying saucers and they were the same as what the Bible calls angels."

"That's what he tells people," Lucille said.

On again off again, on again off again, went the light on Bebb's face as the elevator descended. Then the light came on to stay. The elevator had stopped and the door slid open. Bebb stepped out. There was an enormous circular room that looked like the U.N. Security Council or an operating amphitheater. It was brightly lit from the ceiling, and there were circular tiers of seats radiating out from the clear space in the middle. The clear space was heavily carpeted, and Bebb's footsteps made no sound as he walked across it. He climbed up into the seats and took an empty one about fifteen or twenty rows back. He took off his coat and hat and sat down. In the seat next to him was the man who had remained standing at Herman Redpath's funeral when everyone else got down to pray, or else it was the man's twin brother. He turned toward Bebb and welcomed him with the same gay and youthful smile. He had on a pair of earphones with an antenna sticking up over one ear. Bebb nodded back brusquely as he put on his own earphones.

There is such a thing, I am told, as a *folie à deux,* a state of things where a person's hallucination becomes so intense that he can give it to somebody else like measles and the two of them start hallucinating together. With Bebb away on his errand in New York City, Lucille had been hitting the Tropicanas earlier than usual that morning, and for a few moments out there in the barn, I, who hadn't touched a drop, was drunk as a monkey.

When Bebb's sign finally came, he asked Sharon and me and the boys to come over and see it. Like the Holy Love sign, it was a life-size cross made of opaque glass which could be lit up inside. Like the Holy Love sign too, the two parts of the new church's name were written one on the horizontal member and one on the vertical member in such a way that they shared a common letter. OPEN was written on the cross piece, and HEART came down through it where the E was. To make the lettering symmetrical there was a red heart after the N in OPEN. Bebb switched the light on for us, and we all stood in the spring dusk admiring it. It jutted out over the barn door so that it would be visible from the road.

Bebb said, "Revelations three twenty. 'Behold, I stand at the door and knock. If any man hear my voice and open the door, I will come in to him.' Boys, now you listen to that because it's dynamite. Jesus is cooling his heels right there at the door of your heart, and he's knocking. All you got to do is open up and he'll enter in and sup with you. Talk about your open heart surgery. Why, Jesus has got all the rest of them beat a mile. Once you open your heart up to him, I tell you it *stays* open. It stays open day and night and welcomes all who pass by with open arms—the widow, the orphan, the—boys, it even welcomes your enemy once Jesus gets it open wide enough."

Sharon was standing by the lilac bush. Bebb came over and put his arm around her shoulder. He pointed up at the sign and said, "Honey, how do you like that for the name of your old Bip's brand new church?"

Sharon said, "You've done it again, Bip."

Lucille said, "Bebb, find out what's everybody's pleasure and we'll all go back and have us something out on the verandah."

Bebb was still looking up at his sign. He said, "Starting tomorrow, I've got an ad that's going to run in all the local papers. It says, 'Have a Heart.' It says, 'Open your heart to Jesus. Open your heart to each other. Open your heart TODAY.' I've got my name on it just Leo Bebb, Evangelist. Nothing about Holy Love or Gospel Faith or any of the rest of it. That's ancient history now. Up here I'm starting out with a clean slate. I'm starting out fresh with nothing except Jesus."

A clean slate. A fresh start. The clothes he was booked in returned to him at the warden's office. His bus-fare home put in his pocket. But that was all. Except maybe Jesus. I thought of Bebb starting fresh back then, years before I knew him, after he'd finished doing his time for what they said he'd done in Miami. And here was Bebb starting fresh again now with Open Heart. I wanted to say, "Open your heart to us, Bip. Tell about Miami." I wanted to tell what little I knew about it myself. I wanted to tell Tony and Chris especially because it didn't seem fair for them not to know the full richness and roundness of the man which all the rest of us standing with them under the life-size cross knew in essence if not in detail. It didn't even seem fair to Bebb for them not to know. I wanted to teach Bebb to them like school.

Bebb stood next to Sharon stuffed like a sausage into his dark suit with the lilacs turning to dusk behind him and his fat face full of secrets. I wanted to freeze him there like a slide projected on a screen and give a lecture on him. With the end of a pointer I wanted to touch his mouth, touch under each eye, touch those curves of polished scalp and scrubbed cheek and where the extra flesh made his earlobes stick out.

I wanted to say, "This is Leo Bebb. He is full of beans and bounce. He is afraid of nothing except heights. I have seen him myself approach lions unarmed. He is a supersalesman for Jesus. He has done time. Exactly what it is he did time for and whether or not he was framed, I'm not sure. Only once in my presence did he refer to it directly. He said he had heard about as good singing behind bars as he'd ever heard anywhere."

I wanted to say, or didn't want to say, "Look at the way he's got his breastpocket handkerchief folded. Look how excited he is about his new sign and how he's put his arm around his daughter's shoulder. Could it be that those Miami children misunderstood some innocent gesture? There is no reason why he couldn't have just been taking a leak in the alley thinking he was alone and, when he heard their voices behind him, simply spun around in surprise.

Bebb stopped looking at the sign. He said, "What's your pleasure, folks?" and went around taking our orders.

I had never seen him angry before or speak a harsh word to anybody except Brownie, but after we'd been sitting on the porch for a while having our drinks, both happened.

Lucille was sitting tipped back in her rocker with her feet braced against the porch railing. It was getting dark, and for once she had taken off her black glasses and was staring vacantly out into the twilight when Tony returned with her glass which she had sent him out into the kitchen to refill. She took it out of his hand in a vague way and must have forgotten that it was full again because as she raised it to her lips to take her first deep sip, she slopped most of it down her front. The surprise made her push out with her feet against the railing, and before she could catch herself, she had tipped over backwards in her rocker. Her skirt was up around her waist and her bony legs sticking into the air. One arm was flung out to the side, and she was holding what was left in her glass miraculously unspilled. Her mouth was open in an odd, crooked way as though somebody had hit her in the jaw.

Bebb said, "Get up, Lucille. Get up this minute," and his voice was a frightening thing to hear. When Tony came forward to help her, Bebb barred his way with his arm. "Pick yourself up and go inside," he said.

I did not want to watch her pick herself up, but I watched her. Sharon helped get the chair out from under her, and then Lucille rolled over to one side and took hold of the railing. With this she managed to pull herself up to her knees and finally to a standing position. Her dress was hiked up in back and her thin hair sticking out in all directions. She brushed Sharon aside. With the dignity of a queen she moved off down the twilit porch taking what was left of her Tropicana and entering the house without a word or glance at any of us.

Almost as soon as she had gone, Bebb started talking about her. The anger had left his voice. There wasn't much light left, and such as there was was enough to see by only if you didn't try to see too much. As Bebb spoke, his face became almost indistinguishable from the blue dusk. He said, "First job I ever had was washing dishes in her father's restaurant in Spartanburg. She was a couple of years younger than me, and there was plenty of them after her. I never thought I stood a Chinaman's chance, but her father took a shine to me. It was him that helped me land a job selling Bibles. I wasn't even dry behind the ears yet and never got through high school because my father was laid up in bed a cripple all those years and I had to go to work early. But I knew Scripture backwards and frontwards—Mother, she'd seen to that—and soon I was making enough on commission to pop the question to Lucille. Nobody was more surprised than me when she told me yes. It was hard on her having me on the road most of the time. My territory reached from Louisville clear down to Birmingham, and there was times I didn't even get home weekends. It was hard on her not having a baby right off too. She lost three while she was still carrying them before one finally was born. Little thing didn't only live but a few months."

Tony was perched on the porch railing with his chin on his knee, Chris on the porch floor leaning up against the house. They looked as lulled as I felt lulled myself by the ebb and flow of Bebb's voice coming out of the dusk. He could have told them anything, and they would have hardly noticed. He could even have told them the way the baby had died, and the chances are the sense of what he said would have been lost in the sound. Or I could have told them myself.

Bebb is off somewhere selling Bibles, and Lucille is at home with their colicky first-born. For a week now she has been taking care of him by herself, picking him up, walking him, rocking him at all hours of day and night whenever the pains in his stomach set him howling until his lips turn blue. She is no longer sure whether it is night or day. She's not even sure which is doing the howling, the baby or she. She will be just about to doze off in her lonely bed for the ninth and tenth time maybe when the noise that is somewhere between a sewing machine and a chain-saw wakes her up, and several times she has dragged herself all the way across the room before noticing that she and the baby are making the noise together. On one occasion she finds a hand crawling up the side of her head like a spider and does not know how it got there until she realizes it's her own hand.

The baby is lying in the bathroom where she keeps the crib at night, Bebb's boy. She picks him up under the arms, his head lolling back until she cups it in one hand and holds him tight. She can feel his mouth against her throat, one fist the size of a golfball at her breast. From the bathroom to the bedroom, from the bedroom to the bathroom, until finally he is no longer tense and squirming but heavy and loose and warm and she lowers him carefully into his crib like a loaf and turns him over on his stomach. This time she has a hunch that he is down for what's left of the night and fixes herself a drink to celebrate, then another drink or possibly two, listening to some midnight dance band being broadcast from a hotel somewhere and wondering maybe where Bebb is now and what he is doing and who he is doing it with.

It is the eve of the Second World War, but there in that bedroom in Knoxville, Tennessee, it is the eve of a good sleep and sweet dreams. She doesn't bother to undress, stretches out as she is. She closes her eyes. The bed starts to turn slowly like a display in a department-store window. She lowers one arm so that her fingers touch the floor, and this stops it. Her feet fill with helium and begin to bear her up into the sky. Higher and higher they bear her, her head trailing below through clouds. She is nearing the warm gravitational field of a dream.

She sees the marble counter of her father's restaurant. Down the counter someone is sliding along to her a hot fudge sundae with whipped cream and walnuts on top. The hot fudge starts to overflow, traveling slowly down her belly like fingers, like a voice whispering sweet, dark secrets. The baby is crying in short bursts with equal bursts of silence in between so that she can't tell whether the pattern is white on black or black on white or which is dream. With the corner of her mouth wet against the pillow, she strains to take in the secret of the dark and traveling fingers. Something infinitely sweet is being pulled just out of her reach down the smooth, veined surface.

Bebb's baby is howling. Bebb is off in some cheap hotel room full of Bibles. The dream, the secret, the sundae—it is gone now, the most precious thing she has ever lost although she can't remember just what it was any more as she gets up off her bed so fast and mad that for a moment she thinks she is going to faint. There is a humming in her ears that drowns out the baby, and she has to hold on to the bedpost to keep from falling down. Then she bursts into the bathroom, slamming the door back against the tub. The ugly half-face in the crib, the smell of babyshit, the sight of her own face in the mirror. She grabs up the first thing that catches her eye. It is a long-handled toilet brush. What follows is a kind of Punch and Judy show.

Sharon had gone into the house to make sandwiches for us, and had turned some lights on inside. Bebb and Chris were talking. It was one of the miracles of the space age: Bebb, so round and firm and full of bounce, from Mars, and Chris from whichever one it is that's mainly just clouds of cosmic gas. Bebb was leaning against one of the pillars, a little of the dim, gold lamplight glinting in his eyes. Chris was cross-legged on the floor at Bebb's feet. He had his head tilted to the side and was smoking a cigarette. He was the only smoker among us, and Sharon, who on yoga principles would otherwise have objected strenuously, said he shouldn't give it up. She said Chris needed to smoke as an antidote to his own personality.

Chris was talking to Bebb about a job he hoped to get that summer with a repertory company that put on plays in a theater not far from us in Sutton. He would help with props and paint flats and do errands, and if things turned out as he hoped, he said, maybe they would let him have an occasional small part or walk-on. "I want to make the theater my life," I heard him say. It was the first I could remember having heard of it, this plan for his life, but I had a feeling that he might have made the same speech to me before and I simply hadn't been paying attention. You paid attention to Tony whether you wanted to or not. Just the bang of his footsteps on the stair or the way he left his clothes thrown around his room was vivid and memorable, but Chris was like an over-exposed photograph—indistinct, washed-out. "I want to make the theater my life," he said, this phrase out of *Mary Noble, Backstage Wife,* but no sooner did it slip from his mouth than it faded into the air with the smoke from his cigarette. He was talking about his life and his dreams for the future like a man conjugating verbs, and Bebb sat there listening as if it was the Sermon on the Mount, his expression intense and absorbed and the glow of the lamplight in his face.

Right after Bill was born and they let me in to see Sharon, a nurse came and placed both her hands flat on Sharon's lower stomach and pressed steadily down on it for a few seconds. I'm not sure what the purpose of it was, but she did it with such a measured and professional air that the image has stayed in my mind. I can see her still the way she leaned over the bed in her crisp white uniform and applied what you could tell was a good deal of pressure but not an ounce too much. She had her head turned away from Sharon so as not to breathe in her face, I suppose. She was looking at me. But it wasn't me she was seeing. She was seeing whatever it was that she was supposed to be doing to Sharon's insides down there under the covers. When Chris stopped talking about the job he hoped to get in summer stock—not with a period at the end but his usual semicolon or little row of dots—Bebb did something that brought that scene back to me uncannily. He leaned forward and put his hands down on Chris's shoulders, and although it happened to be me that his eyes fastened on, it wasn't me he was looking at. Bebb kept his hands on Chris that way until Sharon appeared in the doorway to tell us the sandwiches were ready.

Sharon stood looking out at us through the screen. Tony already had his hand on the doorknob to go in, and I could see her face over his shoulder. She opened her eyes as wide as they would go and opened her mouth. Very slowly she stuck her tongue out farther and farther until she looked as if she was trying to touch the floor with it and then she stuck it out a little farther still. She held it there for a while and then slowly withdrew it. At the same time she relaxed her eyes. I recognized it as something her swami called The Lion. It was supposed to be good for revitalizing the face and neck and also served to reduce tension.

6

SOMEBODY left a rose in a hymnal at Open Heart. It was a tight-petaled, crimson rose that looked as if it had just been picked. The hymn that it marked was "Jerusalem the Golden," which was not one of the ones that had been sung that morning. Whoever left it, Bebb said, must have left it as a love offering, and he put it in a glass of water, eventually set it on the altar table with the other flowers and the cross.

The results of Bebb's "Have a Heart" ad were disappointing. He had set up chairs in the barn for a hundred and fifty, but not more than thirty or forty came. More than half of these were women, and more than half of the women were black. A lot of the rich people around Greenwich and New Canaan had black help, and the way Bebb figured it out, they must have felt homesick for the free-wheeling Pentecostal churches they had left behind them in the South and the ad had revived old memories. They were better dressed than most of the whites with their hats and straw purses and occasional white gloves, and Bebb began his service with a special word of welcome for them. He said in Christ there was no east or west and there wasn't any black or white either and Jesus knocked just as hard to get you to open up your heart if it was one color as he did if it was another color.

It was impossible to generalize about the whites who came. There were several young men dressed alike in black suits and black ties with their hair slicked down who Bebb said afterwards were Mormon missionaries who happened to be in the area. There was an elderly woman with hair the color of raw meat who brought some kind of small rodent-like animal in a cage with her and sat in the back row. There was an Italian couple I recognized as the proprietors of a vegetable stand we stopped at sometimes, and a blind man with a white cane and a white linen golf cap which he did not remove during the service. A bearded man who wore short pants and the kind of leather sandals that have thongs you wrap around your ankles came in a pickup truck with some children in back. There were one or two couples who might have been poor relations of the people with the black help. It was not a fashionable congregation. Except for Sharon, the blacks were the only women who had on hats, and of the men present I doubt that more than a handful were wearing neckties.

There had been some talk about Brownie's flying up all the way from Houston to help out at the opening Sunday, but apparently he had his hands full with Holy Love and called up to say that he couldn't make it. Bebb took the news in his stride, but it seemed to be a major disappointment to Lucille and may have helped account for her subsequent behavior that morning. Sharon and I were there, of course, and to my surprise the boys wanted to come too although neither of us had put any pressure on them. And at the last minute the boys' father, my ex-brother-in-law Charlie Blaine, also joined us with his housekeeper, Mrs. Kling.

We were on the point of leaving the house to go over to Bebb's church when they arrived. It was a fresh spring morning, but they had all the windows of Charlie's Buick shut tight and the air-conditioning on. Charlie felt that it was better for his allergies that way. Mrs. Kling was at the wheel. She was a tireless woman with big calves and a big bust who wore a lot of lipstick and always sounded as though she was trying to make herself heard through a closed door. Charlie was wearing an overcoat and a fedora and looked as if the bright sunlight hurt his eyes as he climbed out of the car to greet his sons. He still kissed them when he hadn't seen them for a while, and although Sharon said it gave her the creeps, I admired him for being able to do it so naturally. It has always seemed sad to me that about the only place where American males can embrace one another without incurring the darkest suspicions is on the athletic field. Charlie kissed Chris first, and it was like the meeting of apostles in a fresco, those two faded figures reaching out their arms toward each other in such a Giottoesque and dreamlike way. When it came Tony's turn, Tony gave him a bear hug that almost lifted him off his feet. Mrs. Kling stood nearby presiding over the reunion as though it was some new therapy that she had arranged for Charlie's gall-bladder condition, and when I explained to them that we were on our way to Bebb's inaugural service, she said that a little religion never hurt anybody and they would go right along with us. So the six of us ended up sitting with Lucille that first morning at Open Heart. Chris brought his tape recorder along and recorded Bebb's sermon with it.

Bebb took off from a phrase from Paul's letter to the Ephesians which went *I, Paul, the prisoner of Jesus Christ for you Gentiles.* He said, "You take a little child that's been—let's say he's being punished for something he never even did. They shove him into the closet and turn the lock on him. It's black as pitch in the closet, and there's none too much air to breathe. He stumbles around through the shoes and mothballs. Soft, hanging things strike him in the face, and he thinks there's creatures of darkness in there with him with buttons where their eyes ought to be and no arms inside their sleeves. He hammers his pitiful little fists on the door and begs and hollers for somebody to come let him out.

But nobody comes. There's nobody even answers him.

"You take an animal in a cage. You take a royal Bengal tiger which is —why, Solomon in all his glory was not arrayed like a royal Bengal tiger in his black and gold suit. Up and down the cage he walks in his big velvet sandals, up and down and back and forth, year in and year out. Every time he comes to the end of his cage going one way, he shifts his head around so it'll still be facing out at the bars when he goes back the other way. He's a king, and he wants to look out where the freedom is. People come and throw peanuts at him.

"You take a man in jail. Jails aren't like they used to be—full of rats and bugs with everybody chained up and nothing except bread and water for dinner. Jails are worse now. They're spic and span now, and they smell of creosote. Every week you get your clothes laundered in jail, and they give you soft slippers to put on your feet. The food's not half bad. If you keep your nose clean, you get to watch TV and go to bed most any time you want.

"But brothers and sisters in Jesus, it's *jail*. It's jail worse than jail ever was in the old days because it's like home. For lots of folks it's better than any home they ever knew. It's like home except for only just one thing. It's like that child in the closet. It's like the tiger in the cage. You can't get out.

"Through the windows you see somebody's wife hanging up the wash in the sun. Only you can't get out. From the vegetable garden out back, you can look across the highway to where the Howard Johnson's is. Easiest thing in the world just to drop in and have yourself a cone or some French-fries. Only you can't get out. You can see the folks out driving places with their kids come walking through the swinging door with ice cream cones in their hands. Only you can't get out.

"Fellow sinners, you can take a look at the birds in the sky. You can watch the clouds change shape. You can watch the faces of the guards and think how when they go off duty, they'll drive home through the rain with the wipers going and maybe stop off on the way and pick up something special for dessert. You can tell how when they get home and open the door, they'll smell a smell isn't like any other smell in the world. It's the smell of their wife and kids. It's the smell of their dinner cooking. It's the smell of their own life. Only you can't get out. No, sir. Jail's what you can't get out of. Not for five years, ten years, twenty. Maybe you're never going to get out."

Bebb said, "Right here in Scripture, Saint Paul, he says, 'I am a prisoner for Jesus Christ.' I am in the dark closet. I am in the cage at the zoo. I am in jail. For Jesus' sake. I didn't have to be here. I chose to be here. I'm here for doing like Jesus said. I'm here for baring the naked truth. I'm here for showing my love to the brethren. I'm here for opening my heart. That's what Saint Paul says.

"What did Saint Paul do while he was in prison? Friends, I'm going to tell you what he did. Among his fellow prisoners there was mostly every kind of sinner you'd care to think of. There was murderers and thieves. There were child-beaters and rapists and sodomites. Before he was through, he had led many of them to accept Jesus Christ as their personal Lord and Savior. He had got them singing the songs of Zion. Many's the cell he washed down with the Blood of the Lamb before they finally let him out."

With their profiles overlapping, Charlie Blaine and Mrs. Kling looked like monarch and consort on a coronation medal only it was Mrs. Kling who was the monarch—some early world-conqueror with her heavy red lips and eyebrows penciled in thick and black—and Charlie the shadowy presence at her side. I remember the curve of Sharon's throat and the straw hat she wore with a wide, floppy brim. I remember Tony beside her, his upper lip moist and the muscles of his jaw appearing and disappearing like the spokes of a wheel. And it was at about this point that I first noticed Lucille acting strangely. She kept crossing and un-crossing her legs and rearranging her filmy skirt over her knee. She would open her mouth and put her hand over it as if to conceal a yawn or a belch. The barn was big and dim, and the only light was the small reading light on Bebb's lectern. The pulpit didn't look big enough for him. He rose up out of it like a jack-in-the-box.

He said, "There's more than one way to skin a cat. To be a prisoner for Christ means more than just being a prisoner inside Comstock or Leavenworth or Soledad. Maybe Jesus calls some of us to be that type prisoner just like he called Saint Paul to. But there's another way he calls every last one of us to be a prisoner. He calls every last one of us to be a prisoner right inside our own skin. Why every last one of you sitting there listening to me knows exactly what I mean. There's a royal Bengal tiger in every single son of Adam and daughter of Eve and except you keep the cage door clapped right on him, he's going to get out and tear things to pieces. Tear himself to pieces too, likely as not.

" 'The spirit is willing but the flesh is weak' the Good Book says. That's another way of saying the flesh is strong. Brothers and sisters, the flesh is a mighty beast, and we've got to post guards day and night and put up electric alarm systems to make sure he don't get loose. We got to keep the beast locked up so we can feed Jesus' lambs for him and not feed *on* Jesus' sweet and tender lambs.

"Only listen to this now. We don't have to keep him in the lock-up forever. No, sir. It's not a ninety-nine year sentence. Because the day is coming when the locked up part of us is going to get washed in the sav-ing blood of Jesus same as all the other parts. Amen. The day is coming when the royal Bengal tiger in us will lie down with the lamb in us, and the lion shall eat straw like the ox, and they shall not hurt or destroy in all my holy mountain, saith the Lord."

Several amens were called out. I noticed the black faces especially.

Many of them were smiling and nodding to themselves as if Bebb was showing them pictures of places they recognized from a long time back. Dressed up in their gloves and spring hats like their mistresses, they nodded yes, yes, that was how it used to be. The blind man sat with his white cane hooked around the back of his neck and his mouth ajar. Bebb blossomed out over the constricting sides of the pulpit like a great maroon rose. One stubby white hand thumped a counterpoint to his words.

He said, "Folks, Jesus was a prisoner too. I don't mean Jesus was a prisoner in a prison though the Jews, they booked him there for a few days at the end. But I don't mean that kind of prisoner. And I don't mean Jesus was a prisoner inside his own skin like you and I, because Jesus was Rose of Sharon, brothers, he was Lily of the Valley. He was the royal Bengal tiger and the lamb without blemish both. There was no sin in him, nothing he had to jail up inside. He had the seat of honor in Heaven, and it was through him the earth was made. Only then he come down. He come down from Heaven. From *Heaven!* You ever stop to think what that means? You ever stop to think what it means to come down out of Heaven into this two-bit world?

"Up there in Heaven Scripture says the streets are of pure gold like unto clear glass and the twelve gates are twelve pearls and there is no Temple where people go to worship the Almighty because up there the Almighty is worshiped all over the place and day and night the angels sing praises at his throne. That's the place Jesus left to come here.

"He come down out of the heavenly place to this place. Down, down he come, and what did he find when he got here? He found a place where there's not enough food to stretch round. He found a place where every single night there's little children go to bed crying because that day it wasn't their turn to eat. He found a place where people are scared stiff of each other most of the time and hide from each other and sometimes come out of their hiding places to do hateful things to each other.

"You take your nine-year-old girl found beat-up and raped in the park. You take your old woman shipped off to some cheap-jack nursing home to die of lonesomeness. Jesus found a place where even nature's gone bad. Where babies are born with little shriveled-up arms and young men with their whole life ahead of them get cancers, and there's droughts and floods, and peaches are piled up along the road going rotten to keep the price up when there's people don't have the price of a peach.

"Friends, Jesus come down to a place where every last man, woman and child is living on death row. You'd think the least thing we could do was draw close and comfort each other, but no. Except for a few loved ones, we close the doors of our hearts and bolt them tight on each other."

Bebb's voice grew quieter toward the end. He held on to the sides of his new pulpit with his shoulders hunched up. He said, "This world Jesus come down to, it's got good things in it too, praise God. It's got love in it and kindness in it and people doing brave and honest things, not just hateful things. It's got beauty in it. It's got the silver light of the moon by night and the golden beams of the sun by day. It's got the sound of the rain on the roof and the smell of the rain on the fresh-turned earth. It's got human forms and faces that are so beautiful they break your heart for yearning after them. But coming down from where he come down from, all the good things of the world must have just made Jesus homesick for the place he come down from. Brothers and sisters, the whole planet was a prison for Jesus. He got born here like the rest of us and did the work here he come to do, and he died here. But it was never like it was home to him.

"Same as creatures from some other part of the universe, Jesus was a stranger in this place, and that's another meaning to Saint Paul's words when he says, 'I am a prisoner for Christ.' Saint Paul means this whole planet's my prison because I don't belong to this planet. I'm down here just for your sake same as Jesus was. That's all. I belong to someplace else far, far away. Sometimes I get homesick for it something wicked."

Lucille was on her feet beside me. She had her hand up to her mouth as if she was going to be sick. She was wearing a gauzy dress with lots of pleats and folds that hung low on her skinny legs. She reminded me of photographs I've seen of Aimee Semple McPherson at the Angelus Temple. She wobbled back and forth on her spike heels for a minute and then like some kind of extinct butterfly started weaving her way back up the aisle toward the door.

Bebb could see what was happening, but he remained as cool as he had in the presence of the Joking Cousin at Herman Redpath's funeral. Nothing in his voice or manner changed as she opened the barn door noisily and went rattling out into the spring. I went after her as quietly as I could up the creaking aisle and many heads turned to watch me go, but such was the power of Bebb's oratory that by the time I reached the door, most of them had turned back to him again—those rapt black prisoners' faces looking up at Bebb from underneath their fancy, white-lady hats.

Lucille's heart. She did not open her heart to me when I caught her hurrying home across the lawn. She gave it to me instead and told me to open it for myself later. She pulled it out from somewhere inside the gauzy flaps and pennants and put it into my hand. It was a number of sheets of flowered stationery written on both sides right through the flowers and rolled up into a tube with a couple of rubber bands doubled up around it.

The sun was so bright that you could see her scalp through her thin hair like the curve of a wooded hillside when the leaves have fallen. She said, "Take it. Don't read it now. You'll know when to read it."

I said, "Are you sick? Is there anything I can do for you?"

She said, "Sometimes when he gets going like that, it scares the bejeezus out of me."

I said, "What is there to be scared about?"

Her dress was floating all over the place in the breeze. She had to brush away a bit of the wide collar that had fluttered across her mouth.

She said, "I'm scared he'll get telling too much."

I said, "About what?"

She said, "You name it."

She turned and managed to get up the porch steps in her high heels. At the top she paused, all her plumes stirring. She said, "I got to take something to steady my nerves. You go on back."

I offered to stay with her, but she wouldn't let me.

She said, "Keep it in a safe place and forget I ever gave it to you." At the screen door she paused again as if to say something else, but then she entered the house without a word.

I returned to the barn for what was left of the service as she had told me to, and when it was over, we all trooped back to the house to wait until Bebb had finished shaking hands with the last members of his congregation so we could say goodbye to him and tell him how well we thought everything had gone. Mrs. Kling insisted on being taken into the house to have a look at Lucille. God knows why, but we all went with her right into Lucille's bedroom. Mrs. Kling said, "It looks to me like you've picked yourself up some type of virus that's going the rounds. Your color's lousy. The last thing you should be tanking up on is all that orange juice. There's enough acid in that size glass to burn your radiator right out."

Lucille paid no attention to her or to Charlie either. I don't think she had the faintest idea who they were. She just lay stretched out on her bed with her shoes off and her dark glasses off and her eyes looking little and dried up. She reached out and took Chris by the hand and called him Tony. Poor Chris, he stood there trying to look as though the hand she was holding belonged to somebody else.

Lucille said, "Tony, I was just as good-looking as her once," indicating Sharon. "I weighed ninety-nine pounds, and I had sweet breath, and I could play *The Banks of the Wabash* right through without looking at the notes. I was a virgin up to the day I married Bebb, and that's more than I can say for some people. Sharon, that's some dress you're wearing, baby. If I was to tell everything I know, there's some of you'd say I was smashed. It's no wonder I got to take something to settle my nerves every chance. You hear him say open your heart? If I opened my heart, you'd tell me Lucille, shut it up again. Bebb, if he was to open his heart, you'd think you was dreaming. Ask him about Shaw Hill and Bertha Stredwig. Ask him was he his brother's keeper back in Poinsett days. Ask him what floor he gets off at someday. She's the apple of his eye. Sharon baby, you're the only apple of your daddy's eye that your daddy's got, baby."

She went rambling on for what seemed an endless time. Mrs. Kling tried to take her stockings off but got only one of them peeled halfway down when Lucille kicked out with her other foot and knocked Mrs. Kling's glasses off. If there was one thing in the world poor Charlie Blaine couldn't stand, it was a scene, but he stood through this one as if he was paralyzed. He had his fedora in one hand and the Vicks inhaler that helped him breathe through his allergies in the other, and a lot of the time I think he kept his eyes closed. Lucille kept holding on to Chris so he couldn't get away, but Tony and Sharon escaped into the living room where one of them must have switched the TV on to some Catholic program because Lucille's blurred syllables kept coming through all mixed up with fragments of the Latin mass.

By the time Bebb returned from his hand-shaking, she had dozed off and we were all milling around the porch in our Sunday clothes like relatives after a funeral. Bebb came bounding up the stairs with his maroon robe over his arm and showed us the rose that someone had left in the hymnal. He handed it to Tony, who smelled it and gave it to his father. Charlie took the stem between his thumb and forefinger and made it turn slowly around. Who could have left it? Why? The rose gave us something other than Lucille or the service to talk about for a few minutes. Then Mrs. Kling took it from Charlie and, after inhaling its perfume so vigorously that there seemed some danger of its disappearing up one of her nostrils, returned it to Bebb. We found ourselves suddenly immobilized by a silence as large and sprawling as a collapsed tent.

There was an unmistakable feeling of Sunday in the air. You could hear one of the departing members of the congregation racing his motor somewhere beyond the barn. A peabody bird sang his sad, unfinished song —Poor Sam Peabody, Peabody, Peabody . . .

Bebb broke in finally with a few cheerful remarks about the way things had gone at Open Heart. He was pleased that so many had come and that there were blacks and whites both. He expected more next time. The ads would keep right on appearing. The blind man had told him on the way out that he was a cousin of Harry Truman's.

As we left, I caught sight of him through the bedroom window. Lucille was lying flat on her back asleep among all those yards of Aimee Semple MacPherson gauze. Bebb was sitting on the foot of her bed. He had her bare feet in his lap. I could not see either of their faces.

7

BOTH MY PARENTS were dead by the time my twin sister and I were twelve, and yet even so it always surprises me how few and faded my memories of them are. I have no memory of how one thing we did with them led to another thing, no sense of the time in between times—just a glimpse here and there. It's as if out of miles and miles of home movies the only thing left was a handful of disconnected scraps that had been edited out and preserved by accident. I remember waking up in a room full of green light that came through leaves growing over the window. I remember hearing my father's voice in the hall, and knowing it was my birthday. But of the birthday itself I remember nothing. I remember the door of our New York apartment opening and the bitter, wintry smell of my mother's furs. I remember the chill of her cheek against mine.

One of the fullest memories I have comes from when I must have been around nine or ten and was coming home on the school bus. We were just pulling out of Central Park when across Fifth Avenue I caught sight of my mother and Miriam. They were standing at the curb, and I made the bus driver let me out so I could run across to meet them. We took a taxi straight down Fifth Avenue to the Plaza, where we met my father and all went and had lunch together at Longchamps. I remember my father ordered rare roast beef for me because he said it was good for a growing boy. I remember the stiff breeze and the blue sky and the way the golden statue of General Sherman glittered in the sun with the pigeons fluttering around. I remember the promise of summer vacation in the air and F.A.O. Schwarz just across the way at 58th Street. It is one of the best memories I have because it was such an unexpected thing to have happen, and I thought of it on the spring day, not long after Bebb's debut at Open Heart, when I unexpectedly picked Sharon up at her guitar lesson and we wasted the whole afternoon together. I hadn't planned to pick her up— she called and left word at the Principal's office—and with a pile of papers to correct I certainly had no intention of wasting an afternoon with anybody. The happiest times are always, I suppose, by accident. And maybe the saddest times too.

The *Lear* class had gone better than usual. It was the third act that was up for grabs that day—Lear on the heath with Kent and the Fool, the storm coming up—and nothing could have seemed more remote from our condition, yet there was a moment or two when for some reason it worked, came alive almost, no thanks to me. There they all sat drowsy and full of lunch. There was a gym class going on outside. You could hear somebody calling out calisthenics, *one* and two, and *one* and two. There was a bumblebee softly bumping his way back and forth across the ceiling, but nobody was paying much attention to him. I sat on the window sill in my shirtsleeves asking some boring questions somebody had written in the margin of my copy and wondering idly who had written them there and when and not caring much whether anyone tried to answer them or not. "What evidence do you find in Act Three for a significant change in Lear's character?" was one of the questions I came to, and a fat boy named William Urquhart surprised me by answering it. He was sitting all bent over with his head in his arms on the desk, and I'd thought he was asleep. His voice came out muffled by his arm. He said, "He's gotten kinder."

I said, "What makes you think so?"

The second question coming so quick on the heels of the one he'd just answered was more than William Urquhart had bargained for, and he shifted his head to the other arm without saying anything. You could see where his cheek had gotten all moist and red where he'd been lying on it and there was the imprint of wrinkles from his sleeve.

The ball was picked up by a boy named Greg Dixon. He was the pimpliest member of the class and the least popular. He said, "Well when it starts to rain, he thinks about the Fool keeping dry too. He says it right here someplace. 'Come on, my boy. How dost, my boy?' Here it is. He says, 'Poor fool and knave, I have one part in my heart that's sorry yet for thee.' He's getting kinder to people like Urquhart said."

"Also, he says a prayer for people." It was Laura Fleischman who had spoken up this time. She always sat in the back row next to a good-looking basketball player named Carl West, who, in Tony's gallant phrase, was getting into her pants regularly. Usually she didn't speak at all or spoke with a kind of startled breathiness as if she was surprised herself that anything beside Carl could get a rise out of her.

Somebody horse-laughed not so much at what she'd said, I thought, as at the fact that it was she who'd said it. Carl West sat there beside her with his stocking feet stretched out as far as they could go and his head lolling back as if to watch the bee on the ceiling.

"Nobody says a prayer in my book," Greg Dixon said.

"Line thirty five," Laura Fleischman said.

"That's no prayer," Greg Dixon said. "That's not like any prayer I ever heard of."

I said, "Go ahead and read it out loud, will you, Laura?"

Carl West sat humped way over sideways now as far from Laura Fleischman as he could get. He was staring down at his writing arm, tracing some scar on it over and over again with one finger.

In a small, half apologetic voice with the calisthenic count going on in the background, she read,

"Poor naked wretches, wheresoe'er you are,
  That bide the pelting of this pitiless storm,
  How shall your houseless heads and unfed sides,
  Your looped and windowed raggedness, defend you
  From seasons such as these?"

Every person has one particular time in his life when he is more beautiful than he is ever going to be again. For some it is at seven, for others at seventeen or seventy, and as Laura Fleischman read out loud from Shakespeare, I remember thinking that for her it was probably just then. Her long hair dividing over her bare shoulders, her lashes dark against her cheeks as she looked down at the page, she could go nowhere from this moment except away from it. She still had a long way to go before she left it behind for good, but I felt like Father Hopkins anyway as I watched her—*How to keep back beauty, keep it, beauty, beauty, beauty, from vanishing away* . . .

" 'Expose thyself to feel what wretches feel,' " she read, " 'That thou may'st shake the superflux to them, And show the heavens more just,' " and two, and *one* and two, the voice floated in through the open windows. Carl West had one hand up to his eyes as if to shield them from the sun, the other cupped at his crotch. The bee drifted heavily down from the ceiling and hit the blackboard with a little thud, then crawled drunkenly along the chalk tray.

I said, "Who are these poor naked wretches he's praying for, if she's right that he's praying?"

Greg Dixon said, "We are."

He said it to be funny—they were the poor wretches, presumably, to have to sit there and listen to Laura Fleischman read blank verse when they could be off somewhere having whatever Greg Dixon thought of as fun—but nobody laughed. Maybe I just ascribed my own thoughts to them, but it seemed to me that for a moment or two in that sleepy classroom they all felt some unintended truth in Greg Dixon's words.

Laura Fleischman in the fullness of her time. William Urquhart in his fatness. Greg Dixon with his pimples. Carl West handsome and bored with the knowledge that he could get into anybody's pants in that room that he felt like getting into. They were the poor naked wretches and at least for a moment they knew they were. The pitiless storm.

The *Lear* class worked, in other words. Only for a minute or two, to be sure, with no credit to either me or Shakespeare particularly. Something had worked anyway if only for me, and it was part of what I jogged out to the parking lot with, Sharon's message to meet her at Anita's in my pocket. The weather. The kids. The time of year. My poor dead sister and mother just happening to be waiting there at the curb when my bus came nosing out of Central Park.

I found Anita and Sharon out in Anita's backyard. Sharon was sitting on a canvas camp stool with Anita, gray and intense in her neat slacks and frilled shirt, leaning over her shoulder from behind. She had her hand on Sharon's hand showing her where her fingers should go. They both looked up as I appeared around the corner of the house, but Anita kept right on with the lesson. "Don't mind about him," she said. "That finger belongs on the fourth fret." That rapid, insistent little voice, that intelligent, prematurely wrinkled marmoset's face. Sharon winked at me.

Anita said, "Stretch! Stretch!" and brought her other hand down to help arrange Sharon's fingers in the right position, her head, close-cropped and bullet-shaped, touching Sharon's. If the two of them had been alone, Anita would never have risked it—the touch of Sharon's hair against her puckered cheek, taking Sharon's fingers in hers that way and moving them around. Anita gave me her handsomest smile with wrinkles shooting out like tears from the corners of her eyes. She said, "If I'd just gotten my hands on her a few years earlier, we could have really gone places."

Sharon stood up a good head taller, holding the guitar by the neck in one hand and letting the other hand come to rest for a moment on Anita's crew cut. "So long, Shorty," Sharon said.

In the car she said, "Sometimes I wonder what it would really be like."

I said, "What what would really be like?"

She said, "She'd die grateful for one thing, and it mightn't be so bad either. Like a Swedish massage. Antonio," she said, letting her arm flop out the window as we took off down the Post Road. "Let's get the hell out of here for a while. Let's go spend a lot of money someplace."

I was still on a high from the *Lear* class and the smell of summer vacation in the air so when Sharon sat there with her arm out the window and made her suggestion, I fell like a ton of bricks. We got the hell out of Sutton and drove on to Greenwich because that was the direction we happened to be heading and spent money all over the place.

In the cheese shop we bought a wheel of brie, a Danish gjetost the color of Fels Naptha, a pound of Stilton and two loaves of black pumpernickel. At Meade's, I lost my head in the stationery department—big pads and little pads, a half dozen different colored felt-tips, a vest-pocket adding machine and a self-erasing typewriter ribbon—and Sharon came out with a bag full of paperbacks including *The Yoga Way to Figure and Facial Beauty, You Are All Sanpaku* by Sakurazawa Nyoiti, a book about macrobiotic diets, a manual on vocabulary building, and *Sex and the Single Girl*. In a psychedelic place with huge paper flowers and inflated plastic liquor bottles in the window, we passed up the posters after a long inspection and settled instead on a transparent cylinder full of an oily blue liquid that curled and foamed like waves when you tilted it back and forth and reminded Sharon of the ocean near Armadillo. We wandered up and down the aisles of one of the biggest ten-cent stores I had ever seen and for a while we no more thought of buying anything than in the Louvre we would have thought of buying anything. We just touched things. We touched things made of rubber to look like centipedes and lizards and human eyes. We touched love beads and Tampax boxes, transistor radios, slippery pink piles of ladies' underwear, bags of M and M's like Jack in the Beanstalk beans, checker sets, bicycle lights and electric fans. We watched a clerk with a strawberry fall net a fantail goldfish, put him in a transparent sack with some water in the bottom and then blow it up with her breath and seal it off at the top like a balloon. Sharon said that Bebb's birthday was coming up soon and bought him a framed picture of Jesus like one that he used to have over the offering box at the first Holy Love. For Chris she bought a green eyeshade, like the kind poker players wear in movies, to use when he did his homework outside. For Tony she got a button the size of a butter plate that said Kiss a Toad Tonight. I wanted to find something for the baby, but she said there wasn't anything there a baby couldn't put in his mouth and choke on.

We ended up at a dress shop that smelled like the inside of a purse. It had thick wall-to-wall carpeting and salesgirls fresh out of Bennington or Smith who wore eye liner and lipstick the color of the insides of shells. Sharon tried on at least two of everything. She tried on a long white evening dress with lozenge-shaped holes cut out around the midriff that you could see her suntan through. She tried on a leather skirt and a dress made out of woven ribbons. She tried on a tweed coat that made her look very Round Hill and a suede coat that came to her ankles with some kind of kinky white fur at the collars and cuffs that made her look like a Russian whore. She sampled so many kinds of perfume that she finally ran out of parts of herself to sample them on and dabbed some on me. In the end, she bought herself a rain hat of shiny yellow plastic with ear flaps and a string to tie them under the chin.

It was almost like sex while it lasted. Without a thought in our heads, we were all fingers and eyes and heavy breathing, and when it was over, we drove down to the park where the roses and the duck pond are and sat against a tree in a kind of spent languor watching the ducks. We even dozed off for a few minutes, and I thought how it was too bad that sleeping together has come to mean making love together when it can also mean what it says, just making peace together. When we woke up, we found that the duck pond was full of pink clouds and the sun was starting to go down. I made Sharon drive home and sat beside her with my knees propped against the dashboard and my head pillowed against one of our softer packages. We hardly said a word all the way back.

I have a feeling it's the in-between times, the times that narratives like this leave out and that the memory in general loses track of, which are the times when souls are saved or lost.

When we got back we found Chris in the living room. He had Chopin on the stereo and was sitting on the couch reading. He'd spread a baby blanket out on the floor, and Bill was lying on it on his back playing with his feet. Through the window the sun was setting. The babysitter had had to go home for supper, he said, and Tony had left about the same time saying that a bunch of them were going off to a beach somewhere and not to wait supper for him. The sunset, the Chopin, Bill—it was a comforting scene to come back to after our Greenwich debauch, and Chris presided over it with such gravity that I felt callow and irresponsible in his presence. I wished Sharon had chosen another time to show him our purchases although he seemed pleased with the green eyeshade. He had taken some hamburger out of the freezer to thaw in case Sharon hadn't planned anything for supper. She hadn't.

After we'd eaten, I started correcting the papers that I should have gotten to that afternoon, but by the time I was about a third of the way through I was so drowsy and so irritated at being kept up by them that I found myself filling the margins with angry red exclamation points and finally decided that in fairness to my students I'd better go to bed even if it meant not having their papers to hand back to them as soon as I'd promised. It must have been around ten by then, and Tony hadn't come home yet. Sharon asked if he'd done his homework before he left, and Chris said he'd spent most of the afternoon outside in the sun reading *Playboy*. Sharon said, "He's some playboy all right," and I left them shaking their heads at each other in the living room and went upstairs to get undressed.

Hours later I woke up to a sound that in my dream had been caused by Anita Steen. I had been sitting in her studio where I was supposed to be taking some kind of lesson, but I had come unprepared and wasn't even sure what it was that she was supposed to be teaching me. I told her that I had forgotten to bring my instrument, hoping that her response might give some clue as to what the instrument was, but she just sat there looking at me in a solemn and expectant way. Without looking away, she reached behind her and from the shelves where she kept her collection of primitive noisemakers took down an African tom-tom which she clamped between her knees and started thumping with her flattened palms. Louder and louder she thumped as though it was some secret message that she was trying to drum into me literally. The whole building began to vibrate with it. When I woke up, I discovered that Sharon was not in bed beside me. The bedroom door was ajar, and there was a light on in the hall.

I found Sharon standing underneath the hall light in her nightdress. The thumping was still going on, and when I first stuck my head out of the room, she motioned me to be quiet as though, in some odd carry-over from my dream, she too was trying to decode a message and didn't want to miss a beat. The noise stopped for a few moments, and she said, "Guess what that's all about," and when whatever it was I mumbled didn't satisfy her, she said, "It's that half-assed nephew of yours, that's what it's all about." She said it as though I was the one she was mad at. When the thumping started again, she raised her voice to be heard over it. She said, "It's half past three if you want to know." Her face looked dark and dangerous. She said, "If he thinks anybody's going to let him in at this hour, he's nuts. Let him spend the night out there. It'll do him good."

A voice said, "You better let him in, Sharon. It's gotten a lot colder out, and he could catch pneumonia. All he's got on is his bathing suit."

It was the first time I'd noticed Chris. He was standing halfway down the stairs looking up at Sharon through the railing. He had some kind of white ointment smeared around his nose and chin. I couldn't make out whether he was on his way down or on his way up.

Sharon said, "I don't care if he freezes his balls off. Who does he think he is, tomcatting around till three A.M. and expecting us to snap shit when he comes home?"

Chris said, "You better let him in, Sharon. He's got work tomorrow." He made no move to go either up or down but just stayed where he was, looking up through the banister and waiting for reason to prevail. The baby had started to cry.

I went to the window and looked down. I could see my nephew Tony standing there on the front step. He was barefoot and had nothing on except his bathing trunks and an unbuttoned shirt hanging down outside. His dark hair was plastered across his forehead, and in the moonlight his flesh looked silver. He stopped pounding again and leaned forward with his right arm flattened out against the house and his face buried in the crook of it. For the first time since I'd gotten up, there was silence both inside and outside except for the sound of Bill crying. Then Tony looked up at the window and saw me.

He said, "For Christ's sake, Tono. Open up, will you?" Even in the semi-dark with all that hair in his face I could tell he was close to tears.

I turned and said to Sharon, "I'm going down to let him in," and started down the steps toward Chris.

What I see in my mind as I look back on it is something that I couldn't possibly have seen in reality. I see Tony standing down there on the front step in his bathing trunks with his shirttail out. He is bare-legged and barefoot with the cleft down his chest a dark seam. His face is tipped up to me in the moonlight, the face of my sister's younger boy, who was named after me. At the same time, as though I could somehow have seen them both at once, I see Sharon standing up there in the hall in her nightdress. She is also bare-legged and barefoot. The light from the overhead bulb shines in her hair and on her bare shoulders, but her face is in shadow because it is tipped down to watch me descend past Chris. Tony is outside looking up, Sharon is inside looking down, and yet I see them simultaneously as though for a moment the walls had turned to glass.

Chris flattened himself against the wall to let me by, and Sharon said we could all go to hell. She went back into her bedroom and slammed the door. I don't know what happened to Chris. I suppose he went up and quieted the baby. I unlocked the door and let Tony in.

He was shivering with cold and exhausted, but I made him come into the living room and sit down. We sat side by side on the couch, and I told him that it didn't make any sense to stay out half the night when he was supposed to be getting in shape for track. I told him that he hadn't let anybody know what beach he was going to or whom he was going with. He could have been drowned for all we knew. He had woken up the whole house. I made the speech because I thought I ought to and because I was sure Sharon was upstairs expecting me to, but my heart wasn't in it. I couldn't help thinking that Chris could have said substantially the same things to Sharon and me when we came back that afternoon. And I was as eager to get to bed as he was. All the time I was speaking, he sat looking straight ahead of him, his shoulders hunched, his skin all gooseflesh, his lower jaw shaking.

When I finished, he said, "Honest to God, Tono, she's got it in for me. Anything I do, she's on my back for it. I was out there half an hour begging her to let me in, and she wouldn't do it just for spite. She'd have let me stay out there all night and freeze, Tono, honest to God she would."

I said, "She'd have let you in. You just have got to—" but he wasn't listening. He had his eyes fixed glassily on the rug in front of him, and he couldn't stop talking any more than he could stop his jaw from shaking.

He said, "I know I'm not perfect, but she's not so perfect either. She comes busting into my room just to see if there's anything she can chew me out for without even knocking. I've seen the way she leaves her own room, her clothes flung all over the place. And Jesus, she can be gross, Tono. I mean I've heard her say things that were so gross I wouldn't even say them myself and right in front of guys who hardly know her even. And some of the things she does like coming out to track in that yoga suit. I mean I don't see what she's—" but by this time I was the one who wasn't listening, or rather, I was listening the way I had listened to Anita thumping her tom-tom in my dream. It was the secret message I was listening for behind the thumping, and what surprises me is not that I had already by this time started to hear it but that it had taken me so long.

He wasn't telling me anything I hadn't heard a thousand times before, but at the same time he was trying to get ready to tell me something else, and even though I didn't know what it was yet, I knew how it must feel to be trying to tell it or not tell it and how it was going to feel to hear it if he ever managed to get it out. He was going on about how Chris oughtn't to have to be the one to take care of Bill, all that, and how hamburgers for supper week after week got to be monotonous, and although I still didn't know what he was leading up to, I already knew in some queer way that it was the saddest thing I'd ever heard, and I found myself responding to it before I knew what it was I was responding to. I reached out my arm and put it around his shoulder. He turned and buried his face against my chest. He was weeping. I was patting his shaggy, sea-smelling head like a child or a dog. Of all the words he went on to speak then, the only ones I can remember verbatim were, "I'm sorry, Tono. I'm sorry. I'm sorry." He must have said them a hundred times.

I suppose that I had known all along that he and Sharon were lovers. I had dreamed it and forgotten the dream. It was what Sharon and I had not talked about as we had driven home through the dusk from Greenwich with all the things we'd bought done up in parcels in the back seat. It was itself the done-up parcel that I'd tucked under my head to watch the pink clouds from. I had even planned to talk to my *Lear* class about it when we got to Act Four. "The wren goes to it," I would have read, "and the small gilded fly does lecher in my sight," and Laura Fleischman sitting in the back row next to Carl West would have no more realized what I was talking about than I would have realized it or would have realized just as much. "Let copulation thrive," I would have tossed out into that bee-buzzing room and would have tried to rouse them with it to some feeling for the terrible irony of the old man's fulminations. I would have talked about irony, about inner meaning and outer meaning. Several days later when we actually did come to Act Four, it was Lear's saying, "Give me an ounce of civet, good apothecary, to sweeten my imagination" that I dwelt upon, but by then I knew why.

There was nothing by then that I hadn't imagined. What Tony himself had told me was little enough, his words coming out half smothered against my chest, the few details he gave getting all confused somehow with the details of his giving them, with the salt smell of his hair, the chill, hard thrust of his shoulder against me. But what little he told me turned out to be more than enough, and the scene I constructed out of it was no less rich and full than it would have been if I'd actually been there to witness it.

It had been one afternoon that March apparently, the first warm day we'd had by then with some patches of snow still lying around in the shade like dirty laundry and the track team still doing most of its practicing inside, but there was a suspicion at least of spring in the air. Bill was out in his carriage with a babysitter. Chris and I had both stayed on after school—Chris was helping dismantle the *Julius Caesar* sets, and I had some scheduling changes to work out. Tony had come back to the house alone. He hadn't wanted to stand in line for a shower at the gym so he waited till he got home and took a long, hot one in the bathroom he and Chris shared. He hadn't bothered to shave that morning, so when he finished the shower he thought he might as well do that too, but he couldn't find his razor so he decided to borrow mine. To get to our bathroom he had to go through our bedroom, but it wasn't until the return trip that he saw Sharon was lying asleep on our bed. Or not asleep. What happened then was that they had simply taken each other by surprise again as for years they had been taking each other by surprise ever since he had been a short, fat twelve year old whose zipper was always coming unzipped at the top. They became lovers by accident rather than by design in this version. They were undesigning, accidental lovers.

"Tono, I'm sorry. I'm sorry." The queer feeling as I patted his head with my hand because I couldn't think of anything else to do. How nobody else's hair ever feels quite like hair. My nephew's hair was stiff from the ocean but soft underneath, springy, matted like a dog's coat.

It had happened in March. They had been alone in the house. They hadn't planned to be alone. Neither had known the other was there. Like comedians in a silent film, they had moved about the house always just missing each other. When he went up, she went down. When he entered by one door, she left by another. When she lay down to sleep, he stepped into the shower and turned the water on.

It wasn't he who came into her room. He was in his own room by himself lying on top of his bed after his shower. He was lying on his back with his knees drawn up. His eyes were closed and his head tipped back on the pillow. Awakened from her nap by sounds she possibly couldn't place, she tiptoed barefoot across the hall and pushed the door open on him. He opened his eyes. She came in. Give me an ounce of civet, good apothecary.

They had known all along what would happen as without knowing it I also had known. He as if for a shower, she as if for a nap, they had undressed in different rooms gravely and vaguely, letting the clothes lie on the floor wherever they happened to fall. In robes of air, they had approached each other slowly then, like royalty. It was no longer a house they knew, a time and place they had dreamed about and planned. It was a coronation.

All this I imagined later. With my lips touching his salt-stiff hair, I mumbled into his scalp, "That's all right. That's all right. Things happen, that's all." There in the living room at half past three A.M. I had all I could do just trying, absurdly, to comfort him.

8

THE NEXT DAY was a Saturday, and by midmorning I found myself on a train heading for New York. Bebb was with me. We had caught the express from Stamford. All the seats were full so we ended up in the aisle which was almost full itself by then. Bebb perched sidesaddle on the arm of a seat which was occupied by a little girl with leg braces, and I stood next to him. When the child told Bebb that it was all right for him to sit on the arm of her seat, he gave her one of his cards. It had a head-and-shoulders photograph of him looking straight at you with his eyes bugged out and his eyebrows raised as though he had just made a challenging pronouncement or, as Sharon said, as though somebody had shoved a thermometer up his ass. There were the Open Heart cross and slogans—Open your heart to Jesus. Open your heart TODAY—with *Leo Bebb, Evangelist*, printed in Gothic underneath plus the address and hours of services. The child showed the card to her mother who didn't seem interested but took a red crayon out of her purse and handed it to her. The child colored the heart and then started coloring Bebb red too. Bebb said, "Be careful you don't get it in my eyes, honey. I need those to see with."

I said, "Lucille told Sharon on the phone this morning that fellow Golden has turned up again."

Bebb looked up at me with an expression like the one on his card. He said, "She says she saw him snooping around the barn yesterday in a pork-pie hat and windbreaker. She recognized him by his shape right off. She thinks he's the one left the rose in the hymnal Sunday stuck in at Jerusalem the Golden. She says it was his calling card."

I said, "You'd have noticed him, wouldn't you? He's not one to melt into a crowd."

Bebb said, "Antonio, if that man had've been there, everybody would have noticed him. You didn't notice him, did you?"

I shook my head.

Bebb said, "You can't always be sure what Lucille sees and what she just thinks she sees. When you come down to it, she's not always sure either."

I wanted to keep the conversation going, any conversation, because once it stopped, I started having silent conversations with myself, so I said, "What do you think yourself?"

Bebb said, "I'm not going to say she didn't see him, Antonio. She might have seen him."

I said, "Who do you think he is, Bip?"

The train gave a lurch, and Bebb stretched one arm along the back of the child's seat to steady himself. The sun was coming in through the milky window, and the air was thick with cigarette smoke.

He said, "Remember the fig tree, Antonio. 'When his branch is yet tender and putteth forth leaves, ye know that summer is nigh.' "

"You'll have to explain," I said.

Bebb said, "Antonio, let me put it this way. I've been preaching the kingdom since you were in didies, and there's lots of times it's come out a weak and sickly thing. Why, you can feel it, Antonio. You stand up there in the pulpit and see No Sale written smack across every last face. But," he raised one cautionary finger, "there are other times too, praise God. There are times when your preaching shines out hot like the sun, and the congregation starts putting forth leaves. The young and tender shoots, Antonio. They feel summer is nigh, and they show it."

As Bebb shifted his position, I caught sight of the child's coloring. She had borne down hard on the crayon, but she had been careful about the eyes as he had told her. The face was a deep, waxy crimson, but the eyes were white. He looked badly burned.

I said, "Do you think Mr. Golden's one of your young and tender shoots then who's come north to follow the sun?"

"I'd admire to think that," Bebb said. He gazed at me thoughtfully a few moments, and his trick eyelid fluttered.

I said, "Lucille thinks he's from outer space."

Bebb said, "Antonio, when the kingdom's preached hot, there's no telling what's going to start sprouting. Life starts sprouting, new life. Maybe that means new worlds too. There's no talk about outer space in Scripture, Antonio, but there's angels and archangels. There's principalities and powers in the heavenly places."

"A power called Golden," I said, "a pork-pie principality," and for the first time I found myself thinking about what our mouths were talking about—that wide, flat figure drifting through the high grass in Texas, that queer sub-paunch which for all I knew was where he folded out of sight his spangled wings or Martian appendages. I thought of Lucille's and my *folie à deux* and how Mr. Golden had been sitting there in the subterranean council chamber with his antenna sticking up as Bebb settled down beside him. I might even have asked Bebb about it then and there except that suddenly it was the way it is when you think you've gotten rid of a splitting headache and then you bend over to pick something up and there's a sickening thud behind your eyeballs again: suddenly my nephew was thumping on the door again with his sea-chilled fist, my wife standing under the hall light in her nightdress. I said, "Give me an ounce of civet, good apothecary," but Bebb didn't hear me, not expecting to hear such a thing. He had leaned closer and spoke in a confidential voice.

He said, "Of course I'm not kidding myself. He may just be from the I.R.S. They've been giving me nothing but trouble for years."

The night before when Tony finally pulled himself together and went upstairs to bed, I decided to go to bed myself right there on the couch. If Sharon asked me about it in the morning, I planned to say I just hadn't wanted to wake her up again climbing in beside her. The baby's blanket was still on the floor where Chris had put it, and I pulled it up over me and lay there for a while in the dark listening to Tony taking a shower upstairs. Whatever else you might want to say about him, I thought, you had to admit that at least he took plenty of showers. He took at least one a day and sometimes two, one at home and one at the gym. I don't think I ever actually went to sleep that night, but I wasn't wide awake the whole time either. I spent most of the night in no-man's land and covered a lot of it while I was there.

One of the few things I retain from my Italian mother's sporadic attempts to bring up my sister and me as Catholics is a feeling that you're not supposed to pray for the dead, and I've always tended to avoid it the way I tend to avoid stepping on cracks. But more than once in my life, I've prayed *to* the dead which I suppose is a blacker heresy still. At least I've said things to them in my mind and tried to imagine what they might say back which is maybe what praying is all about anyway. That night, half asleep and half awake, I spoke to my twin sister Miriam.

I said, "What's supposed to happen next if you don't mind telling me?"

I said, "That roly-poly little wop you named after me, the one who told you the plot of *Abbott and Costello Meet Frankenstein and the Wolf Man* the time I brought them up to the hospital to say goodbye to you for the last time, well he's not a roly-poly little wop any more. He's Tarzan the Ape-man and Roger the Lodger rolled into one. He's not Costello any more. He's the Wolf Man. He's been sitting here in his bathing suit blubbering like a ten-year-old. He's antlered me in case you want to know. I'm a twelve point buck now. I am thirty-nine years old and my wife has been screwed by my nephew and my hairline is receding and for the first time in my life I can believe that someday I'm going to get old and die like you."

Conversations with the dead are never very satisfactory. The dead are not very interested in what you tell them and usually don't have much to say. Death is apparently as much of a rat race as life is, and they've got other things on their minds. I don't picture them sitting around in chairs like the cemetery scene in *Our Town* or cooling their heels in God's outer office singing Bach. As much as I can picture them at all, I picture them hurrying off someplace like the White Rabbit in *Alice*. They don't even stop when you speak to them, just look back at you over their shoulders maybe. I could dimly picture Miriam looking back at me as I spoke.

I said, "Say something, for God's sake." But all I could get her to say was, "I'm sorry, Tono." My nephew had already said that, and he'd sounded sorrier than she did.

I said, "What do I do, for Christ's sake? Do I tell her I know or pretend I don't? Do I send him back to Charlie? Do I ask for a divorce? Do I wait till I catch them in the act and take care of them both with one bullet? Do I play it like wop opera or like Noel Coward or don't I play it at all?"

"You're the boss," she said, moving on as if I was after a dime for a cup of coffee.

I said, "What the hell kind of answer is that? Have you forgotten he's your *son*?"

She said, "My son was a little butterball who could never keep his pants zipped."

I said, "That's just the trouble, he still can't," and she didn't even smile, just kept plowing ahead as if she had a life to depend on it. There was moonlight on the rug like snow, the baby blanket up to my chin and my bare feet sticking out. I was boring my dead sister to death.

I said, "You died before you got to meet Sharon, but have you ever seen her from wherever you are? Can you see things from there?"

"Oh God, Tono," she said, "I suppose maybe I could."

"Then do me a favor and see her sometime," I said. "She's something to see, I can tell you. And see me. See him. Help us," I said. "Help us."

She said, "*Ciao*, Antonio." She had places to go.

I was almost asleep again, and couldn't keep up with her any more. "Help us. Help us," I said drowsily.

She said, "*Addio. Addio*, Antonio."

I couldn't keep her there any longer. From the Duchess's tea-party or whatever it was.

A few hours later I made it on stiff legs into the kitchen for coffee. Sharon was there already. She was sitting at the table with Bill in her lap feeding him his bottle and apparently enjoying it. She had her nose and upper lip drawn down a little in a way that made me think of the Virgin in Michelangelo's Pietà. She didn't look up as I came in, holding the bottle tilted down to Bill's mouth with one finger against his fat cheek to tickle him with if he started going to sleep on her. Her legs were crossed, one bare foot in midair throbbing slightly with her pulse. I could see down her neck to where the tan ended and the pale, freckly part began. "The Instant's by the toaster," she said, still too busy with Bill to look up, and it occurred to me that this was the first time I'd seen all of her or at least more of her than I'd ever seen before, or wanted to see. Or this was the first time that it was all of me that was doing the seeing. She was looking down at the baby drowsing in the crook of her arm. One way or the other it was the first time we had met fully.

I thought at the time that it was the turning point of my life, that all our four destinies, Sharon's and Bill's and Tony's and mine, hung on whatever I said next or didn't say right there in that kitchen with the steam from the kettle turning to cumulus in the morning sun. Looking back, I see it as a medieval painting, our three figures motionless in gold-leaf, the words coming out of my mouth like a streamer—*Benedicta tu in mulieribus*. My question at the time was what words would they be, what fatal, sad annunciation? What urbane evasion or Pagliaccian tirade? *Ne timeas, Maria*. We were frozen in the golden air, waiting.

What I said was, "I spent the night on the couch so I wouldn't wake you up." She glanced at me then, her eyes more green than brown in the sunlight. She frowned slightly. The sound of my voice made Bill turn his head. The nipple was still half in his mouth. There was a trickle of yellowy milk on his chin.

It seemed a turning point at the time, but I'm not so sure now. When you think you've reached a turning point, the chances are you've already passed it. It was probably sometime during the night that I'd decided without knowing it that the injuries I'd sustained were critical but that the bleeding was all internal and was going to stay that way. I would see to it that from the outside nobody noticed a thing. Unless Sharon noticed. She hitched the baby over to her other arm so she could re-cross her legs, and the nipple came out of his mouth with a little rubbery pop. Her smile caught me off guard the way it more or less always did, that hang-dog,

Rastus flash of teeth and eyes. Tony had said he was sorry. Miriam had said it. For all I knew maybe Sharon's smile was saying she was sorry too —sorry about my night on the couch, sorry she'd made me believe I was going to get old and die someday—but you couldn't be sure. The rubbery pop of Bill's nipple had a vaguely indecent sound. Maybe she was just smiling at that.

When Tony came down in his Saturday uniform of spectacularly faded jeans and decaying loafers held together with adhesive tape, I watched eagle-eyed from the toaster to see what would pass between them. He said, "What's for breakfast, Shar?" She said, "Cow flops." That's what passed between them.

The rage and tears I'd witnessed that night had happened before, and they would happen again, and I suppose they both enjoyed in one way the time when they were happening and in another way the time when they weren't happening. There was no furtive glance of guilty lovers either, no secret touch as he passed by her, the sole of one loafer flapping loose against the linoleum. Whatever they had been once, and for all I knew might become anytime again, they were not lovers then. Any fool could see it. The furtiveness and the guilt were all mine.

My antlers glittered as I turned my eyes back to the smoking toaster and my enflamed visions. Sharon was tan except where she was pale and freckled like thrushes' eggs. Tony was advancing on her with the jouncing buffoon of his own flesh straining forward to point his way. Every detail complete with close-ups and tricky angle shots ran through my mind like a stag movie as I stood there scraping the black off my toast into the sink. I was the only one of the three of us with something to hide.

Sharon told me Lucille had called to ask if we'd drive Bip to the station because their car was being fixed. He had errands to do in New York, Lucille had said. Also Mr. Golden had turned up again. Tony was sitting between us with his chin in a bowl of shredded wheat and bananas. His manner with me was all Tom Swift. He didn't show even the faintest trace of discomfort or remorse. He'd succeeded in unloading all that on me the night before so that now I was the one who had a hard time looking *him* in the eye.

"Do you mind driving him, Big Bopper?" Sharon said. "This is my Evelyn Wood morning."

As I glanced up at her, I knew that I had to get away that day— their fresh-faced guilt was too great a reproach to my shifty-eyed innocence—and almost before I knew what I was about, I heard myself saying that I had some errands to do myself in New York and might as well keep Bebb company on the train. Maybe I wanted Sharon to ask me not to go. I don't know. She didn't. She took Bill and put him over her shoulder, making circles on his back with the flat of her hand until he produced a small, wet rattle.

9

WHEN THE TRAIN got to Grand Central, Bebb and I went our separate ways. I left him at a freight elevator. He said it would take him down to where the subways were. He stood in it looking grim and preoccupied, I thought, a trussed, bulky package of a man. I watched the doors slide shut on him. The arrow on the button panel lit up red. The arrow pointed down. How far down was anybody's guess.

I had no errands in New York, of course, and had been too busy dreaming on the train to dream up any, so when the doors snapped shut on Bebb, I found myself with no idea where to go next. For a moment I considered taking the next train back. I would return unexpectedly to the house and surprise them in the act. Or I would return unexpectedly to the house and purposely not surprise them in the act. They would find me sitting downstairs and know that I knew what they were up to without having to surprise them. But this was nonsense, of course, because they couldn't be up to anything what with Chris and the baby at home. Only instead of being relieved by that thought, I was depressed by it. It was as if I had gone away with Bebb and left them there not for my sake but for their sakes, and the fact that like me they weren't up to anything only added to my sense of emptiness and loss.

With no goal in mind, I could just as plausibly have walked east from Grand Central or south, but instead I headed north up Park. My sense of the color and character of New York geography dates back to my childhood there, and I think still in terms of my childhood frontiers. South of Forty Second Street is still the old Aquarium at the Battery with its tank full of horseshoe crabs and the statue of George Washington in front of the Treasury Building and a store called Shackman's where you could get the best favors and false faces in the city. West of Fifth is the Natural History museum and the old Met and Riverside Drive, especially the part up around Grant's Tomb, but otherwise it's no-man's land. As a child I never knew anybody who lived west of Fifth, and I'd have to think hard to remember one now. East from Fifth is shops, the romance diminishing as you move from Tiffany's and Schwarz's on Fifth itself to Brooks on Madison, to cigar stores and delicatessens on Lexington. East of Lexington is drunks asleep in doorways and the old El. Park is the lights left on in the Grand Central Building at Christmas-time in the shape of a cross, is apartment building awnings either Rolls Royce maroon or ping-pong table green sheltering doormen in white gloves with whistles and black umbrellas in case of rain. Park Avenue is the rainiest part of the city. And going north on Park is still going home. It hadn't actually been home for thirty years, but north on Park was the way I went that morning of the day when I first woke up to the knowledge that my wife had taken as her lover a child who was named after me.

In the spring, a young man's fancy lightly turns to thoughts of love, the old poem goes, and in a different key maybe, but nonetheless, my thirty-nine-year-old fancy turned the same way. Heading north up Park toward the home we'd shared as children, I thought of my sister Miriam, whom I'd loved. I thought of how I hadn't been able to get much out of her that sleepless night on the couch when I'd tried to tell her ghost what was going on, and I wondered what I would have gotten out of her if she'd still been alive somehow. She would probably have been furious in some predictably Italian way though whether more furious at Sharon for being the seducer (this would have been her inevitable choice among my various versions as I suppose it was also mine) or at Tony for letting himself be seduced or at me for not smelling the rat before it was served up cold at three o'clock in the morning, I could not say. I thought of how year after year one nurse or another in rubber-soled white Oxfords had taken us off to the Park where she conferred with her buddies while Miriam and I roller-skated or drew on the sidewalk with pieces of hard, flat chalk that looked like marble chips or yelled at each other in those vaulted brick tunnels to hear the echo bounce. I thought of how she was all by herself when she died in that awful A-shaped cast with most of her bones broken, but of how Charlie and her two boys and I had all been at the cemetery when she was buried on Christmas Eve day. It was when I realized that I hadn't been back to the cemetery since then that I found the errand I'd been looking for. I would go out to Brooklyn and check in at Miriam's grave, and I would do it not just because I had nothing better to do but because it seemed the right time to do it. But I'd have lunch first. At Forty Ninth Street I thought of the United Nations and my old friend Ellie Pierce, who as far as I knew still did volunteer work at the information desk. My lovely, pre-Raphaelite Ellie with her brocade slipper pumping up and down on the soft pedal as she played Mozart for me or Satie. Ellie, that indefatigable collector of causes, so Vassar and Urban League and Bergdorf's.

A man who has been cuckolded by his nephew is in a uniquely vulnerable state, especially if it happens to take place in the spring when he's vulnerable enough anyway, and the thought of seeing Ellie again gave me a sense of might-have-been as strong as heartburn as I pictured us ambling for an hour or two down some little stretch of the road we had not taken. But when I got to the U.N. they told me at the information desk that she didn't work there any more. They thought she might still come in from time to time to do some filing upstairs, but nobody had seen her for weeks. One of them thought she'd been in the hospital that winter. Maybe she was still there. It was all vague and doubtful, and I'd about decided to give up and have a sandwich by myself when somebody came up behind and tapped me on the shoulder. When I turned around, there was Ellie.

She looked older and more chic than the last time I'd seen her, less pre-Raphaelite and flowing than Edwardian and a little angular. But she looked well too. She had some gray in her hair and was wearing a gray suit with a yellow silk blouse and a yellow rosebud pinned to her lapel. She said, "Tono, I couldn't believe my eyes," and when we kissed each other on the cheek, she smelled, as she always had, of shampoo. I said, "You look terrific. They've been trying to tell me you were in the hospital," and she said, "Oh, that was just for a little repair work." She blushed slightly, I thought, and I wondered if what she meant was a hysterectomy —that most unhysterical of wombs, which had never known any action, out of action at last. "Tell me," she said, with just the slightest hesitation as she found the right name, "where's Sharon?"

I said, "She's home learning how to read."

"Tono, Tono," Ellie said.

I said, "Nobody calls me Tono any more. Sharon says it's too close to her baby word for number two." When was the last time I'd called it number two?

"Well, you can't blame her for that," Ellie said. Then, "What *was* her baby word," which was the last thing in the world she wanted to know but it gave her time to look me over. Did I look older to her, I wondered. My hair had no gray in it, but there was less of it. I wished I'd put on a clean shirt.

"No-no," I said. "She used to call it no-no for some obscure reason."

"Tono Parr," she said, smiling and shaking her head at the same time as though I had dropped something and broken it.

We had lunch together in a French restaurant, my old friend and I. Ellie was the one who knew about it. You had to walk down stairs to get into it, and it was small and smelled of garlic and household ammonia. I had a martini first, Ellie a Cinzano, and she told the waiter what she wanted to eat in her lovely Vassar French. Then she said, "Now tell me what you've been up to, Tono—I can't help calling you Tono anyway. I want to hear everything," and before she was through, she very nearly did.

"Open your heart to Jesus," Bebb's ad said. "Open your heart TODAY," and I wanted to open my heart there to Ellie Pierce not so much so she could see what was inside but so I could. I used to think that to talk about the things that go on in your heart is to take a lot of the bloom off them, and it's true that it does. But it's true too that unless you talk about them, you can't be sure that anything's going on there at all. I said, "Well, we've got this baby for one thing. He's not getting any younger, and he's still bald as an egg." Bill was the last thing I would have expected to tell her about first. Ellie made me tell her more about him, and I wondered again about the hysterectomy and if she still had a womb and what would ever become of it if she did.

I told her about how I was teaching English again and about the wooden thing I had hanging out in the shed. She seemed pleased about the wooden thing because I used to make smaller scrap-iron things during the years we'd known each other. She said she was glad I was still working with my hands by which I suppose she meant she was glad there was still some tangible connection between whoever I had been then and whoever I was now. She said, "Is it supposed to *be* anything, Tono?" She had always liked things to be something.

I told her I didn't think so, and when she asked me to describe it, I was reduced to trying to draw it on the tablecloth with my butter knife. "It looks like a big A," she said, and she was right. I hadn't noticed before, but it did. Was it Miriam's A-shaped cast, I wondered, or A for Antonio which, the way things were happening, might turn out to be a brand new name for number two. "It's the scarlet letter," I said.

She said, "You don't change, Tono."

She looked so understanding sitting there behind her *artichaut vinaigrette,* so handsome and resourceful in her gray suit with the yellow rosebud. She looked as though there wasn't anything I could tell her that she wouldn't find the right place for in her file, nothing she couldn't cross-index so the connections between things would come clear at last— the sea-smell of my nephew's hair, Bebb's face burned crimson where the crippled child had crayoned it, Laura Fleischman's reading "poor naked wretches" out loud in class. I had opened my heart far enough to show Ellie my bald son and the contents of my woodshed. The question now was would I open it far enough to show her the rest. Would I treat her to a glimpse of Lucille wobbling down the aisle of Open Heart in her French heels and Aimee Semple McPherson peignoir? Would I raise for her the apparition of Leo Bebb at this very moment for all I could prove to the contrary meeting in full subterranean council with God only knew what? Would I run off for her the reel of Sharon and my nephew that afternoon in March? Ellie was asking me something about the drug situation at Sutton High School as I reached across the table and took her hand in mine.

It was like when the furnace and the deep freeze happen to come on at the same time so that the lights go dim for a second or two and the TV fades. Ellie hardly hesitated in whatever she was saying, her face barely flickered, and then she was back running normally again. But the risk of overloading the circuits was clear. I gave her hand a comradely squeeze, withdrawing mine to my empty martini glass. I said, "How about telling me about you for a change?" And she did.

She told me how she'd organized a group of tenants in Manhattan House to protest what she felt were discriminatory rental policies. She told me about a museum tour of Greece she had taken. She talked about Mayor Lindsay and the subway strike. She used "we" more than "I" most of the time, but I got the impression it was something more like a committee than a twosome. I kept wondering if I'd been right about the repair work, whether that was what she'd really have liked to be opening her heart about—how it felt to be empty inside, a dead end street. But if she opened her heart to Jesus on the subject, she didn't even take the chair out from under the doorknob for me. We agreed we wouldn't let years go by again till the next time. I would bring Sharon in, and we'd all have dinner and go to the theater. I asked her if I could get her a cab, and she said no, she needed the exercise. We touched cheeks once more out on the sidewalk where the sun nearly blinded us after our dim lunch and then headed off in different directions.

Ellie never found out what was in my heart, and I never found out what was in hers, and maybe it was for the best. Just our failure to was a familiar failure, and it was the familiar I needed that day, not openheart surgery. My only regret after we parted was that I hadn't asked her about my old cat Tom. I'd like to have heard how he was getting on at Manhattan House.

I would also like to have been able to weep a little at Miriam's grave —it would have been a kind of purge for me, and I knew Miriam would have enjoyed it—but it didn't work that way. I've never been much good at tears on demand. At Miriam's death-bed and funeral both, I remained dry-eyed. I cry best when I expect to least. I remember, for instance, when I took Sharon and the boys to see the movie of *Hello Dolly*, which is not what you'd ordinarily think of as a tear-jerker. It was during the big restaurant scene when Barbra Streisand comes sweeping down the grand staircase in her satin and feathers, and everybody starts singing "Hello Dolly" and then the next thing you know, there is Louis Armstrong singing it, Satchmo himself sweating and grinning with his lips wobbling, that face that was turned out back in the days before black was beautiful, just black, and all of a sudden the tears were streaming down my cheeks and I had to stuff popcorn in my mouth. The other time I remember was at a swimming meet between Sutton and Portchester. It was a relay race, and by the time the last relay of swimmers had grabbed the batons and dived in, the noise bouncing back and forth from the tiled walls became so pure and intense that you could hear right down to a kind of distilled silence at the heart of it, and once again I found myself blinded. But there at my sister's grave, I didn't even get a lump in my throat.

At the cemetery entrance they had given me a map with the way I was to go marked out on it, but I missed a turn somewhere and wandered most of an hour down one avenue after another of mausoleums and cenotaphs, old rugged crosses and obelisks and monoliths of every size and shape with just single names cut into them. GALLAGHER, KURTZ, CRUCETTI—with no first names or dates to get in the way they looked like final pronouncements or the presidents of banks. By the time I located the small marker with PARR on it, my first feeling was just relief that I'd finally made it. My parents shared a stone between them, but Miriam had one all to herself. Charlie had picked it out, I think, and it looked rather like him, a faded, canned-salmon-colored granite with the carving of her name still pale and unweathered. Miriam herself would probably have preferred something more on the order of the grieving angel who knelt nearby with a face that reminded me of Liberace. I noticed that though my parents were smooth and level, Miriam had sunk a little, and I decided to speak to the people at the gate about putting in some more sod. It looked forlorn that way, like a fallen soufflé.

I stood there and thought about her and thought about how maybe after a little, a tear might come to make us both feel better, but no tear came. I could not seem to think her into anything much like reality. Even her name the way Charlie had had it carved didn't really seem hers. Miriam Parr Blaine. It made some kind of a career woman out of her, like Helen Gahagan Douglas or Grace Livingston Hill. Then my mind started wandering, and it wasn't long before I wasn't thinking about my sister or about anything else in particular, just staring down at the grass so hard I didn't see it, without a thought in my head.

It's not an easy business to stop thinking, and although according to Sharon it's the whole point of yoga and can be achieved by anybody who works at it, I find it hard to imagine how that can be so. It seems to me that to work at not thinking must be to *think* about not thinking. As I stood there at my sister's grave, my mind was empty not because I'd worked at emptying it but because it had just happened that way, which seems to be how it is with most good things. Despite my mother's efforts to make me a Catholic, I'm afraid that in this regard anyway I turned out Protestant. If there's any such thing as salvation, I suspect it's not through works that we come by it but through grace.

Something else happened there in Brooklyn that afternoon that may have been through grace too although at the time I wouldn't have said so probably. I was still standing there in this kind of empty-headed trance, and then it was like what happens when, just as you're about to go to sleep at night, you seem to trip over something and can feel the whole bed shake under you. I came to, I suppose you would say. Some stirring in the air or quick movement of squirrel or bird brought me back to myself, and just at that instant of being brought back to myself I knew that the self I'd been brought back to was some fine day going to be as dead as Miriam. I knew it not just in the usual sense of knowing but knew it in almost the Biblical sense of having sex with it. I knew I didn't just *have* a body. I *was* a body. It was like walking into a closed door at night. The thud of it jolted me down to the roots of my hair.

The body I was was going to be dead. Through Sharon and Tony I'd finally come to believe it, but through grace alone I banged right into it—not a lesson this time, a collision. You might say that there at my sister's grave I finally lost my virtue, saw the unveiling of middle-age's last and most intimate secret. There in Brooklyn I was screwed by my own death.

I'd taken a subway out, but I felt I needed a taxi going back, and when I got to Grand Central again with forty minutes till the next train, I dropped into a bar and ordered myself a double martini. Standing.

The bar had one of those beach-ball-sized, sequin-covered, revolving globes that scatters light all over the place like snowflakes, and I was sitting there watching it when for the second time that day somebody came up from behind and tapped me on the back. It was Laura Fleischman. "I just happened to look through the window," she said, "and there you were." The momentum of her surprise had gotten her just as far as that, then stranded her there, speechless, in the flurry of light.

I called her by name, knew perfectly well who she was, but it was as if there was something absurdly elementary that I didn't know like who I was myself or whether it was our native language I was speaking; and then "Carl West," I said, of all inanities. "Have you got Carl West with you?" Fitch—Abercrombie, battery—assault, it was the crudest kind of free association, and the moment it was out, I regretted it.

What happened in her face didn't take more than a second or two to happen, but I saw it all. She left her face and retreated to wherever it was she kept Carl West, and while she was inside there with him, the face she'd left behind was totally unguarded.

I've heard it explained that when you sneeze, your soul leaves your body and people say God bless you to keep the devil from slipping into you and taking your soul's place. My impulse was to say something like God bless you to Laura Fleischman for fear that if I didn't, I'd have that face on my conscience for the rest of my life. But then her soul got back on its own somehow. She smiled, and said, "No," by which I took her to mean not just that Carl West wasn't there at Grand Central but that at least for the moment he wasn't there inside with her any more either.

"I've been to the orthodontist," she said, and when I made some fatuous remark about how there didn't seem to be anything wrong with her smile as far as I could see, she said, "It's a molar that's coming in crooked."

It turned out she was waiting for the same train I was, so I made her take the stool next to mine and asked her if she'd have something to drink with me. She said she'd like a 7-Up, which made me feel like a child molester, but by the time the bartender brought it to her with a slice of lemon and a cherry, together with another martini for me, the feeling was past. I was her English teacher again, at least had been once on some other planet.

Sharon sitting in the kitchen that morning with Bill in her lap. My old friend Ellie telling me over lunch about rental policies at Manhattan House. Miriam off there in Brooklyn where I'd forgotten on the way out to say she needed more sod and where the poor echo of her death had been drowned out by the thud of my own (was it really Tony I had heard thumping at the door that night Sharon wouldn't go down and open it?). It had been Ladies' Day for me so far, and each of them I'd sought out to give me God knows what only to come away from them if not empty-handed, at least with nothing in my hands like whatever it was I'd expected. And now Laura Fleischman, whom I hadn't sought out at all, and as we sat side by side on our leopard-skin stools with the light from the globe swarming around us, I thought of that loveliest of all French phrases, *A l'ombre des jeunes filles en fleur*, which Scott Moncrieff renders as "Within a budding grove" when even a plodding literalism would come closer to the loveliness of it—"in the shade of young girls' flowering." John Skelton's "Merry Margaret/As midsummer flower,/Gentle as falcon or hawk in the tower" comes as close to it in spirit as anything I know in English.

In any case, what we talked about was the chances Sutton had of beating Stamford in track and whether seniors ought to be allowed to cut gym in the spring to get ready for finals, but it wasn't small talk. It was big talk because all that we both of us were was in it, and there was nothing left over of either of us to think about anything else while we were talking. And that is how we missed our train.

Laura noticed first. She picked up my hand to get a look at my wrist watch, and I bent forward to get a look at it too, and when our foreheads touched for a second, I noticed it less in my forehead than in my stomach where it felt like when the express elevator freefalls the first twenty floors.

Two things could have happened then of which just one, needless to say, actually did, but to report that one only would be to report less than the truth. A thing can't be both itself and not itself, logicians say, but they must have been thinking of logic rather than reality when they said it, human reality anyway. What we live through in our dreams is no less a part of who we are than what we live through when we're not dreaming, and the events of one leave marks no less deep than the events of the other. Who is to say that what actually happens in a man's life is all that more important to him than what happens not to happen? We missed our train, Laura Fleischman and I. It was an event as much a part of history as Neil Armstrong's landing on the moon or Sharon's telling my nephew there were cow flops for breakfast. There were no two ways about it. But two ways branched out from it. The exigencies of narrative force me to set them side by side. It would be more accurate to present them as a double exposure. The way we took and the way we didn't take.

One way was this. I said, "So we've missed it, so now what?" Laura Fleischman sucked the last of her 7-Up through the straw, rattling the ice. "I've got a timetable here somewhere," she said and started burrowing into a large straw pocketbook that looked as if it might have been her mother's. I saw what she was after before she did and reached in after her to get it out before she buried it again, and there in her mother's straw pocketbook, our hands touched. I might have gotten my hand the hell out of there and used it for smoothing the timetable down on the bar top. Might have. The past subjunctive. That ultimate grammatical subtlety. That capsulized metaphysics. It was the point where the two ways branched.

Let us say I might have but I did not get my hand the hell out of Mrs. Fleischman's pocketbook. I had had two martinis not counting the one I'd had with Ellie at lunch. The revolving globe had made it the last act of Peter Pan where they're up in the tree at night and the fireflies are out. I had run into my own death in Brooklyn and had lived to tell the tale if I felt like telling it. Laura Fleischman hadn't moved her hand. So I folded her hand up in mine and shut my eyes and said, "It takes me back to dancing school."

She said, "What does?" Even if you hadn't happened to be holding her hand yourself, you could have told from her face that somebody was. I had seen her look that way in class when I'd asked her a question she didn't know the answer to.

"Your hand does," I said. "It's damp. Like a dancing-school hand." When you hold a girl's hand and talk to her about holding it, you are holding more than a hand.

She said, "I know. I know what you mean," as though I had explained something that had needed explaining more than anything else in the world. The bartender put a saucer of potato chips between us. When I let her hand go, she moved the potato chips to the side with it and spread out the timetable.

"Like which one can we take," she said, running her finger down the column.

"I'll tell you what Bodhidharma would do," I said. I emptied the potato chips onto the timetable and picking it up with a hand at each side offered it to her. "Take one of these," I said.

She took a big one and broke part of it off with her teeth.

I said, "Now you don't have to take one at all. You've already taken it."

"I've got to be home for supper," she said.

I looked at my watch. I said, "Whoever heard of getting home for supper at quarter of four?"

"Bodhidharma maybe?" she said.

It was in Cocteau's *Beauty and the Beast*, I think, where there was a scene of the beast in a long cape with a high, stiff collar walking down a corridor in his palace. Every time he approached a pair of gilded doors at the end of the corridor, they would swing open and there would be still more of the corridor beyond them, all paneled and mirrored like Versailles, and then another pair of doors. On and on. So it was with Laura

Fleischman and me that spring afternoon after we left the station according to this one of the two ways. Doors opened onto doors and they in turn opened onto other doors until finally we came to the last pair of doors, and they opened too.

I tell her I've thought of people I ought to see in the city the next day and have decided I might as well spend the night there rather than go home and have to come back again the next morning, so Laura Fleischman goes with me to the Gotham maybe or the Plaza and sits off in a corner somewhere looking at *Cue* or at a Van Cleef and Arpels showcase while I register, and going up in the elevator we speak like strangers, which we are, about how the best time in New York is summertime because it's not so crowded then, just the backs of our hands touching, our knuckles, and the way her hair falls, I can see the nape of her neck and the top of her spine, and with her eyes lowered she looks like a girl being lectured by a nun. She has a nun's face herself almost, a slow smile she doesn't use any more than she has to and high, calm cheeks I can see framed in starched linen, embarrassed eyes. It is a white room, and when I open the window, the air has New York in it and springtime and carbon monoxide, and if when I am an old man somebody gives me some of that air to smell, it will either make me young again or kill me sure. A curtain balloons into the room. The sky is a dingy mauve, lights coming on. Laura Fleischman pushes her hair back off her bare shoulders and holds it behind her with one hand. We talk about something at the open window, and this time there is none of either of us in what we are talking about because we are both of us waiting, and what we are waiting for is not just what is going to happen in that room but something farther off than that.

A *l'ombre des jeunes filles en fleur*. In that flowering shade, I can't make out clearly by what sequence of events we have come here. I can't imagine, and I have tried hard to imagine, the things that were said, the doors that had to open around us and inside us to bring us through that final door. I suppose the corridor of the afternoon must have just kept extending before us, and we followed along without ever thinking farther ahead than the next turning. But there at the end there is nothing I can't see. I see the Beast, of course—the moist, imploring eyes, the hairy, furrowed brow and glistening snout, the stiff and arching horn. Beauty is by him. Gentle as falcon or hawk in the tower, Beauty is the shade he rests in and the cool flowering where he gets lost. Somewhere between her pity and her love, within that cleft and confluence, he rises up a prince.

The other way was this. I reached into Mrs. Fleischman's straw pocketbook and took the timetable out. We had just time to pay the check and get down to the track before the next train left. We couldn't find a seat together, but I got one directly in front of hers and talked to her for a while over the back until my neck began to cramp. Then she settled down to a creased paperback of *Great Issues in American History* and I looked out of the window and watched as far as 125th Street and a little beyond until the martinis began to take their effect together with the rockabye jouncing of the New Haven roadbed and I fell asleep. Laura woke me when we got to Stamford. "Mr. Parr," she said, "we're here, Mr. Parr," and opening my eyes to her face bending over me, I couldn't be sure which of the two ways was the one we'd followed and the moment was both itself and not itself, whatever logicians may say. I dropped her off at her house on my way home, and we shook hands in the car as she thanked me for the lift and the 7-Up I'd bought her at the station.

It was dusk when I got home myself. Sharon met me in the hall. She said, "Listen. When Bip got back from the city, Luce was gone, and she isn't back yet. That was a couple of hours ago. She never goes out by herself and their car's busted anyhow. Bip's in a sweat."

She had on her black leotards with some kind of wrap-around skirt over them. It seemed weeks since the last time I'd seen her, and I was about to kiss her hello when I stopped myself and then in a split second stopped myself from stopping myself and kissed her. She said, "I'm glad *you're* back anyway." At Miriam's grave I hadn't been able to make a lump in my throat happen. Here, it was no trouble at all.

10

BEBB DEPLOYED us like troops. Although it wasn't raining, he had on his black raincoat that pulled under the arms and his narrow-brimmed hat. He was carrying a flashlight as long as a nightstick and arrived unannounced while we were having our Saturday night supper. Tony had gone upstairs to get ready for some kind of date he had lined up, and Sharon and Chris and I were having our coffee.

Bebb said, "I'm going to be honest with you, I don't like it. If it was anybody else, you might think she went off to a picture or someplace and just didn't leave word she'd be late. Not Luce. Besides, the car's on the fritz, and she was never one to go in for walking any more than she had to, can't anybody blame her for that. Why Sharon, you know what her balance is like even when she's—Why, in *flat* heels she's not all that steady," he said, bringing the butt of his flashlight down on the table, "and on those spikes of hers she hasn't got a chance. She took off on wheels, that's for sure. What we've got to find out is where she took off for and why she took off."

He gave each of us an assignment. Sharon was to stay home with the baby in case anybody called. Bebb and Chris and I were to make the rounds of railway stations, bus depots, and taxi stands to see if we could find out anything there. "There's no use calling," he said. "I tried that. Right off they think you're out to make trouble for somebody and clam up." On our way we were to drop Tony off at Bebb's house so if Lucille came back while we were away, she wouldn't find the place empty. He didn't say that of the two boys, Tony was Lucille's favorite, but all of us knew it. When Sharon explained that Tony had a date, Bebb yelled up the stairs to him, and he came down in his undershorts with a towel around his neck and his hair standing up in the air from having just been washed. Bebb said, "Tony, I'm asking you to give up your pleasure tonight and help me find my wife because my soul is exceeding sorrowful, and I need you. Will you do it?" and Tony said, "Yes, sir." I had never heard him call anybody sir before. Then Bebb said, "Now we're all going to bow our heads," and none of us was quick enough to grasp what he'd said until he'd bowed his own head and started praying. His bald scalp glistened in the kitchen light. He had his eyes clamped shut and his face screwed up tight.

He said, "Oh dear friend Jesus, who art the hope of sinners and the mender of the broken-hearted, we need thee bad this night. Jesus, thou art the good shepherd of the sheep, and we are here to tell you one of thy sheep is lost. We don't know where to start looking. We don't even know whether she was in her right mind when she wandered off or whether her vexed and troubled spirit had led her to seek comfort in the bottle where she's used to finding it. We don't even know whether she went off on her own or somebody come and took her off by force or guile. There's nobody here knows better than you she's a sinner like the rest of us, but life hasn't been a bed of roses for her either. Please put your love around her like a warm coat so nothing hurtful can get at her wherever she is. And help us go forth now and do our best to find her. We ask it for her sake and our sake, both. And for thy mercy's sake too. Amen." He pronounced amen with a long a.

Bebb's prayer had frozen us all in our tracks like a witch's spell: Tony in his underpants with his feathery hair floating over his head like a black cloud; Chris caught halfway between the table and the sink with his thumb and forefinger in a pair of milky glasses; Sharon holding her face in the V of her hands so her eyes were pulled sideways. I was the only one with open eyes, and when Bebb raised his head from his praying, he looked into them and said, "Antonio, there is more rejoicing in heaven over the one lost one that's found than over the whole ninety and nine that never got lost in the first place."

We left Tony and Sharon in the two different houses each near a telephone and with however many miles there were of night between them. I hadn't arranged things that way. Bebb had. I caught a glimpse of Chris sitting there beside me with just a little glow from the dashboard lighting him up around his father's lashless eyes, and I wondered if he knew about his brother and Sharon and what he thought about it if he did. I decided that whatever he thought about it, he probably didn't think about it as much as he thought about lots of other things, and maybe that was just as well for him or maybe it wasn't. When we got to Sutton, I let him and Bebb out at the bus station, and I drove on down to the railroad.

The ticket window was closed and I couldn't locate anybody in the waiting room or the freight office, but across the tracks I saw what looked as if it might be a porter sitting on a bench under a light bulb. Climbing the moldering stairs of the overpass, I crossed over and described Lucille to him. Skinny with black glasses, I said, pushing sixty, maybe a little unsteady on her feet. Through my description, she emerged as stark as the last name on one of those Brooklyn monuments. CRUCETTI. The man turned out to be a taxi driver. He shook his head and said he'd only been there a few minutes. Then he pointed back across the tracks and said, "Try him."

There was a large man leaning up against the wall under a sign that had MEN on it with an arrow underneath, and when he saw us both turn to look at him at the same time, he raised one arm to us. He had on a pork-pie hat and a windbreaker, and his pants hung loose and baggy on him like sails. I recognized him right away as Mr. Golden.

Just supposing the impossible to be possible, I thought, how did you approach a Principality or a Power or even a man from Mars? With tears in your eyes and excuses on your lips? The way a missionary approaches a Fiji Islander? Did you approach him at all? That one arm raised in salutation—was it raised across the littered tracks only, across the candy wrappers, fruit peels, toilet paper dried and soaked and dried again until it had turned to divinity, seafoam? Or was it raised across light-years, was it raised maybe even across whatever it is (if anything) that separates what is holy from what people throw out of train windows and flush down cans? This side of getting back in the car and telling Bebb I couldn't find anybody to ask, I suppose the prudent thing would have been just to wait there and let Mr. Golden approach me if he felt like it. But curiosity led me on. I mounted once again that dingy Bridge of Sighs, walked a second time past FUCK YOU in lipstick and a place where somebody had tossed his cookies, and wondered if maybe to reach the high angels this was the kind of route you always had to take. Mr. Golden hadn't moved from his place under the sign that said MEN. He smiled as I approached. His teeth were strong and white but you could see that all the back ones were missing. "Mr. Golden?" I said, extending my hand, and he said, "Who he?"

He was dressed as if for work—he could have been a foreman of some kind or a nightwatchman—and his presence at the station suggested that he had some professional reason for being there; but as soon as he started talking, I had the feeling that the clothes he had on were play clothes and his being there at the station was just part of a game he was playing—not a cat-and-mouse game but something like ring-around-the-rosy or flying a kite. A suburban railroad station at nine or ten o'clock on a Saturday night isn't the place you'd normally think of going just for the hell of it, but I had a hunch that this was why Mr. Golden had gone there. He was having fun.

I said, "Haven't I seen you someplace before?" and he said, "If a man keeps his eyes open, there's no telling what he'll see in this world. Think what it would be like to be blind this time of year." With his thumbs in his armpits, he took a deep breath. He said, "I'm crazy about the spring," said it as though he was confessing to some amiable quirk, his eyes sparkling like a girl's. "Just breathing the air gives me the biggest kick. I wouldn't miss it for anything." His voice was on the high side, like a taut rubber band when you pluck it.

I said, "You're the mystery man of the year. Nobody knows who you are or what you're after. What's the story anyway?"

He said, "Can you name me anybody who isn't a mystery man? When you come right down to it, what does anybody know about who anybody is or what anybody's after."

I said, "Does the name Leo Bebb mean anything to you?"

"Lifesaver?" he said. He had taken them out of his windbreaker pocket and offered me one which I accepted. Spearmint. He didn't take one himself but put the pack back in his pocket. "Does the name such-and-such mean anything to you," he said, almost imitating my voice but not quite. "I don't even know if you mean anything to me yourself yet."

I said, "First you turn up at the funeral of Herman Redpath. Then you turn up in Connecticut and are seen hanging around Open Heart. Now you turn up here." He was listening to me attentively, I thought, his lips slightly pursed, but he wasn't looking at me. He was looking up at the sky where way up, too high to hear, a plane was slowly passing over blinking a red light. I said, "Is it any wonder we'd like to know what you're up to?"

He had a lean, fine-featured face, sallow and creased without the faintest trace of whiskers. He had a smallish head and a stringy neck and then this body that looked about six sizes too big for him and this heavy garland of flesh swelling out around his loins as though inside his clothes he had started to roll down some cumbersome undergarment. He could have weighed three hundred pounds, I thought, and yet there was something about the way his pants hung that made me wonder if he weighed anything at all.

He said, "I don't want to keep on giving you smart answers, but do I have to be up to something? Do I have to be some kind of crook or crank or queerie?"

I said, "There's no law that says you've got to tell me anything you don't want to."

He said, "There's laws about everything else."

I said, "If the tables were turned, you'd want to know about me."

"There's no need to turn the tables," he said. "I want to know about you with the tables just like they are now. Tell me about yourself."

Possibly he was an undercover agent for the I.R.S., Bebb had said. Possibly when Bebb preached the Kingdom, he was somebody the Kingdom had taken root in like a mustard seed and who wanted to stay near where the seed had come from, as Bebb had also said. Possibly, as Lucille and Bebb had both said, he was from outer space. "Silvers you might see most anytime if you keep your eyes open and look for the ones has hair and faces the same color," Bebb had told me once, "but goldens are scarce as hen's teeth." Possibly he was a hen's tooth. Whichever he was, I thought, assuming he was any of them, he would have a reason for wanting me to tell him about myself, and for a moment or two, standing there in the night, I almost considered telling him except that I wouldn't have known where to start or where to stop either, so I just said, "Lucille Bebb's missing. We don't know where she's gone."

It was the first time I'd caught him looking directly at me, and all the life there was in him seemed to rise up into those young eyes of his as though seeing was only a small part of what eyes were for.

He said, "Yes. Well, that's how things happen. It's just not the biggest surprise in the world, that's all. She's had to carry that pitiful little death around Jesus only knows how long, and she wasn't exactly a tower of strength to start with. I'm sorry she's lost," he said, and as he said it, the main part of the life drained back down into his face again. His eyes were looking at me now in the normal way of eyes as if to judge how sorry I was myself that Lucille was lost, and I realized that up till now I hadn't been sorry at all much, just interested how we were going to end up finding her—passed out in a corner somewhere or wobbling off into the woods, maybe some friend taking her off on a bender while Bebb was away in the city. I said, "You haven't seen her then?"

He shook his head.

"But you know her by sight?" I said. "You know Bebb."

He said, "Look, do I know this?" He had taken a pinch of his cheek between his thumb and forefinger and gave it a little tug as though to loosen his face, take it off even. "Do I know these?" he said and extended both his hands in front of him, turning them first palms up and then palms down.

"You're old pals," I said, wondering why Bebb had lied, had said maybe the man was this that or the other. All the time Bebb had spent speculating about who or what Mr. Golden might be, inside his shirt he'd probably been wearing a locket with a lock of Mr. Golden's hair in it.

He said, "Pals is your word. I didn't say pals," and I thought Oh Bip, you have been given back to me unstained. He wasn't Bebb's pal, he was just a soul Bebb had saved without their being introduced first, and there he was in his pork-pie hat looking at me through those lovely eyes as though he knew he'd given me something back I hadn't wanted to part with.

I said, "You mean all this time you've just admired him from a distance."

"Oh sweetheart!" he said. "You want to know the distance?" He put his hands in his pockets, and rocking back on one heel all three hundred or zero pounds of him, he swung the other foot forward and took a carefully measured stride. Then he took two more just like it. I thought the fourth stride was going to be the same, but he cut it about in half, scraping a little at the concrete platform with the toe of his sneaker as though to mark an exact spot.

"The front pew?" I said.

His strides had landed him about ten feet away from me beyond the range of the overhead light so I couldn't see his face any more. On the far track a train came through fast without stopping. The draft of it set his pants flapping, and the racing lights lit him up from behind like a statue. All through the train's noisy passage he was evidently talking, gesturing, and when the last car shot by, he kept right on into the soft and sudden wake of silence. It was like the reading you do in dreams—word for word what he said made sense enough, but I couldn't quite make out what it was all about.

"Time and space," he was saying. "You've got all the time in the world and not enough space to swing a cat. Month after month, week in week out," he was saying there in the dark, "all the doo-dah day. Well, you get so after a stretch you know his face better than you know your own face. There's not a point in the world trying to hide anything from each other," he said. "What's the point? The cat's out of the bag anyway. If the cat wasn't out of the bag, you wouldn't be there in the first place. Hide what?" He said, "I set it down as an eternal rule of life that what works just fine on the inside doesn't work a hoot on the outside. Say all you want or mostly want anyway is to chew the fat about the old days, just shake hands again, why not? But the brushoff's what you're like to get. The cold shoulder." He was holding one palm out toward me vertically like a traffic cop, the rails behind him glinting in the moonlight. "Soon as they spot you coming down the pike, they think it's bound to be gimme or else. It's two different worlds," he said. "One of them you're, oh, Peg o' My Heart. The other you're poison. Bad news." He said, "It's one world in and it's another world out." Stepping a few feet forward into the light again with the sweetest, saddest smile, all those back teeth missing or not in yet, he said, "In just a single life there's so many worlds that a man's days stretch out like the Milky Way." He pushed the pork-pie up off his golden brow so I could see that what little hair he had, flat and mashed, was silver. "Worlds," he said. "They leave you old and limp all the worlds you live in before your number comes up."

He had his head cocked to one side and hitched at his belt with one thumb. I was ready for anything by now, ready to see the belt hitched loose, the bolster around his crotch turning out to be folded wings unfolding. They folded out and up in origami folds and pleats and counterfolds the colors of stained glass. They were bigger than he was, and he was big enough. He said, "Tell Leo not to be afraid. It'll all come out in the wash anyhow."

I said, "Why not tell him yourself? I'll be picking him up in a minute."

He said, "I told him already. This afternoon I said, 'Look, Leo. Don't be afraid.'"

I said, "This afternoon he didn't even know Lucille was missing."

A breeze threatened to blow his hat off and he grabbed one side of the brim and held it in close to his wrinkled cheek. He said, "I meant don't be afraid of me."

Ne timeas. I saw him in his windbreaker with a lily in his hand, saw Bebb's startled, fat face looking up at him. Still holding the pork-pie, he ducked his head shyly. "You'll have to excuse me. I've got bladder trouble." He started to move off in the direction the arrow pointed.

I said, "Just one more thing. Is Golden right?"

He paused and glanced back. Closer to the light, his face looked paler, more withery, like a soaked hand. He smiled. "As right as any of them," he said. "I've had so many handles in my day." The two stringy tendons at the back of his neck as he walked away, that huge, flat butt.

I suppose I didn't get who he was then because I didn't want to get it. He'd said it straight enough in his own way. Who wouldn't believe in angels if he thought he could swing it, or visitors anyway from older, wiser worlds? Silvers and goldens. I tried to swing it. I didn't even want to accept bladder trouble at that point. If he had a bladder, I wanted it to be only the kind of bladder you float on, fly with: Mr. Golden drifting along over the rooftops of Sutton calling down *Don't be afraid.*

It was obvious Bebb knew who Mr. Golden was and knew God knew what-all else besides, but I had no intention of asking him about it. Let him keep Mr. Golden under his Happy Hooligan hat along with all the rest he kept there. I didn't even mention the meeting when I picked him and Chris up as they walked down the hill from the bus depot. They'd had no more luck gathering clues about Lucille than I had. We drove on to Stamford and Greenwich and had no luck there either.

On our way back to Bebb's house to drop Bebb off and pick up Tony, Chris said, "Maybe the thing you ought to do now is notify the police."

Bebb said, "Chris, I've thought about that. I may have to turn to the police before I'm through, but not yet. Sometimes the medicine's worse than the bellyache."

I said, "Where do you think she's gone, Bip?"

He said, "By this time maybe she's gone home, and she'll be waiting there for us when we pull in."

Chris said, "I have a hunch she's not."

There was a silence as we rolled on down the dark road in the heavy, quiet way cars have at night. I was driving slowly, half thinking we might find Lucille walking along in the ditch. I kept picturing her suddenly looming up in the glare of the headlights in her French heels and gossamer.

Bebb said, "Chris, do you believe in E.S.P.?"

Chris said, "Yes. Do you believe in it?"

Bebb said, "I believe in it, and I have a feeling she's not home either."

I said, "Can you put yourself in her shoes and figure out someplace she might have wanted to go specially?"

Bebb said, "There was one time years ago the place I found her in was a tree. Sharon and her, they'd had them some kind of a fuss, and she'd got herself up there somehow. She was in a tree reading *Silver Screen*. It was like getting a cat off a telephone pole."

"*Silver Screen*," Chris said.

Bebb said, "There was a time you couldn't keep her out of the pictures. I've known her to take in two double features in a day. There was a place in West Palm she found that showed triples."

"Maybe she's gone to the pictures," Chris said.

Bebb said, "Not any more. Those black glasses she wears, they're because the light hurts her eyes. Even pictures hurt her eyes. She's got so she can't stand light any more."

Chris said, "Who can?" He said it not to be witty but in a dreamy kind of way, wedged in there between Bebb and me in the dark.

Bebb said, "Boys, I'm not going to kid you. I'm worried. I've been worried for many years." He said *boys*, but he was talking to himself and neither of us tried to say anything. I took my eyes off the white line just long enough to glance at him. That face that had looked on Golden plain. That face that had many times gazed down on Herman Redpath while he laid his hands on the old brave's wispy scalp and conjured the sap to rise. That pop-goes-the-weasel, jack-in-the-box face that at any time might spring open or shut on anything. It seemed to have settled, like an old house. The lower jaw had slipped forward. The cheeks hung. The eyes looked loose in their sockets. It was the color of the moon. The next thing he said was, "Chris, what's your opinion of Anna May Wong?"

That Bip, as Sharon was apt to say with a mixture of resignation and awe whenever he did something particularly Bip-like. He worked his plump arm free and slid it around the shoulders of my nephew Chris, that movie fan and Shakespeare buff who dreamed of making the theater his life. With the moon in his face and God knows what in his heart, Bebb talked to him the rest of the way back about Anna May Wong and Leonore Ulric and Erich von Stroheim; and Chris, that ectoplasmic boy, took from it the shape and substance of something like life. We were squeezed together in the front seat, and I could literally feel it happening in him. That Bip.

We found Tony asleep on the couch in Bebb's living room, and when we woke him up, he messed up his hair and threw his shoulders around to loosen them up. He said that nobody had either come or called. Bebb phoned Sharon then at our house, and you could see from his face that she was telling him the same thing.

On my way home with Tony and Chris, we passed Laura Fleischman's house. It was around midnight, and there was only one light on. The light was upstairs, and I wondered if it was Laura's. I tried to picture her in bed there reading *Great Issues in American History*. I tried to picture her hair on the pillow, her nun's face. It was hard to believe that only a few hours had gone by since I bought her the 7-Up. Maybe I had just dreamed it. Maybe I was just dreaming Mr. Golden. It may have been the longest day of my life, and it was hard to believe that I hadn't dreamed the whole thing.

11

THE NEXT AFTERNOON Charlie Blaine and Mrs. Kling turned up for the second Sunday in a row. Spotting them from an upstairs window, Sharon went off like a burglar alarm. Bebb was phoning every hour on the hour to see if Lucille had turned up, which she hadn't, and Sharon said I'd have to take care of my relations by myself, so in desperation I ran downstairs and headed them off before they got into the house. In desperation I took them out to the shed to see my monument. Mrs. Kling gave it a look and said, "It looks anemic. If I was you, I'd paint it."

There it was, turning ponderously on its chain from Mrs. Kling's poke, an iceberg, a theology, whatever it was. The fall of the Roman Empire. Parts of it seemed to turn faster than other parts, little clusters of discs, dowels, knobs, crisscrossing. Ellie had been right. It was basically an A-shape with the pierced crosspiece in the middle that the tongues curved down through. It was the honest, pale color of raw pine, and I liked it that way. I said, "What shade would you suggest?"

She stepped back on one bulging calf, a fist on her hip. She squinnied at it. "Bright ones," she said, as if addressing somebody in the next room. "Bright ones and plenty of them." She turned and stared at me— those heavy mink eyebrows, that tomato-colored mouth. Beside her,

Charlie was the color of smoke in his gray spring overcoat that hung below his knees, a pearl gray fedora. She gave me a push on one shoulder. "Live it up a little," she said.

I said, "My God, maybe you've got something," which was the last thing I'd expected to say, but I saw it suddenly painted like a toy in paint-box colors—putting-green greens and sunflower yellows, fire-chief reds, laid on thick and glossy. Why not?

She said, "How about it, Charlie?" wheeling on him.

Charlie slipped his hand softly down one satiny flank of it. He said, "Well, it might just make it come alive."

And he was right. It might just make it come alive, I thought, and at the idea of painting it I could feel myself coming a little alive—a good brush to get up into those star shapes and crescent shapes, floating the colors down smooth and heavy along the flat surfaces, working them up into the angles of joints and the insides of curves. I said, "It would jazz it up all right, Charlie, that's for sure."

He smiled.

It was one of the better moments my ex-brother-in-law and I ever had together, and we had Mrs. Kling to thank for it.

When I couldn't think of any way to stall them further, I finally brought them into the house. Chris and Tony were off someplace, but Sharon came down after a while, barefoot, with an opaque look in her eye. The first thing she did was tell Charlie he didn't look up to snuff to her. It was the worst thing you could ever tell Charlie, and she knew it. He wouldn't let the subject drop. She said, "I don't know, Charlie. You look a little . . . *winded.*" What followed was one of my worst moments with my ex-brother-in-law, for which in this case I suppose I had Sharon to thank.

He turned to Mrs. Kling as though they were alone in an emergency ward and said, "There, Billie. It's what I've been telling you."

Mrs. Kling said, "There's nothing wrong with your wind, Charlie. You've been all through that with Fletcher, and Fletcher's tops."

Charlie said, "I don't mean shortness of breath. I mean the feeling I get when I breathe in."

Sharon said, "You mean like there's an iron band around your chest?" I managed to give her the eye as she said it, and what her eye gave me back was *shove it,* which was not the most significant exchange we ever had, but what was significant about it was that it was the first time since I'd found out about her and Tony that I'd let our eyes exchange so much as the time of day.

Charlie said, "Oh God, no," with his left thumb creeping up under his left armpit and his fingers starting to work at his wishbone. "It's in my throat. Way back."

Mrs. Kling said, "OK, Charlie. Tell it like it is."

"Physical symptoms aren't the easiest things in the world to verbalize," he said, "but I'll give it another try. When I breathe in, it's as if the air is hitting something it never used to hit before. There's a kind of dry, *cold* sensation. It's like there is something back there the air's hitting against."

"Like a lump?" Sharon said.

"Not a lump," Charlie said, swallowing. "I don't think that's what it is. It's more like a sensation than an actual obstruction."

Mrs. Kling said, "Open up, Charlie, and hold your tongue down." She took his lower jaw in her hand and pushed it in toward his Adam's apple. His eyes were fixed glassily on the ceiling. "I'll tell you one thing," she said, peering in. "You had onions for lunch. And maybe a little cat mess. There's no lump, Charlie."

Charlie touched the corners of his mouth with a handkerchief. He said, "It would be too far back to see anyway."

Mrs. Kling said, "All rightsy, if that's how you want it." She said it with ominous heartiness and swung abruptly around to me. "Give me a flashlight," she said. She held her hand straight out like a statue till I found one in the desk drawer and gave it to her. "Roger," she said. "Have you got a closet big enough to hold three of us?"

"What are you up to, Billie?" Charlie said.

"You're what I'm up to," she said.

I took them to the hall closet. Sharon wanted to come in too, but there wasn't room for four, and of the two of us Mrs. Kling wanted me. "He won't listen to another woman," she said.

Sharon shut the door on us, and Mrs. Kling and Charlie Blaine and I stood there for a few seconds in total darkness. Then Mrs. Kling switched on the flashlight. She told Charlie to put it into his mouth. She said, "Close your lips around it tight, Charlie, like you're sucking a pickle."

The closet smelled of raincoats and shoes and Charlie's onions, and Charlie was lit up inside like a pumpkin. His cheeks glowed the color of fingers cupped around a flame. There was a religious sheen on the underside of his nose. Mrs. Kling's glasses glinted as she leaned toward him.

I wondered what a stranger would have thought, what I would have thought myself if some fortuneteller had foretold the scene. Mrs. Kling and I in that closet with Charlie. Given the people we were, I suppose you could say it was inevitable. Everything was. I found the thought comforting.

Mrs. Kling pushed me with her elbow. She said, "Look at there." Her finger was black against Charlie's translucent beauty. She said, "Boy, is that ever plugged up. See that shadowy part?" Her black finger was moving in the vicinity of his cheekbone. I said I saw it. "Tell *him*," she said. "He thinks I'm giving him a snow-job."

I said, "It looks like you're plugged up all right, Charlie." Charlie tried to say something, but with the flashlight in his mouth it was unintelligible.

Mrs. Kling said, "It's those lousy sinuses. You've got yourself an old-fashioned case of post-nasal drip, Charlie. What you feel in your throat is snot."

Later I found myself sitting on the foot of our bed trying to make conversation with Charlie through the open bathroom door. Mrs. Kling had prescribed a salt solution to be inhaled through the nose and spat out through the mouth. Charlie was doing it. Strapped as I was for something to talk about, I decided against bringing up Lucille's disappearance. Neither Sharon nor I had mentioned it so far. It would only have raised questions that I couldn't answer, plus others that I could. I might have tried talking about the boys, but whenever I did that, he would steer the conversation around to how much a month it cost Sharon and me to keep them, and then whether I actually told him how much or less than how much or brushed the question aside, I always ended up sounding as though I was asking for more. Then Charlie would look nervous and hurt. If I had been made of sterner stuff I suppose I might have talked to him about the boys and sex. I might have told him that it seemed to me sex for Tony was a hydroelectric dam that for the time being was being used for weight-lifting and broad-jumping and hanging African violets around in his jock-strap, not to mention all those showers, but that potentially it could supply the whole town of Sutton with light and heat or blow it off the map and himself with it, not to mention what it had blown off the map already. Or onto the map. I might have told him how it seemed to me that sex for Chris was a shadowy presence in the wings which was maybe why he wanted to make the stage his life. The only shadows on the stage were the shadows you knew about, and the roles were fixed there. Nothing could happen on the stage that wasn't in the script. You didn't have to worry about the wings. But I couldn't talk to Charlie about sex either.

He was bending over the washbasin in his shirtsleeves. In between rinsings, he would straighten up, and we would find ourselves facing each other in the mirror. His eyes looked dimly expectant, and what I found myself coming out with finally was the information that I'd gone out to Brooklyn the day before and taken a look at Miriam's grave.

"Oh my God," he said, and then he was bending over again, cupping the salt solution in his palm and snuffing it up through his nostrils. Here was the man who had married my sister, I thought, whose name she had died with, died of maybe—Miriam on her wedding day with her black hair braided around her head in a wreath, Charlie in his Navy whites with a peeling sunburn on his nose and forehead. I could hear him spitting out into the sink, this man my sister had gone to bed with, as far as I knew the only man. I wondered if he had ever gone to bed with Mrs. Kling and hoped I would never have to hear about it if he had.

"I don't think I could take it," he said. "I'd rather just think about how she was when she was alive."

"Not me," I said. "I like to think about how she is now she's dead."

He said, "What makes you go and say a thing like that for, Tono?"

Maybe because he was the only man my sister ever got a chance to go to bed with. Maybe because Tony was his son. "I don't know," I said. "Do you ever think about being dead someday yourself, Charlie?"

"I guess I do," he said. "I guess everybody thinks about it sometimes."

Some of the solution must have gotten trapped in his lousy sinuses and started to run out unexpectedly because he suddenly doubled over. When his face reappeared in the mirror, I said, "What do you think about when you think about being dead?" Poor Charlie.

"I don't know," he said. "I try not to think about it any more than I have to."

I said, "You should think about it."

"That's morbid," he said. "Do you think about it much yourself?"

I said, "I thought about it when we were all in the closet looking at your head lit up from the inside. I thought about it when what's-her-name told me I ought to paint my masterpiece out there."

"Why did you think about it then?" Charlie said.

"Because I decided maybe she was right," I said. "Maybe I ought to paint it for the same reason they put lipstick on a corpse."

"What's the matter with you?" Charlie said. "You're not even as old as I am. What are you anyway?"

"I'm thirty-nine," I said.

"That's nothing," Charlie said.

I said, "I didn't used to think it was."

"It isn't," Charlie said. "I'm going on forty-seven. Thirty-nine isn't anything."

"It isn't sweet sixteen," I said. "It isn't Tony," at which I stood once again on the threshold of the door that Bebb urged the faithful to open. Charlie was rolling his sleeves back down again, having finished with his sinuses for the time being and also, I'm sure he hoped, with our conversation. I could hear Mrs. Kling downstairs talking over long distance to Sharon and the sound of Bill crying. She'd probably picked him up and was holding him clamped to her bust like a football. *Tony* I'd said, naming his name. I might have said Sharon wasn't the only one in that house he'd screwed and then stood back and watched it start his sinuses running again. He'd screwed me too, screwed me royally and maybe for keeps. I might have said I was planning to nail his balls to the wall.

Charlie said, "There is a book called *The Middle Age Crisis* that's all about what you're going through, Tono. You ought to take a look at it. It's quite an eye-opener." He was standing in the bathroom door putting on his jacket.

I said, "I'm sure it is, Charlie, but right now I'm up to my ears in *The Call of the Wild*."

"That's Jack London, isn't it?" Charlie said.

I said, "Sigmund Freud."

Charlie's lips were slightly parted, and his eyes had gone blank. He was testing to see if he could still feel the dry, cool spot at the back of his throat when he breathed in.

"You ought to give *The Middle Age Crisis* a look-see," he said. "I think it would do you good."

When Tony and Chris came drifting back, Charlie took them out to an early supper with Mrs. Kling. He asked Sharon and me to go too, but we used Bebb's prayer meeting as an excuse. Poor Bebb. The attendance at his morning services hadn't picked up as he had predicted, and he thought if he added an old-fashioned prayer meeting at a different hour, he might attract a different crowd. Even if Charlie and Mrs. Kling hadn't been there to spur us on, Sharon and I would probably have gone anyway just to swell the ranks. At the last one only about seven or eight had shown up including the woman with hair the color of raw meat who ever since the opening service had been one of his most faithful followers. She always brought Mickey with her. Mickey was the gerbil she carried around in a cage. He spent most of his time at church in the exercise wheel. It needed oiling.

Sharon and I arrived early to find Bebb and a policeman about to sit down in the living room. We told Bebb we'd wait on the porch, but he asked us to stay.

The policeman asked the following questions.

Full name: Lucille Yancey Bebb.

Age: 57

Place of birth: Spartanburg, South Carolina.

Hair: Brown, Bebb said, changing it then to auburn.

Eyes: Bebb hesitated. I wondered if like me he'd seen them so seldom because of black glasses that he couldn't remember for sure. Hazel, he said.

Any identifying marks: Bebb said no, then changed it to yes. It was his third slip in a row. The policeman looked up from his yellow pad. Bebb was sitting bolt upright facing him, and his trick eyelid chose this moment to do its trick. Sharon and I exchanged the second glance I'd risked without words to use in case of an emergency. Bebb covered his face with his hands for a moment so that just the tip of his nose stuck out between them. Lucille had some scars on her wrists, he said, reappearing. He said it without a flicker.

Had anybody noticed her indulging in peculiar behavior lately, the policeman asked. *Indulging* was a policeman's word, I thought: peculiarity was indulgence. Bebb's eyelid alone was worth at least a friendly warning. Bebb said he hadn't noticed anything peculiar. He turned to Sharon and asked her. Sharon said, "Have you told him about the Tropicanas, Bip?" She was sitting on the sofa beside him, and when she said it, I noticed her slip her little finger over his little finger on the cushion between them.

Bip said, "My daughter here means sometimes when Mrs. Bebb's low in her mind, she takes a little too much."

Alcohol? the policeman asked, and Bebb said she mixed it with orange juice. Sharon said, "Don't give out the recipe, Bip." It didn't seem to help Bip much.

When the policeman asked what he meant she was low in her mind, Bebb said, "We're Southerners, officer. We're a long ways from home."

It was one of his classical utterances, like *All things are lawful for me* and *I believe everything*. "We're Southerners," he said; all three of them were. It was like a line of great poetry—not that I hadn't always known the truth it contained but that this was the first time I'd ever heard it put into words. There seemed to be nothing it didn't explain: the poor attendance at Open Heart, the grim look on his face as the door of the freight elevator closed on him at Grand Central, all Sharon's lessons. Maybe even Sharon and . . . but I had begun to develop a safety mechanism by then. As soon as my thoughts gave signs of turning the wrong way, it cut them off automatically. They were Southerners. They were a long ways from home. The policeman said he would let them know if anything turned up.

The prayer meeting that followed was less than a success. Only about a dozen showed up including the red-haired woman and the blind man who had said he was a cousin of Harry Truman's. The gerbil's exercise wheel made it hard to concentrate on the praying, and it was obvious Bebb's mind wasn't on it either. The blind man asked us to pray for his sight to be restored. First we all prayed silently together. Then Bebb prayed out loud by himself. When it was over, the blind man jumped up and said, "Praise the Lord! Hallelujah!" but he ended up knocking down several empty chairs and tripped over his white cane. I don't think Harry Truman would have been impressed.

After the service we asked Bebb to come back with us, but he thought he'd better stay home in case anybody called. Sharon said she would stay with him. I could pick her up later. I left them sitting side by side on the porch steps. Sharon had her head on his shoulder. The sun was getting ready to set and had turned both their faces gold.

12

WHEN I got home, I went straight to my desk and took out the rolled-up sheets of flowered stationery that Lucille had given me. They had apparently been written over a period of several months in different colored felt-tips. In some places they were quite difficult to read, and the flowers scattered all over the working part of the paper didn't make it any easier. *Les très riches heures de* Lucille Bebb:

Today I got bread, butter, bacon, baloney, beets. Brownie and Bebb. We should be living in Baton Rouge, Birmingham, Baltimore, Boca Raton, Buenos Aires, or Bethlehem, anyplace where they don't have Indians. I never minded nigger smell too much. It's a lot of it just lemon juice. Indian smell is hair grease and dirty drawers. Bebb says Herman Redpath isn't long for this world but he doesn't look that bad to me. Bea Trionka says half the kids he says are his aren't. They just let on they are to make him feel good. She says that part of him doesn't even work any more, and she ought to know. Bebb must be slipping when it comes to laying on hands.

Bebb went off to a meeting (guess where) and I sat by the fan and watched TV with the sound off. There was an old woman and a young woman sitting in a restaurant talking. The old woman was doing most of it, and you could tell she was making the young one mad the way she kept twisting up her napkin. Finally the young one couldn't take it any more. She got in a couple of cracks and flounced out. The old woman didn't want to let her see she'd made her cry, but soon as she left she got a handkerchief out of her bag and had a good one all by herself at the table. Sometimes it's hard to know what people are talking about even when you can hear every damn word they say.

Maybe Bebb was right. Herman Redpath was hanging his legs into the pool. They looked like sticks of wood. He's gone all yellow [hollow?]. He looks like Papa did when it got into his glands and spread clear through him. I asked Bebb what does he think happens to people after they're dead, and he said as many kind of things happen one side of the grave as the other, just like he knows. I told him when Herman Redpath's time comes be sure to tell me what happens to him and he says it's not always given us to know but if it is he'll let me know too. At supper he ate just the one frank and a bitty piece of lettuce. He's worried what's going to happen after Herman Redpath's gone, will we still have a roof over our heads and stuff and stuff. Who cares?

After Sharon come he never [touched?] me again except once in a while when it was like he couldn't help himself and wanted to get it over with as quick as he could for both our sakes like puking. They all of them got to get rid of it someplace. God knows where he did all those years. I guess it kept building up in him all those years till the cork finally popped in Miami. When I asked him about it through the cage he told me what he . . . right in the eye . . . whispered like he never . . . [At this crucial

point the writing became indecipherable except for a few phrases because
Lucille had scratched out most of it and there was also a bunch of violets
in the way]. *One little girl put . . . he was having* [hating?] *the first . . .
restaurant . . . lonesome . . . burning his hand* [husband?] *like fire*
[fury?] *. . . Sharon . . . face himself again as long as . . . nobody ever
. . . cellmate* [urinate? ultimate? The rest of the paragraph was blocked
out entirely.] *I never saw him bare but only a few times in my whole life.*

He says you got to have something to hold onto. Here are the things
I've got to hold onto. I've got every doorknob in the whole place, the
draw handles, the flusher handle, the stair rail, the TV with green fuzz
down one side of everybody's face, and the Barcalounger and the Digest
and my own teeth mostly and the ice box and the bed post when the room
starts turning and my sun specs and Brownie's hand that's got hair on the
back of it and soft inside like a powderpuff. And a closet full of junk and
stuff and stuff. Shoes. He says store not up for thyself treasure where moth
and rust and so forth.

He says I've got my good memories. Here are my good memories. I
remember a Jack Horner pie made out of a hatbox and crape paper with
different color strings coming out so when you pulled them it shot the pie
all to hell but you ended up with a comb and lipstick set or a ring. I remember Sundays when we closed down Papa let me jerk any flavor I wanted
so long as I didn't make myself sick and cleaned up the mess. I remember
waking up to the noon whistle and there was a letter from Sammy Jackson
set on my water glass addressed just Little Miss Brighteyes, Clover Street.
I remember Cora Bates's fancy-dress. I remember Gloria Swanson, Doug
Fairbanks, Norma Shearer, and Mickey Mouse. I remember the piano. I
remember Sammy J. I remember Tweetybird.

He says count your blessings. When I stopped getting the period, one.
When we got out of Knoxville, two. When we got out of Armadillo, three.

He says you got to have faith. Faith Murphy had the worst breath
in school and ate nosepick. Talk about faith, when I saw the little weasened
thing wasn't moving any more I prayed I would be struck dead if that
would make it move.

They called him Blinky Bebb. He says he doesn't have any control
over that eye to this day or even knows when its cutting up and everybody
has parts like that they don't have any control over such as heartbeat,
breathing, dreaming and so on and so forth. It's all in the hands of God
Almighty he says. I asked him did that mean his eye was in the hands of
God Almighty and he said that was a way of putting it. So its God Almighty winks Bebbs eye sometime and if so why? If all those parts are in
God's hands I asked him what do we have left over we can call our very
own. He said sin right off. Just when he said it his eye cut up. I told him

right then when you said sin your eye cut up. He said I know, can you blame it?

Dear Jesus,

I am writing you this just in case. How come they called you Jesus of all the other names in Scripture? They could of called you Matthew, Mark, Luke or John, they are names with some spunk to them. Jeeezzzus sounds like it had vaseline on it to make it slip in easy. I never liked my own name either. I use to say my name was Ellicul and I came from Grubnatraps. I was a virgin up to the day I married Bebb and for a spell afterwards just like Mary your mother. Later on I killed my own baby, his name was Herman. Sometime I go for days without once thinking about it. Bebb went and got him a swingset even tho he wasn't but a few months old the day he died and when we moved to Armadillo that swingset went with us. Bebb set it up in the yard. Sometimes the breeze clanked the swing around. Once I put my finger in the crack of the door where the hinges are. What happened was the fingernail turned black and after a while it dropped off. I told Bebb it was a accident.

Bebb says underneath are the everlasting arms.

He says surely he hath born our griefs and carried our sorrows.

He says we are all washed clean in the Blood of the Lamb and so on and so forth.

One time what I said to him was Bebb, the only thing I've been washed in is the shit of the horse.

You know what he did? He took the very same finger the nail fell off of only that was years before and I told him it was a accident, and he kissed it. That was when I first thought maybe he was from Outer Space.

Mr. Jesus, is that where you are from too?

Love,
Ellicul of Grubnatraps.

P.S. I haven't said one single thing I wanted to.

P.P.S. Who is the fat man keeps hanging around Holy Love?

They wouldn't let the undertaker take Herman Redpath tho Bebb says theirs a law. They must of got around it somehow. They did it all themselves. Bea Trionka wasn't there, just the men, but Johnson Badger told her what they did. Some of it anyway. They put salt on his tongue and up his nostrils and ears and up his rear end. They painted red and blue designs on his chest, red for the earth and blue for the sky. They buttered his legs. They put moccasins on his feet. They hung an apron on him to cover his private parts. The apron was black to remind him he wasn't to use anything down there till he got where he was going. After they had him in his brown suit they put in his pockets: a box of Sun Maid Raisins, a jacknife, leather bootlaces, a deerskin pouch, some strings of beads, a whistle, a birds wing and ten bran new ten dollar bills. I said to her Bea what do you Indians believe about after a persons dead? She said we don't have to believe anything because what you folks have to believe, we know. She's like all the rest of them.

Its supposed to be a big honor to keep the flies off Herman Redpath. I guess for flies its a big honor to lay your eggs on him. I said I can't do it because Antonio is here and we got to have heap big family powwow. Bebb tries to make out like he doesn't mind Sharon isn't here too.

I woke up and there was Bebb setting in the rocker by the window rocking in the moonlight, he hadn't even taken his tie and jacket off. When he saw I was awake he started talking. I never saw him so wound up, he must have talked half the night. Part of the time I listened and part of the time I dropped off. It didn't make a partical of difference to him which because he wasn't talking to me so much as he was talking to himself or Jesus or whoever he talks to in the night. He talked about the funeral and the hundred thousand and where we're going to go to next and the big things we're going to do when we get there. He talked about Holy Love what's going to happen to it and can Brownie handle things by himself and so on and so forth. After a while I must have dropped off again because the next thing I knew he was talking about something different and he was talking in a different way, slower, like he was reading fine print or telling something he was watching happen out the window while he was telling it but couldn't see too good. He was telling what happened to Herman Redpath after he was dead.

To Whom It May Concern. This is a true account of what Leo Bebb told on the night after Herman Redpath's funeral. He was cold sober and I was sober too it being something like three o'clock A.M. As near as I can remember them, these are the words of Leo Bebb.

Herman Redpath took off his brown suit and set it down beside him where an eagle come and carried it off in his beak to make stars out of it in the sky like the Big Dipper but not stars that will be visible from this planet for a long time to come if ever. Before he took his suit off Herman Redpath put the things he had in the pockets into the deerskin pouch and hung it around his neck with one of the bootlaces. It was cold but the butter on his legs helped keep him warm. The moccasins helped too. Nobody is sure how old Herman Redpath was when he died but he must have taken off a few years when he took off his brown suit because if he wasn't a young man yet he wasn't an old man anymore either. The flesh didn't hang on him like laundry. He didn't have liver spots or breathe through his teeth. He could dogtrot.

He dogtrotted against the wind because that was the direction the eagle flew off in and the place where he dogtrotted was a big wide prairie stretching on and on as far as the eye could see and flat and hard as a paving stone. It wasn't day and it wasn't night and the color of the sky wasn't all that different from the color of the ground which was nothing but scrub and rocks. He could hear his moccasins pounding on it chunk chunk except on the pebbly parts chicka chicka like a rattle, it was the only sounds he could hear because it was all there was, not a snake or a bird or a four-footed creature. He was alone. Till he come up to a big bolder the size of a phonebooth.

Out from behind that bolder raging and screaming there suddenly jumped out a creature was part snake, part bird, part four footed creature and then some. It had its face where its hindparts should have been and it had its hindparts where its face should have been and when it opened any part of itself up you couldn't tell what part it was opening or what it might take a notion to do with it when it was opened. It come tearing full speed at Herman Redpath flapping all the things it had would flap and making the kind of noise a bird would make if it was a snake. Its eyes were rolling around under its tail something wicked and it was hung all over with damp whiskery things where its eyes ought to been. It howled like a coyote would howl if it was a blackwidow spider, and when it saw Herman Red-path wasn't going to cut loose and run it lept on him. It lept on him the way a Royal Bengal Tiger would leap if it was a swarm of maggots. It knocked him to the ground.

Herman Redpath could feel there was something hot and feathery tightning up around his throat from one direction and something icecold and scaley tightning up around it from another direction and down from above something was coming right for him that looked like a concertina and smelled like sewer gas. The mouth of Herman Redpath was chock full of tongue. His eyes were shooting out on stems. He hadn't but only one hope left in all the world. That hope was his deerskin pouch.

The deerskin pouch had got tore off his neck in the scuffle and was laying next him on the ground, the way his neck was twisted he could just see it. Between his hand and the pouch was maybe about 6 inches. The only transportation the hand had was three fingers, two of them having got broke in the fight already, so that hand started in to crawling after the pouch on its three fingers like a roach thats been part stepped on. Somehow that hand made it. Somehow those fingers wrapped themselves around that jacknife and got it open. No clock could measure the kind of time it took, but finally Herman Redpath got so he had raised the jacknife high enough to where it was pointing right down over something the like of a poach egg that grew between what you might have called the creatures sholderblades if it had've had sholders. Not a moment too soon Herman Redpath used up the last ounce of strenth he had left and struck him a good hard one smack into the middle of the poach egg. The sound it made was the sound a blownup balloon makes when you let it go without tying the end off.

Herman Redpath got up. He fixed the deerskin pouch around his neck with another bootlace and took off again. The ground begun to rise after a while and soon he was dogtrotting up hill. The higher up hill he went, the colder it got. The wind blew harder. He was glad for the butter on his legs. Even the small black apron was some comfort. The wind kept blowing it up against his stomack and when he reached down to see could he make it stay put, he accidently touched something he hadn't touched anything like for many a year. It wasn't an old dishmop hanging there anymore. It was a bunch of Concord grapes.

By and by he come to a teepee. There was smoke coming out of a hole in the top and the flap was pinned open. He thought if he could just warm himself in there for a little, he would be able to keep going up to the top of the mountain. He crawled in through the opening, and up near the fire laying on a pile of soft animal skins he saw a woman. She was a young woman with black braids down far as her knees. Like King Solomon said about the Queen of Sheba, her lips were like a thread of scarlet and her breasts like two young roes which feed among the lillys and her belly a heap of wheat.

This woman she welcomed Herman Redpath and told him to come sit down where it was nice and warm. She made a poltice of herbs and dressed the wounds the creature had left on him. She bound up his broken fingers. She offered him meat and drink only he didn't take any of it because something told him he better not. When all this was done, she reached up her arms and showed him how he was to lay down side of her there on the animal skins. She undid the deerskin pouch he had round his neck, and she was fixing to undo the black apron too but before she could undo it, Herman Redpath saw if he was once to lay down with her there next the fire, he would never get up again and he would never make it to the place where he was going. So he reached down into the pouch and pulled out the strings of beads instead. She put one string around her neck and wound the other string into her black hair. Then she commenced making signs at him made him know for sure if he stayed he was a goner. So he took the crisp new ten dollar bills he had in the pouch and handed them over to her too. While she was busy spreading them out by the fire to see how many of them there was he'd gave her, he tied the pouch back on his neck again and took off out of there like greased lightning.

It was a long way to the top of the mountain. He wished he hadn't been so careful about not touching the food the woman had offered him but he put the Sun Maid raisins into his mouth and they took some of the edge off. There was times he thought he heard the voice of the woman hollering sentimental things after him, but he didn't look back once. It might have been the wind. His feet felt heavier and heavier as the ground got steeper. The poltice the woman rubbed on his sore places had set in to itching and burning some. But finally he got to the top and when he got there it seemed like maybe this was the place he was going to settle down and spend the rest of forever in.

Why everything Herman Redpath had ever wanted and hadn't got was there. Everything he'd ever lost and thought he'd never find again was there. All the good times he'd ever had was happening there at the same time and some of the good times he'd never gotten around to having, they were happening there too. There wasn't a person he'd ever given a hoot about that wasn't some way there to make him feel at home. To welcome him back. To set a extra place for him at the table. To laugh and cry with him. To bear his children. To put up with his cussedness. To remember back with him like they'd been there themselves all the best things he could remember out of his whole life clear back to Betty Shortleg with her breath that smelled of apples how she squirted sassparilla at him through the gap in her teeth, back to his greatgrandad showing him the way it was Tecumseh had stood up better than 7 foot tall at Fort Meig with his arms stretched out like eaglewings. All these things and then some were on top of the mountain with Herman Redpath. They were in his ears the way the sound of the sea is in seashells. They were in his eyes the way seashells are at the bottom of the sea. These things were happening alright except the place they were happening in was no place except right there inside Herman Redpath's own head. Herman Redpath was alone.

Herman Redpath stood on top the mountain on his shiny legs with the black apron to cover his nakedness and the deerskin pouch tied around his neck, and there wasn't a solitary thing you could say was truely happening anywhere nearer than a million miles except what was happening on the inside of Herman Redpath. But he had a hunch if he just hung around there awhile, it would all start happening truely on the outside too, all the good dreams of his life coming true together and every last one of the best times he could remember out of his life coming back to life again. He squatted down on his heels with his knuckles on the ground in front of him. He started in taking deep breaths. Then he felt something bumping him on his chest. It was the deerskin pouch.

He opened it up to find out what was in it to make it bump so, and out flew the birds wing. It spun around over his head three times like it was tied to a cowboy rope. Then it took off down into the canyon ahead. Herman Redpath knew he had to follow. He knew even was he to spend the rest of forever on that mountain the only thing he'd ever find there was ghosts.

This was the worst time yet. The mountain face was steep something cruel on the far side. It was so steep when the stones gave way under his feet he'd slip and slide with the mussles in his legs tensing up in a shaky way that made him feel foolish and ashamed. It wasn't getting darker but the air was getting thicker and harder to see through. He couldn't see the horizon anymore. Soon he couldn't see the ground underneath his own feet even, and the only way he knew it was so steep was from slipping and sliding. It got warmer as he went down. After a bit the temperature of the air got to be exactly the same as the temperature of his body and stopped right there. From the time that happened he couldn't feel his skin anymore. It was like either he didn't have skin anymore, or the air was his skin.

Down at the bottom of the canyon the ground stopped being hard. It felt like he was walking in cake flour. He couldn't hear his feet anymore or hardly feel them. He couldn't feel or hear anything else anymore either. Plus he couldn't see anything the air being so thick and tepid. It seemed like because he didn't have any skin anymore he didn't have any shape either or any boundaries. He had a feeling his legs were still working but he wasn't sure he was moving. He could have been just hanging in the air on the end of a string.

Herman Redpath knew the place he was was noplace. He knew the place where he was going was nowhere. And he knew even if there was a way to get from noplace to nowhere there wasn't hardly anything left of him solid enough to get there with. He couldn't think of anything left in the deerskin pouch could help him now, and he was just as glad. It wasn't all that bad being without shape or boundaries. One way of looking at it you weren't anyplace in particular. The other way of looking at it you were everyplace in general. Both ways had there good points. He couldn't even have told you his name if you'd asked him, and he didn't care a pin. He didn't care if he never got to the place he was supposed to get and if you'd have told him there wasn't any such place, he wouldn't have cared a pin about that either. It was very restful.

Then Herman Redpath smelled something. It was a smell half way between peanuts and seaweed. It was a private, historical kind of smell. He couldn't hear or see or feel anything, and there wasn't anything around to know if he could taste it or not. But he could smell. And he figured out what he smelled must be his own smell because there wasn't so much as the ghost of anything else it could be the smell of. By smelling it he got his nose back. It was a start anyhow.

Then he knew what the smell was. It was a smell left over from the time the Joking Cousin had taken a leak on him. There wasn't a doubt in the world but what the smell he was smelling deep down in that canyon was the smell of John Turtle's piss.

Herman Redpath grabbed ahold of that piss smell and pulled himself back into his skin with it like it was a rope. He pulled himself back into a boundary and shape with it. He pulled himself up the other side of the miserable canyon with it. By the time he got up there he could feel the ground solid under his feet again. He could hear the chunk-chunk of his moccasins. It wasn't anything in his deerskin pouch that had saved him this time. It was the piss of that crazy John Turtle. He thought well you never know, and thanked John Turtle in his heart. The air had thinned out so he could see again. The only trouble was the thing he saw wasn't encouraging.

There was a wall in front of him like the wall of a oldtime stockade. It was a wall made of upright peeled logs pegged together so tight there wasn't a crack you could have squeezed so much as the queen of spades through. It was high as the Houston Astrodome and it stretched out to right and left as far as the eye could see. There was just one small doorway through it. In the middle of the doorway there was an old man squatting on his hunkers. His hair was white and hung down his front in two braids. His face was cracked and rutted like a 8 week drought. It took him a few minutes before Herman Redpath recognized the old man was his own greatgrandad the same that had shown him how Tecumseh held his arms out at Fort Meig. This greatgrandad had also been a friend of Tecumseh's brother Tensquatawa the Shawnee Prophet.

Herman Redpath raised his right hand to the old man and the old man raised his. The old man said You smell like you been dawbing yourself all over with peanuts and seaweed, son. So Herman Redpath explained it all out to him about John Turtle. He squatted down on his hunkers like his greatgrandad and they stayed face to face that way chewing the fat for a long time. Herman Redpath did most of the talking but the talk come out with breaks in between the different parts of it for his greatgrandad to get in his 2¢ worth if he felt like it, and there wasn't half as much cussing and shameful language in it as there was toward the end of his days on earth when he was too old and wore out to care what folks thought. When they finished chewing the fat Herman Redpath stood up and raised his right hand again but this time the old man didn't raise his right hand back. He didn't show any sign of moving out of the doorway to let Herman Redpath through either.

Herman Redpath could guess what would happen if he tried tangling there with his own greatgrandad who had Tecumseh and Tensquatawa both for a friend so he asked him polite as you please would he mind moving off to one side to let him pass on through. The old man stood up. There was a lot of rattling, jingling noises when he did it because he was hung all over with wampum and teeth and dried up things that probably he was the only one could give a name to. He was a good head higher than Herman Redpath, and never mind how old his face looked, he had the build of a man in his prime. When he was up, he filled the doorway. When he spread his legs and put his hands out to the sides, he filled it some more.

The old man said to Herman Redpath, Son, before I can let you pass on through you got to tell me two words, one for the earth and one for the sky. It's the rule of the place.

The only thing that Herman Redpath had that was left in his deerskin pouch was the whistle so he took it out and gave two loud whistles on it. The old man didn't budge an inch. He just scrunched up his sholders a little like the sound of the whistle made his ears hurt. So Herman Redpath tried some pairs of words on him. First he would try a word for the earth and then he would try a word for the sky just like his greatgrandad told him.

He tried Fire and Water. He tried Here and There. He tried Bad and Good. He tried Wolf and Eagle and Thick and Thin. He made up some names like Om-pom-poo and Forp and tried them. When Death and Life didn't work he turned it around and tried Life and Death. He tried some long Indian words he hadn't thought of for years like She-who-lies-with-her-ten-toes-up-and-smiles-like-a-planted-field and He-who-lies-with-his-ten-toes-down-and-falls-like-the-rain. But after the first few pairs of words, the old man didn't even bother to shake his head anymore.

Poor Herman Redpath. He had come such a long way. He had run into so many kinds of danger and was still so sore in most of the places where the creature had mawled him. He thought of the kind of thing he might have been doing now if only he'd layed down on the animal skins like the woman had invited him to. He thought of the top of the mountain and Betty Shortleg and all the lost things he would of gotten such a kick out of finding again even if all they were was ghosts. He thought how peaceful it was in that canyon where the air was warm as his own spit and it was like he didn't have any skin. And now his greatgrandad wouldn't let him through the wall.

It made him so mad he thought of trying some bad words just for the spite of it. He thought of trying words like Shit and Fuck and Turd and Fart only he just didn't have the energy. He felt that helpless, all he could do was hang his head and look at the ground. He looked at his moccasins. He looked at his buttery shins. He looked at the black apron. He looked at his belly that didn't sag anymore like an awning full of rainwater but was flat and hard as a washboard. Next thing he looked at was his chest where there was painted on it some red and blue designs, red for the earth and blue for the sky.

The red design was the Indian way of setting down the word for the earth, and the blue design that curled in and out of it like a snake was the Indian way of setting down the word for the sky. The words themselves were too powerful to say outloud so Herman Redpath did them in sign language instead.

The sign for the word for the earth was to get down on your hands and knees and press your two lips on the packed yellow dirt where he and his greatgrandad had been squatting while they chewed the fat. So he got down on his hands and knees and did that.

The sign for the word for the sky was to uncover your nakedness, throw back your head and reach your arms up as high as they would reach and then a little higher. So he took off the black apron that was tied around him and did that.

The old man winked one eye and stepped aside.

*Just for a split second when the old man winked his one eye, Herman Redpath thought of a person he had known back on earth in the old days. He didn't think of him by name because he'd forgotten his name and he didn't think of him by looks or by any feeling he used to have about him in the days when they knew each other because he'd forgotten all that too. The only way he could think of him was by two words which he'd seen written up someplace crisscross with one O in the middle to make do for them both—*HOLY *stretched out crossways and* LOVE *running straight down through it. He thought if ever he run into that person again someday where he was going, as didn't seem likely, he would tell him that the word* HOLY *was a moth-eaten pale-face way of saying the sign for the earth, and the word* LOVE *was a flea-bitten pale-face way of saying the sign for the sky.*

It took Herman Redpath less than a second and a half to think all this. Then he bust out through that door in the wall like nobody's business. He was naked as the day he was born. If his greatgrandad hadn't moved out of the way in time, the old man would have been skewered.

So that's how it was Herman Redpath come to the Happy Hunting Ground. What it was like when he got there and what he saw and what he did, all those things aren't given us to know for now. The only thing that is known about what happened beyond the door in the wall is that it wasn't for years that Herman Redpath found out what the whistle was for. In the meanwhile he kept it hanging around his neck on a leather bootlace so he'd have it ready when the time came.

I believe Leo Bebb truly saw all this with his own eyes. It may be he was seeing it right then while he was rocking in his chair in the moonlight telling me about it. I believe Leo Bebb knows more than he lets on about many many things like for instance about Mr. Fatass Golden. I believe Leo Bebb is from outer space.

Am I crazy, Mr. Jesus?

At the bottom of the last page, one word in each of the five petals of a daisy, Lucille had written in tiny letters MY ONLY FRIEND IS BROWNIE.

13

THE MESSAGE of the daisy petals led me to put in a long-distance call to Brownie immediately. As soon as he answered, I told him about Lucille. I told him she'd left no clues behind and that so far the police hadn't turned up any. I told him I was calling in hopes that maybe she had gotten in touch with him. Maybe he could give us a lead. I didn't mention *Les très riches heures.*

Brownie said, "These are the times that try men's souls, dear. I just don't know what to say. I wish there was something I could do to help."

I said, "Brownie, did she ever let anything drop to you that might give us a clue where she's gone? Has she called you up or written you the last couple of weeks?"

Brownie said, "She and I have known each other a good many years now and we've been through thick and thin together, but we've never been the kind of friends that exchange phone calls and letters. We were never close in that way."

I said, "I happen to know she considered you one of her best friends, Brownie. *Considers* you."

"That is correct, dear," Brownie said. "There's no call to use the past tense. I am sure wherever she's gone and whatever reason she had for going there, she's alive and well. You've got to have faith."

I said, "I'm afraid Bip's desperate."

Brownie said, "He wouldn't ever have gone to the police if he wasn't desperate. You're going to have to help him, dear."

"I wish I could," I said.

Brownie said, "You can help him by telling him you know she's all right."

I said, "I don't know she's all right, Brownie."

Brownie said, "Tell him thou shalt not be afraid for the terror by night nor for the arrow that flieth by day because thou hast made the Lord thy habitation."

I said, "I don't think even Scripture would cut much ice with him at this point."

Brownie said, "Then tell him Brownie says he hasn't got anything to be worried about."

I couldn't be sure it wasn't my imagination, but it seemed to me that Brownie had lowered his voice slightly.

I said, "Do you know something you're not letting on, Brownie?"

There was a silence at Brownie's end. Generally I can't stand telephone silences and will babble any inanity to end them, but I gritted my teeth and made myself sit this one out in the hope that it would eventually force Brownie into giving some kind of answer.

Finally he said, "We are all of us seeking a homeland, dear, even though we have only seen and embraced it from afar. We are all of us strangers and pilgrims on the earth."

I said, "That's not answering my question, Brownie."

"I wish I could lend you a helping hand," Brownie said. "Bear ye one another's burdens—that's what we're all put here for."

More and more it was like talking to a book of Biblical quotations, but I decided to try once more. I said, "For Christ sake, Brownie, is Lucille down there with you or what? Let's cut out Scripture."

Again Brownie paused. Then he said, "Maybe you'd think better of

Scripture if you'd read it clear through to the end. The end of Scripture is Revelation, dear."

"Revelation," I said.

"And the most important part of Revelation," Brownie said, "is the last part."

"The very last part?" I said.

Brownie said, "Give or take a few words, dear."

"I will be sure to look it up," I said.

Brownie said, "You be sure to do that," and with a sigh of relief that was audible all the way from Texas, he said goodbye and hung up.

It was not the first time in my experience that Brownie had tried to communicate with me in Biblical cipher, and I lost no time looking up his reference to Revelation. I was primarily interested, of course, in whatever Brownie was trying to tell me but I was interested too in finding out how the Bible ended. My sporadic readings had never happened to include the last page. It was the first time I'd ever thought of the Bible's actually having a last page, of there being after all those thousands of words one final word.

The Bible I found was a Gideon that must have been in the house when we first moved in. The black binding had gone rusty and was starting to wear thin around the corners. *Placed in this Hotel by the* GIDEONS was stamped on the front cover, and below it there was a circular stain. I pictured some drummer in stocking feet using it as a coaster. Inside, the text was littered with letters of the alphabet to mark footnotes. There were hyphens and diacritical marks to indicate the pronunciation of proper names. Every once in a while an innocuous word like *and* or *is* or *the* would be printed in italics. Reading it was like listening to somebody with a bad stutter. "The grace of our Lord Jḗ'-ṣŭs Chrīst *be* with you all. Ā-mĕn'" was the last verse, but Brownie's "Give or take a few words, dear" led me back to the next to last. Twitching and stammering, it went "He which testifieth these things saith, ¶Surely I come quickly. ʳĀ-mĕn'. ˢEven so, come, Lord Jḗ-ṣŭs."

There could be no mistaking Brownie's message, I thought. He must know something he couldn't say over the phone. Maybe Lucille herself had been in the room as he spoke. Maybe he had promised not to give her whereabouts away. Maybe he thought the operator was listening. In any case, whatever Brownie knew, it could apparently be found out only by going to Texas to find it. There was no time to lose. *Come* was obviously what Brownie was saying. *Come quickly. Come, dear—come* whoever cared enough to find out the truth. Bebb. Me.

But the name in the book was Jḗ'-ṣŭs, Saint John the Divine or whoever it was that wrote Revelations getting stuck on that first syllable so that with his eyes rolled up and his chin bobbing it kept coming out Jḗ', Jḗ', Jḗ', Jḗ', until finally the blessed relief of ṣŭs. Come, Lord Jḗ'-ṣŭs. Maybe that was Brownie's message too, I thought: that the only one whose coming would make any difference in the long run was Jē′ṣŭs. Jē′ṣŭs hopping the plane to Houston. Jē′ṣŭs at the Red Path Ranch. Jē′-ṣŭs knocking at the door to have Brownie open it or Harry Hocktaw or Mrs. Trionka. Maybe Lucille herself. She and Jē′-ṣŭs would sit down over a couple of Tropicanas, her life-blood. Drink up. She would tell Jē′-ṣŭs she never cared for his name. Jē′-ṣŭs would tell her to take off her black glasses.

I had made the call upstairs in our bedroom, and when I hung up, I sat there on our bed with the Gideon Bible open on my knees. I'd told Sharon I'd come back and pick her up at Bebb's. I had Brownie's message to deliver. It was getting late. But I couldn't move for some reason, just sat there staring at the dreary, double-columned page as though exhausted already by the long journey I knew would begin the moment I sat up and started downstairs. *Come quickly*. It was the urgency of the thing that paralyzed me.

I knew I should do something right away, but I couldn't get going. I felt like lying down on the bed—Sharon's and my bed. And Sharon's and Tony's bed too likely enough. That was something else I should probably do something about, I thought, though God only knew what. Talk it out with one of them maybe, maybe with both of them—work it through, work it off. Teach school with it. Lear's lines drifted through my mind, "We two alone will sing like birds i' the cage./When thou dost ask me blessing, I'll kneel down/And ask of thee forgiveness." All three of us kneeling down somewhere, asking of each other something. Come quickly. But for the time being it was more than I could swing. I might even have actually lain down there, shut my eyes on the whole clamoring snarl of things, but then I heard a car drive in. I heard the unmistakable voice of Mrs. Kling. She and Charlie were bringing the boys back from supper. I beat it out down the back stairs.

I rolled out of the driveway as quietly as I could with the headlights off and drove straight to Bebb's. Bebb and Sharon were sitting in the dark living room watching TV, their faces the color of moonlight. I didn't tell them about Lucille's *très riches heures*. I didn't ask Bebb if it was true that he'd told her the story of how Herman Redpath reached the Happy Hunting Ground and if so, how he'd come to know about it. I just reported my conversation with Brownie and quoted from memory the next to last verse of the Book of Revelation.

Bebb said, "Antonio, there isn't a doubt in my mind but what she's back in Houston and Brownie's telling us to get our tails down there pronto. He couldn't say it straight out for fear she'd get wind of it."

Sharon said, "Why did she go, Bip?"

On the TV screen there was a short man in a tuxedo and a fat woman in a sequined evening dress standing in front of a microphone. Somebody came in pushing a wheelbarrow. The laughter crackled like a bonfire, and Bebb got up and turned down the volume.

Bebb said, "Maybe she went to see would we come after her."

"Are you?" Sharon said.

Bebb said, "Honey, I don't just know what I'm going to do." He was still standing by the TV. The fat woman had turned her back to the short man in the tuxedo. He unzipped her dress and helped her pull it off over her head. Underneath she was wearing overalls.

Bebb said, "For many years Lucille hasn't what you might say *moved*. She has set around watching TV and drinking Tropicanas. She has been there when you went out, and when you come back in later, she was right there still. I don't mean she hasn't kept moving in her own way. There's no telling how many miles a day a woman travels just doing her chores. I mean she hasn't moved inside herself. She hasn't gotten any-wheres or even wanted to. For a long time Lucille Yancey Bebb has been stuck."

He was talking to himself, the nutcracker jaw cracking the words out one by one. He was staring down at the carpet, his eyes catching the silvery light of the TV like soap bubbles, pearls. He could have been seeing Lucille herself as he talked about her just the way he could have been seeing Herman Redpath that night as he had talked to Lucille about him: Herman Redpath jogging along with the deerskin pouch around his neck; Lucille stuck year after year behind those black glasses or Lucille wherever she was now, moving wherever she was moving. Behind Bebb I could see that the fat woman in the overalls had gotten the short man into the wheelbarrow and was wheeling him in it across the stage.

Bebb said, "Well, at last she's taken off. It could be a good thing or a bad thing, depending. Say she's gone back to Houston. Then why'd she go there? To get away from something here? To find something there? Brownie maybe. She always took to Brownie. It might be a good thing to chase after her and bring her back. On the other hand it might be just the wrong thing."

I said, "There didn't seem to be any doubt in Brownie's mind any-way."

Bebb said, "Antonio, Brownie's an old woman. Always was and always will be. He'd say you don't take chances no matter what. Brownie'd say as long as Lucille stays put, at least you know where she's at. That's playing it safe. You take Brownie himself. He's played it so safe all his life he's never lived. He's slid his life in under his tail and sat on it. The man's got spiritual hemorrhoids."

Bebb was working one arm up and down as he spoke. He said, "Because thou art lukewarm and neither cold nor hot I will spew thee out of my mouth. Antonio, life is a gamble. If you don't take chances, you're not alive. I promised Lucille Yancey to honor and keep her as long as we both should live. Maybe that means I should go down and fetch her back now before she goes off the deep end. But maybe not. Maybe I honor her most by leaving her go."

Sharon said, "You better do like Brownie says and bring her back, Bip. If anything happens to her, you'll never forgive yourself."

Bebb said, "Suppose nothing happens to her ever again. Can I forgive myself that?"

Bebb switched on the overhead lights and turned off the TV. A young woman holding a different type of denture cleanser in each hand was sucked up into a small bright hole in the middle of the screen and then disappeared.

On the plane to Houston the next morning, Bebb the great gambler, the great believer, was sick. He did it neatly into a paper cup. When he was finished, I could see the tears rolling down his cheeks. He said, "Every time I puke, I cry. I can't help it. Antonio, I've been that way ever since I was a kid."

14

WE DIDN'T LET Brownie know we were coming for fear that if Lucille was down there with him as we suspected and got wind we were on our way, she might clear out before we arrived. We took a taxi from the Houston airport and had it let us off at Holy Love, where Brownie's office was.

The church was open, but we couldn't find Brownie or anybody else. The office looked much as it had when it was Bebb's except that on the wall behind the desk Brownie had hung a much enlarged photograph of Bebb and Herman Redpath that must have been taken not long before Herman Redpath's death. It showed Herman Redpath sitting in a wicker armchair on the lawn in front of Holy Love looking a good deal like John D. Rockefeller in his old age. His bony hands hung down over the ends of the chair-arms as if somebody else had arranged them there. The toes of his high-button shoes pointed slightly in toward each other. He was in his shirtsleeves and wearing a string tie. Bebb was standing behind him in his preaching robe with his hands on the old man's shoulders. His head was directly above Herman Redpath's head, and they were both staring into the camera. They looked like some kind of totem pole.

We had already let the taxi go, so after failing to find Brownie and not wanting to spread word of our arrival by a phone call, we decided to head off for the residential compound on foot. Holy Love was on the fringes of the ranch, so there were several miles of flat, dusty road ahead of us. We had brought a single overnight bag between us which I carried. Bebb had loosened his collar and tie and knotted a handkerchief around his neck to catch the sweat. To keep the sun off his bald head, he put on a

Mexican sombrero which he'd found hanging in the corridor outside Brownie's office. It made him look like part of a nightclub act.

When we came in sight of the stables, some barefoot children ran down to the fence to watch us pass by, but Bebb's sombrero apparently kept them from recognizing him, and he made no attempt to identify himself. I'm not sure he even noticed them. His face looked grim and pale under the jouncing straw brim as he trudged along. He had fastened the drawstring to keep the sombrero on, and the string-ends hung down in a tassel from his knob of a chin. The only time he spoke was when we passed a low cinder-block building where there was a flagpole out front with a flag at half-mast. Bebb pointed to it and said, "Herman Redpath is gone, Antonio, but he is not forgotten."

Except for the children we saw no signs of life until we got as far as the greenhouse. A pickup truck was just pulling out of the drive with pails of cut flowers in the back—white iris, white carnations, long-stemmed roses, and some shaggy yellow species that I didn't recognize. The truck stopped under a tree, and from the shadows of the cab a bare arm shot out and waved at us. A voice called, "Hiya, good-lookin'." Pushing the sombrero back off his forehead, Bebb stopped to watch the driver get out and run across the road to us. I recognized him immediately as John Turtle. He threw his arms around Bebb and hugged him.

He said, "Oh Leo, we been missing you real bad down here. Things aren't the same with you gone anyhow."

Bebb said, "I've had spells of missing you too, John Turtle."

"That's real good," John Turtle said, "the way we both been missing each other, me and you."

"That's friendship for you," Bebb said.

John Turtle was looking at Bebb, but he reached out sideways and poked me in the stomach with his finger. He said, "How you doing, friendship? Gettin' much lately?" His gold-framed teeth glinted in the Texas sun.

I said, "How about yourself, John Turtle?"

"You hear me complaining?" John Turtle said.

Bebb said, "Boys, if I don't get out of this sun for a minute, you're going to find yourself talking with a pool of grease." Sweat was running down from under the sombrero and had soaked through the armpits of his Palm Beach cloth suit.

John Turtle said, "Come on over to the truck and take a load off your feet. Tell me all the things that's been happening anyhow."

"You too," Bebb said. "Tell me what's going on down here, John Turtle."

John Turtle had parked his pickup in the shade. He lowered the tailgate, and the three of us sat down on it with John Turtle in the middle and our feet dangling just off the ground. I have never smelled a body-smell to equal John Turtle's. It was a fourth presence there on the tailgate.

If it had been music, it would have taken the Houston Symphony to do it justice.

"So tell me what's new, John Turtle," Bebb said. He didn't say, "Tell me if my wife's here," didn't even mention her. John Turtle didn't mention her either. They neither of them spoke Lucille's name as we sat there on the tailgate with all those flowers, and yet I had the feeling that it was Lucille they were speaking about the whole time anyway. Their conversation was like one of those trick pictures in which, once you look at it the right way, you discover that the empty space among the trees is really a human face.

John Turtle told Bebb what was new with a number of Indians. He said, "That oldest boy of Harry Hocktaw's, he got caught in the sauna bath playing ring-around-the-rosy with Louemma Pole. I'm telling you there was some awful boo-hoo when all them Poles and Hocktaws got together on it after. I come too. Oh my yes. We work it all out, don't you worry. Harry Hocktaw's boy gonna have him a nice little wife anyhow. He's gonna have sweet-potato any time he feel like it. Louemma Pole, she gonna have a snake in her grass to the end of her born days."

He said, "The day old Maudie Redpath turned a hundred and six, they had some big hoopla. They had a barbecue. They had Lizard Shoptall's hot jazz combo. There was champagne and prizes and balloons. They set Maudie's chair up on a old buckboard and pulled her all over the place. She did a dance on top of there like there wasn't one other soul left alive in the world to remember how you dance it. If you dance it right, you suppose to turn into a blackbird anyhow. That blouse she always wears you can see through, there's some says they could see where her old titties started to come out all over black feathers. Then she had an attack and come near to swallowing her tongue. She say she feel much better afterwards. Live another hundred six years easy."

John Turtle put his arm around Bebb's far shoulder and let his cheek come to rest on the near shoulder. He said, "Lily Trionka lose the baby she was carrying eating too much cherry-vanilla ice cream on a day like this and then riding the exercycle thirteen miles to work it off. You can just guess who she say was the daddy, him in his grave with the butter on his legs not knowing one thing about it. Well, if she's true, then what she was carrying around inside till she went and lost it was her own uncle."

Here John Turtle sang a song that he seemed to be making up as he went along. It had no tune to speak of. With his cheek on Bebb's shoulder still, he could have been singing it to Bebb or to Lily Trionka's lost child or to nobody in particular. It went,

> *"Baby baby don't you cry*
> *All us folks we got to die*
> *Do no good to sob and sigh*
> *Have yourself some cherry pie*

Look for eagle in the sky
See what's up there winks his eye."

Then he said, "Johnson Badger been having bad luck right straight through. That crazy nephew Buck try horsing around with the Electrolux and got stuck so bad they had to take him down to Doc's in town with that thing hanging off him like a gas pump. Johnson's wife Donna she run her golf-cart into a stump and broke the bone in her eye."

When John Turtle showed signs of stopping, Bebb asked him about several other Indians who had been left out. After he had finished hearing the news about them, Bebb told John Turtle the news about himself.

Bebb said, "John Turtle, I'm going to be open with you, you being the Joking Cousin and all. Things haven't gone just like I hoped they would up North. Things I'd as soon not have had happen, some of them have been happening, and things I hoped was going to happen, to be honest with you they're the ones mostly haven't happened—haven't happened *yet*," Bebb said, holding up one finger. His damp face was mottled by the leaf-shadows. " 'Fear not for I am with thee, saith the Lord. Yea, I will uphold thee with thy right hand.' I believe that, John Turtle. I've got to believe that. In the meanwhile my soul waiteth for the Lord more than they that watch for morning. More than they that watch for morning, John Turtle."

Bebb untied the handkerchief from around his neck and used it to mop around under his jaw and at the back of his head. He said, "I was born and bred in the South. I had me a baby boy was born and died here, and when my time comes, I'm fixing to be laid to rest right next to his little grave in Knoxville, Tennessee. I've had bitter times down here same as I've had good times. I've made many bad mistakes here, I'm not denying it for one minute, and I've paid dear for every last one of them. But the South's home, John Turtle. Thanks to the great generosity of Herman Redpath, who was the givingest man it has ever been my privilege to know, I have comforts up North I never had anywheres else. I have a house with four bathrooms. I drive a car with air-conditioning and stereo. When I soil my clothes, there's people will come pick them up at the door and have them back spotless inside twenty-four hours. But there's a woman comes to worship with a sorrowful-looking kind of possum in a cage. There's a wheel in the cage to do its exercise on. That's how I feel up North. It's where I've been called to preach the Cross of Jesus. And I've been going at it hard. I will keep going at it hard. But how long, John Turtle, how long? Until the cities lie wasted without inhabitants, saith the Lord? Until the land be utterly desolate?"

We sat there over his question in silence, the three of us. Across the road there was a bird on the power line. It made a noise that sounded like tightly packed coins chinking in a sack. I decided that since nobody else was going to say it, I would have to say it myself.

I said, "Tell us what's new with Lucille." The remark could have been meant for either of them. That way, I thought, if she wasn't at the ranch, I wouldn't be giving it away to John Turtle that she was missing. He would think I was just asking Bebb to tell him, John Turtle, what was new with Lucille. If Lucille *was* at the ranch, John Turtle would assume that she was there with her family's full knowledge and consent and that we just wanted him to tell us how she'd been getting on since she came.

Bebb, of course, didn't say anything. I could hear the silence he was making not saying anything. John Turtle also didn't say anything. Just the bird on the power line: *chink, chink.* Every once in a while a lovely whiff from the flowers made it through the smell of John Turtle's body. I decided that either Lucille wasn't there or John Turtle wasn't going to let on that she was, and I was just about to say something else when John Turtle finally spoke.

He said, "She didn't look too good anyhow."

Bebb said, "When didn't she look too good?"

John Turtle said, "This morning when I seen her she didn't."

I said, "Where did you see her?"

John Turtle was swinging his legs back and forth letting the heels strike together each time on the backward swing. He was wearing a pair of scuffed black cowboy boots with built-up heels and pointed toes.

He said, "She was over to Brownie's when I seen her the last time. I'll give you a lift."

Bebb said, "Is she at Brownie's right now?"

John Turtle said, "She's not at Brownie's right now, see. She didn't look so hot this morning."

John Turtle was looking down at what he was doing with his feet, and Bebb was leaning forward to see up into his face. Bebb's face as he was looking up at John Turtle was not just expressionless. There was hardly anything left in it to make an expression with.

Bebb said, "How do you mean she didn't look so hot, John Turtle?"

John Turtle said, "I mean she looked kind of cold. She's not over there at Brownie's anyhow. She moved."

Bebb said, "John Turtle, I want you to take us where she moved to right this second. Antonio and me, we're planning to surprise her."

"That's going to be a surprise," John Turtle said. With the toe of one boot, he managed to loosen the other boot at the heel until he could pull it off. He reached down and scratched the sole of his foot, his eyes narrowed in a grimace of relief, his cuff-link teeth showing.

He said, "Lucille, she's kind of dead anyhow."

In connection with her yoga lessons, Sharon once brought home a book about macrobiotic dieting. The book explained that Occidentals need macrobiotics more than other people because they are all *sanpaku*. When a man is *sanpaku*, the whites of his eyes show underneath his irises. That is a very bad sign. It means that you are susceptible to all kinds of diseases both physical and mental. It means that you are apt to come to a sudden and tragic end. It means that you should waste no time taking up macrobiotic diet number seven which consists of eating nothing but brown rice for ten consecutive days.

I had never seen anybody look as *sanpaku* as my father-in-law, Leo Bebb, did at that moment sitting on the tailgate of John Turtle's truck with the pails full of white flowers behind him and the bird on the power line making noises like tightly packed coins in a sack. You could see the whites not only underneath his irises but above them too. This side of hell, they were about as *sanpaku* as eyes can get. I don't think even diet number seven would have helped much.

"You look like somebody shoved a lighted cigar up your ass," the Joking Cousin said. This time he had both arms around Bebb's shoulders.

15

THAT EVENING Bebb, Brownie and I stood shoulder to shoulder in a Houston funeral parlor. Parlor was the word for it—wall-to-wall carpeting, comfortable chairs, pictures. A schooner in full sail. An autumn wood. In one wall there was an alcove. In the alcove there was a box tilted toward us lengthwise like a display of fruit in a grocer's window. Lucille was in it. They had done a pretty good job on her except for the mouth. It was hard to say what they'd done wrong with the mouth except that it wasn't quite what Lucille would have done with it herself.

Bebb said, "They haven't got the mouth right."

Brownie said, "Just remember, dear, what you're looking at is only mortal clay. Mrs. Bebb herself is with her Father in heaven."

"The mouth isn't right," Bebb said. "They've got the wrong dress on her. I never saw that dress before in all my life."

Brownie said, "Donna Badger contributed that dress. They both of them wore the same size."

Bebb said, "They should have used her own dress. That one doesn't look right on her."

Brownie said, "Her own dress wasn't in a state they could use it, dear."

Bebb said, "It was real nice of Donna Badger to make a contribution of that dress, but . . . Why that dress no more looks like a dress Lucille would ever have wore!" He said, "Antonio, you remind me to express my appreciation to Donna Badger for contributing that dress, hear?"

I said, "Take it easy, Bip."

Brownie said, "Let us bow our heads and say together the Lord's Prayer."

I bowed my head, but I did not shut my eyes. I looked at Bebb's feet. One of his shoes was untied. It was a black shoe, and it was still dusty from our walk that afternoon from Holy Love. It must have been untied for some time because the laces had worked loose over the instep so that there wasn't enough of the ends left sticking out to tie. He would have had to start pulling them tight from the bottom holes up in order to have enough at the top to make a bow with. The whole time we were saying the Lord's Prayer together, I was tying Bebb's shoe with my eyes.

When the prayer was over, Brownie said, "Maybe we better go now. John Turtle is waiting in the car."

"Brownie," Bebb said, "you and Antonio go if you want. I'll be along in a few minutes. It's the last time I'll get to see her, and I don't want to rush it."

Brownie said, "It's not the last time. She'll be there on the other side waiting when you get there. She is there right now, dear."

"No, she's not," Bebb said.

"Where is she, Bip?" I said it before I knew I was going to, and it was only as I said it that I realized that I expected Bebb to *know.*

"Tell him where she is," Brownie said. Poor Brownie. I see his face turned to Bebb, his eyes gone all dreamy and pale behind his glasses, his store teeth parted to take in whatever sweet words he thought Bebb was about to throw our way.

Bebb turned on him with his face nearly as red as the child's crayoning on the train. It seemed to swell bigger and bigger like an inner tube through a split tire. He said, "I'll tell him where she is. There's where she is. She's in that box with her mouth on crooked and that miserable dress. She's there with her insides pumped out and something else pumped in. All is left of Lucille Yancey's that poor shell that used to hold a life in it. She's in that box if you want to know where she is. She's a empty box inside that box."

Bebb said, "Brownie, you miserable pissant, why didn't you wait till I come before you let the undertaker have her? Without he'd gone and used his needles and chemicals on her poor flesh, I might have raised her."

He paused for a moment, his face red and his shoe untied. Then as if maybe it wasn't too late after all, he turned to Lucille and said, "*Talitha cumi!*" He said it in the same tone of voice he'd used the time she tipped over backwards in the porch rocker.

For the first time whatever they had done wrong with her mouth seemed to come right. It was the kind of lopsided thing she might have done with it herself if she had had ears to hear what Bebb had just said to her. He said it again, "*Talitha cumi.* Damsel, I say unto thee arise."

For a moment I was certain I could see her flat chest in that borrowed dress start to breathe. The bottom half of the lid was closed over her from the waist down, and I watched for her to start pulling herself out from under it like somebody getting out of a kayak. For a moment it seemed the reason she was so absolutely still was that she was pulling herself together to move. The three of us stood there watching her.

"Brownie, you poor old woman," Bebb said finally, "it might have worked if you only hadn't gone and jumped the gun. Just like it worked when you were laid out there in Knoxville, Tennessee, the color of cement in your underdrawers till the Lord in his mercy gave you back your pitiful life again. She might have rose right up the same as you did. Now there's not enough of her left to raise spit."

There were tears coming down from underneath Brownie's glasses, but all his teeth would do was smile.

Bebb said, "Never mind." The inner tube had burst. He was resting on his rims now.

He said, "She just picked up and went where she felt like she had to go. She's got plenty to keep her busy now without me trying to drag her back against her will. Who knows? Maybe Herman Redpath will give her a hand on the way."

Brownie said, "The communion of saints, dear." He had taken his glasses off to wipe his eyes. When Brownie took his glasses off, you felt you shouldn't look at him.

I said, "Maybe Herman Redpath will give her the word for the earth and the word for the sky."

Bebb said, "She tell you about that?" He was facing Lucille in her alcove with his eyes closed. He said, "One night back there she couldn't get to sleep. I wasn't asleep either. We commenced to talk in the dark. She wanted me to tell her what it is is supposed to happen on the other side and all that. I suppose she might have been thinking about things even back then. Like she wanted to make sure where she'd end up if that was where she decided to go. Of course I didn't suspect anything at the time. I thought she just wanted to find out about Herman Redpath, him having just passed on. So I spun her that yarn to help her go to sleep with. I made it up as I went on, like a bedtime story. The places he went and the things that happened. The things he had to do. It was a kind of lullaby. She went to sleep by and by."

I said, "I think she believed it, Bip. I think she thought it all happened just the way you said."

Bebb opened his eyes and turned to me. For a second I thought his eyelid was going to do its trick, but there was only the faintest tremor. Then it recovered. He said, "Who says it didn't?"

Through the crook of his arm I could see Lucille's forehead with the hair growing out of it. I remembered reading somewhere that your hair goes on growing for a while after you're dead and wondered if Lucille's was. Bebb placed both his hands on the edge of her box. He said, "Goodbye, dear heart." He didn't say it in an emotional way. He said it as if the time had simply come to say it.

When we got back to the car, he told John Turtle we would wait if he wanted to go in and pay his last respects. I wondered if he hoped maybe John Turtle would take a leak on her just in case the going got tough later on.

According to Brownie, what had happened was this. The same Saturday that Bebb and I had taken the train to New York together, Lucille had arrived at the ranch. She had not told Brownie she was coming, just phoned him from the airport when she got in and told him to come get her. She had no luggage and wasn't even wearing a hat and coat. She said when they moved north, she had left a lot of things behind at the ranch that she needed now and nobody would know where to lay their hands on them except herself. Brownie said she kept coming back so many times to this expression of laying her hands on things that it sounded as though that was what she was really there to do—not so much to find the things she needed and take them home with her but just, literally, to lay her hands on them again. He said she talked in a somewhat jumbled way, but it wasn't the first time he'd heard her talk like that and he had an idea she'd probably taken a little something on the flight down. He said when he asked her where Bebb was, she told him to tell *her*. She said wherever Bebb was, he was spending more and more of his time out there and the less said about it the better. When reporting this to Bebb, Brownie said, "She meant outer space, dear. You know how that was always her joke," and Bebb sat there listening to him with his face done up so tight he couldn't have flickered so much as an eyelash.

Brownie said that when he suggested to Lucille that they ought to give Bebb a ring and let him know she'd arrived safely, she didn't offer any explanation but just told him she didn't want anybody to know she was there. She made Brownie promise he wouldn't give her away. Brownie said, "It was the valley of decision, dear. I knew I ought to call you, but she seemed so set on nobody knowing. It was like her whole life depended on it. You at least had Sharon and Antonio. You had your faith, dear. But all she had right then was me. So I promised. When Antonio phoned the next day, I was stretched nearly to the breaking point."

Brownie said, "That was Sunday evening you called. Most of Sunday she spent laying her hands on things just like she said. She hadn't left all that much behind when you moved, but what there was was right where she left it. Nobody's moved in there since you went north. Bea Trionka went over and visited with her a while. Bea says there were only a few drawers had anything in them, but she'd take it out what little there was and sort through it and put it all back again. Some old belts and shoes and some underthings that needed mending, worn out things like what you'd leave behind and never give another thought to. That's mostly all there was, dear. There was a shoebox full of old snapshots and a few keepsakes, but Bea says she didn't make any special feature out of them. She just showed Bea a couple of things she had in there and then put them back. Bea felt like what she wanted to do most was just see her own place again. I guess there wasn't a thing in it she didn't get around to laying her hands on before she was done."

Brownie told Bebb and me all this before we went to the funeral parlor. We were sitting in the big, high-ceilinged room where Herman Redpath's pipe organ was. There was something museum-like about it with just the three of us sitting there. I felt there should have been velvet ropes across all the chairs.

Brownie said, "We had supper together Sunday night, just her and I. I mixed her up a Tropicana first. I had the orange juice on hand, and the gin I got off of Lizard Shoptall. I thought if she wanted to unburden herself of anything that was on her heart, this would be the time. Sometimes it's easier to say things to an outsider, dear. But you know how she always was. She let me do most of the talking. Just once in a while she'd come out with one of her salty comments. I remember I said Sharon's boy must be a lot to handle these days, and she said something about how he wasn't the only boy Sharon was handling these days. It was just the way she had, and down in her heart there never was a kinder soul. She said Mr. Golden had turned up again up North. I asked her could anybody find out what he was up to, and she gave me one of her long looks when you wished you could see behind the dark glasses, and finally she come out and said, 'It's not what he's up to. It's what he's *down* to.' I remember she said, 'Going down, please. Everybody watch your step.' Dear, she didn't say anything different than the kind of thing she always said. She didn't give a clue what must have been in her mind the whole time. She even mentioned something about when she'd be getting home. How could I guess what she meant by home? I'm not sure now what she meant even. Maybe all she meant when she said home was what I thought she meant then. Maybe what happened come as much of a surprise to her as it did to me."

Brownie was wearing his powder-blue suit with the silvery clip-on bow tie which was his usual costume for Sundays. I suppose he had put it on special that Monday for the trip to the funeral parlor. The lenses of his glasses were pink because the pink sky was reflected in them through the window. His after-shave seemed unusually fragrant. Dear Brownie. In many ways he was a breath of spring in that museum of a room.

He said, "After we got the dishes done up, we went and sat out on the porch. It was a lovely, warm night. There was just a little breeze and a new moon. I remember I looked up, and I said, 'When I consider the heavens, the work of thy fingers, the moon and the stars, which thou has ordained . . . What is man that thou art mindful of him?' It is a question I often ask myself, dear. Next thing Lucille, she said, 'Read me some parts out of Scripture, Brownie.'

"You see it was Sunday, and I'd left my Bible out there on the table when I come back from church so it was right there beside me, and there was light enough from the window to read by. Now it wasn't like her to ask to have Scripture read out loud to her. In her heart she was a Christian woman, but nobody that knew her would have expected she'd ask a thing like that, and I should have seen right then something was wrong. But I didn't see it, not even then. I'd just quoted from the Psalmist, and she'd probably seen the Bible laying there on the table. It just seemed natural as could be at that time, and I asked her if there was anything special she'd like me to read. She told me to just let the book fall open in my lap and start reading from the first place my finger touched. So I did like she told me, and the book fell open to Second Kings, the tenth chapter.

"You remember that is a terrible chapter, dear. It tells about how Jehu beheaded all seventy of Ahab's sons and laid their heads together in two heaps by the gate and then put the two and forty of Ahaziah's brethren and all the worshipers of Baal to the sword. It is a very dark Scripture, dear, and I asked her couldn't I close up the book again and try for another. But she said no. She said that was what the book opened to and that was what she wanted to hear. She said maybe it would get more cheerful later on.

"I must have read half an hour or so. I couldn't see her too good in the dark where she was sitting, but I could hear her rocking back and forth in her chair so I knew she wasn't asleep. After a while she said, 'Read me about Jesus, Brownie.' She said it in a kind of drowsy, restful way. It was the last words I ever heard her say, and at that time I was real glad to hear her say them. Second Kings never does get what you'd want to call very cheerful, dear, and I turned to the Gospels with great relief. I opened up to Saint Mark and started reading right from the beginning. I read how Jesus got baptized in Jordan's waters and was tempted of Satan and how he started gathering unto himself the disciples. Then all those miracles, dear. I read how he drove out the unclean spirits and cleansed the leper. How he cured the palsy and the withered hand. All the time I was reading I could hear the chair rocking so I knew she was awake. Anyway, she wasn't a person to let you go on if she wanted you to stop. So I went on and read her how the Savior taught us faith is like a grain of mustard seed which, when it is sown in the ground, is less than all the seeds. The Gadarene swine. The feeding of the multitude. I don't know how long I went on. When I get reading Scripture, I lose track of time. But finally I must have stopped to give my voice a rest. The chair had stopped rocking. She was sitting there with her head back. I thought she just had dozed off, dear."

The smell of Brownie's after-shave. The sky-colored glasses. The gun-barrel sheen of Herman Redpath's organ pipes, and Bebb sitting up straight and stiff in his chair with a plump hand on each knee and his face like something carved out of Ivory Soap. You try to represent the truth of a moment by drawing a line through such points as these. I was sitting next to Brownie on the sofa, and as he paused, I couldn't help remembering that fatal night on the sofa next to Tony: the springy, salt-stiff hair, the *I'm sorry, I'm sorry.* In some queer way, I thought, all moments are one moment. Outside where the sun was going down, there was the sound of tightly packed coins chinking in a sack.

Brownie said, "It was the wrists, dear. All that rocking back and forth—I suppose it acted like a pump. All over her dress, the rocker . . . There wasn't a thing in the world you could do. 'Read me about Jesus, Brownie.' Those were her last words, dear. What a blessing to know she slipped away with the music of Scripture in her ears."

Bebb got up from his chair. He said, "Thank you, Brownie. I'm much obliged."

He walked over to Herman Redpath's organ across the room from where Brownie and I were sitting. He had set his borrowed sombrero down on the bench when we'd come in, and he pushed it to one side to make room to sit down. When he sat down, the sombrero started to fall off the end of the bench, so he picked it up and set it on the back of his head. He pulled out several of the stops and pushed in several others. He settled his hands down on the keyboard and started by pressing out several vague, overstuffed chords.

Then he sang,

> *"Ten thousand times ten thousand,*
> *In sparkling raiment bright,*
> *The armies of the ransomed saints*
> *Throng up the steeps of light."*

There was something about his singing voice that always reminded me of the Gothic radios of my childhood—reedy, maybe one tube a little loose, the amber light of the dial.

He sang,

> *" 'Tis finished, all is finished,*
> *Their fight with death and sin.*
> *Fling open wide the golden gates,*
> *And let the victors in."*

16

SOON AFTER we returned to Sutton, Bebb moved in with us, and Sharon said, "It's like there was a shipwreck and this house is the desert island where everybody gets washed up." We were in bed, and it was raining outside. There was a magazine near the window, and the damp breeze kept lifting the cover with a papery noise.

I said, "You can even hear the palm trees."

Something like two weeks had gone by since the night I found out about Sharon and Tony, and we had been sleeping together all those nights but we had not made love together. It was a long time for us not to have made love. It was not that the idea of sharing her with my impulsive nephew made her less desirable. If I had been thinking in those terms, that might even have made her more so in some dim and unsightly way. It was not that I was out to get even with her by withholding, such as it was, the solace of my flesh, or to get even with myself by refusing the solace of hers—Tony and Sharon continued to live together in that house so much as though nothing had ever happened between them that I began almost to believe that nothing had and that the guilt was therefore mine for having dreamed up the gaudy thing in the first place. I think we had not made love together because getting his horns is only the first stage a cuckold goes through on his way to becoming like the beasts of the field. The second stage is getting gelded. For two weeks making love with my wife had been an occasion to which I simply wasn't able in any sense to rise. In fact it wasn't till her remark about the desert island that the possibility even occurred to me. I suppose it called up all the old business about the girl you'd most like to be marooned with, the old *Esquire* cartoons. Add to that the wet wind rattling the magazine cover and the sound of the rain.

Sharon was lying on her side with her back to me speaking at least half to her pillow. She said, "The Dead End kids, I mean. They got washed up here because their mother kicked the bucket. Because Charlie's sinuses are all he can handle plus Mrs. Kling and her big boobs. And now Bip's gotten washed up. He's like Robinson Crusoe up there on the third floor with his suitcase hanging on the door and his portable TV. It's like he's just roughing it up there till some ship comes by and rescues him."

"The baby," she said. "He's the only one of them that's here on purpose. He got *born* here, for God's sake."

I was lying on my back with my hands folded on my chest. I felt just the way Lucille had looked in her box in Houston. I had an idea there was the same sort of thing wrong with my mouth.

I said, "How about you and me? Are we washed up too?"

I meant washed up marooned, that's all I meant, but it didn't come out that way. I knew it the moment I heard myself say it. Just *washed up* was the way it came out. It was too late to explain. I was like the man who happens to scratch his ear at an auction. God only knew what I might end up paying. I lay there knowing that within seconds I could be taken for everything I had.

Washed up. There wasn't a thing in the world I could do about it except just listen to the rain and wait to see how she'd answer, and then as I waited, and for reasons that will never be clear, there was that about me which after having been for two weeks as good as dead chose this moment to start coming slowly alive again, and there wasn't a thing in the world I could do about that either. Mr. Independence. I've heard that on the battlefield dead soldiers are found—and from the gallows men are cut down—in just such a state as I was in then as I waited in the dark beside Sharon, who lay on her side with her back to me and her knees drawn up. It was a kind of resurrection, I suppose. The crowing cock that puts the ghosts to flight.

"You and me, we live here," Sharon answered finally. "We weren't washed up. We're the native population." I don't know why she took so long to say it. Maybe it just seemed long. Anyway, knowing it or not knowing it, she gave me back my life again.

It might have been Ellie Pierce lying there beside me, I thought, Ellie with her yellow rose, her lovely Vassar French. Or it might have been Laura Fleischman, and for a moment in the lunacy of the dark and the rain I let it become Laura Fleischman, Laura Fleischman *en fleur*, gentle as falcon or hawk in the tower, that child lying there sleepy and shy with her knees drawn up. I remembered a dream I'd had about Laura Fleischman. It was deer season, and I was standing on a hillside. Laura Fleischman came running down the hillside disguised as a deer with antlers tied to her head. I thought what a crazy thing to do, and then I heard a gun go off. Laura Fleischman fell. Soon a real deer appeared, a big buck, majestic and proud. He slipped his antlers underneath her as delicately as though he was picking up a baby and carried her away down the hill on them.

But it was not Laura Fleischman lying there beside me. It was Sharon. Her hair smelled of sleep and home. She said, "We've come one hell of a long way from the Salamander Motel, that's for sure. My God, Antonio."

I remembered the Salamander Motel the way the Pilgrim Fathers remembered Plymouth Rock. At the Salamander Motel she had been Sharon Bebb of Armadillo, Florida, with illegal eyes and a somber mouth, and when I'd reached up and touched the towel she'd wrapped around her like a sari, it had fallen to the floor of the Salamander Motel not with a single movement but with two movements, like a leaf falling. And then like a king returning from long exile, I'd stooped to kiss the earth beneath my feet. "Thou shalt not commit adultery, dear," Brownie would have said, only it wouldn't have been adultery then. We were neither of us married in Armadillo, Florida.

The palm tree rattled on our island. Cartoon castaways—Sharon curled up there like a Playboy center-fold and me signaling for help with my flag in the air.

Sharon said, "How the hell much longer do you think Bip plans to camp out up there? And Tony and Chris, are they going to get married and move in with their wives, for Christ sake?"

I said, "Ah love, let us be true to one another." Always the English teacher. I tightened the muscles in my calves as tight as they would go, and one of them began to cramp on me. I sat up halfway in the dark to work on it.

She said, "Do me a favor, will you? Rub my back. I must have slipped a disc at the swami's this afternoon."

I said, "For we are here as on a darkling plain. Swept by confused alarms of struggle and flight."

"The left shoulder," she said.

So I rolled over on my side and we came together like spoons in a silver drawer, and Sharon said, "Makes me feel all loose like a long-necked goose," which was what the Big Bopper had been singing when I first saw her coming down the steps of the Armadillo manse in her sailor pants. I put my hand on her left shoulder and worked around under it with my thumb. There was the sound of the rain at the window.

After a while she said, "It wasn't his fault, Antonio, and it wasn't exactly my fault either." The words came out slowly as though I was pushing them out with my thumb.

After a while more she said, "Bip says sometimes you've got to take crazy chances. I don't know what he means. Maybe he knows what he means.

"That Bip," she said.

I said, "Is it all over now?"

She said, "God I hope so, Antonio."

She said a few other things too, but I'd have had to be the pillow to hear them.

There were just two more words after that, one for the earth and one for the sky. They were too powerful to say in anything but sign language.

There were two adventures that night of which this was only the first. The second happened an hour or so later. Sharon was asleep, but I was still awake listening to the weather. The rain would almost stop and then it would start again—first a few random drops, heavy, like somebody throwing pebbles at the window, then the sudden rush and clatter of it on the roof. I didn't want the rain to stop. Every time it started up, it gave me back more than just the rain again.

Eventually I heard voices. I heard them first before I could tell whose voices they were or where they came from. It could have been one of the boys talking in his sleep or somebody outside in the wet. Like the rain, they started out slow and scattered, then got noisier. There were two voices, and they came from the hall. Through our closed door, I couldn't make out the words, but I thought I caught my own name. Antonio. One of the voices was Bebb's. I wouldn't have bothered to investigate except that I was afraid it might wake up the baby. I got out of bed without waking up Sharon and stepped into the hall. The light was on in Chris's room, and the door was ajar. I went in.

Chris never opened his window at night, and the room smelled of socks and breath and the medicated ointment he used on his pimples. His bedside lamp was on, and he was sitting straight up in bed. There were white patches of ointment on his face. He looked skinny and pale and scared.

In the center of the room with his back to me stood Bebb. It was the first time I had ever seen him dressed for bed. He had on a seersucker bathrobe with his bare legs sticking out and no slippers. He didn't seem to have anything on underneath the bathrobe. He spun around when he heard me come in behind him. He said, "Antonio, I'm afraid there's been a foolish misunderstanding."

"I was dead to the world," Chris said, "and then I woke up and he was here in my room. I didn't know what was coming off. I thought the house was on fire."

I said, "What's coming off, Bip? Is the house on fire?"

Bebb said, "Antonio, that's what I've been trying to tell him. There's nothing on fire. There's nothing coming off, and there's nothing to get fussed about." Bald, plump, barefoot, he looked like Friar Tuck in his seersucker bathrobe.

"What's a person supposed to think," Chris said, "getting woken up in the middle of the night that way? I was still half asleep. I thought the house was burning down."

Bebb said, "Chris, you're half asleep still. That's the whole trouble."

"So how come you woke him up, Bip?" I said. I closed the door behind me. "For the baby," I said.

Chris said, "You can't blame a person for thinking something must be wrong when he gets woken up in the middle of the night that way. I was dead to the world."

"Nobody's blaming anybody," Bebb said. "Antonio, I'm going to explain it all out to you just like I was explaining it to Chris here when you come in. Your trousers are unbuttoned."

I buttoned them.

There was a desk in the room, and Bebb half sat, half leaned, on it. There was a picture of Miriam on the desk. It was one of those posed photographs they used to take when a girl was coming out, and it didn't look much like her. She was wearing too much lipstick, and they had her looking down over one bare shoulder as though she'd dropped something. The background lighting was what they call in the trade dramatic. I thought that was probably why Chris liked it. The rain was coming down hard again.

Bebb said, "Listen to that rain come down." He tucked the flaps of his bathrobe between his fleshy, white calves. He said, "Boys, watch and pray that ye enter not into temptation, that's what the book says. Matthew twenty-six. I've always been a praying man. There's never been—Now I don't take credit for that," he admonished us, one finger raised. "It doesn't mean you're a better man on account of you pray more. Not necessarily. It may just mean you're a man that's tempted more. I pray nights mostly. I pray for the folks I know, specially the ones that's close to me, the ones I love. Selfish? Antonio, the way I look at it, it's like electricity. You've got a heavier-duty line strung out to the ones you love, that's all. The Almighty can run more voltage through it than he can through the pitiful threads you got strung out to the rest of the world. To pray five hundred amps worth for the rest of the world—that takes a saint, boys. I'm no saint."

He said *I'm no saint* in a thoughtful way as if maybe things might have worked out differently. With luck.

Bebb said, "Tonight I was praying for the folks in this house. I knew the power was running strong. You can feel it when it's running strong. It gets hot inside. Like heartburn. I knew what the Lord was saying to me was Bebb, you get on up out of your bed and go pray for them in their rooms where they're laying fast asleep. He said to me Bebb, don't keep your candle under a bushel but carry it down there to the second floor where they are so it can give light unto all that are in the house. Sometimes even in hotels I've gotten up in the middle of the night and done it like that. It was taking a chance, opening the doors of strangers, but I done it anyway. Tonight it was Chris's door I opened. He woke up. Sometimes it's bound to happen that way. It's the chance you take."

Chris said, "I thought the house must be on fire." He was sitting up stiff in his bed with the white markings on his face.

I said, "It wasn't the house that was on fire."

Chris said, "I was dead to the world, and the next thing I knew, there I was with these cold hands on me."

Bebb said, "Cold hands, warm heart."

"You can't blame a person for being scared," Chris said.

Bebb said, "Chris, nobody's blaming anybody. That's the whole point of it."

"Why me?" Chris said. "Was I the only one you prayed for?"

Bebb said, "No, you weren't the only one. Sharon and Antonio here, I was in there first." His eyelid flickered. He said, "It's a fact when a man's asleep, there's nothing left in his face except the peace and goodness of him. Antonio, you were a real picture laying there dead to the world."

I have thought often since of Bebb's standing there in the dark of Chris's ointment-smelling room. His candle is out from under the bushel. It is burning. And I have thought too of his padding down the midnight corridors of drummers' hotels all the way from Memphis to Tallahassee taking his chances. If he was in Sharon's and my room that night too as he claimed, all I can say is neither of us saw him. But that doesn't have to mean he wasn't there. The way things were, it might be that we just didn't notice him.

Sharon was awake when I got back to bed. I said, "Bip woke Chris up praying for him, that's all. The laying on of hands."

What Sharon said was, "I wonder where to God he laid them."

17

WHEN BEBB announced around the first of June that he had decided to close down Open Heart for the summer and take Sharon and me on a trip to Europe with him, he presented me with a Bell and Howell super eight movie camera with a zoom lens and an optronic eye. He said, "Antonio, time like an ever-flowing stream bears all her sons away, but with a camera like this here, at least you can get a picture of it flowing." When I think of the events of that spring and summer, I think cinematically.

Even with as foolproof an instrument as my Bell and Howell, there are plenty of blunders an amateur can commit. He can overexpose or underexpose by failing to take into account not just the kind of light that's falling on his subject but the kind of light that's falling on him and his hopelessly literal optronic eye. He can get the distances wrong. He can pan too fast. He can forget to trip an important switch or neglect to turn a knob to where the two little black dots meet.

He can take movies of the wrong things, things that aren't moving or things that are moving too fast. A baby in its pen, for instance. He can use up his last twenty-five feet when all it's doing is lying there in the sun like an unbaked loaf and miss the moment of truth when it gets its foot in its mouth. Sometimes when interesting things are happening, he doesn't have his camera with him or gets too interested to remember to use it. Or he uses it and finds out later he forgot to put in the film.

Looking back over the movies I've taken in my life, I find that, as I might have suspected, the scenes I shot are usually not the really significant scenes. On Commencement Day, for instance, I didn't get Laura Fleischman walking across the gym stage with her diploma in her hand—she was wearing high heels and walked as though she was on a tightrope—but got instead fat Bill Urquhart with six inches of white cuff showing beneath each sleeve. The only time Laura Fleischman appears is in a crowd around a bowl of Kool Aid. She is shielding her eyes with a program. You can't even see her face.

I have found out something else which I suppose I might also have suspected but didn't. Although the scenes that I shoot aren't usually the significant ones, they tend to become the significant ones simply because I happened to shoot them. The same thing holds true of my memory. It's usually not the important things I remember best. The things I remember become important because I remembered them.

Take the day we found Mr. Golden in Bebb's barn, Sharon and I. A lot of the things he said have slipped my mind. What sticks is the barn itself. Open Heart. It was dim and shadowy with just a few bright patches where the sunlight hit. Like the Bell and Howell optronic eye, what my memory retains best are those sunlit patches—Mr. Golden's pork-pie hat, for one, the part of one wall that he'd painted red with vertical black lines running through it, the beat-up stepladder where Sharon had put down a spray of lilacs when he first came in. The lilacs stick especially, lying on that paint-spattered rung like wreckage at sea.

We'd driven over to pick up some lumber Bebb had said we could use. He was still living on our third floor with his portable TV and the suitcase hooked over the door, but he said the barn wasn't locked. We could just walk in and take what we wanted. There were some two-by-fours left over from the alterations he'd made, and I needed them for a tripod I wanted to put up for my monument which I'd decided to hang outdoors. Bebb had suggested it. He said, "Why make a thing like that and then leave it in a place can't anybody see it?" Like hiding your candle under a bushel, I suppose. So I dreamed up the idea of setting it up in the backyard where the weather could turn it gray gracefully. It seemed a better idea than painting it the way Billie Kling had suggested. The wind would blow it around and for all I knew birds might build their nests in it and children come and swing on it; but, as Bebb said, you've got to take some crazy chances.

We found Mr. Golden standing on a chair behind the pulpit. He had a can of paint in one hand and a brush in the other. He was in his shirtsleeves but otherwise dressed just as he had been the evening we'd met at the railroad station—the sneakers, the baggy pants, the pork-pie hat. He was making a picture on the wall. There was a kindergarten look about it —the side view of a man sitting in a chair. The head was too big for the body, the hand hung straight down at the side with the fingers splayed out like an udder. There was another man sitting in a chair facing him.

The man Mr. Golden was working on was yellow and the other man was white. They looked as though they had been sitting there facing each other since the beginning of time. There were other pictures on other parts of the wall.

Mr. Golden said, "Leo and me, we're like one of those old-time weather-forecasters with the little house. One man comes out with an umbrella when it's going to rain, and the other man comes out with a sunshade when it's going to be fine. I move in and Leo moves out. That's the way of it."

Sharon said, "Does he know you've moved in?"

Mr. Golden said, "He moved out, didn't he? He moved in with you folks, didn't he?" He stood on the chair smiling down at us with his lovely smile, encouraging us, now he'd shown us how to put two and two together. His face was furrowed and soft like a hand that's been in water for a long time. He said, "If there's anything half so much fun as being alive, I'd like to know what it is."

The barn was dark after the sunshine outside, and the overlapping petals of my memory's optronic eye slide back to let in as much light as possible, but it isn't enough. The reel I end up with doesn't do the scene justice. The walls were covered with Mr. Golden's pictures, but only a few of them show up clearly. The colors seem richer and deeper than they could have been in actuality—blues, greens, reds of stained-glass intensity. Stiff, flat figures are posed in all sorts of ways, but it is hard to make out who most of them are or what they're supposed to be doing. Mr. Golden himself is mostly his disembodied pork-pie hat. He said, "I'm no Michelangelo, but this isn't that whatchamacallit place either. Leo gave me leave to jazz the place up. He didn't care how I did it so long as I kept on doing it and stayed out of his hair. So this is how I did it. There must be twenty or thirty pictures no two alike, and I'm not done yet. What I put them up there to show is the story of Leo Bebb's life."

I don't think we would have known if he hadn't told us: the little flowers of Leo Bebb, in other words—the preaching to the birds, the stigmata, Brother Fire.

Sharon and I were shoulder to shoulder in the aisle between the two sections of folding chairs. Sharon had picked the lilacs by the porch steps and set them on the stepladder when we came in. Her right arm and my left arm, both bare, just barely touched—like a wedding—or the fuzz touched, or the thin sleeves of air that bare arms wear. She said, "My dad didn't mention about anybody staying here."

It was the first time I ever heard her call him Dad. I suppose you didn't call anybody Bip who had his picture upon the wall of a church.

Mr. Golden said, "That one up there by the window is jailbirds, cons. Leo used to give it to them hot and heavy right through the bars." They looked less like birds than eggs the way Mr. Golden had rendered them— rows of shaved scalps like eggs in a box. Bebb leaned out over them big and white with his wings spread. Mr. Golden said, "Sometimes after lights out he'd have the whole row belting out gospel hymns. It was enough to give you goose bumps."

Mr. Golden said, "In that one I'm still working on, it's Leo and me sitting in our little corner of perdition taking each other in the way we took each other in day in day out for five years. After that much time it's a rule of life you even start to look like each other. We used the same bucket for our needs. We worked side by side in the laundry. At night when we were asleep, his breathing and mine, it was like there was only one man breathing. Sometimes they even come in to check."

He said, "Pent up like that closer than marriage in a place the size of a box it gets to where after a while you don't have to *tell* the whole true story of your life to each other. You just catch each other's life from each other like a head cold. We used to play a game to make the time pass. It was a game of imagining. Leo would say something or I would. Let's say it was *raspberry* Leo said. Then we'd both start working on raspberries. We'd work on raspberries till it was like you could feel a raspberry in your mouth with the little red beads of it and the hole in the middle where the stem come out of. We'd work on raspberries till you could taste the true taste of a raspberry which is what a raspberry is, it is mostly a taste and shape in your mouth like summer and like all the raspberries you ever ate in your life. The first one of us that could say he'd dreamed up a raspberry lock, stock and barrel, the whole truth of a raspberry and nothing but the truth, he'd be the one was the winner of that round. You didn't even have to take it on trust he was telling the truth. You could tell from his face whether he was. Then maybe I'd say *sheets*. We didn't have sheets. We had sleazy gray blankets that looked like old newspapers that's been left out in the rain. They had about as much warmth to them as old newspapers. We'd commence working on the feel and smell and all of clean sheets. We'd get so we could hear the sound your toenails make when you slip down between a pair of clean sheets on a cool night. A brass band. A kiss. You name it, we imagined it. The game was to see which of us could get there first. It made the time pass."

A beam of sun turned the crown of Mr. Golden's pork-pie hat gold, a golden crown. He said, "We'd try people sometime. People aren't for beginners. You got to work up to people. You can't just stop at their face either, though even the face isn't the easiest thing in the world to get— their *real* face the way it moves around in life, I mean, not just a snapshot of their face in some one particular look it has. You got to keep going till you can hear the sound a person's voice makes. You got to see how the clothes hang on him and the way he works his hands and feet. The way you know you've got him right is when you've got him so he starts in doing things in your imagination you didn't try on purpose to imagine him doing. Sometimes we'd spend hours on just one person. Once we tried our fathers. There's a picture for you. Two cons in the pitch dark spending half the night trying to dream up their old dead dads."

He said, "You don't have to believe this if you don't want to, but if you dream up a person all the way, sometimes it isn't just you yourself can see him. That picture over there is the father of Leo Bebb the way I saw him though I never laid eyes on him in all my life."

Bebb's father was lying on his back with his arms crooked up into the air and a heavy head of hair spread out behind him. He looked like a fallen tree.

Nearby was what I took to be Bebb raising Brownie from the dead in Knoxville. Brownie's half-sitting figure was outlined in a rainbow of different colors. The outermost band of the rainbow was white, and Bebb was reaching out to touch it with his white hand.

Bebb was selling Bibles. He was driving a pickup truck with the Bibles piled up as high as the roof of the cab in back. The Bibles were red and looked like bricks. Each one had a small cross painted on it.

Bebb was standing under a palm tree with a swatch of blue sea behind him. There was a white balloon coming out of his mouth as though there should be some words written in it, but the balloon was empty.

Bebb was sitting on a bench beside somebody in black glasses with her hair sticking out like a sunburst. There was a baby lying across their laps. Lucille had the head and Bebb had the feet.

Bebb was shaking hands with a red Indian. The Indian had on a feathered headdress that hung down to his heels. The yellow paint of the top feather had dripped down into the blue paint of the one beneath it, and the feathers beneath those had been outlined but not yet colored in.

Above the door Bebb was flying. His arms stretched out straight from his shoulders. His toes pointed directly behind him. His face was round and white.

Mr. Golden said, "Thou knowest my downsitting and mine uprising. Thou art acquainted with all my ways. That's the story of that one."

I said, "Poor Lucille, she always said he was from outer space."

Sharon said, "She'd have gotten a bang out of that one."

"That one," Mr. Golden said, "is a whole lot of things in a nutshell."

Sharon said, "He looks like he's been shot out of a cannon."

I said, "He's got wings." They were small wings sprouting from the knobs of his shoulders and flattened out beneath the crossbeam. They looked inadequate to support his weight.

Mr. Golden had his hands in the pockets of his voluminous pants. He hitched them up, and there was the clinking of coins. It sounded as if he was carrying a small fortune in his pockets. He said, "If I take the wings of the morning and dwell in the uttermost parts of the sea, even there shall Thy hand lead me and Thy right hand shall hold me." With his oversized body and skinny neck, he looked like a turtle craning up out of his shell. He said, "If I ascend up into heaven, Thou art there. If I descend into hell, behold Thou art there."

I said, "Lucille had this crazy theory about elevators too."

Mr. Golden said, "It's a rule of life if a person comes to know as much about you as I come to know about Leo Bebb, sharing near to every living minute with him day in day out up to and including the imaginations of his heart, when you see him coming at you down the pike, you am-scray. It's a natural thing. All I'd have to say is Leo, fork out or it'll be all over town how you and me were roommates for five long years. Either you make it worth my while or I'll hang your downsittings and your uprisings out on the line for every Tom, Dick and Harry to gawk at. He ought to know I'd never say that. I've never said it. But that's what he's afraid of. These pictures, nobody'd know what they were all about unless somebody was to explain them out."

Sharon said, "Well, you can't hardly blame him for being afraid the way you keep tailing him. How come you keep doing it anyway?"

Mr. Golden said, "Take a look at that one over there." Not flying or preaching or raising anybody from the dead, in the one that Mr. Golden pointed at with his delicate hand, Bebb was just standing still. His eyes were closed. He was holding his hands out with the palms turned up as though it was raining and he wanted to feel the rain in his hands. It was the only picture so far that approached being a likeness of Bebb, not just a white shape cut out with a cookie-cutter—the firm, tight H of his mouth on its hinges, the jut of his ear-lobes. But from the waist down he looked like nothing on earth. From the waist down he was a flaming meteor, a Ringling Brothers hoop of fire for lions and tigers to leap through, the concentric circles of an archery butt or wheels within wheels from outermost red through orange and saffron to yellow, to innermost white-hot bullseye. Underneath, his tidy black shoes stuck out like andirons.

Mr. Golden said, "They didn't lock him up for playing tiddley-winks, you know. They didn't lock me up for playing tiddely-winks either."

Up to this point I had thought of Mr. Golden as his face. I had thought of him as that keen, withered, oddly boyish face with that lovely, oddly girlish smile, and I had thought of the rest of him as a kind of cumbersome diversion or disguise. It struck me here that maybe it was his face that was the disguise.

He said, "Leo knows what I was locked up for same as I know what he was locked up for. For every picture I've made of him, he could make a picture of me. He knows my downsittings and my uprisings, and that's how come I'd tail him to Timbuktu if I had to. The way I see it, everybody needs to have a person knows the truth about him, the whole bare-ass truth and nothing but the truth. It's a fact of life."

"Why?" Sharon said.

Mr. Golden said, "Search me and know my heart, that's why. Try me and know my thoughts." On the wall behind him, Bebb was straddling his fire like a flying saucer upended. "See if there be any wicked way in me," Mr. Golden said, "and lead me in the way everlasting."

Sharon said, "You and Bip must have had a ball quoting Scripture to each other."

Mr. Golden said, "Of course this paint's all water-base. It'll wash off easy as pie if he wants to wash it off."

My idea that Mr. Golden was an angel died hard that morning in Bebb's barn. In a way I suppose you could say it never died entirely. Angels have been known to turn up in queerer places than jail, after all. Or he might have been a fallen angel. If Mr. Golden didn't look like an angel in any regulation sense, he didn't look much like anything else in any regulation sense either. I was never sure—and Sharon was no help— whether he was a very old man who looked remarkably young or a man about Bebb's age who looked remarkably old.

I didn't give up easily and to some degree have never given up the idea of Mr. Golden as the Hound of Heaven that poor Bip fled down the nights and down the days, down all the labyrinthine ways, and then some, that were rendered there on the walls of Open Heart: Bip as Happy Hooligan, Foxy Grandpa, Major Hoople, bluffing his way through frame after frame of that stained-glass comic strip which was his whatchama-callit, his life, and Mr. Golden as Mandrake the Magician or Mr. Coffee Nerves relentless in his pursuit, inexorable in his love. Bip on the wings of the morning like Buck Rogers, and Mr. Golden never far behind like Killer Kane in pork-pie hat and sneakers.

The biggest single objection to my theory that Mr. Golden was really an angel is that he did go on and on so that morning, which raises the question whether anybody can be an angel who comes that close to boring you to death. He went on about jail. He reminisced to Sharon and me about the laundry where he and Bebb had worked shoulder to shoulder day in day out drying and folding gray coveralls, about the view of the ice-cream parlor they could get from the exercise yard and how they played their imagining game through every flavor they could think of before they were done—fudge ripple, and cherry vanilla, pistachio, ba- nana, maple walnut. He dreamed up old friends they had had and old enemies until Sharon and I—sitting by then on either side of the aisle in the folding chairs—could almost see them as dreams of our own. Pete Piscatelli baptized by Bebb in the big tub where the blankets were man- gled. Snapper MacFarland who got them all put on crackers and water by dousing himself with cleaning fluid and touching himself off with a Zippo lighter in the mop closet. Young Bobby Cort and Teaser Sprague who came to Bebb one day and asked him to marry them. "Did he do it?" Sharon asked, and Mr. Golden's answer was to point to a kind of triptych where the sun fell—black bars on a red ground with Bebb in the middle and at waist-level, on either side of him, what looked like Kew- pie dolls with big blue eyes and round cheeks and out of Bebb's mouth a balloon that had written on it *Suffer little children and forbid them not.*

Mr. Golden sat down too finally, the Bell and Howell zoom lens retracting until he looked about the size of a Kewpie doll himself, everything around him dark except for the jeweled blur of Sharon's lilacs in the foreground. He talked about his bladder trouble. He told us he couldn't take aspirin because it made him bleed at the rectum. He said Bebb had told him he could stay on there at the house as long as he wanted that summer, but he knew Bebb was going to Europe and he didn't want to stay on past that.

Which brings up the second biggest objection to the angel theory. Does an angel have a rectum? Can an angel bleed?

Whatever the answer to that, Mr. Golden eventually helped us carry the two-by-fours out to the car where the sun must have been too much for the optronic eye because my last shot of him is badly overexposed. Except for the merest suggestion of his withered, boyish face and the pale sand-color of his billowing pants, you can hardly make Mr. Golden out in the storm of light that rages all around him.

When Bebb sent us back to his place to pick up the two-by-fours, he must have known we'd probably run into Mr. Golden. He must have known there was a good chance Mr. Golden would unburden himself to us. He must have suspected we'd find out that he, Bebb, had been pulling the wool over our eyes all those months by making us think he didn't know who Mr. Golden was any more than we did. Maybe he wanted us to find out. Maybe it was just one of the chances he took.

On the drive home we discussed whether or not we should let on to him what had happened. Sharon was for not telling him a word. She said it would be like calling him a liar to his face. I said that by not telling him a word, it would be like showing him that we were liars ourselves. She said he could swallow that better than the other, and I ended up deciding she was probably right. So when we got home, we didn't say a thing. Bebb did.

Some kids had come over to see if I would tell them how they'd done in English before the grades were officially out. Bebb was sitting cross-legged on the front lawn in his shirtsleeves with six or eight of them grouped around him. Tony was there. Bebb was talking in an animated way. Everybody seemed to be listening intently. You could tell he was enjoying himself. When he saw Sharon and me coming up the driveway, he stopped abruptly and waved in our direction. While his listeners' heads were turned, he got up and disappeared around the back of the house. He was moving fast, tripped over the garden hose as he went.

We stopped to talk to the kids, Sharon and I. Laura Fleischman was among them, and I think it was the first time that she and Sharon ever met face to face. It was one of many moments I wish I'd had my Bell and Howell to record. The life and loves of Antonio Parr. I'm not sure they shook hands when I introduced them, but say they did. It was that mo-

ment when their hands touched that I would have zoomed in on—Laura
Fleischman's hand, dancing-school damp, that I had touched for an
instant once in her mother's straw bag at Grand Central. And Sharon's
hand. For a moment it was more than just their two hands that came
together. It was the Salamander Motel and *l'ombre des jeunes filles en
fleur*; it was truth and fiction, earth and sky. What the hands of those
two young women held together in one piece for about a foot and a half
of Eastman Kodak Kodacolor was me. But I didn't have my camera with
me, of course, and I didn't have the grades they wanted either.

I didn't see Bebb again till suppertime. When he didn't answer
Sharon's yell, I went upstairs and found him in his stuffy third-floor room.
He was sitting tipped back in a chair with his feet upon the window sill
looking at a TV aerial across the street.

Without turning around, he said, "I suppose you ran into Golden
this afternoon."

I told him we had.

He said, " 'I was hungry and you gave me food. I was a stranger and
you welcomed me.' Antonio, that's what Jesus said. It's the command-
ment he laid upon us—to treat the stranger just like it was Jesus himself.
Now this Golden, he's some kind of nut. He's been dogging me since I
don't know when. God only knows what he wants. But he has nowhere
to lay his head, Antonio. So I went and took him in like he was Jesus."

I said, "He seems to have a lot to get off his chest, Bip."

Bebb said, "Show me the man that doesn't. Show me the man
doesn't have his whole life to get off his chest when you come right down
to it."

I said, "Have you got everything you need up here?" It was a small,
bare room. There were no curtains at the one window, and the shade looked
like something that might have wrapped a mummy once. I thought of
the picture of Bebb and Mr. Golden facing each other in their chairs
in a room like this, Bebb's hand hanging at his side like an udder.

Bebb said, "You don't want to believe more than half what he says.
He's a lonely man, and he's a wound-up man. He's wound-up something
wicked." He clasped his hands behind his neck.

He said, "You take those young folks I was shooting the breeze with
out there this afternoon before you come back. They're wound-up too.
Those crazy drugs they use—they come right out and told me so theirselves. The desires of the flesh. Don't any of them appear to know that
stuff's dynamite, Antonio. It's enough to blow their life straight to kingdom come if they aren't careful. They go around touching it off with
each other like it was three-for-a-nickel Chinese crackers. Fed up with
school. Fed up with the U.S.A. Fed up with God. They're the hope of
this world, Antonio, and most of the time they don't know their tail
from first base."

He let the front legs of his chair come down to the floor with a thump and swung around to face me. There was more of the old Bebb in him than I'd seen since Lucille's death. A fly lit on his bald head, and he didn't even notice it.

He said, "Antonio, when we get back from overseas sometime round about next—" He interrupted himself and pointed one finger at me as though I was a place on a map he was trying to find his way on. "I'm not kidding myself. It's like I said to John Turtle, Open Heart hasn't panned out like I hoped. It's the right angle, but it's the wrong place and the wrong people. Jesus has not graced that place with his presence up to now. Next fall when school starts, I'm going to start something bran' new. The new generation, Antonio. I'm going to bring the gospel of Jesus straight to the Pepsi generation, hit them right between the eyes with it. That movie house down to the shopping center, I'm going to find out can I rent it afternoons when there's no show on. All that youth and beauty, Antonio. All that pep and pizazz. Kids like Chris and Tony. I'm going to head them out for Beulah Land if it's the last thing I do. I'm going to round me up an organ and somebody knows how to play on it. Maybe they'll let me have Herman Redpath's shipped on from the ranch. I'm going to serve up good things to eat and drink, healthy things. I'm going to have balloons and ice cream and dancing . . ."

He kept on going until finally Sharon came upstairs to say the hamburgers were cold as a clam-wagon, and then he went on a while longer to both of us.

While he talked I thought of Mr. Golden back at the barn painting up the story of Bebb's life. I thought of all those pictures he'd already painted up and of all the ones he'd have to keep on painting up as time went by. Like Flash Gordon or Captain Marvel, Bebb might go on for years. I tried to think of Mr. Golden the way Bebb said he thought of him—a lonely, wound-up Jesus with no place to lay his head, no place to hang his pork-pie hat. And then, not for the first time either, Bebb seemed to read my mind. He spoke Mr. Golden's name.

"Clarence Golden," he said. "I might just put old Clarence Golden on the payroll to stay on and be my new Brownie. I'll need all the help I can get. He may not be Dwight L. Moody or Gypsy Smith, but he knows his Scripture, that's for sure. Leastwise he ought to know it," he said, his eyelid fluttering. "God knows there was a time he heard enough of it. Day in day out for five years give or take a little."

18

SHARON said, "Hey Antonio, guess what. I was changing him in his crib and he was laying there with his little pecker pointed up and when I leaned over to put the powder on, he let me have it right in the eye like a water pistol. Laugh—he almost knocked himself out. Don't tell me he doesn't have a lot of Bip in him. Sometimes I wonder if I was really adopted like Bip says. I mean I was adopted all right, but maybe Bip's the one got my mother in trouble. I wouldn't put it past him. Anyway I hate like hell leaving the poor kid here with Billie Kling to look after him. Having her give you a bath would be like falling in the Electrolux."

I said it would only be for a few weeks and after all Chris would be around too. Mrs. Kling and Charlie had agreed to move in and look after things while we were away.

She said, "With that blockbuster for a mother and Chris for a father —it's going to head him straight for the shrink when he grows up. I think I'll stay home and let you two boys go off by yourselves."

She didn't, of course, but at the time I believe she really thought she would. She'd given herself a shampoo and was on her knees in the back-yard with her forehead on the grass and her hair spread out in front of her to dry.

She didn't give up the trip but she gave up Evelyn Wood and the swami and Anita those last few weeks before we left. She said she needed all her time to bone up on where we were going, which was to be England mostly with a week in Paris at the end. Bebb said England was the place we ought to concentrate on because it was the country our country came from, and Sharon said she didn't know a damn thing about England. She said they didn't tell you a thing about England at Armadillo High because they hadn't heard about it yet. So I gave her books to read which she used her Evelyn Wood on, zigzagging her hand down page after page at a speed that made it possible to cover centuries in an evening. The history of England must have passed before her like those time-lapse movies of flowers blooming or caterpillars turning into butterflies—Hastings, Bosworth Field, Waterloo, VE Day, melting into one continuous free-for-all, kings and queens tottering by on the run like old newsreels. Elizabeth, grainy and out of focus, flickering by with her white horse and her red wig, to inspect the troops at Tilbury on the eve of the Armada. Charles the First stepping, light-struck, out of a second-story window at White-hall and bouncing like a ball up the steps of the scaffold. Victoria giving birth the way a slot-machine gives Juicyfruit, her lumpish successors with their eyes too close together waving to the crowds out of limousines.

After a lot of reading Sharon said, "I don't know a hell of a lot more than I knew to start with. All I know's how much I don't know, and I knew that already."

Which raises the question what *did* Sharon know, if not about English history, then about herself, about me, about the whole comic strip of things that as far as I know may be running serially somewhere.

One day I showed her Lucille's *très riches heures*. I'd never so much as mentioned its existence to anybody before. Evelyn Wood herself couldn't have zigzagged her way through Lucille's handwriting, especially with those flowers scattered all through it, and Sharon read it over, word by word, sitting at the kitchen table with Bill in his playpen drowsing over his bottle and the rattle and whir of a lawnmower from across the street. When she finished, she went back and read out loud the part where Lucille had made lists of things: the things she had to hold on to, her good memories, her blessings.

Sharon said, "Poor Luce. I didn't know any of that. I knew there had to be things like that, but I didn't know what they were. I guess everybody's got things like that there isn't anybody else in the world knows them or wants to know them or who you even want to have know them. When Bip finds out about those pictures in the barn, he's going to have a shit hemorrhage."

Except for the time I was with her in the hospital just after Bill was born, it was the only time I had ever seen her cry. Just her eyes cried. The rest of her face went about business as usual, whatever that was, the shady business of Sharon's face. Her tears might as well have come from the outside of her, like rain, as from the inside of her. She didn't give them the time of day.

She said, "Sometimes when we make it together at night, I think about how it's like when you ride a surfboard. When the water's rough, it can be dangerous as hell if you don't know what you're doing and sometimes even if you do know what you're doing. You better damn well hold on tight if you know what's good for you."

She rolled Lucille's flowered stationery back up into a tube and looked at her bare foot through it. She said, "Sometimes I just shut my eyes and hang on to you in the dark like you're the surfboard."

She knew other things.

When Miriam and I were little, we had a game we often played. You needed two pieces of paper and two pencils to play it. Miriam would take one piece of paper and, closing her eyes, would make some kind of a scribble on it, some haphazard snarl of line or crisscross or whirlamajig. I would do the same on the other piece of paper, and then we would exchange them. The game was for each of us to turn the whirlamajig into a picture, to incorporate the scribble into a drawing that looked like something. It didn't matter what it ended up looking like. The trick was to make it end up looking like *something*.

Our getting married for instance—the sheer fluke of it. Me, Tono Parr (not Antonio in those days because Miriam said it made me sound too much like an organ grinder) taking the Silver Meteor down to Armadillo with a half-baked idea of writing an exposé of Bebb and his diploma mill. Me fresh from the ritual embraces and stately pecks of Ellie Pierce, from the endless box-step of our engagement. Me very Madison Avenue, very Central Park Zoo with all the lions and tigers and crimson-assed baboons safe behind bars. My twin sister in the shape of an A dying under the care of a cancer specialist who looked like Groucho Marx. My cat left to smolder in solitary at the vet's. My fifth of Dewar's in case the going got rough.

And Sharon. Sharon Bebb fresh from God knows what but fresh as the world's first morning in her white sailor pants and bare feet. Her sleep-smelling hair that divided over her ears, those Public Enemy eyes and shattering, hambone smile. Daisy May with all the local Li'l Abners laid end to end at her feet. Jai alai at West Palm. The beach at Fort Lauderdale. Rum and Coke. Sea and Ski. Elvis Presley with green fuzz down one cheek on Lucille's TV. The gift shop next to Holy Love where she worked part time selling shrunken heads, seashell-studded wastebaskets, coconut husks carved into cannibals. Brownie to teach her Scripture through a cloud of after-shave, Bip to take her on occasional trips on the Lord's business to Atlanta, Memphis, Charleston, once to New York, where she saw Marlon Brando getting into a cab. Without knowing it could we have passed each other on the street then?

Bebb, of course, was the one who introduced us. We dallied twice at the Salamander Motel and once in her bedroom in the Manse with Ringo Starr and Oral Roberts looking down from the wall. Later in a moonlight-colored dress she came toward me with her arm in a sling at Herman Redpath's barbecue, and Bebb said, "Behold new Jerusalem coming down out of heaven like a bride adorned for her husband," and for lack of anything better I asked her to marry me, and she did.

That was the whirlamajig. The trick was to turn it into a picture.

All this Sharon must have known better than I knew it. I was the one who located the Sutton house, landed the teaching job, took in my two nephews to live with us, but then all I did was let it lie there like a scrawl on the page. She was the one who tried to make it look like something.

She took up yoga, took up the guitar, took up speed-reading, to fill in some of the empty spaces, I suppose. She drew in a line between Chris and the baby, tried to strengthen the thin curlicue between her world and mine by coming to all those swimming meets and football games and track practices. At first anyway she fitted Tony into the picture by surrounding him with shapes that anyone could identify at a glance—her quick, semi-comic rages over his messy room, his poor grades, his late hours and early loves, followed by precarious reconciliations, interspersed with weepings together over grade B movies and the gags they played on each other, war-games, like the time he hung up the African violets in his jockstrap, the day she filled his Wildroot Cream Oil bottle with Elmer's glue. It wasn't the most artful picture in the world, but granted the scribble she had to work with, it could have been worse. It was a picture anyway, a picture you could live with, at least for a while.

She changed it later. She changed a line here, an empty space there, shaded in areas that had been blank before, darkening them, until the shape that came to enclose her and Tony was a shape that for a while I don't think either of them could identify. When she did identify it, saw the shape of what was probably to come as well as the shape of what had certainly come already, I think she incorporated it into a new and different picture mainly because a *ménage à trois* looked to her more like a living, breathing *ménage* than the earlier, vague tangle had.

Looking back, I give Sharon credit for knowing at some level of her being that in a marriage maybe any shape is better than no shape at all, and I suspect that her infidelity with Tony had a basically geometric impulse behind it, that there was more Euclid than Eros for her in the triangle she put together out of herself, my nephew and me.

What I had put together was also a triangle of sorts, my monument, my Thing, and following Bebb's suggestion and using his lumber, I set it up outdoors before we left for England. Tony helped me. We bolted the two-by-fours together into a kind of tripod and then lugged my masterpiece out of the shed to hang it up. It weighed a ton, and the day was so hot and humid we were dripping with sweat before we were through.

At one point in the process Tony tried to lift it not by the base but by the slender, slatted cross-piece that the wooden tongues curved down through. The crosspiece snapped in his hands and one of the tongues snapped with it.

I said, "Watch it, Tarzan, that's my life you've got hold of," and before I knew it, he was saying again, "God I'm sorry, Tono. I'm sorry," with his face glistening. For the second time, like the night I asked Sharon if she thought we were washed up, I found that I had precipitated by accident a conversation that otherwise I wouldn't have touched with a ten-foot pole.

I said, "Forget it. It's nothing that can't be fixed," and he said, "I don't know what's wrong with me. Everything I touch seems to turn to shit."

I said, "The trouble is you don't know your own strength."

He said, "The trouble is I'm a natural-born yuk."

He said, "You put it together just the way you want it, and then I come along and fuck it up."

I said, "You haven't fucked it up."

There is a piece on the sinking of the *Titanic* that I sometimes used to read my English classes when I ran out of things to talk to them about. It ended with a description of the iceberg itself the way the survivors saw it from their lifeboats. "Tinted with sunrise" is a phrase I remember— the great pyramid of ice as it floated there, glittering and majestic, on the heaving blue breast of the sea. Some such words as that. And there we stood, my namesake and I, looking at my monument swaying idly from its chain with the raw pine turned almost gold in the sunshine and all those knobs and dowels and discs passing each other by as it slowly rotated. It seemed to be involved in some obscure and fearsome action. You hardly noticed the broken part.

"There is no excellent beauty that hath not some strangeness in the proportion," I said. "Maybe you've even improved it."

Tony was watching the thing with the same inward-looking frown that I've seen him run the last lap of a mile with—half St. John of the Cross contemplating the Trinity, half a man when the dentist hits a nerve. He said, "You and Sharon won't have to keep on going away places. I'll be graduating next year. You won't have me in your hair forever."

I said, "The only reason we're going away is Bip asked us."

"Why do you think Bip asked you?" Tony said.

I said, "Why do you think Bip does anything?"

Tony said, "Does Sharon know I told you?"

I nodded.

"Ever since then it's like it never happened. That's almost the worst part," he said. "I go my way and she goes her way and it's like nothing ever happened."

I said, "Maybe nothing did."

"It did," he said.

He said, "If something like that's not important, nothing's important. People oughtn't to be able to just walk away from a thing like that."

I said, "If you'd just walked away, you wouldn't be talking about it now. You don't have to talk about it."

"That night I told you," he said, "you should have thrown me out."

"Would that have helped?" I said.

"I don't know," he said.

My monument had all but come to a standstill, and I reached out with my foot and gave it enough of a shove to set it in motion again, gave us something to look at besides just each other.

Tony said, "Either we ought to be in love with each other or we ought to steer clear of each other, but she's just the same to me as she always was and I'm just the same to her. We came the closest to each other people can come. There isn't any closer than that. It ought to make a difference afterwards. If it doesn't make a difference afterwards, you're not even people, you're animals."

I wanted to tell him that everything you do makes a difference afterwards including even the things you just dream about doing. I wanted to tell him that life keeps piling up till you can no more walk away from it than you can walk away from your own shadow just as at that moment Bebb's life was piling up on the walls of Open Heart. I wanted to say something useful and wise to the roly-poly child my sister Miriam had left me. He stood there with the muscles in his jaw working as he stared ahead at my monument majestic in the spring sun, and I wanted to tell him something that might save him years of confusion if not his soul, but all that came out was, "In one way it doesn't matter half as much as you think. In another way it matters a hell of a lot more."

He said, "I'd do anything in the world if I could make it like it never happened. Honest to God I would, Tono."

"You don't have to do that," I said. "That's for me to do. I'll do it for you."

"But it did happen," he said. "Nobody can change what's already happened. You said so yourself."

I said, "I can't change it for you, but maybe I can change it for me. In time I think I can make it for myself as if it never happened. At least I can make other things happen around it so it won't louse things up. It might even help somehow."

"What do you call that?" he said. Looking at me through Miriam's dark eyes, he stood there stock-still like somebody trying hard not to rock a lifeboat.

"Call it anything you want," I said. "Call it a going-away present."

With a shake of his head, he tossed his hair back. "How about Sharon?" he said.

Hearing him say her name put the whole thing suddenly to the test, seeing his lips shape her name in such a blurred and private way as if he and she were together in one boat and I was alone in another. For a second I wasn't sure I could put my money where my mouth was. *Husbands and wives, little children lost their lives,* the old song ran through my head, *it was sad when that great ship went down.* Then I found I could. Just could. "Sharon will be all right," I said. "You don't have to worry about Sharon."

I don't know what difference, if any, my words made for him, but at least they made a difference in his frown. He was still frowning, but he was frowning out at me now, not in at himself, and he started to say something when the kitchen door slammed and Bebb was there calling out from the back porch. Bebb said, "Antonio, take a squint at these passport photos. Yours makes you look like you haven't eaten a square since Noah."

"Brother, can you spare a dime?" I said.

Bebb had walked out to us by then, and he put one arm around my nephew's shoulder. He said, "Listen, boys, by the time we get back from overseas I won't be able to spare a nickel. I'll be broker than the Ten Commandments."

"That's what you call broke," Tony said.

Months later when I finally got around to editing and splicing together the movies I took of our trip with Bebb's Bell and Howell, this is the scene I would like to have started them out with. I would have superimposed the title on it—OUR TRIP ABROAD in block capitals and behind it a long shot of the three of us just as we were standing there in the backyard: Bebb with his arm around Tony, me with my passport picture in my hand, the dangling monument. More than when the whistle blasted and the SS *France* started to pull away from Pier 92, it was the moment when we actually set off for foreign shores.

19

BEBB fell in love on the boat. She was seventy-five years old, a widow, and her name was Gertrude Conover. She was vigorous and wiry with a habit of tilting her chin down toward one shoulder when she walked so that she always seemed to be moving sideways. She had blue hair, lots of money, and came from Princeton, New Jersey. She had a seat at our table, and the first day out she told Bebb that they had met before. "It was in Egypt," she said. Bebb said that he had never been to Egypt. "That is a matter of opinion," Gertrude Conover said.

Bebb in love. Bebb leaning over the rail of the observation deck mooning out at the receding wake. He said, "Antonio, think if a man was to fall overboard. A ship the size of this one, by the time it got itself swung around and headed back, a man would have drifted off so far it would be like looking for a needle in a haystack. Think how it would be bobbing around out there by yourself in all those acres of ocean with nothing to catch hold of. Think of all those fathoms underneath you full of creatures like the leviathan of Scripture who esteemeth iron like straw and maketh the sea to boil like a pot. The lonesomeness of it, Antonio. The awful lonesomeness of floating around out there all by yourself waiting for the end to come with not another living soul to give a hang whether you sink or swim any more than the ocean gives a hang."

The breeze bounced Gertrude Conover's blue hair softly up and down. She had a way of smiling at you as though what she was smiling

at was not what you were saying but what you were going to say next. She
said, "Whoever put the idea into your head the ocean doesn't care whether
you sink or swim with all that salt in it to hold you up?"

Bebb said, "Salt or no salt, the ocean would just as leave drown you
as wet your drawers. It's the nature of things like the ocean not to give
a hang."

Gertrude Conover said, "Of course they give a hang. Sometimes
people don't give a hang because that's the way people are, but everything else does."

Bebb said, "You're an optimist, Gertrude Conover."

Gertrude Conover said, "I'm a Theosophist."

One day at lunch there was the usual basket of *petits pains* on the
table. After helping herself to one, Gertrude Conover took another,
split it, buttered it, and placed it for Bebb on his butter plate. She did it
in an absent-minded way, not even talking to him at the time, but you
would have thought she'd given him the shirt off her back. He said, "I
never set eyes on Gertrude Conover till the day we come aboard, but it's
like I'd known her always. After she buttered the roll and set it on my
plate, she looked at me and said, 'I don't know why I did that.' What
would make her go and do a thing like that for somebody she doesn't
hardly even know?"

"How about in Egypt?" Sharon said.

Bebb said, "Sharon, you know as well as I do this is the first time I
ever set my foot outside the U.S.A."

He said, "She didn't go and make a big production out of it. She
just went ahead and buttered it so easy and natural it was like I was her
oldest friend."

I said, "Maybe she was just buttering it for herself."

Bebb said, "She'd already buttered one for herself. Besides, she put
it on my plate. Then afterwards she said she didn't know why she'd done
it."

"What's a Theosophist anyhow?" Sharon said. "She's the first one
I ever ran into."

Bebb said, "I'll tell you one thing. If what she is is a Theosophist,
the world could stand a pack more of them."

After dinner the four of us sometimes met in the lounge on the
Pont Véranda to play bingo. Gertrude Conover drank *crème de menthe
frappé* which turned her lips green. Bebb said he'd never seen a lady with
green lips before. Gertrude Conover said, "My, wouldn't your parishioners be glad to hear that."

Bebb asked her once about the time she thought she'd met him in
Egypt, and Gertrude Conover said it had happened ages ago. She said,

"You were a priest of Ptah. Your name was Ptah-sitti. The Pharaoh used to take you on lion hunts with him because he thought you brought him good luck. You got to be one of his pets. You didn't even have to shave your eyebrows off like the other priests, and you had the run of the palace. Then you got into hot water."

They were reclining side by side in their deck chairs with cups of bouillon on their laps. A humid breeze was blowing. Bebb had on a sport-shirt and the kind of sunglasses that look like mirrors from the outside.

He said, "What kind of trouble, Gertrude Conover?"

Gertrude Conover was leaning back in her chair with her eyes closed. She said, "The Pharaoh had a ward by the name of Uttu. He had killed her father in some free-for-all, and he took her in as part of his household. She wasn't pretty, but she was neat and clean considering the age she lived in, and she played the flute nicely. She and Ptah-sitti became inti-mate—they both liked good music and had many other tastes in com-mon—and after a certain amount of time, she found out she was pregnant by him. My dear, when the Pharaoh got wind of it, it sent him straight up the wall. He threatened torture unless she told who her lover was, and though she might have let them torture her to save Ptah-sitti's skin, she was afraid for what it might do to their unborn child, so she gave the poor man away. He was condemned to be impaled. It was an open and shut case."

"That's some way to go," Bebb said.

Gertrude Conover still had her eyes closed. She said, "You were very gallant about it. You said it was little enough to pay for the pleasure of having known Uttu, but luckily you didn't have to pay after all. The Pharaoh was afraid it might bring him bad luck on lion hunts to kill a priest of Ptah so he had the sentence reduced. He had one of your eyes put out instead and called it even-Steven."

Bebb said, "He must have had a heart as big as all outdoors."

I was sitting on the other side of him trying to write a postcard to Chris and Tony, and he turned to me and shrugged. Then he said, "Gertrude Conover, look me in the eye and tell me you're not making this whole thing up."

She opened her eyes and looked at him, but she didn't tell him a word. If she hadn't said she was seventy-five, I would have guessed she wasn't much older than Bebb himself. She had a young mouth, relaxed at the corners. Her blue eyes were faded, but there was plenty of life in them as she lay there looking sideways at Bebb.

"Where were you while all this was going on?" Bebb said.

Gertrude Conover said, "I was Uttu. I died in a papyrus marsh giving birth to the priest's baby. The baby died too, poor little thing."

Bebb said, "I'm sorry."

Gertrude Conover said, "There's no use crying over spilt milk."

* * *

It would be nice to be able to report that the end of Bebb's and Gertrude Conover's shipboard romance was marriage—that after all the centuries that followed on the tragic liaison of Ptah-sitti and Uttu, they finally met aboard the SS *France* bound from New York to Southampton and made it legal. But their romance never had an end in either sense of the word. It had no end in the sense of fulfillment because they never got married. It also had no end in the sense of termination because they continued to keep in touch with each other from that time forward, and if Gertrude Conover's theosophy holds water, they may go right on keeping in touch with each other from one incarnation to the next indefinitely.

A book has an end in both senses. Page follows page, chapter follows chapter, and that is that. The end. And by the time you reach the last page, everything has ended up saying something too. The plot has been unrolled to its full length, the loose threads have been drawn together, and you close the book up with the feeling that the author has made the point which one way or another all authors always make, which is that for good or ill events have a shape. The characters have all *gotten* someplace. Maybe, as at the end of *King Lear*, where the good people and the bad people die, both, and just poor, hapless Edgar is left to stammer the final curtain down as best he can, the place the characters get is really no place and the shape is shapelessness; but that's as valid a way of making the point as any if you can stomach it. Even Lear's story ends, in other words, but Bebb's and Gertrude Conover's never did, and neither did Sharon's and mine, at least not in any sense you can put your finger on. All our lives that summer were less like a book that ends and more like a comic strip where episode follows episode without ever getting anyplace in particular. Or like a home movie where as soon as one reel is through, there is always another reel in the making, where one shot is apt to have as much or as little point as any other and that is probably all the point you're going to get.

When we got to London, we found a letter waiting for us from Brownie. It was full of news. Lily Trionka was pregnant again, and though Brownie was worried about her because it came so hard on the heels of her last miscarriage, he explained that she had given up ice cream and promised not to work out on the exercycle during her pregnancy, and those were good signs. Maudie Redpath had given her blackbird dance another try, and some said that this time the magic was so nearly successful that she was able to fly five or six feet off the ground from the barbecue pit to the swimming pool where she fell into the water and would have drowned if Harry Hocktaw hadn't fished her out apparently none the worse for wear. John Turtle had used some of his inheritance from Herman Redpath to start a Tom Thumb golf course and was making money hand over fist. Holy Love had put in air-conditioning.

In his last paragraph, Brownie wrote, "My prayers are with you folks over there on the other side. Here's hoping you have a well-earned vacation and find rest for your souls. Mrs. Bebb's untimely end came as a hard blow, but lo the rain is over and gone now and the voice of the turtle is heard again in the land. The Lord hath taken away much with His left hand, but with His right hand He restoreth much. Remember Job, dear, and if you get the opportunity, drop us a postcard. Your friend in Jesus, Laverne Brown."

Bebb said, "Sharon honey, remember me to pick up some souvenirs for folks back home like Brownie," and in the course of our travels—sometimes on our own, sometimes with Gertrude Conover in her rented Daimler—we picked up tons of them not even counting the movies I took. Here are a few of them. There could be almost any number more.

Westminster Abbey. Sharon said, "This place gives me the creeps." She was looking tan and hostile in a sleeveless pink dress with a band to hold her hair back. She said, "There was a used furniture place outside West Palm reminds me of it, full of beds and sofas that looked like people had died all over them and stuffed chairs with brown stains. Makes you want to get in here with some dynamite and clean the place up. You take your history, this place stinks of history."

I said, "That's Alfred Lord Tennyson you've got your feet on."

"I wouldn't care if it was William Shakespeare. Jesus," she said, "there's William Shakespeare."

I said, "He's buried somewhere else though."

She said, "He was smart."

The only one in the Poet's Corner who interested her was Thomas Parr. "He must have been kin," she said, and looked him up in the guide.

"He was known as Old Parr," she read, "and lived through the reigns of ten sovereigns, surviving to the age of 152. That even makes Maudie Redpath look kind of sick."

I was reading over her shoulder, and when she turned, our foreheads knocked.

I said, "The wife who outlived Henry the Eighth was a Parr too. It takes a lot to polish us off."

She said, "It better had." We had bought a bag of bullseyes at Boot's, and her breath smelled of peppermint. She said, "I don't want to be a widow. I don't want to end up dyeing my hair blue like Gertrude Conover and being too lonesome to ever stay home."

I said, "You're a long way from home right now."

She said, "You're my home."

Bebb signaled to us. He was standing with his back to one of the pillars in the nave. The bag of bullseyes bulged out of one of his jacket pockets. A pair of binoculars hung around his neck. He had his head tipped back and was pointing up toward the roof.

He had spotted a pigeon fathoms above us. It was perched in one of the arches of the triforium with its wings folded in tight to its sides, a gray bird hard to make out against the gray stone. It was poised up there like a swimmer poised on the edge of a flooded quarry.

There was a crackling in the air as a P.A. system was switched on and a canned British voice began to run through an announcement that once an hour visitors were requested to pause for a moment and join in the Lord's Prayer. The sound alerted the bird and it started a twitchy side-step back and forth on the high ledge. Then it belly-flopped into the brimming dusk and ferried out across the nave sinking slowly, a stone bird. Nobody was paying much attention to the Lord's Prayer or to the bird either.

As it neared the other side, it back-watered with a ruckus of wings and fought for altitude. Bebb had raised his binoculars. The pigeon batted against the clerestory windows a few times on the way up, then shot cockeyed into the topmost ribs of the vaulting. The P.A. system tapered off to a needle-sharp whine and switched out. The pigeon floated in quiet soft as rainwater a hundred feet above our heads.

Bebb lowered his binoculars. "Keep me as the apple of the eye," he said, "hide me under the shadow of thy wings."

Sharon had one bare arm resting on Bebb's shoulder. She said, "That pigeon's smart as William Shakespeare. He wants the hell out of here."

Simpson's-on-the-Strand. Gertrude Conover ordered London Broil. She said, "In Holland I order hollandaise. In France I order French toast."

She said, "Looking at you three just now, I couldn't help thinking to myself those people are complete strangers. For all I know you could be dope-pushers, poisoners, anything. Your appearance is especially un-reassuring, Leo. That queer thing you keep doing with your eye."

Bebb said, "It's never been the same since Pharaoh had it tore out."

"I had forgotten about that," Gertrude Conover said.

Bebb said, "You know what I was thinking while you were thinking about that? I was thinking that for many years I was the number one person for two people. I was the number one person for my wife, and I was the number one person for my daughter. Now my wife's passed on, and my daughter's got herself a husband. That means I'm not anybody's number one person any more."

Salisbury. We motored there in Gertrude Conover's Daimler, and found a letter waiting at the hotel. It was to me from Laura Fleischman.

Dear Mr. Parr,

I am writing this on my 18th birthday. They say what you do on your birthday you keep on doing all year round so I guess you're in for a

lot of letters from me. [Here she had drawn a round, smiling face.] I
didn't get a chance to say goodbye to you at Commencement with all
those millions of people around. I tried to, but you were always surrounded. I wanted to tell you I really enjoyed having you as my English
Lit. teacher, and I think almost everybody in the class did. King Lear
is the most wonderful book I ever read. My favorite line is "The worst
returns to laughter," which I guess means it's always darkest just before
the dawn. That brings me to the main thing I meant to tell you. Carl
West and I have broken up. It was the worst moment of my life so far,
but I can see now how it was bound to happen inevitably. He is a sweet
boy in lots of ways, but he is very immature. He was never interested in
discussing anything. For instance he couldn't stand King Lear. I don't
think he even read most of it. It was a hard decision for both of us, but
maybe it is all for the best. Do you remember the time I bumped into
you at Grand Central Station? You probably thought I acted awfully
childish and dumb, but I was never so surprised in my life to run into a
person. You were so friendly and kind I hated it when the clock struck
midnight and we had to catch the next pumpkin back to Sutton. I'll
always remember our meeting on that occasion.

Well, I guess that's all for now. I hope I haven't made too many
mistakes, you being an English teacher. Have a grand time in Merry
Old England and please give my best regards to your wife if she remembers who I am. Love, Laura.

Sharon said, "I remember who she is. You don't forget a face like
that. There ought to be a law against a face like that. I'm getting damn
old, Antonio."

Soon afterwards she said, "What happened in Grand Central
Station?"

I said, "Would you believe we spent an hour together in a bar and
I bought her a 7-Up?"

"Why shouldn't I believe it?" Sharon said.

I said, "Would you believe a long corridor with a door at the end of
it and then more corridor beyond that and another door?"

As soon as Gertrude Conover had seen our room in Salisbury, she
said it was haunted. There was a Jacobean four-poster, exposed black
beams, and a washbasin with a mirror above it. Gertrude Conover said
to keep an eye on that mirror if we were interested in knowing more
about the room, and before we went to bed that night, Sharon plastered
the mirror over with a wet handkerchief she had rinsed out. It was in the
Jacobean four-poster that I read her the letter.

"Then more corridor and more doors," I said.

She was lying beside me with her hands folded under her cheek and
her eyes closed. She said, "I wouldn't blame you if you shacked up with
her in a hotel. You had one coming."

I said, "Would you believe a room looking out over the Park with the curtains blowing in and these two standing at the window watching it start to get dark outside? Would you believe them standing there wondering not what's going to happen next because in a way what's going to happen next has already happened but wondering what's going to happen next after that? She's left a straw pocketbook she borrowed from her mother on the bed, and she's got her hand at the nape of her neck holding her hair back. It's a queer, formal kind of moment."

Sharon said, "I could believe that."

I said, "I can almost believe it myself. If there really is a room like that someplace, I can believe it's haunted too. Only what's haunting it isn't something that happened there once. It's something that happened not to happen."

Sharon said, "Poor Bopper. That's one that could have been on the house."

The handkerchief dried and peeled off during the night, but when we woke up the next morning, the only thing it reflected was us.

At *Stonehenge* Bebb sat on one of the fallen lintel stones with a shilling guide spread out on his knee. It was approaching sunset, and the great trilithons looked black against the lemon sky. Not far away a family of three was sitting in the grass having their tea—a father, a mother, and their daughter. The daughter must have been twelve or thirteen in a sunsuit with bloomers that hung loose about her skinny thighs.

She was sitting awkwardly half on, half off, her mother's lap. The mother held the girl's cheeks between her thumb and forefinger and was squeezing them into a fishface to keep her mouth open. The sandaled feet and spidery arms wobbled as the mother spooned tea into her out of a plastic cup. From time to time she broke a small piece off a slice of bread and tamped it into the girl's mouth with her finger. Once in a while the girl got a chance to lean forward, and tea and bread would dribble down her chin. She made sounds then, and when she stopped, her mouth would continue to hold the shape of the sounds. The father sat with his back to them reading a newspaper.

Bebb said, "The girl's not right, anybody can see that. It's probably the only way they can get her to take nourishment. She's just skin and bones."

Sharon said, "There's got to be another way than that."

Gertrude Conover had bought a shooting-stick in London and was sitting on it. She said, "Once at Revonoc I had Thomas Mann and Albert Einstein both for dinner. Thomas Mann was visiting in Princeton at the time, and of course Dr. Einstein lived in that little house on Mercer Street for years. Neither of them drove, so when it came time to go, I drove them home myself. I remember thinking on the way that if I smashed into a telephone pole and we were all killed, I would become a footnote to history. Dr. Einstein and Thomas Mann were in the back seat talking German, and naturally there wasn't any accident. When I got back to Revonoc, I fixed a cup of Ovaltine and sat out on the terrace for a while to watch for shooting stars. I thought about all the biographies that would have had my name in them somewhere. I think that was the same year Hitler marched into Paris."

Sharon said, "That's real interesting, but what's it got to do with the price of eggs if you don't mind my asking?"

Gertrude Conover said, "Everything, that's all. Everything's got to do with everything else. Everything fits in somewhere, and there's no power in heaven or earth that can upset the balance."

Still in her mother's lap, the girl had bent double at the waist and was staring at the ground. The mother had put the unfinished bread and tea aside for the moment and was saying something to the father, who was trying to fold his paper lengthways.

Bebb said, "It says here on midsummer day the sun rises smack over that big block of stone and shoots a beam through the middle of the circle. Why it's been something like—" He paused to check his figures, tilting the page to catch the dwindling light. "This place was near to two thousand years old when the little Lord Jesus was born."

A tourist bus was honking its horn, and beyond the trilithons I could see stragglers hurrying out of the postcard place.

Sharon said, "I wonder if they've got a can there. My back teeth are floating."

Bebb was looking off toward where the midsummer sun was supposed to rise. He said, "Those stones have been standing out here summer and winter for three going on four thousand years while mighty empires have come and gone like a dream when it is past. Napoleon Bonaparte, Nebuchadnezzar, Caesar, the whole pack of them. Makes a man feel about as important as spit."

Gertrude Conover said, "I am a rich old woman and, making allowances, I am a happy old woman. If I thought the way you do, I would still be rich, but I would no longer be happy."

Bebb said, "The first time I laid eyes on you, I could see right off you were happy. It made me happy just you being at the same table."

Gertrude Conover said, "I am happy because I believe spit is important. I believe the universe is important. I believe you and I are important. Everything is important because everything is needed to maintain cosmic balance."

Bebb said, "Sometimes things get out of balance."

Gertrude Conover said, "No."

The mother had started to do the feeding again. She had the girl's head wedged back in the crook of her arm and was shoving something into her out of a jar. Her stuffed face was jacked open, and insect-like sounds were coming out of it. One sandal had fallen off. The sunsuit had gotten wrenched around so that it bit into her at odd places.

Bebb rose to his feet and walked toward her. When he got halfway, he stopped. It was as if he had taken Gertrude Conover's words about cosmic balance literally. Stonehenge was like an overloaded tray held on the palm of a waiter's hand. If Bebb had taken one step too many or one step too few, the tray would have started to go. The girl was pinned by her bruised mouth, and the mouth was the center from which her legs and arms rayed out like broken feelers. Bebb had gone about ten feet toward that center. If he had gone nine feet or eleven, it would have been disastrous. The looming stones, Gertrude Conover on her shooting-stick, Sharon with her back teeth floating, the tourist bus, all of it would have begun sliding. The tray would have gone down with a crash.

Bebb stood with his back to us. I could not see what he was doing, but I could see them seeing it, the father first and then the mother. The father slowly lowered his newspaper. The mother relaxed her hold. They looked up and saw Ptah-sitti standing there looking down at them. It would have been hard to say which had been standing there longer, he or Stonehenge. His pants had gotten stuck between his buttocks. What was left of the sun set a bright cap on his bald head.

The girl slid one hand along the grass toward something white. She took hold of it—a napkin, a piece of sandwich wrapper—and held it out in one hand as far as her arm would reach. Then she stretched her other hand out toward it so that she ended up holding it way off there in front of her in both her hands. Ptah-sitti stood his ground as squat and intractable as once in a wild animal preserve called Lion Country in Armadillo, Florida, I had seen him get out of his car and stand among lions.

One of the best movies I got, the last before we boarded the *Queen Elizabeth II* for home at Le Havre, was at the Eiffel Tower. First a shot of the whole great uncial taken from below, that soaring initial printed against a cloudless Parisian sky. Then a shot traveling up one of the legs in an elevator the size of a boxcar. Finally another shot not from the very top—you had to wait in another line for another elevator to get there—but from the platform halfway up where the restaurant is. Bebb and Sharon are standing against the railing. Bebb has moped around a good deal since we said goodbye to Gertrude Conover at Victoria Station. She said, "Don't be blue. We're all number one people. He has numbered even the hairs on our heads they are so dear," but it didn't seem to help much. Bebb said, "I don't have any hairs on my head, Gertrude Conover." But in Paris he got another letter from Brownie, which brought him to life again. Brownie wrote that the Federal Trade Commission had proposed new guidelines for private vocational and correspondence schools, and a Texas legislator had announced that nothing stood in the way now of ridding the Lone Star state of every fly-by-night diploma factory within its borders. A man had already been around to Holy Love to check on enrollment and tuition figures, Brownie wrote, but in Bebb's absence he had refused to give them out. This is what Bebb is talking about as I zoom in on him there at the rail somewhere between earth and sky.

He is saying, "That was a piss-poor move to make. Brownie ought to showed them every last figure he had. There's not a thing we do isn't open and above board just like it's always been. We don't have a particle to hide, and that pitiful Brownie knows it same as I know it myself—maybe," he says, breaking in on himself, "maybe he knows it, or maybe he's been up to some tricks since I took off overseas."

For emphasis he wags the ice-cream cone that he bought down below. He says, "Holy Love is in trouble, but we're not going to get into a sweat about it. Holy Love's been in trouble from the word go. But we got the First Amendment to the Constitution on our side. And we got Herman Redpath's great fortune too."

He looks straight into the optronic eye, and his mouth snaps shut on its hinges. Then it opens for the last time, and he says to Herman Redpath or whoever else, if anybody, happens to be listening, "Forget not the congregation of the poor forever, for the dark places of the earth are full of the habitations of cruelty," as the purr of my Bell and Howell breaks into the steady clicking that indicates the fifty feet have run out.

LOVE
FEAST

For my mother

1

THERE WAS A TIME when it was out of sight out of mind. A day, a week, a year ended, and when it ended, that was the end of it. But then they invented home movies. Before we left for Europe one summer, my father-in-law, Leo Bebb, gave me a Bell and Howell super-8 with a zoom lens and an optronic eye, and for anyone with a piece of equipment like that, the past may drop out of mind the way it always used to but out of sight never. It is always around to sight any time you feel like sighting it, thousands of feet of it wound up in reels and stowed away in cans. Baby's first steps, the picnic on the beach, some lilac bush tossing its dowager plumes in the spring breeze someplace—even if you don't take it out and look at it very often, you know it's available. Bebb's septuagenarian paramour and traveling companion Gertrude Conover, who is a Theosophist, claims that this reflects a cosmic truth. Maybe so. What I can attest to is only that, cinematically speaking if not cosmically, the song is over but the melody lingers on.

My father-in-law Leo Bebb, my wife Sharon and I at the Eiffel Tower, for instance. For all the ground we have covered since and will go on covering for better or worse until finally the ground covers us, there we continue to stand on that first platform the elevator lands you at, the one where the restaurant and the souvenir shop are. It is one of the best shots I got that summer. Bebb is leaning against the guard-rail with an ice cream cone in his hand. His bald dome glints like a second Sacré Coeur against the clear Parisian sky. His firm, fat face looks fussed and sweaty. His gaze is aimed straight at the optronic eye, and he is gesturing at it with his ice cream cone. His mouth is snapping open and shut like a change purse. My Bell and Howell has no sound attachment, but I remember his words anyway. Not surprisingly they are from Scripture. "Forget not the congregation of the poor forever," he is saying. I zoom in on his face until it all but fills the screen. His trick eyelid flutters half way down, then up again. "For the dark places of the earth are full of the habitations of cruelty." His text and my fifty feet run out almost simultaneously.

What happened next I had no film left to immortalize, but I remember it well enough. He gave the ice cream cone an upward swipe with his tongue and said, "Antonio, you've got to hand it to these Frenchies. They don't say flavor like we do, they say perfume, and they're right. Without you can smell what you're putting in your mouth, it might as well be pencil shavings." He must have worked the ice cream loose with his tongue and the gesturing because as the three of us stood there looking down, he tipped the cone inadvertently, and the ice cream fell out. It hit one of the diagonal struts on the way down and hung there. It gave me a queasy feeling in the groin to watch it. Bebb was in a pensive mood. "It looks like a blob of pink spit," he said, "and below it . . . Down there below it lies Paris, France, spread out like a crazy-quilt. The City of Lights." Part of the ice cream slid down the strut and fell off onto the next one below. "It's got a long way to go before it makes the City of Lights, Antonio," Bebb said. "We all of us do."

Holding onto the rail with both hands, Sharon straightened her arms and pushed back away from it as if she was pumping on a swing. She said, "There's a sermon in that, Bip."

Bebb was as eager as the next man to believe that to get away from things for a while was with luck to make them disappear, and when he invited Sharon and me to go to Europe with him that summer, we leapt at it with no less optimism. God knows there was plenty to get away from. There was Open Heart for one thing. Open Heart had never panned out, at least not the way Bebb hoped, and he knew it.

He said, " 'When two or three are gathered together in my name, I will be with them' saith the Lord, and I don't doubt for one minute that he keeps his promises. He was with us at Open Heart, all right, but he was with us in a special way. The Good Shepherd doesn't always just stand around and let the sheep graze wherever they take it into their heads. Sometimes he drives them on to greener pastures, and that's how it was at Open Heart. He was there the whole time only he was there telling us to move on out to a place he would show us. He hasn't showed us that place yet, but he will. He's never let me down yet, Antonio." So for Bebb our European summer was a matter of getting away from the black help, the cousin of Harry Truman, the lady with the gerbil in the cage and the handful of others who gathered together Sundays to hear him preach the Kingdom in the wrong place and at the wrong time. The right place and the right time would turn up when they would turn up. Bebb had no doubts about that. He said, "It's like Christopher Columbus, Antonio. To discover the New World, you got to scrap the Old."

As far as you could name it, I suppose what Sharon and I were getting away from was Tony, the younger of my two nephews who was named for me—that muscle-bound jock as Sharon called him in one of their turbulent encounters, that seventeen-year-old track star and Lothario who glittered in the waters of our domesticity as harmless as a beach ball until you touched him the wrong way, or the right way, and he went off like a mine, scattering wreckage for miles. It was late one night when I unlocked the door to let him in from some spring adventure that he told me that he and Sharon had become lovers, and later in her own way Sharon told me too. It had happened by accident apparently, catching both of them by surprise no less than it caught me. Neither of them had any plans to let it happen again, but even a little adultery goes a long way and although our marriage survived, it survived barely. With the hull stove in, the engine room flooded, and Bebb at the bridge, we limped to Europe for repairs. Tony and his brother Chris plus our son Bill were packed off to spend the summer with their father, Charlie Blaine. And then there was the death of Bebb's wife, Lucille. We were all three getting away from that. Poor Lucille. The dead, by and large, are harder to get away from than the living. I see her at the Manse in Armadillo, Florida, sitting in front of the color TV with her black glasses on and a Tropicana at her side—half gin, half orange juice—the way she'd been when I first met her. I see her listing down the aisle of Open Heart in her French heels and Aimee Semple McPherson gauze. I see her laid out in Bea Trionka's dress with her hands crossed at her breast so that the wrists she'd spilled her life out of wouldn't show. I don't suppose her name was mentioned more than a half dozen times all the weeks we toured southern England in Gertrude Conover's rented Daimler, and yet the silences between us were again and again hers—those long, askew silences that had always been her primary means of communication, that slight dropping of her lower jaw that was her smile. I wondered often what she would think of Bebb's romance with Gertrude Conover, and there were times when I had the strong sense that she was telling me. Bebb and Gertrude Conover at the rail of a Thames ferry with Traitors Gate looming dark behind them. Bebb and Gertrude Conover in the maze at Hampton Court, Gertrude Conover with her Baedecker in hand reading to Bebb through the box hedge the secret of how to get out. What did Lucille think? *There,* I all but heard her saying with a deflection of her black glasses toward them. *You tell me.*

There was no getting away from any of the things we were trying to get away from, but somehow the trip worked anyhow. When we took the Golden Arrow for a final week in France before sailing home, we left Gertrude Conover behind in London, and Bebb moped around for a while, missing her, but Paris restored him. We stayed at the Hotel Voltaire where according to a plaque Jan Sibelius, Richard Wagner and Oscar Wilde had all preceded us. I pictured them arriving as a threesome, standing there together at the concierge's desk. Our rooms were in front, and the noise of the traffic that went on all night made it like sleeping in the Lincoln Tunnel, but the view was spectacular. From our shallow balcony you could have tossed a croissant over the book stalls into the Seine, and directly across on the right bank was the Louvre. From the start Sharon had disliked London. She took it personally. "Those crazy English," she said, "they're too damned hung up on history. All their old churches and castles and beat-up you-name-its, they remind me of those things they used to make out of dead people's hair. Luce had one had been her Grandma Yancey's, a whole lot of wreaths and flowers that the moths got into. The French, they've got as much history as anybody else has and then some, but they can take it or leave it." Paris, unlike London, met with her full approval, in other words, and it was she who showed us the sights. She got a lot of circulars from American Express, and there wasn't much we missed.

The day before we sailed for home we took the train to Versailles, and if I had to choose one moment to stand for the best that happened to us that summer, Versailles would be the moment. The precariousness of our marriage, the failure of Open Heart, Lucille's death, as always they were as inescapably part of the gear we carried with us as Bebb's binoculars, my Bell and Howell, and Sharon's *Guide Bleu*, but Versailles taught us something about how to carry them. The little grotto where Marie Antoinette hid when she heard that the women of Paris were marching out to storm the chateau. The room where Louis XV died in a stench of gangrene. The *Salle des Glaces* where the treaty was signed that solved nothing in particular. The past clung to the place all right but as a proud and even festal garment—history not as mould but as glitter. Sharon wangled us tickets to the *Jeu de Son et Lumière* in the evening, and although the *lumière* was less than what my optronic eye needed to operate at top effectiveness, there was enough to let it record at least some of the more incandescent moments such as the grand finale when all the fountains were turned on full force which even in their heyday were put into action only when the Sun King was known to be coming around the corner. Great floodlit plumes pulsed high into the dark from pool to pool all the way down the whole range of terraces, light bursting apart into water, water falling apart into light. Over the loud speaker system came the *son* of Charles Boyer's narration against a background of the *Marseillaise* sung by a chorus of thousands with drums, trumpets, cannons, and I don't know what-all else. Behind us, with only its foundations in shadow, the great chateau floated a few feet off the ground.

Bebb sat there like something carved out of soap with the binoculars pressed to his eyes. Sharon was between us in a sleeveless dress. I had my arm over the back of her chair, my hand on her bare shoulder where I could feel both the coolness of her skin and the warmth of her life beneath it. There wasn't one of the three of us who didn't wear some kind of cockeyed crown.

Several weeks after we got home, when all my twenty-odd reels of film finally came back processed from Eastman Kodak, I sat down to the task of editing and splicing them. It was the first time I had had the chance to see them, and my fingers literally trembled with apprehension as I set about cranking them through my viewer. My fingers trembled because although I had every reason to believe that our trip had been a success, I couldn't escape the fear that if for some reason the movies didn't turn out, it would prove that with all its deadly accuracy the optronic eye had seen dark things that I had failed to see or that the bright things that I thought I'd seen had been only the fictions of my longing for bright things.

Nothing is ever clear-cut, of course. The movies had good parts and bad parts both. For every successful shot like Bebb with his ice cream cone on the Eiffel Tower or Sharon and Gertrude Conover on a fallen lintel stone at Stonehenge, there was a failure—the Queen's Horse Guard blowing across the screen like autumn leaves because I'd panned too fast or a sunny morning of feeding the pigeons at Trafalgar Square turned into a dim and moonlit swirl of ghosts because I'd inadvertently switched the exposure control knob to manual.

So for all the preservative powers of cinematography; in the long run maybe the past is just as elusive as it always was. I snipped out all the bad parts and with little bandages of splicing tape mended what was left into an unbroken sequence of good parts. The worst is lost forever. Only the best remains. With possibly one exception.

As the Q.E. 2 steamed up the Hudson toward New York Harbor, it looked for a crazy moment as though the great stacks couldn't possibly clear the Verrazano Bridge. My movies end with an overexposed view of Bebb on the open deck bracing himself for what seemed inevitable catastrophe. His plump fists are clenched at his sides. His tipped-up face is a bright and featureless blur. You can't go home again said Thomas Wolfe. What my parting shot seems to say is that, at your own risk, you can.

2

WHEN WE GOT BACK from Europe, we found that Open Heart was gone. The barn that housed it had burned down so completely that there was nothing much left but some charred beams. One day Bebb poked around through the wreckage for a while in the hope, I suspect, that he might find his big preaching Bible miraculously preserved from the flames, but of course he didn't. Everything was gone including the murals Bebb's friend Clarence Golden had slapped up all over the walls—a kind of Sistine comic-strip that told the story of Bebb's life as Mr. Golden had come to know it during the time, years before, when they had been cell-mates. I was still open to the possibility that as Lucille had often darkly hinted, Mr. Golden was a creature from outer space.

The same day we found out about the fire, we found a note left under the kitchen door. It read:

Friend Leo, in Hebrews 12:29 it says by FAITH they passed through the Red Sea as by dry land so when you land back safe and sound from the other side you know what you got to thank for it is the same as what we all of us got to thank for everything we have or ever HOPE to have worth more than two pins. My sugar is back down where it belongs, and when I wasn't wrestling it out with Guess Who I had a real rest cure at your place. Thanks for the hospitality. Its the wide blue yonder for yours truly now and there is no telling the next time our paths will cross, if not in this world then in a better world to come, Amen. Leo let the dead bury the dead. You got your work cut out for you down here like we all do and don't you worry but what without ceasing I will make mention of you always in my prayers same as I count on you making mention always in yours of your fellow sinner in Jesus and old chum without ceasing, F.

P.S. Remember Bull Litton? He's signed me on as night watchman so whatever happens you'll know I'm there watching. Smiles.

Bebb said, "I'll tell you one mistake he made. Anybody knows Scripture knows it's Hebrews *eleven* is the big chapter on faith. It was Hebrews eleven twenty-nine he ought to put down, not Hebrews twelve twenty-nine. He ought to know better than that."

Sharon said, "I'll tell you another mistake he made. His name is Clarence Golden, and he signed it F."

Bebb said, "Fats. Back when I first knew him, a lot of them called him Fats. So that's no mistake. F is Fats Golden. But the other one, that's what you call a mistake. Hebrews twelve twenty-nine. Who'd have thought Clarence Golden would go and make a mistake like that?"

Later on with nothing else to do except unpack her bags, get food in for supper, arrange about bringing the baby back from Charlie Blaine's and so on, Sharon took out the rusty Gideon I had acquired somewhere and checked Bebb out. She said, "That Bip, he sure knows his Scripture. The part about the Red Sea *is* eleven twenty-nine."

"Just for kicks," I said, "see what it says in twelve twenty-nine."

I remember she was sitting on the stripped mattress of our bed with one bare leg crossed over her lap in what looked like one of her yoga positions, the Gideon propped against her calf. She said, "Jesus, you're never going to believe this. You know what twelve twenty-nine says?"

She kept her finger on the double-columned page, but she looked at me as she read it. She said, "It says, 'Our God is a consuming fire,' that's what it says. Before Open Heart burned down, Fats Golden wrote us our God is a consuming fire."

I said, "*Maybe* he just got the number wrong."

"Smiles," Sharon said.

I said, "I wouldn't tell Bip if I were you. He's got enough on his mind."

She said, "Listen, we've all of us got enough on our mind."

Even at that early point maybe part of what we both had on our minds was the knowledge that for better or worse something was coming to an end between us.

Charlie Blaine was a hypochondriac, and it always surprised me that he had as much time left over as he did for his educational TV. What kept him busy was not so much his various sicknesses themselves—as far as I know, not one of them ever seriously incapacitated him—but trying to work out in his mind how to describe his symptoms to the doctor. He told me once that to put a pain into words for somebody who has never felt that pain is as much of a challenge as to put the colors of a sunset into words for somebody born blind. I suppose that trying to put his pain into words was the story of his life. Maybe it is the story of all our lives.

Not long after his wife, my twin sister Miriam, died of myeloma, a form of cancer that attacks the bones, Charlie thought he had it. Even assuming it was contagious, he could hardly have caught it from Miriam since they had been divorced for several years before her death and such communication as there was between them had taken place almost entirely over the telephone. But Charlie was sure he had it anyway. Because I had seen a lot of Miriam from the early stages of her sickness right up to the end, I knew as much about it as anybody, and on a number of occasions Charlie tried out on me various ways of describing his symptoms. The pain was not localized, he told me; in fact he suggested that maybe *pain* was too much of a word at that point although *sensation*, on the other hand, didn't strike him as quite word enough. But whatever you called it, he said, it seemed to affect him all over. He told me how once when he was a child there was a strange and apparently sourceless rumbling sound in his family's house that led them to believe for a while that they must have a ghost until they discovered eventually that what they had was a community of squirrels in the hot air ducts of the furnace. What he felt was something like that, he said. The problem was to locate those fatal ducts of his being where the squirrels had taken up residence. He also told me that whenever he got up out of a chair or sat down in one, a peculiar thing happened. He could feel his muscles doing all the things muscles do when you get up or sit down, only then, as soon as they had finished doing it, he could feel them doing it all over again like a kind of echo. It was as if he had two bodies, he said, a substantial one and an insubstantial one. Death like a ghostly comedian was following him everywhere, aping each of his most basic and life-like movements. Or maybe it was all in his mind. Even Charlie was sometimes willing to admit that possibility.

The symptoms of my failing marriage were no less obscure and uncertain, and even at that early point my attempts to describe them, if only to myself, were no less time-consuming. Something was rumbling in the hot air ducts. We went through the motions of our life together much as usual, Sharon and I, but I sensed that in the background, dimly, we were perhaps also going through the motions of our death together.

How did it all start? When did I first become aware of the sensation if not the pain? Many times I tried to trace my way back to the earliest symptoms. Maybe it started when Bebb moved out of our house a few months after we all got back from Europe and it didn't do much good for any of us let alone for Bebb himself.

Moving out was his own idea. He left his portable TV in the small third floor room he had been living in, telling Tony and Chris they could go up and use it any time they felt like getting away from things. Everything else he owned he managed to squeeze into two dog-eared suitcases with straps around them, relics of his days on the road as Bible salesman. Sharon said they looked like the kind of suitcases you find torsos in in vacant lots.

Bebb the far-darter. I remember him standing at the airport in his Happy Hooligan hat and tight-fitting black raincoat saying goodbye to us. He said, "I'd as soon drive a nail through my thumb as go up in one of those things, but then I ask myself what am I saving myself for, Antonio?" It was a November afternoon, raw and wet.

He said, "I've got something here to remember me by. Luce, she run it up for me on her machine to use at Open Heart, but seeing how there's no such place as Open Heart any more I want you to— Here. It's a keepsake." Out of his raincoat pocket he produced a brown paper bag. In it there was a piece of white linen which, when unfolded, turned out to have the words OPEN YOUR HEART TO JESUS stitched in red along one edge—an altar cloth—and as he stood there in the drizzle holding it out for us to see, a small contingent of demonstrators happened to come off the air field toward us. They carried banners and placards with peace signs and anti Viet Nam slogans, and a boy with a pony tail and a Robert Louis Stevenson moustache spotted Bebb's keepsake and came over.

He said, "Man, you a Jesus Freak?"

Bebb said, "I'm behind Jesus a hundred per cent, and I've been called a lot worse things than freak in my day if that's what you mean." His trick eyelid did its trick. He said, "What can I do you for, son?"

"We surely could use that flag in our army," the boy said. "We'd fly it high and wide for peace."

"Jesus was for peace," one of the girls said. She had a World War II overcoat that reached almost to her ankles and a Day-Glow headband.

Bebb said, "Honey, Jesus is the Prince of Peace. Where there isn't any Jesus, there isn't any peace worth a nickel."

Lucille's altar cloth must have been about six feet wide. The girl took it by one corner, and Bebb still had hold of the other, so they stood there with it spread out between them. The air was chilly enough to see their breath in.

"Go on and give it to them, Bip," Sharon said. "We don't have any place for it home."

They called Bebb's flight number over the loudspeaker, and his face went as pale as the cloth either from the necessity for a quick decision or the imminence of his departure.

Finally he said, "I'll tell you one thing. I don't go in for dope or you-name-it sex or walking the public streets got up like Hallowe'en and knocking the U.S.A. every chance you get, but I believe in Jesus and I believe in peace so if you'll treat this thing with respect and do like what it's got written on it, you can have it and welcome."

So in the end all we got to remember him by was the brown paper bag. At the gate his last words were, "Even rigged out like crazies and hair all over their faces, there's no two ways about it. They're beautiful. They're beautiful and they're young, and it's like the Book says, 'It shall come to pass that your sons and daughters shall prophesy and your *young* men shall see visions.' That's how come I let them have it, Antonio."

As he walked up the steps to the plane, he bent over with his handkerchief to his mouth, and Sharon said, "Sometimes even before he gets on board he pukes."

Although the reason Bebb gave for going back to Houston and Holy Love was that it was time for him to rejoin the laborers in the vineyard, even then I had a feeling that the real reason was that he sensed the ghostly rumbling in our marriage and thought we might stand a better chance of exorcising it without him. I think he knew perfectly well before he got there that the vineyard at Herman Redpath's ranch had all the laborers it needed.

Brownie had everything well in hand. He had put in air-conditioning. He had installed a more powerful carillon in the tower so that there was no part of the ranch beyond the Sunday strains of *The Old Rugged Cross* and *I Need Thee Every Hour*. And Herman Redpath had left Holy Love such a handsome endowment in his will that not even Bebb's remarkable money-raising skills were needed. So for the better part of a year after Bebb left us, he rattled around down there. He got Brownie to let him preach once in a while. He helped the two fat Trionka sisters put the files of Gospel Faith College in order and read some of the 8½ x 11 book summaries submitted through the mails for advanced theological degrees. He signed diplomas. He helped arrange such tribal festivities as what Maudie Redpath claimed was her hundred and tenth birthday at John Turtle's Tom Thumb golf course. But his heart wasn't in any of it. Nobody down there really needed him the way Herman Redpath had, and he knew it.

So Bebb ended up leaving the ranch and joining forces with Gertrude Conover in Princeton, New Jersey. He became a world traveler. Over the course of three years or so they visited together every continent except Australia, and some of them they visited more than once. They went on a photographic safari in Kenya and sent back snapshots of themselves in pith helmets sitting side by side on the mountainous rib-cage of a drugged elephant. After a cruise through the Greek Islands, they spent a week at Delphi where through theosophic channels Gertrude Conover established contact with the ancient oracle whom she had apparently done business with in an earlier incarnation.

One spring they went to Egypt and took a taxi out to see the Sphinx. As they stood there between its paws, Bebb said that for a moment or two he had a feeling that this was not the first time he had gazed up into that great ruined face. Then, he wrote, "It come over me in a flash the reason the face of the Sphinx looked so familiar was it was a dead ringer for the face of George Washington on the front of a one dollar bill. When I told it to Gertrude Conover, she asked me what it was put it into my head the U.S.A. was the only country George Washington was ever the Father of."

In between trips Bebb returned occasionally to the Red Path Ranch and once in a while visited Sharon and me for a few days in Connecticut, but when not traveling he spent most of his time with Gertrude Conover at Revonoc in Princeton. Revonoc was a large whitewashed brick house with stone lions at the entrance to the drive and a broad terrace in back that looked out over a sweep of putting-green lawn and a heated swimming pool protected on three sides by a yew hedge. Whatever some people said, you couldn't accuse Bebb of using his friend for her money. With most of the hundred thousand dollar bequest from Herman Redpath still intact, he had all the money he needed. And he was no toady either. He was always interested in finding out more from her about her theosophy, but he gave no signs of believing much of it himself. He made no attempt to be like her Princeton friends. He kept on wearing the same kind of gents furnishing suits and pointed shoes and painted ties he'd always worn. He didn't try to improve his grammar. Often he would take the train into New York by himself on errands that she knew nothing about. There was no sense in which he seemed to have sold out to Gertrude Conover and the placid rhythms of Revonoc, and yet I couldn't escape the feeling that those years with her were somehow lost ones for him.

I remember seeing him once when he didn't know I was anywhere around. It was during a weekend I spent at Revonoc one winter. I was walking down Nassau Street on some errand or other when I suddenly happened to notice Bebb walking slowly along in the same direction on the other side of the street. It was late afternoon and snowing. On my side, the lights of the shops made everything look comforting and Dickensian, but on Bebb's side there was only the massive stone shadow of the Firestone Library dimmed by the tumbling flakes. Bebb had on his habitual black raincoat with a lining buttoned in which made it look even tighter than usual but which probably wasn't enough to keep him warm. He had on his hat but no galoshes, no gloves. He looked somehow diminished walking along through the winter, and the sadness I felt as I watched him was mixed with a sense of disillusion.

He moved independently enough through the landscape Gertrude Conover provided him, but it wasn't his landscape any more than the snow was his snow. Bebb belonged closer to the sweaty heart of things. He belonged where the lions were not stone like the ones at Revonoc but hairy, horny, cantankerous like the ones I had seen him stand unafraid among on the scrubby plains of Lion Country near Armadillo. He had let down the congregation of the poor he had talked about half way up the Eiffel Tower, had let himself down, and I had the feeling Sharon and I were somehow to blame.

If she and I had been more each other's, Bebb would have been more ours, more his own—not that he would have necessarily stayed on living with us, I suppose, but that, humanly if not geographically, we instead of Gertrude Conover would have been the base he operated out from. And with us as his base, I felt he would have operated more in his own peculiar way, toward his own peculiar ends. Instead of making it easier for us to exorcise our ghosts by leaving us, he became one of our ghosts himself. We were haunted by the Bebb he used to be, the Bebb who except for us he might have kept on being.

3

IN WHAT WAY wasn't Sharon quite mine in those days? Maybe she had never been quite mine from the beginning and it was only when we were left alone together that I began to notice it. Bebb and my nephew Chris cleared out within a few months of each other, and Tony cleared out within a few months of that, so that within the space of about a year the house was empty except for Sharon and the baby and me.

Chris, that pimply, pale, and stage-struck boy who was endlessly exploited by Sharon as resident baby-sitter and maid of all work. After graduating from Sutton High, where I taught English, he was accepted at Harvard, where he went with every intention of becoming Elia Kazan if not Tennessee Williams only to become instead Merrill, Lynch, Pierce, Fenner and whoever it is rolled into one. He started a typing service his freshman year, branched out into Xeroxing as a sophomore, and by the time he was a junior was earning more than his tuition and switching his major from Drama to Economics. Vacations he took to spending with his father and Billie Kling and summers he worked as runner for a Wall Street brokerage so that Sharon and I rarely saw him. His complexion cleared up, his hair grew thinner, his neck and shoulders filled out enough to take away some of his Bunthornian willowiness, and by the time of his graduation he could have been taken for an assistant dean. "I want to make the theater my life," he had said once to Bebb in the accents of *Mary Noble, Backstage Wife,* and maybe Moneymaking Prodigy was only another role he was trying on for size. What sneak previews were going on behind that dim, well-organized face were anybody's guess. Sharon's guess was simplicity itself. "What that Chris needs," she said, "is to get laid."

Tony had no such problem, but he had others. He graduated from High School the year after his brother and partly through disinclination and partly through poor grades didn't go to college. Instead, he joined me on the staff of Sutton High the fall after his graduation in a variegated capacity that included helping coach track and swimming, running the manual training shop, and doing such grounds work as operating the snow-blower in the winter and one of the power mowers in the spring. "A jock of all trades" was what one of the faculty wags called him, and after the dazzling spring of his senior year when he broke three school records in track and virtually singlehanded brought Sutton out ahead of Port Chester, Rye and Greenwich, his return that fall was like Lindbergh's coming back the next morning to sweep up the ticker-tape. He let his dark hair grow thick around his ears and down the back of his neck so that he looked more than ever like something out of the Elgin Marbles when, stripped to the waist, he would work out with his weights in the back yard to keep himself in shape; but with no more records to break or cups to win, he must have asked himself the question what he was keeping himself in shape for, because after a while he gave the weights up and spent most of his free time in his own room playing his cassettes with the door locked.

Except for the night he confessed to me about himself and Sharon, the only time we ever risked touching directly on the subject again had been one spring afternoon just before we left for Europe when I remember his saying to me that he would do anything if he could only make it as if it had never happened, and my answering him—for lack of anything else to say—that maybe we could at least make things happen around it that would make it not matter so much. Actually we did a better job of it than I had any reason to hope, and the reason was that by some miracle of grace the kind of things we made happen around it were pretty much the same kind of things we'd been making happen always. Tony and Sharon went on fighting the same wild battles they'd been fighting since he first moved in with us—his slovenly room versus her slovenly housekeeping, his nocturnal adventures that kept him out till all hours versus her yoga, speed-reading, guitar lessons that kept her from . . . and so on. In between such assaults there were as usual the equally passionate truces when they would sit together in front of the Late Show red-eyed at Paul Henreid leading Rick's bar in the *Marseillaise* right under the nose of Conrad Veidt and his

Nazis, or at Leslie Howard, fresh from the arms of Ingrid Bergman, seeing the child he had abandoned for her struck down by a car as she ran toward him across the street. And in much the same old ways I went on being me with them and they themselves with me until finally among such familiar happenings it came to seem to all three of us that nothing so outlandish as a man's wife cuckolding him with his nephew could possibly have happened except perhaps on the TV screen. Thus it was not by taking pains with each other that we saved the day, or almost did, but by being as shiftlessly congenial and inconsiderate as ever. The slightest gesture of sympathetic understanding, the faintest *effort* toward some sort of civilized accommodation, would have spelled our doom.

I think it was that locked door that spelled it finally or at least the early stages of it. Doom like the mystic syllable Om is not just the sound you hear but the silence at either end. Tony would come back from school in the afternoon and maybe polish off a can of beer or some unnamable thing Sharon had left in the ice-box. He might fool around with our son Bill for a while or tell us about something that had amused him that day like the time he was taken to task for saying to somebody that an affable senior named Bruce Hurley was the biggest prick in school when what he'd actually said was the simple locker-room statistic that Bruce Hurley *had* the biggest prick in school. Then he would thump up stairs in his disintegrating loafers held together with adhesive tape and put on the Stones or the Airplane or whatever. From below you couldn't hear the tune very well, just the beat, but you could hear him shut the door. And if you listened, you could hear him lock it.

Every time it happened, it sent Sharon up the wall. "What's he do in there all the time with the latch on, play with himself? Does he think we want to break in and watch him for Christ sake?" I remember the first time she said that, I thought of how Brownie might have said if we would go in and really watch him for *Christ's* sake, maybe he wouldn't have to play with himself any more but would come out and play with us, play and make merry before the Lord. Sharon said, "He doesn't need to lock it. I wouldn't go into that hole if he paid me, the way he leaves it. You could cut the air in there with a axe."

The bed unmade, the pajama pants accordioned on the floor where he'd stepped out of them. There was a wedding picture of his parents on the dresser—Charlie in his Navy whites, my sister Miriam with a little too much lipstick, a little too much lace, looking very Italian, at his side. There were his track shoes, a framed award Charlie had received for some TV series, a brassiere hanging down from the ceiling light. There was a button the size of a butter plate with *Kiss a Toad Tonight* on it. There was a stack of old *Playboys* and a picture of Jesus Bebb had given him which had eyes that looked closed until you looked at them hard and they opened. There was his cassette player. "That poor bastard," Sharon said once, standing in the midst of it one morning when he was away.

"Maybe he's not locking anybody out. Maybe he's just locking himself in with his treasures." But the next time he locked it, she carried on the way she always did although never to him for a wonder, only to me, as if I were the one who locked the door or it was because of me he locked it. Maybe it was. Anyway, his locked door prepared the way so successfully for the day he told us he was moving out that we weren't even surprised when it happened. He'd rented a room in a boarding house on the other side of town, he told us. He didn't give us any special reason why, and we didn't ask him because to all intents and purposes he'd of course moved out already.

Bebb walking along through the snow down Nassau Street. Chris turning into J. Paul Getty in Cambridge and not coming back for vacations any more. Tony off on his own at a boarding house. Looking back at the early symptoms of what went wrong between Sharon and me, I have the feeling that with each departure there was, if not a pain, a sensation at least of something lost beyond the loss of the one who had departed. Life went on as usual in our increasingly empty house, our schedule or lack of it continued basically unchanged, but as in the case of Charlie's muscula-ture, there began to be an echo. Even making love at night we were both who we were and also who we either could have been or maybe never could.

Then, not long after Tony left, Sharon started a health food store with her guitar teacher, that grizzled little marmoset named Anita Steen. They called it the Sharanita Shop and handled the regular line—variants by the dozen of every known vitamin and combination of vitamins, seeds and seaweeds, yoghurt and brown rice, everything so unrefined and natural that even the paperbacks of Adele Davis, Sakurazawa Nyoiti and Euell Gibbons were such, Anita said, that if you got tired of reading them, you could always eat them. Anita took care of the business end and the order-ing, and most of the time Sharon ran the shop. She would leave in the morning when I did, taking Bill with her, and often she didn't get back until just in time to throw something together for supper. From the start business boomed. There were days when we hardly met except in bed.

Whatever the fatal disorder was that we'd caught, though, there were periods of remission, and out of bed as well as in it we continued to have good times. There were afternoons on the beach with a length of clothes-line attached to Bill's harness so we didn't have to keep an eye on him every minute as he staggered around after the sandpipers. We had people in. We went out. We had a few evenings in the city. Sometimes Bebb and Gertrude Conover, in between voyages, would come in from Princeton to have supper with us. We had our good times, Sharon and I, and to have heard us together even when we were alone together, nobody would ever have guessed that anything was wrong any more than most of the time either one of us guessed it. But it wasn't what we talked about that told the tale. It was what we didn't talk about.

First what we didn't talk about was the sad things that had happened like poor Lucille's death and not seeing Tony and Chris much any more and Bebb's losing most of his bounce off there somewhere with Gertrude Conover. Only then by a process no less subtle than the process by which a sensation turns almost imperceptibly into a pain, it got to where what we didn't talk about was no longer the sad things that had happened but the sad thing we both of us more or less knew was getting ready to happen next. Little by little the silences between us changed their shape the way clouds do with an upheaval so vast and furious and slow you hardly notice it.

One evening in October Sharon asked Anita Steen for supper, and in place of the usual corned beef hash or frozen chicken pies, she put together a real meal for once which we ate not in the kitchen but in the dining room with wine and candles. After supper, with a girl from school to clean up and put Bill to bed, Sharon and Anita set up a card table in the living room and got down to the business of the evening which was to go over a month's worth of sales slips and check them off against the last inventory. I had a batch of themes to correct which I set about doing at my desk in the same room. There was a wind, and you could hear it stirring through the dead leaves at the side of the house.

I remember the way the two of them looked sitting there at the card table by lamplight—Sharon in a peasant skirt and low-necked, puff-sleeved blouse, Anita in her usual grey flannel slacks with a white shirt that had frilled cuffs and ruffles down the front like a matador's. I remember the grey crew-cut and bullet head of Anita Steen and that stunning cascade of wrinkles that was her smile, that flaring of nostril and baring of teeth like a horse on a merry-go-round. Her sharp yellow pencil, her half-moon spectacles, her king-sized cigarettes—everything she touched seemed part of a trick proving that her hand was quicker than every eye except her own, those quick brown eyes of Anita Steen's that were always busy with something other than whatever was busying the rest of her.

And Sharon. I remember Sharon sitting there with her elbows on the table and her chin in her hand. I remember the way, looped at the wrist, her long hair fell, the shadow of her eyes as she gazed down, lazy and bored, at the record of all the good health she'd sold that month. I remember that Renaissance face always so somber and deadpan until with a sudden Bojangles grin she let the cat out of the bag and made even her sternest judge her partner in crime. The gaudy crime of Sharon's smile. She hadn't lost her summer tan, and you could see the low-cut boundary of it still, could see down to where it turned pale and freckled like thrushes' eggs. Sitting there looking at her with my red pencil in my hand and those feckless themes, I could see in my mind the whole cool and moonlit landscape of her flesh as I had come to know it the first time we made love together at the Salamander Motel in Armadillo. It was the landscape where I had lost my way never really to find it quite again, or her either, and I thought how the way I would describe my symptoms as I sat there watching her would be to say that it wasn't exactly a pain but it wasn't a picnic either. It kept changing: sometimes a choked feeling when I started to speak, sometimes more like a lump in the throat, sometimes just the shiver you get when a rabbit runs across your grave.

She said, "Go get Shorty and me a Coke, will you, Bopper? You don't look like those papers are grabbing you anyway," which God knows they weren't, the usual catalogue of plane crashes, suicides, drugcrazed knifings I was used to getting from my tenth graders who always stirred a strong mixture of death into their literary efforts to make up for what they knew was a fatal absence of anything much like life.

Anita Steen said, "Get it yourself, you spoiled beauty," and then to me, "You better take this brat in hand," only taking her in hand herself, catching Sharon's neck in the crook of her arm and pulling her over sideways till for a moment their heads just touched and Sharon popped her eyes and tongue out at me, strangling to death, then *Shit* as she knocked a week's worth of sales slips off the table with her bare arm. As she ducked down under the table to pick them up, the eyes of Anita Steen and my eyes met roughly at the place where Sharon's face had been, and instead of meeting there as enemies, we met for the first and only time in our lives as old war comrades coming together in an empty place where some crucial battle had taken place while both of us were looking the other way. Anita Steen tried flashing her brigadier wrinkles at me, but for once they failed her, just rocketed like tears from the outer corners of her eyes and fizzled out in the shadowy no man's land where her smile should have been. Sharon was the prize we both were battling for, and with our eyes we told each other we both had lost.

After she left that night, we had a battle about her, Sharon and I. Sharon was lying on top of our bed in a pair of my pajamas and I was still in the bathroom where through the open door I said something mostly fatuous about how anybody could see the whole Sharanita enterprise was just an elaborate maneuver for getting Sharon into the sack with her, and Sharon said if I couldn't accept Anita Steen for what she was, it was time I wised up and stopped being such a tight-assed square. I said I could accept Anita Steen for what she was without much sweat but didn't know whether I wanted to accept the way Sharon led her on, getting all fancied out for her plus candles and wine and letting her paw her whenever she felt like it, and Sharon said anybody thick enough to think Anita Steen wanted to play grab-ass with her was thick enough to think she wanted to play grab-ass with Anita Steen. She said Anita Steen had long since leveled with her about what she was but had told her she didn't have to get uptight about it because Sharon wasn't her type, and I said if I was Anita Steen that's just what I would have said too.

My accelerated pulse and labored breathing, the sense I had that my vision must be going back on me because the air between us had somehow gotten bent and what I was seeing was not Sharon herself but some re- fracted image of Sharon—all my symptoms grew to the point where I could no longer believe they were just in my mind because they were sure as hell working now on my vital functions themselves so that what had been up to then only a sensation had turned into a five-star, technicolor pain that even Charlie Blaine could have been proud of.

There was Sharon, my heart's desire and shipmate, stretched out like a *Playboy* center-fold in a pair of my drip-dry pajamas on that six by eight raft that was the bed where we had ridden out many a dark storm, cling- ing on to each other for dear life; and the pain I felt as I saw whatever my failing eyes could see of her there had nothing whatever to do with Anita Steen. It was Anita Steen we were yelling at each other about above the high wind that filled my mouth, but at the heart of our howling there was a silence as at the eye of the storm there is a failure of breath, and that was where the pain came from, the unbreathed knowledge in both of us that this time it was Davy Jones almost for sure and that part of what we were howling at each other for was help.

No help came until such as there was in Sharon's finally rolling half over on her side to grab a cigarette from the night table and light it be- hind the veil of her hair as at the same time my drip-drys pulled apart enough to show her tanned belly and she said through a lamplit puff of smoke, "Jesus, Antonio, why don't you get your balls out of here," which if not a life-line was at least a line to leave on. Just as I was, with only a towel wrapped around me and the toothpaste still unrinsed from my mouth, I went upstairs and spent the night with a group of dead flies in the stuffy third floor room where Bebb had left his portable TV. He had also left a copy of Billy Graham's *The Jesus Generation*, but I couldn't keep my mind on it and spent most of what was left of the night watching the wind in the telephone wires and the leaves.

Breakfast the next morning went normally enough. The Cream of Wheat boiled over, and Bill kept up a steady patter which like bad hand- writing you could understand only so long as you didn't stop to figure out any particular word. Sharon and I had no more and no less to say to each other than we usually did at that hour, and whatever it was we said was neither more nor less historic, but the air I saw her through was still bent air and the sound of her voice came to me from across water. That after- noon I let my tenth graders out of class early and drove downtown where I made arrangements to rent a room for myself and my balls both at my nephew Tony's boarding house.

Among the paperbacks you could buy at the Sharanita Shop was one called *Sweet and Dangerous: the new facts about the sugar you eat*. Sharon had left on the kitchen table the copy of it that she was reading, and I propped my note against that rather than pinning it to the more tradi- tional pincushion upstairs. I said that if too much sweet was dangerous, maybe too little sweet was dangerous too. I told her where I was going and how to get hold of me in case she needed me. I asked her to tell Bill that I would come back to see him the first chance I got. I signed with just the single initial A, that letter that in one form or another has haunted me for years. A as the shape of the cast my poor sister died in with most of her bones broken, and as the shape too (quite unintentional on my part —it was my old girlfriend Ellie Pierce who first pointed it out to me) of the outsize wooden mobile I'd made and with Tony's help hung from a tripod in the back yard where it had weathered to a silvery grey covered with bird droppings. A as the Eiffel Tower where the ice cream had fallen out of Bebb's ice cream cone marking for him no less than for Sharon and me the end of one era and the beginning of another. A for Adultery, *Andiamo*, Amen. A for A *rivederci*, Antonio. I signed the note, packed my bag, and left the house with a kind of dazed efficiency.

It was only when I was in the car driving toward town through the Hallowe'en-colored maples that I found my face wet with tears almost as if it was somebody else's tears and somebody else's face. A for delayed Adolescence. A for that deep-drawn ah-h-h of mingled regret and relief with which we tend to greet the death of even the people we love most; maybe even, in the last analysis, the death of ourselves.

4

POOR BEBB. The news of Sharon's and my separation hit him hard, coming as it did at a time when he was in so many ways separated and at loose ends himself. He drove up to Sutton when word first reached him and saw us both. Separately. With Sharon he tried prayer. He told me about it later. Right there in the same kitchen where I'd left my note, he laid his plump hands on her head as in the old days he'd laid them on Herman Redpath and tried, in his phrase, to raise the whole mess to the Lord.

I have seen busboys in restaurants do much the same, crouching down by the service table to get their right shoulder and the palm of their right hand underneath a tray piled high with dirty dishes, then struggling to their feet under the weight of it and trying to make it out to the kitchen without losing balance and dropping the whole thing. Bebb must have risked a spiritual hernia straining to get us off the ground with his prayer —not just Sharon and Bill and me but Tony and Chris and in some measure himself too as they were all involved in our mess with us. I picture the sweat running down his bald head and his eyes bugging out as step after precarious step he tries to make it to where the Lord can take over in the Big Kitchen Up There and wash us all clean in the blood of the Lamb.

Bebb ascribed the flop of his prayer not to any lack of interest on the part of the Lord but to Sharon. He said, "Antonio, she didn't even let me get as far as—why I'd hardly more than shifted out of second before she busted in. She said, 'Bip, I might just as well lay it on the line. Whoever you think you're talking to, I've never seen him or heard him or felt him, and I've never tasted or smelled him either. As far as I'm concerned, you're just beating your gums.' Antonio, it pulls the rug right out from under a prayer to have somebody come out with a crack like that. To be honest with you, I feel like I've had the rug pulled out from under me in more ways than one. I don't have the zip I once did. When a miserable thing like that happens, I don't snap back like I used to."

With me, he didn't try prayer; in fact he seemed to lose track of his mission of reconciliation altogether in a fog of melancholy reminiscence. He talked about the old days in Armadillo and about Holy Love and how maybe he and Lucille would be there still if only he'd played his cards differently. With the mark of Sharon's lipstick on his cheek, he stared out at the grey sky, looking as though he'd forgotten whatever else he'd come to say. In any case, he drove back to Princeton that evening with no reason to think that he had done any good at all in coming to see us. All he took back with him for his pains was the knowledge that Sharon had cut loose not only from me but from whatever it was Bebb had thought he was praying to in the kitchen as well.

I think that in many ways it may have been his bleakest hour up to that point because whereas five years in the pen and the débacle of Herman Redpath's ordination and even Lucille's suicide had all been events he could steel himself to, this new phase of his life was hardly an event at all but more just a falling apart, a gradual gathering of darkness. It was Gertrude Conover who caused the light to shine for him again, a light that for a while blazed down as hot and bright as any Bebb had ever sweated under before.

She was pushing eighty at the time, but there was something very female about her still, something almost seductive. When she walked, she had a way of tilting her chin slightly down toward one shoulder so that she seemed always to be coming at you sideways. It was as if, although the general drift of her life was in another direction altogether, she was nonetheless determined to tack her way somehow to you because theosophically speaking, it might be eons before you got reincarnated together again, and it would be ridiculous not to make the most of it while you could. There was no telling in what quaint ways you might be useful to each other. She herself told me months later how it came about that she was able to be useful in rescuing Bebb from the dark night of his soul.

The two of them had returned from shopping one November afternoon, she said, and since there were too many packages to carry into the house all at once, Bebb went back to the car to get the ones that were left. When he hadn't reappeared after a half an hour or so, she got worried about him and went out to see what had happened. She found him sitting in the front seat of the car with the packages forgotten in his lap and staring out the window with such a morose expression, the light through the tinted glass giving him such a grim pallor, that she asked him what on earth was the matter. When Gertrude Conover asked you what on earth was the matter, you felt she really wanted to know, and instead of ducking the question, Bebb more or less told her.

"He said he was homesick," she told me. "My dear, he sat there all crumpled up over the groceries, and his voice sounded as though it was coming out of a deep hole. I asked him what he was homesick for, and he said, 'Gertrude Conover'—because you know I'm never just Gertrude to him but always this Southern thing of both names together—he said, 'Gertrude Conover, I don't know. I'm homesick, but I don't know what I'm homesick for any more than you do.' Poor soul. He was so blue. What does a person say? I said everybody gets homesick like that sometimes. I quoted Wordsworth about how the soul that travels with us, our life's star, hath had elsewhere its something and cometh from afar. He's always quoting Holy Writ to me, and I like quoting *The Oxford Book of English Verse* back at him, but you could see he wasn't listening. Blue? I've never seen him bluer. You get so you can actually see the color of it, you know. The astral body. So I tried another approach. I said, 'Come out of it, Leo. Think of other people for a change. Thanksgiving's only a few days off, and the University's full of young people who won't be getting home for it.' I said, 'For all their long hair and so forth, they're probably every bit as homesick in their way as you are in yours.' I said, 'Why don't you think about what you can do for *them?*' You know, it worked like magic. He said to me, 'Blessed art thou among women, Gertrude Conover,' and right there in the front seat of the Lincoln he blossomed like a rose."

Suppose that there had been no second load of packages for Bebb to go back to the car for, or that it hadn't been that close to Thanksgiving, or that Gertrude Conover had just quoted Wordsworth to him about his homesickness and let it go at that. On such slender chances hang the destinies of us all, unless Gertrude Conover is right that there is no such thing as chance. Anyway, Bebb caught the ball that she tossed in his direction. His astral body shifted from blue to a positively sunrise pink as he decided the thing to do was throw a free turkey dinner for any Princeton undergraduates left on campus who wanted to come, and Gertrude Conover helped him for all she was worth as at that point she would surely have helped him for all she was worth if he'd wanted to stage a mass baptism in her heated swimming pool behind the yew hedge.

As for my own Thanksgiving, Charlie Blaine asked me to come out with Tony for the weekend, but not feeling up to the window-rattling cor-

dialities of Billie Kling, I had reconciled myself to staying at the boarding
house alone when Bebb phoned and invited me to Revonoc, describing his
plans for the free turkey dinner with such enthusiasm that I couldn't resist
being on hand to watch them unfold. I drove past our house on the way
out of town and saw Bill riding his tricycle on the driveway. I thought of
stopping by for a moment to make sure Sharon was keeping an eye on him
from inside, but considering the risks both ways, I decided against it. I
thought at one point that Bill had seen me, and I waved at him out of the
car window, but he must have been looking at something else. He had on
a rainbow-colored tam with a pom-pom, and his small, fierce face was
thrust out over the handlebars as he charged a pile of dead leaves.

I arrived at Revonoc the day before Thanksgiving and was given a full
description of all the preparations that I wasn't there in time to observe
for myself. Bebb showed me one of the posters that he had put up at the
U Store, Murray Dodge, Freshman Commons, and other strategic spots all
over the campus. He and Gertrude Conover had lettered them themselves.

*The Rev. Leo Bebb, Evangelist, and Mrs. Harold Conover invite you to
join them in giving Thanks at a Turkey Dinner at 1 P.M. Thanksgiving
Day at No. 17, Gouverneur Road (off Bayard Lane). Sign up below and
Come as you are. BLESSED ARE THEY WHICH DO HUNGER
AND THIRST AFTER RIGHTEOUSNESS FOR THEY SHALL BE
FILLED (Matthew 6:5)*

Bebb had made the rounds several times a day to check on how many
had signed up, and the results were somewhat disappointing. Not counting
Chairman Mao, Mary Poppins, Angela Davis and Judas Iscariot plus others
that were either illegible or the work of small children, there were only
about twenty-five signatures all-told; but Gertrude Conover checked with
friends at Nassau Hall on the number of students who were expected to
remain on campus over the holiday, and she and Bebb decided that there
would be a good deal more than twenty-five who would probably come
whether they bothered to sign up ahead of time or not.

Trestle tables were set up in the spacious front hall of Revonoc with
several extra ones in the adjoining solarium in the event of an overflow. On
the landing of the main staircase chairs were placed for a four-piece orchestra. A caterer provided china, glassware, silver, and white tablecloths
twenty feet long. Frozen turkeys were rounded up. Extra help was signed
on. From an old family recipe Gertrude Conover personally prepared an
enormous claret punch that called for *violettes de Parme*, which she had to
send to New York for, and Appollinaris Water, for which she substituted
Saratoga Vichy. Chrysanthemums, white, yellow, and copper-colored, were
arranged in vases all over the house. The tables were decorated with wicker
cornucopias of vegetables and fruit waxed and rubbed to a high polish.
The whole house was cleaned from the billiard room in the cellar to the

maids' quarters on the third floor. The gravel drive was raked. The stone lions out front were hung with wreaths of laurel around their necks. Signs were put up at either end of Gouverneur Road bearing the single word REVONOC plus an arrow, a heart, and, in an effort at contemporaneity, the circular peace symbol with the upside-down Y inside.

The preparations reached a crescendo around ten Thanksgiving morning when the tables were being decorated and the caterer's truck arrived followed shortly by the waiters and the four musicians with their instruments. Bebb in shirtsleeves helped carry the small, night-club-sized piano to the landing, and I remember him standing there staring down over the bannister at all the activity he had precipitated. His face was flushed and his eyes almost feverishly bright, and I thought how different he looked from the time he had watched his ice cream fall slowly down toward the City of Lights. "He's really come into his own," I said, with a bowl of raisins and mixed nuts in my hands, and Gertrude Conover turned to me with those weathered blue eyes and said, "Let's hope this time his own will receive him" not as if she thought they wouldn't but as if, thumbing back through the earlier lives of Leo Bebb, she had come upon some times when they had and other times when they had not, and she hoped that this time in Princeton, New Jersey, would be one of the former. Behind Bebb on the landing, the pianist was giving the violinist a note to tune up by.

By one o'clock only about a dozen students had arrived. One of them must have been close to seven feet tall with a bad case of acne and an Abe Lincoln beard. There was a fat, effeminate boy who turned out to be the grandson of somebody Gertrude Conover had known as a girl in Cleveland, Ohio. A pair of blacks arrived together, one of them wearing a striped black and terra-cotta kaftan and the other a grey flannel suit with a Tattersall vest and a large Afro. There was a boy who said he was there to do a story for the *Daily Princetonian* and a girl in vinyl slacks who had come with the understanding that there was to be a peace rally. There were also two or three of the kind that I suppose Bebb had dreamed of—fresh-faced undergraduates straight out of Pepsi Cola ads with their pink cheeks and strong white teeth.

Bebb and Gertrude Conover greeted them all as they straggled in. The claret punch was passed around, and most of them accepted it except for a few like the black in the kaftan who declined on the grounds that he was a Muslim and a swarthy man in a jump-suit who looked ten years older than the rest of them and asked for a dry martini. The orchestra on the landing played things like *Tea for Two* and *Smoke Gets in Your Eyes*. White-coated waiters who almost outnumbered the guests moved among us with trays of canapés. Gertrude Conover, in a green wool dress with yellow chrysanthemums pinned at her waist, tried to keep conversation going among the few who had gathered around her, and I did the best I could with the ones around me except that I kept losing track of what we were talking about in my effort to see how Bebb was making out.

He stood near the foot of the stairs with a group that I was glad to notice included the Pepsi Cola contingent, and although I thought I was able to catch him glancing at the front door from time to time to see if any more were arriving, there was nothing in his manner to suggest that he found anything wrong. He was doing most of the talking himself, everybody listening with what seemed more than merely polite interest, and I remembered wondering what if anything of a person carries over from one year to the next let alone from one life to the next? What if anything makes the man who begets a son, say, the same as the man who waves at him, unnoticed, from a car window? Were the Bebb standing there among the undergraduates and the Bebb who had once stood unarmed and unafraid among the lions of Lion Country, the selfsame Bebb, or was Gertrude Conover right that the self is a will-o-the-wisp and the carryover from one moment to the next as indefinable and insubstantial as whatever carries over when one candle is lit from another? Such metaphysical speculations as these together with my attempt to hear what Bebb was talking about made it difficult to focus very satisfactorily on the future of the Prospect Street eating clubs which as nearly as I can remember was the subject my group was tossing back and forth. I know only that by about two o'clock there can't have been more than at most twenty people waiting with increasing restlessness to start eating a meal that had been prepared for ten times that many. When I saw Bebb climbing the stairs and gesturing to the orchestra to stop playing, I was sure that he felt the time had come to settle for the ones who were there, write off the ones who were not, and give the signal to start digging in.

As soon as the music stopped, the talking stopped too, and everybody looked up at Bebb on the landing. His tie was a metallic silver shading down into midnight blue. His round, white face was packed tight with confidence.

He said, "Welcome to Revonoc, folks. In case anybody hasn't noticed it yet, Revonoc is Conover spelled backwards because this place where you're standing is the home of Mrs. Gertrude Conover, who is the salt of the earth backwards and forwards both and has a heart so big it must wear her down sometimes just carrying it around. The two of us, we're real glad you college students have come out to return thanks with us today, in fact you're part of what we got to be thankful for most. I know there's lots as don't go in for your long hair and your beards and all that, but like I said to Gertrude Conover the other day, Gertrude Conover there was a time the boys used to go around looking like cowboys and moving picture stars. Nowadays they go around looking like Jesus. Boys, I'm here to tell you for my money that's a change in the right direction."

You could smell the turkey. Several waiters had come in with water pitchers, and you could hear the velvety rattle of ice against silver. Gertrude

Conover stood beside the black in the striped kaftan. Her slip was showing. I wondered if Bebb was just making it all up as he went along.

He said, "Friends, I know you're all waiting for me to wind this up so you can take a seat and get down to business, but first let me unload something I've got on my chest. Gertrude Conover and me, we expected a bigger turn-out today, a lot bigger. There's no point in the world trying to pretend different. Why, we got gobbler and gravy and candy yams out there enough to feed this pack for a week and still have enough left over for a church supper. We got ice cream in special that's made like turkeys and pilgrim hats. Even if we all was to eat up till we burst, it wouldn't hardly make a dent on what's been laid out here today. What a waste of good food! What a waste of a warm and loving heart like Gertrude Conover's who put this spread on! Most of all, what a waste of a day the Almighty made on purpose for sharing together the bread that strengtheneth man's heart and the wine that maketh it glad."

Bebb took a quick, deep breath, and I thought I saw something falter inside his face as if for the first time since he had started, he didn't know what he was going to say next—or do next—and for one moment there arose within me a vision of Bebb there on the baronial staircase of Revonoc once again exposing his final secret—opening, sharing, shriving himself down to the naked and nethermost truth to the Pepsi generation. He did not.

"There's a story in Scripture Jesus told. You know the one I mean," Bebb said, wiping the back of his neck with his handkerchief. "It's the story of the great supper. Luke fourteen sixteen. Jesus, he told it. He told it one Sabbath at a Pharisee's house. The way Jesus spun it out, seems there was a man once that decided to throw a big do. He invited everybody he could think of and some others he'd never of got round to thinking of except he wanted to make sure there wouldn't be a soul left off the list by accident. He got in the food and fancied up his house. He hired a band to play through dinner. Finally the day come round just like this Thanksgiving day did, and the man waited for the company to start turning up. Only it never did. All that turned up was a batch of excuses. There was one sent word he couldn't make it on account of he'd bought him a herd of cows he had to look after. There was another couldn't make it seeing as how he'd just got married and the bride didn't want him to leave her high and dry on the honeymoon, and so on. So the man took all that kind of thing he could take, and then he just flared up. He called in his servant, and he told him to go out into the streets of the town and haul in whoever he saw didn't look like they had anything better to do. The servant did like the man said, and you never saw such a pack as he brought back with him, but there was party hats and snappers to go round, and everybody had the time of their life. That was how the great supper finally come off.

"Friends," Bebb said, and he was glistening now where his sideburns would have been if he'd had sideburns. "Friends, there must be ninety and nine places in this room with nobody to sit down in them, and Princeton, New Jersey, must be full as any town of people who don't have a place on earth to go for Thanksgiving. So what are we waiting for?

"Folks," said Bebb, spreading his arms so wide that his jacket strained at the single button that held it, "let's see can we round us up a houseful and be back inside the hour."

If it was partly the power of Bebb's oratory that made the thing catch fire, it was partly also the power of Gertrude Conover's claret punch. One cup packed the wallop of two martinis, and during the long wait before Bebb's speech many cups had been emptied. Bebb deployed us like J. Edgar Hoover—some to the campus and some to the Seminary and the Westminster Choir School, some to upper Nassau Street and some as far down as Jugtown, others to Witherspoon, Mercer, Prospect, and so on. Even the musicians and several waiters volunteered to join in the search. Bebb took as many as Gertrude Conover's Lincoln would hold and dropped them off here and there along the way before proceeding on by himself to cover the hospital, the Junction, and God knows where-all else. Those with assignments closer went off on foot, some of them running. The reporter from the *Daily Princetonian* stood out on the front steps getting action shots. Gertrude Conover stayed behind to see if she could round up anybody by telephone. Somehow the turkeys were kept warm.

As for me, I ended up by the Palmer Square tiger full of claret and half convinced that either I was dreaming the whole thing or was having a nervous breakdown. How did you invite people to a parable? Whom did you invite?

There's been this mix-up on Gouverneur Road . . . There's this rich lady named Gertrude Conover . . . I know it sounds crazy, but . . . . One after another I tried out various approaches in my head as I started off down the square. November, that bleakest of all months—in October Englishmen shoot grouse, in November themselves, as the grim French jest goes—and never was it much bleaker than just then with the streets virtually empty and the raw, grey air. There was a family of three coming down the steps from the Nassau Inn—a mother and a father and their teen-age son—but using the excuse that they looked as though they'd just had their dinner, I decided against approaching them. On a balcony over one of the shops a woman in a polo coat was setting out two pots of dead ivy, but she had disappeared inside by the time I got close enough to call up to her. There was a man sweeping the floor inside the liquor store and I knocked at the window, but he thought I wanted to come in and buy something and shook his head at me. Farther down, a boy and a girl were standing in front of the Playhouse reading the announcements of coming attractions. The girl had a long orange and black scarf wrapped several times around her neck, and the boy had hair down to his shoulders and was holding a fox terrier on a leash. I tried to explain to them what I was after, but they got it turned around somehow, or I did, with the result that they thought I was asking for a handout instead of offering them one, and although they were very nice about it, they indicated they were broke themselves. It wasn't until I reached the big parking lot at the bottom of the square that I finally succeeded in getting my pitch straight, and of all the people in New Jersey I might have found to make it to, the one it turned out to be was Nancy Oglethorpe.

She was climbing into one of the parked cars so that the first view I had of her was of a pair of fat legs seen from behind with the stockings rolled up six inches or so above the knee. She had on a poison green coat with fur collar and cuffs, and she was carrying an enormous black patent leather purse. She had some kind of black scarf tied around her head and under her chin, but in the process of getting into the car, she knocked it off and it fell to the ground. Stepping back out again, she picked it up and placed it between her teeth while she dug in the big purse for her keys. When she turned around to do this, she still had the scarf in her teeth, which meant that my first impression of her frontally was of a woman with a luxuriant black beard. It was only when she removed the scarf from her teeth that I could see her face.

Those soft, dark, football-shaped eyes, that small scarlet seam of a mouth and milky skin, it was the face of some Sumerian soubrette or Babylonian beauty queen. Her black hair was teased up into a giant beehive except where silken sideburns descended flat about her ears. Even under the folds of her green coat the hanging gardens of her bosom jutted verdant and proud, her hips swelling like the bass fiddle at Belshazzar's feast, and yet for all of this, she tapered down to surprisingly shapely calves and ankles and a pair of almost dainty patent leather feet. Lachaise could have sculpted her or Michelangelo laid her on over eight square feet of Sistine ceiling, but to do her full justice it would have taken some ancient near-Easterner working on a sun-baked wall in Ur. I was about to speak to her through the braided wire parking lot fence when in a voice that sounded as though she might never have been nearer the ancient near east than Canarsie she spoke to me instead. "Pardon me for asking," Nancy Oglethorpe said, "but do you happen to know if there's any place still serving lunch?"

"It's a funny thing you should ask," I said, "because it just happens that—" and so on, with the chill breeze swaying her beehive and making my nose water while in the background the dreaming towers of Princeton went on with their grey November dream. It was almost too easy, and as soon as I'd finished explaining Bebb's problem to her, she made it easier still.

She said, "This is positively providential, and I accept with pleasure I'm sure. I was supposed to meet a gentleman at the Nass, but he didn't show, and by the time I decided to go in without him they told me the dining room was closed, wouldn't you know it. We can take my car if you want and maybe pick up some others on the way. Believe me, this town is full of displaced persons."

And so it was that I ended up in Nancy Oglethorpe's Chevy with the shocks gone and a tubercular rattle under the hood, looking for strangers to fill out the ranks at Revonoc. She drove, and I looked. We cruised down Witherspoon as far as the hospital, then threaded our way back through a lot of narrow side streets. After hearing me bumble my way through the first couple of solicitations, Nancy took over the talking. An old Negro inching his way along John Street in an aluminum walker, a woman with a child coming out of a laundromat, a graduate student with a bad stammer whom Nancy Oglethorpe turned out to have done some work for once, a pair of nuns who were attending an ecumenical conference at the Seminary—her approach with each of them was the same. She would pull up to the curb, roll down the window, and then make a brief statement of which the opening gambit was "Do me a favor" and the closing one "Do yourself a favor" and sandwiched between them a synopsis of the situation on Gouverneur Road presented with such breezy eloquence—those Assyrian eyes, that hanging garden—that by the time we hit Nassau Street again, we had a full car.

Most of the others had returned before we did, and the hall of Revonoc was crowded with people. By three thirty or four the somber afternoon had started deepening to twilight, and lamps were lit, the chandelier that hung down from the top of the stairwell seeding the waxed fruit and polished glasses with pearls of light. The orchestra went back into business with musical comedy—*Hello Dolly*, *The Rain in Spain*, *Vilia*. The punch bowl was replenished. Young and old, black and white, town and gown—"Antonio, it's Noah's ark," Bebb said to me at some point. "We got two of everything, only here it's the clean and the unclean both." He was in his element, standing near the door to greet as many as he could when they first came in. *The heart of Gertrude Conover's as big as all outdoors. You young people are the hope of the future. It's a great school, a great town, a great time to be alive.* Bebb's cheeks swelled out as if with the effort to hold all his phrases in his mouth at once while he popped them out one by one like watermelon seeds. *Praise the Lord, brother, Halleluiah, sister,* and chattering in the overexcited cadence of flood victims in a Red Cross soup kitchen they eddied around through the turkey-laden air. Gertrude Conover had had some success on the phone, and there was a fair sprinkling of blue hair and pearls among what was a mostly young to middle-aged miscellany with the young predominating and decidedly more Elizabethan than Edwardian, more Woodstock than Gouverneur Road. Ants and anteaters, cats and dogs, lambs and lions, they were all stabled together there in uproarious harmony while outside the chill sky darkened.

The elation of Bebb was contagious as he moved around like the bouncing ball in the movie house sing-alongs of my youth. He was pulling something off and he knew he was and everybody there would know it if they stopped to think back on it later. I knew it myself except that I couldn't help knowing too of how even the great feast was a less than adequate substitute for the supper of my small son and estranged wife sitting in Sutton with the TV on top of the icebox going, the breakfast dishes still unwashed in the sink, and a combination of smells in that cluttered kitchen that were like no other smells on earth because they were for better or worse the smells of my own life.

In a way Bebb spoke to this when the time came, among the other things he spoke to. The time came more or less when the ice cream did, the turkeys and pilgrim hats Bebb had mentioned earlier, only starting to go a little soft and shapeless by the time they finally made it to the table. Bebb rose from his seat and spoke from there rather than climbing up to the orchestra landing as before. On one side of him sat the old black whose aluminum walker we had managed to squeeze into the trunk of Nancy Oglethorpe's Chevvy, on his other side a man in a Norfolk jacket who presumably had come with one of the blue-haired ladies.

Bebb talked a long time—it must have been five years since the last time he had had a congregation that big and who knew how long it would be before he had one as big again—but they listened to him, you could tell—listened to him partly, I suppose, because what he said, he said in his high style and partly because, although as a teetotaler he hadn't touched a drop of Gertrude Conover's claret punch, he was drunk on the occasion and spoke in such a disconnected way that you had to listen if only to hear what he was going to bounce to next. I remember in fragments what he said because he said it in fragments.

He said, "The Kingdom of Heaven is like a great feast. That's the way of it. The Kingdom of Heaven is a love feast where nobody's a stranger. Like right here. There's strangers everywheres else you can think of. There's strangers was born twin brothers out of the same womb. There's strangers was raised together in the same town and worked side by side all their life through. There's strangers got married and been climbing in and out of the same fourposter thirty-five, forty years, and they're strangers still. And Jesus, it's like most of the time he is a stranger too. But here in this place there's no strangers, and Jesus, he isn't a stranger either. The Kingdom of Heaven's like this."

He said, "We all got secrets. I got them same as everybody else— things we feel bad about and wish hadn't ever happened. Hurtful things. Long ago things. We're all scared and lonesome, but most of the time we keep it hid. It's like every one of us has lost his way so bad we don't even know which way is home any more only we're ashamed to ask. You know what would happen if we would own up we're lost and ask? Why, what

would happen is we'd find out home is each other. We'd find out home is
Jesus that loves us lost or found or any whichway."

The room flickered like the scratched print of an old newsreel, the
hands of Bebb jerky as Woodrow Wilson laying a wreath on the tomb of
the Unknown Soldier. Shadows. Faces. Afros like puff balls of dust under
beds, more air than hair. Grainy, light-struck blizzarding of old film.

Bebb said, "Eating. Feeding your face. Folks, I've eaten my way
'round the known world. I've eaten snails out of their own shells in Paris,
France. I've eaten octopus in Spain and curry in India so hot it makes your
eyes water and the skin on your head go cold as ice. I've eaten hamburgs
pitiful and grey like the sole of your shoe in greasy spoons from here to
Saint Joe. I've eaten the bread of affliction, all of us has. We got to eat or—
food, it's life, but all the food in the world, all the turkey and fixings plus
your ice cream the shape of hats, it's not life enough to keep you alive
without you eat it with love in the heart.

"Dear hearts," Bebb said, "we got to love one another and Jesus or
die guessing."

Bebb said, "I wasn't born yesterday. I'm not kidding myself what we
got going here is a hundred percent guaranteed to last forever. There's
nothing in this world lasts forever. That's the miserable sadness of it.
Time will be when the party's over. Time will be when all the good times
of our life is over because they are like grass which in the morning it
flourisheth and groweth up and in the evening is cut down and withereth.
Time is the enemy, and the tick of the clock is the sound his toenails
make pattering up on us for the kill. Friends, while we're still sitting here
feeling good let us promise to remember how for a little bit of time we
loved each other in this place. Even when the party's over, let us remember the good time we had here with Jesus."

Where did Bebb's speech begin? Where did it end? The whole gathering was Bebb's speech, his parable, and everything that happened and
was said there by anybody was in a way part of what Bebb said. I don't
know who started the singing, but there was singing. There was *Onward
Christian Soldiers* and *Going Back to Nassau Hall* and *We Shall Overcome*. There was *Swing Low Sweet Chariot*, *The Orange and the Black*,
Roll out the Barrel, and *Blowin' in the Wind*. There was a toast to Gertrude Conover proposed by Bebb and followed by a great deal of whistling
and table-thumping during which Gertrude Conover stood up in her green
dress like a small, lopsided Christmas tree. There was Bebb's saying that
before we got up from the table we should all join hands and sing *Praise
God from Whom All Blessings Flow*. When this worked as well as it did,
he proposed that we follow ancient procedure and exchange with the
neighbor to our right the kiss of peace.

There was a moment's hush, a silent passing of the angel of death
over our heads, and then Bebb turned to the old Negro beside him. He

took that black face between his hands, held it for a few seconds like a mirror he was studying his own face in, and then tipped it forward until at some particular point in time which for all I know was a point appointed before the world began, those tight, relentless lips and that corrugated black forehead met. Then everybody got into the act.

If you added together all the hugging and squeezing and shoulder-pounding that have taken place on Gouverneur Road since the Continental Congress sat in Nassau Hall, I doubt you would have come close to what took place at Revonoc during the next five minutes or so. Boys who looked like Jesus kissed blue-haired ladies and girls out of Charles Addams cartoons, kissed other boys who looked like Jesus. Old tigers with prostates and hearing aids kissed short order cooks and retired policemen. Nuns kissed Daughters of the American Revolution and stammering grad students. Jump-suited martini drinkers and teeny boppers with fly buttons down the outside of their flies kissed Abe Lincolns welted with acne, Midwestern fairies, and vestals from Miss Fine's and Westminster Choir. Seen from the landing it must have looked like some D. W. Griffith Bacchanal with lions roaring from the arena below and Claudette Colbert taking a bath in mother's milk.

Nancy Oglethorpe. Somewhere out of the maelstrom Nancy Oglethorpe rose up, and at the sound of her voice the room grew still. "Jesus . . . *Jesus!*" she called out. She made it sound as though Jesus was taking his time in the washroom and a taxi was waiting outside with the meter on.

There were people long afterwards who said that Nancy Oglethorpe was a plant and that she and Bebb had cooked the whole thing up ahead of time. I do not believe that. On the other hand what happened couldn't have worked out better for Bebb if they had cooked it up. With her eyes lowered, her towering beehive tilted slightly forward, she looked as though she was saying a prayer except that she seemed to be saying it to us rather than to Jesus and in a voice that sounded less like Saint Thérèse of Lisieux than like a New York telephone operator. There was something of the TV commercial in the way she did it: first the real-life scenes of irregularity—the headache, the irritability, the loss of pep—and then the helpful friend with the knowing smile and the family-size remedy.

The first thing Nancy Oglethorpe did was tell her story. She said she was thirty years old. She was unmarried. She had to work for a living. She had started out as a public stenographer at the Pennsylvania Hotel in Manhattan, but she was attracted to Princeton because of its rich cultural opportunities and decided to try her hand there instead. I remember thinking of her immersing herself in the rich cultural opportunities of Princeton like Bathsheba settling down into the tub where King David first laid his eye on her: Nancy Oglethorpe signing up for the chamber music series at McCarter; Nancy Oglethorpe auditing a graduate course in cultural anthropology; Nancy Oglethorpe in flat heels and a corduroy jumper exchanging views on Kafka and women's lib at faculty cocktail parties.

She said that as time went by she found that the greatest call for her services came from the Grad School—dissertations to type, footnotes to check, bibliographies to compile—and since much of this required the presence if not of her employers themselves at least of their books and index cards, she made it a practice to come to their rooms to do her work. Like Florence Nightingale moving through the wounded with her lamp, I pictured Nancy Oglethorpe entering the kind of academic squalor I remembered from my own university days—the unmade bed and mad scientist desk, the glutted ashtray, the petrified coffee at the bottom of plastic cups—and there in the midst of it Nancy Oglethorpe standing in a cloud of patchouli with those eyes as sweet and dark as stewed prunes. She unties the scarf from around her head and pats the beehive back into shape. She removes the poison green coat like the seventh veil and drapes it over the back of an eviscerated armchair.

At this point in her narrative Nancy Oglethorpe paused, and the level of silence in the great hall of Revonoc clicked up a notch. You could hear it. All those faces turned toward her. That whole hymn-singing, yam-stuffed mob frozen in their tracks. Bebb with his neck twisted like a cruller so he could see her over his shoulder. A lady with pixie glasses and a hare-lip. Prince Valiant smoking a joint. Uncle Remus in a sheepskin Afghanistan vest trimmed with sequins and yeti fur. The dowagers of Gouverneur Road and Lilac Lane.

"I was a mere child. I didn't know what I was getting into. The flesh is weak. I started having affairs," Nancy Oglethorpe said. "I have been leading an extremely promiscuous existence ever since to say the least." I pictured her on that unmade scholar's bed like a great mound of yoghurt, her electric typewriter forgotten on the littered desk.

"But that's all a thing of the past now," she said. "I'm making a clean breast of it to you. I'm making a clean breast of it to Jesus."

I tried to imagine Jesus watching her the way I was watching her as she stood there in the glitter of Gertrude Conover's chandelier. In the event that he had answered her summons and was present there on Gouverneur Road with the rest of us, would he see whatever the bees inside that hive were up to that had prompted her to this public confession? And how would Nancy Oglethorpe see Jesus, I wondered, remembering from catechism class a homily to the effect that if Shakespeare were to walk into a room, everybody would automatically stand up whereas if Jesus did, everybody would automatically kneel down. Would Nancy Oglethorpe melt to the floor like ice cream, the nuns, the Afros, all of us?

Nancy Oglethorpe was saying, "I haven't been able to look myself in the eye for seven years. I wanted to sever connections with the past and make a fresh start, but psychological factors having to do with long-term patterns of behavior and the unfortunate reputation I have acquired in

certain circles plus the fact that my professional work is constantly exposing me to situations that are too much for me to handle, these have all
contributed to making it problematical at best that I could ever change.
I have been like a rat caught in a trap. Then out of the blue I got invited
here. I've never been a religious person vis-à-vis church and Jesus et cetera,
but right here in this room it hit me like a bolt out of the blue."

Nancy Oglethorpe paused and smiled. It was the first time I'd seen
those tiny teeth. "Frankly," she said, "what did Jesus ever mean to me
before this? This whole schmier about the blood of the lamb and what
have you, to be perfectly frank I never related to it."

Her voice got smaller and more precise then as if she was working
on a stencil and didn't want to have to go back and make corrections.

She said, "The gentleman I had a luncheon date with today didn't
have the common courtesy to show up. It's like cold water in the face
when a thing like that happens. There I was, dressed up in clothes appro-
priate to the occasion only to have the props kicked right out from under
me. Then this total stranger appeared and asked me here, and I confess my
motives in accepting him were extremely mixed, because the flesh is weak
like I said. But it's like Reverend Bebb has so well expressed it. Nobody's a
stranger. That stranger who came up to me in the parking lot was no
stranger. He was Jesus, as it were. Jesus sent him there to pick me up."

She clasped her hands at her bosom as though she was going to sing
the rest. "Jesus has come into my life to stay," she said. "I am through
with the past. I am through with not daring to let my right hand know
what my left hand is up to. Jesus did it for me, and I want to give him and
Reverend Bebb some small token of my appreciation. I want to give
thanks, and I think I have found the way. I think the way is we should
go on having get-togethers like this on a regular basis. I think we owe it
to Jesus to share with other persons this salvation-type experience we have
had here today.

"I think," said Nancy Oglethorpe, slowly sweeping the room with
her glance, "I think we should try to make Princeton, New Jersey, one big
love feast for Jesus."

There is no power on earth, they say, that can stop an idea when
its time has come, and there at Revonoc that November afternoon there
was no power that even tried to stop it. After the failure of Open Heart,
the burning of the barn, and those four sad and footloose years that followed it, Bebb had finally managed to open a heart to Jesus, and partly
because the time was ripe but partly also because the heart he opened
was Nancy Oglethorpe's heart, history was made that day on Gouverneur
Road.

5

LIFE MUST GO ON, so they say, and by the same token I suppose death also must go on, the two of them hand in hand like old playmates. Life was Bebb, it seemed to me then—Bebb launched on a brilliant new career with Nancy Oglethorpe and Gertrude Conover both beside him at the tiller, Bebb poised to evangelize Princeton, New Jersey, to set up the Supper of the Lamb in the groves of academe. And death was me returning to Mrs. Gunther's boarding house in Sutton, Connecticut, was me driving to school past the house where my wife and son lived as if I had died there. As a ghost I was more haunted than haunting since if either of them marked my spectral passing at about quarter to eight every morning, they gave no sign of it. If from deep inside the house they saw me, I had the feeling that what they saw must be as transparent as the reflection of my own face in the car window that I searched for them through. My arrangement with Sharon was that for the time being we would not see each other, but in my case anyway that seemed a redundance. Even if she had wanted to, I couldn't believe there would be enough of me for Sharon to see. I was free to see Bill whenever I liked, but it was weeks before I felt substantial enough even for that.

Tony and I had rooms side by side at Mrs. Gunther's and shared the bathroom with one other boarder, a retired schoolteacher named Metzger, who spent most of his time in his room watching television. Metzger lived in fear of having a heart attack and made arrangements with Tony and me that if ever he was stricken, he would summon our help by pounding three times on the wall. He tried it on several occasions in the middle of the night just to see if we were on our toes, and it was after one of these false alarms that Tony and I found it possible to talk for about three minutes about something more than what was new at Sutton High.

In T-shirt and undershorts, he sat smoking a cigarette on the foot of my bed and said, "Honest to Christ, Tono, I feel awful about you and Shar. If I thought it was my fault, I'd shoot myself," and I said, "Save your ammunition."

He said, "Are you ever going to get back together again? I mean like this way it's not either one thing or another. It's a real nothing situation."

I said, "I wish you'd tell me," and I remember thinking maybe he could—my own flesh and blood telling me about my own flesh, my own blood; this boy whom my sister had named after me and who, having lived with us since the beginning, not to mention having bedded my wife, was the world's greatest living authority on our marriage, impressed upon

it like a seal and with its seal impressed upon him. If anybody could en-
lighten me, I thought maybe he could.

He said, "It must take real guts."

"Being married," I said.

"I guess," he said. "Being married to her. Only being here like this
too, living in this dump all by yourself after all those years of having her
to live with. It must take guts. I couldn't do it myself, I mean having had
it all once and then not having it any more."

"Having somebody to live with and then having nobody to live with.
You're right," I said, wanting him to be right, wanting somebody to be
right. "I suppose it takes guts both ways."

"Having somebody to live with," he said. "And having somebody to
sack out with," and I remember the little jolt of almost schoolteacherly
satisfaction I felt, as if he was in my English class and had spotted something in a book that I hadn't spotted myself: the guts it took literally to
sack out, *sleep*, by yourself, to let yourself drift alone into dreams, pass
unaccompanied into the night.

"Sometimes I get horny as hell," he said, sitting there with his cigarette in one hand and his bare foot in the other, and my schoolteacherly
satisfaction vanished as I suddenly saw that all he had meant was that it
must take guts to have nobody to have sex with, which was the least of
my worries as of course it was among the worst of his. I could hear old
Metzger flushing the can across the hall while before my eyes my wise
friend and counselor turned into a child dressed up to look like a man
with hair on his chest and the muscles working in his stubbly jaw as he
avoided my glance by looking down at the bare floor.

"You should try cold showers," I said. I had never felt more alone. I
was a middle-aged man surrounded by children and death.

Death was there not only in the form of Metzger ready to thump
three times on the wall any minute—maybe his flushing was a signal for
all I knew—but death was downstairs too, laid out in glass cases for me
to walk through on my way out of the house every morning, death spread
out on the tops of every table and shelf in sight. Our landlady, Mrs.
Gunther, was the widow of an undertaker who, following the custom of
his trade, had over the years accepted payment in kind for his services so
that Mrs. Gunther had gone into the antique business with a house full
of the lockets and brooches, the beads and spoons and assorted fripperies
of the bereaved.

Children also surrounded me—not just Tony, whom I saw every
day, and Bill, whom I saw more clearly for not actually seeing him at all,
but the children I taught whatever it is you try to teach in English—why
Brutus joined the conspirators, the difference between a mixed metaphor
and a dangling participle, how to use the language of Shakespeare and
Milton more like a precision tool than a blunt instrument. But such matters as these can be dealt with for only so long at a time, and then there

you are with maybe half your fifty minutes still left to fill up with something else. If you're good at it, you hold your tongue and wait to see what the class will fill it up with themselves. You let a silence endure until one of them can't stand it any more and says something out of the depths of his discomfort and then another says something else if you're lucky, and before you know it who can tell what queer, instructive thing may happen. But I have never been good at silences myself. In the classroom I am always the uneasy host to whom the absence of chatter spells disaster, and there is no end to the disastrous things I have said just to keep the party going, things that later I could have bitten my tongue for saying.

Not long after the fateful Thanksgiving at Revonoc, for instance, I remember going on at excessive length to a group of ninth graders about what *irony* meant. I think most of them understood it well enough before I started, but just to keep the silence at bay I rattled on about it anyway. I talked about outer meaning and inner meaning. I said that an ironic statement was a statement where you said one thing but to people who had their ears open said another. I explained that when Mark Antony in his funeral oration called the Romans who had murdered Caesar honorable men, he was being ironic because his inner meaning was that they were a bunch of hoods, and when that remark didn't seem to get anything started, I waded in deeper still. I said that in addition to ironic statements you also had ironic situations. Their silence deepened. I remember then a small, fat boy named Stephen Kulak. He was young for the ninth grade and looked it with a round, pink face and the judicious gaze of a child. He said he saw how something you *said* could mean two things but he didn't see how something that *happened* could, so I reached down into my own silence and pulled out the first example that came to hand. I said suppose you had a bride on her wedding day. Suppose she was all dressed up in her white dress and veil, and then on her way back from church a car ran into her and she was killed. That was an ironic situation, I said. It was ironic because on the same day that she started out on a new life, her life stopped. Two things. Now did he see what ironic meant? I remember watching him as he sat there at his desk in a Red Baron sweat-shirt trying to puzzle through my lugubrious illustration until finally in some dim and memorable way his pink face seemed to change and he said, "I get it now. It's a kind of joke," and I could see that he really had gotten it, that there in a classroom with the Pledge of Allegiance framed on the wall and Christmas wreaths made of red and green construction paper Scotch taped to the window panes, Stephen Kulak had learned from kindly old Mr. Parr, who had a hard time keeping his mouth shut, what irony was, and jokes, and life itself if you made the mistake of keeping your ears open. Once you get the reading and writing out of the way, I suppose what you teach children in an English class is, God help you, yourself.

Death ready to thump on the wall or flush the can whenever you least expected it, and Mrs. Gunther, that blondine pelican whose cry was "You don't find them like that much any more," meaning the mortuary napkin rings, lapel watches, christening mugs and souvenir spoons from Grand Rapids, Niagara Falls, the Chicago World's Fair, that she sold in the front parlor directly under the room of that lonesome, horny child who was my nephew. Death leaping out of my own mouth like the frog in the haiku, PLOP, into the primeval pond of dozing innocence that was Stephen Kulak. You never knew when death would come at you or from where. The children at least you could usually see coming. But not always.

I did not see Laura Fleischman coming, for instance, and how could I have seen her? You do not see the first day of spring coming either. Sharon forwarded me a printed notice from the dentist that it was time I showed up for my annual prophylaxis, and I went for the appointment resigned to yet another meeting with Darius Bildabian, whose chairside manner is perhaps best represented by the way he would wait till you had your mouth full of spit-drainers and cotton wadding and then as you were mumbling with pain under the repeated blasts of cold air that he shot into the living heart of your cavity would say to whoever his nurse happened to be at the moment, "What do you suppose Antonio is trying to tell us, Miss X? Maybe it's something funny that happened in school today," his own exorbitant teeth flashing above you terrible as an army with banners.

Waiting in his outer office that December afternoon, I was deep in an article on diseases of the mouth which included the color plate of a tongue covered with matted, black hair when I was summoned into one of the treatment rooms to discover that the hygienist who was to do the preliminaries was Laura Fleischman—a child whom I had not only failed to see coming but whom there would probably have been no way to prepare for even if I had.

She had graduated from Sutton High the same year as Tony, and I had had her as a student in senior English. She was a shy, dark-haired girl with high cheekbones and something fragile about her smile, like a nun on holiday. The year that she was my student, we had met by accident once in a bar at Grand Central, and in my mind at least, certain things had become possible that day—certain doors had half opened which, I suppose because we had not passed through them, had never fully closed so that in a way some shadow of me had stayed waiting in front of them ever since. Sometimes the things that do not quite happen in your life count for more than the things that do.

I had not seen her since the day she graduated, and there she stood now in a white dress and white stockings with her hair caught back in a silver barette. The first thing she did was anoint the corners of my mouth with a fingertip each of some white lubricant that made me feel like the Tin Woodman when Dorothy oiled his hinges to keep his tears from rust-

ing them, and such conversation as we had took place for the most part
with her hands in my mouth—the little whirring wheels of rubber and
emery, the gritty pink dentifrice, the squirts of tepid Lavoris. She had
seen my name in the appointment book so she was ready for our meeting
as I was not. Was *King Lear* still my favorite play? Did I ever see so-and-so
or so-and-so from her class? What did I think were Sutton's chances in
track that spring? How were Mrs. Parr and the baby? She had come with
questions enough to see her through the whole session whereas I was
empty-handed of course and with my mouth jacked open and my eyes
fixed glassily on Darius Bildabian's dental school diploma hanging on the
wall considered telling her the truth about Sharon and me but decided
not to, said just that Mrs. Parr was still every inch herself but the baby
was no longer a baby. None of us was. The one question I could think to
ask her in return was about Carl West, the boy she had been going steady
with when I'd last known her, a handsome, laconic basketball player who
according to Tony was making out with her in those days any time he
felt like it, which I could only imagine was often.

"Oh, I haven't seen him for ages," she said, "not since we broke
things off my senior year." She had turned to get something out of a
drawer when my question stopped her. The silver barette held her hair
away from her head in back, and as she stood gazing down into the
drawer for whatever she would start looking for again when she remembered what it was, the nape of her neck looked bare and vulnerable. She
said, "I wrote you a letter about it. You were in England, and I wrote you
things were over between Carl West and I. I wrote you on my eighteenth
birthday."

I said, "I remember," not remembering. I wondered if I had ever
answered the letter.

Out of the drawer she took a long-handled dentist's mirror that caught
the light like a star in her hands as she turned back to me. "Carl always
said I had a school-girl crush on you," she said.

With pick and mirror she poked her way around my lower jaw while
I watched her face for signs of what she was finding. At twenty-two she
could have been my daughter, I thought, could have made me in my
forties a grandfather by now as for all I knew maybe she already had
although she wore no ring. I wondered if Tony had been right about her
and Carl West. She frowned as though she was reading my teeth like a
palm, my character as well as my cavities lying open before her, my future
as well as my past. I dreaded the moment when she would remove her
mirror long enough to tell me that she had seen the first tell-tale signs of
fuzz on my tongue, a suspiciously soft spot near the gum line of my marriage. I could see the pulse at the base of her throat, the open white
collar and shoulder straps of her white slip as she leaned over me. "Rinse,"
she said, handing me a pleated paper cup of warm water which I tried to
spit out with the urbanity of a wine-taster.

"Did you?" I said as she came at me again, and it stopped her mirror in mid-air.

"I'm sorry?" she said as though I had caught her attention wandering in senior English.

"Have a crush," I said.

"All the girls did," she said. "Open, please," hurrying back from the spree of her smile to telling my teeth again like beads. She made a pencil mark on the chart of my lower jar. "Everybody thought you were out of this world, your name being Antonio and everything. You know how girls are at that age. You seemed so much younger than the other teachers. You didn't treat us like a bunch of dumb kids like most of them did. Remember the time you spent the class before the prom showing the boys how to tie a bow tie? We thought—" Sharp as a needle, her pick had found something to reckon with in one of my back molars. It kept getting stuck in it as though the molar was made of wax. The edge of her hand was cool against my lip. She said, "Naturally we knew we didn't have a chance, I mean the girls. We used to see your wife when she came out to watch track practice. Everybody said she looked like a Hollywood star. Carl West said—" Some fragment of the molar suddenly chipped off and the pick hit pay dirt with a squill of hot pain that I could feel down to the soles of my feet.

"You'll need Novocaine for that one," she said as she marked it down on her chart.

I said, "I'll need last rites," and there was death again because every pain is a kind of rehearsal, I suppose, for the final pain, the loss of each snag of tooth, each inch of hairline, a foretaste of loss itself as John Donne knew, that grim wag with his puns on dying: dying as death, dying as orgasm, because every time you fire forth the stuff and substance of life, your life itself is somehow less, somehow lost a little. Death, sex, a child named Laura Fleischman, all staring me down together as I reclined there with a rubber bib under my chin and Darius Bildabian's fluorescent klieg bright in my eyes. CASTLE, it said on the light—the seige perilous.

"Mrs. Parr and I," I said. "Maybe you've heard. We're not together right now."

"Golly, Mr. Parr. I didn't know," Laura Fleischman said. Golly . . . gee whiz. . . "I'm awfully sorry."

I'm sorry. It had been Tony's phrase the night he had told me through chattering teeth that he and Sharon were lovers, burying his face in my shoulder, his salt-stiff hair, and saying it over and over again. When a child says *I'm sorry*, the sorrow becomes yours to hear the child have to say it. It was Stephen Kulak all over again—the sorrow mine for having exposed inner meaning to a child for whom outer meaning was puzzle enough. Irony is a game primarily for grownups. A form of solitaire. Laura Fleischman waited beside me in first communion white as I looked for some way to make light, to make white, of the whole thing.

I said, "You know it may be for the best. You fall in love and get married and have kids—all of it in such a blind rush the way things go. Maybe somewhere along the line there's got to be a pulling apart so you can pull back together someday with your eyes open. I haven't given up by a long shot."

"You mean it's not a legal separation or anything," Laura Fleischman said.

I said, "Separation is always illegal as hell."

She was looking down at the lilypad tray where her instruments lay and the chart where she'd marked down the worst. She said, "They say it's always darkest just before the dawn."

I said, "There are always lots of good things like that left to say."

" 'The worst returns to laughter,' " she said. "When Carl and I split up, I wrote you that was my favorite line in *King Lear* because it was so hopeful. I never dreamed I'd be using it someday to cheer you up."

I said, "You've cheered me up already."

Once in my life I had held Laura Fleischman's hand. It was the time we had happened to meet in the bar at Grand Central, and with a couple of martinis under my belt I had done it then almost by accident, before I knew what I was doing. This time I was dentist chair sober and knew what I was doing what seemed centuries before I got around to doing it. My hand was still holding the arm of the chair it had grabbed onto when the pick struck home, and her hand was near enough mine for me to feel the little warmth of air between them. In distant cities mothers unaccountably gathered their children to their skirts and stray dogs showed their teeth as I reached out and took her hand in mine. I said, "You've given me back my Pepsodent smile."

The *irony* of the thing as I look back on it, the outerness and innerness of what took place there in Bildabian's office. What was outer was the hands themselves, was the diploma on the wall and the jet of water circling in the basin at my elbow, was those white stockings and trig white nurse's dress she wore, with her dark hair gathered back at her neck, and my grey flannel legs stretched out at full length, my scuffed cordovans toed out on the footrest. What was inner was not just the puzzlement of flesh our hands had failed to solve—in the comic-strip balloon of my forty-three year old fancy I saw her of course not in white but in nothing, the slimness of her fragrant and shy as John Skelton's midsummer flower, gentle as falcon and hawk of the tower. What was inner was mostly the sense of history, her history and mine, the history we were making. The irony of the present is that it has a future. The irony of a hand is all it stands both to hold and to lose.

"Poor fool and knave," I said, like Bebb quoting Scripture, "I have one part in my heart that's sorry yet for thee."

Darius Bildabian said, "Long time no see, young fella. What's the bad news?" He pushed through the curtained door with a round mirror strapped to his forehead like a miner, the sound of his voice cleaving our hands like a pick. He took the chart from Laura Fleischman, studied it, humming, and then pushed the mirror down to where he could peer through the hole in the middle and see into the open secret of my mouth. Later, when the drilling started on my back molar and I lay there making strangled noises at the sheer metaphysics of the thing, he said, "Maybe it's the one about the traveling salesman, Miss Fleischman. Maybe it's one Antonio picked up in the locker room at Sutton High," and when I stood up eventually to leave—he had his arm around my shoulder and part of my face was dead and cold—Laura Fleischman said, "I'm still living with my mother in the same old house, so if you ever feel like a home-cooked meal, you just let us know," which meant among other things that before I left the office, I had to explain everything to Darius Bildabian, or almost everything.

My face was just starting to come back into its own when later that same day of death and children I drove over to Sharon's to pick up my son Bill and take him to a restaurant for supper, just the two of us. It was to be our first meeting since my departure some three weeks before, and I had arranged it with Sharon over the telephone. It was also the first time I was to see her, or so I assumed until I rang the doorbell—how did the stray dogs of the world respond as I stood there on my own doorstep wondering whether to ring or just walk in?—and it was answered not by Sharon but by Anita Steen. It was like taking a drink of ice-water only to discover it isn't ice-water but Gordon's gin. Or vice versa.

Anita Steen looked like a kind of child herself in a way, a short, wrinkled child in velvet slacks and a frilled shirt, a child grown old before its time trying to get somebody to adopt it. She said Sharon had had to stay late at the shop and Bill was still upstairs finishing his bath. She asked me to come in and sit down while I waited. She offered me a drink, which I accepted. She leaned forward with her elbows on her velvet knees and talked to me through the smoke of her king-size Winston.

She said, "Big boy, I'm going to give it to you straight. I don't like what's going on one bit. This kid you're married to is going through hell. She'd shoot me if she knew I was saying that, but I'm saying it. When you brought her up here from Squatville, Florida, did you ever stop to think what you were letting her in for? Did you ever stop to think *who* you were bringing up here, for God's sake? Maybe she's picked up how to look like Westchester County, but she's straight corn pone just the same. She doesn't say manure, she says horseshit. She doesn't read *The New Yorker*, she reads *True Confessions*. If her tail itches, she scratches it, and she wouldn't call it her tail either. I don't mean she doesn't try like hell. What do you think all these lessons are about—speed reading lessons and yogi lessons and studying Adele Davis as if it was the holy damn Bible? Why do you think she came to me for guitar? The point is it doesn't work. She's a fish out of water. You name me three friends she's made up here on her own. I don't mean people you know together. I mean people she knows all by herself. She's made one friend, and you want to know what her name is? Her name is Anita Steen, and that's not exactly what you'd call hitting the jackpot."

She said, "Listen, it's time you learned something about loneliness from an expert. If I was the bad fairy at the christening, you know what I'd leave by the cradle all wrapped up in pink ribbon? I'd leave loneliness, that's what I'd leave—the straight, hundred proof, bonded stuff. I'm going to tell you something. That bourbon you're drinking isn't any of the stuff you left here when you pulled out. I happen to know you left three fifths of Jack Daniels when you pulled out, and that's not one of them because the last of the Mohicans was carried out of here feet first days ago. Somebody told me this morning just breathing the air in the Sharanita Shop was enough to give you a buzz. Maybe she's not off the deep end yet, but she's climbing up to the high board."

She said, "I'm going to tell you one more thing, and then I'll shut up. You better make *mucho* big effort to patch things up between you two or it's going to be too late. For Christ sake, come down off your high horse, Antonio Parr, because pardon my French, but don't you believe you're the only thing in pants that's rung this doorbell since you left, and I'm not referring to Anita Steen either." Whereupon, as if on cue, my five year old son arrived. He was wearing corduroy overalls the color of tomato soup and an Irish sweater put on backwards so that it crowded him under the chin. His feet were bare and lobsterish from the bath, and he was carrying his sneakers in his hands. He said, "Guess what, I made a pee in the tub and nobody even knew a thing."

DURING THE WEEK, I lived in Sutton—lived in my room at Mrs. Gunther's where I corrected papers, slept and ate my solitary breakfasts of tap-water instant coffee and dry cereal wet down with milk kept cold on the window-sill, lived in my classroom at school, lived in the diner down by the station where I had supper sometimes with Tony or Metzger but usually alone. Tony went his own way, and I leaned over backwards not to pry because the same footlooseness which was purgatory for me was a kind of potential paradise for him, the first time in his life he had been on his own, and I didn't want him to think he had to carry his uncle on his back. Most of the time I didn't know much about whom he saw or where he went, knew only that he kept late hours. Once in a while I would happen on him talking over the phone under the stairs when I came in. At my approach his slow murmur always turned clipped and informational, and no matter how many steps at a time I tried to make it up to my room, he had invariably hung up by the time I got there. Metzger had no such involvements as far as I knew, but supper time, he explained to me, was prime time with Perry Mason leading on to Walter Cronkite leading on to Truth or Consequences and thence to the crescendo of Dean Martin or Laugh In so most of my suppers I ate by myself.

I spent the weekends at Revonoc. There were faster ways of making the trip there, but I always took the way I had known as a child—the old Merritt Parkway, the Henry Hudson, the West Side Highway, and then on under the river through the Lincoln Tunnel to New Jersey. I loved the view you got of the George Washington Bridge at dusk when it came alive with the tiny lights of cars, that great fragile web thrown across to the Palisades in a way that always made me think of Walt Whitman's noiseless, patient spider launching forth filament, filament, filament out of himself in the hope that it would catch somewhere, O my soul, on the far side. I loved the looming hulls and silent stacks of the liners moored at the piers along the West Side Highway, and I loved rolling like a Tinkertoy down the ramp into the tunnel. When I was a small boy, my father told me once that we were traveling under the river and if I kept my eyes open I might see fish swimming by, and that mild whimsy has so stuck in my mind all these years that every trip I've ever made through that tunnel since has given him back to me again for a moment or two, my poor young father who died before I got around to knowing who he was. Whenever at night I dream about tunnels, I'm sure it has nothing to do with what Freud would say but that it's my father I'm dreaming about, and I suppose Freud would have something to say about that too. You can't be too careful what you tell a child because you never know what he'll take hold of and spend the rest of his life remembering you by.

I went to Revonoc for the weekends because I needed to see Bebb, needed to have someone I could talk to about Sharon—especially after Anita Steen's broadside—and about the life I was leading without her, to use the word *life* loosely, and about the life she was leading without me or that was leading her. It wasn't that I needed Bebb to give me advice so much as I needed him simply to give me his attention—to reassure me, simply by listening to my story, that it wasn't just a story, wasn't just something I had dreamed up, but something that was actually happening to me, something that had had a beginning and was having a middle and that someday, I hoped, would have like everything else an end. The irony of the thing, as I might have explained it to Stephen Kulak, was that Bebb hardly noticed my need. My need and his not noticing. Two things.

It was Gertrude Conover who explained Bebb to me. Bebb himself was off somewhere, and she was giving me tea in her upstairs sitting room.

She was stretched out on a chaise longue with her feet up and a Siamese cat in her lap. She said, "Leo is round. He has always been round. The things that man has done with his life—all his lives—and the things his life has done to him, they have made him round as a ball. They have made him the shape of a boulder, the shape of an apple."

What I wanted to say to her was that Sharon was hitting the Jack Daniels, that Anita Steen and I weren't the only things in pants that had rung her bell since I'd moved out, that all through my supper with Bill I had had to sit on my hands to keep from pumping him about her, listening instead as he sat there over his congealing hot roast beef sandwich looking at me through his mother's eyes, more green than brown, and chattering on about what he wanted for Christmas as if it was the most natural thing in the world that we weren't all living under the same roof any more. But Gertrude Conover either didn't notice what I wanted to say any more than Bebb did or else she was approaching it, as she walked, sideways. She said, "You know those tops they have for children, those boxes with the lids cut out in diamond shapes, star shapes, cross shapes and so on so that the child has to pick out the right shape block to get it into the box through the right shape hole? That is the law of karma in a nutshell. The shape you make of your life this time around has everything in the world to do with the shape of your life the next time around. If it is an angry, jagged shape, the only life it will fit into next time will be an angry, jagged life—a wolf, perhaps, or somebody like that awful New Hampshire journalist who made poor Muskie cry."

I said, "Bip is a ball?"

She said, "He even looks like a ball. You can see it for yourself, Antonio. You don't have to be a theosophist. He is tight and solid and round. He rolls like a ball. He bounces like a ball. He is hard to get hold of like a ball because a ball has no corners or edges to get hold of it by. In all his lives his karma attracts him to round, ball-like people like round Nancy Oglethorpe. Everything she's got is round. And to round places. You were with him at Stonehenge. Why do you think he was so much in his element at Stonehenge? You saw the way he looked there—as if he'd come home. My dear, Stonehenge is a circle. And now Alexander Hall. Don't think it's an accident that Leo Bebb found his way to Alexander Hall. Besides there are no accidents. That's karma for you. In a nutshell."

Alexander Hall, that roundest and most Bebbsian of all University buildings, that great mound of rough-hewn pink brownstone with its round Romanesque arches, its fat, round turrets with their conical roofs, the bulging sides of its circular, glassed-in arcade that you have to pass through to enter the rotundity it encircles, that omphalos of varnished oak and Homeric mosaic where public lectures, concerts, Roman Catholic masses, and other such miscellaneous University activities take place. Alexander Hall was where, by accident or otherwise, Bebb and Nancy Oglethorpe came to preside over their Love Feasts for a while. Gertrude Conover helped arrange it through her Nassau Hall connections, thus making herself the agent of karmic potencies.

The article in *The Daily Princetonian* was what started the ball rolling, to use yet another expression of roundness that Gertrude Conover would have said was no accident. It hit the front page, and there were pictures. Bebb standing beneath the stone lions of Revonoc. Waiters, musicians, guests hurrying down the front steps on their way to invite in the uninvited. Nancy Oglethorpe making her apologia under the chandelier. The reporter played his story straight for the sake of laughs, but there were no laughs of the kind the reporter had played it for because right from the start Bebb was taken up like Tiffany glass or Art Nouveau, not as something to laugh at but as a base from which to laugh instead at the kind of people who would find him laughable. If Bebb had appeared in beard and beads playing Jesus rock on an electric guitar, the chances are Princeton wouldn't have given him the time of day, but he came in his gents' furnishings suit talking about the blood of the Lamb as if it was delivered to his front door by the quart every morning, and Princeton lapped it up with an enthusiasm that I think caught even Bebb by surprise.

Bebb gave much of the credit to Nancy Oglethorpe. He said, "Antonio, that woman is a powerhouse. I don't care spit how she used to tomcat around out there at the grad school, she came clean about all that the first feast we ever had. Though your sins be as scarlet, they shall be white as snow, Antonio, that's how clean she come, and she's been giving her all to Jesus ever since. Why she's better than Brownie ever knew how to be, and she's no kind of pussyfoot like Brownie is either. The trouble with Brownie is that life threw such a scare into him from the word go, he never lived it, just stuffed it inside his drawers and sat on it. That Nancy Oglethorpe, she's lived. She knows what she's talking about when she talks. And she knows what I'm talking about too."

Knew what Bebb was talking about and with her organizational skills and convert's zeal saw to it that what he was talking about was given maximum coverage and distribution by peeling those original Thanksgiving banqueters, whose names and addresses she managed to get down in shorthand before they left, to a hard core which she deployed through the town and campus like Vigilantes armed with flyers announcing each subsequent Love Feast as it came along and suggesting the menu. *Put your hand in the hand of the man who fed five thousand. Eat your troubles away at the Supper of the Lamb. Ho, everyone that thirsteth, come!*

And they came, more and more as the weeks went by, until finally Revonoc wasn't big enough to hold them, thirsting for God (if anybody) knew what and fulfilling the dream Bebb had gone to sleep on all those years of gypsying around the world with Gertrude Conover and fulfilling too, I suppose, some round, Babylonian dream of Nancy Oglethorpe's. She too came into her own in that round of feasting, found herself for the first time not dictated to but dictating, not typing but typed at last as some kind of camp Magdalen forgiven much because she loved much. Bebb was the master of the feasts and Nancy Oglethorpe the caterer who saw to it that there was more than enough of everything to go around including herself.

Who came? In an interview in the *Prince* Nancy Oglethorpe was quoted as saying, "Being as how I took psychology at Hunter College and it has been a life-long interest of mine ever since that time, I am more psychologically oriented than Bible oriented vis-à-vis the so-called Love Feast movement here in town, and though we end up meaning the same thing I would use a different type language than Leo Bebb to describe what's going on. Mr. Bebb says the individuals we are relating to are lost sheep, and I say more they are like myself lonely and insecure persons with the kind of self-destruct hang-ups you got to expect anywhere this day and age but especially in a cultural scene like Princeton which attracts a basically introverted and egg-head type of individual. Who comes? You name it, at Love Feasts we got it."

What did they find when they got there? The detractors of the movement—because of course detractors were inevitable and when they came, they came not without ammunition—the sour mouths, nitpickers and malcontents said that at any given Love Feast you could find whatever you were looking for, meaning the worst, needless to say: winos finding winos, acid-heads acid-heads, fairies fairies, victims victimizers, and so on, everybody confessing his sins and then cozying up afterwards to the ones who had a taste for the same kind of sinning he did. Whatever the truth of that, enthusiasts and detractors alike agreed that what they found at those Love Feasts was essentially each other.

The original turkey and claret punch gave way to simpler fare. While Revonoc was still the scene of operations, they experimented with various possibilities. They tried Kool Aid, milk, and a combination of ginger ale and Welch's grapejuice. They tried Slim Jims, Sultanas, Fritos. It was Bebb the teetotaler who said he didn't care much what there was to eat but thought what there was to drink should have some kick to it. He said it over Nancy Oglethorpe's objection that if word got around alcohol was being used, it might attract the wrong kind of people, to which Bebb said, "Nancy, it's the wrong kind of people Jesus *wants*. Why, that's the whole thing about Jesus. And he wants the right kind of people too. I was raised a Baptist, and a Baptist takes to spirits like Satan takes to holy water, but I can't help that. It's spirits helps oil the hinges between the wrong people and the right people, and it's spirits Jesus served the night they come to take him, not soda pop, though there's Baptists would tell you different." So what they ended up with was a kind of punch that was partly for Jesus' sake and partly too, I think, for Lucille's sake because like the Tropicanas that Lucille had drowned her sorrows in and finally herself, there was a lot of orange juice in it, only then, in place of the gin and in far less majestic proportions, a dry, white wine. It even tasted like Tropicanas if you didn't think too hard about it. "Here's to Jesus," Bebb would say, raising his paper cup high to start things off, and then with their Tropicanas in hand, everybody would turn to his neighbor and say, "Here's to you." That was the way the Love Feasts opened. They closed, as on Thanksgiving, with the kiss of peace.

And what went on between? In between the toast to Jesus at the beginning and all the kissing and squeezing at the end, there were not only all the people who might be corralled in off the streets—because at each Love Feast Bebb sent out a deputation for that purpose—and all the people also that the ones who were corralled in might in turn corral in themselves, and so on, world without end. Whatever you found at Bebb's Love Feasts, you could be sure it would be more than you had bargained for.

And you could be sure, of course, that there would be Bebb himself, that *round* man, that snowball gathering substance somehow as he gathered momentum, growing rounder and fuller as the weeks went by until you felt that the time would come when his tight skin, his tight face and raincoat, must surely split. No wonder he failed to notice the obscure needs I brought with me from Sutton. Once in a while, he tried. If I mentioned Sharon's name, he would sometimes glance my way over his shoulder as a miler might at the shout of a familiar voice from the bleachers—"You got to keep the wires open between you and her, Antonio. You got to keep them open between you and Jesus," profundities like that —but then on back to the relentless dash and downhill barrelling again. He had his hands full.

The Love Feasts were feasts, which meant anybody could propose a toast, propose anything. There was an instructor from the History Department, for instance, a man named Roebuck, with a handlebar moustache and combat boots. He came regularly. When he spoke, you could see his teeth through his moustache. There was something antiphonal about the public propositions and counterpropositions that he and Bebb exchanged.

"Every place I look I don't see Jesus," I remember Roebuck's saying once. "Where is he?"

"Wherever two or three are gathered together in his name, that's where he is," Bebb said.

"Can't see him," Roebuck said.

"He sees you," Bebb said.

"We have this twelve year old, this sick one. His hands don't work," Roebuck said. "He wears a little helmet with a piece sticking out from the forehead with a Magic Marker attached to it. That's how he writes his name."

"Jesus said suffer the little children to come unto me and hinder them not," Bebb said. "You bring him on in here next time."

"You will make him all better," Roebuck said.

Bebb said, "Lord, I believe, help thou mine unbelief."

Roebuck said, "You will give him the use of his hands and fingers. You will make it so he can walk like a human being."

Bebb said, "There's nobody knows the grief in your heart save only one. It's like your grief is his grief."

Roebuck said, "Since Thomas Aquinas, the fattest of all the saints, there have been five classic proofs advanced for the existence of God. There's the ontological proof, the teleological proof, the proof from consensus, and so forth. Do you have a favorite?"

Bebb said, "I never got past grade school. I wasn't much bigger than your boy when I took my first job so I couldn't prove the six-times table. Jesus, he believed God existed. That's the best proof I got."

"Of course there's one place I haven't looked for God yet," Roebuck said, "or Jesus either."

"Where's that you haven't looked for him?" Bebb said.

Roebuck stood there in Alexander Hall with the bottoms of his trousers bloused out over his combat boots. "Up my bleeding ass," he said.

Or Bebb on power: "The American Free Enterprise system couldn't never so much as been if it wasn't for Jesus. The Christmas trade alone is a for instance. Right here in Princeton, New Jersey, more gifts are being bought and wrapped up this minute in the name of Jesus than in any other name in the Yellow Pages or the whole telephone directory. That's power for you."

Or Bebb on confession: "It's not like Jesus doesn't know all the things you ever done that are wrong without you telling him about them. But until you lay your cards on the table and level with him, they're the great gulf fixed between you. It's only when you tell it to Jesus like it is that they become the Golden Gate Bridge."

Or Bebb on travel: "All the roads in the world are one road when you come right down to it because your dirt tracks, your superhighways, your Park Avenues, the place they all end up at is the same place, and that's the funeral parlor. We all got that to look forward to before we're through, and we all got rough places and smooth places both till we get there, so in the meantime this cup I'm hoisting to Jesus, it's one for the road."

And there was also, of course, Nancy Oglethorpe. Like Superman, her true identity remained hidden from the majority of mankind. She went right on with her career as itinerant stenographer, and nobody would have looked twice to see her misfiring up the hill to the grad school in her black Chevvy with her electric typewriter on the back seat, her Corrasable Bond and sharp yellow pencils, to enter those ravaged scholars' rooms armed now with the breastplate of righteousness and the helmet of salvation to fend off temptation. Like unassuming Clark Kent, who only when he stripped down to his acrobat's tights and waist-length cape revealed the superstrength that enabled him to fly through the air like a bird and batter down steel walls with his bare fist, it was only at the Love Feasts that Nancy Oglethorpe was seen for what she truly was.

She presided over the distribution of the Tropicanas. She organized the rescue squad that followed Scriptural precedent by combing the streets for the uncombed. She handled press releases to the *Daily Princetonian* and, as word spread, to the *Trenton Times* and *Newark Evening News*. She did the mimeographing and sent out the notices and when the practice started of collecting love offerings at each feast, managed the banking and bookkeeping of that too.

Bebb was crazy about her from the start. Partly, I suppose, it was because hers was the first heart he gave himself credit for opening since the old Holy Love days and partly because she was the first to suggest that the original Love Feast should be perpetuated. I think too that Bebb was impressed by her beehive, her French heels, her poison green coat and found it all far closer to his idea of *haute couture* than Gertrude Conover's muted woolens, far closer to what he thought might catch the wandering eye of the Pepsi generation. Or maybe Gertrude Conover was right and what attracted Bebb to her most was that like him, like Stonehenge and Alexander Hall, she was round. She was also, as she put it, psychologically oriented, and from Hunter College days she brought certain encounter-group techniques and ploys which in time Bebb came to adapt to his own ends.

She said, "It's got to be more give and take, Leo, not just you giving and them taking all the time. Nobody can relate to a father figure indefinitely. Everybody wants a piece of the action," so there came to be feasts where instead of preaching to them, Bebb would simply stand up on the platform and throw words out to them. The words he threw out were old sawdust trail words like *salvation* and *sin* and *faith*, and his congregation would come back at him with whatever words first entered their heads, sometimes a word at a time, sometimes a whole barrage of words at once.

JESUS Bebb would wing at them like a big league pitcher, and *Christ* they would bat back at him, *Christ* and *cross* and *crutch*, *cripple* and *couple* and *two*, *one*, *win*, *wine*, *waste*. HEAVEN he'd send sizzling down toward home plate, then duck to avoid being clobbered by *sky*, *pie*, *day*, *night*, *light*, *dark*, *dreaming*, *Daddy*.

I heard PEACE get him *sleep*, get him *sack* and *sex*, *languor* and *anger* and *fight*, *truce*, *truth*, *together*, *tomorrow* and *sorrow*; LOVE get him *lost*, *found*, *food*, *full*, *feel*, *heal*, *holy* and *Hell*. Sometimes the words sailed up between them like birthday balloons.

And sometimes I watched him up there calling out old names that he had lived with all his life and getting nothing back at all. *Beelzebub, Cherubim, Goshen*. They would hang suspended in the echoing silence of Alexander Hall while he stood up there on the same platform where Eleanor Roosevelt and John Mason Brown had stood before him.

It was Nancy Oglethorpe also who introduced a new method of confession into the Love Feast liturgy. Originally confessions had been made
the way Nancy Oglethorpe had made hers at the first Love Feast—one
person would stand up when he felt like it and say his piece. I remember
a seminarian with all his hair shaved off and a loose-fitting grey sweat-shirt
saying that he stole on the average of a dozen books a week from the U.
Store. I remember a varsity tennis player with a golden beard telling how
he had corrupted a twelve year old girl on the shores of Lake Carnegie. I
remember a janitor with the face of a Supreme Court justice describing
how in Normandy in 1944 he had for no reason he could explain shot a
child out of a tree like a squirrel.

But later Nancy Oglethorpe said, "I'm asking you, how many got
what it takes to stand up and do it like that? Six or seven maybe? Ten
out of a hundred? You need guts to come clean in public like that, and
if you had that kind of guts, you probably wouldn't have sinned in the
first place. It's a vicious-type circle." So again she persuaded Bebb to do
it so that everybody could get into the act, and the way she taught him
was this.

When Bebb gave the word, everybody was supposed to pick out a
person to confess to so that there was a lot of milling around and changing places, and for a while it looked like a bargain basement with everybody trying to find the one it would cost him least to spill the beans to—
townie dropouts and varsity jocks, Aquarian potheads, coed madonnas
with ironed hair, butterfly-crotched peace-freaks who put flowers in the
barrels of ROTC rifles. When everybody was finally coupled, the Ogle-
thorpian rite was simple. Your partner held his hands up side by side,
palms out. You made believe his hands were a mirror. You looked into that
mirror and described out loud what was wrong with your face. Then your
partner described in turn what was wrong with his face as he looked into
the mirror of your hands. When you were both finished, for absolution
you fed each other the sacramental elements. If crumbs got into your beard
or Tropicanas slopped down over your love-beads, Nancy Oglethorpe
said so much the better. It helped break the ice. An ice-type breaker.

The only time I gave it a try myself was soon after my conversation
about Sharon with Anita Steen. It was the first Sunday the moveable feast
had moved into Alexander Hall and when Bebb gave us the word to
choose our partners, I felt a hand on my shoulder and turned to find
Nancy Oglethorpe standing in the aisle asking me in effect if she could
have the next dance.

Looking into her hands, I did the best I could. I said, "They say
husbands and wives get to look like each other after a while so part of
what I see in my face is my wife's face. The hitch is my wife and I have
split up so the part of my face that's got her in it has split up too. It
won't work any more anyway. When I took our little boy out for supper,
just the two of us, I couldn't make it work worth a damn. I'm afraid

that's all I can see in my face right now, Nancy, but it'll have to do. You're
next. Amen."

I raised my hands quickly then to have them there to hide behind
before Nancy Oglethorpe had a chance to lower hers. I just made it. Over
the tops of my fingertips I could see her beehive bending so near me that
if my hands hadn't been between us, we would have been eyeball to eyeball. I didn't know what she was up to. Some confession so dark that she
had to come this close to whisper it? Some unspeakable encounter-group
ploy like suddenly spreading my hands apart by the thumbs and taking
my nose between her teeth? Instead what she did was this. Taking my
hands by the wrists, she planted a moist, pneumatic kiss dead in the
center of one of them. I can feel it there still.

Was it to absolve me? I don't know, but the next moment there we
were like a bride and groom feeding each other the first piece of wedding
cake. I took a sip of Tropicana from her Lily cup. She broke off a piece
of my Ritz cracker with her tiny teeth and swallowed it, unchewed, like
the true host.

Maybe she wasn't absolving me with her kiss at all. Maybe she was
just making a pass. But maybe too the lines can't be drawn as sharply as
that, and as I drove back to Sutton that evening, drove north past the
Cloisters and the piers of the great bridge, it occurred to me that one way
or the other maybe her kiss was as close to the kiss of peace as any I was
likely to find anywhere else just then. Things being what they were.

7

THE WEEK after I got back from Princeton was the last one before vacation, and I spent the afternoon of the final day of classes helping straighten
up the gym after the Christmas book fair. In the overheated world of
Sutton High it is always mid-August and under the bright overhead lights
of the gym in their wire cages it is always high noon so that during the
hours I spent packing the unsold books back into cartons and lending
a hand with the tables, I lost all track of what the weather was up to
outside. It was only when I stepped out into the parking lot around five
that I discovered that about four inches of snow had fallen, and it was
still coming down hard.

The damp linen smell and coarse-woven silence of the snow. The
fan-shapes of light from the gym windows and the sight of my car almost
unrecognizable as it crouched there lonely and white. To teach school is to
catch from the children you teach not only their colds but a little of their

childhood too, and I stood there at the gym door with a panic in my stomach no less sweet and wild than Stephen Kulak's, say, at the thought that school was out and vacation had begun, at the unexpected sight of the snow. In the fullness of time, the Scriptural phrase goes, and for a moment or two it was as if, filled to bursting, time had split apart at last, and there at the heart of it was the mystery laid bare. It was time to go home, or the heart of time *was* home, and I had been there all along without knowing it just the way all that hot, bright afternoon of dismantling the book fair I had been part of a snowfall without knowing it. Then Ralph Milliken, the Principal, thrust his way out through the door at my back in his clinking galoshes and velour cap with ear-flaps saying, "Plan to be home for Christmas?" as he pushed on past me, and with my briefcase heavy in one hand and my portable typewriter heavy in the other, I realized that home was Mrs. Gunther's and vacation was watching Dean Martin ham it up as Santa Claus on Metzger's TV. For the time being anyway, I couldn't face either and drove downtown instead.

Most of the stores were open late for Christmas, and the lights were on in the Sharanita Shop. From the other side of the street I could see the shelves laden with vitamins and the revolving stand of paperbacks. There were open barrels of things like brown rice and sunflower seeds, nuts and dried fruit lined up in apothecary jars. Only Sharon, if she was there, I couldn't see. With no clear intention of going in but just to touch base at the sight of her, I crossed the street and, standing off to one side, looked in through the plate glass at where she usually sat behind the cash register. The chair was empty, but over the back of it was a sweater I recognized. It was a camel's hair cardigan she had bought at Sevenoaks the day we drove down in Gertrude Conover's rented Daimler to see Hever Castle because it was where the Boleyns came from and of all Henry's wives, Anne Boleyn was my wife's favorite. The sweater had pearl buttons down the front and was too long for her, and I remember telling her it made her look like a Nanny. In the ashtray her cigarette was smoking, and over a doorknob hung a canvas bag that must have gone back to Armadillo days. It had *The Sunshine State* and a palm tree stenciled on it. Even your worst enemy's belongings, left defenseless and alone that way, can be more eloquent than the Gettysburg Address, and it was that cardigan that made me open the door and step into the empty shop. The smoldering cigarette was two thirds ash, and I stubbed it out.

I studied the paperbacks for a while. There was *Drink Your Troubles Away: the Health Cocktail Habit* by somebody named John Lust and *The Miracle of Vitamin C* with a reproduction of Michelangelo's God creating Adam on the cover. There was *The Hidden Menace of Hyperglycemia* and *Overfed but Undernourished*. I had just put back *Magnesium, the Nutrient that Could Change Your Life* and picked out a copy of *Vigor for Men Over Thirty* when I heard a thump and rumbling in the plumbing, and in a moment or two a door into the back of the shop opened, and Sharon came out. She was wearing a wrap-around crazy-quilt skirt over the black leotards she wore to yoga class. If she was surprised to find me there, she gave no sign of it. Just a moment's hesitation at the door as she pulled the skirt around at the waist to make it as straight as her face.

"Hey," she said.

I said, "Merry Christmas."

We didn't shake hands or anything, just faced each other there over the health foods and life-enriching vitamins, and I knew it was a mistake to have come, maybe even to have been born. She took her usual seat behind the cash register so that it was from above I saw her, like a teacher proctoring an exam—her cheekbones, the glimmer and dividing of her hair.

"I was fixing to give you a call one of these days," she said, lighting what I took to be one of Anita Steen's king-size Winstons. "Bip's got me worried half sick."

"Bip's fine," I said. "He's the belle of Princeton. There's nothing to worry about."

She said, "Did he tell you the new one he's pulling on the IRS this year?"

I said, "He doesn't tell me the time of day any more. He's too busy with the Pepsi generation."

"You're lucky," she said. "He's been on the IRS shitlist for years, and this time he's really stuck his neck out. He was so tickled he called me up special just to read it out over the phone."

I said, "Read what out?"

"His tax form," she said. "He's filled out his tax form this year like he wasn't filling it out for himself but he was filling it out for Jesus. Right down the line, that's how he's done it. Like where it says put down your first name, he's put down the first name Jesus, and where it says last name, he's put down, 'I am the first and the last, says the Lord.' "

She said, "The place where it says wages, he's put down 'The wages of sin is death.' He's filled out that whole thing with words out of Scripture like it was Jesus filling it out, 'Render unto Caesar' and all that stuff. He says all his income, it's going out for Jesus, so why not send it in like it was Jesus's income. He was pleased as punch when he read it over the phone.

"This time they're going to get him," she said. "They're going to jail him sure. The best he can hope for is they'll pack him off to the funny farm."

"He's been in worse spots," I said.

She said, "I remember the time they jailed him before. I was just a kid myself. I was playing in the yard with a cat name of Mercy that Brownie gave me. I remember Luce came out in a wrapper half stoned and told me. She told me they were fixing to lock my daddy up five years for doing something that hadn't hurt a soul and was just his nature, and right then when she told me, I was sick all over that poor cat Mercy."

She said, "Way back when Luce first started hitting the Tropicanas, the most either of us ever had was each other, Bip and me. Even if he's from outer space like Luce said, he was always real good to me. I never heard him say a mean or spiteful thing, and he never took a strap to me all those years though there was plenty of times he should of. He took me on trips with him soon as I was big enough to take, and he told me his troubles, some of them, same as I told him mine. He made a fuss over me like he was trying to make it up to me because I wasn't his own flesh and blood. Sometimes I used to think I really was his own flesh and blood though he told me different—not Luce's, but his—and there's still times I'm not sure. There's lots nobody knows about Bip. It didn't seem like I was ever going to get over them locking him up in jail five years."

I said, "I guess it wasn't the easiest thing in the world, being Bip's daughter."

She said, "I never thought about it like that."

I said, "Don't think about it." I could hear a car trying to get unstuck out in the snow somewhere, the panicky sound of tires spinning. "Your life isn't something to think about too much. You just live it the best way you can."

She said, "When you start thinking about it, you're sunk." As she raised her head, some vague fragrance reached me that could have been perfume or bourbon or something fruity she'd had for lunch. She said, "It's like Mickey Mouse, the way he can walk off the edge of a cliff and go walking right on in thin air without thinking a thing about it. Soon as he looks down and starts thinking about it, that's when he starts falling."

"Mickey Mouse always comes through in the end," I said.

She said, "When I come through in the end, I'll let you know."

She said, "How about you, Bopper? Is everything OK?"

"I'm OK," I said.

She said, "You go out and have yourself some fun, hear? There oughtn't to be any time you can't find some way at least to have some fun in it."

"How about you?" I said. "Are you having any fun?"

She said, "Not one hell of a lot if you want to know," and then the bell over the door tinkled, and a black girl came in with snowflakes in her hair.

She said she was looking for Mu tea, and while Sharon was hunting around for it, I stood there by the brown rice and sunflower seeds wondering what I had come looking for myself. Somebody to go to bed with again as lovers do and friends do, both—a lover to make the most of darkness with, a friend just to let the dark be dark with until it covers you up like snow? Somebody to say no when I said yes and never when I said now, to give a shape and edge to the emptiness of things even if it was a cutting edge? Maybe all I was looking for was just somebody to grow old along with me like Rabbi Ben Ezra so I wouldn't end up traveling around the world like Gertrude Conover to make myself believe I had a home to come home to that I was homesick for. I thought about walking out of the gym into another world and about what Bebb put down for Number of Dependents when he was filling out his form 1040 for Jesus. I suppose what Bebb put down was Everybody. For myself I would have to put down Nobody.

Several more customers came in while Sharon was making change for the black girl with snowflakes in her hair, so I picked up a brown bottle with a pink label on it and took it up to her to pay for it before the others got ahead of me.

"The miracle of Vitamin C," I said, and I thought of Michelangelo's God on the paperback cover reaching down out of his cloud to touch Adam who is stretching out his hand in such a languid way to receive the gift of life that you wonder if he really wants it. Maybe he had an inkling of all the strings attached.

Sharon wouldn't take my money.

She said, "It's a Christmas present," then leaned over the cash register and breathed into my ear, "Shove one of these up three times a day and you'll feel like new." This time there was no doubt it was bourbon.

I'm coming home, I thought of saying, thought of leaning forward and burying my face in her sleep-smelling hair as the customers waited their turn. The trouble was my symptoms were the reverse of Charlie Blaine's. Charlie Blaine complained that after each move he made, he could feel some shadowy presence inside him making the move all over again, a death inside him echoing his life. For me, it was the shadow that came first, a dim impulse to reach out, to touch, that I had nothing inside me substantial enough to carry out because I had the idea it was my death that was real, my life the echo.

In Alexander Hall Nancy Oglethorpe had fed me from her Lily cup and in the Sharanita Shop Sharon had made me a present of Vitamin C, but neither of them was powerful enough to bring the roses to my cheeks. I said, "Maybe it's magnesium I need, the nutrient that could change your life," but by that time a man in a ski parka had stacked his purchases on the counter, and Sharon was starting to add them up for him, tapping them one by one with the eraser of her pencil, so I drifted back out into the night again like snow and wandered around town the better part of an hour with a frozen carrot for a nose and two thumbprints where my eyes should have been.

8

IT WAS BROWNIE who unexpectedly saved Christmas for me. He phoned me at Mrs. Gunther's the morning after my meeting with Sharon at the shop and invited me to spend Christmas with him at the Red Path Ranch. He said, "I have heard from Mr. Bebb these are troubled times for you, dear, and I want you to know that the latch string is always out."

"Brownie," I said, "you don't know the half of it," and standing there under the stairs in my bathrobe and slippers with Mrs. Gunther's mortuary curios gathering dust all around me and my tap water Maxim keeping warm on the radiator in my room, I told him I would catch the first plane I could get. Tony had already left to spend the vacation upstate with his father and Billie Kling, and Metzger, after all, had both Mrs. Gunther and his TV, so it wasn't as if I was abandoning anybody.

The last time I had seen the ranch was some four years earlier soon after Lucille had died there to the sounds of poor Brownie, all unaware, reading Scripture. The residential compound of tile-roofed mission houses, Herman Redpath's swimming pool, Holy Love built to look like the Alamo with its carillon that sent *Lead Kindly Light* and *When I Survey the Wondrous Cross* trembling out over the scrubby flatlands as far as the greenhouse and John Turtle's Tom Thumb golf course—it all seemed much the same to me. Going on a hundred and eleven, Maudie Redpath was still in circulation looking as though it was only her peekaboo blouse that held her together. She was none too steady on her feet, but she still got where she wanted to go in Johnson Badger's electric golf cart. Bea Trionka had lost seventy-five pounds, she said, but she still looked as much as ever like a pan-fried Pope John the Twenty-third. Harry Hocktaw, that moon-faced tabby cat, met me at the airport in huaraches and a Harry Truman sport shirt. And John Turtle was there, the Joking Cousin himself. He was the one who was on hand to greet me at Brownie's house when I arrived from the airport—Brownie was down at Holy Love signing mail-order diplomas, he explained, with his gold-framed teeth flashing—and he was the one with whom I spent the most memorable part of my first and only Texan Christmas Eve.

Brownie was living in the house that had once been Bebb's and Lucille's and invited all the Indians in for supper. Lizard Shoptall was there with his jazz combo so there could be dancing. The Johnson Badgers were there with their troublesome nephew Buck and Maudie Redpath wearing a gardenia behind an ear that looked like a smoked oyster. Bea Trionka came with her three daughters and their husbands and children, and there was a wide representation of Poles and Hocktaws. Harry Hocktaw and his sons set off some fireworks out on the terrace, and through the picture window we watched skyrockets, pinwheels, and clouds of different colored smoke light up the sultry Texan night while Lizard Shoptall and his boys belted out some of the racier carols like *I Saw Mommy Kissing Santa Claus* and *All I Want for Christmas Is My Two Front Teeth*. There was a tree, of course, decorated entirely with things to eat like strings of popcorn and cranberries, kumquats and marshmallows and braids of red licorice. For the cocktail hour Brownie had put together a temperance eggnog which looked and tasted like Wildroot Hair Oil, but when some of the Indians brought along whiskey, Brownie raised no objection. He spent most of the time before supper out in the kitchen getting things ready, and I joined him there after a while not because all the noise in the living room was too noisy but because there kept being moments when it made the silence inside myself seem too silent. He had on a frilly apron that must have been left over from Lucille's day and his sleeves rolled up so that his pale, hairy arms were bare to the elbow. There were dark sweat stains under his arms, and every time he bent over to stir something or peer into the oven, his smile looked so precarious I was afraid it might turn up somewhere in the supper later like a favor in a Jack Horner pie.

He said, "It's a little hard to remember what day this is, isn't it, dear? It's hard to think of the Savior's birth except in northern climes where there's a fire crackling on the hearth and the snow is coming down."

I said, "Even up north it's not always that easy, Brownie."

Brownie said, "How's Sharon, dear? How's the baby?"

I said they were great.

"Some ways," Brownie said, "Christmas is a sad time for all of us. The snows of yesteryear."

When suppertime came, Brownie gave a blessing with a lot of peace on earth in it and tidings of great joy and glory to God in the highest, and everybody started popping snappers at each other and blowing out long paper buzzers with feathers on the ends.

To eat, there was chile and tortillas and tamales and a huge trough of green salad full of honeydew balls and slices of onion and beefsteak tomatoes. There were lots of other things too, Indian things with names I had never heard of, some of them corn on the cob yellow and sweet, some of them bitter and dark. But the main thing was one of Roland Birdbear's piglets. Lily Trionka brought it in on a platter and set it down in front of Brownie. It had its small, fat legs tucked in under it with the trotters cut off, and its chin rested on a pillow of parsley and aluminum wrap. Its eye-sockets were empty and puckered up, and in the silly little grin of its mouth there was a silver dollar. Its rubbery snout was scorched on the underside, and it looked so much the size and shape of a baby that when Brownie started in to carve it, I looked the other way. There was plenty to look at.

When Roosevelt Pole arrived dressed up like Santa Claus with a clothes mop beard and his paunch swelling out over a pair of skintight red bathing trunks and the fuzz on it parted down the middle, the sack he carried over his shoulder turned out to be full of dry ice and cans of beer so cold it made your throat ache. For the children he had sarsaparilla and frozen bananas dipped in chocolate and grated peanuts, and some of the children put pieces of dry ice in their sarsaparilla so that billows of milk-white vapor slid out over the table like ground mist. Old Maudie Redpath got so carried away she threatened to try dancing herself into a blackbird again, but Harry Hocktaw, who had been the one to pull her out of the swimming pool the last time she'd tried it, talked her into singing a song instead. It consisted of one series after another of very high, rapid notes that sounded like a bosun's whistle with Harry Hocktaw filling in the silence between series by shaking his dried gourd full of seeds.

John Turtle took over while the dishes were being cleared off. He had brought along his guitar, and against a background of chords that had a tendency to flatten out and slide like the mist from the dry ice he sang a number of carols, some of them straight and some of them not straight. He sang *O come all ye faithful* and *God rest you Mary Musclebound*. He sang *The first Noel* and *It came upon a Greyhound bus.* "Silent knife, holy knife, all is man on top his wife," he sang with the veins on his neck standing out. Everybody who wasn't doing something else joined in on *I'm dreaming of a white Christmas,* and then he did a solo of "We three strings of Turtle's guitar. Ho ho ho, and har har har." Brownie asked for *O little town of Bethlehem,* and when John Turtle finished that he went off into "Away in a manger, so little and so sad, the little lord Jesus he tried to be glad." Brownie whispered to me, "You have to remember they're just children, dear. They don't mean a bit of harm."

Then Brownie said, "How's Sharon?" not remembering that he'd already asked me that, and this time I decided I'd tell him something different. He looked so pillaged and distracted sitting there over the wreckage of the meal with most of the Indians on their feet and milling around by this time that I figured he probably wouldn't hear me anyway. I said, "Brownie, she's not in all that good shape if you really want to know."

He said, "You know the old prayer. 'Keep me ever restless until I find my rest in thee.' "

"She isn't restless for rest," I said.

"Rest doesn't mean a nap, dear," Brownie said. "It means peace."

I said, "What is peace, Brownie?" I knew I sounded very cool and Ivy League, but on the inside I didn't feel cool at all and asked the question in hopes that maybe he had an answer.

He was scraping dirty plates as I passed them up to him, and he paused with one of them in his hand, looking down at it as though maybe what he was looking for lay buried in the scraps.

He said, "Whatever peace is, we know it best from the empty place in our hearts where it's supposed to be. Until we find it, dear, we're all strangers and pilgrims on the earth."

"I hope you find it, Brownie," I said.

Brownie reached over and pressed my hand. He said, "I think of you as one of my dearest friends." But for all the kindness of his words, I felt the part of his heart they came from was not so much the part he loved his friends with as it was the empty part.

Later on that evening, by the time my son Bill would have pinned up his stocking and gone to sleep with the Charlie McCarthy that Tony had given him, I put through a long distance call to Sutton, and while it was ringing once, twice, three times, and as clearly as I could see the bare hall where I stood, I could see Sharon come out of the bathroom in the terry cloth beachrobe she wore for a wrapper and walk across to the table by my side of the bed where the phone was. I could see the way she sat down on the bed, tucking one bare foot up into her lap, and the way her hair fell as she leaned over to pick up the phone. Just as her fingers touched the receiver, I hung up.

Some of the Indians had gone home or passed out by then, but there were still plenty of them in the living room watching TV, dozing, playing cards and so on, and out in the kitchen the big clean-up was still going strong. Brownie and the Trionkas were doing the lion's share, and the air was so steamed up from many runs of the dishwasher that the black hair of the Trionkas hung down their fat necks in damp ringlets and you could see the outline of Brownie's underwear where he had soaked through his shirt. John Turtle had taken his shirt off and was sitting naked to the waist at the kitchen table where the slops for Roland Birdbear's pigs were piled high in front of him. His hairless, brown chest was ribbed like a washboard, and he was drinking a can of beer. He called out to me in the hall to come take a load off my feet, and I went into the kitchen and took the chair opposite him.

John Turtle smiled at me in a penetrating way and scratched himself in one cavernous armpit. He said, "Joy to the world, cousin. Time for puff-puff now."

Out of his pants pocket he pulled a small pipe. It was made of clay like the kind they sell on Saint Patrick's Day, only around the bowl the white of it had turned yellow from use. He also pulled out a small leather bag with draw strings and filled the pipe out of it with something that looked blacker than any tobacco I was used to, more like tea. He tamped it down hard with his thumb and then added a little more.

He struck a long kitchen match and, waiting for the sulphur to burn off, lowered it with care to the bowl of his pipe. The mixture he was using was so dry that when he sucked the flame down into it, there was a little bubble of fire mixed in with the first cloud of smoke. It made him sneeze, a loud, wet sneeze that caught the light in a transcendental way as it sprayed out over the slops. Then he took a long drag and with his eyes shut held it in for a while before letting it flare slowly from his lips and nostrils. The second drag he held in an equal amount of time but then with his cheeks puffed out like the South Wind on an old map blew it toward me in a blue stream. "Like that smell?" he said.

I said, "It smells like somebody set fire to a wig."

He said, "OK, Wig. Now you go puff-puff," and held the pipe out to me across the table.

God knows it was the last thing in the world I felt like, but remembering about peace-pipes and Indians and not wanting to give a Joking Cousin offense, I took it from him and held the wet bit to my lips.

"Two puff-puffs," John Turtle said. "One for earth and one for sky." He sat there picking his nose and looking at me in an amused and curious way.

The first puff I took burned my tongue and brought tears to my eyes, and as I exhaled it, the inside of my head felt mentholated and foolish and the ends of my fingers went numb.

"Don't forget earth," I heard John Turtle say as if from some distance, and at the second puff a cloud of nausea swelled up from my stomach and my face turned cold. First I thought I was going to be sick, and then I thought I was going to die. Then I thought I was dead.

Along the side of big roads you sometimes find a billboard painted on something like a Venetian blind so that when the slats are tilted one way, there is one picture, and then, when by some inner gadgetry the slats are tilted the other way, there gradually appears another picture, and that is how it happened there in Brownie's kitchen. First I was looking at one thing, then I was looking at another.

John Turtle and I were walking along together across a broad, motheaten looking plain that reminded me of some of the back country around Armadillo, Florida. The sun was directly overhead and the sky had a bleached-out look from the heat of it. There were some spindly palm trees off in the direction we were moving, and a few white cattle-egrets picking around among the cowflops. John Turtle was kicking up the dust with his bare feet as we walked and at the same time whistling a song that he matched roughly to the rhythm of his stride.

I said, "There's something following us, Joking Cousin." I didn't want to look behind either for fear I'd see it or for fear I wouldn't see it, but I wanted John Turtle to look behind. He didn't. He was holding his left shoulder with his right hand and his right shoulder with his left hand, and he shimmied from side to side as he walked.

"Listen," I said. "Do you hear anything?"

We both of us stopped, and John Turtle let go one shoulder and cupped his ear with his hand.

He said, "I hear something all right." He crouched down to a squat and I thought maybe he was going to flatten his ear to the ground like a scout. Instead he fumbled around in the dust with his long brown fingers and poked out a pebble the size of a nut. He put the pebble in his mouth and rolled it around so I could hear the clicking of it against his teeth.

I said, "How come you did that?"

"That stone was thirsty something cruel," he said.

I turned and looked over my shoulder. The view behind us was just like the view ahead of us—miles of empty plain, an egret or two.

"What you see, cousin?" John Turtle said. He said it thickly with the pebble still in his mouth bulging out one cheek. He was still squatting in the dust, and he had a feather stuck in his greasy black hair.

I said, "I don't know as I see anything." I remembered somebody telling me once that the way to see things far off is to look above where you think they are because you can see more out of the corner of your eye that way than you can looking at them head-on. I tried letting my gaze travel slowly from left to right just a little above the horizon, and once I thought I saw a small, dark shape moving along close to the ground maybe a mile or so away, but when I lowered my eyes to look at it directly, it wasn't there.

John Turtle took the pebble out of his mouth and held it in his fingers. It glistened like a pearl with his spit on it. He put it back on the ground, covered it over, and messed the dust up all around it so you couldn't tell where it was any more.

We walked quite a long way in silence then, and it was such a restful, warm day and the walking was so easy along that dusty scrub that for long stretches at a time I quite enjoyed myself. Every once in a while, however, I remembered in the midst of all the pleasantness of it that something hard and sad was bearing down on me from behind, and every time I remembered it, my stomach turned over inside me. I didn't mention this feeling to John Turtle, but maybe he sensed it because he started reeling off a lot of old jokes.

He told me the one about what the Indian said to the mermaid and another one about what the big dog said to the little dog and a few others which I've forgotten, and at one point we both of us got to laughing so hard that we leaned on each other with our arms wrapped around each other's shoulders, and the smell of his sweat was so much like chicken broth and the smell of his breath so much like honeydew that I buried my face against his slippery, warm neck and I thought that if whatever the small, dark shape was that was following us showed up just then, the chances are I wouldn't even notice it.

Then John Turtle said, "You know what the little piggy went to market say?" and I told him I didn't.

John Turtle said, "He say Wee wee wee all the way home," and at that point I wasn't laughing any more and my stomach didn't turn over so much as it turned inside out because I suddenly knew what that small dark shape was I had seen out of the corner of my eye. It was the pig Brownie had served us for supper.

I could see the way it had looked when Lily Trionka brought it in on the platter with the silver dollar in its mouth, exactly how it had looked without one detail spared me. I could see its little puckered up eye sockets and its cut-off feet. I could see the turned up corners of its mouth. I could see the scorched, rubbery snout. I hadn't been able to get much of it down —the meat had a sweetish taste to it and was so tender that it tended to fall apart in your mouth—but I had had my share right along with the rest of them, and I knew it was after me now with a vengeance. As clearly as I could see John Turtle, I could see it scuttling along through the white birds and moving as fast as it could on what was left of its hoofless stumps. I could see its gay, appalling little smile.

"Isn't there some place to hide?" I said to John Turtle as if my life depended on it because I was absolutely certain that it did.

He said, "Which place you want anyhow?" and "That one," I said. "I want that one over there."

Not more than a few hundred yards ahead of us there was a high fence made of heavy wire mesh such as you find in zoos, and there was a set of gates in the middle of it standing wide open. Leaving John Turtle in my dust, I sprinted through them.

There was a stream across my path, and I ran down into it sending great fans of water dazzling up into the air as I splashed my way to the far bank and clambered out on all fours. I tore off down the path on the other side not daring even to think about looking back and followed it on through a grove of palmetto and yucca and straight ahead till a big out-cropping of tan rock barred my way and I had to loop around it. It was on the other side of those rocks that I came out into a place I knew I'd seen before.

It was a mangy, zoo-colored place, roughly circular in shape, and the yellowish earth of it was packed down velvety hard. Around the fringes of it there were some scraggly palms and a few other trees I couldn't iden-tify that had trunks that looked like cement and greenish brown leaves as big as picnic plates. From the trees, the ground sloped slightly down toward the center, and in the center there was a wide pool with some patches of high grass growing here and there around the edge. It reminded me of pictures I've seen of African water holes, and then I remembered what the place was and when I had been there before.

It was Lion Country. The last time I'd been there was way back when I first met Sharon, and it had never crossed my mind that I'd have occasion to see it again. Standing there looking at it now I thought to myself, well, there it is, and in a lazy, semi-tropical kind of way the place seemed to be saying the same thing to me. Well, there you are. Then I saw the lions.

It was like seeing old friends. A pair of them was sauntering along the far shore of the pond with their narrow hips and heavy, sunflower heads. A lioness with half-closed eyes was suckling some cubs under one of the cement trees. An old male with its tail out straight like a pump handle was taking a crap. Another was crouching by the pool to drink, and ripples drifted slowly out over the water from his lapping tongue.

Out toward the middle of the pool something was moving toward me that I thought at first might be a water lily cut adrift or the snout of an alligator, but as it drew nearer I could see it was somebody swimming. All I could see was just the head and every once in a while one of the hands when it broke the surface of the water as the swimmer sculled slowly backwards. When the figure was still some five feet from shore, it stood up, and I saw that it was a woman. When the woman turned around, bending over sideways first to shake some water out of one ear, I saw that it was my mother-in-law, Lucille Yancey Bebb. She had on a two-piece bathing suit that hung loose about her flat chest and skinny thighs, and on her head, with the flap over one ear turned back, she wore a bathing cap covered all over with rubber petals. She had on her dark glasses, and when she made it to dry ground, she paused for a moment to take them off and wipe her eyes underneath. Then she put them back on and padded her way up the hard-packed yellow earth toward me.

I have learned from sad experience that when you run into the dead in your dreams, it is just as well not to try engaging them in conversation. They almost never seem as glad to see you as you are to see them, and if you go up with your arms outstretched and years' worth of gossip on your lips, more often than not they won't even try to look interested. So I just stood my ground while Lucille approached, dripping water at every step, and when she finally reached me, I didn't say a word, and she didn't say a word either. She just let her jaw drop slightly in what I knew from ex-perience was a smile and reached out to take me by the hand. In silence she led me up to one of the largest of the palm trees and showed me I was to sit down. Then she peeled off her petaled bathing cap and sat down near me. I can still remember the peace of that moment with the trunk of the palm tree between my shoulder blades and no need to run any more. John Turtle was lost somewhere in the outer fringes of Lion Country, and the lions themselves were going about business as usual as though there wasn't a human being within a thousand miles.

I don't know how long we sat there, Lucille and I, until out of the corner of my eye I caught sight of some movement and turned my head to find my sister Miriam standing not far away. Her hair was tied back with what looked like a piece of florist's lilac-colored ribbon, and because the long, burnoose-like robe she was wearing reached the ground, I was afraid for a moment that maybe underneath they still had her in that awful

A-shaped cast she'd died in and that she couldn't move. But when she saw I had noticed her, she came over to me and this time it was more than I could do not to say anything so I said her name. She said, *"Ciao, mio caro,"* in a rather hushed way and sat down on the other side of me from Lucille.

Everything was quiet. The lion at the pool's edge finished drinking, and the surface flattened out. The lioness who had been suckling her cubs was also through. She had one of them between her front paws and was washing him with long, upward sweeps of her tongue. A low-hanging, brown palm leaf gave a papery rattle above my head, but otherwise there was no sound to speak of.

After a while, I saw two figures approaching from behind the outcropping of sand-colored stone. I had no trouble recognizing who they were. The taller one in back was John Turtle. The shorter one in front was Herman Redpath. They were both naked, and Herman Redpath was carrying a shoulder-high staff with a bunch of feathers fastened at the top.

Herman Redpath wasn't all dried up and wizened the way I had known him, with the skin of his face pulled so tight he couldn't get his lips closed over his teeth right. Instead he was shiny and supple like a piece of well-oiled leather and I would have said he looked years younger except that years younger would mean he still had old age ahead of him, whereas the impression he gave me was that he had it somehow behind him as if it was a nut that had split open and the Herman Redpath I was looking at was the meat inside. He walked up to where I was sitting between Lucille and my sister and then stopped. John Turtle squatted down on his heels a short distance behind.

Herman Redpath raised his feathered staff and planted the end of it squarely in the center of one of my shins.

First on that shin and then on the other he drew with his staff a series of little dots like the markings on dice from the knee down to the ankle. "Those are wolf tracks," he said. "They're so you won't ever get wore out."

Then on the insteps of my two bare feet he drew a small cluster of x shapes from the ankle down to the toes. "Those are dragonflies," he said. "They're so you won't ever run into more trouble than you can handle."

He paused for a moment then, and looked at me as if maybe now it was my turn to do something, but not knowing what he expected, I didn't do anything, and he continued. With his staff he tipped my feet up so they were resting on their heels, and on each of the bare soles he drew an upside-down v. "Those are mountains," he said. "They're so as you can walk from hill to hill without ever bogging down in the valleys."

While all this was going on, John Turtle picked up a dried gourd like Harry Hocktaw's from the ground beside him and started shaking it. Chicka-chicka, chicka-chicka went the seeds inside.

Herman Redpath turned his staff the other way round and aimed it roughly at my heart. With the feathered end this time he drew a large circle on my chest starting from the pit of my throat, around the outside of one nipple, down almost as far as the navel, and then up around the other nipple to the throat again. "That is the teepee circle," he said. "It's so you won't never want for a place to come in out of the rain."

Chick-chicka, chicka-chick-chick went John Turtle's rattle in a slower, more elusive rhythm. Like priests turning to face the altar, he and Herman Redpath had both turned around to look at the water hole as I was. Herman Redpath reached up and took hold of a small whistle I had noticed hanging around his neck on a leather bootlace. He raised it to his lips and gave two sharp tweets.

And there it was—the pig, the same pig Lily Trionka had carried in on a platter. It appeared on the other side of the pool, hesitated for a moment, and then came trotting around the shoreline skirting the patches of high grass. Its stumpy legs and dainty hooves were a blur, they moved so fast. Its rump waggled from side to side with its tail curled up like a Greek alpha. Its oversized ears were cocked forward, veined and rose-colored with the sun shining through them. Its snout was close to the ground. Its eyes were demurely lowered and its long lashes the color of flax. When it reached where I was sitting, it settled down on its hind-quarters and raised its head a little. I reached out with one hand and touched the end of its snout. It felt cool and wet and gritty, like Lava soap. Then it opened its mouth and dropped into my hand the silver dollar.

On the dollar there was something written, and—how do I say it? What was written on it wasn't Antonio Parr or Tono or Bopper or Sir or any of the other names I've been called by various people at various times in my life, and yet it was my name. It was a name so secret that I wouldn't tell it even if I remembered it, and I don't remember it. But if anybody were ever to show up and call me by it, I'd recognize it in a second, and the chances are that if the person who called me by it gave me the signal, I'd follow him to the ends of the earth.

I came to at the kitchen table with my cheek cradled in a slippery green wedge of honeydew rind. Brownie's smile hung low above me like a new moon. He said, "He should never have made you try puff-puff, dear. You've been sick all over your nice Christmas suit."

soon after I got back to Sutton, there was a thaw. The temperature rose into the fifties, and off and on for two days it rained until the only snow left was in a few front yards where you could see the remains of what had

once been snowmen. The earth looked as bare and vulnerable as I felt—
sodden, olive drab grass, dog-droppings, mud. They kept Tony at school
late helping lay down wooden duck-walks to the students' parking lot and
the science lab. Mrs. Gunther's cellar flooded. Then it got cold again, and
ice froze on Metzger's TV aerial so that his reception went from bad to
worse and he lost UHF almost entirely. He said, "UHF was my Ho Chih
Minh trail, and now all that comes through is ghosts. If CBS goes, I've had
it. CBS is my goddam umbilical cord."

There was a note waiting for me from Sharon when I got back. It said,
"Bill and I are taking off for a while to rest up after Christmas. Anita says
she'll keep an eye on the furnace and the mail. Bip's been trying to get in
touch with you. I guess things are closing in. Keep an eye on him for me."
She signed it, "Mickey Mouse."

Tony seemed morose. His vacation with his father and Billie Kling
had been a flop. He said, "You know Dad. This time it was his eyes. They
gave him a test for glaucoma and told him he was in great shape only the
pressure in one eye was a hair higher than the other so he's sure he's going
blind. Every half hour he'd ask me if I noticed the light was getting dim,
and then he'd make me let him feel my eyeballs to see if they felt any
harder than his did. I mean Jesus, Tono, what kind of vacation is that having somebody feeling your eyeballs the whole time? Besides the skiing was
lousy, and I was too broke to go anyplace else so most of what I did was
eat. Like I've gained ten pounds if you want to know the truth."

I think it was his weight that depressed him more than anything else.
Every evening before he went to bed he worked out with his barbells,
and mornings he'd do jogging in place until Metzger complained. What
bothered Metzger, I think, was that if he started having a coronary, nobody would hear him give his three thumps on the wall above the thumping of my nephew's bare feet. So Tony took to jogging outside instead,
four times around the block before breakfast every day in his grey sweatsuit with a towel around his neck, fair weather and foul. He had turned
twenty in November and felt the pressure of the years. "Once you hit
twenty," he said, "even a jock like me doesn't stay in condition unless he
works at it," and I remember his inward-looking frown as he said it. It was
partly the frown of a man who knows that staying in condition is uphill
all the way and partly, I thought, the frown of a man who, after three
years of Phys. Ed., shop, and maintenance work at Sutton High, isn't sure
just what he's staying in condition for.

I knew I ought to talk to him about it—his prospects at Sutton in
particular, his future in general—and I suspect he would have been grateful if I had, what with nobody else much to talk to, least of all his father.
At the faintest sign that somebody wanted to talk about something that
might make waves, Charlie Blaine would either go upstairs for one of his
longer naps or get Billie Kling to taxi him down for an electrocardiogram.
I should have talked to my namesake more about things that mattered, but

I was gun-shy, I suppose, afraid always that he would tell me more than I wanted to know. It was a way he had. When I told him Sharon had gone away for a while, for instance, he said, "I told her she ought to fly, but she said the only way they'd ever get her on a plane was if they let her drag her feet, so she took the bus. I told her it was a crazy way to do it, but she got me to take her to the bus station anyway."

He and Sharon had been seeing each other, in other words. There was no reason why they shouldn't have. He'd never given me any reason to believe that they weren't. But I'd never stopped to think about the possibility before, and I didn't want to stop to think about it now. But Tony kept charging forward. "They're in Armadillo," he said. "She said she felt like seeing her old buddies again. You can't blame her, Tono. It's no life for her up here by herself."

I thought of the phone calls I had interrupted him at under the stairs and of how Anita Steen had told me I wasn't the only thing in pants that had rung the doorbell since she had been there alone, and now whether I wanted him to or not, he was putting two and two together. We were sitting in my classroom where I'd stayed late to correct papers, and it was raining outside. Tony was leaning up against the blackboard. He had rung the bell, and Sharon had heard it. He had come in, and she had come down. He had said something, and she had laughed maybe or not laughed, had gotten him a beer, turned on Johnny Carson, told him to take his cruddy feet off the coffee table—God only knew what they had done. As for me, I didn't want to know. All I knew was that once two people have made love, a door is opened between them that not even years of noblest resolve can ever entirely close again because the flesh has a pitifully weak sense of time and honor both, and old wounds throb like new again at the approach of rain. That day in the dentist chair, for instance, my hand had found its way to Laura Fleischman's hand so easily for the simple reason that it had been there before and knew the way even though I myself had forgotten it. And Tony and Sharon had also known the way, and whether they had followed it again in my absence and where it had led them if they had, I had no wish to find out.

"Where's she staying in Armadillo?" I asked because it was a question that took her out of the house and away from the sound of his ringing and put her about fifteen hundred miles south. She was staying at the Salamander Motel, he told me. She'd left him the phone number if I wanted it.

"She's been there before," I said—I hoped enigmatically. It was my attempt to end our exchange with a story I chose not to tell him rather than with one I chose not to have him tell me. It ended nothing.

He said, "She gave a going-away party the day before she left, and I drove down from Dad's for it. It was New Year's Eve. Anita was there, natch, and some of her yoga class and a few health food freaks thrown in for good measure—nobody I knew especially. She and Anita played the guitar and there was dancing and booze and vitamins. I don't know when old Bill got to sleep. He sat up at the top of the stairs with his legs through the rail, having a ball watching. Everybody had a ball," he said. "The only rough part was when Sharon got sick."

"Feel free to make a long story short," I said.

"Not booze sick," he said. "Sick sick. She was off booze into some kind of health juice. She said maybe that was the trouble with her. She said you can stand only so much that's good for you, and then you start needing something that's bad for you, and if you don't get it, then you start being bad for yourself. She looked awful, whatever it was. It was after everybody had gone home. She was upstairs trying to get rid of it only she couldn't. She said it was because what she was trying to get rid of was herself. She scared hell out of me."

He took a piece of chalk and drew a line on the blackboard with such a sudden, fierce stroke that the chalk snapped and fell to the floor. He said, "You gone, Bip gone. All her friends gone that she didn't know all that much better than I did so they wouldn't have done her much good even if they'd stuck around. I was all she had. I couldn't just walk out and leave her. Christ.

"I spent the night," he said.

I remember the rain at the windows. They were the old-fashioned kind that open at the top with a long pole, and I took the pole and closed them because it was starting to rain in a little.

"You want a lift home?" I said.

He was standing with his shoulders against the blackboard, the line he had drawn going through him like an arrow. He said, "She just needed somebody to hang onto, that's all. The next morning I put them on the bus for Florida. I wanted to tell you, Tono."

I found myself thinking vaguely of Stephen Kulak, the pudgy ninth grader I'd once explained irony to in that same classroom where now the rain was drumming softly at the window. Irony as two things, Stephen Kulak. My nephew's wanting to tell me and my not wanting him to.

Tony had his ankles crossed like Nijinsky as he looked at me through the dark and operatic eyes of my twin sister.

I said, "You're a good man, Charlie Brown."

He said, "I'm a dumb, overweight jock."

"I didn't say that," I said. "You said that."

He said, "I'm sorry as hell, Tono."

"Just give me an ounce of civet, good apothecary," I said, "to sweeten my imagination."

She didn't come back that week, Sharon. I called the house from time to time, but there was no answer, and from various places of concealment across the street I could see on various occasions that it was Anita Steen, not Sharon, who was minding things at the Sharanita Shop, that withered little Fauntleroy sitting behind the cash register in a cloud of what I assumed must be the kind of cigarette smoke that puts apples in your cheeks and helps stave off the hidden menace of hyperglycemia. Sharon didn't come back that winter at all. She wrote me that she had decided to stay on in Armadillo. She said she could think things out better down there and the people at the Salamander Motel had given her and Bill special rates. Anita had told her that she would look after the shop while she was away.

Sharon didn't come back. Tony didn't tell me any more stories I'd just as soon have passed up. The weather didn't change for better or worse but continued to ice up by night and turn to mud by day. It was a winter when nothing particular happened one way or another out where you could see it but only inside, I suppose, where luckily or unluckily you couldn't see it unless you were Gertrude Conover with an eye for karmic stirrings, an ear for whispered cues from the prompter's box. And that was fine by me. I needed to have nothing happen for a while, and that was why, although I knew Bebb was trying to get hold of me, I made no effort to get hold of him. A number of times that winter he called at Mrs. Gunther's while I was in, but each time I got Metzger to tell him I wasn't. Metzger didn't even ask me why, and I didn't spend much time asking myself why either, let alone feeling guilty about it. Whatever Bebb wanted, I didn't have it in me to give. Whatever Bebb had to give, there wasn't enough of me just then to want it with.

And then one day in early spring he turned up—at a time when I least expected him, Stephen Kulak, which was also the time when I had most reason to expect him because part of the *roundness* of Bebb was always, like the ball in a pinball machine, to pursue his goal no less relentlessly for all the bumpers, buzzers, baffles and blinking lights put in his way.

I came back from school late one afternoon to find him in my room. He was lying on my bed in his shirtsleeves with his tie loosened and his shoes off. He had hung his jacket neatly over the back of the desk chair with his hat perched on top of it and his shiny, black shoes lined up on the floor where his feet would have been if he had been sitting there, so that at first glance it was as if there were two Bebbs, the natty one at the desk and the mussed one on the bed. It was as if, waiting there in my room with nobody around to bother about, he had taken a break from being himself. The effect was startling.

He said, "It's a day of trouble and of treading down, Antonio. That's why Gertrude Conover gave me the loan of her Lincoln so I could drive up. The fat's in the fire, and I need a sharp young go-getter like you to help me figure it because I'm not as young as I once was. There's been goings on in Princeton, New Jersey, you should have been there with your Bell and Howell to get pictures of. If you've got a few minutes, I'll run them off for you."

The first scene he ran off took place in the office of the Internal Revenue Service in Trenton, New Jersey.

Bebb said, "There was a bunch of us got letters ordering us to show up at the same time, and I was the first one to get there and the last one to get seen. Antonio, I cooled my heels the best part of three hours while one by one everybody else got called in ahead of me. There was a pane of crinkled glass like a men's room, and I watched the whole pack of them through it getting their business done in there and coming out again. I looked at every wore-out magazine and dog-eared newspaper there was till finally all I had left to look at was the plain fact I was being put in my place. By the time they finally got round to calling my name it was the middle of the afternoon and I hadn't even had my dinner yet. Inside there was a agent sitting at a big desk name of Connor. He wasn't much taller than a parking meter and he had eyes rolling around in his head like marbles and a breath on him you could have got money for in a package store. He made me stand there must have been five minutes while he diddled around with some papers he had, and then he looked up at me and said, 'Do I have the honor of addressing the King of the Jews?' That miserable little pen-pusher, I gave him as good as he gave me. I said, 'My kingdom is not of this world,' and he come back at me quick as a water moccasin. He said, 'Well, maybe your kingdom isn't, but your form 1040 sure as hell is.' He had a secretary in there with a mouth painted on her didn't have any more to do with where her real mouth was than the map of China and she set in to snickering. I told them I was a U.S. citizen, one, and a ordained minister of the Gospel, two, and if they thought I was going to stand there and let them use me like that, they were mistaken."

I said, "Sharon told me about your 1040, Bip. I'm afraid you asked for it."

"I asked for a hearing," he said. "I didn't ask to be held up to shame and ridicule."

He said, "Antonio, it's no secret I've been having trouble with the IRS for going on forty years, and you want to know why? It's not on account of I've cheated on my income. I've got an income. I never once let on I didn't. My finances are an open book. The love offerings, the Gospel Faith tuition fees, the nickels and dimes coming in every Sunday year in year out plus all the weddings and funerals I'd as soon have done for nothing except what a man doesn't pay for he doesn't value. And the great generosity of Herman Redpath, Antonio. I'm including the hundred thousand too. Why, averaged out I've had more income out of serving the Lord than most anybody I know in this type of work, and being pretty much a one man operation save for Brownie, I never had much overhead either."

He said, "Antonio, I got an income but I also got an outgo, and I'm going to tell you where my outgo goes to. First off, I'll tell you where it doesn't go to. It doesn't go to Leo Bebb. Leo Bebb hasn't got any stocking full of fifty dollar bills stuffed up the chimney. He hasn't got any blue-chip securities or life insurance, and he hasn't got any pension plan either. Blue Cross? The only cross I've got is the cross of shame and glory. No sir, except for the clothes on my back and the incidental expenses of living, everything I've got goes to the church. This side of starving to death, my income and my outgo are dollar for dollar the same as each other because everything I got coming in goes out to Jesus. Right down to the last dime, it all goes out to feeding his lambs just like he told us."

I said, "The trouble with that, Bip, is you don't have a church any more," and he said, "Antonio, I am a church."

I am a church, he said, this new pronouncement, and I thought how in a way he looked like a church—some sprawling, bald-domed Hagia Sophia or chunky, sun-bleached seamen's Bethel—as he lay there on my bed with the room smelling of his feet.

He said, "I did the best I could to explain it all out to that pitiful little Pontius Pilate how come I filed in the name of Jesus like I did and the point I was trying to put across doing it that way. He was just about as interested as he was whether I put on clean drawers that morning. They're going to investigate me, that's the long and the short of it. Connor and that Jezebel with lips painted on her wouldn't fool a blind man, they're going to go through every record I got clean back to the creation. They're going to have me up for malfeasance and contempt and willful attempt to defraud the U.S. Government.

"Antonio," he said. "They're going to nail me up."

That was the first scene Bebb ran off for me. The second took place at Princeton, in the Nassau Hall office of some assistant dean. The assistant dean himself was there with a beard and one of the denominational chaplains with a turtleneck and a pectoral cross. Unlike the experience at the tax office, here Bebb was treated very well. The chaplain offered him a cigarette which he refused. The assistant dean showed him a clapper that had been stolen from the Nassau Hall bell in oughty something. The assistant dean inquired after Gertrude Conover, whom he knew socially. The chaplain told a little joke about a Black Muslim and a southern Baptist meeting at Saint Peter's gate.

I wondered as Bebb described it if he had recognized in that office the terrible advantage he had—the advantage of Armadillo over academe, the bush leagues over the Ivy league. I could see them so clearly, the dean and the chaplain—not crew-cut and gray-flanneled as in my day but the dean with his beard, the chaplain with his turtleneck, trying no less to be all things to all men as with Bebb they undoubtedly fell all over themselves trying to be Bebbs. I could see them searching for prepositions to end their sentences with—*this is where we're at, Mr. Bebb*—scratching themselves where it didn't itch, wishing they'd boned up ahead of time on Uncle Billy's Whizzbang and the language of the sawdust trail. Bebb being Bebb wouldn't try to be anything else because he couldn't if he wanted to, just sat there in Nassau Hall as he would have sat on the can while they dithered around him.

Bebb said, "They came down to it finally, what they'd called me in there to say. You could see they didn't want to. They'd been put up to it. It was that plain.

"They have closed the doors of Alexander Hall to me, Antonio. They have closed them and bolted them tight."

There was the mess for one thing, they told him. Love Feasts no less than fish fries left litter—crumbs and wrappers, paper cups and Tropicana stains. Even after the supper of the Lamb somebody had to pick up the pieces. The dean laughed at the sheer triviality of the thing, his feet propped upon an open desk drawer, but there had been flak from the janitorial staff, and good janitors were harder to find than good deans. Or good shepherds, the chaplain said. Besides which there was the eternal question of precedent, the dean said, striking while the iron was at least lukewarm. It was one thing to make Alexander Hall available to a group like Bebb's for what had it been now—six weeks, two months?—but to perpetuate the thing beyond that was not only to give it official University endorsement which was something the trustees might be as hesitant to offer as Bebb to accept—*It's the kiss of death around here these days*—but also to open the door to you name it. Gay Lib, Leary's boys, Jehovah's Witnesses, Transcendental Meditators—if the University wrote Bebb a blank check, on what basis could they justify writing anything less for the Honorable Elijah Mohammed?

"Antonio," Bebb said with his head sunk back on my pillow, gazing out at Metzger's aerial against the grey sky, "there's plenty I could have said, only I didn't say it. Nancy Oglethorpe, she's got a clean-up squad goes over that place after every feast so there's not a janitor in the business could find fault with it. And talk about your sodomite societies and your Hindu jamborees, they're no more like—Antonio, Love Feast isn't some kind of Lodge or Clam Bake. I'm not asking the Nassau Hall crowd to do any more for me than that chaplain's asking them to do for him. I'm there to preach the good news to the poor, I'm there to give a cup of cold water to the least of these my brethren, these fine young brethren they've got there at Princeton University that are the salt of the earth except that they're tempted every whichway by things like drugs and sex and knocking the American way of life."

Bebb didn't say that at this point in the interview the dean lit his pipe, but even at that remove in time and space I could smell it—could smell that whole world of deans and pipes and stolen clappers that I had known myself in the early fifties. God knows times have changed and maybe people don't come as young as they used to, but even so I can't help believing—because with part of me anyway it's of course what I want to believe—that for everything I knew then there is still at least a reasonable facsimile going now: the tipsy labyrinth of a football weekend and the jolt of bouncing your first check to discover that life goes on anyway; courses in things like *Love and Death in Nineteenth Century Fiction* or *The History of History*, with titles so enchanted that not even taking them could ever quite break the spell. I wanted to believe that it was because the young still accepted all the ancient verities as basically unassailable that they could afford to assail every last one of them with the abandon of apes. I wanted to believe that they too believed, just as I had once believed, in the endless procrastination of old age and death, the lifetime guarantee of boyhood friendships and the inevitable victory of the martini over the Manhattan, Mozart over Mendelssohn, marriage over masturbation. In any case, as Bebb evoked that whole never-never land by his account of his brush with it at Nassau Hall, what moved me was not the thought of how it had menaced Bebb but of how Bebb had menaced it and what a fragile thing it was.

Bebb said, "The chaplain told me how way back in the twenties sometime there was a group like Love Feasts got started on campus where everybody collected together and confessed things in public that were better left private. Sex things, Antonio. He didn't come right out and say sex things, but it was what he meant mostly. He said how it got out of hand and a lot of loose talk and loose living come out of it, and it gave the place a bad smell. I told him that wasn't the kind of show we were running at Alexander Hall and what was coming out of it wasn't loose living, it was souls saved for Jesus. Well, the dean, he put his oar in again. He said all they had to go on was what they'd heard tell from people who had been there. So I asked him what people, and that stopped him. He said he didn't want to get into personalities. He said there was no point naming names. And I'm going to come clean with you, Antonio. He was right. There was no point naming names because I knew what the name was without anybody had to name it. Roebuck, Antonio. From the first time I laid eyes on him, I knew Roebuck was out to get me.

"I went to see him," Bebb said. "That same day after I finished with the Nassau Hall boys, I went straight to that little hole-in-the-wall Roebuck's got him for an office over to McCosh Hall and put it right to him. He was there all by his self in those Army boots of his and a saucer full of cigarette butts. I said, 'Roebuck, you never made a secret of how you feel about me, and I never held it against you. Every man's got a right to come to Jesus in his own way, and if my way's not your way, there's no hard feelings. But you've kept on coming to the Love Feasts anyhow, and no matter what spiteful things you said, I never meant you anything but good. But all the time I was meaning you good, you meant me evil, Roebuck, and now you've gone and turned this place against me. Roebuck, Roebuck,' I said, 'why persecutest thou me?' Then he took me by surprise, Antonio. I'll give him credit for that.

"He said, 'I believe we've met somewhere else, Mr. Bebb.' I didn't know what he meant, and I told him so. 'Let me refresh your memory,' he said. He doesn't look you in the eye when he talks to you. He looks at you up around where your hairline is, if you've got a hairline. He makes you feel like you've got another pair of eyes up there you never thought to use before."

Those two Bebbs. The one sitting at my desk straight as a chair-back in a Tyrolean hat and a pair of Thom McCann shoes not saying a word, buttoned up tight. The other one spread out on my bed like the stuffing of the first one.

Bebb said, "That man knows his history, Antonio. It's his special subject, and he knows it inside and out. He reeled off a whole list of times and places where he said we'd met before. He told about the days they had children eight, ten years old and up working in mines like pack mules maybe twelve hours at a stretch till their pitiful little bodies were nothing but skin and bones and they couldn't hardly see in the daylight while people like me went on looking the other direction and preaching thy kingdom come. He told about the days they tore the living flesh off people with red-hot tongs and broke their legs with hammers because they didn't believe like they should about doctrine. He went on how those old-time crusaders used religion for an excuse to rape women and raise hell and how back in slavery times there was ministers of the Gospel owned slaves just like everybody else and proved out of scripture it was the way things was meant to be. I don't suppose there was a single miserable thing anybody ever did in the name of Jesus that Roebuck didn't spell out chapter and verse before he was done. He enjoyed it. You could tell from the way he worked his face what a good time he was having.

"He said each one of those times and places I was there, Antonio, and that's where we met before. He said I wasn't the type that beat the slaves and raped the women and tortured the heretics because I didn't have the balls for it. No, I was the type just closed my eyes to it and helped other people close their eyes to it by telling them a lot of fairy tales about Heaven. This trick eyelid of mine that goes shut on me sometimes without me even knowing about it, Roebuck said you didn't have to be a expert psychologist to explain that. He said that eyelid was a dead giveaway how the only way a man like me can go on believing in Almighty God is by pulling that eyelid down like a window blind between me and all the shit in the world that proves there isn't any Almighty God and never was or will be.

"You take a word like shit, Antonio. A preacher isn't even supposed to know there is those kind of words, and Roebuck, he thought he'd throw me a curve just using it. I said, 'Roebuck, you think I don't know about shit? What you've been telling me about isn't even a millionth part of all the shit there is because you've stuck to just the religious shit, and that's only one kind of all there is because piled up right alongside it there's a million other kinds. You take your big business, your politicians, your high-class colleges like Princeton. You take your haves and your have-nots both, your whorehouses and your W.C.T.U.'s. You take not just your red-neck nigger-haters but your N double A's and your civil rights parades, not just your hard-hat flagwavers but your peaceniks and C.O.'s and love-ins. You take anything people have ever done in this world, and the best you can say about any of it is that it's maybe one part honest and well-meant and the other nine parts shit. If I close my eyelid down on all the shit there is in the world, I've still got to face up to all the shit there is in me, because I'm full of it too, Roebuck. I'm not denying it. And you're full of it. It's the shit in us is part of what makes us brothers, you and me.' I used that word shit to him till it begun to sound like I invented it.

"He caught me by surprise. I caught him by surprise. A preacher talking about things like—Antonio, shit is what preachers have been talking about since Moses except the word they're more like to use is sin. Only Roebuck didn't know that. It shut him up for a minute. Then he said, 'If the world's mostly shit, Bebb, where's God?' Just like that—where's God? As if I could say, 'Look, there he is, Roebuck, He's squeezed into one of those books you got on your shelves. He's out there a zillion miles northeast of the Milky Way. He's catching forty winks over in Alexander Hall till the next Love Feast gets off the ground.' That Roebuck was like a bird floating in the sky asking where's air, only I didn't say that then because I didn't think of it till later.

"I said, 'I'll tell you about shit, Roebuck. Take it from an expert. There's two main things about it. One thing is it's stink and corruption and waste. The other thing is if you don't pile it up too thick in any one place, it makes the seeds grow.' I said, 'Roebuck, God's where there's seeds growing. God's where there's something no bigger than the head of a pin starting to inch up out of the stink and dark of shit towards the light of day.' I said, 'Roebuck, God so loved the world he sent his only begotten son down here into the shit with the rest of us so something green could happen, something small and green and hopeful.'

"Roebuck said, 'I don't even know what you're talking about, Bebb,' but I could see he knew more than he was letting on just like all of us do, Antonio. A man that believes in the Almighty knows worse than he's letting on and a man that doesn't believe in the Almighty like Roebuck knows better, but we all of us know more. I said, 'Maybe you don't know what I'm talking about, Roebuck, but I know what you're talking about. All this about God and ancient history and so on, down deep what you're talking about is that boy you got home can't use his hands and feet. That's the main shit the world tossed in your direction, isn't it, Roebuck?'

"He said, 'Bebb, he can't even take his pecker out when he needs to make a leak. All his life he's going to have to have somebody around to take it out for him or just let go in his pants. Maybe someday he'll learn to hold a pencil in his asshole like that girl that draws Christmas cards. That's the only green and hopeful thing he's got.'

"Antonio, there's a whole mess of scriptures that has to do with things like Roebuck's boy, the pointless, dirty things that make you wonder if life's anything more than a popcorn fart. My ways are not thy ways, saith the Lord. Fear not. I could have rattled off a dozen of them without batting an eye only I didn't have the heart to, and it wouldn't have made a dent on Roebuck if I had. There wasn't a solitary thing I knew to say that I felt like saying, and it seemed as though Roebuck had run out of ammunition too. We both of us just sat there staring at each other. Then I saw something I didn't notice up till then. It was one of those little signs they have on desks with your name on it. Virgil M. Roebuck it said. All I knew up till then was just Roebuck, and then seeing that sign I thought to myself how this wasn't any old Roebuck. This was the Roebuck they'd settled on calling Virgil. This was the special Roebuck they'd pinned that special name Virgil onto and raised up to amount to something special, and here he was, not one of your big time professors that get their pictures in the papers but just Virgil Roebuck that smokes two, three packs a day if he smokes one and has this boy he's got to take his pecker out for him every time he needs to take a leak.

"Antonio, I busted in there mad as a hornet, but you can't stay mad when you start thinking things like that. Once you commence noticing the lines a man's got round his eyes and mouth and think about the hopeful way his folks gave a special name to him when he was first born into this world, you might as well give up.

"I said, 'Virgil, the night is dark, and we are far from home.' How come it was the words of that old hymn popped into my mind just then to say? I don't know, but it did. I said, 'The night is dark, Virgil Roebuck, and home's a long ways off for both of us.'

"He didn't say a word for a while. He just sat there at the desk in his Army boots and his cigarette between his teeth the way he does. Then he cupped his hand up over one eyebrow and tossed me one of those two-for-a-nickel highball salutes they used to do. He's out for my scalp, Antonio. I'm sure as I'm sitting here he's the one talked them into kicking me out of Alexander Hall. But he saluted me, Antonio, and it wasn't just to mock at me either. That salute was him saying maybe we're in two different battles. Maybe we're on two different sides. But when you come right down to it, the war we're in is the same war. Antonio, we're far from home, all of us are. Who's going to judge which of us has got the farthest way to go through all the shit and the dark?"

Bebb swung his legs over the edge of the bed and sat up to describe the last scene to me. His shirt had come untucked in back from the way he'd been lying and his trouser legs were hiked up baring his white calves. He leaned forward with his elbows on his knees, and I had the impulse to plump him into shape like a pillow and stuff him back into his tight-fitting jacket where he belonged.

He said, "It never rains but it pours. As if it wasn't enough to have the IRS and Nassau Hall both on my neck, I got a letter last week from the insurance company that handled things back when Open Heart burned down. Of course the people we rented from was the ones that had the insurance, but being as I was the tenant when it burnt, I had to fill in some forms and explain how I'd been using the barn for a church and so on. Everything was open and above board, and the people got money for a new barn without a hitch. Only now, four years later, the company's opened the whole business up again.

"Somebody's been telling tales out of school, Antonio. Back when the fire happened, it never come out Clarence Golden was living in that barn. I never made a feature of it because to tell the truth there didn't seem any cause to. I never set his name down in those forms because Fats Golden, he's had his share of hard knocks in this world and then some, and I didn't want to lay any more on him. It wasn't like he was doing anything he shouldn't have, just camping out there because he didn't have anywheres else to lay his head. Inasmuch as ye have done it unto one of the least of these my brethren, ye have done it unto me, Antonio. That's why I told him he could bunk down out there while we were overseas. I didn't see any point stirring up the insurance company over a thing like that. Well, they've been stirred up.

"They wrote me somebody's gone and sent them an anonymous letter. Somebody's written a letter they didn't have the crust to sign their name to telling how the summer Open Heart burned down, there was a friend of mine living in it that once a long ways back did time. I expect you know Clarence Golden did time once, Antonio. He never was one to make a secret of it. So they're reopening the case on the grounds the fire that burned down Open Heart wasn't necessarily an accident. They didn't come straight out and accuse anybody, but they said they've got their lawyers working on it. They want me to come answer some questions.

"My nose is clean, Antonio. I wasn't there when that fire happened, and even if it was set on purpose, I didn't stand to make a dime out of it. I lost a lot of property including the pulpit and the fold-up chairs and the hymn books and that big preaching Bible I wouldn't have taken any kind of money for. It wasn't me that collected on the insurance, it was the people that owned the place, and there's not a lawyer in Christendom could prove any different. But there's two things that keep me awake nights, and I'll tell you the worst one first.

"A man has enemies. In my line of work, it goes with the territory and you got to expect it—you even got to be thankful for it. Blessed are ye when men shall revile you and persecute you and shall say all manner of evil against you falsely for my sake. It's a honor to have the same kind of enemies Jesus had. Like that banty rooster tax collector, that Connor who's trying to force me to render unto Caesar what isn't Caesar's because it's Jesus's and I've told him so to his face. Or Roebuck. Roebuck's just the latest, souped up model of the fool that saith in his heart there is no God and is out to nail anybody that says different because deep down he's scared of the competition. Roebuck's scared. Why do you think he wears

those boots of his like there was a war on? But whoever wrote that anonymous letter and didn't sign his name to it, that's another kind of enemy. I
don't know who it is, Antonio. I don't know why he's out to get me. He
could be a stranger. He could be somebody I've done some deep and hurtful thing to without even knowing it. He could be anybody, and there isn't
hardly a person I know or ever did know I haven't tried fitting his face
onto just for size. Even in dreams. He's a enemy without a face that follows me even into the dreams where a man goes to find rest and guidance
for the days ahead.

"The second thing is Clarence Golden. There's some ways Clarence
Golden's the—*five years*, Antonio. Him and me, we were together five
years day in day out till there wasn't hardly any closer two people can come
this side of matrimony. I'm not saying there aren't times he's an awful
pain in the tail. You never know when he's going to turn up or what way
he's going to find to devil you about something. Like the way he covered
the walls of Open Heart with pictures straight out of my life, private
things, Antonio, I could no more have left up there for the world to see
if that fire hadn't happened than I could have stood up and preached the
Kingdom buck naked. But he's my old friend, and I don't want any harm
to come to him, and now he's in worse trouble than I am, and it's on my
account he's in it. When those insurance lawyers start looking into things,
they're going to look into Clarence Golden."

Bebb had been staring down at his feet all this time, but at this point
he looked up at me.

He said, "Antonio, Clarence Golden is a firebug. What those lawyers
are bound to dig up about him is the thing he did time for way back was
arson."

Thus the woes of Leo Bebb. He stood up, ready by then to move out,
go somewhere, and I stood up too, ready, God knows, to have him go. He
threw his arms up over his head in a monumental stretch, groaning and
making faces, tossing his fat shoulders around to loosen them up, and I
found myself echoing his gesture so that we stood there facing each other
for a moment both with our arms in the air.

Our woes met, Bebb's spoken and mine unspoken because how was I
to speak to him of Sharon and Tony holding on to each other for dear
life? It was like a high sea at the beach when the waves rolling in and the
waves rolling out collide with a teeth-rattling slap and sky-high explosion
of foam—Bebb's speech and my silence meeting head-on with such a jolt
that it had us both on our feet like fans at a touchdown.

Connor. Roebuck. The writer of the anonymous letter. The possibility
that they would all somehow get together to overthrow Bebb if in some
subterranean way they hadn't gotten together already, weren't in fact all
three the same person in three clever disguises. Bebb wasn't there for either
my advice or my condolences, however, and whatever fumbling combina-

tion of the two I started to serve him up he literally turned his back on as he vigorously set about putting himself back together again—tucking in his shirt, tightening up his tie, putting back on his jacket and shiny black shoes, until there was only one Bebb again, as buttoned up and battened down as ever.

He was also apparently not there to inquire into the state of things between Sharon and me. At the diner later, where he insisted on paying for my supper, he made at least a stab at raising the subject but waited until I had my mouth full of cheeseburger to do it and by the time I'd swallowed enough to choke out something about how there wasn't really much new, he was off into plans for a student demonstration against Nassau Hall for exiling him from the campus. I don't know why Bebb was there. All I knew was that not even the rock of ages can cleave for thee very well when it's round as a pumpkin and rolling downhill at seventy-five miles per hour.

10

"LAURA?" I said. "This is Antonio Parr." Not Antonio. It was too soon for that. Not Mr. Parr. It was too late for that. I was using the phone underneath the stairs. The kitchen door was open, and I could see Mrs. Gunther opening a can of Puss 'n Boots. She had the radio on with the dial set somewhere between the six o'clock news and the bagpipe version of *Amazing Grace*. Upstairs Tony was taking a shower. Metzger was alone in his room reading the evening paper out loud. The cat Mrs. Gunther was fixing supper for was stretched out on the glass top of a display case full of hat pins and souvenir spoons with one paw hanging over the edge.

"Oh my goodness," Laura Fleischman said. "I thought I recognized your voice."

I knew where everybody in the house was at that moment, and looking back on it, I picture where everybody else was at that moment too.

Sharon is at the gas station across the road from the Salamander Motel. There is a sandwich machine out front, and she is standing in front of it in a halter and shorts while Bill reaches up to drop the money in. The sun is blinding on the white stucco gas station wall and on the white road.

Spring has come to Gouverneur Road, and Bebb and Gertrude Conover are coming home from a drive with Gertrude Conover at the wheel. She sits with her chin pointed down toward one shoulder and seems to be gazing as much out of the side windows as through the windshield so that even while driving she looks like a passenger. As they turn into the driveway of Revonoc, Bebb reaches out through the window like a Chinese emperor and breaks off a sprig of forsythia.

Nancy Oglethorpe is typing out a dissertation on The Civil Service Reforms of Chester A. Arthur, and as she leans forward to make an erasure, her breasts crush against the keys and trigger the tabulator which slams the carriage back to the farthest margin and rings the bell.

Charlie Blaine is walking slowly from the garage back to the kitchen porch. He steps on a crocus without knowing it and skins his bare arm against the side of the house. His eyes are closed because he is checking out what it is going to be like to be blind.

Darius Bildabian has stayed overtime at his office to make some denture repairs. With an upper plate in one hand and a lower plate in the other, he holds them out at arms' length through the curtained door of the waiting room where his twelve year old son Mardik is waiting for him. He clacks them up and down to make them say, "What's up, Doc?"

Roebuck, a red bandanna handkerchief tied around his forehead like a pirate, is playing squash with a colleague from the Philosophy Department, and after a long day at the shop, Anita Steen is soaking in a hot tub with a bourbon on the floor beside her and a copy of Rod McKuen in one dry claw.

I say, "Does that invitation for a homecooked meal still hold?"

"You mean tonight?" Laura Fleischman says. In the background I can hear a noise like a car going over railroad tracks. "Let me turn the washer off."

At the unmistakable sound of Mrs. Gunther's setting the plastic dish down on the linoleum, the cat drops lightly to the floor and starts toward the kitchen hugging the wall with her tail in the air. A thump overhead makes me wonder for a moment if Metzger is signaling for help at last, but craning out as far as the telephone cord will let me, I catch a glimpse of Tony's bare rump as he stalks heavy-footed to his bedroom and think to myself that it is not given to every man to behold with such Olympian detachment the nakedness of his wife's lover.

"Look," Laura Fleischman said, "I just checked the ice box, and I mean if you don't mind taking pot luck, I can whip up something if you want to come over. Mother had to go to Toledo because her sister's dying, so there's just me."

"And we will take upon us the mystery of things," I said for lack of anything else. "As if we were God's spies."

The mystery of things. To year after year of Sutton High seniors I have explained that what the old king seems to mean is that only God and his spies see that it is the things themselves that are the mystery—all the people there are, in all the places there are, doing all the things they are doing at any given moment of time. While I stood there under the stairs making my call, at the same moment Mrs. Fleischman's sister was dying in Toledo and upstairs Tony Blaine was studying his young flesh in his dresser mirror for signs of advancing age. All the people in the world are always doing something, somewhere, and for all I know the dead are too—

Lucille floating like a water lily in the lion's pool and Herman Redpath with his whistle around his neck. In a classroom smelling of steam heat, chalk dust, flatulence, pencils, hair spray, breath—themselves all part of the mystery—I tried over the years to explain that to see things the way Lear says God sees them is not so much to see through them to some mystery beyond or within as just to see them as they are. As mysteries go, that is staggering enough for anybody. I clipped my fingernails. I put on a clean shirt. I took two of the vitamin C pills Sharon had given me. I picked up a fifth of Dewar's on the way. Ripeness is all.

I had never been in Laura Fleischman's house before, the chief mystery of which was that for a house that had seen all twenty-odd years of her comings and goings, it seemed to have left as little mark on her as she on it. The nubbly wall-to-wall carpet of swimming pool blue, the Barcalounger in homespun vinyl, the cataract stare of the TV which wore like an old lady's hat a foil-wrapped pot of African violets on a crocheted doily and the what-not shelf of Reader's Digest condensed books with a tinted photograph of the late Mr. Fleischman on top—to have an eye for the kind of things that mark the boundaries between classes in a classless society is curse enough let alone to blunder into marking them sharper still as I knew I had the moment I produced my fifth of Dewar's and set it down on Mrs. Fleischman's sewing table. A drink before dinner—I had grown up in a world where that eloquent little semicolon between the clauses of a day was as inevitable as day itself. Even alone at Mrs. Gunther's I had my evening drink as at Revonoc Gertrude Conover did and elsewhere all the blue-haired ladies and the old Tigers and Elis they were married to. More than the clothes we wear or the language we speak, it is the final shibboleth that will give us away when the African violets and tinted photographs of the world rise against us at last, and all I can say is that the poise with which Laura Fleischman stepped out into the kitchen for glasses and ice was remarkable.

Unlike the day when she had caught me by surprise at Bildabian's office, this time we had both come prepared with conversation enough to see us through and to spare, but if forewarned is forearmed, it is also foredoomed, or at least foredoomed to stick to your conversational guns until the last round you have come grimly supplied with has been fired.

Her job with Bildabian, and her plans for the future; her sick aunt. The old days at Sutton High, the prospects in track that spring, the wet weather. Salvo after salvo, we shot them all off, each from his own emplacement, until I despaired more and more of the moment's ever coming when like opposing troops on Christmas eve we could crawl out and meet like brothers in the no man's land between. I sat on the couch with my feet on the coffee table. Laura sat across from me on a leatherette ottoman with her bare arms and shoulders tanned by some burst of sunlight that must have happened that week while I was looking in the other direction. Facing us was the Barcalounger of Mrs. Fleischman and the tinted likeness of

Mr. Fleischman from the shelf with the condensed books.

She was thinking of leaving Bildabian, she said, because there were things about the job she didn't like, then maybe moving in with a friend in New York and trying to find a new job there. I said I thought Sutton stacked up pretty well in racing but didn't stand a chance in the javelin or shot put. I said there had been a lot of changes at school since her day, but there were most of the same old faces on the faculty. I had two scotches to her one, but each swallow left me only soberer than before to the point where my despair was so great by the time she got up to go check on supper that I asked if there was a john I could use less because I needed to use it than because, like getting up and walking around the card table, I thought the move might change our luck. It was upstairs, she said. The second door I came to.

I opened the first door I came to instead and found myself in her room. *Blue night* was what my son Bill called twilight in those days, and blue night lay light as snow on the ruffled tester of the four-poster bed and the white nurse's uniform on a hanger hooked over the closet door. A muslin curtain floated out on the damp air, and on the wall near me hung a photograph of her graduating class, the girls in their long white dresses, with a slip of Palm Sunday palm tucked in behind the frame. The bed was opened with her nightdress laid out over the foot. There was a desk in the corner and on the desk a copy of her class yearbook. I had brought my glass of Dewar's with me, and setting it down on the desk, I turned on the lamp and took the yearbook up in my hands. Downstairs I could hear the sound of the ice box being opened and shut, the click of china, and I thought of how the labor of our conversation-making must have left her as tired and sad as it had left me, and of how once we had eaten our supper and I had stayed out my time and gone home, this was the room that she would come home to. I pictured her reaching up into the night-dress she had laid out for herself like her own nurse, pictured her reading herself to sleep in that cool bed. Like a child on his way to the principal's office, I thought how in a few hours I would also be, if not safe in my own bed because maybe there is no place on earth less safe, at least re-prieved in it for a while as I looked back through closed eyes on the failure of our evening together.

I opened the year-book at the page that was marked, and on that page there was a picture of myself frowning into the sun in my baggy sweat suit complete with clipboard and stopwatch. Marking the page there were two things—a red plastic muddler from the Grand Central bar where we had once met by accident and a note I had apparently written from France, some five years before.

It said, *Dear Laura,*

Congratulations two weeks late on your 18th birthday. 18 is a good age to be as ages go, and I hope you will hang on to it as long as you can. I read your letter at an inn where they say Sir Francis Drake got word that the Armada had been sighted off Land's End, and a theosophist who was traveling with us said our room was obviously haunted. Can you tell me a room that isn't? I am writing this from a hotel in Paris where the armada of traffic under our window all night makes such a racket that it's like sleeping in the Lincoln Tunnel. The only ghost that's with me at the moment is yours. I can see you sitting at the back of the classroom in your usual seat trying like a waiter not to catch my eye for fear you'll be the one I call on if you do. I should be haunted by ghosts like that more often. I'm sorry to hear about you and Carl West, but I'm glad you're taking it philosophically if not theosophically. Never mind, someday all in green your love will come riding, and in the meantime thanks for your letter and think kindly once in a while of your old English teacher and friend, Antonio Parr.

That cumbersomely avuncular note enshrined there like a piece of the true cross—I replaced it with the muddler between the pages where it belonged and had turned to go back downstairs when I found Laura Fleischman standing at the door.

"So now you know," I said. "I'm one of God's spies."

"I told you we all had a crush on you," she said. "Every paper you ever wrote a comment on I kept put away somewhere. You must think I'm an awful fool."

I said, "The fool that wrote that letter was an awful fool. I don't even remember writing it, if that's any excuse."

"I remember getting it," she said. "I bet I read it fifty times the day it came."

I said, "Maybe it starts to grow on you after a while."

"Anyway," she said, "supper's ready. I was afraid you'd given up hope," and I said, "Everything but," and switched off the lamp on the desk so that the room turned into blue night again.

She said, "I feel so stupid sometimes when I'm with a person like you, talking a blue streak about a lot of stuff I'm not even all that interested in myself. Maybe it's my job that's made me such a chatterbox. When you've got your hand in somebody's mouth, the only one that's left to do the talking is you."

We were both standing together in the doorway now, and as she turned around to go, I put my hands on her shoulders and turned her back again, and that was how we finally met face to face in no man's land.

The Chinese Emperor places the spray of forsythia in a glass of stale water threaded with bubbles while full of tubes and needles the sister of Mrs. Fleischman dreams of walking along a beach at low tide. Sharon slides a five dollar bill through the window, and a pair of tickets leap up at her like tongues, a pink for her, a green for Bill. Billie Kling places the thumb and forefinger of one hand on the eyeballs of Charlie Blaine,

and in the voice of somebody making a transatlantic phone call tells him
he has nothing to fear but fear itself. Alexander Hall is dark and empty,
and under one of the pews a single potato chip lies like an autumn leaf.
The mystery of things.

"And what more shall I say," wrote Saint Paul in a passage that I
heard Bebb hold forth on more than once. "For the time would fail me
to tell of Gideon and Barak, of Samson and Jephtha, of David also and
Samuel and the prophets. These all died in faith, not having received the
promises but having seen them afar off, confessing that they were strangers
and pilgrims on the earth." I put my hands on the shoulders of Laura
Fleischman, and in that room with the curtains afloat and the blue night
deepening, one thing led to another thing until at the end of all the things
that happened, I received the promise, received from that twenty-two year
old girl what would have stopped David himself dead in his tracks and
made all the prophets drop their shaggy jaws.

The girls in their long dresses waited with their backs to the wall.
The white tester trembled above us like a coif. The headlights of cars
drifted slowly across the ceiling. To the consternation of Samson, there
came a point where I was afraid my strength would fail me and I would
have to be content like the rest of them with having only seen that promis-
ing land I could not enter. It nearly came to that, I don't know why—less
the scotch, I think, than my sense of history—but in the end it didn't. I
was spared that lesser, fleshly failure for the sake of a ghostlier and greater,
which is to say that I made my entrance straight and tall only to find that
even then I was still afar off, a stranger and a pilgrim to that fragrant
earth.

I remember lifting her hair, weightless, in my hand and finding that it
weighed about what blue night does or rain. I remember remembering
that to make love is to make nonsense of opposites like soft and hard,
chill and warm, swift and slow; it is no longer either-or but both-and,
each a pair of ways to speak a single truth. Desire and despair.

I remember that after a while we slept for a little with only a fringe
of light from the hall to cover us, and when I woke, she was asleep beside
me like a pool of shadows except where the light made her islands in a
pool, and I was all gooseflesh in the cool air, trying to withdraw to some
deep place inside my skin, or to the warm places where our skin touched,
to keep from shivering her awake. She was asleep with one arm unfolded
across me, and I thought of all those months I had watched her at the
back of my classroom, that girl who from the highest flight of her beauty
could go nowhere, I thought then, but away from it, away from me, but
who lay there asleep now at my side while downstairs our uneaten supper
lay in ruins, the sherbet melting into the fruit salad. I dreaded the moment
she would open her eyes and I would have to say something, pick up
somehow and go home when I had no home to go home to and knew she
was not my home either any more than I was hers as she was bound to

know too as soon as she opened her eyes, if she didn't know it already. Only she didn't open her eyes. She spoke with them closed so that for all I knew she'd been awake the whole time too.

She said, "We used to have a bet to see which of us would be the first to kiss you, and Lois Kinney almost won. You were leaning over to correct her paper once, and she said she came so close to it she almost died, only at the last moment she chickened out. You probably didn't even know."

She said, "You don't have to worry this was my first time or anything like that because my first time was with Carl West. I didn't want to, but he wanted to so much I let him. That time you and I met at the station, I knew the moment you touched my hand that I would with you too, if you asked me to. Afterwards I used to think about it going to sleep at night, thousands of times. I'd think where we'd have gone together and how it all would have happened. I knew it was bound to happen someday just the way I always dreamed it would."

With her eyes still closed and her words more breath than sound in the hollow at the base of my throat, she said, "I just want you to know I wanted it to happen, and I'm glad it happened the way it did, and I don't want you to worry about anything because it was the way I wanted it."

I tried to say something, but I was stuttering with cold by then, Stephen Kulak, and it was like every joke you'll ever live to hear about the green bridegroom on his wedding night because I rolled over on my side to face her closed eyes then and ran my hand down between her shoulder blades and the length of her spine to her cold little tail for all the world as though no one had ever explained to me that there was any more to it than that, and when to my slapstick dismay I found myself rising again to the very occasion I had every cause to shrink from, time again would fail me to tell of the sadness and loneliness of my pilgrimage. To make love with so nearly a stranger usually fans the spark of an old lecher's heart, but to make love when he is himself the stranger is to turn the heart to stone. This time we both fell asleep, and when I woke again, it was daylight, and Laura Fleischman was gone.

When I went downstairs, I found her in the kitchen making breakfast. She had on her nurse's uniform with her hair brushed back into the silver barette, and I was unshaven with my teeth unbrushed, my hair in my eyes. I said, "The man who came to dinner," and she said, "I had to throw the dinner out. It wasn't much anyway."

She said, "I was just about to come up and wake you. I knew you wouldn't want to be late for school," and I wondered if that was really what she had been about to do and how she would have gone about doing it and how things might have turned out differently for us both if she had. In her place, I would probably have sneaked out the back door with as little noise as possible.

She was standing at the counter in her white dress, her white stockings and shoes, pouring milk into a pitcher like a girl in a Vermeer, and I said, "What time are you supposed to be at Bildabian's?"

"I'm supposed to be there like about ten minutes ago," she said with her back to me still, "but I always arrive a little late so the appointment girl's sure to be there first. I don't like being there alone with him."

"Is he after you?" I said.

She said, "That's why I'm quitting," and as she turned toward me with the pitcher in her hand—frowning at the thought of Bildabian's toothy advances, I suppose, of quitting her job and moving to New York—for a moment it was no longer she in one place and I in another place and the emptiness between us a place that wasn't home for either of us, but both of us were together in the same place, and it was a place I was afraid I might be homesick for for the rest of my life if I had to leave it now. As she came toward me frowning that way with her eyes lowered, I was for a moment her teacher again and she was my student, and within the protection of that old relationship I felt secure enough to face the possibility that for better or worse I could never leave her again at all. But only for a moment, because as she sat down at the table and looked up at me finally as if it wasn't the easiest thing she'd ever done in her life but not the hardest either, she was not my student any more but a girl I hardly knew in a world where there was no protection, and the only way I dared to play it was to play it safe.

I said, "Listen, I'm not Bildabian, but I'm not Prince Valiant either. I'm a nice place to visit, but you wouldn't want to live there. I had a dream at Christmas time that all these years I haven't even known my right name, and even after they told me what it was, I couldn't remember it."

She said, "There's nothing you have to be sorry about. You don't have to say anything you don't want."

I sometimes think that all the major dramas of my life have taken place in kitchens, and maybe that's because in kitchens there's always something else to fall back on if the going gets tough, like cooking or eating or doing the dishes. And maybe that's the real drama after all—just keeping yourself alive day after day and cleaning up afterwards. I remember watching Laura Fleischman pour milk out of the pitcher into her dry cereal with the rustle of autumn leaves. I remember sunlight on her bare arm as she reached out for the sugar, and I remember the bitter taste of my coffee. We were keeping alive.

I said, "Do me a favor, will you, and be happy for God's sake? I mean right now I could list all the happy people I know on the back of a six cent stamp, and I'm not even sure about them because it takes one to know one."

She looked at her watch and said, "Bildabian's not going to be happy. I've got to take off." So it ended up that I was the one to see her to the door instead of the other way round, and there in the hall, with Mrs.

Fleischman's Barcalounger facing us from the living room, what I kissed goodbye was more than just a girl who smelled of breakfast and Ivory soap.

I read an article in the *Times* once on the stages that the old go through on their way toward death, and somewhere along the line they apparently go through one called *decathexis*, which the *Times* defined as "an emotional detachment from life." Ordinarily this stage comes on gradually and toward the end of the line, but for me it came rather abruptly and no nearer my end than I was as I stood just inside the Fleischman's screen door.

As I kissed Laura Fleischman goodbye there in the hall, my heart wasn't even in the goodbye let alone in the kiss. There was nothing I had to let go that I hadn't let go already, and though I suppose that if the loss hadn't mattered at all, I wouldn't have noticed it, all I can say is that it didn't much matter to me that it mattered. With hardly a pang I watched her swing out of the driveway and drive off in the direction of town. Decathexis.

After she'd gone, I went upstairs to get my jacket and tie, and while I was at it, I made the bed too, made crisp hospital corners and smoothed the white spread flat with the palm of my hand. A feather came out of one of the pillows as I plumped it, and before I left, I opened the year book on her desk and laid it between the proper pages. Then I closed the book and went on back to Mrs. Gunther's to wash up and shave.

11

AT BEBB'S INSISTENCE I went down to Princeton the following Saturday to be on hand for the historic march on Nassau Hall protesting his eviction from campus because to let go of your life does not mean that your life necessarily lets go of you. I've heard it said that in great office buildings even after the boss has gone home and the doors have been locked behind him, the self-service elevators continue to work off the uncompleted calls of the day, those empty cars moving relentlessly from floor to floor for hours afterwards. So in answer to Bebb's summons I set out again on the well beaten track past the great bridge, Grant's Tomb, the West Side piers, and down under the river through my father's tunnel.

It was the first really lovely day of spring we'd had and nowhere lovelier than at Princeton when I arrived. The magnolais were out at Revonoc. The swimming pool was full. A negro with cotton in his nostrils was mowing the lawn, and the house was full of the fragrance of newly cut grass. Gertrude Conover met me in the hall and greeted me with such an unusual air of distraction that I wondered if she had sent her astral body off on an errand somewhere. She said that Bebb had already gone on to Alexander Hall where the marchers were assembling, and if I wanted to be on time, I'd better hurry.

She said, "I don't need to tell you this isn't the first of his incarnations I've known, and in every single one of them he's gotten himself mixed up in something like this. His aura gets bright as a hundred watt bulb, and the rest of us are drawn to it as moths to a flame. That time in Egypt when he was a priest of Ptah, for instance. Don't think for a minute that I was the only one to get burned. Even the Pharaoh is still paying the price, a man who had every reason to expect that by this time he would have made a nice little advance toward cosmic consciousness. And look at him now."

I said, "Where is the Pharaoh now?"

"His name is Callaway, and he is mowing the grass," she said. "His second wife has left him with seven children to support, all of them under ten. They have a cold-water flat on John Street."

"How much does he know about his previous incarnation?" I said, and it was moments before she seemed to hear my question as she stood there on the black and white tiles like a threatened queen.

Finally she said, "All that poor man knows is that he's been having nosebleeds ever since Leo moved in. He thinks it's some kind of allergy. Imagine it—a man who once held the power of life and death over thousands right in the palm of his hand.

"Here," she said. "Leo is going to want this for the march. Do you mind taking it to him?" It was Bebb's maroon preaching robe which lay draped over the bannister, and by the time she'd picked it up and handed it to me, I think she'd forgotten why.

Bebb was delighted to get it. I found him—that hundred watt bulb and despair of Pharaohs—standing in the midst of some hundred or so followers who were milling around in front of the glassed-in Romanesque entrance to Alexander Hall. His bald head was pearled with sweat in the spring sun. He had on the kind of dark glasses that you can see through only from the inside. He was in his shirtsleeves and pale with excitement as he threw his arms around me and hugged me to him. He said, "Antonio, this is the day that the Lord hath made. Let's you and I rejoice and be glad in it," and when I'd helped him into his robe and he stood there larger than life in the red of martyrdom with mirrors for eyes, he could have been the god Ptah himself.

In describing the great march and everything it precipitated for Bebb and all of us, I lean heavily on a special issue of the *Daily Princetonian* which was brought out the next day under the banner headline BEBB EM-BATTLED: THE FALL OF THE HALL. For all his excessively alliterative and telegraphic journalese, the undergraduate reporter did his homework thoroughly and supplied a wealth of detail including the *ipsissima verba* of various eyewitnesses which help convey the overall sweep of the thing better than I could, who was caught up in my own particular backwash. Backwash is the word. Two cups of coffee have always had the effect on me of two quarts of beer, and having foolishly not taken time to relieve myself after leaving Sutton that morning, I was so preoccupied with my own inner distress that everything I saw was colored by it. I suppose a man's view of history is always colored by something, and if I saw the gaudy events of the day primarily in terms of the occasion they might or might not offer for satisfying my homely need, the undergraduate reporter seems to have seen them in terms of conspiracy. Whereas what I saw behind every tree was a potential haven for myself, what he saw was new evidence that Bebb had planned everything out with extraordinary foresight and cunning. I don't think this view is correct. I think many of the things that happened happened by chance. But who knows? Maybe right from the first day I ever laid eyes on him, Bebb was more cunning than I ever gave him credit for. Or maybe Gertrude Conover's theosophic dictum is right and there is no such thing as chance anyway.

Be that as it may, the *Prince* begins with a verbatim transcript of Bebb's address to his followers before the march began as Nancy Oglethorpe captured it on her tape recorder, holding the small black microphone up at him like an enema tube. They had all gathered on the blacktop between Alexander and the Presbyterian Church carrying their homemade placards and bedsheets lettered with slogans like *Love is a Feast* and *Tell Your Troubles to Jesus, Ban the Bomb not Bebb* and *Nassau Hall Go Home.* There was a Campus Cop named McCartney on duty in his little kiosk right in the midst of them, but he gave no sign of being particularly disturbed by what was going on all around him, and there seemed to be no reason why he should have been. In their jeans and bell-bottoms, their shorts and bare feet, they looked no more menacing than the usual bunch you might find queued up at the movies any night of the week. There wasn't so much as a water pistol in sight, and such shenanigans as there were could hardly have been more pastoral and innocent. Some flower children presented Officer McCartney with a daisy chain, and a black track star scaled one of the squat turrets to scatter a bag or two of paper rosepetals, and that was about the length of it. Officer McCartney apparently phoned in a routine report just to play it safe, but the Proctors' Office didn't even bother to investigate. "In Nassau Hall business went on as usual," as the *Prince* put it. "President's secretary typing out honorary degree citations. In University Chapel, choir rehearses *Also hat Gott die Welt Geliebt* for Sunday service. Dean Borden is home sprucing up for alumni dinner in Allentown, Pa. Rainbow colored Frisbees tossed among sun worshipers in nearby Holder court."

It was somewhere around eleven when Bebb finally mounted a green wooden bench and delivered his marching orders. He took his text not from Scripture for once but from the annals of the American Revolution. He said, "It's going on two hundred years since General George Washington struck a great blow for liberty right here in Princeton, New Jersey, and today we're going to follow in his footsteps and strike us another one. You and me, we're going to march on Nassau Hall and ask for the liberty to keep on having our Love Feasts here in Alexander Hall where we've been having them right along. That's the whole show in a nutshell. I've got a petition in my hand signed with near on to three hundred John Hancocks, and I'm fixing to put it personally right into the hand of the President himself. Folks, we're not asking for the moon. All we're asking for is the liberty to keep on saving souls on this historic campus just like they're supposed to be saving them over there to the University Chapel."

Bebb launched forth then into a rather rambling account of the Battle of Princeton and the events leading up to it. He told how Washington had first struck at Trenton while the Heinies were still hungover from Christmas, and how he had taken it as easy as taking crackers off a shelf. He told how then the British in their fancy red jackets and tight pants had hotfooted it down from Princeton to win it back the next morning and how Washington had outfoxed them by marching around their lines under cover of darkness and striking at Princeton the next day while it was virtually undefended.

According to Virgil Roebuck, who was interviewed by the *Prince* later, it was in this section of the speech that Bebb had tipped his hand as to the foxiness he had in mind himself. "You got to hand it to that mother," Roebuck was quoted as saying. "He as good as gave the whole show away when he told about the Princeton campaign, but who the hell learns anything from history?" I'm not sure about that. As things turned out, it is undeniably true that Bebb employed some of the same tactics as his famous predecessor, but it is hard for me to believe that he was playing cat and mouse in his oration. If he was tipping his hand, I don't think he knew that he was. If he was making any comparisons, I don't think it was a comparison of tactics with tactics but of himself with Washington—both of them down on their luck, beleaguered, up against terrible odds. I remember the emotion in his voice as he stood there with the sweat running down and describing how Washington crossed the Delaware "with cakes of ice the size of refrigerators on every side," how he resisted all temptation to "head back for Virginia where the future First Lady of the land was waiting to welcome him with open arms."

Then "Boys," he said. "Boys, we got the Father of our Country on our side and we got our Father who art in Heaven on our side too, and that's a hard combination to beat. Let's move off to Nassau Hall for Jesus." So Jesus, God, General Washington, and maybe the Sphinx too if he remembered Gertrude Conover's theory that the Sphinx was only the General in an earlier avatar—I believe it was they, rather than any elaborate stratagem, that filled Bebb's heart as he led his followers forward, with me and my distended bladder keeping up as best we could.

From Alexander Hall to Nassau Hall is no distance at all if you take the direct route, but in order I suppose to give the thing maximum exposure, Bebb followed a very indirect one. We headed toward Witherspoon first, and from Witherspoon off toward the Blair arch where with our shoe leather clattering like applause down the enormous flight of stone steps we descended into the lower campus. The marchers must have numbered well over one hundred and fifty by then, and needless to say they attracted a good deal of attention as they snaked slowly along with their hymns and placards. Faces appeared in dormitory windows, and bodies choked the entryways. Sunbathers abandoned their transistors and six-packs to fall in behind. Passers-by stopped dead in their tracks, and some of them fell in behind too. Bright as a Kentucky redbird against the grey Gothic stone, Bebb strode along at the head of the long procession like a visiting head of state, but he kept breaking ranks to shake hands and exchange pleasantries with the onlookers, then hoisting his skirts to catch up again at his fat man's light-foot trot. The column was stretched out at such length that sometimes a hymn would rise up from one segment of it and something like *Going Back* or *Crash through that Line of Blue* from another. Nancy Oglethorpe and her aides kept fanning out to distribute flyers that showed a mug shot of Bebb with the astonished stare of a man shot out of a cannon—above him WANTED, below him FOR BRINGING THE GOSPEL TO GOMORRAH. All of this in the loveliest spring imaginable with only a few clouds gathering on the horizon, a kind of children's crusade with Bebb as Peter the Hermit or an overstuffed Pied Piper.

Ambushed by Atheists was the subhead under which the *Prince* reporter described the single untoward incident that marred the otherwise leisurely, picnic air of it all, the only foreshadowing of trouble to come. The way it happened was this. The marchers wound their way around past the lower battlements of the gym, then up the sloping road that leads back to the heart of the campus again where it turns sharp right past those twin Greek temples, Whig and Clio, and on toward the library and the Chapel. The rear of Nassau Hall loomed up on our left like the Promised Land, massive and ivy-covered, and we could have approached it from there, but Bebb's idea was to make his grand entrance at the front instead so we continued on past it until we reached Murray Dodge, and it was there that the incident took place.

An undergraduate group that called itself Atheists for Democratic Action had set up a roadblock. There must have been fifteen or twenty of them all told. Some of them were holding up a huge placard that showed a caricature of Bebb as a fat convict in prison stripes with a halo over his head and the legend *Back Behind Bars with Bebb*. Others had stretched an American flag out across the road where the parade had to pass with an atheist at each corner to hold it down and several others

armed with cameras to record the desecration in case Bebb chose to lead
the faithful over it. The procession came to a halt. There was a certain
amount of catcalling back and forth. The atheists set off some firecrackers
when Nancy Oglethorpe tried to approach them with a handful of flyers.
Bebb walked forward with his right hand extended to offer peace. The
rear portions of the procession had crowded forward to see what was going
on, several of them got their hands on the flag, and the next thing I knew,
a scuffle had broken out.

It never turned into a free-for-all luckily—the action was pretty much
limited to where the flag was—but both Bebb and Nancy Oglethorpe were
caught up in it. Neither of them actually gave battle as far as I could tell,
but I could see their heads bobbing around in a sea of heaving shoulders
and flying elbows. I remember Bebb's flushed and desperate face, his robe
pulled half off one shoulder, and I wondered if like Washington he was
tempted to give the whole business up and go home to the open arms
of Gertrude Conover and the peaceful terrace of Revonoc. But "I am a
church" he had said that dreary time in my bedroom at Mrs. Gunther's,
and I suppose that meant to him that you took things as they came
whether they were the ravening lions of martyrdom or this sweaty Mardi
Gras of ponytailed Princetonians most of whom didn't give a hoot in hell
whether the church stood or fell flat on its face. Anyway it didn't last long.
The Atheists for Democratic Action were vastly outnumbered. The Love
Feasters captured the flag, and the next time I saw it, Nancy Oglethorpe
had it draped around her shoulders like a beach towel. With her beehive in
tatters and her face streaked like a Comanche's with her melting pancake,
she started the march going again. It was at this point that, unable to
contain myself any longer, I ducked into Murray Dodge to find a can, and
by the time I came out again, hysterical with relief, the mob had disappeared around the far end of Nassau Hall to take up their vigil out front.

There must have been close to three hundred of them by then gathered out under the regal elms. The atheists had joined them and so had
brunchers from the Student Center and scholars from the Firestone stacks.
Shoppers had drifted in off Nassau Street and so had a flock of Lawrenceville seniors on a tour of Revolutionary War sites. Some townie girls had
commandeered a sprinkler and were horsing around with it by the Dean's
house, but most of them had crowded around the steps of the main entrance, a few sitting astride the bronze lions that stood guard there. Bebb
had already entered the building with a few of his principal lieutenants
to present their petition to the President, and Nancy Oglethorpe, still
swathed in the Stars and Stripes, was trying her best to lead a pray-in outside while the rest of us waited for Bebb to reemerge and announce the
outcome.

If anything substantiates Roebuck's theory that like Washington in
1777 Bebb had his whole stratagem planned out well in advance, it was
the events of the next half hour or so, and since like everybody else I

spent that time waiting under the tall elms, I must rely entirely on the researches of the *Prince* for what took place place behind the scenes.

The first thing that took place was that the Proctors' Office received an anonymous phone call to the effect that if Bebb was thwarted in the attempt to deliver his petition to the President in person, or if the petition was turned down flat, his followers were planning to enter Nassau Hall by force if necessary and stage a sit-in in all the major administrative offices. Whether this actually was the plan or, if not, whether Bebb wanted the authorities to think that it was and thus to that end contrived the anonymous phone call himself, remains among the hidden things of history, but in any case, whoever baited the hook, the Proctors' Office lost no time in snapping at it. Within minutes all the proctors and Campus Cops that could be contacted were ordered to take up battle stations at Nassau Hall including, significantly, Officer McCartney, who left his post at the kiosk by Alexander Hall and proceeded to join the rest of his colleagues on the double.

While this maneuver was going on, inside Nassau Hall Bebb and his deputation made their way to the President's office where they were received by a secretary who said that the President was in an important conference and asked them to take seats and wait for him. This step is one that Bebb obviously couldn't have planned, and thus it seems to me to knock at least a small hole in Roebuck's theory. The next step, however, is something else again. Instead of waiting in the President's outer office with the rest of them, Bebb asked the way to the washroom and left.

Alerted by the proctors to expect a possible sit-in, most of the office staff had closed and locked their doors, and for that reason the *Prince* was unable to locate anybody who actually saw what Bebb did next. That he went to the washroom is attested to by the discovery there later of a sheaf of flyers left on the edge of a washbasin, but how he proceeded from there is anybody's guess. It hardly matters. Somehow—either by one of the side doors or possibly, I like to think, through a ground floor window —he managed to leave the building undetected, and while everybody including by then the entire security force of Princeton University was waiting for him to appear on the front steps of Nassau Hall, he hightailed it instead to Alexander Hall where Officer McCartney's kiosk stood empty except, reported the *Prince*, for a well-thumbed copy of *Penthouse* and a half-eaten swiss-on-rye. If Bebb's followers had founded a new religion in his name, I suppose they would have started their calendar with the Year One as the year of this historic flight, this hegira that Bebb made unseen by human eyes from the one great hall to the other.

Officer McCartney was not there to greet him, but others were. Gertrude Conover was there for one. She had arrived in her low-slung Continental driven by her black gardener Callaway. En route to the U Store with a malfunctioning typewriter, an undergraduate named Max Briden-

baugh happened to be there also, and Bridenbaugh was the *Prince*'s source
for all this.

A handful of Love Feasters who had not been along on the grand
march had gained entrance to Alexander, and as soon as Gertrude Conover's Continental drew up, they ran out to help Callaway unload. According to Bridenbaugh the back seat was piled high with gallon jugs full
of Tropicana, bags of potato chips, paper plates, paper cups, and a huge
silver punchbowl bearing the Conover arms. All of this was rushed into
the building, and Bebb and Gertrude Conover and the handful of Love
Feasters followed, locking the glass doors behind them.

Holding his blood-stained handkerchief to his nose, Callaway revved
up the Continental, parked it near the entrance to Holder, and left the
campus on the run. Max Bridenbaugh shoved his broken typewriter into
the abandoned kiosk just in time to prevent its being trampled to pieces
by the hordes that almost immediately started streaming in from Nassau
Hall, myself among them. Bridenbaugh, whose opinion as chairman of
the Ivy bicker committee was given considerable weight by the *Prince*,
stated that the whole operation was carried out in a way that suggested
split second timing and a degree of coordination that bordered on the
supernatural.

There was something aquarium-like about the scene that followed
with those few pale faces floating dim and ghostly on the inside of the
glassed-in rotunda and everybody else on the outside. The proctors had
formed a cordon around the doors, exhorting the crowd to disperse and
threatening disciplinary action if it didn't. There were more older faces
mixed in with the others now. Except for Virgil Roebuck, who had arrived with his son in a wheelchair that looked several sizes too big for
him, I didn't recognize many of them, but the *Prince* identified such
notables as Stanislaus Fuchs, the Nobel laureate in physics, and James
Ingram, that year's poet-in-residence. Somebody told me that the enormous man in the white beard and pith helmet was Dean Emeritus Nelson
Higby Ackroyd.

The *Love is a Feast* and *Ban the Bomb not Bebb* posters were as
much in evidence as ever and the hymns kept coming, but holy hell had
all but swallowed up what little was left of a holy cause when word flashed
around that Dean Borden had arrived, and the crowd divided like the
Red Sea to let him through. It was one of the great encounters surely—on
one side of the glass Dean Broadus Borden, Philadelphia-born former
Rhodes Scholar and holder of honorary degrees from Harvard and Lafay-
ette dressed for his Allentown dinner in pearl grey dacron and regimental
stripes, and on the other side of the glass Leo Bebb, sweat-stained and
grim with his trick eyelid doing its trick like a broken window shade. They
made a brief attempt to communicate through the dusty panes like a
Head Curator and a blowfish, but when this failed, Bebb gave the word

and one door was unbarred just wide enough for the Dean to squeeze through sideways, scraping his glasses off in the process.

In a few minutes the door opened and the Dean came out again with one lens missing, the other cracked, and Bebb came with him. Like Eisenhower at a fund rally, the Dean held his arms up high above his head, the mob fell silent, and into that silence he dropped the terms that he and Bebb had agreed upon. The marchers were to be permitted to enter Alexander in an orderly fashion to conduct their feast, and in return Bebb guaranteed that afterwards they would disband peaceably and abide by whatever decision the President reached on their further use of University property. The Dean then turned to give Bebb a symbolic handshake, and as though in token of divine endorsement, there was a clap of thunder, and the rain started coming down in sheets as the two lords, spiritual and temporal, retreated into the Hall with the nimbleness of vaudeville hoofers to avoid being crushed to death by the advancing horde.

There was a rumor that the Tropicanas that were served inside were spiked with something stronger than the customary white wine, and an unidentified freshman was quoted as saying, "Man, like that stuff was a real *bomb*," but in her own interview with the *Prince*, Gertrude Conover denied this. She said, "It is a scientific fact that matter can be converted into energy. It is a spiritual fact that energy can be converted into matter. It was the karmic energy of Jesus Christ at the Cana wedding that turned the water into wine, and I believe that it was the karmic energy of Leo Bebb that had a similar effect on the Tropicana punch." When they asked her to comment on the rumor that an empty case of Mr. Boston gin was discovered among the wreckage later, she said simply, "I have already given you my comment." As for how the last Love Feast unfolded, the *Prince* account proceeds as follows.

Picture Alexander Hall crammed to capacity. Picture J. A. Holzer mosaics of Homer and his Heroes looking down on seething bouillabaise of believers and unbelievers, faculty and undergrads, cops and catechumens.

Picture rainforest atmosphere, soggy and steaming. Bodies soaked to skin. Flesh glistening pink through sopping garments as downpour continues outside. Some strip to bare essentials. Shirts and blouses scuttled. Air heavy with scents of spring, sweat, wet clothes, wet hair, orange juice and karmic gin.

Parrot squawks and primal screams rend jungle miasma as mob jostles for seats in pews. Balcony packed with BACK BEHIND BARS WITH BEBB *poster draped down over railing.*

Cops and proctors form cordon with shoulders to stage apron. On stage Dean Borden broods with head in hands. Miss Oglethorpe mans massive punchbowl while aides prepare paper cups and platters of potato chips. Atheists for Democratic Action chant God is Dead *to block-that-*

kick cadence from balcony while Westminster Choir belts out When the Saints.

Varsity halfback helps History Department's Virgil Roebuck hoist son in wheelchair to position of safety on stage. Bebb lends a hand. Light in auditorium Götterdämmerung dim as rain rattles windows. Enthroned in central panel, Homer goggles down blind as faith as Bebb mounts lectern and calls for order.

Bebb's voice bursts through overcharged PA system like atomic blast: "Come unto me all ye . . ." (triggers feedback YE-E-E-E-E of such lethal pitch three hundred pairs of hands shoot up in chain reaction to three hundred pairs of ears as system cuts out). "Who labor and are heavy laden . . ." (sifts out unamplified and floats down soft as radioactive ash over stunned survivors). "And I will give you rest," intones Evangelist Bebb in hushed Gospelese. You could have heard a pone drop.

Bebb raises paper cup to propose toast: "Here's to Jesus." Bends elbow. "Here's to you." Bends elbow again. Places potato chip on tongue and swallows sacramentally. Crowd quiet. Oglethorpe committee starts distributing holy elements.

Chaotic clamor rekindled as karmic concoction passed around. Dean Borden booed when he refuses. Booing billows as proctors follow Dean's lead. Turtlenecked chaplain almost chickens out too but then chug-a-lugs. Crowd roars approval. A.D.A. recommences God is Dead chant as Bebbites battle back with God is Good to same beat. Transubstantiated Tropicanas guzzled by gallons. Bebb Buddha-like at lectern. Campus Cops brace for action.

Human pyramid formed in back pews. Stripped to jockey shorts black feaster shinnies up to tear down Back Behind Bars banner. Slugfest breaks out on balcony and starts to spread when Bebb at mike raises arms and blasts out, "Little children, let us love another" as cue for Kiss of Peace.

Pandemonium! Agape vies with Eros as Gott-und-Ginvertrunken cultists rise in pews embracing with dionysiac abandon. Aisles aswarm with sweating, rainsoaked bodies. Barechested boys and bra-less coeds tangle. Beardless frosh hug hairy-legged lettermen. Even atheists amorously aroused as inhibitions wilt in steamy atmosphere of Turkish bath or Methodist massage parlor. No holds barred in multiple clinches. Ejaculations, pious and otherwise, pierce humid air of Bebbsian bacchanal.

Topless teenybopper seen riding piggyback on grizzled custodian. Miss Oglethorpe heaved from hand to hand like huge blanc mange. Prone on stage turtlenecked chaplain titters in tongues as barefoot nymphet treads his shoulders free of knots. Tab Hunter and Jane Fonda lookalikes finger each other like blindmen reading braille while overstimulated undergraduate upends punchbowl into pith helmet of Emeritus Dean and serves it round as loving cup.

Comments seminarian, "The question isn't was it an orgy or was it a sacrament? It was a sacramental orgy, that's what it was. All I can say, if God is dead, it was one hell of a wake."

"When Bebb started dancing," states another, "I knew the age of miracles hadn't passed."

Two hundred pounds of cornfed evangelist are bouncing like giant beachball. Pearshaped blur of white flesh spins like top. Like cotton candy in cotton candy machine spiritual leader seems to whip up substance from surrounding celebrants and waxes bigger as he whirls. Circle clears around him.

As spinning slows, sweat-spangled moon-face comes in focus. Bebb opens mouth as wide as crater to shoot forth moon-mad Pig Latin incantation: INNYNAY MADGEEZERS RYZENWOCK. Points plump finger toward rim of circle. Stage silent.

INNYNAY. Points at what? Whom?

MADGEEZERS. Points at aluminum and leather rig with glittering wire-spoked wheels like spotlit circus unicycles. Invalid son of History's Roebuck throned there.

RYZENWOCK. Broken boy bends forward in chair. Shaft of moonlight shoots from Bebb's finger. Boy fights one foot free of footrest. Thrusts with back to push to front of seat, all sinews straining. Second foot follows as Bebb repeats command in mothertongue.

"In the name," Bebb bids,

"Of Jesus,

"Rise and walk!"

Boy has risen, stands stiff. Takes step, toe trailing. Takes step, toe just clearing floor. Third stiff step lands him half the way to Bebb at circle's center.

Robed now in sacrament-stained Revonoc tablecloth, Bebb spreads great wings wide in welcome, baring whalebelly pale barrel-chest and God knows what-all. Moby Dick? Boy's knees start to buckle but braces them and falters forward.

Hall mesmerized by miracle. Romanesque rotunda rocked with whoops and whistles. Halleluiahs. Then:

BLAM! BIFF! POW!

Borough Police bursts through doors at rear. Tear gas threatened. Everybody ordered out. Mass exodus starts as Campus Cops join Keystone contingent in keeping exits clear. Stage emptied in seconds. Love Feasters leapfrog pewbacks. Atheists stream down balcony stairs. Proselytes pour out on rain-slick blacktop and disband.

Damage to Hall estimated at $1500.00 and massive clean-up underway as *Prince* goes to press. Love Feast leaders booked on charges of disturbing the peace and up for suspension by Nassau Hall. President turns thumbs down on petition. Miss Oglethorpe in Princeton Hospital with fractured collarbone incurred in flight from stage. Mrs. Conover called to police headquarters to answer questions. Evangelist Bebb sought for *inciting to violence and rumored also to be wanted for Income Tax evasion and insurance fraud.*

Bebb's present whereabouts unknown. Last seen shielding Roebuck boy in arms as all around them stage surges like chorusline of Hair. Missing Conover Continental found abandoned at railway parking lot suggests guru may have made mad getaway on P.J. & B.

Interviewed at Revonoc, lanky, olive-skinned son-in-law Antonio Parr admits to mystification. When asked his estimation of Bebb, High School English prof Parr quotes Browning:

> *We that had loved him so, followed him, honored him,*
> *Lived in his mild and magnificent eye,*
> *Learned his great language, caught his clear accents,*
> *Made him our pattern to live and to die.*

So much for the *Prince.* I stayed on at Revonoc for what was left of that shattered weekend because Gertrude Conover asked me to. She took to her bed as soon as she returned from the interrogation at Borough Hall, and I did not see her again before I left, but she wanted me on hand to take care of the telephone and handle the press. Beyond that, her theory was that by remaining under the same roof, our auras would combine with that of the Pharaoh in his current incarnation and provide a kind of beacon light by which Bebb could find his way wherever he was going.

As she mounted the stairs to her bedroom, her blue curls hanging limp from the day's exertions, she paused with her hand on the bannister to explain this to me. Then she said, "Events he did not anticipate have shaken him loose from his karmic field. For the time being the gravitational pull of his destiny has no more effect on him than a magnet on an egg. If we stand by him now, you and I and Callaway, it is just possible that this time Leo Bebb may break free once and for all and rise to cosmic liberation like a balloon."

12

BIP, I said. PRINCETON. TROUBLE. GONE . . . shouting all the key words so that it was like hearing them for the first time myself, getting my own bad news. I might as well have saved the cost of the call for all Sharon could hear over the terrible connection, she at the Salamander Motel, I at my usual post under Mrs. Gunther's stairs. But she got the gist of it well enough, her voice crackling back at me like the sound track of an old movie: *Jesus. That Bip. Hand.* You had to hand it to him?

Home. It was like one of Bebb's free association sermons. *Bill. Bus.* There was a thunderstorm blowing across from the gulf, she said. I could almost hear the palmettos and cabbage palms rattling, the lions with their backs to the rain by the riffled pool as the lightning clove our talk in two. She would come. I would meet her. Then *I miss you*, I said. MISS YOU.

Afraid she'd be struck, she hung up as I was saying it, the blips and pizzicati of connections being disconnected becoming the small Bronx cheer of the dial tone so that again my message ended up being for me. I missed her.

I did what I could to get the house ready for my wife and son. Junk mail lay in drifts under the slot, and I waded through the importunities of congressmen and missionaries, catalogues full of nose hair clippers, early American fondue forks and personalized pencils. Ice had gotten in under the flashing during the winter, and there was a damp stain on the dining room wall as though a firing squad had finished off the Czar and his family there. A pot of petrified Cream of Wheat stood in the kitchen sink. Nobody had bothered to take out the Christmas tree, and I found it in the living room, a ragged brown scarecrow in a pool of needles.

I opened some windows and picked up the mail. I plugged in the refrigerator and filled the trays. I ran water into the Cream of Wheat and left it to soak. Before I was through, there wasn't a room I didn't enter, not a door I didn't push open half expecting to find something mouldering in a corner behind it. When I opened the door of the little attic room where Bebb had lived, I wondered if what I would find would be Bebb himself hiding out in a pool of dead flies, as sere and pillaged as the Christmas tree. The room was empty. In Sharon's and my room, the bed was unmade, last slept in, I suppose, the New Year's Eve when she had gotten sick and Tony had stayed to comfort her.

More even than to keep the weather out, the purpose of a house is to keep emptiness out, I thought—to box ourselves off from a sky that is too spacious, a horizon too far-flung, to carpenter for ourselves a space we can handle and feel at home in. But something had gone wrong. Instead of boxing emptiness out, those abandoned rooms had somehow boxed it in, emptiness not as an absence but as a presence: our house so filled with emptiness that it was hard to imagine there ever being room again for anything else.

Later that day I drove to Stamford to meet them, and I can see them still as they got out of the bus, Sharon carrying a string bag of grapefruit she'd bought on the trip and Bill in a straw hat with an alligator on it. Spotting them before they spotted me, I saw for a moment how they looked when they didn't have me around to look at, how they must have looked all those weeks without me in Armadillo or would have looked if

I'd been lying in my grave instead of standing there by a cigarette machine watching them without their knowing it. Sharon had her hands under Bill's arms to lift him down from the bus steps, and it must have tickled him the way he was cackling as she swung him down to the street. That was how they looked, and having seen it, I found myself not wanting to see any more, shifting my position so that the cigarette machine stood between us.

When I kissed Sharon, she kept hold of me with her cheek pressed against mine just long enough to make me wonder why, but it turned out to be only because her gold hoop earring had gotten snagged on my jacket, and having that to fuss about was as good a way to get through the moment as any. Bill gave me a wet smacker on the chin and handed me something done up in a Kleenex and a rubber band. It was a sand dollar.

"Hey, Antonio," Sharon said.

There was no lack of conversation on the drive home. It was as if they had simply been away on a vacation and wanted to catch me up on how things had been with them. From the back seat Bill told about a cat named Shell who went into the closet when you were away and made messes in your shoes. He told about a beach where he'd worked his treasure finder to locate an oarlock and a pirate's tobacco can and about a man who had hair in his ears and chewed up live shiners for chum. Sharon said she'd gotten her old job back part time at the souvenir stand where they sold shrunken heads and carved coconut husks and rugs with sunsets and palm trees on them. She said that a boy she used to know had turned the building where Holy Love used to be into a seafood restaurant and that the house where she had lived with Bebb and Lucille was vacant now and up for sale. She had gotten the key from the real estate agent and taken Bill through it one day—Lucille's TV room out back, the pull-chain john with the varnished brown seat, the gingerbread verandah where Herman Redpath had stood to have his picture taken the day Bebb had ordained him and all hell broke loose.

As they chattered on I tried to imagine what it had been like for them; I tried to get the feel of finding a cat-mess in your shoe or entering again that Charles Addams manse where I had first seen Sharon coming down the front steps in white sailor pants and a raspberry shirt as Bebb had leaned on the horn to hurry her. I tried to hear between the lines as they spoke, to search their words for some clue I could find my way back to them with; and all the while I was doing it, my son from the seat behind me was exploring me with his hands. He was reaching around and tracing the line of my jaw, my lips, running his fingers against the grain of my beard, and it occurred to me that in his own way he was trying to do the same thing. It was as if he was searching my face for something buried there, for secret treasure he maybe even half knew was a clue to the secret of himself as every time I drove through the tunnel where my poor father had told me once to keep a lookout for fish I half knew it was my own secret I was tunneling toward.

I thought of all the things I could tell them, when my turn came, about how life had been for me while they were gone. I could tell about puff-puff, how there by the lion's pool where I had seen Herman Redpath again and Lucille and Miriam, Brownie's suckling pig had rooted me out, that *porcus Dei*, dropping into my lap a name that lay deep beneath all my other names, my true and hidden name which I had never since been able either quite to remember or quite to forget. I could tell about Laura Fleischman and how in the blue night I had been granted my heart's desire only to discover that something less than my heart was in it. More than anything I could explain about decathexis—how the habit, I suppose, of keeping too sharp an eye on your own life can precipitate you prematurely into that geriatric state where life itself becomes a kind of spectator sport in which there is nothing much left either to win or to lose that greatly matters.

Bill with his treasure-seeking hands on my face—if anybody was to find there some scrap worth salvaging of the life I'd let go, surely he was the one, my child. He owed me that, or I him. I could have told him that too. Instead, I caught one of his fingers between my teeth the next time it came near enough and held him by it for a moment, his alligator hat knocked cockeyed against the back of my head. Then I let him go.

"That didn't hurt," he said, sinking back into his seat, and I said, "That's what you think."

What I actually did tell them about when my turn came was mostly Bebb's adventures—the march on Nassau Hall, the final Love Feast, Bebb's mild and magnificent eye as Roebuck's boy had staggered those few steps toward him across the stage. It became a kind of comic strip the way I found myself editing it for Bill's consumption, and I left until some other time the job of filling in for Sharon the little clouds that come puffing out of people's heads with the light bulbs and question marks in them.

After we'd eaten the sandwiches I'd gotten in and put Bill to bed, Sharon stood in the hall for the first time in four months looking up those empty stairs. She said, "I wish I had a dollar for every time I've dreamed about this place. It's the same dream every time. I'm back here again just like now. Everything looks normal as hell. I check it all out. Then the same thing always happens. I open some door or turn a corner, and all of a sudden I'm looking at a part of the house I never saw before. I think what a queer thing it is that all the years we lived here there was this whole bunch of rooms we never used because we didn't even know they were there."

Then "Today it's like coming home for a funeral," she said, "only nobody's died."

I said, "Speak for yourself."

She stood there with one hand on the banister and with the other reached over her shoulder to unhook her blouse at the top.

She said, "Listen, I know there's a whole mess of things we've got to hash over, but it seems like we were six months on that Greyhound, and my tail's dragging. If it's OK by you, I vote we sack out. We can start out even in the morning."

The business of bags, supper, bedding down Bill had given us a common ground to meet on, but without warning she pulled it out from under us now. She stood with one foot on the bottom stair, her unhooked blouse showing where her tan ended, and I stood under that same hall light where once Tony had hung up his jockstrap with a pot of African violets in it. It was no longer the last few months we had to contend with suddenly but the next few minutes.

What could we do to help Bebb? Was our marriage washed up permanently? If so, how about Bill upstairs asleep in his alligator hat? They sounded like subjects for doctoral dissertations compared with the one she'd dropped naked and quivering between us. Sack out *where* became the only question with flesh on its bones—she upstairs in our unmade bed and I back at Mrs. Gunther's or, if I stayed, in Tony's or Chris's room or up in Bebb's attic with the dead flies? It was left to me to answer somehow, and she did nothing to make it easy, watching me in silence with those somber eyes.

"It's OK by me," I said. "Mind if I stick around and play a few hands of solitaire?" Then, without warning again, her smile.

The secret of most faces is the look they have in repose, turned inward on where the secret is, but with Sharon it was always that minstrel-show flash of white teeth that let the cat out of the bag, made anyone she flashed it on a party to the secret of who she was.

"Be my guest," she said. "Just do me a favor first, hear? Get that tree out of the sitting room before you come up. It gives me the creeps."

"And piss on the side of the bowl," she said.

So she went upstairs with her brown back showing down to where it wasn't brown any more and her long hair streaked by the Armadillo sun and her tail dragging, and I went into the living room to deal with the tree. Every time you touched it, a million more needles fell to sweep up, and I had to unscrew the stand and roll back the carpet, but I got it done eventually and dragged the tree out back to the compost heap.

There was a sharp-edged white moon overhead and stars thick and quiet as dust, the *silence éternelle* that scared hell out of Pascal but to me has always seemed a somehow plumed and floating hush over the scariness of things. Near the compost was that great A-shaped wooden contrivance of knobs and dowels and slotted laths that I had put together during the first years of our marriage and with Tony's help had set up in the back yard. It hung on a rusty chain from its tripod the worse for wear and weathered silver, broken here and there by the weight of snow, the kids who sometimes came and fooled with it. I gave it a little shove with my foot and watched it as with a gallows creak it turned ponderously in the moonlight, the slow passing behind one another of its parts giving it the look of movement within movement. I thought of the Hayden Planetarium where Miriam and I had been taken as children and of that crouching, two-headed machine that projected the stars onto the domed roof as now it seemed to me this old toy of mine was projecting them in all their colossal pointlessness and beauty. I stopped it with my foot to make the stars stand still. The light was on in our bedroom.

Everything stands still, the old riddle goes, and motion is in the eye of the beholder if it's anywhere at all. A comic strip, an arrow in flight, a life—like a movie, they are all a succession of stills, a parade of unmoving moments that only seem to move. No matter what happens next, everything that has happened is for keeps. No matter how long Orphan Annie goes on, each frame along the way remains intact. My monument on its chain, for instance. The Christmas tree on the compost heap. I stand beside them to this day wherever else I've found to stand since. There is a cloud coming out of my head as I stare up at our lighted window, and Sharon is in that cloud. She is looking the way she did the first time we made love together in the Salamander Motel the winter before we were married. She has just come out of the shower, and the towel she had wrapped around her like a sari lies at her feet where it fell when I reached up and touched the tucked-in place at her shoulder. Light comes in through the slats of the Venetian blind. She is wearing only water. In that frame too I stand to this day, and so does she.

She was asleep by the time I got upstairs, the light turned off, and talk about your comic strips—Daisy Mae lying there on her side as warm and loose as silk beneath the moon-drenched sheet while with slapstick caution Li'l Abner climbs in beside her all gooseflesh. Frame after frame he lies there not daring so much as to gulp.

In bed at night, shadows have a way of turning into substance, thoughts into things you can catch your toe on so that you feel the bed shake as you literally fall asleep when that time comes. My day was drifting back at me as I waited for sleep there—the tour of our empty house, the bus, Bill's hands on my face—and the sadness of it got all confused with a dryness in my throat, desire confused with the pillow under my head, something that wouldn't lie flat. There was a scent of hair-tonic on the pillow—Tony's?—that I kept dimly trying to break like a code which promised to make sense of everything.

Then the phone. I heard it first as the ripping in two of something with writing on it and reached across Sharon for whatever it was, whatever I was, knocking the receiver off the hook in the dark and feeling her move beneath my arm as I fumbled for it. It was Bebb's voice I pressed to my ear, Bebb telling me who I was: Antonio?

"That you, Antonio? Now listen real close. I got to talk fast."

He said, "The hour is at hand, Antonio. The powers of darkness are on the march, and time's running out. Here's what I want you to do. I'm in New York City, never mind where for now. There's things better not said over the wire."

He said, "There's a place in the park where they serve sandwiches and soda pop under beach umbrellas. It's down a flight of stone steps. There's a pond at the bottom has a stone angel in it. You know the place I mean?"

When I told him I knew it, he said, "If you can make it round four P.M. tomorrow, don't be surprised to find a certain person there can guide you to me. Can you make it, Antonio, Sharon and you both?"

I didn't ask him how he knew Sharon was back or if he knew also that at that moment I was leaning across her to get at the phone. I told him just that we would make it, and his relief was audible. I pictured him squeezed into a streetcorner booth somewhere with his black raincoat buttoned to the chin and the brim of his Tyrolean hat pulled down.

He said, "Meantime you tell Sharon Bip said not to worry about anything. Tell her we all of us just got to hold tight to Jesus."

Somebody else evidently said something to him then, and he must have covered the receiver with his hand as he turned to answer. All I could hear was a burst of muffled laughter. I don't know that I ever heard Bebb laugh before, and the incongruity of it stayed in my ears long after the harried tone of the rest had faded. That hushed and conspiratorial s.o.s. and then that solitary, fat man's laugh so rich and abandoned. It was as if beneath the secret of his whereabouts lay a deeper secret still which only by accident I had heard an echo of. Then all was gravity again as he came back.

"Hold tight to Jesus," he said, "because he's the only one there is won't never let you down." Then "Tomorrow four o'clock, Antonio. Meantime don't take any wooden nickels," and he hung up.

"It was Bip," I told Sharon. "He says we've got to hold tight to Jesus."

"Jesus who?" she said.

I had started to roll back to my side of the bed and tell her the rest of what he'd said when she slipped one arm around my waist. She said, "A person's got to hold tight to something."

Sex education is known as Human Relations at Sutton High, and among those of us who are pressed into teaching it each year to small, glassy-eyed groups of freshmen and sophomores, the party line is that sex for sex's sake is at its best not much. If only your bodies meet and the human beings that happen to inhabit them don't, the chances are you'll only compound the problem you shacked up together to solve. It's not a bad rule of thumb as rules of thumb go, and by and large I'm willing to stand by it myself. But there are exceptions.

I didn't have the faintest idea who was inhabiting Sharon's body that

first night she got back. The very familiarity of her outer presence beside
me there only deepened the inner mystery, and she had no reason to be
any better informed about me. So it was only our bodies that met that
night, those two old reactionaries going off half-cocked as usual, and by
all rules it shouldn't have added up to much. Except that it did. I suppose
you couldn't say we made love together, being in inward ways too far apart
for that, but at least we made a kind of stopgap peace together. Human
relations notwithstanding, even the flesh has its own cloddish wisdom.

When we were through, I remember she said, "That one was on
Bip," and when I told her about his smothered laugh, she said, "You
never can tell about Bip. Maybe that's what he woke us up for."

13

THE RAIN HAD DWINDLED to a fine grey mist by the time Sharon and I arrived at the Bethesda Fountain in Central Park. The place was nearly
deserted, the umbrellas taken in. Only one of the tables was occupied.
There were two middle-aged Japanese sitting at it. One of them looked as
though he might have been part of a U.N. delegation. He had on a
Humphrey Bogart trench coat and a tweed golf cap with the visor un-
snapped. The other was plumper and shabbier with a *Daily News* unfolded over his head like a small, peaked roof. They were sitting side by
side facing out across the water. They both wore glasses and seemed to
have their eyes closed. The terrace was littered with shallow puddles,
and under one of the empty chairs a few pigeons pecked half-heartedly for
crumbs. The whole scene had an oriental feeling—only the tops of the tall
buildings visible in the distance, the two old friends, the single grey of
water and sky. The only spot of color was the yellow plastic rain hat
Sharon wore. We stood just inside the arch that the wide stairs descended
through. From the refreshment booth farther back under the arch a scent
of coffee floated out into the damp city air. On the chance that one of
the two Japanese was Bebb's emissary, we walked to the edge of the basin
where they could see us. Neither of them seemed to notice.

On the fountain, the angel was striding forward in a purposeful way
with his head bowed. One hand was at his side as though to keep his
long skirts from blowing, the other extended out over the pool.

A pigeon sat on one of the angel's outstretched wings, and under his
stone hand the water lay flat and still. A paper plate floated upside down,
an unfurled rubber filmy and vague as a dead fish.

Sharon said, "You sure he said four? It's nearly half past."

A young couple appeared down the stairs and stood in the archway looking out in our direction. The girl had a Bonwit's shopping bag and the boy a camera strung around his neck. There was something foolish and abandoned about them, like actors taking their bows to an empty house. After a while they came out and sat down at one of the tables.

Sharon said, "Maybe it's some kind of trap."

She had picked me up after my last class and driven me straight to the train where we couldn't find seats together, then the quick dash from Grand Central to the park so we'd hardly had the chance to exchange a word since the night before and didn't dare exchange more than a few at a time now for fear of missing what we'd come for.

The boy got up from the table and came over. He said, "Sir, I wonder if you'd mind doing us a favor and taking a picture. You've just got to line us up in the window and push that jigger down."

"Honeymooners?" Sharon said.

The boy said, "I guess you could call it that."

He went back to the table and sat down, and I crouched to my heels on the wet terrace in front of them moving the camera around to get the background right. What followed was pure Alfred Hitchcock—the missing finger on the stranger's hand, the old lady turning around and not being Dame May Whitty. Beyond the lovers' heads, standing on the balustrade above the archway, a solitary figure appeared in the viewer. He was wearing a green rubber raincoat that almost touched the ground and a porkpie hat. I couldn't make out his face very well, but I didn't need to. That great heap of a body lumping out in the wrong places as though it was several people gotten up to look like one, that scrawny neck—there was no mistaking him. It was Mr. Golden. He raised one arm and with a single backward sweep motioned us to follow him.

By the time we made it up the stairs, he had crossed the road and traveled a surprising distance away from us through the wet grass. The way the raincoat hid his legs, he never seemed to be running, but we had to rush to keep from losing sight of him in the mist. He didn't stick to the paths but took a crazy, zigzag route as if he was trying to shake us instead of lead us. Once we saw him clamber up a slippery outcropping of rock so nearly on all fours that he looked like a giant turtle. Once we had to dodge traffic to follow him across a road only to find that he'd doubled back to the other side and was heading off in a new direction. At a dip in the ground where several paths intersected by a drinking fountain, we lost him completely until Sharon spotted him up in the air beyond some shrubbery.

He was standing on the topmost rung of a slide in a children's playground, and I half expected him to hoot out *Ally-y all-y in come free*— the sense I had that he was playing with us, leapfrogging the hills and dales of Central Park like some enormous child. It must have been the way he set his fires, I thought, touching them off for the sheer sport of it, that great shambles of a man dancing around with his beautiful, withered smile lit up by the flames. As we ran toward the playground, he slid down the slide like a basket of laundry and bounded off through a gate in the fence. I remember him silhouetted at the far end of one of those brick-lined underpasses that smell of dead leaves and piss. I called out his name, the echo bouncing back and forth between the curved walls, and raising his porkpie hat, he waved it at us, then off again up the steep path beyond.

We had started out south from the fountain, but after all the back-tracking and crisscrossing we ended up going north till we found ourselves entering the zoo. A cloud of pigeons clattered into the air as Mr. Golden plowed down an avenue of cages with a lead of about fifty yards. A llama was still gazing after him with a look of superb hauteur as we came along in his wake, a red fox pacing back and forth with his clever face always turned toward the bars.

When we reached the open plaza where the seals are, we saw Mr. Golden on the far side of the tank. He had bought a white helium-filled balloon that bounced above him on its string as he disappeared around the corner of the old armory. Starting up the stairs to the street level, we had just time to see him spring into the frontmost of several cabs drawn up at the curb and take off down Fifth Avenue with a sizzle of tires on the wet pavement. Sharon and I piled into the next one. FOLLOW THAT CAB I said.

Somewhere between Park and Lexington we lost him in the traffic. Sharon was for giving up, but I had the feeling she was only matching my classic charge to the driver with a classic of her own—the moll who turns chicken when the heat's on and has to be slapped back into commission. So we kept inching east through the honking jam of red tail-lights and glistening fenders until we ended up first in line at the light on Second. Halfway down to the next side street, a cab was double-parked on the avenue with Mr. Golden's head stuck out through the back window. He had his thumb in his ear and was wagging his fingers at us. A few blocks farther down Second he turned east, but we missed the light again and had to wait at the corner. When we finally made the turn, there was no trace of him so we kept going till we hit First.

The block between First and York was almost empty. There were tenements on both sides with fire escapes out front and bars at the lower windows. An armchair with the springs falling out stood abandoned by a litter basket as if the last inhabitant might have sat there evenings before he finally pulled out with the rest of them. There was a brownstone garage with a corrugated portcullis rolled shut and EAT SHIT chalked across it less as a call to action, I thought, than a kind of parting confession. The steam from a manhole cover flattened out in the moist air, and over-head the hazy sky had gone brown with the approach of dusk.

A few doors beyond the garage, the cab of Mr. Golden had drawn up with the motor running and its yellow flanks steaming as we cruised up behind it. The driver jerked his thumb toward the building across the street, then with a death rattle of valves shot off toward York. The building was a great windowless pile of sootstained brick with a sign on it that said *Bull's International Fireproof Storage.*

It was like entering the great pyramid of Khufu and I wished we had Gertrude Conover with her memories as Uttu the Pharaoh's ward to guide us. We passed several doors, but they were locked. The one marked Office had a bell beside it, but the sluggish buzz failed to raise anyone. If Mr. Golden had preceded us, he had left no trace. The corridor ended in what seemed to be a blank wall but turned out to be the latrine-grey doors of an elevator. The only sounds were the ones we made trying not to make any. Then as we stood there, Sharon in her yellow hat and I clammy as the sweat cooled between my shoulderblades, a dime-sized light above the elevator button came on red, and from deep below we could hear the rumble and slap of cables. I said, "We've still got time to go home."

Sharon said, "We came to see him, didn't we?"

It was less a reproach than a real question. Bebb on the skids, Bebb down and out in the fireproof depths of Bull's storage—maybe we didn't want to see him. I thought of the fatness of his laugh over the phone, pictured him bleary and unshaven with his eyelid now at permanent half-mast. Maybe we'd better go home while we still had our illusions intact. The latrine-grey door shuddered, and as it started to slide open what we saw through the inner grille was that the elevator was empty except for the white balloon resting against the ceiling with the string hanging down. We got in and rode down as far as it would go.

"With trembling hands I made a tiny breach in the upper left hand corner and peered in," Howard Carter writes in his account of discovering the tomb of Tutankhamen. "Surely never before in the history of excavation had such an amazing sight been seen—objects, some familiar but some the like of which we had never seen, piled upon one another in seemingly endless profusion—two life-sized figures of a king in black, gold kilted, gold sandaled, the sacred cobra upon their heads . . . a heap of curious white oviform boxes, a beautiful lotiform cup of translucent alabaster, a confused pile of overturned chariots . . . Somewhere in all this magnificent panoply of death we would find the Pharaoh lying."

Sofas on sofas, chairs and tables stacked higgledy-piggledy with their legs in the air like sacrificial victims, translucent refrigerators, cardboard packing cases big enough to hold a Pharaoh each and coil upon coil of sacred carpet, lotiform lampshades, gilt frames, fire screens, old wardrobe trunks humpbacked and multi-stickered, headboards, bookshelves—we picked our way through a vast, dim basement down narrow paths piled higher than our heads with the debris of generations. If you'd dug deep enough, you would have come to stone knives, potsherds, the bones of extinct species. I'd brought the white oviform balloon with me from the elevator, and it floated above us like a cloud full of question marks.

Then, before we saw Bebb, we heard him, and I can hear him still as his voice came echoing toward us through the subterranean dusk. "Strait is the way and narrow is the gate which leadeth unto life, Antonio, and few there be that find it."

You think of Bebb squeezed into his gents' furnishings suit or buttoned up to his chin in his black raincoat. You picture his neck bulging out over his tight-fitting collar and that pint-sized hat on his head. But here was Bebb untrussed and overflowing, Bebb with the stays unloosed and the lid off. He had on a pair of loose-fitting paisley pajamas and a huge red dressing gown with satin lapels and a tasseled cord at the waist. His face looked firm and vigorous as though he'd just stepped out of a cold shower. His bald scalp was polished to a high sheen. When he spread his red arms to welcome us, he was like the sun rising.

He said, "Rejoice with me for I have found my sheep which were lost. Put rings on their hands and shoes on their feet and bring the fatted calf and kill it."

Sharon said, "This is some hideout you got here, Bip," and wrapping his arms around her he said, "Sharon honey, I'm through hiding. There is nothing hid which shall not be manifested nor anything kept secret but that it shall come abroad."

He took both my hands and said, "The winter is past, Antonio, and the sound of the turtle is heard again in the land." I suppose he could have gone on entirely in quotations from Scripture if he'd wanted to.

I said, "You're looking good, Bip," and Bebb said, "Antonio, you look like you've had a dose of monkey glands yourself."

He said, "Follow me."

We proceeded single file still deeper into the labyrinth of Bull's International Fireproof Storage, Bebb leading the way with the pajamas flopping about his ankles and Sharon and I following along behind, damp and disheveled by our chase through the park. Sharon said, "You better leave go your balloon. It looks like we escaped from the funny farm," and giving it its freedom, I watched it rise to the ceiling and stick there. We passed through several more acres of buried history.

What we came to finally was more of a cage than a room—three wire-mesh walls and a wire-mesh ceiling built out from the rear wall of the building like something to keep out rats. It was so much brighter inside than the rest of the basement that it took a few minutes to make it all out.

There was a large roll-top desk, a filing cabinet and some folding chairs. There was an electric hot plate on top of the filing cabinet, some coffee mugs and a bag of Hydrox cookies. A girlie calendar dated 1957 hung over the desk and beneath it a standing phone of an even earlier vintage. Hooked here and there through the wire walls were a number of hangers with clothes on them—an overcoat with a Persian lamb collar, a

Mandrake the Magician opera cape, some double-breasted suits and a Chinese kimono. I pictured Bebb whiling away the days down there trying them all on. There must have been a whole MGM costume department stashed away somewhere.

The rear wall of concrete was decorated with a crudely painted scene which from its resemblance to the murals that had burned up with Open Heart I recognized as the work of Mr. Golden. There were a lot of feather duster palm trees in it, a bright blue sky with birds flying across like black checkmarks, some overstuffed white clouds—a scene not unlike the ones on the rugs that Sharon sold at the novelty shop in Armadillo. Beneath this tropical paradise was a cot, and stretched out on it on his back with his raincoat folded under his head for a pillow and not even breathing hard was Mr. Golden. On his low-hung bolster of a paunch a small transistor radio was balanced, and he had it plugged into one ear by a cord. His eyes were closed, his expression serene.

Sitting down in the swivel chair at the desk, Bebb clasped his hands behind his head and gazed at us with the look of a parlor magician who's just taken fifty cents out of somebody's ear. He said, "Fats and me, we spent five years in a place no bigger than this. I'm going to be honest with you. In some ways it's been like coming home."

Sharon said, "Jesus, Bip, you can't hole up here forever."

I said, "That was some chase you gave us, Mr. Golden," and with his eyes still closed, Mr. Golden said, "I'm a nightwatchman that sometimes watches with his eyes and sometimes watches with his ears, but the point is I'm always watching. There's a woman calling in who says she's got a alligator pear pit with a plant coming out of it better than four foot tall."

That was the way our conversation began, and in many ways it is characteristic of all that followed. To the best of my recollection, our four statements followed in the sequence I've given—home, Jesus, chase, alligator pear—but you could rearrange them any other way, and they would hang together as well or as badly. Possibly chase came first, then alligator pear and home, and only then Jesus. We had moments, of course, when the sequence was as unalterable as knocking and opening, but it seems to me that much of the time we said what we wanted to whether it fitted in or not, and that's the disjointed way I will set it down here. Sharon and I, Mr. Golden and Bebb—each of us had a particular set of words to get across, and at the heart of each set was one special word so deeply buried in the others sometimes that you had to be a Howard Carter to dig it out without having it fall to dust in your hands.

Bebb, for instance. It took Sharon to explain to me his special word. I hadn't gotten it on my own, so lodged it was in everything else. She said, "He was telling us *goodbye*, you poor peckerhead. Couldn't you even hear?" It was days afterwards that she explained it, standing out on a potatofield in New Jersey as the sun started to go down, and I knew she was right though at the time Bebb was actually saying it I hadn't heard it. Goodbye is such a sad word, and by comparison all his other words in that cage seemed bright and hopeful.

Twirling and untwirling the tassel of his robe around his thumb as he spoke, he said, "Antonio, I've been in the ring for Jesus going on forty years, and I've been beat up something cruel. Spiritually speaking, I've been—why, this pitiful soul of mine, it's got lumps the size of an egg all over and a pair of cauliflower ears and a jaw on it looks like raw hamburg. I'm a walking grocery store the way the powers of darkness have worked me over all the way from Miami Beach as far north as Princeton, New Jersey, and they're not done with me yet. Only they're not the ones I'm scared of. It's the darkness in here I'm scared of," he said, tapping his chest with his tasseled thumb. "The shameful things a man does with his life. The shameful things don't anybody know about but him. I've been down for the count more times than you could shake a stick at. I'm not denying it. But the ref's never gotten farther than nine yet. Jesus, he's always propped me back on my feet somehow. He's always had me back in there slugging it out for him again."

I said, "Did you ever think of retiring from the ring for a while, Bip? I mean you're pushing sixty-five and there's nobody on your back a good lawyer couldn't square you with. Why not just get the hell out— you and Gertrude Conover take a trip somewhere. Think of all the places you've never seen—museum tours, South America cruises. . . ." I all but had the travel brochures out on the desk in front of him, and I remember the acceleration of my pulse as I spoke, my mounting excitement at the thought that if I could only persuade him to let go, we could somehow all of us let go. I suppose what I wanted Bebb to do was wash decathexis itself in the blood of the lamb.

He said, "Antonio, I've had thoughts like that myself sometimes. A man dreams dreams. This isn't the Ritz Hotel, but I've got Fats to bring me food and drink and keep watch nobody comes around asking embarrassing questions. I could be snug as a bug down here laying low till things blow over. The IRS, they've got bigger fish than me to fry anyhow and so's that insurance company I've got on my tail. When the heat's off, maybe I could take off someplace like you say." His eyelid fluttered shut as if to hold his dream in for a moment, like the smoke of a good cigar—he and Gertrude Conover watching the moon rise over the Acropolis, taking a boat trip up the Amazon.

"Why not just get the hell out, Bip?" I said.

He said, "Because getting the hell out, that's what hell is, Antonio. I've got to gird up my loins for the next round. I've got to move on."

"Where you going to gird up your loins to move to next, Bip?" Sharon said.

Bebb said, "Up. Holy Love, Open Heart, Love Feast," he counted them out on his fingers. "I've burned all my bridges. Up's the only place I got left."

Mr. Golden gave a little grunt and cradling the radio against him so it wouldn't fall, rolled over onto his side.

Bebb said, "He's awful big on those talk shows. Seems like the world's full of lonesome folks dying to talk."

Mr. Golden said, "The world's full of sickies. A man's sounding off how the people that hand out trick-or-treats with razor blades in them ought to have their private parts cut off with a razor blade."

Sharon said, "What's with this insurance company you've got on your tail?"

Bebb said, "Somebody wrote them a letter the fire at Open Heart wasn't any accident."

Mr. Golden said, "The good thing about fire is it burns your bridges, and a man's got to burn his bridges so he can move on. It's a rule of life, if a man don't keep moving on, he's good as dead. Every time you cross a bridge, burn it."

Bebb unclasped his hands from behind his head and stretched them high into the air. With the trace of a yawn in his voice, he said, "So when you expecting the baby, honey? You picked out a name for her yet?"

Sharon said, "I never said I was expecting any baby."

Bebb said, "I know. You weren't planning on saying it either."

Sharon said, "I'm not saying it. You're saying it."

Bebb said, "I kind of hoped you might call her after your mother. She'd set a lot of store by that, poor soul."

I said, "It's true? You're having a baby?"

Sharon said, "You tell him, Bip. You've got all the answers."

Bebb said, "It's going to be a girl, and she's going to name it Lucille after her mother. It'll have its father's eyes."

Sharon said, "It better have somebody's eyes."

"What if it's a boy?" I said.

Bebb said, "It's a girl."

"What if somebody'd been tailing you?" Mr. Golden said. "You think I was leading you all around Robin Hood's barn just for the fun of it?"

"It crossed my mind," I said.

Sharon said, "What if we'd have lost you?"

Mr. Golden said, "Where's your faith? Where's your ding-dong faith?"

"I don't have any," Sharon said.

Mr. Golden said, "Then you didn't have anything much to lose."

Bebb said, "Sharon, nobody that doesn't have faith ought to feel too bad about it. Even the ones that have it, it's not like they have it permanent, like a face-lift."

Mr. Golden had propped himself up on one elbow. He said, "Here today, gone tomorrow, that's faith for you."

Bebb said, "The Apostle Paul wrote faith is the evidence of things not seen. Now if the only evidence a man's got is something he can't see, you can't blame him if sometimes he—when a thing's not out where you can see it, sometimes you have a hard time believing it's there."

Mr. Golden said, "If a thing's not out where you can see it, there's a fifty-fifty chance it's not there, period."

"It's a chance you got to take," Bebb said.

"You think there's something there, Bip?" Sharon said.

She said, "Forget all the preacher talk. Just say it like it is. If you had to bet everything you've got there's something there, would you do it? When it comes right down to it, would you bet your tail, Bip?"

Bebb said, "Remember that thing your mother wrote before she passed on? She wrote what she was washed in, it wasn't the blood of the lamb. It was the shit of the horse. Show me a son of Adam doesn't have days he feels like that."

"Would you bet your tail, Bip?" Sharon said.

Bebb said, "Sharon, there's been days I wouldn't even bet my green stamps."

"This day, now," Sharon said.

Bebb drummed his fingers on Mr. Golden's desk. There was a clipboard with a bunch of inventories in it, and he worked his finger in under the clip till it was caught there. He said, "When the time of testing comes, I'll just have to say, Savior, let thy grace be sufficient. Jesus, take pity on this wore-out old tail of mine that's all I got left to bet with."

Mr. Golden said, "Flying saucers have landed." He was frowning with concentration, his hand held up for silence and his transistor still plugged into his ear.

"This lady was walking home from the pictures after dark when she saw something she took for a fire hydrant. It had a little round hat on it and it didn't come up any higher than her knee. Then the hat commenced to glow red like the end of a cigar when you take a pull on it, and she could see it had a queer kind of face to it like a balled-up handkerchief. Just before it took off, it said something. Just as plain as day she heard it. It said, 'Don't be afraid.' Soon as it said it, it shot up like a rocket."

"Think of it," Bebb said. "A creature that size come all those millions of miles just to offer a word of comfort."

Mr. Golden said, "They're all heart, those small-size ones."

Bebb was smiling. "All heart and a yard wide," he said. "Sometimes wider."

Mr. Golden had lovely white teeth, but when he returned Bebb's smile, you could see all the back ones were missing. His face had a puckered look like a hand that's been in hot water too long. He said, "The big ones too. They'd give you the shirt off their backs if they had a shirt."

Bebb said, "If they had a back."

Mr. Golden said, "They come in all sizes and shapes and flavors like ice cream though there's some you couldn't tell from humans unless you were one of them yourself. You could tell then easy enough."

"If you felt like telling," Bebb said.

Mr. Golden said, "They're the same breed of cats as the angels of Scripture. They've been paying us visits since the beginning of time."

Bebb said, "They carry messages for the Almighty down through all the moons and stars and Milky Ways of outer space."

Mr. Golden said, "There's not a doubt in the world about it."

Bebb said, "Not if there's an Almighty anyway."

"Right," Mr. Golden said. "Not if there's an Almighty and he has messages to send out."

"Like Having a wonderful time, wish you were here," Bebb said. "Or Keep in touch. Love to everybody."

"Or Don't be afraid," Mr. Golden said.

Bebb said, "Don't be afraid for the terror by night or for the arrow that flieth by day."

"Our God is a consuming fire," Mr. Golden said, "but don't be afraid of him either. It's just if we won't burn our own bridges, he burns them for us. It's a rule of life a man's got to move on."

"I don't know as I ever happened to see one myself looked just like a fire hydrant," Bebb said, and I remember still the sound of their laughter —Bebb's like wind whistling down a chimney, Mr. Golden's like somebody cracking kindling across his knee.

Mr. Golden said, "A yellow dog that answers to the name of Ed slipped his collar in front of the Public Library on 42nd and Fifth. It doesn't bite. There's a reward out. It's five dollars; no questions asked."

He seemed to be listening to his radio and talking at the same time. He said, "The man that runs the show, he says not a yellow dog runs off but Guess Who's eye is upon him."

Mr. Golden got up off his cot and stretched. His bulk was mostly width, from shoulder to shoulder, hip to hip. In terms of thickness he was oddly flat as though, like a playing card, if you looked at him edgewise, you'd see almost nothing. He passed around the bag of Hydroxes.

He said, "I wasn't always a mole like you see me down here now better than twenty feet underground and more. It used to be I flew the wide blue yonder with the best of them, wheeling around up there in the clouds with my wings stretched out like a red-tail hawk. You take your roughest ocean, up there it looks like the wrinkles of old age. It looks like you can pick up whole cities and put them in your trouser pocket."

Bebb said, "They used to call him Josephine back then. Remember 'Come, Josephine, in my flying machine'?"

"*Up, up, a little bit higher!*

Watch out! The moon is on fire," Mr. Golden sang the old song out in a voice that was unexpectedly high and sweet. "The things I've been called in my time you wouldn't half believe."

Bebb broke his Hydrox in two and gave half each to Sharon and me. He said, "You take it. If I lose my figure, what have I got left?"

Mr. Golden said, "Technically, I was ground crew, a grease monkey, but on test runs they shoved me the stick fast enough. Inside and out, nobody in the outfit knew those ships better than me."

Bebb said, "Antonio, they figure I'm through. That miserable little Connor of the IRS and Virgil Roebuck with his combat shoes and those fingers of his that's all over nicotine—even down here in the bowels of the earth I've heard the echo of their rejoicing. Ever since they broke things up at Alexander Hall, there's been dancing in the streets of Princeton, New Jersey. Back behind bars with Bebb. Well, I'm not behind bars yet. I've still got me an ace or two up my sleeve."

He had gotten up to offer coffee around and stood with his back to the wire-mesh wall, his red bathrobe and polished scalp bright against the dim cavern that loomed behind him. Lucille had a theory about certain mysterious elevators which, if you knew their secret, took you down to levels deeper than the deepest basements where people from outer space met to lay plans, and I thought how if she could have seen Bebb and Mr. Golden there in the vaults of Bull's Storage, it would have confirmed her wildest suspicions. As Bebb stood there like a routed general on the eve of a great comeback, it crossed my mind that hidden among all these acres of junk behind him there might be battalion after battalion of God only knew what—fire hydrants, angels—ready to follow him to victory.

I said, "Bip, the first thing you need is a good lawyer. You can't just—" Raising his hand, he interrupted me.

He said, "Antonio, we're past all that, Fats and me. Wrangling things out in court, having them rake up a lot of stuff that's over and done with and better to leave lay. I'm through trying to fight them on their own ground where they're the ones know every hill and valley of it."

Mr. Golden said, "When you got wings, why stick to the ground, period? Ever hear of a bald eagle scrapping it out on his feet?"

Bebb said, "All I've done up till now, it's been small potatoes. A soul here, a soul there. . . . I reached out far as I could. The unchurched multitudes I tried to catch with the mail order ads of Gospel Faith College. The great whore of the North I set up Open Heart to wean away from the cup of her fornications. The Pepsi generation, how I made to stay them with flagons and comfort them with apples for I was sick with love, Antonio, and I don't know as I'll ever get over it. None of those things ever come to as much as they should of maybe because I never gave much as I should of to them. I thought small, and I reaped small. Sharon, the time's come to think big. This may be the last round coming up, and your old Bip's going to shoot for the moon."

"*Up, up, a little bit higher!*" Mr. Golden sang with chocolate Hydrox blacking out most of his teeth. "*Watch out! The moon is on fire!*"

Sharon said, "Do me a favor, will you, Bip? This time keep all your buttons buttoned."

Bebb said, "What God hath joined together, let no man put asunder. That's number one. Number two is like unto it. What Bebb hath joined together, let no man put asunder either. I joined you two together. Way back in Holy Love days I fixed the whole thing up in ways you never knew. Antonio, first time I ever laid eyes on you, I could see you were right for each other. You were a tree without apples. Sharon, she was apples without a tree. She was the apple of her daddy's eye, but what kind of future's that for a girl? She needed a branch to grow on same as you needed her to put out leaves and fruit on the shiftless branches of your life. Without you'd had each other, you wouldn't have either of you amounted to spit."

He said, "Why, if you couldn't stand the sight of each other, that's one thing. If you treated each other like dirt and went around saying cruel and spiteful things and cheating on each other every chance you got, that's one thing. Sometimes maybe a divorce is made in heaven same as a marriage even though it don't say so in Scripture. But you've been through thick and thin together, and it's made you the best friends either one of you's ever like to find again. Even if you split up and get married off each one to somebody different, you'll be forever phoning each other long distance and trading the kids back and forth. Antonio, he'll be coming round every time there's a birthday or somebody's took sick. They'll all of them say isn't it something how those two get on so friendly even so.

"If there's one thing makes me want to puke, it's a friendly divorce," Bebb said. "If it's got to be, give me a divorce that's hateful. When you're friends, stay put. So what if it's not all moonlight and roses? What is? Stay put because if you don't, you'll spend the rest of your life looking to find each other in the face of strangers."

Sharon said, "All my life I listened to you, Bip. Even down home this winter, everything I did I could hear you quoting Scripture about it."

"Don't listen to me," Bebb said. "Listen to your own self."

Sharon said, "It got to where sometimes I thought maybe the reason

I ran out on Antonio was because you picked him for me just like you said."

Bebb said, "Sharon, you'd have picked him anyhow. Gertrude Conover, she'd say it was on account of there was some other life you used to love him in. It's not doctrine, but who knows? Nobody's got a corner on the God's truth, and there's nobody has the right to dump on somebody else's version of it."

Sharon said, "What is it makes people want to dump on you, Bip? Your whole life they've been dumping on you."

Bebb released the clipboard far enough to get his finger out. There was a red line across the knuckle. "Jesus never let on it was going to be any different," he said.

Sharon said, "Far back as I can remember, they were dumping on you. Right from the time they picked you up in Miami."

She said, "I always dreamed you'd be like Oral Roberts someday. I wanted them to run your picture on TV and name a college after you. Only every time you almost had it made, somebody dumped on you. How come, Bip?"

"I took some crazy chances," Bebb said. "Sharon, the way I figured it, if a man was to lay bare all the hurt and shame in him out where folks could see it, might be somebody'd come along someday who'd make it right." You could see he'd forgotten Mr. Golden and I were there, only Sharon.

He said, "Take what happened down there in Miami, for instance. Those kids. Talk about your angels, why the eyes those kids had, they were the eyes of angels if I ever saw one, and their kid faces and their bare feet and the way they were hollering around out there in the sunshine—they were having them a time like all the good times a man ever had when he was a kid himself rolled into one. A *good* time, Sharon, a time with goodness and fun and bare feet skittering all through it. I was watching them play niggerbaby back of that seafood place, and it come over me all in a minute. I had this feeling if just one split second those kids would have turned those eyes they had onto me the shameful way I was laid bare in front of them and not gone and mocked at me or tore off home, just looked at me with all that fun and beauty they had in those eyes of theirs, why I'd have walked away from that place a saved sinner.

"It was a fool thing to do, a crazy chance," Bebb said, "and I never two seconds running held it against anybody things went and turned out just like they did."

I'd only seen Sharon's face wet with tears twice before—once just after Bill was born and once when she read the long letter Lucille wrote Jesus on that paper of hers that had flowers blooming all over it. Both those times it seemed to me her tears had more to do with just her face than with whatever was going on inside her face like the tears if you smell an onion or Bildabian hits a nerve, but this time she looked as though they were rolling down on the inside too.

She was sitting beside Bebb with her hand resting between both of his on his knee, but she withdrew it when he finished speaking and pushed back a strand of hair. The act of twisting around to see her at such close range next to him bugged Bebb's eyes out so that his face looked dangerously overinflated. Reaching out to take her hand back again, Bebb raised it up and as though he suddenly had an unbearable toothache pressed it against the side of his face like a poultice. Or else it was her hand where the unbearable pain was, and the poultice was his plump, white cheek. He didn't say anything for a while, just sat there with his eyes bugged out and Sharon's hand pushing his mouth crooked where he'd pressed it to him.

Finally he said, "Honey, you know what's the last word of all the millions of words there are in Scripture not counting the Amen at the end, which one it is that comes at the tail end of the whole shebang?"

Sharon shook her head.

Bebb said, "Well, it's 'Come, Lord Jesus.' Just as plain and straight as that. I always figured it put pretty near the whole thing right in a nutshell. Just 'come.'"

Sharon said, "All I can say is he better come on the double then.

"If he's coming," she said.

He in his bathrobe, she in her raincoat with her head resting against his shoulder—I don't suppose the light in that cluttered cage of a room changed in the slightest, but the way they were sitting there propping each other up, it was as if they were watching a sunset.

On the wall behind them the palm trees stand stiff and motionless as the clouds turn pink. The checkmark birds become a flock of spoonbills. They are flying back from a long day's fishing on the flats. They circle around once or twice through the tinted sky, then float down to settle for the night in the place where Sharon and Bebb are sitting.

From my first meeting with Bebb years earlier, the picture I remember best is at the entrance to the Lexington Avenue subway. I had walked him there in the rain, and half way down the stairs he turned and looked back at me over his shoulder. He had on his black raincoat and Happy Hooligan hat, and he said, "All things are lawful for me, but all things edify not. One Corinthians ten." Oddly enough, the picture I remember best from this final meeting is something like it except that in this one Bebb is going up instead of down.

When it came time for Sharon and me to leave, he led us to a handier elevator than the one we'd arrived by, a large freight elevator so packed with furniture there was barely room for two of us to squeeze in together up front. He said he wanted to see us safely on our way so Mr. Golden and I waited below while he and Sharon took the first ride up. The only door the elevator had was a folding grate you could see through, and that is the last picture of him I have kept.

Over his pajamas he is wearing the overcoat with the Persian lamb collar, but he has on that same original hat. He is looking neither to right nor to left but straight ahead through the grating of the door. His mouth is snapped shut on its hinges, and as the elevator starts to move, I think I see his trick eyelid flutter, but maybe this time it is a genuine wink. The elevator rises slowly—first his head disappears, then his Persian lamb collar, then those two plump fists hanging stiff at either side. Finally all that is left are his feet in what I suspect are the same black shoes I mentally tied for him while he said the Lord's Prayer over the remains of poor Lucille laid out in a Houston funeral parlor. Then nothing is left but the empty shaft with the cables looping down like shroudlines. As things turned out, it was the start of a record-breaking flight.

14

WHEN Brownie flew on from Houston in a cloud of after-shave, he brought John Turtle with him, and my heart sank at the memory of the abominations he had committed at the funeral of Herman Redpath and at the thought of what he might go on to commit now in that potato field north of Princeton where we all gathered—Sharon and Gertrude Conover and I, Tony and his brother Chris, Charlie Blaine and Billie Kling, Nancy Oglethorpe, and Anita Steen of all people, Anita Steen looking the most stricken of all and in a dress for once instead of her usual slacks. She wore the rusty black dress and black stockings of an Italian peasant, her face puffy with grief. I hadn't even realized she'd known Bebb, but she had apparently, from the days when she used to come to the house to teach Sharon guitar.

She said, "Listen, religion's not for Anita Steen, and he knew it, but we always got on anyhow. Maybe it's because we were both queer as three dollar bills," and then the wrinkles of grief started to shoot across that fierce, orphaned face like a cake of ice when you hit it with a pick, so when she asked if she could come along with Sharon and me, we agreed to drive her down with us from Sutton.

Brownie did his best to reassure us about John Turtle. He said, "John Turtle is not here in his official capacity as Joking Cousin because Mr. Bebb was never a member of the tribe, dear. He's here to pay his respects like the rest of us, and I don't look for any trouble from him."

And Brownie was nearly right. John Turtle didn't interrupt the

prayers with blasphemies or carry on indecently during the Scripture readings, and he didn't take a leak in the coffin either, because of course
there wasn't any coffin, just that sprawl of blackened debris with one
corkscrewed wing jutting up and the neat furrows scorched the color of
toast in streaks that shot out starwise. The only trouble he caused, if you
could even call it trouble, was after Brownie had finished and we were all
standing around like a ruin, and before anybody realized what he was up
to, John Turtle had kicked off his saddle shoes and moved as far in
toward the wreckage as he could without hurting his bare feet on the
shattered hardware.

He was wearing a double-breasted checked suit with built-up shoulders, and his black hair was greased down so flat it looked as if he'd
painted it on. With his arms crooked at the elbows, he held his fists up
around his ears, threw back his head, and did a dance. It seemed to me a
rather restrained dance with a lot of bending over double in it and
straightening up again, the legs moving mostly from the knees down,
the feet never leaving a circle not much bigger than a steering wheel. He
didn't sing any of his songs while he did it or make any other sound, and
after a few minutes we almost forgot to watch him the way we might
have forgotten to watch a black crow pecking around for potato bugs.

But then he left his small circle and came toward us with a crouching step, his legs wide apart, his arms curved out to the side and wobbling
like a crab's claws. His gold-framed teeth glittered as he swayed from side
to side on his haunches, and then suddenly he leapt forward and with
the delicacy of Rudolph Nureyev seized Gertrude Conover by the waist
from behind and raised her off the ground. You might have thought they'd
rehearsed it.

If Gertrude Conover was taken aback, she gave no sign of it but
rose up in his grip as light as a bird, her expression unchanging as she
gazed out straight ahead, her black pumps dangling in the air. The Joking
Cousin held her there maybe two feet off the ground, that small woman
with not a feature or a blue hair out of place. He circled around with her
a few times, his bare feet padding softly up and down through the
scorched furrows. It was as if he was searching for just the right spot, the
right vantage, and when he found it, he straightened out his arms so that
she was raised that much higher still and stopped dancing then, just held
her there as far as his arms would reach like a man at a parade hoisting
a child to see the elephants pass by.

Her dress had gotten hitched up in the process, and I remember how
her white slip showed, beneath it her thin, beige legs. I remember the
little exclamation she gave as though what she could see from up there
was both a surprise and an end to surprise, the way she brought her
hands together palm to palm in front of her face like a diver.

Nancy Oglethorpe's beehive, the grey crew cut of Anita Steen, the
fedora Charlie Blaine wore in fair weather and foul because of his sinuses,

we were the skyline John Turtle raised her to see beyond—beyond us and
the wreckage we'd gathered by, to the flat acres stretching out behind it;
to a blue silo dazzling in the sun, to the horizon where swollen grey
clouds were crowding each other like elephants. Like the time I stood
out by the compost heap looking up at Sharon's lighted window the
night she came home from Armadillo, it is one of those frames where all
of us who were there go on standing forever.

"Widow lady, oh my," John Turtle said, his cheek pressed tight
against Gertrude Conover's behind. "Window lady, oh my." Considering
all he might have done and said, I figured we'd come off remarkably well.

"My dear, have you ever been to a Princeton reunion?" Gertrude
Conover had said that morning out on the terrace of Revonoc with an
espaliered quince spidering out on the wall behind her. "Let me tell you I
have lived through a great many of them. They are Walpurgisnacht. They
are Vanity Fair. Well, they are a disaster. I remember when Harold
Conover was still alive going with him to the forty-five year tent one
evening. There were two elderly men at one of the tables pouring pitchers
of beer over each other's heads. They were both of them bishops. Suburban housewives with brand new permanents and too much lipstick.
People's children in little T-shirts with tigers on them throwing up and
getting lost. And my dear, the P-rade. The P-rade is the climax of the
whole thing. Matadors, Mickey Mouses—each returning class is dressed
up to look like something different, and they all carry comic signs and
bottles of one thing or another. They come from the far corners of the
earth."

She said, "Naturally Leo Bebb chose the P-rade just the way he chose
the Pharaoh's court in days gone by and just the way he will choose who
knows what spectacular arena in days yet to come. If there are to be days
yet to come for him. I like to think perhaps he has burst the fetters of his
karma once and for all and can slip off now into cosmic consciousness
like a drop of water slipping back into the ocean. It's only selfishly I don't
like to think that," her blue curls bobbing in the spring breeze, the
Pharaoh tying back some red roses across the lawn by the swimming
pool. "Selfishly, I don't like to think of never running into him again.
Even at his bluest he was . . .

"Leo Bebb was always good company," she said.

The color blue. Red roses for a blue lady, as the old song goes; the
blue hair of Gertrude Conover; the wide blue yonder where Mr. Golden
had winged it with the best of them in his time; Bebb at his bluest. As
though I'd been there myself I can see him appearing like a bolt out of
the cloudless blue sky over Nassau Street. The band in their ice cream
white flannels and orange blazers. The old grads with their hearing aids
and straw boaters. The young grads gotten up to look like Martians, like

castaways. I see the flash of the trombones, the revolving blue lights on the cars of the cops blocking traffic, hear the bum-boom of the big drums, all that.

Then *Come Josephine in your flying machine*—coming in over the squat turrets of Alexander Hall and the Presbyterian Church a low-flying spit-and-glue flivver laying balloons like eggs, hundreds of them, and leaflets, LOVE IS A FEAST, with a shot of Bebb on each. It was the same shot Sharon said made him look as though they were taking his temperature rectally, his eyes popping out of his head, his mouth clamped tight on a cry for help.

It buzzed the whole length of Nassau Street from Palmer Square to Jugtown and back with the engine roaring like Armageddon and the wings a-flap, so low that in many places the marchers scattered and children clung to their mothers' skirts. They say you could feel the wind of the props, that dogs ran wild, that Charles Willson Peale's Washington fell to the floor in Nassau Hall and cracked its frame.

I see Fats Golden at the stick like the Red Baron—his scarf streaming out behind him, his leather helmet, his goggles, that lovely, wind-swept smile. I don't see Bebb because he is swamped in balloons, the whole fuselage stuffed with them—they must have spent days blowing them up—Bebb himself a balloon as he shovels them out into the sky.

On the return flight when they hit Palmer Square for the second time, Mr. Golden must have given it everything he'd got. They say you could see rivets popping, seams straining, sweat breaking out on the scarred silver belly, as it hovered for a moment like the sun at Gideon, pulled itself together, then shot straight up into the wide blue. At about three times the height of Holder Tower it leveled off and spoke—two streamers spilling out from the tail in a long line, two twenty foot pennants trailing out behind in tandem, one of them HERE'S TO JESUS, on the other one HERE'S TO YOU.

Gertrude Conover said, "It was his parting shot, his One for the Road, circling around up there over the town the better part of an hour doing all kinds of crazy stunts, climbing and swooping and what have you. They found out the plane had been stolen from the Princeton airport, and there were troopers out there waiting for them to land. They called me to find out what I knew. I knew absolutely nothing. The last time I saw Leo Bebb was at the *débacle* at Alexander Hall. The last time I spoke with him was when he phoned me late one night just a day or so ago. He said he'd left his red preaching gown in the back seat of the Lincoln and would I have it dry-cleaned for him. He said that portable television he keeps in his room wasn't working properly and asked if I'd get the repair man up before the guarantee expired. They seemed queer things to be calling up so late about. I believe they were his way of letting me think he was planning to come back. I knew he wasn't, of course."

I said, "He'd burned his bridges behind him."

Gertrude Conover said, "His friend Clarence Golden burned them for him. That remarkable man came to see me one day. I'd never even heard his name mentioned before, and there he was strolling across the lawn with his hands in his pockets like my oldest neighbor. I recognized him almost immediately. He was one of the great eighteenth century *castrati*, a man by the name of Serafico Veluzzi. I was myself a provincial *contessa* visiting in Rome at that period, and more than once I heard him sing so beautifully in St. John Lateran that the Pope himself was in tears. Serafico sat on this very terrace and told me I was not to let Leo Bebb come back here even if he wanted to. With the sweetest smile in the world, he told me that if I did, he would personally notify the Internal Revenue people and the Borough Police to come get him. He told me he'd seen to it he couldn't go back to you in Sutton either. It seems he was the one who wrote that anonymous letter to the insurance company about the fire there to make sure that sanctuary too would be unavailable. He said, 'We've got to keep him from getting sidetracked this time, Mrs. Conover,' and then he went drifting off across the lawn again like a cloud of steam. What I wouldn't have given to have heard him do just a bar or two of the *Miserere*. They say that once or twice even the statue of the Virgin was seen to wipe her eyes."

Here's to Jesus . . . Here's to you . . . trailing circles through the blue sky as Gertrude Conover watched from Gouverneur Road. The police waiting at the airport. The P-rade getting underway again. Then a spasmodic hiccoughing from deep in the vitals of that antiquated machine—a belch of tobacco-colored smoke from the exhaust, a long expectoration of flame. It fought for altitude, stalling and rattling itself to pieces, and set out on a mad, zigzag course roughly north. Like the Keystone Cops when the steering wheel comes off in their hands, I picture Mr. Golden and Bebb squeezed into the cockpit with what's left of the balloons, and the controls gone haywire—Ptah-Sitti the priest and Serafico Veluzzi. I picture them with their arms wrapped around each other, their Red Baron goggles clacking together as the green world wheels and turns upside down. I picture those two old cons locked in fiery embrace as the world hurtles up through the blue air to embrace them.

What I want to picture next is this. They bale out. Their chutes pop open, and swinging side by side in their harnesses they float slowly down through the sky like toys. They hit the ground together in a tangle of ballooning silk and scramble to their feet. I see them then from up where the abandoned plane is burning to death, two small, round figures, Tweedledee and Tweedledum, tearing off across the acres of potato land. They are already half way to the horizon when the plane hits.

There was no evidence that any such thing took place. Nobody saw them come floating down, and no chutes were discovered on the ground afterwards. There were several witnesses to the crash, and all of them agreed that while the plane was still high in the air, it was gloved in flame and fanned to fury by the long, fast fall. The only evidence for their escape was the negative evidence that there wasn't the slightest trace of anything that could be identified as either Bebb or his friend in the wreckage afterwards: not so much as a button or a tooth let alone a charred porkpie hat thrown clear or a partly melted lapel button with Holy going across and Love coming down through the single O. But that was not considered significant since there was hardly anything else in the wreckage that could be identified either. The fire was so intense and its destruction so complete that some said it could have been caused only by somebody's soaking the old crate with gasoline and then touching it off with a match. That is not incompatible with the escape theory, of course, and might even be used to support it—Mr. Golden touching it off precisely in order to account for the absence of any identifiable remains. But no one ever advanced such a theory officially, and even I advance it only in a tentative and wishful way.

In any case, it was because there was no body to bury or even any ashes to scatter with the assurance that they weren't just the ashes of leftover balloons that Brownie suggested he hold the service at the site where, if anywhere, the dust that had once been Leo Bebb lay. The farmer who owned the field gave his permission with the understanding that we keep it small. He didn't want his potatoes trampled any more than he had to, and the rest of us were just as glad, not wanting a horde of former Love Feasters or any more trouble with the authorities. So just the handful I have already listed came, and Brownie kept things short and, needless to say, sweet. Dear Brownie. He must have had his store teeth especially buffed up for the occasion. I have never seen his relentless smile so bright.

He started off with *I am the resurrection and the life*, then read two or three psalms including the twenty-third, and when he came to the part about preparing a table before me in the presence of mine enemies, I remember wondering with what homiletic ingenuity he would have explained away that always rather discordant and to me unedifying note. I suppose he would have said something to the effect that the table was a kind of smorgasbord to which the psalmist had every intention of summoning his enemies too as soon as he got around to it.

He read the part where Jesus says that in his father's house there are many mansions, and I could not help thinking of it as rather like the Red Path Ranch outside of Houston with all those flatroofed stucco buildings and the new Holy Love Herman Redpath had built for Bebb to look like the Alamo, not to mention John Turtle's Tom Thumb golf course, Bea Trionka's exercycle, the greenhouse, the swimming pool, and so on—something there for every taste. There was no eulogy, just a prayer which Brownie had written specially with lots in it about fighting the good fight and death where is thy victory and how when the heavenly city comes down at last, there will be no sorrow or pain in it because God himself will wipe away the tears from all our eyes.

I don't know for sure that anybody wept at the service. Out of the corner of my eye I could see that Charlie Blaine had his handkerchief out, but it may have just been his sinuses, and Nancy Oglethorpe's eyeliner ran some, but I had seen it run on other occasions when she was at her most cheerful. I noticed Tony's brother Chris standing there pale but dry-eyed in a beautifully cut gabardine suit and thought how with the exception of Gertrude Conover he could probably already buy and sell us all. Sharon was beside me, but the way her long hair fell all I could see was the rim of one ear and the bridge of her nose, so I couldn't tell about her. But she had already said goodbye, after all, in the basement of Bull's International Storage when Bebb had tried to explain to her about Miami Beach, when they had sat there at sunset and watched the spoonbills home.

Brownie came up to shake our hands afterwards. He said, "What the Lord taketh away with one hand he giveth back with another. I understand you're expecting a blessed event, dear," and when he had moved away to shake some other hands, Sharon said to me, "There's one thing I've got to put you straight on, Bopper. It's not on account of the baby I'm willing for us to give things another try, and I hope it's not on account of the baby you are either. I wasn't even going to tell you about it till Bip pulled the rug out. And there's something else about that baby I've got to put you straight on too, about who that baby is," and just as she was getting ready to tell me, I reached out and laid my hands over her mouth.

I said, "Let me put you straight on something instead. It doesn't matter who that baby is. Maybe it matters to God, but it doesn't matter to me. Maybe it ought to matter to me, but it doesn't. So don't you let it matter too much to you either."

She moved my hand away as far as her cheek and said, "It wasn't his fault. I made him stay. I didn't know but what I was pregnant anyhow so it didn't seem like that way it made much difference. It was New Year's, and I was feeling so low in my mind. He was too. He was having this nothing vacation with Charlie and Billie. I couldn't let him go home alone. So maybe it's your baby, and maybe it's not. I'm not even sure myself, if you want to know the truth."

I said, "Well anyway, at least it's all in the family," and what she said was, "That Bop"—not That *Bip* for once but That *Bop*, with the same mixture of admiration and disbelief, saying it about me as though there was somebody else there to say it about me to as she stood among the scorched star-points slowly shaking her head. That Bop.

Nobody was sure whose baby it was, and when it finally came and was a girl just as Bebb had predicted, we named her Lucille although what we ended up calling her was Lucy. My nephew and I looked enough alike in a general kind of way—dark-haired, dark-eyed, like organ grinders—so that even if she'd turned out to look like one of us, it could just as well have been a form of looking like the other. The way it worked out, she didn't look like either of us. She looked like Sharon—the same somber face, the same giveaway smile.

If Tony had any suspicion that she might have been his, he never let on that he did unless perhaps by the fact that soon after she was born, he gave up his job at Sutton High and moved in with Chris in New York as though that small geographical gesture would clear him in everybody's eyes including his own. The best thing that happened to him in New York was that he started seeing a good deal of his old classmate Laura Fleischman there, and when they were married about a year later and I stood up for him as best man with Sharon and the baby among others looking on, I thought how it would take God himself to sort out the tangle. But the point is that it was a tangle which somehow bound us life to life as though what we'd variously found in each other's arms was maybe not the home we'd been after but at least a place to get our bearings by.

On our way back from the wedding reception in the wall-to-wall living room of Mrs. Fleischman, Sharon put it this way. "It's like the man says, Antonio," she said. "The family that lays together stays together," and as she said it, I could almost hear that gusty, smothered laugh of Bebb's the night he rang us up in bed.

I have never dreamed about Bebb since the afternoon of Brownie's service, and if in one way I'm sorry about that because it would be nice to catch a glimpse of him again, in another way I'm just as glad because like all the others you run into that way, I suppose he would give me the brush-off, indicating that he had miles ahead of him still and no time to stop and palaver with old friends. But if I do not have dreams about him anymore, I still sometimes have daydreams.

When the Joking Cousin put his hands on either side of Gertrude Conover's waist and lifted her up as high as he could reach, she could see a good deal farther than the rest of us, of course, and in my daydreams it's her eyes I see through, which is the only reason I can think of for why John Turtle called her Window Lady. Beyond the blue silo and the tree-line at the edge of the field, beyond the horizon itself, up and over what King Lear called "the thick rotundity o' the world," I see where it is that Bebb and Mr. Golden escaped to after safely bailing out.

It is a tropical isle. There are palm trees and pink beaches on it and jungle pools where in the daytime brown-limbed natives swim and at night the beasts pad down on velvet feet to take their ease and drink. The natives have made Bebb their king. What else could they do with him? I see him naked as the day he was born only even more so if possible because this is a nakedness of his own risking. Night after night he presides at the great tribal feasts. The food is laid out in heaps—parrot-colored fruit to eat which is never to thirst, wine made of yams and citrus and sassafras root to drink which is never to hunger. Bebb himself is a great pile of fruit glinting the color of pearl by the light of the moon as he dispenses himself. Mr. Golden also is there like an oddly shaped swarm of fireflies, the keeper of the flame, and of their kingdom there shall be no end unless that day should come when it seems time to end it, and against that day there is always the flame that Mr. Golden keeps, another bridge to burn for the sake of another bridge to cross.

Which brings me finally to decathexis and myself. I will not pretend that something didn't end for me during that sad time when Sharon sent me packing or that the life that was left me wasn't a life I was ready enough to let go when that time came. Call it my youth that ended, a capacity for ignoring irony like Stephen Kulak, a taste for certain flavors of hope. Did I let it go because it had ceased to work for me, or did it cease to work for me because I had let it go? I don't know the answer to that, but I let it go anyway, and why not? A man has the right to let go the life he was born with and never asked for in the first place. Better to let it go and admit you no longer feel what you used to feel than to go on keeping up pretenses like old Metzger, thumping three times on the wall as if the death that approaches is the death of something that isn't already dead. In any case, I let it go, that first and original life that comes with the territory, and if once in a while I feel regret, I no longer feel remorse.

But the second life is another story. Out of the wreckage of things I picked up a kind of marriage again, a daughter who by one route or another at least has my blood in her veins, a capacity if not for rising above irony like the saints, at least for living it out with something like grace, with the suspicion if not the certainty that maybe the dark and hurtful shadows all things cast are only shadows. This second life is the one I chose for myself, and this time there will be no decathexis if I can help it. Because I have made this bed, I will sleep in it, and this time I will not let go until the Shadow itself wrests it from my grasp, or if there is any truth at all in some of the more rotund and apocalyptic utterances of Leo Bebb, not even then.

TREASURE HUNT

For Bob and Betty Clayton

1

GERTRUDE CONOVER turned on her cassette player, and over it came the unmistakable voice of Leo Bebb. It said, "The trouble with folks like Brownie is they hold their life in like a bakebean fart at a Baptist cookout and only let it slip out sideways a little at a time when they think there's nobody noticing. Now that's the last thing on earth the Almighty intended. He intended all the life a man's got inside him, he should live it out just as free and strong and natural as a bird. Now you take your—"

The speaking cut off into a noise like a vacuum cleaner, and Gertrude Conover pushed the re-wind button. Backwards at top speed, Bebb's voice became the falsetto dither of Disney mice.

Gertrude Conover said, "That was the last part, but it doesn't matter which part you start with because the thing's a regular patchwork quilt. He must have fiddled around with it off and on for weeks."

She said, "It makes you feel awfully blue to hear that voice again, doesn't it? I've been on two cruises since this was made, and I might as well have saved my money for all they helped cheer me up. I've never been one to rush from one life to the next, but there have been times I thought that without Leo Bebb to pep things up, this one couldn't end too soon to suit me."

I said, "He took a lot of the action with him when he checked out. There's no question about that."

Sharon said, "I've got a question. How come you never played this thing to us before? It's been a whole year."

Gertrude Conover said, "My dear, I was only told about it myself last week. I immediately asked you two down for the weekend to hear it."

It was a Saturday afternoon in June, and the three of us were out by Gertrude Conover's swimming pool in Princeton, New Jersey. Gertrude Conover was sitting in a canvas deckchair wearing one of those transparent green eyeshades that I associate with poker players in old gangster movies and holding the cassette player on her knees. Although she was in her early eighties, she looked closer to sixty-five or seventy. Sharon was lying flat on her back on the hot slates with her wet hair drying to her shoulders like seaweed, one long leg stretched out straight, and the other drawn up at the knee. I was lying on my stomach beside her. In the background you could hear the sound of the hand mower that Callaway was using to trim around under the lilacs—the hectic forward rattle and languid backward sigh that reminded me always of the long summer naps of childhood.

Sharon said, "Who was the one told you about it, Gert?" and Gertrude Conover said, "I'll play it for you first and answer that afterwards."

I suppose that under different circumstances it would have made me feel blue, as Gertrude Conover predicted, to hear Bebb's voice again when I'd thought for sure that he'd stopped talking permanently. The way things were, however, it wasn't the blueness that struck me so much as the oddness of the coming together of many different things at once like the voice of Bebb and the smell of the lilacs, the sound of Callaway's mower, Sharon stretched out beside me in all her glory with the top of her bathing suit untied so her shoulders would tan properly. And there were all the different kinds of things Bebb had recorded too, a kind of oral doodling he must have killed time with at odd moments during the last weeks he had lived at Gertrude Conover's before the combined hostility of the Princeton Police, the fire insurance people and the Internal Revenue Service had forced his sensational departure.

There were a number of dead spots on the tape, passages of Bebbsian silence that buzzed like bees through the silence of our listening to him all those months later. There were noises, some that weren't identifiable and some that were—rattling papers, creaking chairs, a radio or a TV muttering away in the background. You could hear Bebb clear his throat a few times, hum, make sigh sounds. Once there were a couple of loud blasts that I took to be honking, as if he had gone out for a drive one day and taken the little machine along with him for something to talk to. Most of the time I listened to it with my eyes closed, and as each section came along I found myself picturing him as he made it.

Plump and pale he sits on the edge of his bed in his shirtsleeves with his chin in his hands not noticing that outside there is a wet spring snow falling and a cardinal on the bird feeder.

It is early morning, but he is fully dressed in his gents' furnishings suit with all four points of the handkerchief showing from his breast pocket. He is staring at his Tweedledum reflection in the dresser mirror. There is no sign that his bed has been slept in.

His bald head glints in the moonlight as he stands looking out the dark window. In the rapid hush of a man at his prayers he is saying, "Robe to the cleaners. Check out the TV guarantee. Contact Fats. Read up on Battle of Princeton. See does Rexall's carry rhubarb and soda. Hemorrhoid salve. . . ."

I reach out to touch Sharon's bare foot with mine, but she does not touch me back. Through my one open eye I see that Gertrude Conover's eyeshade has turned the upper half of her face green. Some scraping sound Bebb made a year before startles a dragon fly off the diving board.

It skims the turquoise water and then up across the slope of lawn toward the broad terrace of Revonoc.

As for the tape itself, to me it was all fascinating—even the lists, the pauses, the unfinished scraps of things—because it was all Bebb, and Bebb speaking from another world, and Bebb speaking to himself, which meant that for all I knew he might at any moment lay some secret bare, some shadowy corner of those last days of his life when he recorded it. But objectively speaking, most of it was of no great significance, and I preserve here only a fraction of all there was: first, some notes he made for one of his Love Feast sermons at Alexander Hall presumably, then a couple of letters, and finally—just before the already quoted words about Brownie—a kind of testamentary passage which was to have the most far-reaching consequences for all three of us and others. I think not just of the whole crazy journey south in Gertrude Conover's Continental but all the ambiguous epiphanies, the apocalyptic confrontations, the scandalous revelations. *Had we but known*, as the old come-on goes, but of course we didn't know. We just listened to the voice of Bebb rattling on out of the past as though it was in no sense a matter of life and death at all.

The high points were as follows.

SERMON NOTES   Bebb says, "The kingdom of heaven, it's like unto treasure hid in a field the which when a man hath found it, he hideth it and for joy thereof"—Bebb comes down so hard on *joy* it makes the machine rattle—"he goeth and selleth all he hath or ever hopes to hath and buyeth that field. Well, it's like you're poking around a junk shop, and inside a old humpback trunk with the lid half stove in you come across a pack of letters somebody's great granddad tied up with a string from a chum back home name of Abe Lincoln that's worth a clear five thousand bucks each if they're worth a dime. Now you tell me what a man would give to lay his hands on that trunk. Why he'd give his bottom dollar. He'd give his right arm for a treasure like that, and for the kingdom of heaven —Listen," Bebb says, "he'd give ten years, twenty years, off his life. You know why? Why because the kingdom of heaven, that's what it is. It's life. Not the kind of half-baked, moth-eaten life we most of us live most of the time but the real honest-to-God thing. Life with a capital L. It's the treasure a man spends all his born days looking for, no matter if he knows it or not. The kingdom of heaven, it's the treasure that up till a man finds it, every other treasure that comes his way doesn't amount to spit."

Bebb says, "The kingdom comes by looking for it. The kingdom comes sometimes by not looking for it too hard. There's times the kingdom comes by it looking for you."

Then one of the buzzing silences, and at the end of it, breathily, as if he's holding the microphone to his lips, "Maybe it don't come at all. Period."

LETTERS   The first one is to the IRS agent named Connor, who initiated proceedings against Bebb for filling out his form 1040 in the name of Jesus instead of his own name, putting down things like *the wages of sin is death* where it asked for wages and *I am the first and the last, saith the Lord,* where it asked for last name.

Bebb says, "Friend Connor, I call you friend because like the Apostle Paul said, 'Let not the sun go down upon your wrath,' Ephesians four, and the sun's going down here in Princeton, New Jersey, in more ways than one. You and that woman you got working for you have used me hard from the word go. You kept me cooling my heels in that waiting room till I missed my dinner, and when you finally let me in, you uttered all kinds of evil against me falsely. I know you can't help it hardly. You are a undersize man trying to add cubits to your stature being spiteful and mean, and that woman she is a plain woman trying to make up for it painting a pair of lips on her wouldn't fool a blind man. Connor, I'm no lily either, but I'm not a cheat. I filed like I did because every nickel of income I ever took in, I took it in for Jesus, and every nickel of out-go I ever laid out, I laid that out for Jesus too. Connor, life's too short to stay enemies. Your friend in Jesus, Leo Bebb."

The second letter is to a member of the Princeton history department who was instrumental in getting the university authorities to stop letting him stage his Love Feasts in Alexander Hall.

Bebb says, "Roebuck, that cripple boy you got you say he can't take a leak without somebody comes and pulls his pecker out for him, don't you let this spite you got for the Almighty on account of that stop you asking him to make that boy whole whether you believe the Almighty's up there to hear you asking him or not. Ask him anyway. Roebuck, all the believing a man's got to do is believe it's worth the chance. Say it's only a one in a million shot there is a Almighty, what you got to lose talking to him, Roebuck? Yours truly, Leo Bebb."

I remember wondering as I lay there with the sun hot on my back if Bebb had ever gotten around to mailing the letters. I never got a letter from him myself; in fact as far as I know, I never even saw his handwriting. I never saw him asleep either, or cry. I never saw him naked. We must have shaken hands dozens of times over the years, but I have no recollection of what his handshake felt like. Once he hugged me, and I recollect that. It was when he was hiding out in the basement of a storage warehouse in lower Manhattan, and though I didn't know it then, it was the last time I was ever to see him. Bebb knew it. He had on a fancy red dressing gown he'd dug up somewhere, and throwing his arms around my shoulders, he gave me a squeeze that almost knocked my breath out.

In any case, it was at some point during the tape of the letter to Roebuck that something happened to make Gertrude Conover turn off the machine.

"Jesus," Sharon said, "what's bugging Callaway?" and I looked up to see him come running out from behind the lilacs with his head tipped back as far as it would go and a white handkerchief pressed to his black face. Sharon had sat up in such a hurry that she forgot she had undone the straps of her bathing suit top, and I remember how startled and white her breasts looked, like another pair of eyes. Callaway was in too much of a hurry to notice them as he came tearing past, and when Sharon herself noticed, she made no big production of it, just reached up behind her neck and tied things back in place again.

"He hasn't had one of his nosebleeds for ages," Gertrude Conover said. "Sometimes all it takes is the mention of Leo Bebb's name although Callaway himself is no more aware of the connection than he is aware that in an earlier life he was the Pharaoh. Who would think to look at him now that there was a time when he had only to snap his fingers and both the Lower and Upper Kingdoms would dance attendance?"

"He's come a long way since then," Sharon said.

Gertrude Conover said, "My dear, we all of us have."

When the tape started to play again, I hoped that maybe Bebb would say something that might shed light on the climactic events of the preceding spring. The march on Nassau Hall to protest his expulsion from the Princeton Campus and the historic seizure and siege of Alexander Hall that followed it; the balloon-scattering flight in a stolen plane over the heads of the Reunion P-rade as it moved down Nassau Street; the fiery crash in the potato field—I hoped especially that Bebb might give some clue as to how much of it all he had planned out carefully in advance and how much was just happenstance. Failing that, I hoped he might reminisce about some of the other events in his life that I had always wanted to know more about. I would like to have heard him expand on how he and Lucille had come to adopt Sharon after their own baby's death or on the five years he had spent in the pen, not to mention the event that had landed him there which I had only the most fragmentary picture of: the sunlit stucco wall out behind a Miami Beach seafood restaurant; some barefoot kids playing niggerbaby with a tennis ball; Bebb with something pale and shapeless nestled in his hand.

Bebb had never told me much about himself except a glimpse here and there, and he had never encouraged me to tell him much about myself either though God knows there were times I would have given my right arm to. The winter that Sharon and I had split up for a while, for instance; if he'd given me the faintest sign, I'd have started unloading things on him then that I'd probably be unloading on him still if he were still around to unload them on, but he never gave me the chance. Bebb was always in a hurry. You felt he couldn't let anything sidetrack him, not even the sad things that were happening that winter to his daughter Sharon, who was the apple of his eye, the one he loved more than all the rest of us put together.

It was to Sharon that the most important part of the tape was addressed and also to me, but this time it wasn't a letter. Bebb said, "Sharon, honey, this is your old Bip talking. Antonio, I'm talking to you too. I'm talking to the both of you sitting there side by side again like the Almighty intended. Little children, let us love one another because he that loveth not abideth in death. Amen. That's the whole of Scripture in a nutshell. Gertrude Conover, you're welcome to listen in too. There's some ways you're the best friend I ever had, and if things had turned out differently, well who knows." It was an uncanny business, and I could feel Sharon's muscles tightening where our bare arms touched.

Bebb said, "All my life I wanted to do something big for Jesus only nothing I ever did amounted to scratch. Could be the best thing I ever did for him was back when I was on the road selling Bibles where folks could read up on him for theirselves, but that wasn't big enough to suit me. I wanted to be up there in the head office—gospel-preaching, healing, revivals, the whole shebang. Talk about your missions, I set up Gospel Faith College and put in paid ads all over creation. 'Put yourself on God's payroll,' they said. 'Go to work for Jesus now.' A racket? The way they—"

Bebb broke in upon himself. He said, "Listen, was it a racket Jesus saying lay down your fishpole? Leave go your buck-saw, your manure fork, you name it, and follow me. Two-bit whores, crooks, sodomites—Jesus didn't ask for any credentials, and I didn't either. I ordained anybody answered that ad and sent in his love offering. Gospel Faith's still in business, but it's small potatoes. Everything I ever did, it was small potatoes. I'm a small potato my own self, and that's the truth of it. A man does what he can."

I could see Callaway up by the far end of the terrace. His face was tilted to the sky like a drought victim watching for rain, and he was holding his nostrils pinched tight together with one hand. Sharon was sitting with her knees clasped to her chest and staring somberly down at the ground.

Bebb said, "The grass withereth, the flower fadeth. There's no man lives forever. Whether he's done big things in his life or just small, pitiful things, the time comes like a thief in the night when the show's over. A man thinks about after he's gone. He thinks about the things he never got around to doing and he wonders will there be anybody to pick up where he left off."

A tinkling sound stirred faintly in the background of the recording, and I pictured Bebb sitting there with his back to the TV which was turned on low across the room. It was playing a little song about false teeth adhesive or a gentle but effective laxative.

He said, "All the money I've got after bills and taxes if that sawed-off little penpusher in Trenton, New Jersey, leaves me with two red cents to rub together, all that, it's to come straight to you two and your kids, no strings attached, and that's that. I thought some about passing it on to Holy Love, but Herman Redpath, he pumped enough into Holy Love to keep it afloat till kingdom come, and Open Heart, well it burned down, and Love Feast, let's face it, those love feasts they're not going to last any longer than me if that long. So all the money, that's yours free and clear. But there's something else.

"There's a piece of land outside of Spartanburg, South Carolina, that belongs to me. It's down there in a place name of Poinsett that's where I was born and raised, and there's a house on it that's mine too. I don't suppose anybody's lived there going on twenty-five, thirty years, but far as I know it's still standing. It's the house I first saw the light of day in. Up till the day I got married and moved out, it was home. Now what I want to say to you is this."

As Bebb got ready to say it, something must have gone wrong with his machine because the speed was suddenly cut way down, and his voice started coming out twice as deep and half as fast so that he sounded drugged or like a man trying to talk in the midst of a paralyzing yawn.

Dragging each word out to inordinate length, he said, "Antonio, I'm leaving that place to Sharon and you. The land and the old homestead. Both. I'm not laying anything on you what to do with it. You can sell it and use the cash. You can give it away. You can turn it into something. Any whichway. But you mind this.

"An . . . to . . . ni . . . o . . ," Bebb said, and the way my name came inching out, it was as though I was hearing the full, painful truth of it for the first time. "I want you to do something nice with that old place. And I want you to do it for Jesus."

Those fateful words.

Then the part again about Brownie's life-style being like a repressed fart. The vacuum cleaner noise cut it off in mid-sentence, and Sharon said, "Why Bopper, you're crying."

I thought she was crazy. I have never cried easily, and I wasn't crying then. I wasn't even feeling as if I might cry given half a chance. It was queer and sad in a way to hear Bebb's voice again, but it was nothing that made me feel like breaking down. I told her that.

Gertrude Conover said, "Then what's all that running down your cheeks like rain?" and she was right. I put my hands to my face, and it was wet.

She said, "It's Leo Bebb. He has apparently affected your eyes much the way he has affected poor Callaway's nose."

"Like an allergy," I said, and even as I said it, I could feel a new hot trickle start down. Then Gertrude Conover. It was an eery thing to see. First her eyes seemed to be swelling in size, getting goiterish and glittery in the green light of her visor, and then there we were, the two of us, looking on the outside as though our hearts were breaking whereas on the inside we were both of us going on with business as usual.

Gertrude Conover dropped the cassette player back into her knitting bag and took out a Kleenex to dab at her face. She said, "The karmic energy of that man is something to write home about. Just the sound of his voice has an effect not unlike that of peeling a Bermuda onion."

"Not on me," Sharon said, and Gertrude Conover said, "That's what you think."

Even as Sharon had spoken, it had started happening to her too; then right in the midst of it that sudden shattering, shattered smile of hers. "You've got to hand it to old Bip," she said.

That evening Gertrude Conover drove us for dinner to a place across the river in Pennsylvania not far from New Hope, and as her Continental rolled along through the green countryside, I remember thinking about the name New Hope and all the other lovely old names we have in this country and what a pity it is we've long since stopped hearing what they meant to the people who christened their towns with them—not just hope but *new* hope. Providence. Concord. A new *haven* safe from the high seas and punishing winds of the world. Anyway, the restaurant where she took us turned out to be in the branches of an enormous tree. There were platforms fanning out at different levels among the leaves, and tables on them with checkered tablecloths, and candles burning like fireflies. It was up there somewhere, over our *coq au vin* and beaujolais that Sharon said, "Gertrude Conover, you never did get round to telling us who it was put you on to where Bip's tape was."

Gertrude Conover looked at her in that encouraging hopeful way she always had as though she expected you to go on and say something even better than what you'd just finished saying, but when Sharon didn't say anything more, she finally just answered the question. She said, "There's no point beating about the bush. The one who told me about Leo Bebb's tape was Leo Bebb himself."

Sharon leaned forward. She said, "You mean his ghost?"

Gertrude Conover said, "It was not a ghost."

I have never seen Sharon's face so still. It was still like a top when it's spinning so fast you can't believe it's spinning. She said, "He didn't die in the crash then?"

It was what I'd always wanted to believe, of course. That he'd bailed out somewhere or been thrown clear. That he'd found his way to some southsea paradise where the natives had crowned him with parrot feathers and made him their god or their king. The plane had burned up so completely that no trace of him was ever found, not so much as a gold filling or the sole of a shoe, so it was possible after all. I hung on Gertrude Conover's next words.

She said, "He never went into all that. He was obviously more interested in the future than the past, and as usual he seemed a little pressed for time."

It was a mild evening, and you could see the moon through the branches. There were several broad, shallow stairways leading down to the ground, and a waiter was sitting at the foot of one of them with his head in his hands. A bunch of eleventh grade English papers were waiting back home to be corrected—the Sutton High commencement was only a few days away—and there I was, up in a tree listening to an octagenarian theosophist with blue hair who might be telling the truth, or making it all up as she went along, or suffering from hardening of the arteries.

Gertrude Conover said, "It was after I got back from the Budapest concert at McCarter last week. They'd done the first Razoumovsky, which is my favorite. Dee dee *dum*, dee *dum*, dee *dee*. Well, it takes the wrinkles out, that's all. I was sitting out on the terrace letting the music wash back over me under the stars with a cup of hot Ovaltine and some graham crackers when suddenly I heard this voice beside me saying, 'Long time no see, Gertrude Conover,' and of course I knew in a second who it was. I would recognize that voice anywhere. I said, 'Leo, you're a sight for sore eyes,' and he said, 'I could use one of those graham crackers, Gertrude Conover, if you've got one to spare.' "

I said, "Do you mean he was alive like you and Sharon and me, the way the three of us in this tree are alive right this minute?"

She said, "Oh I would say a good deal more alive than that. Under certain circumstances, the cosmic batteries can recharge very rapidly."

I said, "How did he look?" and she said, "Not a bit fuzzy around the edges, if that's what you mean. Round. Clean. Much the way he's always looked. I had several grahams left, and he ate them all."

"What did you talk about?" Sharon said, and she looked at me as she said it and narrowed her eyes at me, just the merest flicker with nothing else in her face moving.

Gertrude Conover said, "He did most of the talking, and it didn't last long. He told me the tape was under the Hudson Bays in his old closet, and it was. He said he knew you didn't even know the South Carolina place existed because he never got around to listing it separately in his will, and he's got his heart set on your doing something about it, you especially, Antonio. He said he should have gone down there himself years ago, but he never got around to it. If you ask me, the trip would have stirred up a lot of old memories he'd as soon have let be. The childhoods of Leo Bebb have almost never been happy ones, and I could tell he was relieved as soon as the subject changed. We parted soon afterwards."

I said, "I'm trying to picture it, Gertrude. I'm trying to see him walk away across the lawn or get into a car and drive off."

She said, "Well I'm afraid I can't help you with that because I was the one who left first. What with the Razoumovsky and the Ovaltine and the surprise of seeing him, I suddenly felt so exhausted I said good night and went straight up to bed. He understood perfectly. Besides, he'd done what he came for."

"Did you shake hands goodbye?" Sharon said. "Did you ever the whole time he was there touch him with your own two hands, Gertrude Conover?"

A little gust of air rustled the leaves and bent the flame of our candle sideways. Gertrude Conover took a sip of her beaujolais and then said, "My dear, a great many lives have come and gone since the last time I touched Leo Bebb with my own two hands."

I said, "What was the last thing he said before you left?"

She said, "The last thing he said before I left was 'See you in the funny papers.' Within ten minutes of that I was in dreamland."

2

BEBB HAD SAID, "Antonio, I want you to do something nice with that old place. And I want you to do it for Jesus." The question was what was I supposed to do with it? When was I supposed to start? How could I be sure Jesus would approve?

Beyond that, there were cloudier questions. Was Gertrude Conover reporting an actual encounter with Bebb in the flesh? There were the graham crackers after all. Or was it Bebb's ghost unable to rest in peace until the Poinsett matter was settled to his satisfaction? She never saw him arrive or depart; as nearly as I could tell, she hadn't actually *seen* him very well at all. Or was she just wandering in her mind? Sharon said, "Antonio, she can't hardly even get the seams of her hose straight any more. Sometimes when you try and talk with her, it's like she's a million miles away."

Yet the last time we saw her before setting off for Sutton, she gave no such impression. She spread a road atlas out on the library table and showed us the route she had marked in with red crayon. She said, "We could take the Chesapeake Bay Bridge and go by way of Washington. We could spend the night there and see the sights. Then we could proceed at a leisurely pace through the Virginia countryside. The horses. The old houses. Have you ever visited Monticello? Well, we could take our time and see anything we felt like. Callaway would enjoy driving us. He is a southerner born and bred." Gertrude Conover was a world traveler as well as a theosophist. Together she and Bebb had climbed the Acropolis by moonlight, had dangled head down like bats to kiss the Blarney Stone.

She said, "As for the Jesus part, why couldn't you get Brownie to join forces with us? He might have some good ideas about the sort of thing Jesus would approve of."

Later that day on the way back to Connecticut, Sharon said, "I don't know, Bopper. The whole thing seems like a wild goose chase to me. Bip said himself nobody's lived there going on twenty-five years. You ask me, all that's left is just a hole full of old corncobs where the outhouse was. I vote we sell out like he said and give the money to UNICEF. Why wouldn't that suit Jesus just fine?"

I got my papers corrected finally. I sat through Commencement watching the girls in their long dresses and high heels teeter up for their diplomas, the boys in their bell-bottoms and Elizabethan tresses. Our six year old son Bill gave a terrible cold to his baby sister Lucy, who treated us all to a week of sleepless nights during which I spent so much time helping walk her back to sleep that all day long for a while I tended to break into the same bouncing stride. I spent the first day of vacation working on my six foot mobile. One of the legs of the tripod it hung from had split, and I had to replace some strips of lathing. I hated to see it drop slowly to pieces before my eyes.

Life went on much as usual, in other words, but off and on I kept thinking about Bebb and the mission he'd charged me with. I dreamed about him once, or at least he made a brief appearance at the end of a dream about something else. It was raining, and I was standing out in some kind of roughly circular field trying to dig a hole, but every time I took another shovelful, the rain and mud started filling it back up again until my arms got so tired I could hardly make them move. Then suddenly, way off in the distance, I saw Bebb. He was strolling along in his tight black raincoat. I called out to him, and I could tell he'd heard me because he stopped and looked in my direction, but when I called out to him again to come give me a hand with the digging, he started walking away. I tried to follow him, but by that time I was up to my knees in the hole I'd been working at. Then I noticed that Sharon was there beside me in her yellow plastic rainhat. She said, "It's just like I told you, Antonio. You're just digging your own grave." It came out like the punchline of an old family joke. Every word of it was rich with comic associations, including the two occurrences of the word 'just,' and I laughed so hard that laughter became the bridge I got out of the dream on. When I woke up there were tears of it in my eyes.

That same week I also saw a home movie that had Bebb in it. It was a reel I'd taken the summer he took Sharon and me to Europe with him, and I ran it off one of the nights when I was taking my turn with the baby. The projector was still set up from the last time I'd used it, and sitting with the baby over my shoulder like a hot water bottle, I started the past flickering away through the 3AM dark.

There was my nephew Tony in chewed-off blue jean shorts and no shirt working out with his weights in the back yard. There was my son Bill strapped onto a merry-go-round horse at Playland, that small, bewildered face spinning around and around through the gilded shadows. Sharon was sitting on the green grass in her black leotards. With both her arms stretched out sideways like wings, she leaned forward farther and farther until finally her forehead touched one knee.

Then Bebb.

He is standing at the door of Open Heart. Above his head the life-size glass cross is lit up inside. He is wearing his maroon preaching robe and shaking hands with the congregation as they come filing out. I recognize the man with the white cane who said he was a cousin of Harry Truman's and the woman with red hair who sometimes brought a pet gerbil in a cage to the services. There are also some black women in white gloves and Sunday hats. Bebb suddenly notices me taking his picture and starts to wave. As he does so, he unknowingly knocks one of the black ladies' hats crooked. I zoom in on him at this point, and the nearer he comes, the wider my Optronic Eye opens until his face on the screen becomes not only much bigger than life but about ten times brighter. At the farthest reach of the zoom, the features slip out of focus and the face turns into an incandescent blur that nearly fills the screen. It is so bright that the baby stirs on my shoulder. Then a grid-shape snaps across it, branding it like a waffle iron. The reel ends.

Sharon is behind me in a pair of my pajamas and reaches down to lift the warm baby away. She says, "You're fretting yourself sick over this, Bopper. Do like Gertrude Conover says and go see Brownie, hear. That way you can settle what to do once and for all."

A dark snake-like thing starts uncoiling down in one corner of the screen as the projector bulb scorches a hole in the film, and I switch it off just in time to keep Bebb's face from going up in flames.

* * *

I couldn't have picked a worse time for my visit to Brownie although when I suggested it over the phone, he said I couldn't have picked a better. It was to be the weekend of Rose Trionka's wedding to Johnson Badger's problem nephew Buck, and all the way from Texas I could hear the emotion in Brownie's voice as he told me that it promised a new era of peace and harmony for the Indians of the Red Path Ranch. Brownie told me that for years there had been bad blood between the Trionkas and the Badgers and that was what made the union of Rose and Buck so providential. He said, "It is providential that you will be there to give them your blessing too. It is the Montagues and the Capulets all over

again, dear." As water to a fish, so sweetness and light were to Brownie
—sweetness like his after-shave, light like the light that flashed from his
glasses with their tortoise shell brows.

He met me at the Houston airport in a Hawaiian sport shirt, sandals
and bobby socks, and on the drive back to the ranch I told him about
how we had discovered the existence of Bebb's property in South Carolina
and how I hoped maybe he could give us some tips on the kind of thing
Jesus might enjoy having us do with it. I told him how Gertrude Conover
had suggested maybe some of us could drive down and look the place over.
I was on the point of telling him also about Gertrude Conover's report
that she had actually *seen* Bebb the night she had come back from
hearing the first Razoumovsky with her wrinkles taken out, but I thought
better of it. Brownie listened sympathetically enough, taking his hand off
the wheel from time to time and pressing my arm to show me that he
was with me all the way, but I had the feeling not only that his mind
was on Rose Trionka's wedding but that he was making some sort of
effort to keep it there. I had the feeling that the things I was telling him
were somehow a threat to his peace, so I stopped short of telling him
that maybe Bebb was still alive and let him turn the conversation back
to the wedding instead. I remember the royal blue sport shirt he was
wearing with a tangerine sunset printed on it and dark sweat stains
spreading out from under his arms like the approach of night.

We entered the Red Path Ranch through the two totem poles on
either side of the main gate and stopped first at the greenhouse to pick up
a basket of white gladiolas because Brownie was afraid there mightn't be
enough at Holy Love. Then on past the concrete service buildings, past
John Turtle's Tom Thumb golf course, and on to the sauna bath where
there were two or three naked Indians asleep on deck chairs out front.
Brownie said, "They're like children, dear. They don't mean any harm
by it." We drove straight on through the stucco and tiled-roof residential
section without stopping, but I recognized the house where Bebb had
lived. I recognized the house that had once been Herman Redpath's
with its two-story living room to give height for the organ pipes. A skinny
boy with a flower between his teeth was driving an electric golf cart toward
Herman Redpath's swimming pool and waved at Brownie as we drove by.
Brownie said, "That's Noah Seahorn's boy, Elk. He's a rainmaker."

I said, "Have you ever seen him make rain?"

Brownie pulled slowly into the circular drive that led to Holy Love
and said, "There's lots of things down here I've learned to close my eyes
to."

Four or five Cadillacs were pulled up out front and a red carpet had
been rolled down as far as the bottom of the stone steps where a couple
of Indians in shorts and T-shirts were sweeping the walk before rolling it
the rest of the way. There were men on ladders stringing crepe paper
streamers over the entrance and down from the tops of the taller cedars
like maypoles. In one of the Cadillacs some hard rock was turned up high,

and by his pussycat moustache I recognized Harry Hocktaw as the one who was stretched out on the hood with his bare feet flat against the windshield, keeping time with a gourd full of dried seeds. Chock chuck chuck chick-chick, chock chuck, chock.

Brownie had barely gotten out of the car when Rose Trionka's mother Bea swept down on him with her hair up in rollers and a yellow Mother Hubbard that fell from her fat shoulders like sunshine down the Capitol dome. She said, "Violet's puked on the altar. Lily says she stuck her finger down her throat for spite. Put it down, you dumb fart!" Her great breasts tossing like a shipwreck, she elbowed her way to a tub of azaleas that was moving along on brown legs.

Brownie said, "Violet's the oldest Trionka sister and the only one not yet married, but she would never have done a thing like that for spite." His smile hung at half mast as he paused to let two men carrying a harp pass between us. He said, "Sometimes just heartbreak is enough to make us puke, dear. I better go see."

I followed him into the church but hung around under the balcony while he squeezed down the center aisle past the men vacuum cleaning. The chancel was crowded with flowers—drifts of them bordering the shallow steps and ropes of them twined around the columns of the pulpit. With a wreath of white chrysanthemums around its neck, the big altar cross looked as if it had just come in first at Hialeah. The fragrance was overpowering, but it did not quite drown out Violet.

As I stood there waiting for Brownie, someone came up behind me and with a surgeon's deftness grabbed the top of my underpants and gave them a sharp, upward tug. It was John Turtle, his black hair plastered down flat, his teeth framed in gold like cufflinks. I said, "You haven't lost your touch, Joking Cousin."

"Hey there, cousin," he said. "How the hell you been anyhow?"

"Win a few, lose a few," I said. I was still trying to dislodge my underpants. "What you been doing with yourself?"

"Same old thing," John Turtle said. He gestured vigorously with his right hand.

I said, "Big wedding today."

"Big Rose," he said. "Big tits." He reached out and put both his hands on my shoulders. He cocked his head to one side and gave me a glassy, clinical stare. "Nice seeing you, man," he said. "Last time was old Leo's funeral."

"You danced," I said. Crouching and barefoot on the potato field, he'd padded around and around like a dog circling in for a crap. I had never seen John Turtle perform at a wedding before.

I said, "I hope you're going to behave yourself today, Joking Cousin." With his hands on my shoulders, his face was so close that it was hard to see it whole, just separate parts of it—a bony, indented cheek, a narrowed eye.

He said in falsetto, "I hope you're going to behave yourself today, Joking Cousin." He drew me a little closer to him, and even in competition with the flowers and poor Violet's puke, his smell was something to be conjured with. Hair oil, sweat, horse were only the outer edges of it. Then he changed the position of his hands on my shoulders.

He switched the hand that had been on my right shoulder to my left and the hand that had been on my left shoulder to my right so that his bare arms made an X of flesh between us. He didn't say anything. He just let the smell sink in and the X of his crossed arms and the feeling of my underpants, which were not yet entirely unwedged. One of his gold-framed teeth glistened. Whatever the Joking Cousin's joke was, I got the idea that it was very old and famous and deadly serious. Over his shoulder I could see Brownie beckoning me to join him down front.

Everybody came to the wedding, of course. Badgers and Trionkas, Hocktaws and Seahorns, Shoptalls, Redpaths, Turtles and Poles—there wasn't a pew with as much as two inches to spare. Undertaker chairs were set up in the side aisles, and even the balcony was overflowing. While people were getting seated, music was produced by Lizard Shoptall at the organ and Louemma Pole riding the harp sidesaddle—*Indian Love Call, Rose Marie, The Anniversary Waltz.* The stained glass windows blazed in the afternoon sun. Old friends hailed each other. Escaped from their families, small children toddled up and down the aisle. Babies drowsed or wailed at their mothers' breasts. Maudie Redpath, going on one hundred and twelve, was wheeled to her place in a chair with red, white and blue streamers laced through the spokes. Bea Trionka in tangerine satin was led down the aisle by John Turtle and sank into the front pew on the Trionka side like the setting sun.

The bridal procession entered to *Lohengrin.* The bride's two sisters came first, Lily about eight months gone and Violet still pale and unsteady with her circlet of gardenias slightly askew on her slippery black curls. They carried dozens of long-stemmed roses the color of frozen custard, with English ivy trailing as far as their knees, and the aisle was just wide enough to accommodate the two of them abreast. Rose herself followed on the arm of an elderly man who at first glance could have been Herman Redpath risen from the dead but was identified for me as his cousin Seahorn Redpath from Laguna Beach. He didn't stand much taller than Rose's armpit and like his late cousin had skin drawn so tight that he couldn't get his lips to close properly over his teeth. As he hesitation-stepped forward, the overhead lights swam across his shiny brown scalp like goldfish. And beside him Rose, but Rose so heavily veiled in virginal white on the arm of her tiny escort that it wasn't until later that I saw her plain. Surrounded by braves at the altar steps, Buck Badger awaited her up to his crotch in flowers.

Brownie prefaced the ceremony with a short homily based on the text "It is better to marry than to burn." Robed in white with a robin's egg blue stole around his neck that had Holy embroidered in silver down one side of it and Love embroidered in gold down the other, he explained that the text was almost universally misunderstood as a slur on matrimony. On the contrary, he said, diligent study revealed that *burning* did not refer to unsatisfied lust as commonly supposed but had to do with the practice of making burnt offerings. According to Brownie, what the Apostle Paul was saying was that although to make burnt offerings got you high marks in heaven, for a young couple like Rose and Buck to offer themselves to each other in holy matrimony got higher marks still. Brownie said, "Taking it back to the original tongue, what this scripture really means is not just it is better to marry than to burn but it is *even* better."

Brownie gazed down at the wedding party as he finished, but his glasses were so steamed up that it is doubtful he could see them.

He then proceeded to conduct things in the regulation manner. Lily took Rose's bouquet for her and placed it beside her own on the great protrusion of her lavender chiffon belly. John Turtle gave the bride away with a face so straight it was crooked. Bea Trionka muffled her emotion in a corsage the size of a cabbage, and as she thrashed around I could see where in her distraction she had forgotten to take out one of the rollers. Buck Badger got the ring on his bride's finger without fumbling it, and then, as flash bulbs went off all through the congregation, he raised her veil like the flap of a tepee and kissed her.

What happened next happened so quickly that I could not see how it was done, but all of a sudden the Joking Cousin scrambled up the steps from one side and Buck Badger closed in from the other side, and the next moment there she was, all three hundred pounds of her, floating in the air above us. I can still see her enthroned there, piled high in the air like whipped cream, like pastry. I see still that round, flat face with the black hair looped down over one eye, that dim, crazy little smile. The whole front of the church was ablaze with her. Ushers and bridesmaids staggered backwards shielding their eyes. Stained glass windows shook in their frames. It was the sheer featherbed whiteness of her that was so dazzling, all those tumbled flounces and petals of bosomy white that were Rose.

For a moment the whole church held its breath. Then Lizard Shoptall at the organ and Louemma Pole at the harp struck up *Que Sera, Sera,* and waving and smiling and squealing Rose Trionka Badger came down out of the chancel adorned for her husband like the heavenly city itself and went floating up the aisle a good six feet off the ground. I suppose there must have been people carrying her, but I swear I can't remember any. As far as I could tell she floated up through that canyon of Indians as much under her own power as white clouds in a summer sky.

* * *

That evening Brownie said, "I wish I could believe that somehow Mr. Bebb was looking down from the hereafter and saw it all," and I said, "I thought you could believe two or three things like that before you even had breakfast, Brownie." As soon as I said it, I wished I hadn't.

I remember a Halloween pumpkin we kept on the mantle too long one year, and how after a while the face started to go lopsided and the lid caved in and pumpkin juice started rolling down the cheeks. And so with Brownie. The smile stayed relentlessly in place, but all around it everything else started falling to pieces. He said, "I wouldn't want it to get around, dear, but the truth of it is I'm afraid I've lost my faith."

We were sitting out on his porch in our shirtsleeves. It was a breathless, heavy dusk, and the ice in our iced tea had all melted so that it was tepid and watery and tasted like snuff. From off in the distance the electric carillon of Holy Love sent *Now the Day Is Over* drifting toward us.

Brownie said, "I never had a child of my own, but it always seemed as though maybe having faith wasn't all that different a thing. It seemed as though faith was like somebody to take care of you when you got old. A shoulder to lean on when the shadows lengthened and your work was done. A hand to hold. Now it's like I had a child once but it's died. There are times I don't know as how I can keep on going."

I said, "How did it happen, Brownie?"

He mopped around under his chin and back of his neck with his paper napkin, then leaned back in his rocker and I wondered if it was the same rocker Lucille had died in. He said, "It came on gradual, like cancer. First a little pain here, a little dark spot there. I made out like it wasn't happening. Maybe if it had been caught in time, something could have been done about it. I don't know."

"Maybe something can still be done about it," I said, but Brownie wasn't listening.

He said, "Of course when Mr. Bebb passed on, that was part of it. He raised me from the dead in Knoxville, Tennessee, dear. That was many years ago and you know the story. He was forever telling me he should have saved himself the trouble. He said I never really lived the life he'd gotten back for me, just shoved . . . just shoved it up my you-know-what and sat on it. He said hurtful things like that for my own good. He was my Rock of Gibralter, and when he went, it seemed like he took my faith with him."

It was like driving past an accident. I tried not to look at Brownie as he spoke, but most of the time I couldn't help myself.

He said, "Another thing. I have carnal desires like everybody else, dear. Maybe you wouldn't believe it to look at me, but I've had many opportunities for backsliding in that direction here on the ranch. These Indians, they don't mean any harm by it, but lots of times they don't care a fig what they do or who they do it with just as long as they get a chance to do it. It's like when you've got a healthy young appetite, you'll take anything that's put before you. I've always resisted these temptations because of my faith. I've passed up things that . . . joys. . . ." He took off his glasses and rubbed his eyes with his thumb and forefinger. He said, "Now I ask myself this question. All these precious things I've given up for Jesus, what have I got to show for it?"

I said, "Brownie, your interpretations of Scripture bring lots of people comfort and hope."

He said, "Scripture says, 'Cast thy bread upon the waters for thou shalt find it after many days.' I have cast my whole life upon the waters, and it's sunk out of sight like a stone."

"Nobody knows you've lost your faith, Brownie," I said. "You can keep on helping people anyway. That way you might get it back again."

He said, "You don't know how it feels to say things you don't believe any more. It's like a woman with a dead baby inside her."

It was *Abide with Me* that came fluttering dimly toward us through the deepening twilight now. By this time Brownie's face was little more than a pale blur.

He said, "Scripture says where your treasure is, there shall your heart be also. The trouble is my treasure's turned out to be a bad check. Spiritually speaking, I don't have a nickel left to my name."

I said, "You've still got your warm and generous heart, Brownie."

Brownie reached out and softly squeezed my arm. "I shouldn't burden you with my problems, dear," he said. "You've got problems of your own."

We sat in silence for a while, just the creaking of Brownie's rocker and the distant bells. I thought of Gertrude Conover out on the dark terrace of Revonoc and how suddenly Bebb had appeared. I thought of the way Bebb would have worked Brownie over if he'd appeared there to us—*Brownie, the most faith you ever had was just one part faith to nine parts Aqua Velva. No use to cry over a pitiful thing like that.* It would have given Brownie another pain to take his mind off the pain he was rocking away with in Lucille's chair. But Bebb's way wasn't my way, and I couldn't think of any approach of my own to use on him instead until it occurred to me that I still hadn't told him how Gertrude Conover thought she had seen Bebb, so I told him. I tried to tell him in a way that would leave it up to him, as Gertrude Conover's account had left it up to me, to decide for himself whether it was Bebb or Bebb's ghost she had seen, and when he questioned me on the point, I said, "Brownie, I asked her the same question. I said did she mean he was alive the way she and I were alive, and all she said was she hoped he was more alive than that. You take it from there."

It stopped Brownie's rocking anyway, and I pressed my advantage.

I said, "Brownie, you need a change. You need to see new places and new people, and you need to stop taking your spiritual temperature all the time." I thought of echoing Bebb's image and talking about shoving a spiritual thermometer up but decided against it.

I said, "The trouble with your faith is you've tired it half to death just worrying about it. Come on down to Poinsett with me. We'll go for Bebb and Jesus both. We'll make a vacation of it."

I was so carried away by my own persuasive powers that for the first time I felt something almost like enthusiasm for the venture myself. Sharon could come too. We could park the children somewhere. It would beat just hanging around Sutton all summer putting my six-foot mobile in shape and keeping the grass mowed. If Brownie's problem was that he'd lost his faith, mine was more or less that I'd never had one to lose that amounted to much, so like the man who hit pay dirt plowing his field, maybe we'd both stumble on something down there. But I could tell my words hadn't grabbed Brownie. He still wasn't rocking, but that was about it. Then I was inspired.

I said, "Who knows if she really saw Bebb or not. Chances are she's not all that sure herself. But just suppose she did. Stranger things have happened. And if so, it could be what we'll find in Poinsett if we go is Bebb. Maybe that's why he wants us down there."

Bebb holing up in the cellar of his mouldering homestead, broke and friendless. Bebb in disguise, the Man with a Thousand Faces. For all I knew, Bebb as the Phantom of the Opera, disfigured, crippled even, by his narrow escape from the burning plane. No such fantasy had crossed my mind before—I was summoning it up purely for Brownie's sake—but once summoned, it came to life for me.

I said, "Jesus, Brownie. Suppose he's in bad trouble and needs our help?"

Brownie's face kept changing shape like ectoplasm as I tried to read it through the darkness. When he spoke, he fitted his words to the sound of the old hymn. "When other helpers fail and comforts flee," he said, "Help of the helpless, oh abide with me."

I said, "How about it, Brownie?"

I could hear the sound he made taking a swallow of his watery, tasteless tea. He said, "Let me put it this way, dear. I don't suppose I've got anything to lose I haven't lost already."

3

I DON'T SUPPOSE that my life before I got married was ever as simple as it came to seem afterwards, but the way I remember it anyway, if I felt like doing something in those days, I just got up and did it. I had no job to tie me down—my various stabs at novel-writing, journalism, the construction of take-apart scrap-iron sculpture, gave me if nothing else the advantage of being able to drop them at a moment's notice. So if it had been back in my bachelor days that I decided to take off for Poinsett, South Carolina, I would have just packed my bag and taken off. But those days were long since gone and maybe never existed in the first place.

"*This is the dog / That worried the cat / That killed the rat / That ate the malt / That lay in the house that Jack built*," the old rhyme goes, and in much the same way one complication led to another as I tried to organize my departure. There was the question first as to whether or not Sharon would come along, and just in itself, let alone in what it gave rise to, that was complicated enough. There was a time when she would have leapt at any excuse for dropping like hot potatoes such few motherly chores as she actually attended to—Miriam's older boy, Chris, who lived with us for a while, took such marvelous care of Bill as a baby that Sharon was free to devote herself almost entirely to her yoga lessons, speed-reading lessons, guitar lessons and so on—but after the rapid sequence of our six month separation, the death of Bebb, and the birth of Lucy, all of this changed. She gave up her lessons, gave up her share of the health food shop that she'd started with that grizzled little well of loneliness, Anita Steen, and grabbed on to motherhood like a raft in a storm. So for her own sake as well as for the children's she hung back for a while from letting go, and at the same time I hung back from urging her to. More complications. I wanted her with me, that sleepy-limbed, somber-eyed girl with the caught-red-handed smile, wanted her to battle with, bed down with, keep my bearings by, but at the same time I didn't for one minute want her to think I was setting too much store by it. When a marriage cracks like a plate and is glued together again, of all the things you've got to be careful about, the first is to look as if you aren't being careful about any of them. So she held back from saying she'd come and I held back from persuading her until it was finally Bebb in his way who brought us together just as he'd brought us together the first time in Armadillo, Florida. She said, "You know something, Bip never told me an awful lot about who his kin were or where he came from any more than he ever told me about me and where I came from if he even knew. So to hell with it, I'm going to go down with you and have a look for myself. There's got to be somebody who'll mind the kids while we're gone," though the question was who. Another complication.

The ones we finally hit on were my nephew Tony Blaine and his wife Laura, who lived in Manhattan. We asked them if they'd come stay while we were gone, and when they said they'd love to, it sounded as if they really meant it. What could have been less complicated than that? Except that it was complicated. To start with, Laura had a good job as hygienist in the office of a Park Avenue dentist and would have to commute back and forth from Sutton, but that raised no problems because she'd be there to get breakfast and back in time to get supper and in the meanwhile Tony would be able to keep an eye on the kids since it so happened that he was between jobs. That was what raised the problems. Poor Tony, my namesake and nemesis, that handsome, feckless, star-crossed boy who had risen to dizzy heights as track star, bon vivant, and man about town his senior year at Sutton High only to drift more or less earthwards ever since. In the year since he'd moved to New York and married Laura, he'd worked as a supermarket stock boy, a clerk in the necktie department at Brooks Brothers, an orderly in a Presbyterian old people's home, and on the side had gotten an occasional job modeling things like terrycloth jump suits, Irish gillies' hats and sunglasses for good measure. At twenty-four he could still think of himself as looking the field over till he turned something up that really suited him, and with Laura's salary together with what I always suspected must be an occasional handout from his older brother Chris he could tell himself that he could afford to keep on looking things over indefinitely. But I had a feeling these illusions would be harder to sustain in the workaday reality of Sutton than in the dream-spawning city. Laura would leave for work, and Tony would not leave. She would go off to earn money cleaning people's teeth, and he would stay home to deal not only with the children but with the hard fact that if he and Laura were ever to have children of their own, he would have to settle down to something permanent so they could afford it. "Christ, Tono," he said to me once, "what's an ex-jock like me good for? The best offers I've had are from some of the queers you run into in the modeling scene. One of them offered me a hundred bucks an hour just to pose for him bareass and don't think there haven't been times I've considered it."

So he was the man all tattered and torn, I suppose, with Laura the maiden all forlorn, and so on back to the rat, the cat, and finally the house that Jack built which was our house, Sharon's and mine, the place where the final complication lay buried. This was the possibility that the true father of our daughter Lucy was not me but Tony.

I don't know how much this was something Tony brooded about, but when he and Laura arrived with their bags the evening before Sharon and I were to set out for the South, I can't believe that it didn't at least cross his mind. We led the two of them upstairs to show them where they would be staying, where the dirty diapers went, and so on, and we had just started trooping downstairs again—I see us suspended there between floors as between incarnations with Sharon leading the way and Tony bringing up the rear—when all of a sudden our son Bill came staggering down the hall with his baby sister cradled precariously in his arms. Tony leaped to the rescue. He ran back upstairs, snatched the baby up, and stood there looking down at her with his face gone all haywire and x's where his eyes should have been like Krazy Kat hit with a brick. "Well, I'll be goddammed," he said, "I'll be goddammed" and it was only after he'd said it two or three times more that I realized it was probably the first time he had ever actually held her. Then Sharon said, "Hand her on down to her mama, hear," and I remember the awkward way I had to lean sideways as he conveyed her down over the banister. I remember how Laura and I were compressed together there for a moment or two beneath the London Bridge of their reaching arms.

It was an awkward evening generally, as I look back on it, and partly at least because before it was over, our roles got turned around somehow. Sharon and I with our bags all packed to make our early start the next morning became the guests, and I had the sense of Tony and Laura marking time like restless hosts until we were gone. There was an awkwardness too in Laura's having known me for so long as Mr. Parr that she had a hard time calling me either Tono the way Tony did, or Antonio or Bopper like Sharon, so that most of the time she called me nothing at all, which made me feel all the more ghostly and guest-like. Bill was the only one of us who seemed to have his feet on the ground, and even as he tottered around sleepily among us in a space helmet after supper, his presence was so stabilizing that I found myself dreading the moment Sharon would take him up to bed. When the moment finally came, she was already half way up the stairs with him when he called down that he wanted Tony to carry him the rest of the way and Tony was off like a shot, the whole house rattling as he pounded up after them. This left Laura and me alone together in the living room with poor Laura having no name to call me by when she finally said, "Maybe it's time we let you and Sharon go to bed now too. You've got a long drive ahead of you tomorrow," and I said, "I hope you'll like it here while we're gone. It will be a change anyway," and she said, "A change is always nice, and then it's nice when you get back home again too." It was like trying to play tennis without a ball.

I said, "Bill shouldn't give you any trouble. He's also pretty helpful if you have any trouble with the baby," and she said, "Oh I don't think it's any of it going to be like any trouble."

She was sitting across the room by a bridge lamp with the light of it in her hair, and she was looking down at her hands as she talked, frowning at them with her eyebrows raised as though there were several things about her hands that puzzled her. I thought of all the months she had sat at the back of my classroom looking much the same way with her lashes dark against her cheeks, not wanting to catch my eye for fear I'd ask her some question she didn't know the answer to.

Upstairs there was the sound of Sharon's voice followed by Tony's locker-room laugh snapping through it like a damp towel, the patter of Bill's bare feet across the ceiling and a thump in the pipes as a faucet was turned on.

"It makes me think of *Dear Brutus*," I said. "Remember that one?"

She said, "I remember the title. It was Sir Peter Barrie, I remember."

"Sir Peter Pan," I said. "Sir James Barrie. It was the one where everybody got a chance to—"

"Now I remember," she said and, knowing an answer finally, raised her eyes. "It was this enchanted forest and they all had a chance to see how things might have turned out if they'd done something different in their lives."

"Like those two upstairs a couple, and you and me down here a couple. It was just something that crossed my mind," I said, but as soon as I'd tossed it across the empty place between us, it became more than I'd ever bargained for. For a moment or two then there was no empty place between us with her looking across at me out of her life and me looking across at her out of my life, the separate lives we had each of us lived touching awkwardly in that room where we were both uneasy guests the way they had always touched. Instead it was as if the life we might have lived together had become the life we had really lived, and we were looking at each other across a place filled with houses we had lived in together and babies we had borne and love we had made, fights we had fought. There was no need to ask each other any more questions or to explain anything to each other because for the moment there was nothing about each other we didn't know and hadn't always known.

She said, "I never told anybody," and I knew what she meant just as she'd known I'd know, meant she'd never told anybody how during that same sad time when Sharon and I had split up, I had asked myself to her house for supper once because I was bored and lonesome and though we didn't have much in common, we at least had Sir Peter Barrie and Ethan Frome and King Lear in common and I was at the point where I would have settled for a lot less. What she had never told anybody was that the evening had been a tongue-tied disaster until in the First Communion hush of her bedroom between sheets blue with dusk we ended up making love together not all that less awkwardly than downstairs we had made conversation together but with the difference that from the little death of that second failure, a life branched off deep inside me which was no less alive for my having not only never actually, year-in-year-out, lived it but not even thought about it all that much, the way things go. A few months later when Laura married my nephew, I suppose we both must have thought about it separately, she and I, but at different moments and in different ways so that it was only that evening in Sutton when Tony and Sharon were putting the kids to bed and the pipes were thumping over our heads that we both thought about it together and it came alive for both of us at once.

A dying man's whole life passes in seconds before his eyes, they say, and to the extent that the whole life I might have lived with Laura passed then before mine, I suppose in a way I was dying myself. I felt the whole life I lived in that house with my real wife and real children shudder under me like an earthquake, and since the other life was not substantial enough to bear my weight either, for a moment it was as if an abyss had opened beneath me. I didn't even trust myself to speak for fear of what it could pitch me headlong into, so I might be sitting there still with cobwebs in my hair and my mouth choked with silence if my son Bill hadn't come to the rescue. He piped word down that he wanted Laura and me to come kiss him goodnight so all I ever got around to saying to her before we went on up was "Dear Brutus," I think, "Dear Brutus, dear Brutus"—breathing it more than saying it out where I could be sure that she'd heard it—but even that was enough to tremble its foundations again, the house that Jack built, before we reached the security of the second floor.

Sharon and Tony and Laura and I—I remember the four of us standing there around the bed where my skinny son lay so sleepy he was drunk, so drunk he hardly knew it when one after the other we kissed him, strange deputation that we were. Sharon and I were to be on our way before he was up the next morning so our goodnight was really our goodbye too although he was in no state at that point to know it or care much, and I wasn't either as I look back on it. When I whispered goodbye into his small, sweaty ear, I didn't let myself mean any more than just goodnight by it. Goodbye, goodbye. If you really stopped to think about it, I don't suppose you would ever say it.

4

MY CHIEF TROUBLE with Callaway was that most of the time I had no clear idea what he was talking about. If I stopped to puzzle it out word by word, like bad handwriting, I was lost. The most I could hope for was the general drift, and even then I got it wrong as often as not. To cut short both my frustration and his, I would sometimes finish off what I thought was going to be his sentence only to find him swatting the air between us with his shapely black hand as if a bee was attacking him. What stung him, of course, was not my failure but his own. He knew he wasn't getting through and his desperate eyes told me he knew, his black face glowing with the misery of it like a coal. The misery made him talk even faster than he was talking already, the heavy, sweet Southern syllables getting all gummed together in odd clusters at that breakneck Northern speed. *Mustapha zigzag compustuck silo*, he would say. Something like that. Gertrude Conover claimed that over the years she had learned to understand him, but I had my doubts. She would tell me what he had said, either a verbatim translation or a loose paraphrase, but even when he bobbed his head around in endorsement, I suspected that it was less because she had rendered him right than that he admired her version for some special quality of its own.

"Whimsal ah humbleseep duggasick toe moe juffle," he said on the steps of the Lincoln Memorial with the sun blinding bright on the marble and a stiff breeze ballooning Sharon's skirt.

He said, "Tie mudruss begga dandyfay roesah." He was frowning up toward the rotunda where you could just make out the great figure enthroned in shadows. "Summa sot," he added in another voice, quieter, as if it might be a melancholy footnote to the rest. Summer's hot? Somersault? Gertrude Conover's hairnet had come loose in the breeze, and she had reached one lizard green arm across her face to fasten it. From under her arm she said, "When he was the Pharaoh, he had temples many times the size of this one, though some were not." The repairs completed, she lowered her arm to find the hairnet dangling from her bracelet. She yanked it loose and slipped it into her purse. "That's enough out of you," she said.

Callaway was standing several steps above us in black trousers, shiny black shoes, a dazzling white shirt open at the collar and a green Agway cap with a visor. I wondered whether she had made the observation on her own or had been quoting him and, if quoting him, whether she had quoted him right. Did Callaway know of his former glory, remember temples he had presided over that made the Lincoln Memorial look like two cents?

When he turned around to gaze back across the Mall over our heads, his bony face under the visor looked like a black keyhole.

It was Gertrude Conover who had insisted on seeing the sights in Washington on our way south. Somewhere in Maryland with Callaway at the wheel and Sharon and me on either side of her in the back seat, she said, "No wonder it's taking me so long to work my way to cosmic consciousness. There are so many places I've never been, so many things I've never done, so many fascinating people I've never met. I simply can never resist another rebirth, even though I know perfectly well where it will get me in the end and where it won't get me, too. It's like eating salted peanuts. The more lives you live, the more lives you crave. I'm afraid I'm the eternal sightseer."

"Why not?" Sharon said. "You always seem to get the red carpet treatment. Back when you knew Bip in ancient Egypt you were a princess, you told him."

Gertrude Conover said, "Technically no. My father was only a Nubian tough who had the bad luck to get himself killed in a border free-for-all. It's true the Pharaoh took a shine to me and made me his ward, but I was not a princess of the blood."

"Six of one," Sharon said.

I said, "In the eighteenth century you said you were an Italian contessa."

Gertrude Conover said, "I've never seen a century drag the way that one did. There were times I thought it would go on forever.

"But yes," she said. "I've always tried to keep my karma in good repair, and of course the pay-off has been that more often than not I've been born with a silver spoon in my mouth. Though not always, of course. When the Aryans were spreading out all over creation with their bad teeth and their impossible language, I starved to death in the Punjab, and at the time of the Viking raids on the English coast, I was witness to barbarities that would make your flesh crawl. Generally speaking, though, I don't deny what you've said, my dear. By and large I've traveled through history first class."

"Do you remember all those lives?" Sharon said.

Gertrude Conover said, "That's like when people ask me if I've read all the books in the library at Revonoc. I say what on earth would I want to do a thing like that for?"

I said, "In the ones you remember, did Bebb always turn up?"

"I always hoped he would," she said.

She was gazing out the car window as we talked, her face turned away from me, but I could see her eyes reflected in the glass, and beyond them, through them, the landscape racing by like the centuries.

She said, "You forget so much between lives—of course it would be unthinkable any other way. Just imagine remembering a thousand first loves, a thousand sets of children you bore and raised, a thousand wars. But Bebb I never forgot. In every new life I lived, there would come a moment when I remembered him. Something would happen to remind me or maybe I would catch sight of him waiting for me on the fringes of some dream I was dreaming. And then I would hope like anything that our paths would cross again. Sometimes they did, sometimes they didn't. And when they did, I won't say that it was all moonlight and roses, but one way or another, every time Bebb turned up, he made it a red-letter life."

She said, "It was his not turning up that made the eighteenth century such a flop—just one baby after another for years, not to mention the awful damp and people throwing their slops right into the public street."

I said, "Bebb must be an eternal sightseer too."

It made a good picture, I thought—the two of them touring through the ages together, meeting, parting, meeting again. She would know him by the way he sacrificed his unblemished lamb or shouldered his flintlock or blinked that trick eye of his under the velvet cap of some Renaissance shyster.

"Not Leo Bebb," she said. "You remember the summer we were all in England together, how restless he was—always in such a hurry to move on to the next place? It was never the sights that kept him moving—he hardly noticed them—and it has never been the sights that have kept him returning to this earth so many times either."

"How come he keeps doing it then?" Sharon asked.

Gertrude Conover said, "It is the nature of the man."

She said, "As long as there's anybody left to return to down here, Leo Bebb will always return to them. Return *for* them might be a better way of putting it."

She pulled a tourist map of Washington out of her purse and unfolded it across her knees. She said, "Leo Bebb is an always-returner, and that is the long and the short of it."

Once we arrived in Washington, something happened which made me believe for a time either that he had returned yet again or that as far as this particular life was concerned, he had never left in the first place. Our tour of historic landmarks had taken us to the Library of Congress where we drifted off into different sections of a large exhibition room, and I was wandering around only half seeing the things they had set out in the glass cases. I remember a matching set of white beads and white earrings that Mary Lincoln had apparently been partial to and a photograph of Harry Truman standing under a rack of neckties in the days he ran a haberdashery. I remember thinking how if you didn't happen to know about all the sleaziness and double-dealing that have gone on in Washington over the years, you might never guess it from the kind of shabby, sad things it chooses to treasure or from the look of the stately, hopeful Federal buildings with their soaring columns and Justice, Liberty, Truth, all the great abstractions, carved into their facades like New Year's resolutions before the hangover sets in. It is a very touching, very vulnerable city to me, and I can never return to it without feeling a lump in the throat. It affects me like that scene in *Ruggles of Red Gap* when Charles Laughton recites the Gettysburg Address in the saloon and the faces of the crowd go still and soft at the sound of it and the faces of the audience watching it years later go stiller and softer yet at the sense of a time gone by when the Gettysburg Address could mean so much. In other words I was thinking wistful thoughts as I drifted through that place, and in that sense I suppose you could say I was ready for what happened next although in every other sense I was not ready at all. What happened next was that I stepped through a small door and found myself standing on a balcony looking down into the rotunda of the main reading room below.

It was an enormous, lamp-lit cavern of a place with its ornate marble walls, arches, balustrades, and soaring sky-lit dome, its mighty circulation desk and curved ranks of file drawers with a card each for all the books ever published in the universe. Except for a vague rustling sound, people dwarfed by the balcony's height moved noiselessly across acres of floor or sat at long tables lost in their reading. It was the living heart of the library that I'd stumbled on, and I had the sense of great pulse and purpose, of librarians with their hair in buns telling the Dewey decimal system like beads, of the unscuffed soles of statesmen heavy on the thick carpet, of congressmen and scholars grave and quiet as carp in the depths of their concentration. Then I thought I saw Bebb.

I saw a shiny pink scalp set atop a pair of thick shoulders anyway. I saw a plump hand turn a page. On an empty chair beside him I saw what looked like a black raincoat and a Tyrolean hat. And then as suddenly as I'd seen him, I lost him again.

A woman in a green dress holding a child by the hand moved between us; there was a shifting of positions; for an instant a shape blotted out the light of the reading lamp, then withdrew again, and in the dazzle of it I saw that Bebb was gone. Unless a figure I could only partly see crouched at a lower drawer of the card catalogue was Bebb. I leaned out as far as I dared to see if it was but couldn't. I would have shouted down to him if the great size and hush of the place hadn't stopped my mouth, would have jumped down to him if it had been twenty feet instead of what seemed a hundred.

Dear Bebb. What was there about him? It is hard to say exactly. He never had that much time for me, not even when he must have known I most needed him. He was always in a hurry, always so intent on the next thing he had to do, as Gertrude Conover pointed out in the car, that you felt he wasn't entirely with you even when he was. He was by no means the wisest person I've ever known or the most eloquent or the most warmhearted and heaven knows he had his shadow side like the rest of us. Not even counting his five years in the pen, or his smog-bound finances, or the ambiguous nature of his various evangelical enterprises, you had the feeling that during his life and for all I know during innumerable other lives thrown in he had moved through dark and painful places that had left that one gimpy eye of his needing to flutter closed every once in a while to shut out the dark and painful memory of them. And yet, what was there about him that made me miss him more than any man? Even at his lowest and bluest, there was a life in him that rubbed off on you, that's all. You might feel better or you might feel worse when Bebb was around, but in any case you felt more. There was more of you to feel with.

So there in the Library of Congress I was prepared to do almost anything. If Bebb was down there, I had to get to him. There was somebody crouching half out of sight who might be Bebb, and if it was, he might have seen me, might be looking up surreptitiously at me even as I stood there looking down at him. He might not want to give himself away to me for fear that in my excitement I might give him away to God knows who, so I tried signaling to him in a way that I thought would catch nobody's eye that wasn't on me already, tried wagging my hand back and forth at chest level and then pointing down into the reading room to show him I'd be down there myself in no time flat and to wait.

As I rushed back through the exhibition room, I noticed Sharon and Gertrude Conover off looking at things in a corner, but I not only didn't have time to tell them what I was up to, something in me didn't even want to tell them. For fear they'd think I'd gone off my rocker maybe, or maybe, beneath that, the fear they'd come along and somehow dim for me a moment that all my life I'd been waiting for without knowing I was waiting for it.

I clattered down a flight of marble steps, two at a time, raced through corridors, and finally found myself at a pair of swinging leather doors which I pushed my way through to find that I was in the great reading room at last.

It took me a few moments to get oriented. I spotted my balcony, the circulation desk. The woman in the green dress was standing at it listening to a man with spectacles pushed back on his forehead telling her something soundlessly. Beyond her was the table where Bebb had been reading, if it was Bebb, or pretending to read, if he was pretending. Beyond that were the curved ranks of the card catalogue. I made a rapid tour through all of them, but there was no longer anyone crouched at the lower drawers, and I recognized nobody. My heart leapt when from behind I saw a bald man reaching for a volume of the Cumulative Book Index, but when I positioned myself to see his face, it was comprehensively not Bebb's—a flabby, tired face with a small pink moustache.

The woman with the green dress had seated herself at one of the long tables and was filling out some kind of form while beside her the child, a boy about eight, was goggling up at the skylight fathoms above us in the dome. I went up to the woman and explained my problem. From a distance I thought I had recognized an old friend sitting near her. Did she by any chance remember a stout man with a bald head, sixtyish, clean-shaven I was about to add but didn't then. For all I knew he'd grown a beard. For all I knew he'd grown another face. Did an always-returner always return looking the same?

"You notice anybody looked like that, honey?" the woman said to the little boy.

The boy said, "There was a man that winked his eye at me," and again my heart leapt.

"A bald man?" I asked.

"He had a hat on."

"You remember what kind of a hat?"

"Just a plain hat."

"Fat?"

"Hat," he said. "He had on a hat, and he winked at me."

I said, "You didn't happen to notice where he went, did you?"

He pointed at the skylight. "Up there's the tallest window in the whole world."

"You don't happen to see him anywhere in this room still, I suppose."

"I seen his eye wink," the boy said. "He winked like this." He screwed up one whole side of his face to get the eye closed.

I thanked them for their help.

I didn't tell Sharon and Gertrude Conover what had happened because I wasn't sure if anything had happened. Gertrude Conover was buying postcards, and Sharon was sitting on a radiator with one bare foot in her hand. I asked her where Callaway was.

"He went to the can," she said. "He seemed like he was in a real hurry."

I said, "He wasn't having one of his nosebleeds, was he?" At the thought of that telltale nose of Callaway's, my heart leapt a third time.

She said, "I didn't ask him what he was going to do in there."

Gertrude Conover appeared with her postcards fanned out like a bridge hand. She said, "The Folger Shakespeare Library is only a skip and a jump away. It's the largest collection of first folios in existence."

Sharon said, "Gertrude Conover, did you ever run into Shakespeare in one of your other lives?" She was leaning forward to fold her toes back and forth, and her hair covered half her face.

Gertrude Conover said, "My dear, Shakespeare was a nobody. He pronounced his r's like w's and couldn't even spell his own name properly."

"No shit," Sharon said. She seemed genuinely interested.

When Callaway reappeared, I asked him if his nose had been giving him trouble. He seemed to find my question amusing and smiled broadly. "Joppa dill," he said. Then, taking his handkerchief out of his pocket and holding it balled up to his nose, he said, "Possum," and laughed.

Since Gertrude Conover had already headed out through the revolving door for the Folger, she was not there to interpret for me.

5

SHARON SAID, "No wonder Bebb hightailed out of here first chance he got. Jesus."

Poinsett, South Carolina, was less a town than an intersection. There was a dry cleaner, a package store, a quonset hut converted into a V.F.W. headquarters. The post office, we eventually discovered, was in a store that sold groceries, drugs, drygoods, sex magazines, and personalized compacts with names like Earlene and Cindi and Kimberly on them. Over the cash register was the first strip of flypaper I'd seen in years, all gummed up with flies that looked as though they might have landed there during the Hoover administration. There were two big gas stations with plastic pennants and revolving signs. There was a Baptist Church with a triangle of dead grass in front of it and a bulletin board that read "Redemption Center—no green stamps required." A railroad track cut across the road we entered on, and we had to wait for an endless freight train to pass by. Callaway counted the cars while we waited, and when the caboose rolled by, he said "Sixty-two" so loud and clear that for once I understood him perfectly. Between the two gas stations there was a Chicken in the Basket place made of white tile like a men's room, and even with the windows of Gertrude Conover's Lincoln closed tight and the airconditioning on high, we could smell the frying fat. It must have been ninety in the shade if there had been any shade instead of just miles of flat red farmland, peach orchards, a trailer park. Off toward the horizon was a hazy stack of buildings that was Spartanburg.

I tried to picture Bebb there fifty years earlier, tried to remember what little he'd told me about his life there. He'd said his father was a house painter who'd been crippled by a fall and spent most of the rest of his life in bed. He'd spoken of a hard-working mother who had managed to keep the family going and had been the one who started him off on the sawdust trail. Somehow he conveyed the impression to me that she herself had never followed it far enough beyond faith to make it to charity but had bogged down somewhere just short of hope. The first job he'd had was washing dishes at a restaurant in Spartanburg where he had wooed and won the boss's daughter Lucille Yancey. From there he had gone on to selling Bibles. The only building I could see that looked as if it might have been standing in those days was the grocery store—post office where we went to ask the whereabouts of the old Bebb place.

I marvel at the figure we must have cut as we filed in—Gertrude Conover in her blue hair and white shoes, dressed for cocktails on the terrace at Revonoc; Sharon with dark glasses the size of butter-plates, bellbottoms, and her shirttails knotted in front to keep her midriff bare; Callaway looking more like a chauffeur than usual except for his Agway cap. A bell over the screen door announced our arrival but it might as well have saved itself the trouble. Everybody looked our way as the man behind the post office grille repeated our phrase back at us a few times—old Bebb place, old Bebb place—sweeping his eye around the store to make sure nobody was missing anything. Nobody was. There were a couple of youths thumbing through the magazines, a girl with a bad complexion waiting on an old man in the grocery department, a few others. The postmaster was all Adam's apple and teeth as he leaned his forehead against the bars.

It had never occurred to me to work out a strategy, but under his gaze I found myself not wanting to go into details. I didn't want to tell him any more than I had to about why we were there and what we were after—partly, I suppose, because when you got right down to it, we weren't all that sure ourselves what we were after. Gertrude Conover said, "We were motoring by and just thought we'd like to see where a dear old friend was born. Well, it is a kind of sentimental journey," and I felt that like me she was reluctant to say who the dear old friend was as though at the sound of his name they might all rend their garments and the crops would fail. As a result the man rambled on about Bebbs in Greenville, Saluda, Tryon, speaking in one of those Southern accents that's less of a drawl than a sly little pussyfoot patter up near the front of the mouth, and I found myself not wanting to cut him short for fear of putting him in some queer way on guard. I felt he was looking at us queerly enough as it was and remembered all the movies I'd ever seen about Yankees getting locked up in just such a Dixie backwash as this for conduct no more suspicious. I thought I could see him wince inwardly at the free and comradely way Sharon rested her arm on Callaway's shoulder as she leaned over to take off one shoe.

Then it was Sharon who finally came out with it. She said, "Anybody here know a place where a man use to live by the name of *Leo* Bebb?" and the old man buying groceries set his bag down on the counter as if he could handle only one thing at a time and said, "Leo Bebb, he used to buy scratch off me back when I had the feed store. He'd come say Sam, let me have a hundred, didn't say a hundred this or that. Seemed like he was always in a hurry, couldn't only say but a hundred, Sam. Course I knew it was scratch. Always *was* scratch," which wasn't much in the way of a souvenir and yet "Ah did you once see Shelley plain," I thought, "and did he stop and speak to you?" those same watery old eyes goggling out at a Bebb unimaginably young and untouched but even then in a hurry.

The man behind the bars finally got around to saying there was only one Bebb place he knew in Poinsett—he pronounced it Points—and showed us how to get there on Callaway's map. Babe's place, he said. Babe Bebb? He didn't seem to want to go into details either. Back in the car again Gertrude Conover said, "There was something about that old man having known him. He put his thumb right on my heart."

It wasn't the place of our dreams when we got to it, at least not of my dreams—no silvery clapboard, sway-back roof and forlorn, abandoned windows, no waist-high grass at the busted porch steps. There was nothing Andrew Wyeth about it, just a big, square two-story house like a child's drawing of a house. It had black asbestos shingles with a white trim and was set not far off the red clay road. The grass out front was mowed to within an inch of its life and by the front door there was a tractor tire painted white with nasturtiums in it. There was a birdbath supposed to look like antique stone, a Chipmunk Crossing sign and two plastic flamingos, one looking skyward, one pecking for something to eat in the scorched grass. By the side door stood a couple of gas cylinders screened behind white palings and nailed to the palings a sign that read:

UFORIUM
OPEN DAILY
LECTURES SATURDAY—ALL WELCOME
CONSULTATIONS BY APPOINTMENT

"Looks like there's Bebbs here all right," Sharon said. Nobody answered the bell if it even worked, but the door was open and we went in.

The Uforium. Just inside the door you ran into a partition blocking your way with a rainbow-colored painting of a flying saucer on it. The saucer had a low crown and a wide brim like a cardinal's hat, and it was tilted toward the earth at a rakish angle as if the cardinal might have had one too many. The door in the crown was flung wide, and out of it a comic strip balloon streamed up into the toy-blue sky with the message "*Hurry Aboard! It's later than you think!*" lettered on it. On a table in front of it was a contribution box, a book to sign, and a glass with some of the nasturtiums in it. Behind the partition was the Uforium proper.

It was the light that struck you first, a yellowish, extraterrestrial glow that came through the fly-specked window shades that were all pulled down to the bottom. There were pictures of flying saucers on the walls, photographs mostly, some with portholes, some spoked like wagon wheels, some just streaks of light on the horizon or dots in the sky that an amateur might have mistaken for birds. There were pictures of people who had seen flying saucers and pictures that these people had evidently made of what they had seen. One of them showed a figure with a head like a radio tube and one big eye where his navel should have been. Around the room under the windows there were exhibition cases with glass lids, and in one of them there was an enlarged Kodacolor close-up of a human mouth. Next to it in the case were some small pellets that looked like mouse droppings. The mouth was wide open so you could see the teeth, and on the crown of each tooth was a dark spot that looked like one of the mouse droppings. Sharon said, "Hey Bopper, want to see some outer space cowflops?"—some flat, roughly circular objects about the size of dinner plates. They seemed to be plaster casts of something.

In the center of the room on a large, low table like the kind F.A.O. Schwarz used to display electric trains on at Christmas time there was a relief map painted psychedelic green with different colored pins stuck in here and there all over it—yellow pins for landings, a card explained, red ones for sightings, blue ones for hearings. On a sloping hillside there was a question mark made up out of pins of all three colors. Around the edge of the table were burned places where people had apparently left their cigarettes and forgotten them. Sharon came over and breathed something in my ear. She said, "I've just had a sighting," and pointed to the far end of the room where there was a door standing ajar. Through the door you could see part of a window and part of a table. On the table you could see part of a human being. It was a hand. As I approached, I saw a puff of smoke drift down towards it.

The hand belonged to a fat woman who seemed long since to have forgotten it. She was sitting there gazing out the window with her back to me, a flyswatter on the table beside her. She had bare, fleshy arms and a pink ribbon tied in her grey curls. Except for the tangle of cigarette smoke, there was such stillness about her that she could have been part of the Uforium, the waxwork of a flying saucer captain's wife watching the sky for saucers. There wasn't much for her to see through the window, just the stretch of red clay road we'd come on and our car parked out front with Callaway drowsing behind the wheel. I had to speak twice before she turned around.

I remember still the way she looked that first time I ever laid eyes on her, before I even knew her name—that plaintive, fat face as she bit the inside of her lip crooked, her forehead dimpling like a child's desperate to go to the john but scared to ask, those eyebrows she'd tried to pencil on where she didn't have any eyebrows of her own. You could see the thick grey curls were a wig. She didn't have a real hair on her head. Her cigarette was in her mouth and one eye squinnied up against the smoke, her small features huddled together as if for protection behind it. Was she Mrs. Bebb, I asked. Was she Mrs. Bebb? Twice.

I had the impression that she wasn't answering right off the bat because for a moment, come upon suddenly that way, she wasn't sure. I had the impulse to take the cigarette out from between her lips for her the way they do in the movies for dying soldiers, but she managed with it still in place finally, talking around it like a thumb. Whispering almost.

I still remember too the first time I heard that breathy little babydoll voice she had that turned everything she said into a tiny question she sounded afraid to ask, afraid there was no answer to. "I'm Bertha Bebb?" she said. "Babe's downstreet?" then that hand that still didn't seem to belong to her bringing the swatter down hard on a fly on the window sill. The working end of the swatter was baby-blue like a rattle.

I could see her face register the appearance of Gertrude Conover, who came edging into the doorway beside me, her voice coming out under my armpit like an inaugural address compared to Bertha Bebb's. She said, "We're looking for an old house that hasn't been lived in for years. You've had your Uforium here long?" Hearing it spoken for the first time, I heard it *euphorium*.

Bertha Bebb said, "Want to see the moonrocks till Babe comes?" When she got up out of her chair I saw she was wearing men's shoes and bobby socks, passing through the door as vague and shapeless as weather. She carried the swatter in one hand and the cigarette in the other. She didn't look at Sharon as she passed, just said "Hey" to her. Sharon said, "Hey." Bertha Bebb said, "Here's the *moonrocks?* Don't touch them barehanded. They're all over moongerms?" She poked at them with the swatter, her forehead still puckering in hectic, worried ways. The moonrocks looked like bits of broken cinderblock.

"I thought all the moonrocks were in places like Washington, D.C.," Sharon said. "Where'd you get these moonrocks from?"

"From the moon?" she said. She said, "Every step you take you bounce higher than a kite. Babe says he broke wind once? He was twenty minutes walking back to where he took off."

Sharon said, "Bip would have gotten a bang out of that one." Bertha Bebb wasn't getting a bang out of it. She looked afraid she'd said something wrong.

Gertrude Conover said, "Has your husband been to the moon, Mrs. Bebb?" Been to Cincinnati, been to the barber's? The fathomless imperturbability of Gertrude Conover.

Bertha Bebb raised a glass lid and took out something that looked like a badly charred pair of football shoulderpads. She said, "It's all there's left of his *space* suit? It burnt the minute the air hit it."

"Oh dear, what a shame," Gertrude Conover said, running her fingers down one dangling strap. "I hope he wasn't wearing it at the time."

Bertha Bebb said, "The air's different up there. There's more room in it? Babe saw a pack of them bigger than him in a space he couldn't hardly squeeze into, his ownself, here on earth."

"What's a hearing?" Sharon said.

Bertha Bebb took a puff on her cigarette, letting the smoke come out helter-skelter with her words. She said, "There's one," using her swatter to tap the case with the open mouth and the mouse droppings in it.

Sharon said, "You hear with your *mouth?*"

Bertha Bebb said, "Not my mouth."

Despite the earlier warning, Gertrude Conover had picked up a moonrock, but I noticed that she had slipped on one of her white gloves first. She said, "There are some that you hear then, and there are some that you see. . . ." She waved the moonrock toward the photographs on the wall. "Tell us about the ones that actually land, Mrs. Bebb."

Bertha Bebb said, "The horses go crazy sometimes, near to kick the stalls out." It was the most positive she'd sounded yet, as though at least about the horses she was reasonably sure. She said, "Sometimes they climb right out and poke into things? They've been doing it since Bible times."

"Bip always said they were the same as the angels," Sharon said.

"Silvers and goldens," I said. "He said goldens were scarce as hen's teeth."

"Don't hold your breath till you see your next silver either," Sharon said.

Bertha Bebb said, "Babe's been aboard? They gave him things? He'll show you some if you have a consultation."

Gertrude Conover put the moonrock back where it belonged and peeled off her glove. She looked quite young in the smoky, yellow light. She said, "Well you see it's not a consultation we came for. We just hoped he could help us locate the place we're looking for."

Bertha Bebb said, "He helps anybody he can lay his hands on?"

There was a sound of raindrops on the roof, the first unevenly spaced drops of a rain just starting, and then Sharon said, "Was there ever anybody lived in this place years ago by the name of Leo Bebb?" Letting the suspicion drift out as easy as the name: that these Bebbs were squatters, that beneath the black asbestos shingles and white trim was the weathered clapboard of my dreams, this very room the room Bebb had come back to the sadder and the wiser from the old lady with sticking plaster on her mouth at the Spartanburg depot.

Sharon stood on one side of the map and Bertha Bebb on the other, and I remember thinking there should have been a new pin stuck somewhere into the hills between them to mark the hearing that took place then as the name of Leo Bebb was spoken and heard.

"Has he passed?" Bertha Bebb said as soft as the sound on the roof, *passed* in the sense of passing by, passing through, I thought, until Sharon said, "A year ago this spring."

Bertha Bebb was still holding the charred shoulderpads, and she went to put them back. From the way she lowered the glass lid over them with her fat shoulders humped forward, her grey curls shaking, you would have thought it was made of lead. Her back was turned. After a while, she said, "You kin?"

A whiff of wet came wafting into the Uforium. A fly buzzed three circles above us before landing on a lamp by the door.

"He was my daddy," Sharon said.

Bertha Bebb turned around, pushing the smoke aside like a curtain. She said, "Lucille's baby?"

Sharon shook her head. "Bip adopted me."

Bertha Bebb's voice was so quiet now I couldn't hear what she said, but Sharon heard.

"It's Sharon," she said.

Bertha Bebb said something else.

"If he knew, he never told me," Sharon said.

Then after a long pause, the quietest thing of all from Bertha Bebb. I don't think anybody heard it, not even Sharon, but from the way she stood there with the smoke sliding up her fat wrist you could tell that it was a question and that it had to be answered, so for lack of anybody else I answered it. I said, "Leo Bebb," then just stood there and watched the landing the name made, soft as rain, on that great moon of a face.

She noticed the fly on the lamp eventually and let him have it with her baby-blue swatter. It was a glass lamp that broke in two when it hit the linoleum. The fly escaped unharmed.

6

SHARON SAID, "You look enough like him to be his twin brother. My God."

Babe said, "Honey, I am his twin brother."

Sharon said, "I never heard him tell he had any twin brother."

Babe said, "Child, you ever try making a list of all the things you never heard your daddy tell? You ever try catching a summer breeze in a bag?"

Sharon said, "You had the same mother and daddy and you were raised on the same place?"

"Rat," Babe said.

"This same house?"

"Rat," Babe said.

To his wife he said, "Don't you mind about this, hear." The broken lamp dangled from his hand by its cord, head down like a dead chicken. With his arm around her shoulder he gave her a squeeze that undimpled her forehead, her small features unhuddling enough to let a smile slip through. Her step was light as a girl's as she left, the grey curls bouncing. "That's my Shirley Temple, my own sweet love," he said.

Only then, starting with Sharon and clutching out from her, did he manage to scramble his arms around all three of us at once in a great football huddle embrace smelling of plastic and rain, his words coming out half muffled, "Oh I knew you were coming. I knew you quick as a wink." When he took his arms away, we came apart like a barrel.

Except for his damp red hair all clumped and ragged, he could have been Bebb if you didn't look too hard—Bebb in a fright wig, Bebb having gained a few pounds and aged a few years. He had less the look of Bebb's hard-rubber bounce to him than of something with give to it, comfier, his plump Bebbsian face a New Year's Eve balloon on New Year's Day, but bug-eyed and jazzy like Bebb with no neck to speak of, a tight-lipped Kewpie-doll H of a mouth. There was a lot more cracker in his voice. His *right* came through *rat*, his *I* the sound you make around a tongue depressor when they tell you to open up wider and try again, but his mouth snapped open and shut on his words like a trap the same way, the same scrubbed look of a fat nun. It was like seeing somebody in a dream who's died and you're so glad to see him again that you can hardly stand it, yet all the time you know deep down that it isn't really who you think it is because there's some emptiness inside that the sight of him doesn't fill the way food doesn't fill you in dreams either. It was almost but not quite Bebb there, Babe instead with his spikes of rainy red hair and his see-through plastic raincoat that you could see his sleazy slacks through, his rolled up shirtsleeves, his pot swelling out over his belt in a way Bebb's never would have. Bebb was always too buttoned in, trussed up for that, almost always. Babe didn't seem in a hurry like Bebb, seemed looser, pinker. And there was nothing wrong with either of his eyes. I kept watching for a telltale flutter. There was nothing.

To Sharon he said, "Child, your daddy and me we sprouted up from seeds in the same womb. The first thing I ever touched was your daddy tucked up next me in the same dark. First thing I ever heard was him holler out when they whumped the breath of life into him five minutes after they left off whumping me. It wasn't just the same milk we drunk out of the same teats, it was all the same first sights and smells and sounds of life. You take a pair of chimps humped up together in a cage with their big scared eyes watching out through the bars, that was your daddy and me to a T. Watching the sky turn black as thunder. Watching our cripple daddy staring out the window at us with his unshaved whiskers. Watching the fearsome things shadows do on the ceiling nights if somebody bumps the bulb and hearing our poor, wore-out mama say bitter words made her wish she'd bit her tongue out soon as she said them. We were a pair of comical-looking little fat chimps hanging on to each other for dear life while the world come bearing down on us like a express train." A flying saucer hovered above him like a hat and above that the sounds of Bertha moving around upstairs looking for flies.

Sharon said, "Bip never talked about it. I couldn't ever picture him being any different than the way I knew him, and all the time I knew him he looked the same. Luce said she bet even in his crib he used to lay there fat and bald-headed in his double-breasted suit."

Babe said, "The only toy we had between us was a beat-up old Erector set with a wind-up motor they give us out of the missionary box because they were ashamed to ship it off that way to the heathen. It use to set over there under the moonrocks. Daddy use to lay on a sofa next the stove. If the hens weren't setting right, Mother she'd bring and lay eggs up around him where the warmth would hatch them out. Didn't he use to cackle his head off just to spite her when the Eastern Stars come," and then "Bawk, bawk, bawk, *begawk*," Babe went with his head rocked back like a man gargling, "puck, puck, puck, *petawket*," with tears of amusement welling up in his eyes. "Laugh? I . . ."

"No wonder Bip never made a feature of talking about it," Sharon said. She traced a raindrop down the wavy pane behind her.

He said, "Honey, he just turned the lock on those times and threw out the key. He was a bag stuffed full of times he didn't talk about. He made out like the only time it ever was was the present time and you better make the most of that before it got stuffed in the bag too. He cleared out of Points first chance he got because Points was those two little sad-sack chimps with a setting hen for a father and a bitter blow for a mother plus a few other things besides he'd stuffed away and sat on the lid on.

Now I stayed put. Maybe I just didn't have the get up and go. I didn't try to make out like things never happened that happened. Maybe I should of. I moved right in on those things. I took over this pitiful place all stunk up with the old days like they were something crawled in between the walls and died, and I moved the future in like furniture. What you're looking at it's the future," he said, including the whole Uforium with the sweep of his arm.

"Friends," he said, "there's lots of kooks and phonies in this business, but what we've got here, it's treasure from on high. It's the hope of the world come true."

When he mentioned moving in and taking over, I thought the moment had come to bring up for better or worse the whole delicate business of what we were there for, but as soon as he started in on the Uforium, I decided that it would be like passing the plate during the elevation of the host.

Gertrude Conover said, "You said you were expecting us and you recognized us right away. Those seem very remarkable things, Mr. Bebb."

Babe said, "I've seen things and done things that make recognizing you folks look like a card trick."

"It's interesting you should say that," Gertrude Conover said, "because I believe in remarkable things myself. All my life I've hungered after them the way other people hunger after money or God. I am an old woman, but I have never given up the hope that before my time comes, I will see something truly remarkable. If your brother were here he would quote Scripture to me. My dear," she said, turning to Sharon, "what's the part about the man who saw Jesus as a baby and said now at last he could die happy?"

Babe waited while Sharon shook her head. Then he said, "Lord, now lettest thou thy servant depart in peace, for mine eyes have seen thy salvation, Gertrude Conover." He said both of her names together the way Bebb always had, and you could see that it had its effect on her as she stood there with the one white glove that she'd put on for protection against moongerms.

"I thought I had gotten over the worst part of missing him," she said. "You must miss him too."

Looking down at his wet shoes, his eyebrows raised, he said, "For forty years we didn't give each other much as the time of day."

Later, when the show came, it came without warning. It had started to rain hard, and standing in the streaming doorway Gertrude Conover tried to signal Callaway to come in if he wanted to, but he didn't see her. Of all the things we were there to talk about we talked about none of them but the rain instead, the trip down, a place to stay nearby. Like a great wave, the discovery of Babe and who he was had carried us so far so fast that when it receded we were left high and dry, gasping for anything to say that would disguise what utter strangers we were. And then out of the blue he said, "Now you just watch this," and with a snap of his wrist sent something spinning through the air, then another and another until there were as many as three or four of them moving slowly through the air at once. Some landed on the relief map where he seemed to be aiming them, some clattered to the floor, slid off into corners. There was a whole drawer of them apparently—flat, round, colorless—and like an overfed discobolus he half crouched there in the dim light with his see-through raincoat touching the floor as he skimmed more and more of them out toward the map.

At the same time he must have thrown some switch because in addition to the flying saucers, the air was filled with flying saucer noises, the blips and beeps of electronic sound, insect-like chirpings. Lights came flashing off and on, little pinpoints of light, flotillas of them, spinning around the room with the saucers and saucer sounds until I began to lose all track of the fly-specked shades, the photographs, the rain, and it was as if Sharon and Gertrude Conover and I were floating through outer space ourselves. The strobes made constellations of us, the Blue Curls and Bare Midriff taking their place with the Big Dipper and Orion as there slowly floated to the surface of all the other sounds the sound of Babe's recorded voice sonorous and crepuscular like the travelogue narrator of my youth bidding his sunset farewells. "They're coming," he said, "just like we always dreamed they would. They're falling soft as goose down. They're twittering like birds in spring. The sky's ablaze. The heaven's afire."

"Old folks in nursing homes look up," Babe's voice said, "and folks in hospitals with tubes running through them and needles under their skin. Poor folks look up that can't afford shoes for their children's feet. The children look up—the little one with the harelip on him, the one her daddy twists her little arm off nearly when he comes home drunk and out of work. The whores with their painted lips and the sodomites look up. The rich folks with their treasure stored up where moth and rust doth corrupt and thieves break through and steal. And the thieves look up through the lonesome bars of their cage. Folks, we're all looking up at where hope comes from, and there's not a pair of eyes that isn't wet with tears."

Like a plague of locusts the cosmic chirpings grew in volume, then subsided again. Babe's recording said, "They're better than us up there. They're a zillion times smarter. Where we've got shots against measles and whooping cough, they've got shots against death. They don't war and raise hell with each other because they don't have to. They've each one got all they want and then some. They got us on their minds, friends. They're all heart, and they're set on bailing us out soon as ever they can. There's a few have paid us visits already. All we got to do is show them we're ready, and that's where SOS comes in.

"First there's S for signals. The wrong signal's worse than none. Find out how to signal from your own place right. That's how they know they got friends down here waiting.

"Next there's O for outerspace-watch. If we don't keep a watch on day and night, we'll never know when they're coming. Then too it's the way we know when one of them touches down for a look-see. Sign up for outerspace-watch.

"The last S is Saturday meeting. At Saturday meeting we get to find out who our friends are. We swap sightings. We listen to hearings. Folks, the most important part of Saturday meeting is we all get together just to plain *look up*.

"So that's SOS.

"Shove Off Soon.

"Send On Spacemen.

"Save Our Skins. Meantime if you've got a SOS needs attending to out of your own life, sign up to see Babe Bebb. Consultations by appointment only."

The canned speech, the beeps, the lights, they all ended as suddenly as they had begun, and into the fresh silence Sharon's voice fell small and flat as a coin. "Jesus," she said. "It's Bip all over with the Gospel left out."

With her loveliest souvenir of an eighteenth century smile Gertrude Conover said, "Lord now lettest thou thy servant depart in peace."

When Babe looked at me, I couldn't think of a thing to say. We'd run out of Dewar's and by now the package store would be closed up tight. We had no place to spend the night. I'd never been persuaded even by Bebb's eloquence that the Gospel was for me, but when it was left out, I missed it. The floor was littered with what I could see were some sort of plastic container lids. They said Sunshine on them. I had the kind of headache that clamps down tight like a football helmet. I forced some sort of ghastly smile, and even as I felt it turning to stone, Babe reached out with his plump hand and touched my cheek the way he might have reached out to straighten a picture. "Why you're all wore out, boy," he said. It would be impossible to overstate the effect of his diagnosis.

You put up a brave front in this world, especially if it's the world I was born into. No matter what sad thing happens, you go on with business as usual if for no other reason than that it would never do to let down in front of the help. You go on teaching your ninth graders the difference between *like* and *as*. You keep the lawn mowed in the summer and the walk shoveled in the winter. When you find out your wife has been cheating on you with your muscle-bound nephew, you don't throw them out but get out yourself. You move into Mrs. Gunther's boarding house where after a while things work themselves out somehow and you get back together again so almost entirely as if nothing had ever happened that it might as well not have, for all you take away from it that might have saved your soul. When at an odd, disconnected moment in your life you shack up with a girl like Laura Fleischman only to drift through it like a ghost, you don't either mourn your lost youth or make a wild stab at recapturing it. You must reconcile yourself to spending the rest of your middle age making the best of things because you can no longer make the most of them. When your father-in-law goes up in flames on a New Jersey potato field, there goes up with him what's probably the only chance you'll ever get to make a fool of yourself worth making.

With his smile shimmering like a moonlit ruin, Brownie tells you he's lost his faith.

Tony picks up what may or may not be your daughter Lucy and says, "Well I'll be goddammed."

"Why you're all wore out," Babe said, touching my face. He said, "Why you're all wore out, boy," and it was like hearing my name spoken in a place where I thought there was no one who knew it and I'd all but forgotten it myself.

When Callaway appeared at last, running through the rain with a piece of newspaper over his head, Babe moved us all on into the living room which turned out to look much as I imagine it must have in Bebb's day—a slippery horsehair sofa with an oval photograph over it of what might have been Bebb's grandparents standing shoulder to shoulder like a police line-up. They looked goiterish, overupholstered and mentally unsound.

There was a parlor organ with pieces of worn carpet on the treadle, a plastic poinsettia plant, a wastepaper basket stuck all over with seashells. From where I sat the stairway was visible through the door and I could see the socks and shoes of Bertha Bebb sitting at the top of it. The very air smelled of the nineteenth century and there must have been things in there that hadn't been touched since nineteenth century fingers had touched them, and yet I remember thinking that for all I knew contacts of Babe's from outer space might have padded across those rag rugs and looked at the same things I was looking at through whatever they used for eyes.

Bebb had left the house to Sharon, but Babe was living in it. Bebb had told us to do something nice for Jesus with it, but Babe was already doing something with it which, though maybe it wasn't just what Bebb had in mind, had at least a quality to it that he would have found not uncongenial. Even with the Gospel left out, there was lots of hope in it, and I felt sure Bebb would have liked the part about everybody looking up—the sodomites, the sick people with needles under their skins. So I think if I had had my way I would have simply let well enough alone and started heading for home as soon as we decently could. But not Sharon.

Sitting next to Babe on the horsehair sofa she told him the house he was living in was her house, and if she didn't say that she was planning to put him out on the street, she didn't say she wasn't either, but all of this in such an easy, loose-limbed kind of way, with whatever Southern accent she'd lost up North coming back as if she'd never lost it, that there was nothing Babe could have gotten hold of to hit her back with even if he'd felt like hitting her. Whatever came to matter to her later on, what mattered to her then, I think, was not that Bebb had left her a house but that he'd left her a past, a background, an origin. As an adopted child she'd never known the family she really belonged to, and in Sutton, Connecticut, she never found anything she belonged to either—the Sharanita Shop, the yoga, the Evelyn Wood Speed Reading had all come and gone. But whether she chose to take it over or not, she belonged here. That was what I felt she wanted not just Babe but all of us to hear. The asbestos shingles, the nasturtiums, the scorched lawn, it was less that they belonged to her than that she belonged to them, and she had Bebb's will to prove it. "To his surviving children is what it says," she said, "and I'm the only children he ever had as far as he ever let on anyway."

"I don't guess surviving was all that easy either, honey," Babe said, and the way he turned around to look at her beside him there, his plump neck contracted awkwardly by the closeness of the range, reminded me more of his brother than anything I'd seen him do yet.

"I'd never have made it without Bip," Sharon said. I remember her sitting beside Bebb that way in Armadillo once with the Holy Love cross blinking on and off over their heads, the setting sun turning their faces to gold.

Babe said, "He had a way with him, your old Bip, there's no two ways about it. It's why this place come to him instead of me in the first place. Why there wasn't a birthday Mother ever had he didn't remember her, and even when it wasn't her birthday he'd send things. There'd be picture postcards from the drummer hotels, and he'd ring her up, all that. For years it was me and Bert that looked after her hand and foot, but it was him that got the credit. Funny thing. You might think it would of been him that got the blame for not being there to look after her his ownself, but instead it was me that got the blame for not being him. His whole life long he fell on his feet that way."

Sharon said, "Except when he fell on his ass."

Babe clamped his jaws tight on that one. He raised both hands and let them drop to his knees. He said, "Bad news travels fast, and it travels far." He gave a fat man's sigh, like a tire going flat. He said, "I know he did time, and I know what he did it for. He had his shameful side to him the same as everybody else. The thing about your daddy was he could wink his eye at it better than the rest of us."

Sharon said, "He was always winking that eye of his," and it was at that point, without warning, that Babe did an imitation of it that made my scalp go cold because it was both so like and so unlike the real thing.

He let both eyes flutter closed, then open again, as though they had a life independent of the rest of him, but whereas with Bebb you felt that it was the rest of him that was in the driver's seat and the eye just momentarily getting into the act, with Babe it was the other way around. Just for an instant I had the feeling that it was only when I saw those eyes flicker that I'd caught a glimpse of whatever it was that was doing the driving inside Babe.

The last part of our conversation that rainy afternoon had to do with Jesus. Gertrude Conover was the one who explained how Bebb wanted us to do something nice for him down there, and Babe said, "Well, Leo was always big on Jesus," and Gertrude Conover said, "It was an enthusiasm I'm afraid I could never share."

She said, "Jesus was one of the great bodhisattvas, there's no argument about that, but I always felt he was a little bit of a snob. If you weren't a prostitute or a crook of some kind, he never had much time for you. He was the first person most people would have thought of turning to for comfort back in those days, but I never felt that way myself. The one I always thought I would like to turn to was Pontius Pilate. He was a very civilized man for his day, and he gave you a great sense of resourcefulness and strength, not unlike Nelson Rockefeller."

"Maybe so," Sharon said, "but it's still Jesus that Bip wants us to do something nice for," and we all thought about it in silence for a while.

Callaway, who had been standing against the wall as narrow and dark as a grandfather's clock was the first to speak. He said, "Yucca mollentow cumble walla baptree," and I nodded thoughtfully right along with the others.

Gertrude Conover said, "Maybe so. Or perhaps there could be some kind of a playground for children. Or a vegetable garden. The vegetables could be given to the poor."

"Or you could set up a big screen and call it the Jesus drive-in," Sharon said, "Babe here could get some of his spacewatchers to watch if there's anything going on in the back seat."

"There's one thing while we're thinking," Gertrude Conover said. She had taken off one glove and was fanning herself with it. She said, "You never did explain how it was you knew to expect us, Babe."

What with the rain and the approach of dusk, it had gotten so hard to see that Babe went to the fringed lamp to turn it on. "I had a hearing on it," he said. He reached up under the fringe for the switch.

"A hearing?" Sharon said.

He turned on the lamp, and his face was lit up from beneath. "From outerspace," he said.

Gertrude Conover said, "You mean they actually come all the way down here to give you a special message like that?"

"They transmit them special," Babe said. Then, "Look."

Opening his mouth up as far as it would go and stretching it out sideways with his two forefingers, he leaned over the lamp so that it would

light it up as much as possible. There was no doubt in my mind that it
was the same mouth that we had seen the photograph of in the Uforium.
As far back as you could see, each tooth had a black dot in the middle of it
about the size of a mousedropping.

7

WHATEVER THE TRUTH is about visitors from other worlds, we all of us
visit back and forth enough between worlds right down here, heaven
knows. There is the public world, the world of things which happen more
or less out in the open where people can see them. Babe's eventually
explaining to us about his teeth, for instance; his insisting that we stay
there at his house instead of putting up at a motel with Callaway; Brownie's somewhat disheveled arrival by air the next day, and so on—the sort of
things that would get into your biography if anybody ever decided to write
one. And then there is the private world, the world of things which happen inside your skin or which, if they happen out in the open where
people can see them, are the kind of things that nobody would be apt to
pay much attention to. Much of the time you hardly pay much attention
to them yourself, and yet they are the things which make the difference
between a good day and a bad day, things which in the long run may
even have more to do with the difference between a good life and a bad
life than the job you work at or the person you marry. I think of things like
landscape and weather, things like the fact that there was only one bathroom at Babe's which we all five of us had to share, plus the subfact that
the john seat wouldn't stay up on its own so you had to hold it in place
when you were taking a leak, and how these things cast a faint but significant shadow over our whole stay. I think of the sound of Bertha's fly
swatter. Like a newly grown moustache or the hum of a refrigerator, you
got so used to it in time that you were hardly conscious of it, yet something
inside you was always waiting like a fly itself for the next time it struck one
of its deadly blows.

And I think of things more elusive still than those, though perhaps
related to them. I think of a persistent feeling I had, for instance, that
things both were what they seemed and yet were something else too, the
way on the eve of our departure from Sutton I knew of course that Sharon
and I were married, had had children, had come apart and together again;
yet at the same time when Laura Fleischman and I were alone together for
a moment, it was somehow she and I who were married all those years so
that my unlived life with her and my lived life with Sharon challenged

and menaced each other in unsettling ways. Babe was Bebb's twin brother, not Bebb, and yet there were moments when, right in the very act of looking at him and cataloguing the differences between them in my mind, I would find that it was Bebb I was looking at. And Gertrude Conover. The more she tended to talk on about her earlier lives—often her accounts were much fuller than I have recorded them here, the parallels she drew between Pontius Pilate and Nelson Rockefeller, for example, going on at considerably greater length—the more I was inclined to believe that, as Sharon put it, the bulb was starting to go dim. Her stocking seams were not always straight any more, an occasional hairpin was left dangling from her blue curls. Yet who was saner than Gertrude Conover? Who better than she knew all the best short-cut diagonals to the heart of things: coming right out and asking if Babe had been to the moon, or coming toward you with that sideways tack of hers, looking at you half over one shoulder, which suggested always that she was taking the most direct route, the alternatives to which might involve two or three more lives to travel, two or three thousand more miles. Nightmarish is too strong a word but dreamlike may be not quite strong enough to describe this feeling I kept having, and I sometimes think, looking back, that what triggered it was that moment before we left home when my nephew Tony for the first time held Lucy in his arms and in a single instant I knew that she was both my daughter and possibly not my daughter at all.

Brownie's arrival became another case in point. He got off the plane in Spartanburg looking just like himself if not more so—his Harry Truman sportshirt dark with sweat at the armpits, his sky-blue slacks, his white suede loafers—and almost before I saw him, I smelled him, the usual sweet strain of after-shave adapted for full orchestra, positively Tchaikovskian, as he came pushing through the glass doors with his smile hung out in the sun like laundry. Just Sharon and I were there to meet him—Gertrude Conover was making the most of our absence by taking a bath while the coast was clear—and Brownie embraced us both with if anything more than his usual warmth. He was full of his flight from Houston.

He said, "It was so peaceful there up above the clouds. I thought how when it's storming down here, up there the sun's always shining. It's like fairyland, and all the sad, cruel things that happen, they're like they never happened. If a man could stay up there long enough, it might give him back his faith again."

He listed slightly to one side at this, and I thought it was just the weight of his bag which he'd refused to let me take, but then I noticed how pale and clammy he looked and, despite the after-shave, the unshaved stubble on his face. When I tried to steady him, he pushed me gently away and setting down his bag took off his glasses and wiped around under his eyes with his monogrammed handkerchief. Brownie without his glasses is always an unsettling sight—like a nun out of her habit—and the more so because the heavy frames across their top keep a kind of lid on his smile which without them you're afraid a strong current of air might carry away and Brownie with it.

He said, "I'll be all right in a minute, dear. I'm afraid I took a little something on the plane when the girl offered it. It's gone right to my head."

Sharon's voice rang with admiration. She said, "Why Brownie, you're smashed," and immediately I could see she was right, but if on one level it made sense of things—the pallor, the starboard list, the after-shave so strong that he'd probably gargled with it—on another level, in the same near-nightmarish way, it threatened sense itself. Brownie smashed? Black white? Up down?

Sharon said, "Listen, Bip always said flying scared the piss out of him too. If a couple of belts help, why not?"

Brownie had sat down on his suitcase with his hairy bare arms folded in his lap and his glasses lying over one sky-blue knee. People had to walk around him like furniture. He said, "Oh I'm not scared of flying, dear. That's not the problem. When life doesn't mean much to you any more, death doesn't mean so much either."

It is not an easy thing to look miserable when all your teeth will do is smile, but it was one of Brownie's accomplishments. He said, "I had a talk with John Turtle before I left. I told him right out how the reason I haven't put on a service at Holy Love since Rose Trionka's wedding is because I'm not a believer any more. I can't preach faith of our fathers living still, dear, when my own faith's curled up inside me and died."

A porter wheeling a cart piled with luggage had to back and fill to get around him, but he didn't seem to notice. He said, "I take something every chance I get to help me forget."

So my private world as it existed down there in Poinsett for a while was a world marked by a kind of double vision not unrelated for all I know to the doubleness of having to use the john and hold the seat up simultaneously, a world in which I kept seeing a single, solid person like Brownie or Babe or Gertrude Conover pull apart somehow into two, the way if your stereopticon gets out of whack, the single 3-D view of the Grand Canyon, say, turns out to have been all along two views which only your gullible eye has given the illusion of unity. Brownie, that sugar-coater of all the bitterest pills of Scripture, his faith as ineffably sweet as his after-shave, went so queerly out of focus that beside him on his suit-case sat Brownie the godforsaken with his smile gone pale and clammy in the Carolina sun. It was with a great sense of relief that on the drive home from the airport, we moved back into the public world again, the world of getting from one place to another place, and I listened to Sharon describing to Brownie, who had the window wide open and the wind ballooning out his Harry Truman shirt, the solid, historical events of our arrival in Poinsett and our discovery of Babe. I don't know how much attention Brownie paid, but I paid plenty, held on tight to the reassurance that

Sharon and I had both of us experienced more or less the same thing. It is when the public world begins to pull into two like the private one that the real nightmare starts. Irony is another word for it, I suppose—the good turning out to be the bad, the real the unreal. It is one thing to talk about it, but to run into it head-on is something else again.

Sharon was saying, "Like I mean you've got to hear this Babe to believe him. You don't know if he really believes it himself. How could he believe it?"

She said, "The UFOs, that's one thing. Lots of people believe in UFOs. They believe in them because they want to believe in them the same as they want to believe in ghosts or Scripture or real-life monsters. Bip was like that. He said to me one time, 'Honey, I'm a born believer. You tell me anything you want makes this world out to be crazier than it already is and one gets you ten I'll be believing it in less time than it takes you to tell it.' I'm the other way. I don't believe a quarter ounce over what I've got to. Life's a whole lot simpler like that, and it saves you being disappointed."

In the mirror I could see Brownie looking up at the bleached-out, hazy sky where he'd taken whatever it was he was only now paying for. He still hadn't put his glasses back on, and his face looked blown clear by the rush of hot air through the window. Beside him Sharon was so wrapped up in what she was saying that she didn't seem to care whether he was listening or not. Her hair had blown across her cheek and a strand of it into her mouth, but she didn't seem to care about that either.

She said, "Now Babe, he doesn't just believe they've landed. That's kid stuff. He believes there's millions more fixing to land any day. He believes they're going to come and take away everybody that signs up at the Uforium to a place where they wipe their tails with hundred dollar bills and there's shots you can get against death. He believes they've picked him out to be head of the whole show, and he's got this room full of moonrocks and burned up space suits to prove it."

Brownie let his head flop sideways on the seat-back, and taking advantage of his momentarily facing in her direction, Sharon pressed her point home. She said, "Brownie, that man's got him a special radio set right in his mouth. He showed it to us in his own front parlor. I thought I was going to have a hemorrhage. Would you believe teeth with transistors in them no bigger than that? Creatures from outer space installed them for him special. They wired old Babe up for stereo so they can ring him up any hour of day or night and tell him what's new on Mars. Jesus. I said, 'Babe, you've got to be putting us on,' so he opened up real wide and told us 'Listen.'"

We had all of us sat there in that parlor and listened. Callaway with his back to the wall, Gertrude Conover as if she was listening to the Budapest Quartet do Beethoven at the McCarter theater, Sharon like a lion tamer with her head almost in the man's mouth. The grandparents stared down bug-eyed from their oval frame over the sofa. The rain blew against the asbestos shingles. Somebody's stomach growled.

Sharon said, "Of course if you listen real hard, even nothing's got a sound to it. Only this wasn't just nothing. It was a kind of hum like a power plant. It was like what you hear inside a shell. Bopper, how do you think Babe made a sound like that come out of his mouth?"

I said, "I didn't hear it. I can believe it, but I didn't hear it where I was."

Sharon said, "Well, I heard it, but I can't believe it. I can't even believe Babe believes it."

I said, "Gertrude Conover heard it."

Sharon said, "Gertrude Conover's like Bip. She wants to believe stuff like that. It's how she gets her kicks."

Like a man coming out of ether, Brownie said, "What did the message in his mouth say?"

She said, "Not a damn thing. He said there was nothing coming through right then. Like the sound the TV makes before the Mickey Mouse starts."

I said, "What do you think about it, Brownie? UFOs. Martians. The whole scene."

Brownie had put his glasses on by now, and they helped to pull him back into one piece again, the frown of the frames and the jubilation of the teeth coming together into the single 3-D Brownie I'd always known. He said, "Luke seventeen, dear. 'As it was in the days of Noah, so shall it be also in the days of the Son of Man.' It was the last sermon I preached at Holy Love. When the end is coming, you can expect many peculiar things to start to happen.'"

"You still believe the end is coming?" Sharon said.

Brownie said, "I would like to believe it. I would like to believe it will all end soon, and there are signs. There are many similarities between our time and Noah's time. I will mention only a few." To be talking about Scripture again after so long seemed to put a little of the color back into his cheeks.

He said, "For example, in Noah's time it says that men went away from the presence of God, and all you have to do is any Sunday of the year take a look at your ball parks and race tracks, your Disneylands and so forth to see that most people in this world just aren't very interested in God any more. Also it says it was in Noah's day that men started marrying two wives, and when you stop to think about what goes on in our own divorce courts these days, why two wives per man doesn't seem like anything to write home about. Noah's time was a time when Scripture tells us all flesh was corrupt, and I don't have to remind you what goes on in massage parlors, dear, or in porn palaces where they show things on the screen that give people ideas they would never have had on their own in a thousand years."

"Speak for yourself," Sharon said.

Brownie said, "There shall be signs in sun, and moon, and stars, dear. Maybe the UFOs and everything are one of the signs."

He waited until we'd arrived at his motel and Sharon was out of ear-shot to say what I suppose must have been on his mind the whole time. He said, "When you were there at Rose Trionka's wedding, you said something to me that's had me mulling it over in my mind ever since. You said Mrs. Conover told you she'd had a chat with Mr. Bebb—since he passed on, I mean—and you said as far as you knew, there was no way of telling whether it was just in her mind or whether—"

I remember him standing there in that cave of a motel room with the picture window at one end, the wall to wall carpet, the Hollywood beds, and hesitating when he reached that point. On the wall behind him was a big reproduction of a painting in colors that made your eyes ache. It showed a millpond with the mill reflected in it, weeping willows, blue sky, a boy sitting on the grassy bank fishing with his dog beside him. If I hadn't been somehow taught from the cradle to think that a picture like that was the last gasp, I might have thought it was the most beautiful thing I'd ever seen. I had a feeling Brownie might find it a comfort when he got around to looking at it later.

He said, "You thought maybe there was one chance in a million Mr. Bebb was still alive, and maybe if we came down here it could just be we'd find him. You said it might be he was hiding out down here from all the people who were after him those last days and maybe he needed our help. It's why I came, dear. Just that one in a million chance."

With technicolor greens and day-glo yellows the artist had painted the woods stretching off into the distance on the far side of the pond, trees beyond trees fading away into a golden haze like a king's treasure, and I wondered what was so bad about an artist showing a world I would have traded this world for in two seconds flat.

Brownie was almost whispering now. He said, "I don't suppose you've seen anything that makes you think he's still alive." At such close range the after-shave was no longer enough to camouflage whatever he'd had on the plane. He had reached out and taken my hand to steady himself. There were pinpoints of sweat on his upper lip.

I could have mentioned the man I'd spotted from the balcony in the Library of Congress and Callaway's nosebleed. I could have confided in him some of my more fanciful thoughts when Babe first came bouncing into the Uforium in his see-through raincoat, but any of that would have been to paint the kind of picture I'd been brought up to look down my nose at, so instead of a golden haze, I brushed in a cool, grey wash. I said, "I don't think so, Brownie. You'll have to see what you think yourself."

Out of the bathroom came Sharon's voice. She said, "Hey, Brownie. Guess what. They've got a blue light in here that sterilizes the seat in case of moongerms."

Brownie's smile glinted in the shadows, and he released my hand. He said, "You can't be too careful these days."

He said, "If you don't mind, dear, I think I'll just lay down for a few minutes and rest my eyes."

That motel room of Brownie's became our secret meeting place, our haven, as the days went by. Callaway's next door was just like it and just as convenient, but it was Brownie's we always ended up in. Maybe it was the boy fishing in the millpond that did it. In any case the effect of our staying under Babe's roof was to make it virtually impossible to talk privately among ourselves about what we'd come for, and Babe didn't seem in any hurry to bring it up himself. He made little jokes about it instead. *See will Sharon let you turn on her dishwash, hear?* or *It don't do to rile up Sharon or you'll come home some night to find the door latched on you.* Little jokes about Jesus. *Where you reckon Jesus wants this sack of groceries put? Gertrude Conover, I've got a notion Jesus might be tickled pink if we dug us a swimming pool out back and asked the black folks over for a dip.*

The first morning we were there started with a joke about Jesus. It was still very early and I was dimly aware of chicken noises outside when I heard Babe softly calling my name in the hall. By the time I'd pulled on a pair of pants and made it out of the room without waking Sharon, he had gone downstairs. Peering over the bannister, I saw him standing there in what I took at first glance to be a space suit but turned out to be a sweatsuit that covered him from wrists to ankles with the hood tied under his chin and his big pink face swelling out of it like the sewed-on face of a doll. He was a man-sized kewpie doll beaming up the stairs at me with his hood going up in a point and his flimsy grey legs.

He said, "There was a fellow down here in a beard and sandals and a hatbrim made of sunshine asking after you. Said you were fixing to do something nice for him. Come take a little jog with me and could be he'll turn up again." So much for the joke, but in any event it was how it happened that the first time Babe and I had alone together was somewhere around 6 A.M. dogtrotting off across the scorched yard where the chickens skittered out of our way and then padding on down the hard-packed, tomato soup-colored road.

I am a track man from way back and have coached it for years at Sutton High, but I was no match for Babe when it came to condition. Long past the point where I could handle any more than a few gasped syllables, he was still able to handle short sentences. He pointed out sights—shanty town, a pig farm where he and Bebb had worked as boys, a stretch of dusty hillside that he said was a favorite landing place for saucers. He talked about saucers, puffing, his eyes bulged out but the words still coming. He said, "There's some say I'm cuckoo. A phony. You name it. So what? Sticks and stones. It's the wave of the future. Hope of the world. Most folks I don't tell the half of it. Come see me in the office sometime and I'll show you things. Blow your mind."

He talked about Jesus. He said, "You thought I was funning you about Jesus. I was and wasn't both. Know something? Someday Jesus'll climb out of a saucer. Sunshine in his hair. Gather his own up just like it says. Only he's a spaceman, that's what. You'll see."

More for my sake than for his, I thought, he slowed down a little after a while. From a distance the sweet-and-sour smell of the pig farm was sweeter than Brownie's after-shave in the early morning air. We'd turned off the main road and were trotting through a pine wood, the needles so thick and soft you could hardly hear us. To make up for the reduction in speed, Babe was raising his knees higher, pumping his arms harder. He named names—*Red bud*—*Fat pine*—busting open with his ankle-high sneaker a mouldering stump all gold and henna and turpentine smell inside. *Stredwigs*—two or three squat, pitted gravestones inscribed Stredwig and set at crazy angles within the remains of a barbed wire fence, a couple of rusted-out cans. "Bert was a Stredwig," he said. "My poor old Shirley T. My sweet, hurt love."

He said "Thought the world of Leo. Close to killed her when he passed. The way she carried on. Snuck off to the mall after dark. Smashed Western Auto's window all to hell. They didn't press charges, thanks be. Some folks are all heart, and that's the truth."

He talked more about truth. He said, "Truth is it broke me up too when Leo passed. My own flesh I hadn't seen for years and now won't ever see. I had this dream. Leo was on a kid's swing. Funny thing. Says, 'No hard feelings, Babe.' Two times like that. 'No hard feelings, Babe.' He'd got this all-day sucker in his mouth so the words come out crooked and wet. He was the one named me Babe even though I drew breath five minutes sooner than him. 'Oh Babe,' he said. He tried to touch me only the swing pulled him out of reach. Farther and farther. 'Oh Babe,' he said."

He said, "The truth hurts. This will he left. When I heard he'd shot the place clean out from under me, it hurt. Not just the place. There's other places. But him being the one shot it. What if I didn't have a nickel to my name? What if I was sick and didn't have another place to go? I could have passed before him for all he knew and Bert left without a roof over her head. Her that always thought the world of him and him of her."

He said, "Well, a man's got to do what he thinks, and that's the truth. He left it to Sharon. Why not? She's his only surviving children like she said. Lucille Yancey never could have another one of her own. After what happened to that one she had." Babe stepped up the pace again. Through the trees you could see a black man in a white T-shirt hitchhiking to work, a woman dumping a pan of water out a window.

Babe said, "Death leaves a awful mess," jogging around what could

have been a squirrel once or a cat or part of one of the Stredwigs. "Hell,
so does life." The sweat had soaked through his sweatsuit leaving a Ror-
schach-shaped stain between his shoulder blades.

Not slackening his speed, Babe said, "There's some might fight a will
like that. Take for instance where's the papers? Was Sharon adopted legal?
You got to have papers. There's ways to fight if a man wants to fight. Feel
the old ticker ticking. Pumps the poison out. Who wants to fight? Kin
fighting kin. Only a man can't help thinking. Sharon got proof she was
adopted legal? Got papers?"

In sight of home again—we'd come a rough circle—he slowed down
and wheeled on me, bouncing around me like a ball with his head cocked
sideways and his guard up, jabbing at me with his right, that steaming
tub of a man gotten up like a kewpie, a gnome. I made some kind of
pathetic show of jabbing back. I could feel my pulse in my ears, my teeth.
I said, "Don't worry."

I said, "Won't throw you out. Got our own place. Lousy shape. I've
had it."

We'd stopped at the back stoop and I leaned over double to wolf
enough breath to finish. I said, "Just needed the vacation. Plus what Bip
said. The Jesus thing."

Babe had pushed off his hood and run his hand through his hair so
that it stood out in rays like the sun on old maps. He said, "You hold on
to Jesus, boy," and winked at me, blinked would be a better word for
distinguishing it from what Bebb did. Bebb did it with one eye, not even
knowing it; Babe did it with two eyes, knowing it well.

The blink of Babe. Over the years I've seen it done by other people,
other times. I've even done it myself. You catch the other person's attention—your son in the rear window of the car, for instance, and you on
the front steps to see it drive off with him. Then you squeeze your eyes
shut on the sight of him. It is more deliberate than a wink and takes
longer, says more. It says *You and me, kid.* It closes everybody else out
and that one person in. So Babe to me anyway.

Eyes open again, he shrugged one shoulder high against his cheek to
mop it. He caught my neck in the crook of it, and we were cheek to cheek
there for a moment so brief it almost didn't happen. It happened. The
rust-colored chickens clucking around our feet. The smell of coffee through
the kitchen screen.

So what if he weighed two fifty, had farted on the moon, said rat for
right? When he winked his wink and put his arm around my neck, it was
like the time he said, "Why you're all wore out, boy."

Sharon wasn't the only orphan, after all, and for a moment there Babe
was my father and my mother both, and I would have followed him to the
ends of the earth. Then he let me go, and I went begawking off like one
of the chickens.

What I first thought I saw through the kitchen window was a balloon, a white balloon such as they print *Playland* on or *Happy Birthday*. What was printed on this one were the small, cramped features of Bertha Bebb. She was leaning over the counter getting breakfast. She hadn't put on her wig yet.

Sharon said, "I almost flipped when I busted in on her, but she didn't bat an eye." This was on our drive to meet Brownie's plane that afternoon. "She said it gets awful hot with it on summers. Just like that. She's not as freaked out as you think, Bopper. Soon as she spotted you and Babe tear-assing out of the woods, she said, 'You stand up for your rights, honey. Nobody loves you like yourself.' It's the God's own truth too," Sharon said with her elbow sticking out the window and her hair full of wind.

Like Babe, she spoke of the truth as single, 3-D, not something that pulls apart into the two little Grand Canyons of the stereopticon slide, the right hand and left hand of the God's own truth.

I said, "Did Bip ever tell you anything about what went on when he adopted you? Did he ever happen to mention papers?"

"He didn't like to talk about it," Sharon said. "Like Babe said, Bip was a bag stuffed full of things he didn't talk about."

8

CALLAWAY HAD another nosebleed. He was driving Gertrude Conover someplace, and it started to happen so hard and fast that he had to pull over to the side of the road and stop. She said, "It's the worst I've ever seen him have. It was torrential. He has a trick of pushing up on that bone between the nostrils, but that wouldn't stop it. Nothing would. He needed his hand to hold the handkerchief so he couldn't drive, and I couldn't either, of course. I've kept my license up over the years, but I've lost that part of my nerve. Well, we were stuck there high and dry. What to do? Callaway said sometimes ice helped. Where to get ice? We were in the middle of nowhere. The only building in sight was a brick one with flat roofs and a smokestack like a crematorium. It was the local school. There were a couple of cars parked out front though school must have closed weeks ago, so I told Callaway to sit tight, and I would see what I could find. My dear, I found everything. A very helpful woman, ice beyond the dreams of avarice, a dishtowel to put the ice in. It worked like a charm. The nose was fine again. But now listen to this."

She said, "Do you know what those people were doing in that school? They were setting things up for a Well Baby Clinic, that's what they were doing. Of all the places Callaway's nose could have started to bleed, the one it chose was practically on the front steps of a place where in a very short time all the babies of Poinsett will be gathering." She paused to let this sink in.

Back of Babe's house there was a glider, the two benches facing each other with the little awning over them and the slatted floor you could push with your feet to make it swing. We weren't swinging, but that is where we were sitting, Gertrude Conover on one bench with Sharon and me facing her on the other. Babe was in the Uforium holding consultations. He said there would be people coming in and out most of the day, and it was true—maybe as many as a dozen or so during the course of the morning. It would be hard to generalize about them. A few were black. Some came with children in tow. By and large they looked like country people—leathery, faded, cleaned up for the occasion—but there were several I thought could have been Spartanburg gentry. There was a cadaverous man who was driven up in a pickup truck and had to be helped down out of the cab. There was a black woman on crutches. I had been sitting there in the glider just watching the parade go by when Gertrude Conover started talking about the latest nosebleed, and it wasn't until her portentous pause that I started paying serious attention.

She said, "Of course you can never tell about the always-returners. When it comes time for the man in the street to be reborn, the matter is out of his hands. Everything depends simply on the shape of his karma. If it is a jagged, dangerous shape, say, he will be reborn as a Doberman pinscher perhaps or a juvenile delinquent. If he has unsatisfied desires to work off, the shape of those desires will tell the tale. The timid little soul with dreams of glory will keep being born until he gets to be a Richard Nixon or the head of I.B.M., which is why so many of those high-powered people have timid little souls inside them and have to go to psychiatrists on the sly."

Without looking up from her reading, Sharon pushed her bare feet forward on the slatted floor and started the glider gliding. Gertrude Conover's chiffon scarf fluttered over her shoulder.

She said, "Well, the always-returner is a horse of a different color. He is so full of cosmic consciousness that he doesn't have any more shape than the air we breathe. What little karma he has left wouldn't cover the head of a pin. That means when it comes to rebirth, he is in the driver's seat. He arranges to be born wherever and whenever the fancy takes him. My dear, would you mind? It is making me feel a little giddy." She reached out one foot and placed it on the ground.

She said, "I do not believe in coincidence. I believe Callaway's nosebleed is telling us that Leo Bebb has chosen to be born again in Poinsett, South Carolina, heaven only knows why. I believe there is every reason to expect that one of the babies that will be brought to that clinic today will be him."

I said, "How will you know which baby?"

Sharon said, "There never was a baby born that didn't look a little like Bip till he got some hair on him anyway."

Gertrude Conover said, "Well, we will take Callaway with us. He is the canary in the coal mine. And we will take Brownie if he has recovered from his flight. I'm sure if Leo's there, he will find a way to make himself known to one of us."

Bert had appeared on the back porch and was scattering scraps of bread and lettuce to the chickens. "Heekie, heekie, heekie," she said in her tiny voice. With the sunshine on them, her arms looked as white as the bread. She had a pink ribbon to tie back her curls. "Hey," she said to Sharon, and Sharon said, "Hey, Bert." She looked as if she wasn't a hundred percent sure who Gertrude Conover and I were.

Brownie had recovered. We found him and Callaway having a beer in front of Brownie's TV at the motel, but they seemed glad enough to be interrupted. They had met only once before at the time of Bebb's funeral in the potato field, but it seemed to have been enough to establish a bond between them. Callaway had on an orange and lemon sport shirt so much like the kind Brownie favored that I wondered if he could have lent it to him. The way it set off his black face and spear-shape of bony black chest, I was able for the first time to imagine how he might have looked as a Pharaoh. Gertrude Conover didn't explain her purpose. She just said that we were going to have a look at some babies. As if making a libation to Ra, his face aglitter, Callaway raised his beer in the air and said, "Home fome bayseed tuffa," and then Brownie said, "Suffer little children." A translation? He made a stab at raising his beer too but faltered en route and drained it off instead. "For of such is the kingdom of heaven, dear," he said to nobody in particular, wiping the foam from his upper lip.

We spent a good part of that afternoon looking at babies—babies of all shapes and sizes, babies teetering in under their own steam, carried in, wheeled in. There were clean babies and dirty babies, tragic babies and comic babies. There were creamy, sleek babies and babies with violet circles under their eyes. There were little old men and women disguised to look like babies. There were ladies with sharp yellow pencils and soft Southern voices to write down their health records, nurses and a doctor or two to test the hearing and urine, to examine the vision and blood of babies. There were classrooms set aside for each operation with the dwarf-size desks and chairs pushed off to the side where someday people like me would teach the wind out of their baby sails with maybe nothing worse than such somber verb forms as *if you had, might have been, will have gone*, let alone the grim metaphysics of irony, the helpless babbling in the presence of the unspeakable that is metaphor, the specter at the great feast of language that is spelling and grammar and the four major rules for the use of the comma.

Since Bebb's plane had crashed just about a year earlier, any baby older than a year was automatically disqualified, so we ended up looking at only the ones that didn't show signs of five o'clock shadow with me hovering near the main entrance where they all came in and Sharon lingering between blood and vision and Gertrude Conover moving about pretty much at will, although she kept a weather eye on the parking lot as if suspecting that some baby might get only that far before losing its nerve. We all, of course, kept a constant check on Callaway's nose, and I made a special point of not losing track of Brownie either. I had a feeling that if anybody was to stumble on the reincarnation of Bebb it would be Brownie if only because it would comfort him so—a round, bald baby with a gimpy eye to look after and then finally, in his old age, to look after him.

I was struck by the way every baby has a whole collection of faces that he keeps trying on like party hats and how there's no way of knowing which is the face he'll eventually settle on for the long party of his life. There were one or two babies who looked vaguely like Bebb to me but there were times when they looked vaguely like a dozen other people too, so I made nothing of it. It wasn't long before, like wallpaper samples, they all started to look alike to me, and I stepped outside for a breath of fresh air.

There was a girl sitting on the parking-lot steps in skin-tight shorts and a halter with her hair up in rollers. She said, "You find the one you were looking for all right?" and then, when my only response was a blank stare, added the one word "Babe," which I heard as just plain babe, baby, the baby that in our madness we were looking for back inside that baby-filled school. She *knew*. So just for an instant the whole thing pulled apart again into two things. One thing was this local Daisy Mae splitting out of her pants and as much a part of the real world as the simmering black-top and the glare from the windshields of the parked cars. The other thing was the oracular utterance that had just come out of her moist little mouth like a comic strip balloon which seemed to confirm the reality of a world where messages from outer space were transmitted dentally and dead evangelists turned up in diapers to have their fingers pricked.

She said, "I heard you asking after him at the store," and the two things blessedly came back together again. She was the girl who'd been waiting on the old man when we'd asked directions and "had I found Babe" was all she meant. Even if she had given me back only an illusion of the oneness and solidity of things, it was an illusion I fell all over myself to grab hold of. Not having to explain the crazy business I first thought she'd been asking about, I leapt at the chance to explain everything else. Yes, we had found him. We were staying at his house. We were having the time of our lives. And "It's a shame about his wife," she said, only shame came out *shime*, wife *waff*, as she pulled a pack of Winstons out of her cleavage and lit up with a clink of her Zippo.

She said, "They do say she's getting worse. That poor man. Most everybody feels real sorry for him. It's a crime, the things that happen."

Crime came out *cram* as she pouted out her lower lip to flip the smoke up toward her rollers.

I said, "Lots of people know Babe around Poinsett, do they?" except that I made it Points instead of Poinsett. Anything. Lots of people knew Babe. Lots of people had been to the Uforium. Lots of people had seen him toss his frisbees, had handled his moonrocks. I was like my hypochondriac ex-brother-in-law Charlie Blaine, who, if the electric lights happen to dim, makes sure lots of others have noticed it too so he'll know he isn't going blind or crazy.

She said, "There's other Stredwigs that were peculiar besides her. There was one of them used to set fire to people and lived under a bridge. Bertha doesn't set fire. She just creepycrawls around nights like a coon after trash. If she does anything real peculiar, folks don't make a fuss out of respect for Babe. Most everybody in Points knows Babe Bebb."

"And the Uforium," I said. "I suppose they know about that too."

She said, "They surely know about the Uforium." Leaning back on her elbows against the stair railing, she gave me a long look. She said, "They surely do know about that."

Then Sharon said, "She's got him spotted. You better come quick." Shoving the school door open with one arm, she almost dragged me in with the other. "Jesus," she said. "Over there by the water cooler."

He wasn't a well baby, he was a blind baby. His eyes were deep-set and flat like the eyes a child might push into clay with his thumb. He looked about a year old to me, fat and pasty and dressed in skimpy shorts that his diapers hung down out of and a washed-out Donald Duck shirt that didn't quite cover his belly. He didn't look any more like Bebb to me than a dozen other babies I'd seen that day. He looked more like W. C. Fields if I'd had to say somebody. With one fist he was digging at his cheek as if it was something he wanted to get rid of, and his flat little eyes went all fluttery with the effort. Gertrude Conover was seated on a bench beside the water cooler, and the baby was on her lap. She had her arm around him, and I remember how tanned it looked against that rubbery little leg, how bright her gold bracelet. She said, "I know it's the one. The minute I saw him, the tears spouted out of my eyes," and Sharon said, "Honey, that poor little thing's enough to make tears spout out of anybody's eyes."

It's not just beauty, of course, that's in the eye of the beholder but friendship, love, everything that matters is there, and I suppose that's why in the twinkling of an eye they can vanish. What I mean is there was Gertrude Conover, that dear lady, to use the Wasp phrase, that one person in all of Poinsett who spoke my native language and came from the same Wasp world I came from and about whom my feeling was that if she was slipping, as Sharon said, it only went to accentuate the heights she still had such a long way to slip from—and then in a twinkling this all van-

ished and there instead was old, rich, dotty Gertrude Conover sitting by the
water cooler as irrelevant as grape shears. As she looked down at that poor,
starch-fed child in her lap whose diapers I could tell even at that range
were in desperate need of changing, what she saw was a bodhisattva because that was a more manageable sight to see. It was myself, of course,
that I lashed out at, my own similar distaste for reality as two-faced and
double-crossing to the last drop: a baby, one, and blind as a bat, two.

I said, "When you're dead, you're dead. Christ. Bebb's dead. That's
not Bebb that's crapped in his pants because the dead can't crap any more.
People don't get to come back, and flying saucers haven't landed, and let's
get the hell out of here." But of course my tantrum was in the eye of the
beholder too, and the next thing I knew it also had vanished and for an
instant it was given to me to see Gertrude Conover more or less as maybe
she actually was even when there weren't any eyes around to behold her—
an eighty year old white woman with blue hair and crooked seams and a
baby who looked a little like W. C. Fields asleep with his head against her
throat so she had to hold her chin awkwardly high to accommodate him.
There was a faintly strangled look about her.

She said, "What you say may be true, Antonio. We won't know till
the curtain comes down on the last act. But in the meantime I'll tell you
what I feel." She was talking very quietly so as not to wake the baby, and
I had to bend down to hear her above all the clinic noises going on in the
background. She said, "I'd rather be wrong about all those things I believe
in and more or less alive and interested than right as rain and bored half to
death."

It brought me to my knees or at least the baby did who without warning arched his back so violently that he would have fallen if I hadn't
grabbed him. I took him under the arms and hoisted him up to where he
was lying against my shoulder with my hand under his shirt to smooth his
sticky, bare back. The smell of him was even more overpowering than his
squawling. Gertrude Conover said, "You see. You're doing it too. Just like
the time by the swimming pool."

Except that unlike the time by the swimming pool I knew that I was
doing it. Even before she spoke I had felt myself doing it, the hot trickle
down the side of my nose and around the nostril to where with a sad little
burst it dissolved into the taste of salt. Only it was not because I believed
the baby was Bebb that I was doing it; it was because I couldn't believe
it was Bebb.

Gertude Conover said, "There will be so much less to distract him
being blind. Well, he'll find other ways to see, they always do. He will see
things that are hidden from the rest of us like buried gold."

She said, "All the lives I've met him in before, this is the first time
I've ever held him in my arms. It makes me feel very humble. Just think of
it. The rest of us will all make a break for cosmic consciousness the first
real chance we get, but not his kind. They keep coming back as long as

there's a single straggler left down here to come back for, and you know how long that means, I suppose."

Brownie and Callaway had wandered up by then, and the five of us were all grouped around with the baby and me more or less in the middle so that you might have thought it was some kind of screwball baptism what with the water cooler right there and the way we were so quiet while everybody else was milling around dragging babies into classrooms to have their oil and water checked. You could have heard a pin drop if one had happened to drop from Gertrude Conover's blue hair as she rose from the bench, smoothing the wrinkles out of her lap. She touched the baby lightly on the sole of one foot with her finger. She said, "My dear, what it really comes down to is the Leo Bebbs of the world keep coming back forever."

The mother turned up not long afterwards—a washed-out looking woman with big ears and a transistor radio around her wrist. Before she left with her baby, thanking us for minding it, Gertrude Conover got her name and address and the baby's name. The baby's name was Jimmy Bob Luby, and the last we saw of him was being dragged away backwards in one of those strollers that has a canvas seat you stick your legs through and a tray that comes down in front. He was sucking on the remains of a Milky Way, and like the broken clock that comes right twice a day, his fluttery little eyes looked just right with his expression of mingled apprehension and rapture. ·

We didn't get back to Babe's till dusk, having stopped on the way to drop Brownie and Callaway off at the motel where at Brownie's suggestion we paused to take a little something before supper. Once again we tried to figure out what if anything we could do or try to get Babe to do for Jesus before we started thinking about packing up and going home again. But nobody seemed to be able to keep to the subject very well— partly because of Jimmy Bob, I suppose, and partly, I think, out of a kind of unspoken sense that our simply having come to Poinsett was in itself such a major step on the way to doing something for somebody that we could afford just to coast along on it for a while. And the bourbon and ginger ale slowed us down too, of course, that sickening combination of Brownie's which, as a strict Dewar's-on-the-rocks man myself, I would have ordinarily gagged at but which, its sweetness fading into the sweetness of Brownie's smile and Brownie's smell and the golden haze of trees in the millpond picture, lulled me sweetly.

Bebb was dead, I had said to Gertrude Conover in my moment of exasperation, and Jesus was dead, and though the exasperation was long since gone, the fact was with me still. The dead didn't care whether you did something nice for them or not, and there in that shadowy, wall-to-wall cave with my bourbon and ginger in my hand and vacation in my heart, I didn't much care that they didn't care. I had signed up with Babe for a consultation the next day—he had promised to blow my mind and I was interested in picking his—but I didn't much care about that at the moment either and found myself offering the consultation to Brownie instead. Having arrived only the afternoon before, he hadn't met Babe yet, and it seemed as good a way as any. He said, "That would be very nice, dear."

He was sitting on the foot of his bed with his glasses over his knee again only this time it didn't bother me especially—we were all of us nuns out of habit at that point I guess. "All those babies," he said, shaking his head slowly from side to side. "It's almost enough to restore a man's faith—like little love-notes from Heaven."

Sharon said, "Down the old rat-hole, Brownie," touching his glass with hers, and no rat-hole ever came with so pearly and radiant a facade as the one Brownie raised his glass to.

So by the time we got back to Babe's there wasn't much daylight left and the peepers were peeping and when we pulled up in front, we just sat there in silence for a few minutes taking in the soft and twilight peace of it. The flamingos looked almost real on the front lawn and the asbestos house almost handsome with the pinewoods dark as a dream beyond it and the slope of hillside where maybe someday the celestial armada would land. I put my arm around Sharon's bare shoulder beside me in the front seat, and part of what my arm meant was that it was hers, this place, whether she ever chose to claim it or not, and I was hers too under the same conditions. It was a good moment, in other words, with Gertrude Conover dozing in the back seat, a faint whiff of woodsmoke drifting in from shantytown. All hell broke loose then.

There was a shrill barnyard squawk from the hen house out back, a terrible thump and scuffling as the whole brood panicked, the coppery hens and cocks begawking out of there like the feathery end of the world. Then Bert—that bulky figure looming up behind the chickenwire, that massive grey head charging out of there with such force that the very air thudded out from her in rings.

By the time we'd pulled ourselves together, she was gone, and by the time we made it into the house, she was gone again if the house was where she'd charged to. Only Babe was there. He was in the kitchen, up against the refrigerator as if somebody had stacked him there like luggage. His face looked taken apart and put back together again by somebody who'd never seen a face. The mouth was on crooked, and the eyes were inside out.

He said, "She must have took a spade to it. It was the favorite one she had." By one yellow leg he was holding what could have been some ragged, rusted thing he'd mopped the cellar with.

9

IT WAS BABE, needless to say, that I went to sleep thinking about that night, but it was Bebb I woke up to somewhere around three o'clock in the morning with his daughter asleep at my side and the old house where he'd been born mumbling in the dark. It was a dream that woke me, a dream about Bebb.

He was sitting in a rowboat in the middle of the millpond in Brownie's picture. The light had the rich, golden quality of late afternoon, and the trees were glistening as though there had just been a rain. Bebb was in his shirtsleeves with the oars pulled back through the oarlocks so that the blades stuck up in the air on both sides, glistening and wet like the trees. There was a picnic spread out on the seat beside him. It was a white picnic laid out on a white napkin—peeled hardboiled eggs, sandwiches made of white bread, two glasses of milk. As though he'd been waiting for the right moment to do it, Bebb carefully picked up one of the glasses of milk and leaned forward to hand it to his companion sitting in the stern of the boat. His companion was Jimmy Bob Luby. The glass was all the child could hold, and he needed both hands to hold it. It was filled right up to the brim, and he had to lower his lips to it to take the first sip without spilling any. Bebb sat watching him with great interest. It was only then that I noticed the name of the boat printed across the stern. It was *The Venerable Bede*. I called across the water to him, "You mean the Venerable Bebb, don't you?" and it was the sound of my own laughter at what struck me as the richness of my joke that woke me. Bebb was laughing too. I suppose it was the creaking of the house that had worked its way into my dream or somebody flushing that one communal john.

The Venerable Bebb. It is appalling how few memories I retain from the catechism class of my Catholic boyhood and how still less I have tried to refresh those memories since, but a few hard facts remain. I have always remembered, for instance, that you are a venerable as soon as they start seriously considering you for promotion but that before you can make it all the way to the top there are three qualifications you have to meet consisting of a reputation for sanctity, the heroic quality of your virtues, and a few blue-chip miracles. It was these arcane matters and their possible application to the case of my late father-in-law that I whiled away the time with before I finally went back to sleep again. Thinking is an even queerer business than usual at that hour, of course—thoughts drifting off into sound or touch or flickering through your mind like somebody else's home movie, disjointed, sunstruck, leading nowhere—and my thoughts about Bebb kept turning into pictures of Bebb, hazy conversations with him in which the sound of his voice got confused with a crick in my neck or the sound of my pulse in my ear when I lay a certain way on the pillow. He sat there in his rowboat in the middle of the golden pond eating a sandwich so when he laughed at my joke, he almost choked, the white crumbs spraying out of his mouth like rice at a wedding and his eyes popping, then swallowing hard but with some sandwich still left unswallowed so that when he spoke it was like Callaway speaking—*vesper humdrum keyhole*—which made me smile into the crook of my arm at this second joke.

I thought, if you can call it thinking, of Bebb as venerable, a saint-in-the-making, and of the reputation for sanctity he enjoyed—would he have enjoyed it?—and what it rested on if it could be said to rest on anything. God knows there had been other saints before him who were queer as Dick's hatband, and a whole flock of them went cackling through the night like Bert's chickens—flagpole-sitters, leper-lovers, middle-aged celibates in barbed wire underwear, virgins floating in the air like birthday balloons, grown men preaching to yellow-bellied sapsuckers or naked and cruciform in subzero cells. So why not Bebb with his penchant for baring something maybe not all that unlike his soul, that holy lover of Trionkas, Redpaths, Badgers, Turtles, opener of suburban hearts, chief caterer and catalyst of the great Princeton feasts? If Bebb had run afoul of the law for his pains—the IRS, the Borough police, the fire insurance people—so had the others and fouler still, after all, for worse pains: sawed in half, grilled, tossed to the lions. I thought of Bebb and Mr. Golden a thousand feet up in their spit-and-glue flivver trailing *Here's to Jesus, Here's to You*, over the Nassau Street P-rade like restaurant ads, then the fiery martyrdom that ended them up corkscrewed into those starwise-scorched furrows.

The sanctity of Bebb was like a fish I was trying to hook, and I drew my legs up like a fishline so the knees touched Sharon, who moved in her sleep. I angled for the heroic qualities of Bebb's virtues that were moving drowsily, like carp, just below the surface. He hated heights, but I have a movie of him eating an ice cream cone on top of the Eiffel Tower as if it was his own back stoop. I remember how when old Herman Redpath lay dry and brown as a smoked herring in his coffin, before the Joking Cousin took that leak on him which legend has it was his golden clew out of the abyss, Bebb spoke of him getting back on his feet again like Gene Tunney after the Long Count, and when I said to him, "Do you believe it, Bip?" he said, "Antonio, I believe everything," and when I said, "The way you say it, you make it sound almost easy," he said, "Antonio, it's hard as hell." So he was heroic in that department too, hoisting his faith off the ground grunt by grunt like an overweight weightlifter, the eyes bulging, the sweat rolling down. There was hardly anything worth believing that Bebb did not believe.

From far off in the night there was the sound of a shantytown radio or a breeze in the dark pines. Bert's chickens were mourning their tragic loss

in silence, and miles away Connecticut floated in sleep like a raft with
Lucy and Bill aboard, the puzzling, moonlit faces of my children. They
were all right. Before we went to bed I called, and my nephew Tony said
they were. He said also, "That Lucy, that Lucy" so I could all but see the
marveling shake of his head, the Krazy Kat smile, as he spoke of my daughter or niece, his cousin or daughter, whom he couldn't resist naming to me
twice that way—*that Lucy, that Lucy*. He said Charlie Blaine, his father,
had dropped by on his way to a New York specialist. It was a ringing in
his ears this time, or a sound like crickets or the hissing of damp logs, which
he could get rid of only by shutting himself up in small windowless places.
Tony said, "Christ almighty, Tono, he spent half the time he was here in
the hall closet," and I said, "Good God," thus exchanging long-distance
blasphemies with my horny namesake who'd given me horns. Sharon mur-
mured in the dark as though her young lover had wormed his way out of
my dream into hers.

Bebb said, "Antonio, it's the enemies a man's got inside himself are
a man's worst enemies."

He said, "There's dark and shameful things a man keeps hid that if he
don't get them out into the sunshine they'll drag him into the dark." He
stood there against the blinding stucco with his shame like a bunch of
white grapes in his hand and pierced in a thousand places by the sun's arrows as the children skittered off barefoot through the seafood slops. He
said, "It was a fool thing to do, a crazy chance, and I never blamed anybody it turned out like it did," landing him in a room not much bigger
than the hall closet where he and Fats Golden spent five years imagining
their way through black raspberry, burnt almond, pistachio, all Howard
Johnson's flavors and then some. The Venerable Bebb. The crumbs flying
out of his mouth. The glass of white milk he handed to Jimmy Bob Luby
with such care.

I tried to remember his miracles then, counting them off like sheep.
How he raised Brownie from the dead in Knoxville, Tennessee, unless
Brownie wasn't as dead as he thought he was, and how he believed he
might have raised poor Lucille too if the undertaker hadn't already done
a job on her. How he restored the potency of Herman Redpath or such
was the old Ojibway's boast and he claimed he could produce eyewitnesses.
How he told the crippled son of Professor Virgil Roebuck of the Princeton
History Department to rise and walk, and the boy managed a kind of
fractured turkeytrot from his wheelchair to the center of the Alexander
Hall stage where he fell into Bebb's arms like an armful of sticks.

Could Bebb have walked on water if he'd taken a mind to, climbed
out of the rowboat and padded across the golden pond to me, turned the
white crumbs into butterflies or restored the sight of Jimmy Bob? I said,
"Old friend," skipping the words across to him like flat stones, "old father,
old fart . . ." When they went zigzagging slowly down to the bottom, I
drafted a letter instead: "Dear Bip, Even if you never worked a miracle,

you were a miracle, and that's what counts. I'll tell the *advocatus diaboli* to put that in his pipe and smoke it. I'll tell the *advocatus diaboli* we are going to do something nice for you in Poinsett, South Carolina. We are going to make a shrine to you where little girls in white dresses will sing the songs of Zion, and there will be piles of wheelchairs, wigs, dentures, white grapes," and I thought of Bert's poor chicken being carried into the shrine on a stretcher and of the way Babe had been stacked up against the refrigerator, then added to my letter *Diabolus, dillabolus, babilobus, babebulos*, pure Callaway again. Even I didn't know what I was talking about. I knew nothing else from then on either until I knew Sharon was leaning over me with her hair in my face saying, "Rise and shine, Bopper. It's time to get up." It was time to get up, the morning of what turned out to be one of our fuller days.

At breakfast Bert's face looked like a child's labored drawing of nose, mouth, eyes on a white page too big for them, and as the day before I had tried to read ahead from the faces of babies to their grown-up faces, so I tried there in the kitchen to read back from the overgrown face of Bert to what she'd been when she still had all her marbles and her hair, when she'd first known Bip. Then SMACK went the baby-blue swatter even as I sat there eyeing her over my Special K, and another redskin bit the dust. If you could have trimmed the page down to fit the drawing, I thought, it mightn't have been half bad—not pretty quite, but interesting, alive, clever even. Tipped there to the sunny window, it was white as the page it was drawn on, blue-lipped. She said, "Luby? Luby?" Gertrude Conover had asked about them. She said, "You know what her name is? Ruby Luby?"

It was the first time I'd seen her smile, as much a surprise as Sharon's smile. She said, "They're foodstamp people. And all those babies? No wonder there wasn't eyes enough to go round?" Like heekie, heekie, heekie, everything she said was tiptoe questions there were no more answers to than there were chickens in her coop that could answer them.

It was also the first day I really got a feeling for what it must have been like to live out a life in that house—the bare bulb hanging in the upstairs hall that had scared the wits out of the fat twins when somebody knocked it at night, the rusty claws of the bathtub's feet, the narrow back stairs steep as a ladder with old newspapers piled along the walls. Most of the wallpaper looked as if it went back to Bebb's childhood or beyond. In our room there was a diamond-shaped lattice with faded pink roses and brown dampstains that themselves blossomed into bigger, handsomer brown roses. Riding the same currents of air they'd ridden for years, cooking smells drifted along the same angled passageways and bald carpeting, through the same shadowy, varnished doors. Sharon showed me a room that Bert had shown her, tucked in behind the backstairs like a box with brown matchboard walls and ceiling as shiny as the doors and full of shelves. There were stacks of old magazines on the shelves, and brown-paper bags, blankets, linen, mason jars, hats and shoes and paint cans and suitcases, everything so neat and rich it could have been *trompe l'oeil* with the shadows like painted shadows, the spaces between things only the illusion of space. Sharon ran her finger across the front of one of the suitcases and in a startling imitation of Bert's tiptoe whisper said, "It's my treasure in there? She likes me, Bopper. She wants to show me her treasure."

I said, "Where her treasure is, there shall her heart be also."

"That's Scripture," she said.

Then after breakfast that morning I drove to the motel to pick up Brownie for his consultation with Babe, and it wasn't till he appeared dressed as if for a first communion in white shorts, white socks, a linen cap with perforated sides, that I realized what an occasion it was for him to meet Bebb's twin for the first time. He said, "Mr. Bebb never mentioned a brother to me. He never spoke about his family to me, and he never asked me about mine. We were not close in that way," and I said, Tell me about your family, Brownie."

He said, "I never knew my father, and my poor mother had to put me in a foster home when I was eight. It was not a happy childhood, dear," and he looked so unhappy as he said it that I questioned him no further, just left him in the Uforium with two or three others waiting in undertaker chairs to see Babe.

Bert was hanging wash out on a line near the chicken coop as though it had nothing but the happiest associations for her, and almost as soon as I had introduced Callaway to her he started to help her with it. It was an odd thing for him to do without being asked to do it, and you could see the oddness of it sinking into her face like quicksand until it was gone. From that moment it was so much as if they were old friends that I sometimes think nothing less than Gertrude Conover's theory of reincarnation can adequately account for it—as if when Callaway was Pharaoh, Bert was a favorite concubine or a great white mare he rode if Pharaohs rode mares. There in the sunshine with their arms in the air they seemed to be hanging from that line like laundry themselves, he a long black stocking, she a sheet ballooning out in the summer. Hidden behind the *New York Times*, my one line left open to reality, I could hear the sounds they exchanged if not the words, Egyptian words, for all I know, her anxious little question-marks, his dark syllables that stilled them like a hand.

A man came out of the Uforium carrying an open carton with what looked like a few of the moonrocks in it, and I wondered if Brownie's turn would be next. At some point Babe appeared in the window for a moment. He had pulled the yellowed shade to one side, and I could see his round face peering out as if he was counting the house before curtain time. If he saw me, he gave no sign of it, but I could see him see Bert and Callaway. It was a long look he gave them like a time-lapse movie of an egg hatching—Bert first, Callaway second, then Bert and Callaway together, third. Then he blinked at them as he had blinked at me the morning we jogged: both eyes at once, deliberately, as if he was taking his movie and storing it away for some special showing at some special time. Then the shade fell back in place again, and it can't have been long afterwards that Brownie and he had their first meeting. Brownie told me about it at some length later that day, told me on a ferris wheel, the way things turned out. It wasn't an ordinary ferris wheel but a double-threat one with a wheel at each end of a single spoke so that not only did each wheel turn on its own axis but, as the spoke also went around, they were turning on its axis too, first one on top and then the other a dizzying height above the ground.

It was a county fair—part agricultural, part honky-tonk—and Babe had an exhibit at it, one booth in a great barn full of vegetables, farm machinery, handcrafts and 4-H demonstrations, where he had on display among other things the moonrocks that I'd seen carried out, the charred space suit, many UFO photographs and some round, flat things that Sharon called moonflops which were billed as plaster casts of outerspace footprints. Babe himself was on hand, like a life-size doll in his green jump suit, to answer questions and hand out flyers with his picture on them and a message entitled *There's Room for One More*, whose general drift was that when the saucers finally landed en masse for the great rescue operation, there would always be room for anybody who had gotten ready by participating in the Uforium SOS program—Shove Off Soon, Send On Spacemen, Save Our Skins.

We all went to the fair with him including Bert who I felt sure wouldn't have made it if it hadn't been for the fact that Callaway would be there too. She was dressed like a girl of sixteen in a skirt too short for her, saddle shoes and bobby socks, the usual ribbon in her hair. Babe said, "Keep an eye on her for me, old buddy," and I did for a while, on her and Callaway both side by side in the bingo tent among electric toasters, giant pandas, pink plastic cake-covers. But up there on that wheel I had eyes only for Brownie squeezed beside me on our swinging cradle as we revolved slowly through the stratosphere.

He said, "When I first laid eyes on Babe, I thought I was seeing a ghost. The blood drained right out of me and I must have looked like death because he took hold of my arm and helped me into a chair. He brought me a cup of cool water, and he said I wasn't to try to talk till I felt better. He said, 'Laverne, you look like you've been to hell and back.'"

Brownie said, "Nobody's called me Laverne for a hundred years, and how he knew I've been through hell, I'll never know. The tears started to come. I couldn't help myself when he called me by my right name instead of Brownie and showed me he knew what I've been through since I lost Leo Bebb and Jesus both in a single blow. He didn't hold my tears against me. He just turned away to the window so I wouldn't be embarrassed having him stand there watching me."

Up, up we went around the great, slow arc as though we were aboard a saucer already and bound for the stars. The light was beginning to fade, and earth seemed far below us. Brownie said, "Babe told me many things this morning, dear. He told me about Jesus. He says Jesus was from outer space. He says he was a man just like us but from an advanced civilization. He says he came down to get us ready to go back with him to the world he came from, and when we wouldn't listen, he had to go back all by himself. Babe says the resurrection was really a spacelift. Jesus was the only passenger on a spacelift that was supposed to take the whole world."

I said, "Think of it, Brownie." What else could I say? For the first time in a long while Brownie's voice had something of the lullaby sweetness to it that it used to have when he was interpreting Scripture, and I didn't want to say anything to mess it up for him so I just said think of it and then tried to think of it myself. I thought of Jesus dressed up like Neil Armstrong for a moonwalk, rattling around in an empty saucer on that long trip home with all those empty seats that could have accommodated the rest of us. I thought of all the uneaten meals, the little paper bags with nobody to be sick in them. I pictured him sitting at the controls in his fishbowl helmet with his head tipped sideways like that da Vinci study for the Last Supper where he looks so tired and Jewish and some of the paint has chipped away.

Brownie said, "It's enough to make your head swim. Babe says Leo Bebb believed the same thing only he wouldn't let on he did because he thought people liked the old Gospel way better."

I said, "Do you think that's what Leo Bebb believed, Brownie?" I remembered Bebb in the basement of Bull's International Fireproof Storage, which was the last place I ever saw him. Bebb told Sharon that the best words in all Scripture were the three last ones, and when Sharon said she didn't know what the last ones were, he said them out to her—"Come, Lord Jesus"—and I wondered now if what Bebb had had in mind was Jesus coming back in his saucer some day hardly gray around the temples yet thanks to those shots they had up there against old age and death and in the meantime communicating with this world through the fillings in Babe's teeth. And if that wasn't what Bebb had in mind, then I wondered what he had had in it. All the time I'd known Bebb, I'd never tried drawing him out much on what he believed. I'm not sure why, but I suspect maybe it was because though I was never much of a believer myself, I needed Bebb to be. I think I was afraid that if I asked too many questions, he'd turn out to have the same doubts I did plus a few more I'd never thought of because I didn't have that many beliefs to be doubtful about. I remember Sharon's asking him once if he had to bet his tail on whether the whole business about God was true or not, which way he'd bet it, and what he said was, "Honey, there's days I wouldn't even bet my green stamps." It was enough for me to get by on, the suggestion that there were other days too, but just enough, so I was grateful that the subject never came up in my hearing again.

Brownie's face had already started to recede into the dusk as though he himself was receding, so to reestablish contact I said, "What do you believe yourself, Brownie?" He heard me this time and just as we reached the top of the arc and started down the far side, he turned to me and said, "Babe gave me a life-ray treatment this morning, and I believe it has already started to work."

If Sharon had been squeezed in between us when the life-ray was mentioned, she and I could have exchanged a glance and all would have been well, but up there in the air with nobody aboard but Brownie it seemed a tossup whether he was off his rocker or I was. So I just said, "Tell me about it," and he told me.

He said, "You have seen for yourself the things Babe has in the Uforium, but they are just a small part of all the things he has. He says he's got things that if they fall into the wrong hands it could put the whole world in danger. And he's got other things he says ordinary people wouldn't understand the use of any more than a caveman would under-stand it if you showed him a copy of Scripture. He would just think it was something to start a fire with or throw at a dinosaur."

The sound of acid rock came floating up from the midway and a few lights had started to go on in the buildings where the agriculture exhibits were. The wheel stopped to let on passengers below, and we were stuck there about half way down the downward arc, dangling out over nothing.

Brownie said, "Has he showed you his life-ray yet, dear?"

I said, "There've been times I could have used a life-ray, but nobody's ever shown me one."

Brownie said, "It's not at all what you might expect. It's not like a death-ray gun out of Buck Rogers. It's more like a hairdryer. If you know what a colander looks like, it's like an upside-down colander covered with different colored wires coming up out of the holes like the inside of a TV. There are some dials on it, and there's an antenna on top. Babe adjusts it on your head and then stands behind a special screen because he says you can get too much life just like you can get too much x-ray. He turns it on with his voice, dear."

I said, "What did he say to turn it on, Brownie?" and Brownie said, "All he said was just, 'Don't be scared, it's not going to hurt, Laverne.' "

I could tell that he was very moved, and for a few moments we sat there in silence while the wheel cranked down another spoke or two, then stopped again. He said, "It isn't a feeling you can put your finger on because it's more on the inside than it is on the outside, but let me put it this way. When I first started going to grade school, I was always very nervous the days I knew Mother was off working someplace. It seemed like I was lost and nobody was ever going to find me again the rest of my life. But there were other days I knew she was home because it wasn't her day to go out working, and those days I had a wonderful feeling I was safe and everything was going to be all right. Dear, the best way I can describe the life-ray is when Babe turned it on with his voice, it gave me that same feeling. For the first time in many years, I knew Mother was home."

I said, "Do you think the life-ray really did it or do you think it was just in your mind?" and Brownie said, "I know the life-ray did it, dear."

I said, "How can you know a thing like that, Brownie?" and Brownie said, "Because I've got proof."

He said, "You've probably never noticed it, but I wear dentures, dear." It was like Toulouse-Lautrec saying I'd probably never noticed it but he had this problem with tall girls. I had the feeling I was setting him up for some marvelous gag that I was the only one not to see coming.

I said, "I've always admired your smile, Brownie."

He said, "I don't expect to be wearing them much longer. Babe says very often the life-ray makes a person grow a brand-new set of teeth, and I think mine have already started to come in."

"What makes you think so?" I said.

He said, "I can feel them with my tongue, dear," and though I could not be sure in what light there was left, I have a suspicion that he did something then that caused his whole smile to drop an inch or two so he could get his tongue in under it and take a reading. At that point, having picked up a full complement of passengers I suppose, the wheel gave a lurch and was off in earnest not just on its own axis now but on the central axis too so that, revolving as before, we were caught up in a greater revolution still that carried us so high we stopped talking. Not even the sky seemed the limit any more.

For want of a nail the shoe was lost, for want of a shoe the horse was lost, then on to the rider, the battle, until in the end the kingdom was lost, as the old rhyme goes, because of that one lost nail. On such slender threads hang the destinies of us all. If it was true about Brownie's teeth, I thought, then it was true about the life-ray; if it was true about the life-ray, it was true about Babe, and what Babe said about Jesus was true, and it was true the resurrection was just a spacelift, then on until finally the Kingdom would be lost with a capital K. Thy-Kingdom-come itself would never come because there was no place and nobody for it to come from anymore except some other planet where a fart might carry you a hundred yards if you weren't careful. If Brownie was right about his teeth, I thought, then those days when Bebb wouldn't even bet his green stamps on God would turn out to have been the only days he wasn't backing a loser. If Brownie was right about his teeth, then what was lost was in the long run all of us because saints and sinners, wise men and fools, we were all of us all dressed up with no place finally to go except death if we were lucky and a world where they had shots against death if we weren't.

And of course if Gertrude Conover's theory of reincarnation turned out to be true, even if we made it to the grave, we still wouldn't be home free.

What a metaphysical ride it turned out to be up there in the Carolina sky with Brownie so full of new hope and me beside him with hopes dashed that I'd never even thought I had. The wheel became the great wheel of death and rebirth itself, the same vicious circle that had carried Gertrude Conover all the way from Pharaoh's Egypt to Nixon's USA, that had picked Bebb up out of the New Jersey potato field and deposited him in the womb of big-eared Ruby Luby to emerge with those flat little eyes I'd watched flutter as he gummed his second-hand Milky Way in the stroller. If Gertrude Conover was right that Bebb was an always returner, then never had he seemed more venerable to me. What sinister facts could the *advocatus diaboli* put in the balance against a man who postpones his own freedom in order to ride the great squirrel cage until he has rescued the last squirrel, which means postponing it forever? Around and around we wheeled with the bingo games, udder-pinchings, pie-tastings, moonrock-viewings, and skin shows going on beneath us, and when finally a man with a beer-belly and a five cent cigar raised the safety bar so we could get out, I could have knelt down and watered the red clay with my tears.

Sharon was there looking harried with a pink plastic cake-cover in her hand. She said, "Either of you know where Bert is?" and Brownie with the fate of mankind hanging on that porcelain smile said, "I could have kept going around up there forever."

Sharon said, "Babe's having a hemorrhage. He says she oughtn't ever to be left alone."

"She was with Callaway the last time I saw her," I said, and Brownie pointed up at the wheel where about seven or eight spokes above our heads a child with a stick of cotton candy was leaning out over the side. Brownie said, "Watch out, dear. I think he's going to be sick," and he was right. I stepped out of the way just in time. It reminded me of the time the ice cream fell out of Bebb's cone on the Eiffel Tower and we watched it drip its way down from strut to strut as Bebb said, "Forget not the congregation of the poor forever."

10

PART OF WHAT gave our search urgency was that when Lucille disappeared in the same unexpected way, by the time we found her days later she was laid out in a Houston funeral parlor with her mouth on wrong and a dress that didn't fit her all that well either. God only knew what had become of Bert. She could have been anywhere—trapped in the Haunted House among jets of air and spiders dangling, or flattened out against the seat of the Arctic Bobsled as it gunned around to the screams of the Grateful Dead, or being sampled in the judge's tent like pastry.

Callaway was missing too, and Gertrude Conover, Sharon, Brownie and I fanned out to look for them. Babe stayed with his moonrocks because that's where she would come back to if she came back, he said. His eyes were round as marbles and his smile was out of synchronization with the rest of him. He told us to try the ring toss, shooting gallery, cake raffle and so on because she loved prizes more than anything, but she wasn't at any of them or at the skin show either where two naked women were lying on their backs with their hands on their hips and their butts in the air tossing a beachball back and forth with their yellow-soled feet. We tried the chickens, such chickens as I'd never seen before, wild-eyed ones with Fiji headdresses, beige and tan herringbone ones, chickens with huge pantalettes and scarlet feet and lipstick-colored combs, but Bert wasn't among them, or at the hot dog stand, or resting her feet with her saddle shoes off outside the ladies' room, so after a while we went back to Babe's, but she wasn't there either and neither was Babe.

He had left Brownie to keep an eye on things for him and hand out the flyers. Brownie told us he'd driven home to see if she'd somehow made her way back there, and Sharon and I decided to go back and investigate for ourselves. Gertrude Conover was going to come with us, but Babe had taken his car and Callaway had apparently taken hers so we had to walk and told her we'd come back for her as soon as we could. We left her drinking a cup of coffee that Brownie had gotten for her somewhere, and I remember how game she looked perched there among the moonflops with her cashmere sweater over her shoulders and the paper cup in her hand. I suppose when you have survived the barbarities of Viking raids and died giving birth to a priest's child in a papyrus swamp, an unexpected change of plans at a county fair is not apt to count for much.

It was dark by the time we reached the house, but there were lights on inside and Babe's car was there so we went in the back door and found Babe in the kitchen. He was sitting with his back to us and spoke without turning around. He said, "Your boy brought her home. She was here when I got here. I just got done putting her to bed."

He was sitting at the kitchen table in his shirtsleeves with a cup of black coffee and a piece of chocolate cake with chocolate frosting. He stretched his hands out, one for each of us, and we each took one because it was impossible not to. He held us there for a moment, and I remember the black circle of his coffee against the white enamel table top and the larger black circle of the cake with his one piece missing. He said, "No hard feelings." When he spoke, you could see where the chocolate had blacked out some of his teeth. He said, "Like the man says, it's all well that ends well." He was still having trouble with his smile. It kept flaring up unexpectedly on him like a fire you'd thought was out. It wasn't till he said no hard feelings that I realized he'd held us responsible for Bert's disappearance, so I was afraid I was out of synchronization myself, and the conversation got off to a wobbly start.

He said, "She was all shook up. I could tell right off something had happened. She was sitting in here with five or six cigarettes smoking away in different parts of the house where she'd laid them down and forgotten. It was like they were parts of herself she'd left laying around all over the place so all that was left out here was an empty shell."

I said, "I guess the fair was too much for her," and Babe said, "It wasn't the fair." He cut us each a piece of dark cake and poured us coffee, sliding them across the table to us as though he was putting something together for us of which his words were one part and the things he was moving around with his hands another part.

He said, "Seeing her like this makes you think back. She wasn't ever Carole Lombard or anything in that league, but she had a sassy way of talking that beat all—nothing smart-ass but just all kinds of fun to her and a gleam in her eye bright enough to read by. There wasn't anybody in town that was better company than Bertha Stredwig back here forty years ago," and I wondered if he'd ever tried his life-ray on her and if it would start her hair coming back again the way Brownie said it had his teeth. He said, "There was a time she could have handled what happened here tonight like nothing at all. There wasn't anything or anybody she couldn't handle."

"What happened, Babe?" Sharon said.

He said, "Tell me about this boy of yours. What's he call himself?"

I said, "He calls himself Callaway."

He said, "What do you know about Callaway?"

I said, "He mows lawns and drives and has nosebleeds. Gertrude Conover says he has a lot of kids, and I think his wife left him."

Sharon said, "Tell him what he used to be in the old days, Bopper."

I said, "You tell him."

Sharon said, "Gertrude Conover says he used to be the Pharaoh. She says back in ancient Egypt he used to rule over cities that would have made places like Washington D.C. look like a whistle-stop."

He said, "Callaway brought her home because she said she wasn't feeling good. She shouldn't have ever gone in the first place. She was all wore out like I knew she'd be. Callaway followed her on into the house, and of course she didn't know what to do so she sat down someplace, her wanting just to go up and lay down on the bed. Then he plunked himself right down alongside her and set in comforting her. There's nobody can touch the colored folks for comforting people. They get it from their mammies. It's in their blood. The next thing he had a arm around her telling her never mind and she'd be better in no time. I'm not saying he meant any harm by it. I'm not one of those that say they're all of them no better than an animal."

As he talked, I tried to test the truth of how he said it was by picturing to myself how it might have been, and I found I could picture it well enough—the two of them propping each other up somewhere, those dense grey curls cradled against that bony black cheek, the rumble and creak of their voices.

Babe said, "Excuse me a minute." The phone was ringing and he went into the hall to answer it, which didn't put him far enough away for us to say anything but far enough away for Sharon to place both hands palm down on the table in front of her and look at me with her eyebrows raised as high as they would go. When he came back, he said, "That was space-watch. They've spotted one up over Shaw Hill. Low, like it might be getting set to land. They're all excited it might be the big show."

I said, "Do you think it's the big show, Babe?"

He said, "Antonio, when the big show starts, it'll be like a golden rain. It'll be like the fourth of July of the world." He was looking up at the ceiling as though it had already started and in his face anyway you could almost believe that it had—that plump red face tilted upwards, those skyrocket eyes.

He said, "What happened was while he was doing his comforting, that hand of his started moving around places where it hadn't ought to move. She took to him the moment she set eyes on him, I saw that my ownself, but when he started cozying up to her that way and she could see signs he had more on his mind yet, it threw a scare into her. She tried to shove him off her, and there was a scuffle. She hollered out, and that time it was his turn to get scared. He was coming out of here on two wheels when I drove up, and my poor Shirley T., I found her in here with part of her shirt tore open and her wig knocked crooked, that pitiful grey wig she's got where once she had hair on her as long and pretty as Sharon's here."

He said, "There wasn't any harm done. I got her tucked in upstairs now. He'll be the hell and gone in no time and she won't ever have to lay eyes on him again. I'm not going to breathe a word, and don't you breathe a word either. There's no point making—" and then Gertrude Conover walked in looking a little haggard and chilly with her sweater buttoned up under her chin. "Another pot of coffee," he said, finishing his sentence, "unless Gertrude Conover here wants some."

She didn't, poor soul, having already had coffee enough back among the moonflops where we'd forgotten all about her as Babe had unfolded his tale. Callaway had brought her home, she said. It was a lovely, starry night and she had thoroughly enjoyed herself though she was glad she'd brought along her sweater. She and Brownie had handed out a lot of the Uforium flyers, and when Callaway showed up to get her, he had helped them for a while. Sharon asked her about Callaway then—in a guarded way, as the expression goes, and I remember thinking how there was hardly one of us she wasn't somehow guarding.

She said, "Callaway mention how he was the one that took Bert home?" and Gertrude Conover said, "She got a little overtired and weepy, poor dear, and it was Callaway she turned to. He was very proud. You'd have thought she'd given him the shirt off her back. What a world it is."

Sharon was formulating a new and even more ponderously guarded question when Babe intervened. Gertrude Conover was standing behind his chair so she couldn't see him give a microscopic shake of his head to silence Sharon as effectively as if he'd clapped his hand over her mouth while Gertrude Conover continued with what a world it was.

She said, "Well, I saw Ruby Luby again, that name. She must have had six children with her, all obviously hers with those big ears and all under six years old, I would swear. It was far, far past their bedtime, of course, and you've never seen such a miserable little contingent dragging along behind her, their faces all smeared up with soda pop and ghastly candy bars. Except Jimmy Bob," and over Babe's red head she faintly narrowed her eyes at us so that this time it was about Jimmy Bob that we were silenced, a whole new set of secrets guarded.

She said, "He was as grimy as the rest of them, but he was radiant. He was enthroned in his little stroller like the Dalai Lama with all the sacred marks upon him and his face positively giving off light like the moon. He is blind as a bat, poor thing, but you can tell by just looking at him that he sees things the rest of us don't even dream. I bowed my head to him as his mother wheeled him by, and I know in some way he saw me. He turned his little head toward me and nodded back so gravely it was as if he was saying, 'There you are, Gertrude Conover.' My dear, it was as if I could actually hear him say, 'There you have always been, Gertrude Conover, and there you are again.'

"Well," she said, "I am getting a little overtired and weepy myself, and this is as good a time as any to have my go at the bathroom before the line starts forming."

Later that night, in bed among the brown roses, I decided that what Babe had been doing with all the words he had spoken and the things he'd moved around the table was less putting something together than burying something for us to find when the time came, less telling us about something that had happened than telling us about something he wanted to happen so bad he could taste it like the chocolate on his teeth. It was why he couldn't keep a lid on his smile. I woke Sharon up to explain it to her. I said, "He wants us all the hell out of here, that's what he's saying. He's saying it doesn't matter about any will. It's his place and we've hung around long enough. He's using Callaway to get rid of us, and it doesn't matter whether Callaway really went ape or not. I say we get the hell out before we get caught in the fourth of July of the world."

Sharon said, "I say it's my place, and I'll get the hell out when I'm ready to get the hell out."

"What's the point?" I said, and Sharon said, "There doesn't have to be any point. Bip left me this place, and maybe there's something here I can use. Maybe we'll even find something nice to do for Jesus after all."

I said, "Maybe the nicest thing we can do for Jesus is get Callaway out before they string him up."

She said, "We don't string them up so much anymore, Bopper."

I said, "Do you think he really did it?"

"With Bert?" she said. "Listen, that Babe's got it in his head everybody's some kind of kook. He said plenty about Bip too after you went up."

"Such as," I said.

"He said Bip didn't get his kicks like other people," she said, "and when I asked him what else is new, he said he didn't just mean he was a flasher, like what they sent him up five years of his life for. He didn't come right out and say so, but he let on there were some that thought he and Brownie had a thing going way back. He said the reason Luce started hitting the Tropicanas was because she knew about it. Jesus."

I said, "Do you believe it?"

As she moved her head toward the window, her cheek turned silver, and she placed the back of one hand against it. She said, "There was lots about Bip I didn't ever know or see. Like I never saw him bare but once in all my life. Once when Luce was smashed she said she never saw him bare except a few times in all her life either. It was winter the time I saw him. I went into his room to look for something, and he was laying there naked as the day he was born. I thought he was dead, and I don't know to this day what he was up to. It was cold in that room, and he was staring straight up at the ceiling with those jellybean eyes of his. He had dimply knees and not a hair on him except a little where you'd think and not much else there either that showed anyway with the pot he had on him. It was so cold in there I guess he'd all just shriveled up. He had his arms down stiff at his sides and his legs out straight like he was made of snow. I was still a kid, and I went running downstairs and said, 'Oh Jesus, Luce, they got my daddy laid out dead on his bed,' and Luce said, 'That's what you think.' Half the time I don't think she knew what he was up to any more than I did. There wasn't anybody knew all there was to know about Bip."

"Including Babe," I said.

She said, "If there's things to know about Bip that Babe knows, I want to know them. It's like maybe that's the main thing he sent us down here for."

I said, "Maybe Babe was the one thing he didn't have the guts to flash till after he was gone."

"That Bip," she said. "Nobody could ever tell what he was fixing to do next."

"Babe too," I said. "Poor Callaway."

"Poor Bert. Poor everybody," Sharon said. "Poor Bip in that stroller saying, 'There you are again, Gertrude Conover.' "

"Forget not the congregation of the poor forever," I said, and lifted a ribbon of silver hair from the glistening silver cheek where her hand lay.

11

BROWNIE SAID, "I've got good news and bad news, dear," and I said, "Better hit us with the good news first, Brownie," and then Brownie did for sure the same thing with his smile that I'd suspected him of doing on the ferris wheel the day before. The whole smile dropped about an inch, and suddenly it was not Brownie any more but Lon Chaney changing from Dr. Jekyll to Mr. Hyde with this terrible maw of fangs hanging out over his lower lip. My double vision again, one pulling apart into two.

Fortunately the others couldn't see him from where they were sitting in that dark cave of a room where the only bright and cheerful thing was the golden millpond above Brownie's bed. It seemed a crime to be inside on the loveliest day we'd had yet—clearer and cooler for a little rain the night before, the red roads a deeper and less dusty red, the greens greener —and of course it was the question of Callaway's crime that had brought us together there to conspire like criminals at a safe distance from the innocent Babe, who, even as we'd slid out of the drive on muffled wheels, had been putting on one of his shows. The Uforium blinds were all drawn, and you could hear the extraterrestrial blips and chirpings, the canned voice starting out on its spiel as the lights spun.

Brownie said, "They have definitely started to come in. I can feel them with my tongue. The life-ray is working, dear. It won't be long until I have to stop wearing my dentures because they won't fit down over the gums anymore." All of this came out thick and clattery like an eggbeater, but then he snapped the smile back in place again. He said, "It may not mean much to you, but it is very good news to me," and I said, "It means more to me than you know," because what it meant, of course, was that if the life-ray worked, then Babe worked, and if Babe worked, then Jesus was Neil Armstrong and Thy Kingdom Come was a five hundred yard fart and an anti-death shot in the ass on the Planet of the Apes.

Sharon said, "You better lay the bad news on us too, Brownie," and Brownie said, "Maybe I better let Harold tell you about that himself." I don't think even Gertrude Conover could think for a moment who Harold was until he started talking. Harold was Callaway. Harold Callaway. It was like being at a christening.

Callaway said, "Buffa. Waffle. Tomtom. Kudzu. Clapper," short, heavy syllables that came thumping out like footsteps as Callaway sat there on the foot of one of the twin beds staring down at the wall-to-wall carpet with his head in his hands. I have never seen a shirt as gorgeous as the one he was wearing—a fireman's red covered with psychedelic green cabbages or brains that Tutankhamen himself would have been pleased by let alone Harry Truman. Out of his breast pocket he pulled a piece of paper which he unfolded and handed to me.

The paper showed a crudely drawn picture of a naked black man. Around his neck hung something that looked at first glance like that ancient Egyptian symbol of life and happy days, the *ankh*, but that proved to be the parts of himself that should have been located at his crotch. What was located at his crotch instead was a kind of madman's tu-tu of dark, heavy lines scrawled around and around as if to obliterate some unforgivable mistake. In one place the pencil had gone through the paper. Underneath was written in block letters NIGGER GO HOME, and Brownie said, "He found it slipped under his door when we got back from breakfast." Then Callaway said something, and Gertrude Conover said, "Maybe somebody booked it in advance," and Callaway shook his head. Brownie said, "I said he could move in with me if his was spoken for, but the man said he couldn't allow it because this isn't a double room. I told him it has twin beds in it, but he says that doesn't matter. He says when a room's got just one person in it, that makes it a single room and he can't put two people in a single room. We got talking in circles, dear. It's as plain as the nose on your face they're throwing him out."

I don't remember ever having seen Callaway smoke before, but he had lit up by then and was sitting there with a king-size cigarette expertly angled up from his lips to keep the smoke at a distance. In contrast to the dead white of the cigarette, the whites of his eyes looked like meerschaum. It was Sharon who asked him the unaskable then and asked it in front of Gertrude Conover and Brownie, neither of whom had heard a word of Babe's charges either, so that she was confronting all three of them at the same time. She said, "When you took Bert home last night, Callaway, did anything happen between you and her that might have made things turn out like they have because Babe said when he got home she was all shook up with lighted cigarettes smoking all over the house where she'd left them."

It was a long, unraveled sort of sentence that ended up somewhere between a question and a statement, and it was as hard a thing as I suppose she had had to do up to that point. I remember thinking that as recently as a week before I couldn't have imagined her doing it and that maybe the reason she was able to do it then was that for the first time in her life she had a base to do it from. She was asking about something that had happened in a house that was her house because Bebb had left it to her, and in some queer way I suspect that Babe and Bert may have been her base too. They were hardly a pair to give you a sense of security, but they were more in the way of a family than she'd ever known she had before, and I think that counted for a lot with her. She sat on the edge of Brownie's dresser among the deodorants and after-shaves while he and Gertrude Conover and I waited in various kinds of silence for Callaway to answer.

He had risen from the bed and stood in profile at the picture window with his hand on his hip and the scurrilous drawing in his hand so that it projected forward not unlike the way the kilts of pharaohs are depicted on sun-baked walls as projecting forward, which I have read somewhere is supposed to indicate that those ancient fathers of their people were so potent as to be in a perpetual state of erection. He stood there all black and bony and fireman's red against the parking-lot view and for a few moments said nothing at all. Then he said something short and deep and the texture of plaited straw at the end of which he raised the drawing in both hands and with ritual precision tore it in two and then each of the pieces in two and then dropped it in the basket by the door.

Such was the power of the gesture that even without the faintest idea what he had said, I could not doubt his innocence of Babe's charge, and it was obvious that none of the others doubted it either. Gertrude Conover said, "The reason I have always called you Callaway was not to demean you but because, as you know, my husband's name was also Harold, and when he was still alive it was confusing to have two Harolds around at the same time. The alternative was to call my husband Conover."

Following on what had just passed, Callaway's handsome smile came as a special gift. "Thalassa jubal," he said, and this time it was Gertrude Conover who smiled. "It's quite true," she said. "Sometimes I did call him Conover."

In other words unless either for reasons of her own or out of the depths of her confusion and unreason Bert had lied to Babe about Calla-way, then Babe must have lied to us about him. And now both the drawing under the door and the threat of eviction seemed to prove that he was spreading the lie around. Why? To get us all the hell out. Why? Because we'd been there long enough. I thought of Babe's see-through raincoat through which you could see nothing but the next garment down, and I thought how there was probably nobody anywhere who wasn't both what you could see he was and also what you could not see he was.

And I thought of the faith Brownie had lost and the new faith in Babe he had found to take its place so that to launch a counterattack against Babe for having borne false witness would be to risk demolishing the only radiant thing Brownie had left, inside or outside, except his smile. So I didn't launch anything and neither did the others, still vibrating as they were from Callaway's eloquence. Instead, like the man at the complaint desk, I said only that there must have been some mistake and it probably wasn't anybody's fault, and Sharon said the hell it wasn't, and Gertrude Conover said if this motel forced Callaway out, she was sure there must be other motels that would take him in, and Brownie said, "I think the root of the trouble is Bertha Bebb herself. For years she has gone around breaking things. Now she is taking a turn at breaking people. It isn't her fault, it is just the way the poor soul is. I'm sure Babe will be able to straighten everything out."

Maybe it was because I suddenly found myself hoping against hope that he was right on both counts that I said I would go see him immediately myself and have the consultation I had already put in for. At the same time, though I wouldn't have threatened Brownie's faith for anything, I couldn't resist at least holding it up to his own inspection. I said, "I wonder why he hasn't ever given Bert a go-round with his life-ray," and Brownie said, "Oh, but he has. He told me about it."

"What did it do for her?" I said, and Brownie said, "It made her hair fall out, dear."

Babe said, "It's the Plymouth Rock of the future. It's the first place they'll set their foot down. It's the spot where the new world's going to start at." It was Shaw Hill, the slope where spacewatch had logged its sighting the night before. Babe looked pale and squinty in the bright sun. He was wearing a T-shirt, a voluminous pair of khaki shorts, and sneakers without socks. He was leaning against the post of a broken-down barbed wire fence, and I was leaning on my elbow in the grass. I had told him about the drawing and what it showed hanging around Callaway's neck like an ankh and about the circular conversation Brownie had had on the subject of what constituted a double room and about how Callaway had protested his innocence. It placed the ball as squarely in his court as a ball can be placed, I thought, but instead of lobbing it back at me, he merely pocketed it with that slow, two-eyed blink of his as if he was putting it away to be dealt with later, or putting me away. Then he said his piece about Shaw Hill's being the Plymouth Rock of the future and left me to conjure up visions of whatever creature would be the first to set spacefoot on it or webfoot, claw, golden sandal, to inaugurate the new age.

Then he opened his mouth wide enough to reveal the mousedroppings and said, "Don't fret over Callaway. All things work together for good to them that love God, Antonio," and immediately two things worked together for me with a force I can't overestimate. One thing was that his lips didn't seem to move while he was speaking, and the other thing was that the voice he spoke in was Bebb's voice.

For the moment I could think of only one explanation, and that was that Babe was Bebb.

I didn't see how it was possible, but every alternative seemed impossible. Babe had been Bebb right along. He was Bebb now. He was quoting Scripture. He was playing a game I didn't understand, but that was the kind of game Bebb had always played. The only thing that couldn't be Bebb was the hair because Bebb was bald as an egg. The hair couldn't be real. As surely as I knew he was Bebb, I knew that that rusty hair must be, like Bert's, a wig.

Before either of us knew what was happening, I reached out and took hold of a spike of it and gave it enough of a tug to pull the wig off and expose that bare and shiny scalp I knew so well. It was an act of madness, and even as I was doing it, I knew it was, knew that I had finally fallen apart into two myself: both a madman and a man watching himself be mad. Time stopped in its tracks, and the moment fell clear like a frame from a comic strip—the round, pale man leaning against the post, and me with a spike of his hair in my hand and a comic strip balloon over my head full of exclamation points and question marks.

The hair didn't come off, and the voice that spoke wasn't Bebb's. It was Babe's. It said, "Got my own teeth too." I said, "Who are you anyway for Christsake?"

I said, "Do you expect me to believe you've been to the moon and had little green men put transistors in your teeth? Do you even expect me to believe you believe it? Do you think I'm crazy? Are you crazy yourself?"

He said, "They're not green, and I'm no crazier than the next man, and as for you, Antonio, I don't know what I think exactly about you. I'm just a country boy. The moon? Listen," he said. "I'll tell you something. The moon's nothing next to the places I've been. Hell, they're not even places like the moon's a place or this hill's a place. Is a dream a place? Is there a place inside you where you live and watch the world out of through your two eyes? Are the things a man remembers out of his life a place he goes to like you go to the pictures Saturday night? I've been where there's no maps to show the places they're at because they're no more places than tomorrow's a place. I tell about the moon because there isn't a mother's son would believe it if I told the truth about the other places I've been and the things I've seen there that don't have a shape or edges to them like a stick of wood."

Opening his mouth, he stuck two fingers in it to spread the lips apart and pulled it sideways. Like a man talking to a dentist, he said, "Do you think I just went down to old Doc Hansel on Henrietta Street and said, 'Fix me a black filling in each one of these here so I can bluff a bunch of dumb rednecks?' Listen," he said, taking his fingers out, and once again, without any apparent movements of his lips, Bebb's voice came out.

It said, "Everything's going to end up making sense. You'll see. There's a time coming when the wolf and the lamb will feed together, and the lion shall eat straw like the bullock, and dust shall be the serpent's meat."

It said, "Antonio, there'll come a day they shall not hurt nor destroy in all my holy mountain, saith the Lord."

I said, "What are you, some kind of outerspace ventriloquist?"

I said, "I asked you about Callaway. That man's innocent as the day, and you're spreading it around he tried to jump your wife."

Babe said, "Listen," and again there was the sound of Bebb's voice. Bebb's voice? There wasn't that much difference between the two voices really—Bebb's a little quicker, crisper than Babe's with not quite so much Poinsett in it, but nothing a twin brother couldn't handle if he half tried. As for the lips not moving, I've seen any number of amateur Edgar Bergens do as well. Yet it wasn't just the way it sounded that was like him but the things it said.

It said, "And God shall wipe away all tears from their eyes, and there shall be no more death, neither sorrow nor crying, neither shall there be any more pain, Antonio, for the former things are passed away," and I said, "Jesus, Bip, don't think I wouldn't believe it if I could," and he said, "Antonio, you'll believe it when he comes," and I said, "Oh shit, Bip"—*shit* not as an expletive but as a cry of longing and despair that welled up not just out of Callaway's getting screwed but out of the whole world's getting screwed, out of all sadness, failure, loss. "Poor everybody" Sharon had said among the brown roses, and Brownie, Jimmy Bob, my nephew Tony with the baby in his arms, everybody ·vas included in my excremental lament. I said, "He's been coming two thousand years, Bip, and he hasn't made it yet."

"He'll make it," Bebb said. Then Babe said, "Hi-yo Silver," and then "Brrrrum brrrrum brrrrum bum bum" in strenuous imitation of the overture to *William Tell* by Gioachino Rossini.

I suppose what happened next can be put down to a number of causes of which the life-ray, however it's to be finally understood, has got to be one. Babe hadn't brought the upside-down colander with him that Brownie had described to me on the ferris wheel, but he said he didn't need it. He said they'd built the life-ray power into him the same way they'd built the transistors into him, and all he had to do was activate it. Then right there on Shaw Hill, that Plymouth Rock of the future where they shall not hurt nor destroy in all my holy mountain saith the Lord, he activated it. He fixed me with those gumdrop eyes of his and reached both his hands out toward me with the fingers arched over as if he was taking hold of a pair of doorknobs, and activated it with the same words he'd used on Brownie. "Don't be scared," he said, and I wasn't.

In the candlelight voice of Liberace at the keyboard, Brownie had said it made him feel Mother was home, and it made me feel as if I was home myself. I felt the way I used to feel when my sister Miriam and I were children in New York in wintertime, and it was dusk, and many stories below on Park Avenue the traffic was honking its way slowly home from work like cows at milking time. And there was the smell of supper in the air, and there was nothing bad or sad anywhere in the world that could ever get at us. That was how the life-ray made me feel when Babe activated it by saying, "Don't be scared" and turning two invisible door-knobs in the air.

It was Babe who'd planted the Lone Ranger in my mind and Babe, of course, who was zapping me somehow. I was aware of it even as he was doing it and thought, well, he is a ventriloquist and an impersonator so why not also a hypnotist, but just as in a dream you can know it is a dream but keep on dreaming, my knowing what Babe was up to did not affect his power to be up to it. Then his mouth came open again, and Bebb's voice came out with the lips not moving, and I remember thinking that now Babe was doing all his stunts at once. Out of his mouth Bebb's voice said, "A fiery horse with the speed of light, Antonio, a cloud of dust and a hearty Hi-yo Silver." Then there was the Lone Ranger himself.

I can see him now riding up over the brow of Shaw Hill in his white Stetson with his half-mask in place and a handkerchief knotted around his tanned throat. I can see the smile on his lips that would have turned Tom Mix green with envy and kept John Wayne awake at night. He was mounted on Silver with a rope at his saddle and a pair of pistols at his hips, and there was no doubt in the world who he was. He was the great champion of the down-trodden himself. He was Kemo Sabe or Faithful Friend, faithful to the task of bringing law and justice to the lawless plains at last. At his side was Tonto, and Tonto was John Turtle with his hair hanging down long and black and oily from his headband. He had his left hand cupped over his right shoulder and his right hand cupped over his left shoulder so that his fringed leather arms were crossed at his chest.

Bebb said, "I saw heaven open, and behold, a white horse, Antonio, and he that sat upon him was called Faithful and True, and in righteous-ness he doth judge and make war."

The Lone Ranger went galloping across the plain as tight to the saddle as though he and Silver were one, and little puffs of dust sprang up at each beat of the thundering hooves. Tonto followed along behind at an equal pace but jouncing up and down in his saddle with his elbows flopping like wings and his long hair streaming.

"Come on, Silver. Let's go, big fellow," the Lone Ranger called in that stern but reassuring baritone that had so often been a comfort to Miriam and me when we were left by ourselves in the New York apart-ment, and then the great Walkure shout of the Old West as he called out "Hi-yo Silver. Awa-a-ay!" and the steaming flanks gathered themselves together for a sprint up the side of a hill.

At the top of the hill the Lone Ranger and Tonto paused to scan the horizon, the masked man's gaze cutting east to west like a two-edged sword and Tonto shielding his eyes with one hand while with the other he kept knocking two of the bones around his neck together like castanets.

Chicka-chock, chicka-chocka, chuck-chocka they went. The horses tossed their heads eager to resume the chase. Far off in the distance there was a railroad train winding its way through the rolling landscape. Clouds of steam trailed out from its stack, and if you strained your ears, you could just make out the wail of its whistle. Herds of buffalo scattered at its approach.

"Look, Kemo Sabe," the red man said, pointing.

The Lone Ranger said, "We haven't a moment to lose, Tonto." He had only to give the lightest touch of his heel and they were off again, heading down the far side of the hill like wind.

It is a race against death as well as against time because bound across the railroad track, directly in the path of the hurtling locomotive, is the body of a man. It is my nephew Tony Blaine, who has been trussed around from head to toe with heavy rope. His arms are pinned to his sides so that he looks as if he is in a cocoon. I can see the white clouds in his eyes as he cranes to catch sight of his approaching doom, and when our eyes meet, we both acknowledge the impossibility of my helping him in any significant way.

He says only, "I'm sorry, Tono. I'm sorry," as if it is his fault that he is there or his fault that, to make life simpler for everybody including himself, he has not been there before this. When I ask him how he ever got in such a mess, he comes as close to shrugging his shoulders as he can, bound hand and foot, and that seems as good a way as any of saying that maybe it's not all that different from the mess he's always been in. Not so very far away now the train lets out another wail, and you can feel the faint trembling of it in the tracks.

I put my hands under his head so he won't have to keep holding it up all by himself, and his hair feels springy and matted the way it did the night he first confessed to me about himself and Sharon when by some strange reversal of roles I ended up being the one to comfort him. He has relaxed so that I can feel the full weight of his head in my hands now. It is surprisingly heavy, and I am afraid that if I should let go, his neck will break. He says, "That's some baby you've got, Tono," and as he says it, his eyes turn into x's again, and then the train is upon us, the terrible clatter and hiss and fiery brass of it, and I take the head of my namesake and cradle it against my chest just as the Lone Ranger comes galloping down the hill toward us.

There is no time to dismount, and he is hanging so far to the side from his saddle that I can't see what keeps him from falling. He has his six-shooter in his hand and is aiming it at the big hempen knot at Tony's feet. The rush of air is whipping his kerchief against his cheek, and through the eyeholes of his mask I can see his eyes narrowed against the blast of it.

Only a split second before it is too late, he fires. A silver bullet.

Zing! The knot is shattered. The rope uncoils like a serpent. The boy springs free and heads off across the plain as the train shoots by.

I hear the voice of Bebb. He is saying, "My beloved is like a roe or a young hart. Behold, he cometh leaping upon the mountains, skipping upon the hills. He feedeth among the lilies until the day breaks and the shadows flee away."

Bebb says, "Antonio, that boy of Virgil Roebuck's, he couldn't even take his own pecker out when it come time to make a leak. All his whole life he'll have to have somebody take it out for him or just let go in his pants. When I said, 'Hope, Roebuck. Roebuck, there's always hope,' Roebuck said, 'Someday maybe he'll learn how to hold a pencil up his ass like that girl that draws the Christmas cards, and that's all the hope that boy's ever like to have.' "

Ruby Luby is lying outside in a canvas deck chair which has one bad arm. She is wearing a two-piece bathing suit, and her head is covered with tight little curls held flat to her scalp by bobby pins. She is asleep with her arms folded back over her head, and there is a pale blueish tinge to her shaved armpits. Her transistor radio is going full tilt on the ground beside her, but it has drifted to a point somewhere between a ball game and somebody singing country western through his nose.

Jimmy Bob is sitting cross-legged in the dirt not far from her feet. He has nothing on but diapers and a pair of pink rubber pants that have a few spots of what looks as if it might be dried ketchup on them. From the waist up he is the color and shape of an unbaked loaf of bread. He has a pacifier in his mouth made of the same kind of translucent brown rubber that I associate with the bathing caps nurses used to wear on the beaches of my youth, and he is chewing on it like a five cent cigar. He is playing with a snake which, like Jimmy Bob, seems to be blind. It keeps raising its head and lowering it in apparently random directions. It is a dark, nondescript-looking snake, but inside its mouth it is the color of marshmallow whip.

Not far away the Lone Ranger is squatting on his heels looking on. The sun glitters from his silver spurs, and under the dark shadow of his Stetson you cannot tell his face from his mask. In a voice so quiet and even that it comes out almost like silence, he says, "Hold it, Tonto," and John Turtle stops in his tracks. He has been crawling forward on his knees and lower arms with his butt in the air and a gummed-up looking turkey feather tucked into the back of his headband. He is naked except for a strip of rawhide around his waist and two small flaps in front and back for modesty. In his fist he has a tomahawk which he had already raised to strike at the snake when the masked man stopped him.

After several unsuccessful tries, Jimmy Bob finally locates the snake and clasps it around the neck with both hands, the rest of its long body dangling limp as a jumprope. He raises it slowly up to where he can huddle its head against him so that he and the snake end up both facing forward, cheek to cheek, and then at almost the same moment the snake opens its snowy mouth wide and Jimmy Bob, with his eyes going crazy, opens his mouth wide too, and they look for all the world like a pair of old drinking companions launching off into *Show Me the Way to Go Home.*

Bebb says, "Antonio, there are three things which are too wonderful for me, yea four things which I know not, the book says. There's the way of an eagle in the sky, the way of a serpent on a rock, the way of a ship in the sea, and the way of a man with a maid. Plus there's a fifth one too that's not in the book, at least not in the same part. It's the way of that man when he comes riding into the world on his silver horse with justice on one hip and mercy on the other."

He says, "Antonio, he comes like a thief in the night, like a bridegroom to the bride he's got waiting for him with flowers in her hair. You should see how they turn pale when he comes, some of them. The cheaters of widows and orphans, for one, and the lawyers they pay to make it legal. The flag-waving politicians with their hand in the till. The folks that run the sex movies and the smut stores that poison the air of the world like a open sewer. The whole miserable pack of them. He doesn't do a thing in the world to hurt them because just standing there seeing him go by is hurtful enough, all that glory galloping by they missed by being spiteful and mean. Their hearts just break against the sight of him the way waves break against a rock."

Bebb said, "But it's the others that's the real sight to see, the ones that aren't any better than they ought to be but not all that much worse either. That means all of us pretty near. He comes riding up so fast on them there's no time to put on their Sunday suit and go wait for him in the front parlor with the Scriptures laying open on the table. The midwest farmgirl that run away from home and don't have any other way to make ends meet, she's sitting all painted up on a bar stool trying to look like she knows the difference between a martini cocktail and a root beer float. The middle-age drummer that hasn't made a sale all day is stretched out on his bed in a cheap motel staring at the ceiling with the TV on. The big-time executive is bawling out his secretary for coming back from her dinner ten minutes late, and the old waitress with varicose veins is taking the weight off her feet a few minutes in the help's toilet. Of that day and hour knoweth no man, Antonio. Therefore be ye also ready, for in such an hour as ye think not the Son of Man cometh."

"Brownie," Bebb said. "That pitiful Brownie, like as not he'll be off someplace trying to make the Book of Job sound like a Mothers Day card. Sharon's twisted herself into a knot doing yogi, and I can hear Gertrude Conover explaining it out to somebody how it was to be a short order cook back in ancient Rome. Antonio, the first time they all of them hear him holler out Hi-yo Silver, the place to watch is their face."

Bebb said, "You ever looked at somebody's face sitting in the window watching for his folks to come home? Say it's gotten dark and the roads are slippery and there's been some bad accidents come over the radio. One by one he watches the headlights of cars come winding up the hill. He's got his heart in his mouth hoping this time for sure it's going to be the one to slow down and pull into the yard, but one after the other they all just keep on driving past till his face goes grey waiting for what looks like it's never going to come. Antonio, that's the face we all of us got when we're not doing anything special with our face. You look at somebody the next time he's just sitting around staring into space when he doesn't know anybody's watching.

"Then finally when he's about given up hope and maybe dozed off a minute or two, he hears the back door open. He hears footsteps in the kitchen. He hears the voice out of all the voices of the world he's waiting for call out his name. Then you watch his face. Antonio, all over the world there'll be faces like that when the rider comes."

Then Bebb said, "I saw an angel standing in the sun, and he cried with a loud voice saying to all the fowls that fly in the midst of heaven, 'Come and gather yourselves together unto the supper of the great God,'" and the angel was Mr. Golden. He stood there with his queer, low-slung paunch and his porkpie hat. His withered face was lit up by his lovely girl's smile that showed his back teeth all missing. He had his arms up in the air as he spoke, and with the sun behind him they cast long shadows down over the sage-covered slope where he stood. He said, "Blessed are they which are called unto the marriage supper of the Lamb."

It was the marriage supper of Rose Trionka, only Rose coming down out of heaven this time instead of down out of the chancel of Holy Love in Houston, Texas. She was vast, white, glittering like a turreted city with pennants flying from the battlements and bunting streaming from the windows, and when she landed light as a summer cloud, the hillside blossomed all over with roses, and the Lone Ranger stepped up to take her by the fingers and lead her to the great feast.

Everybody was there. Lucille was there in a filmy, long-waisted dress that Irene Castle might have danced the Charleston in, and my sister Miriam with a circlet of orange blossoms in her dark hair. Herman Redpath was there in a headdress of snowy egret feathers that reached to the ground and Maude Redpath in silver fox and French heels. My nephew Tony was there with Laura Fleischman, his bride, and they were dressed as they'd been at their own wedding with Tony in a rented cutaway a little skimpy at the shoulders and Laura in white tulle and sweetheart lace. Sharon's old partner at the Sharanita Shop, Anita Steen, was there in tights and ruff like Sarah Bernhardt doing Hamlet, and Metzger was there, my erstwhile neighbor at Mrs. Gunther's boarding house, the one who arranged a three-rap signal on the wall between us in case he should suddenly start having a heart attack. My dentist Darius Bildabian was there and so was my ex brother-in-law Charlie Blaine and his nurse-companion

Billie Kling with her mink eyebrows and bullhorn voice.

And of course Bebb was there. He had on his maroon preaching robe with his scalp polished to a high sheen, and he came toward me bringing two people with him whom at first I didn't recognize. He told me their names, and it was only then that I saw they were my father in his World War One uniform and my Italian mother. I had just started toward them with my ams outstretched when suddenly everyone stopped talking and looked up toward the crown of the hillside where we were all gathered.

The Lone Ranger and Rose Trionka were standing against the sky. The Lone Ranger reached out and raised the veil from his bride's face. Then he reached up and took hold of the corner of his mask. When he pulled it off at last, the light was so overwhelming that for a few moments, like Emily Dickinson "I could not see to see."

When I could see again, it was Babe I saw—Babe the ufologist, ventriloquist, hypnotist, impersonator, in his T-shirt and jumbo shorts but dozing now in the afternoon sun, slumped over at the middle like a grain sack with his mouth ajar. He was a trickster and a slanderer, and by his own admission he believed the Gospel was just a way of putting things to people who weren't ready yet for the headier truths of Ufology. But insofar as he was the creator of my dream, I think he created it because with part of himself he would have liked to dream it too. I suspect that for Babe not believing may sometimes have been as hard as Bebb said believing was.

Anyway, when he woke up and fixed me with those saucer-spotting eyes again, he said, "I've got to make a living same as everybody else, Antonio. I usually get ten bucks for a consultation and five for a life-ray treatment, but seeing as you're kin, I'll make it ten even," and the way he said it, sitting there so fat and crooked and unabashed, I could see how if you didn't have anything else handy to put your faith in, you might be tempted, like Brownie, to put it in him.

12

A NUMBER OF THINGS happened elsewhere while I was having my consultation with Babe. Callaway found himself locked out of his room and his extra pair of pants, his beautiful shirts, his Agway cap, and everything he owned thrown into a heap in the place where the ice machine and the trash bin were. Gertrude Conover wanted to force a showdown with the manager then and there, but Callaway dissuaded her. He made a long speech which Sharon said even she had a hard time understanding, but apparently he got very excited in the course of it and at one point made a gesture of such violence that it knocked Brownie's glasses off and badly cracked one of the lenses. The result of the speech was that Gertrude Conover insisted they find another motel for Callaway and Brownie both, and the four of them set out in the Continental, dropping Sharon off at Babe's on the way because she saw it as an opportunity to wash her hair while nobody else was waiting for the can. She was on her way upstairs to do it when she nearly fell over Bert, who was sitting on the top step in her saddle shoes and bobby socks with her flyswatter on one side of her and a suitcase held together with clothesline on the other. She told Sharon she had been waiting for her and had a place she wanted to take her to and some things she wanted to show her. So Sharon put off the shampoo, and carrying the suitcase between them they walked up into the pine woods where Babe and I had jogged and kept going till they reached the place where the little collection of Stredwig gravestones stood among rusted out Sterno cans and the remains of a fence. The largest of the stones lay flat on the ground, the inscription long since garbled by weather, and while Babe and I were journeying into the future on Shaw Hill, Bert and Sharon sat down on the stone, the suitcase across Bert's knees, and started out on a journey of their own. The suitcase was of course the one that Bert had first pointed out in the little varnished room at the top of the back stairs, the one where she said she kept her treasures.

Apparently Bert did very little talking at first, and when I think of the scene, I think of the place in *Hamlet* where Polonius quizzes Ophelia on what the Prince said to her, and Ophelia answers with the speech in which she describes no words he spoke but goes on in some detail about what he did with his hands, arms, shoulders, eyes, face, to which Polonius then replies, "This is the very ecstasy of love." That's the way I see Bert sitting there among the graves beside Sharon, not saying much but moving the way clouds move, which is to say so slowly and subtly you can hardly see what is happening until little by little it has happened. As one by one she pulls her treasures out of the suitcase on her lap, small things go on in her face that make big differences. The forehead puckers, the eyes go puddled and dark, the cheeks melt in places like snow. I see her whole bulk shifting—a saddle shoe toeing slightly inward, a grey curl trembling, as she hands things to Sharon in whatever order she happens to come on them.

There were photographs with no shadows in them—a woman walking away from a square car with a paper bag in her arms, two men in straw hats sitting in rockers with water behind them, a woman with the top of her head gone. Once in a while Bert would say something. "This is the summer I turned nineteen?" she said. She said, "That's the one they called Fiddling Sam? Played at our senior hop?" She said, "When she took sick the last time, they forgot and left her in the hammock the whole day. She was all over honeybees when they found her? All that cologne, they thought she was a rosebush?" She said, "That's your daddy?" and Sharon said to me, "When she was handing me the ones of Bip, she pressed her lips together and hummed little tunes." There was Bip in knickers. There was Bip in an open roadster holding up a copy of Scripture in each hand. There was Bip with his face so faded out his features looked like bird tracks in the snow.

Sharon said, "I said, 'Bert, you want me to read this?' She took it out of the envelope and spread it out on my lap for me. You'd have thought I was a big doll. She put her hand on my head and bent it like a doll's so I'd read it."

Sharon read it to me. It said, " 'My own sweet honey love, I was in tears for you last night. What's it mean when a man's heart's so full he cries tears? If God is love like the book says, then the love God is is tears because that's what it is for me most of the time we're apart and I have to pretend like I don't care. Every time he says you two this, you two that, my heart skips a beat. I'll be there the same time tomorrow anyhow no matter if you come or not. If God is love there's no love doesn't have some God in it along with all the rest it's got in it too. You are my love and tears both, and there's nothing God doesn't wash whiter than snow in the end though it makes his love cry tears too. Sweet dreams to my own sweet honey love.' " Bert's face slowly tumbled together like clouds, a stray wisp disappearing into the sky. Her nostrils swelled out with the tune she was humming, Sharon's head bent like a doll's beside her.

Sharon said, "I said, 'Jesus, Bert. That's a moonflop.' It was wrapped up in pink tissue with a rubber band and it was about the same shape as a moonflop only littler. It was a round piece of hard clay with this little bit of a hand-print pressed into it like they do in grade school. It had a hole in it to hang it up, and it had a name scratched in with a match it looked like. Bert said, 'He went and stole it for me?' and I said, 'You're asking me, Bert?' She said, 'I'm telling you, honey.' "

Sharon said, "She said Bip went and stole it away from Luce and mailed it to her. She said she never saw him after he married Luce and moved to Knoxville but sometimes he'd write her a line or two. She's got them all saved. Sometimes all he wrote were words out of Scripture. He'd write her things like 'Damsel, I say unto thee arise' and 'Let him who is without sin cast the first stone' and 'Lo I am with you alway, even unto the end of the world.' "

Sharon said, "She had things in there too she'd found laying around the house from when he was growing up in it. There was his lunch pail he took to school with him that's got his name still scratched on the lid and a piece of scorecard where he'd got Babe Ruth to sign his name on it when he came through Spartanburg once. She had a diary in there he'd kept for a while. It was lots of it just how he laid out five cents for phosphate or fishline or something and how he took in a quarter drawing stove wood in his wagon, but there were places he'd list off his sins for the week. He wrote he copied off of Emma Missildine's paper, and he and his buddy caught them a bullfrog and played toss with it till one of its legs came off. He put down the times he used bad language and things like *sassed Mama* with a number after it. Bert said there were plenty of good deeds he could have put down too, but I told her when you do a good deed, you're not even supposed to act like you notice it."

"He raised a sigh so piteous and profound," Ophelia says, "as it did seem to shatter all his bulk," and I picture Bert's shattered bulk as she turns to Sharon there among the fallen stones and hands her a snapshot of herself as she was before her features started huddling together for protection and she put on all that flesh—a flapper with her hair flat to her cheeks and her stockings rolled below the knee. She and Babe are sitting side by side on some porch steps and behind them a woman in a long skirt with her head and shoulders lost in the shadow of the porch roof. She says, "That's Babe's mother?" She says, "That's the year I lost my baby?" and Sharon says, "I didn't know you and Babe had a baby," and Bert says, "It wasn't Babe's baby I had." Then that profound and piteous sigh that shook the grey curls, the fat arms, cracked the face down the middle in an ecstasy of love.

Sharon said, "I mean Jesus, Bopper, what could I say? 'Whose baby?' I said, 'Take it easy, Bert.' She had all that stuff out of the grip scattered around her and more stuff still to go, and she was sitting there making that little sound she makes to the chickens heekie, heekie, heekie. I just said, 'Take it easy, Bert,' and after a while it came out piece by piece like she was counting out money.

"Bip did it again," Sharon said. "He and Luce weren't married yet, but Babe and Bert were. She said there was a time they were both of them courting her together, and for a while she couldn't choose between them, but she fixed on Babe finally because Bip was already starting to get into selling Bibles and Babe was home more. She and Babe got married and lived with the mother, and Bip would come home weekends some. She and Bip would go off together berrying. Babe got sun-rash so he didn't go, just the two of them with their pails up there on that hill where Babe says the UFOs are supposed to land. I guess that's why he wants them to land up there so he'll have something else to remember that hill by. When Bert was telling about it, she was like a saucer herself getting ready to land. She'd tell about it as far as the hill, and then just when she was going to come out with it, she'd make that chicken noise again and shy off. And pulling more stuff out of the grip the whole time. Like those notes made up out of Scripture that sometimes didn't even have Bip's name signed on them. Sometimes they'd just be words of hymns like 'The night is dark and I am far from home' and 'I need thee every hour.' "

Sharon said, "She finally made a three point landing and told it like it was. She said it finally happened she and Bip made it up there in the berry bushes and the clouds while Babe was back home taking care of his sun-rash. It just about killed them both afterwards, the shame of it, and they vowed they'd never let it happen again. Bip went and married Luce to make sure it wouldn't. Then Bert found out she was going to have Bip's baby. She tried to make out at first like it was Babe's, but Babe knew it wasn't and finally wormed it out of her whose it really was. He had his suspicions from the start. She said he carried on so it almost made her lose her baby. Babe said when the baby was born he wouldn't have it in his house, and he went to Knoxville and raised hell with Bip over it. There was this terrible row, the two of them rolling around on the floor pounding each other to pieces and poor Luce there watching. She was pregnant with the baby that later on died so there were these two women both of them pregnant by Bip, and Bert says part of what sent Babe clear out of his head was he couldn't make anybody pregnant himself. It seems like he was the twin that got the hair and Bip was the twin that got the balls, and he all but killed Bip, beating on his head till his eyes were so swelled up one of them never did work right again from then on. Jesus, Bopper, the way she sat there telling it all with her treasures scattered around her like a picnic and the sweat rolling down out of her wig."

It was later that night that Sharon told me and in the kitchen, of course, that room that has always been the Oval Office of my life, the place where the great crises sizzle and snap like bacon, where most of my major decisions have been made like breakfast. The events of the day had been such that we were divided into two hostile camps by then, and everybody except Sharon and me was trying to get some sleep before what was bound to be some kind of showdown the next day. The only light was the little one over the stove, and it was both very peaceful and very charged in there with the fireflies twinkling outside like enemy campfires. We were sitting at the kitchen table, and Sharon was looking down at it, tracing circles with her finger where the evening before Babe's black coffee and black cake had made circles.

"Poor Bert," she said. "She lost Bip and Babe both. She lost her hair. She lost her baby. It was a girl."

"Died?" I said.

She said, "Adopted. Babe swore he'd kill it if she ever brought it home."

I said, "Has she ever seen it since?" and she said, "She's seen it."

"Bip's own flesh and blood floating around somewhere," I said. "It gives you a queer feeling."

"Queer as hell," she said.

I suppose it was the lateness of the hour that had slowed me down, not to mention the lingering effect of the life-ray and the anticipation of bloodshed to come, but up until then I had thought it was Bert she was mainly telling me about. Then she glanced up from her circles with a look on her face that I don't think I had ever seen there before. Up till then the only opening I had known into the secret of her face was that sudden flare of a smile she had, but as I looked at her now, her whole face was flickering with secret like a candle though there wasn't a smile within miles—just those guilty eyes, that somber mouth—and I said, "Who adopted Bert's baby anyway?" and she said, "I'll give you three guesses," and it was only then that in the balloon above my head the lightbulb came on the full five hundred watts worth at last, and I said, "Jesus Christ. I don't believe it."

She said, "You better believe it, Bopper. That's the truth of it," and I said, "You know, it's a funny thing, but there's someplace in me where I've always known it was." She said, "Put her there then. I've always known it was too," her hand coming at me over the white table. Then right there in the Oval Office with everybody else asleep I shook hands with the flesh and blood of Leo Bebb and for the first time in my life knew for sure that that was who I was shaking hands with and knew a lot of other things besides.

The present is always up for grabs, of course, and the future, who knows, but at least the past you think you've got salted away where neither moth nor rust doth corrupt nor thieves break through and steal. Then the first thing you know, the past starts playing tricks on you too. Like coffee that's spilled on page one hundred and stains its way back through page twenty-five, the revelation of Sharon's true identity—the strawberry mark on the left shoulder, the coronet on the baby blanket— changed the shape of events I'd thought were safe long since. I think of that evening barbecue at the Red Path Ranch when I proposed to her, for instance—how as she came walking toward me through the firelit Indians with her arm in a sling and wearing a moonlight-colored dress, Bebb appeared behind me and softly spoke words into my ear to the effect that she was mine for the taking. What he was inviting me to take, of course, was not just the apple of his eye but the flesh of his flesh, the breath of his life, and it was not until all those long years later that I understood she was more precious to him than he could possibly tell without impossibly telling at the same time the whole unseemly tale of his dalliance with Bert among the clouds and berry bushes and the terrible time in Knoxville, Tennessee, when those two roly-polies tried to destroy each other at the feet of poor, pregnant Lucille.

And I think of the last time Bebb and Sharon ever saw each other in the basement of the storage warehouse where Bebb was hiding out from his enemies. Sharon had her head on Bebb's shoulder, and they both of them had a kind of dreaming look in their eyes as though they were looking at a sunset. The truth of it was that what Bebb was looking at was the knowledge that this was the last chance he'd ever get to tell her who he was and who she was and that he was never going to tell her.

And Lucille and Bert, Bebb's two great loves—in the new light I saw them both in new ways too. Lucille sits in front of the color TV with her dark glasses on and a Tropicana in her hand; and the TV, the dark glasses, the Tropicanas, all three are what she uses to hide behind from everybody including herself. Why did she develop her taste for gin and orange juice? Why did what happened to her baby happen? Why did Bebb marry her in the first place? She drops her lower jaw in what it takes an expert to spot as a smile. "You tell me," she says with that Foster Grant blank where her eyes ought to be. She looks like someone watching a total eclipse of the sun.

The first time we meet her, Bert says, "Has he passed?" Passed out, passed through? She is holding Babe's charred shoulderpads in her hand. Rain falls on the Uforium roof. Her face is the moon, and when I answer that he has passed indeed, I watch my answer make its historic landing there, and I think at the time that it's only Babe's brother we are talking about, a man it's been years since she thought of last.

Thus Bert's graveyard disclosures as Sharon reported them to me late that night cast light on many things, but nowhere was the light they cast more illuminating than on the garish event that had taken place only a few hours earlier to make of that day the Hallowe'en of my life, as I look back on it, with false faces falling off and the truth beneath the white sheet turning out to be a truth to make the hair stand on end.

It was after I had had my life-ray treatment on Shaw Hill and after poor Bert had spilled the beans to Sharon in the woods. Around five or so Gertrude Conover came back from her tour with Brownie and Callaway bearing the news that there wasn't a motel to be found that would take them in. She bore the news also that Callaway had had another nosebleed. The two facts were not, in her estimation, unrelated. Theosophically speaking, she said, no facts were unrelated. The motel keepers' intransigence, suggesting that Babe's slanders had spread like the plague, was the problem, she said; and the nosebleed, suggesting what it always suggested, pointed to a solution. The solution was that we should seek out Bebb. Having gotten us to Poinsett in the first place, he was the logical one for us to turn to for help. There was no question in her mind where we should look for him. She had the address in her pocket where she had put it when Ruby Luby gave it to her at the Well Baby Clinic. It was Lola's Trailer Court. She said that since in his present incarnation Bebb was only a year or so old, it might take something to jog his memory about who we were and what we needed him for, and luckily, anticipating some such eventuality, she had brought along a relic that should do the trick nicely. It was Bebb's maroon preaching robe, the same one that he had led his famous march on Nassau Hall in, and although Jimmy Bob would not be able to see it, of course, she felt that just its presence should be sufficient. Babe was not around when we left, only Bert, resting upstairs, and Sharon slipped a note under her door telling her where we were going just in case she needed us.

In my normal state of mind I don't think I could have set off on such a crackpot errand without cracking up in the process somehow myself, but by then I was not in my normal state of mind. Beginning, I suppose, with the experience of thinking that I'd seen Bebb in the Library of Congress reading room and proceeding from there to the moonrocks, the transistorized teeth, Jimmy Bob, the life-ray, the Lone Ranger, I had moved step by step to a kind of panicky openness to almost any possibility, which I suspect must be, if not the same thing as what people like Bebb would call faith, at least its kissing cousin. Sharon and I, Callaway and Brownie and Gertrude Conover, there we were, all five of us, piled into the Continental with the maroon preaching robe folded up in Gertrude Conover's lap like the flag they give a soldier's widow, bound for a trailer-court interview with the reincarnation of a dead evangelist, and although I thought even at the time that it was folly to believe anything could come of it, I thought too that it would be a greater folly still to believe that nothing possibly could. In a world where we are often closer to the truth in dreams than anywhere else, who is to say what is possible and not possible, true and not true, any more than in dreams you can say it? Callaway drove with Brownie beside him, the two ladies and I in back, and I thought of Gideon and Barak and Samson and all those others who are said to have spent their lives dreaming of a homeland which they had had only a glimpse of from afar and not all that clear a glimpse either. I mentioned them to Brownie as we set off just to see what he would say, and I remember him still as he turned to look at me over the back of his seat through his cracked lenses and said, "They were the great heroes of the faith, dear, but they died still guessing just like the rest of us."

Lola's Trailer Court was a raw, jerrybuilt-looking place right off the main road across from a drive-in movie. The trailers didn't seem to have been parked in any special order but just abandoned at various angles around a one story cinderblock building with a Kwik Wash and a Coke machine and an office where presumably Lola herself did business. There were some lines strung up with wash hanging on them. There were some trash-filled oil drums. There was a man with a bottle wrapped in a brown paper bag who pointed out where the Lubys' trailer was. It was out on the edge of things, and we moved our car to a place nearer to it where there was a stand of pines and some bird-spattered picnic tables.

It had turned overcast and much hotter since the freshness of the morning, and the light was hazy and dim with a sense of thunder in the air. Gertrude Conover looked pale and older than usual standing by the picnic tables with the robe over her arm. Her hair had lost much of its blue and didn't have the same bounce to it. Her upper lip was moist with perspiration. Her spirit, however, remained undampened as she explained her strategy to us. It was not uncomplicated.

We would all go to the trailer, she said, but only she would go in, because she didn't want to scare the Lubys out of their wits right at the start and there wouldn't be room for all five of us anyway. The rest of us would wait outside where the combined force of our karmic fields would, even through the trailer walls, start stirring in Jimmy Bob memories of the life he had once lived among us. It was important, Gertrude Conover said, not to stir them too much or too soon because she wouldn't want the child to reveal anything in front of his parents that might alarm them or lead them to suspect that there was anything unusual about him. "He will have a hard enough time in that family as it is, poor thing," she said, and for the same reason she would not bring the maroon preaching robe in with her because with all its rich Bebbsian associations she expected it to open the door wide in him that our combined karma would have barely pushed ajar. We would leave it in the car instead, she said, and after spreading it out over the front seat, to increase its power to awaken Jimmy Bob, she pinned to it one of the flyers that had been passed out during the same famous march in Princeton. Just to make sure. "Ban the Bomb not Bebb" it said, in reference to the University's eviction of the love feasts from Alexander Hall, and there was a head-and-shoulders mug shot of Bebb with his eyes bugged out and his mouth clamped shut that Sharon said made him look as if he was having his temperature taken rectally.

The trick, Gertrude Conover said, would be to get the baby to the robe without his parents. She said, "I will explain that we were just passing by and happened to recognize the address she gave us. She will remember how I took an interest in the child at the clinic, and I will tell her I wanted to see him again before we left. Maybe I will tell her I have some little present for him in the car, or maybe I will ask to take him for a stroll in his pushcart while the rest of you stay by the trailer to distract her. Well, I will depend on the inspiration of the moment. We will see what we will see."

Sharon said, "How do you figure he's going to be able to help us, Gertrude Conover? He can't see the hand in front of his face and he probably doesn't have ten words he can say together in a row."

Gertrude Conover said, "Who knows what he can see? As for helping us, he has helped us already. He has given us a point to rally around when we're all at sea about what to do next. My dear, he has given us hope."

Brownie said, "A little child shall lead them, the prophet says. The trouble is where is there to lead us to when we're all lost in the dark together?"

He said, "It's the blind leading the blind, dear. We can't any of us see much more than the hand in front of our face. Nobody knows for sure there even is a hand." I could hear in his speech that he must have taken a little something before we left, and I wondered if Mother was home still and how the new set of teeth was coming along. I wondered how rough a time he was having of it now that the Babe he so admired had turned against the Callaway he so loved and how he would ever be able to choose between them if the time ever came when he had to choose.

Gertrude Conover led the way to the Lubys' trailer, and the rest of us followed along in single file. The bodies of the trailers were silvery and dim in the fading light. We could have been threading our way through wrecks at the bottom of the sea.

It was Ruby Luby who answered Gertrude Conover's knock. There was a smell of frying food as she stood in the doorway with children peering out from behind her skinny legs. Gertrude Conover did the talking while the rest of us hovered around in the background radiating karma. In a few moments they disappeared into the trailer together, and the door closed behind them. Then Callaway had a recurrence of his nosebleed.

It wasn't one of his worst ones by a long shot, but it was enough to keep us occupied while we waited for Gertrude Conover to reappear with Jimmy Bob. Brownie walked back to the Coke machine and returned with a cold bottle which Callaway pressed to his upper lip while at the same time somehow holding the handkerchief in place. I wondered how much he understood of what we were there to accomplish and whether Gertrude Conover had ever explained to him her theory about his nosebleeds, and then finally the door opened again and Gertrude Conover came out with Jimmy Bob in her arms. Ruby came out too in some kind of Sears Roebuck sunsuit. Then a T-shirted man I took to be her husband came with a beer belly swelling out over his belt and a disagreeable face with the upper lip caved in. They stood there on the steps for a moment as though posing for a photograph, and then suddenly Gertrude Conover pointed out over our heads to where we had left the car. "Good God," she said, and my first thought was that it was part of her ruse for getting Jimmy Bob to the preaching gown. It was not.

It was Bert. Even at a distance and through the dwindling light, I could recognize the grey curls, the shapeless bulk. Like the time at the hen house, there was something violent going on though at first it was hard to see what. She was standing at the car with her back to us. Her shoulders were heaving, and you could tell she was doing something that required great strength and great concentration. She could have been a medieval executioner gutting a felon. There was a wrenching, rasping sound. She was getting her back into it. Something gave way, and for a moment she almost lost her balance. Then one arm shot up, and something flew glittering through the air. It was the side-view mirror that had been torn from its socket. She did the same thing in half the time with the aerial. She took some weapon I could not identify and like Casey at the bat swung it full force against one of the side windows. There was a sound of shattering glass. She flung the door open and the horn blared as she must have hit it leaning in. Something flashed red, then redder and bigger as she held it out wide. It was Bebb's robe with his picture pinned to it, and eyeball to eyeball they must have stared at each other for a moment or two as I pulled myself together sufficiently to start running toward them. Even as I ran, the most furious part of the attack took place.

It must have been recognizing the picture and seeing whose robe it was that triggered it. She ripped at the robe, yanked it, punched it, for all I know took it between her teeth and gnawed at it. She threw it to the ground and leaped on it. Like Oliver Hardy demolishing a Model T, she jumped up and down on it with her arms flung wide, her head bent low, her legs pumping. There was terror in it and comedy in it and a deep, twilit silence in it that heightened them both because from where I was anyway she made no more noise in her rage than she would have made in a dream about rage. Then I reached her and there took place the final falling apart into two of things, the refusal of things to stay put, stay simple and unitary and true enough for a man to put his trust in and get his bearings by. I grabbed her by the shoulders and spun her around, and it was only then that I saw that the person standing there in that tent of a dress with the massive grey wig knocked crooked was not Bert at all. It was Babe.

It was Babe looking the way he had that night by the refrigerator with the dead hen in his hand, Babe with his face shattered like the window of the car and put back together by a creature from outer space who'd never seen more than a rough diagram of a face. He gave me one wild, searching look and then broke loose from my grasp. Clutching his dress in a knot at his groin, he ran back toward the trailer as best he could where the others were still standing too flabbergasted to move. Then back toward me again. Then he stopped dead in his tracks for a moment, his bare legs milky pale beneath his trussed-up skirts.

"Laverne!" he shouted in a windy, faraway voice like the voice a child hears calling him home when evening comes, and with all the other thoughts running through my mind, the one that outran the lot was the thought that this was Brownie's moment of truth. Did he go to Babe or did he stay with the others by the trailer? Gertrude Conover was the only one of them left on the trailer steps. She stood in the open doorway with Jimmy Bob in her arms. He was a big baby, and she was standing at an awkward angle so she could support part of his weight on her hip. He had one hand in the air in front of him, the palm facing out. Though he was straddling her hip, his face was turned in the same direction hers was. If he hadn't been blind, you would have said he was gazing toward Babe like the rest of us, maybe even signaling to him.

Once more the sound of Brownie's name went drifting through the air, and this time Brownie responded. I can see him still as he moved slowly away from his friends. I couldn't see his face from that distance, but if I could, I would have looked the other way. I suppose it was Mother who was calling him—Mother in drag, with her curls knocked cockeyed, the sweat rolling down. All around us the dim hulks of the trailers glimmered. By the mutilated Continental, the red robe lay stamped into the red dust and what was left of Bebb's face on the flyer goggled up at the darkening sky. In the arms of Gertrude Conover, fluttering his small, flat eyes, maybe Jimmy Bob said something, but if so, nobody heard him.

Nobody did anything. We all just watched as Babe and Brownie moved off through the dusk together with their arms around each other somehow, holding each other up. They headed for the picnic tables. They disappeared into the pines where the branches swallowed them up, babes in the woods. I was the only one who had been close enough to see who the car's attacker really was, but I didn't want to say anything about it in front of the Lubys, and when I finally did say it on the ride home with Callaway at the wheel—his dignity intact despite the raw, twisted scars where the aerial and sideview mirror had been and the cobweb-shattered window—I don't think they really believed it. Even I didn't entirely believe it.

As soon as we got home, the four of us filed upstairs to Bert's bedroom, a stunned and silent deputation, and there she was, as fast asleep as when Sharon had left her note. She was lying in bed bald as an egg with her suitcase on the floor beside her. The clothesline was tied back around it. We did not wake her.

There was so much to say that nobody had the energy to try to start saying it. Gertude Conover was the one who seemed the most done in. In addition to everything else, there had been her long, unsuccessful search for a new motel for Callaway, and she looked exhausted. Her walk was unsteady, her seams crookeder than usual, more loose hairpins dangling. Nevertheless, before retiring for the night, she pulled herself together and made a small speech.

She said, "Well, it was a disappointment. Why pretend it wasn't? I am getting old. I am getting old. I am old as the hills already. I know my theosophy must seem far-fetched and dotty to you. There are times when it seems far-fetched and dotty to me. Do I remember my past lives, or do I just dream them up? Maybe the past is always something you just dream up. Who can be sure of anything when you come right down to it? I had such high hopes. A little touch of Leo in the night. I had hoped that Jimmy Bob might give some sign. Well, he didn't. It has left me feeling very blue. I feel very blue and old and dumb.

"And yet," she said, her hand on the varnished bannister, "Thank your stars there is always *and yet*. This side of Paradise, perhaps it is the best you can hope for. Jimmy Bob gave no sign, but think of it this way. If it weren't for him, what happened this evening would never have happened. If it weren't for him, we would have gone on thinking that it was poor Bert playing Yahoo tricks all these years when all along it was Babe. I don't believe for a moment this was the first time. Obviously the man is mad. So maybe what happened this evening was itself the sign. And what didn't happen was a sign too. It was a sign saying not to look for miraculous signs because we wouldn't see them even if they were served up to us on a silver platter. My dear, everything that happens is absolutely seething with miracle, and who sees it? Who even wants to see it most of the time? Life is confusing enough as it is."

She went about half way up the stairs, her slip showing. The bannister creaked as she leaned on it. Then she turned once again and looked back at us over her shoulder. "One more thing," she said, "and then I will shut up and go to bed. It is just this. I held him in my arms again. You don't have to be a theosophist to see what a wretched time he is going to have growing up in that family. You should have seen the inside of that trailer, and I shudder when I think of the meanness and ignorance in the face of his father. Leo Bebb has always had frightful luck with his fathers. But when I held him in my arms, all those sad things seemed to melt away. All the things that menace him seemed to draw back like wild animals from a fire, and all the things that menace me too. I could feel it in my bones, and I know he could feel it too. He laid his little head against me, and you can call it dotty if you want, but for a moment I believe even death itself drew back. There was nothing in heaven or earth that could hurt us. I believe that for a moment we achieved cosmic consciousness, my dear old friend and I, and not even death and all his minions could touch us with a ten-foot pole."

She said, "I am going up now. It has been the longest day of my life. When I'm finished with the bathroom, I will leave the door open. Sweet dreams."

I asked Sharon two questions before we finally went upstairs ourselves. The first question was what had happened between her and Bert when she first found out she was her mother, and Sharon said, "It wasn't like we made a big fuss over each other or anything like that. It was more like it made us strangers all over again. I could feel my face go all frozen and queer on me. Neither of us said much. What can you say? She had all that stuff to put back in her grip again, and I helped her. We lugged it home together through the trees. I didn't kiss her even, or her me. It wasn't till I looked in on her before we left for Lola's that I kissed her just once on top of her old bald head, and she didn't even know it. I could have been kissing Bip the way it felt. It was like when I used to kiss Bip on top of his old bald head the same way."

The second question was why, when she'd found the truth out that afternoon, she'd waited till then to tell me about it, and she said, "I used to lay awake nights wondering who my real folks were, and when I finally found out, it was like I wanted to just keep it to myself a while. For a few hours there wasn't anybody in the whole world that knew Bip was my father and Bert was my mother except me and Bert. Not even you, Bopper. I guess it was the closest I ever got to a family reunion."

Then she said, "She gave me this out of her grip the last thing she did before she closed it up again. She told me it proved who I was in case

I ever had to prove it, and I could have it if I'd keep it safe somewhere and never lose it."

It was written in Bebb's hand on the back of a Light of Truth Bible Company order blank, and it said, "Dear One, I went and picked her up today where you said and brought her home to Luce. Luce was laying on the sofa tuned in to Major Bowes on the wireless. She's been listening to that thing day in day out for weeks. I guess it takes her mind off things. When I set the baby alongside her on the sofa, she didn't even look like she noticed, so for a while there I just about died. Finally she reached down and poked the blanket back with one finger so she could see what it looked like inside, and there was that pitiful little bundled-up thing watching her with those big eyes she's got on her like she knows the secret of life. It was like I'd given her her own baby back she'd lost. She picked it up and cuddled it against her, and things started in to happen all over her whole face you could tell she's got a chance again now to join the human race. Before, she was a goner if I ever saw one the way she was just laying there day after day on the sofa with the wireless going. So you see you've done the right thing letting her take the baby.

"Bert, my ways are not thy ways, saith the Lord. You'd think that baby was the love of God incarnate the change she's made for good in Luce's poor broken heart always thinking back on the awful thing she did when she was out of her head with drink. You don't ever have to worry again our baby won't have all the love a baby ever had in this world. Luce has fixed on giving her the name of Sharon. I guess you know the name I would have given her, but it's all the same anyway.

"Bert, let's never forget what was pure and good that we had between us, and let's never remember more than we can help it what was shameful. The judgment upon us is we'll never set eyes on each other again this side of glory, and Sharon she'll never know who we truly are to her till then either. It's not the way we either one of us would have ever picked, but there's not any way on this earth doesn't lead to the throne of grace in the end if that's where you've got your heart set on going. Farewell, my own dear heart. I won't ever forget. Remember me in your prayers the same as I'll always remember you, and remember our little one.

                                                                    Leo Bebb."

13

SINCE BABE still had her wig, wherever he was, Bert had to make do the next morning with a hat. It was an old-lady straw-colored straw hat with pale blue and green paper roses at the brim, and she came down to make breakfast wearing it and a sleazy, flowery dressing gown to go with it that fluttered when she moved, a whole bank of flowers nodding in the breeze. Sharon said later she looked like a garden party at the funny farm, but if so, one of the great garden parties, her face more at rest than I'd ever seen it, blooming almost, the features no longer so crowded, the forehead unpuckered. Of course it was the first time I'd ever seen her as Bebb's dark and secret love, more even than Lucille and Gertrude Conover the real love of his life, I suppose, not to mention the mother of Sharon, the grandmother of my children whom she didn't even know existed, my own mother-in-law. All of it came at me full force for the first time as she moved around like late spring putting breakfast together. She said, "Where's Babe?"

It was her only question up to that point, the day so drowsy still with early sun, so unopened, that there'd been no time yet for other questions. It was the one I dreaded. I didn't want to tell her about Lola's Trailer Court and went at it in such an oblique way it's a wonder she knew what I was talking about. I told her about parking the Continental by the bird-spattered picnic tables and how the trailers looked like sunken ships. I slipped it in about somebody's appearing out of the pines while we were waiting for Gertrude Conover to come out. I alluded to his doing something strange and violent to the Continental. I mentioned that in the dwindling light it was hard to make out just who he was, and then in that little toy voice she said, "It was Babe?" and I didn't have to answer for her to know the answer.

She said, "He have on my wig and things?" and when I nodded, she said, "I always knew it was Babe."

I said, "Why didn't you tell people it was Babe for God's sake?" and she said, "Who'd believe a Stredwig?" So all in a moment I saw her not just as Bebb's dark and secret love but as the bearer of yet another secret of her own—that year after year she had sat there bald as an egg while Babe went out in her grey curls smashing things, and that swatting flies and smoking cigarettes she had known year after year that he was doing it.

It was my turn to ask the questions then, and her answers came with question marks after them the way everything she said came with a question mark after it to indicate that if you found what she had to say not to your liking for any reason, you were free to change it to anything you liked better just as Babe was free to dress up in her clothes and Bebb was free to adopt their baby and never tell her who she was for fear the shame of it might be too much for them all. "Who'd believe a Stredwig?" she said, as if she wouldn't be apt to believe herself even unless you gave her special leave and encouragement. There she was, known for the first time for who she truly was and what she truly knew, yet that didn't seem to shield her any better from the world than her sleazy wrapper or paper roses shielded her. Her little question-answers came pitter-pattering out.

"He's not to blame?" she said. "After what I did, I had it coming?

It was a shameful thing? Leo and me we never planned it to happen like it did. It just happened a little at a time up to where one day Leo said, 'Bert, I don't even know my right name any more. I don't even know Jesus any more. You're the only one I know for sure out of the whole world, Bert. You're the only one I need to know.' It's scary, that kind of loving? It gives you the power of life and death?"

I thought of Bebb as she quoted him, how part of what he treasured inside that fat, buttoned-up face was the memory of the time he no longer knew the name of Jesus, how part of what he had bared in Miami Beach like a wound for the flummoxed children somehow to heal must have been the shame of it.

Bert broke six white eggs into a white bowl and beat them with a fork, her roses trembling. She said, "Every year there'd be windows broken? There'd be flower-beds stomped and trash cans pushed over. A privy'd catch fire? A chicken's neck wrung? My poor heekie. I always could tell by when my wig was gone. Babe's smart? He knows I'd sooner die than go out bald-headed. That way there wasn't ever a chance of two of me showing up at the same time?"

She said, "Folks in Points think a lot of Babe but they're scared too? Him and his life-ray? Nobody ever did anything if they saw crazy old Bert doing crazy things come sundown. They no more mentioned it to him than if I was a harelip he had or a crooked leg. I didn't either? I never once said, 'Babe how come you're doing it?' I couldn't shame him, saying it out like that."

"Why did he do it, Bert?" I said.

She said, "What man would ever look twice at a woman that knocks down pea-fences at night? Children poke each other when they see me. I don't go downstreet any more hardly, except the dentist? He wants me like one of his moonrocks. He does it so nobody'll get too close for fear of moongerms. That's why?"

She said, "Sometimes I talk to him in my mind? I say, 'Babe, you ever going to be done revenging yourself?' He says, 'Bert, I'm not revenging anymore.' He says, 'I'm keeping you safe, Bert. I'm making it so there won't ever anybody get at and hurt you again.'"

"Jesus," Sharon said. She said, "You're going to get the hell out of here, Bert. You're going to pack your things and come home with us. You tell her, Bopper. She can't stay here with that sonofabitch," and I remember still Bert's face wilting as she said it.

She said, "He was taking a big chance doing it there at Lola's in broad daylight?"

I said, "Bip used to take big chances. Maybe it's in their blood."

"The hell you say," Sharon said. "Bip took chances there was a god in heaven and angels on earth with gold and silver faces on them. The only chances Babe ever took was nobody'd catch him out a liar—all that shit about going to the moon."

Bert said, "That's not shit, honey? He's told me about the moon till it's like I've been there my ownself?"

The coffee was perking and upstairs you could hear Gertrude Conover and Callaway moving around. In the grey light from the window, Bert's face became the moon she was thinking about. She said, "Babe says it's all over little round stones like goat turds. It's just miles and miles of goat turds far as the eye can see. Babe says it's got this awful odor to it too? He says it's so strong it seeps in through your space helmet? He says the whole moon smells like where it needs mopping up around the toilet, all musty and sharp like stale wee."

"The other planets have it too?" she said. "Babe says the creatures live on them have to keep plugs in their noses it's so bad."

"That's where they're going to spacelift us to?" Sharon said. "Jesus."

Bert said, "They've got shots against death there, honey?"

"Hot damn," Sharon said.

I said, "You believe it, Bert?" and her answer was as uninterrogatory as any I ever heard her make. She said, "Everybody's got to believe something."

Suddenly, out of nowhere, a new voice spoke. It said, "That is true, dear," and we all wheeled around to find that it was Brownie, of course. He'd come in through the front and was standing behind us in the doorway.

It was Brownie's voice and yet not Brownie's voice just as it was Brownie and yet not Brownie. It was Brownie grown twenty years older. He was leaning against the jamb with a silvery stubble on his chin and his clothes all wrinkled as though he had slept in them. It was Brownie without his teeth.

To come upon a man without his teeth is an unnerving business under any circumstances. It not only changes his face but changes all faces in more or less the same way so that, like mongoloids, every man without his teeth looks much like all other men without their teeth. My dentist Darius Bildabian has a habit of leaving his treatment doors open, and I have stumbled into more acquaintances than I care to remember in just such a state. But in Brownie's case the change was even more unnerving still because without his teeth he was without his smile. And Brownie *was* his smile. I never realized how much so until the grotesque and tragic moment when he tried to smile for me when he had nothing in the world to smile with. It was like seeing a man try to walk without legs.

Sharon said, "Brownie, what's happened to you?" and he said, "It's my teeth, dear. A third set is coming in so they don't fit anymore." Then you could see him steeling himself for what he had to say next.

"Babe's outside," he said. "He says if you all aren't out of here by noon, he'll get the sheriff."

I shudder to think what it must have cost Brownie to bear such a message and how almost lethal a dose of life-ray Babe must have used to get him to bear it. He staggered as soon as the words were out, his face ashen, and then it was like that scene from *On the Waterfront* where Marlon Brando's brother pulls the gun on him and Marlon Brando goes so mumbly with grief and disappointment and embarrassment for his brother that the gun might as well not exist, much as Brownie might as well not have delivered his terrible message the way Sharon totally ignored it in her grief and disappointment and embarrassment. She helped him into a kitchen chair and hung over him like Mother herself. Brownie said, "It's nothing, dear. I just haven't had my breakfast yet."

I said, "We're your friends, Brownie. How could you ever side with him?" and he said, "He's got the life-ray, dear. He's given me a new lease on life."

Sharon said, "You look like death, Brownie."

Brownie said, "It's like Bert said. Everybody's got to believe in something or somebody."

I said, "Brownie, he goes around in drag and sets fire to shit houses." He was all but down for the count and yet even so I had the compulsion to use words like *shit* on him.

He said, "Maybe he's got reasons he can't tell us. He gets hearings sometimes he won't tell about to a soul. All I know is when he turns the life-ray on me, I can feel the cares just melt away."

Sharon said, "It's not like he just hits the bottle or cheats on his wife. They could send him up ten years for the things he's done."

Brownie said, "There's things about him I don't understand just like there are things about God. You've just got to have faith, dear. It's like somebody calls you in the dark and you pick up and go even though you can't see where to put your foot. Scripture is full of dark places a man can't understand."

I said, "There was a time you could explain them without half trying, Brownie."

He said, "The trouble was I couldn't explain the dark places in myself, dear. I prayed 'Lead us not into temptation but deliver us from evil' for many years, and he never delivered me. It was something I could never understand."

I said, "You're a good man, Brownie, and if there's a heaven, you'll get an aisle seat. The trouble is you give up too easily."

"Oh don't think it was easy," he said.

Outside it had started to rain, a feathery grey rain with a grey mist rising. It fell on the roof of the hen house and on the hood of Babe's car, and I thought of it falling all over Poinsett—on Shaw Hill and shantytown, on Lola's Trailer Court. I pictured Jimmy Bob Luby in soiled diapers by the trailer window listening to it fall, the drops no more in number than the lives he had lived, had yet to live.

Sharon was the one to speak finally. She said, "You can tell that old fart I've got a letter proves the will's legal and it's my house. I'll give him twenty-four hours to get his moonflops out of here, and if he shows his ass around here after that, I'll blow it off."

A tear ran down Brownie's cheek. The kettle started to whistle. Callaway appeared in the doorway, as narrow and dark as a doorway himself. "Frumbo digga awning," he said. Then Gertrude Conover. She looked refreshed and ready for the worst. She picked Brownie's hand off the table where it lay and shook it. She said, "Stay for a coffee, Brownie. I've been watching Babe from upstairs. He is in a cataleptic trance."

Brownie again did the best he could in the way of a smile. It was like something ancient and unrecognizable in the back of the refrigerator. He said, "I'm feeling a little under the weather. I better not," and from the stove Bert said, "There's eggs ready?" said it more to Callaway than to anyone else. There were dark bloodstains on the front of Callaway's shirt from his last nosebleed, and he sat with his face turned away from her, his black chin in the V of his coral palms.

There was a single, sustained blast from Babe's car which someone else might have been sounding for all Babe so much as blinked an eye, sitting out there like laundry in the wet. Then he gave a short second blast, then another.

Sharon said, "Do like I told you, Brownie. Tell him I've got a letter proves Bip's my daddy. Tell him to go to hell."

So Brownie headed off into the rain in his rumpled shorts and bobbysocks, and the rest of us sat down to watery scrambled eggs and bitter coffee, resisting the temptation to gawk out the window to see how Babe would react to Sharon's answer to his ultimatum. His trance seemed so profound that it was hard to think of his reacting much at all, hard to think of him as the same man who had done a dance of rage and despair on his brother's relics.

While we waited, Gertrude Conover said, "This is a sad business. Well, it is a mess. But think of it this way. If the great wheel is to keep turning, part of it must be turning downward so the rest of it can be turning upward. Downward, upward, sad things and happy things, it's all one. It's all just the wheel going round, round, round." Her gold bracelet rattled as she traced several revolutions in the air with her finger. She said, "My dear, the whole point is to get off the wheel. That is theosophy in a nutshell. It is also common sense."

I said, "It is also Ufology. Spacelift will carry us off to a better world."

"That would be only out of the frying-pan into the fire," Gertrude Conover said. "One world is as much part of the wheel as another part."

I said, "At least this one doesn't smell of stale piss."

Sharon said, "That's what you think."

I said, "At least they let you die in this one. It's not much, but it's something."

Gertrude Conover said, "Die and be born, die and be born. It's just back to the wheel again through the same old door. Death isn't all it's cracked up to be. It's like life that way."

She had a forkful of scrambled eggs she was about to eat but then lowered it slowly to her plate again. She said, "When I stood there in the twilight with Jimmy Bob in my arms, for a moment or two I felt neither life nor death could lay a finger on us. I will never forget it as long as I live. Neither life nor death. I suppose it was the peace that passeth all understanding. I could tell the baby felt it too."

Bert said, "You ever have any babies of your own, honey?"

Gertrude Conover said, "When I married Harold Conover, I was fifty and he was going on seventy-three."

Sharon said, "They're getting out of the car."

They were. Callaway leapt to his feet and went to the window. He kept so far off to the side that from outdoors the most you could have seen of him was a single eye, a single sliver of bony black cheek. Brownie and Babe were standing in the rain discussing something, Babe had a large brown-paper bag in his arms. He was wearing his see-through raincoat, but he was bareheaded, his hair standing out in damp red spikes as it had the first time we'd met. Brownie gestured limply toward the house.

Callaway said, "Rootabaga mushseed. Alpha slope." He said, "Gunner flaymole. Mowdown. Limbo," dark, solemn words that clouded the pane with his breath. Beyond him I could see Babe and Brownie walking slowly out of sight around the front of the house.

Bert laid one hand lightly on Sharon's bare arm, and it occurred to me that it might be the first time she'd touched her that way since the day Bebb had taken her away in a blanket to turn over to Lucille where she lay on the sofa listening to Major Bowes. She said, "Don't be scared, honey? You got the letter." There was the sound of the front door opening, footsteps in the hall.

The wagons were drawn up in a circle, in other words, every eye cocked toward where the attack would come from. There was a humming in the air. The refrigerator coming on? Saucers landing? The life-ray? My life was in my throat. Brownie was the first to appear on the horizon. He stood in the door with that one lens of his glasses cracked like a saucer. Babe pushed in by him. What landed was the brown-paper bag with a wig in it and a big, sweat-stained, polka-dot dress with rips under both of the arms. It landed in Bert's lap where Babe tossed it. The humming of the tracks as the locomotive steamed along its deadly way?

The womenfolk were steely-eyed and indomitable, not a green rose or a blue curl stirring. Sharon's thin smile was tight as a bowstring. Callaway and I stood our ground behind where they sat at the round table. Babe and Brownie had us surrounded. Babe said, "It's my house, rat? It's my wife, rat? The law's on my side, rat?" His words ricocheted past us as he stood there in his see-through raincoat seen through by all of us but as though it was a cause for pride instead of shame.

Bert had her wig out of the bag in seconds, slipping it on with her fingers inside to ease it down over her shiny scalp like a bathing cap. She said, "My dress is all tore?"

Babe said, "I'm giving you today to clear out. I'm giving you twenty-four hours to git." He was never more Bebbsian, that plump hypnotist, impersonator, space-traveler who had held his nose to the stench of planets offering us time like prairie flowers. He was playing his pair of deuces like a royal flush. He said, "No hard feelings. I won't make trouble for your boy here if you go quiet. If Leo left you cash money, take it and welcome. All I want's what's mine by rat."

"It's mine," Sharon said. "It's mine to do something nice for Jesus with or any damn thing I want."

Babe said, "It's mine mine mine mine mine," a gibbering parody, his face all screwed up, his shoulders hunched to his ears. Then he said, "The trouble with Leo, he thought he was Jesus his ownself half the time. He preached the Kingdom like he was the king of it. That two-bit diploma factory, he turned out ministers like they were candy bars. All the miracles of Scripture, they looked like peanuts alongside his miracles," and Brownie said, "It's true, dear. I was laid out for dead in Knoxville, Tennessee, and Mr. Bebb raised me. He told me to stand up in Jesus's name, and I stood up."

Babe said, "Let me tell you about Jesus."

It was Jesus the spaceman I was prepared for, Jesus with a noseplug stepping out of his saucer to the rescue, and I think that was the Jesus Brownie was prepared for too. You could see he wasn't looking forward to it, but at least he knew he could live with it. It turned out to be another Jesus.

Babe said, "I know my Scripture same as Leo knew it. Why shouldn't I? We got it shoved down our throats like tonic from the time we could pee standing. Right there in the Gospel it reads, 'Jesus wept,' and if I had a nickel for every time they've preached on that one, I'd be riding around in a Cadillac sedan. Jesus, he was the best old weeper of all time. If they was to give a prize for weeping, he'd win the kewpie doll, hands down."

He said, "The sacred heart of Jesus. The R.C.s they've got them pictures of it looks like a tomato done up in barbwire. The world's in one hell of a way, and Jesus weeps till his sacred heart near to pops. Hell, he's been at it since the year one without a coffee break. There's miseries in this world enough to make a stone weep." He pulled out a dishtowel and rubbed his hair with it.

He said, "There's a pile-up on the interstate rips the tits off a teenage girl. There's old folks in nurse homes they don't even change their drawers when they let go in them. There's crooks and half-wits loose in the streets and phonecalls at midnight to wake folks up with awful things they never dreamed could happen, not to them anyways, six year old kids some pervert stuffed into a sack after they did things their own mother wouldn't recognize them."

Gertrude Conover had her head turned sideways as if one ear was all she could bear to listen with, and there were tears rolling down poor Brownie's cheeks that would have made even Jesus look to his laurels. Babe shied his horrors out like the plastic lids with Sunshine on them. He said, "They're starving and fighting and dying of cancers the whole world over, and all the weeping Jesus ever did since Lazarus hasn't helped more than a bucket of spit." His hair was a red feather duster from the rubbing, a fright wig. "You think I wouldn't believe if I could? You think that—Listen," he said, breaking in on himself. "Leo was all the time preaching hold tight to Jesus, hold tight to Jesus. It's like a drowning man holding tight to water. The day I'll believe is the day I see him coming across the waves with his hand stretched out. It's the day I hear him say, 'You look all wore out, Babe,' and I take a hold of his hand. Hell, there's been times I held my hand out in the dark till it went pins and needles on me waiting for him, and he never come yet. I never seen him yet, and Leo Bebb never seen him either."

Gertrude Conover said, "How do you know what Leo Bebb saw?" and Babe said, "The dark and shameful things he done showed he was lost in the dark like the rest of us, that's how I know."

Gertrude Conover said, "Leo Bebb could see in the dark. He was never lost. Even blind, that man could see."

I stood there like a rube at a high-wire act until without warning the old acrobat had me up there with him. For the first time he raised his glance to me, said, "You ever seen Jesus, Antonio Parr?" He was close enough to smell as he said it, the smell of him rain, plastic, a whiff of peppermint. He was sucking on something. He blinked at me, and *you and me* his blink said. He said, "Father, Son, and Holy Smoke, you ever laid eyes on that crowd, Antonio Parr?"

I have read that men shot down in battle who've lived to tell the tale tell that there comes a moment when you rise high in the air above your own body and look down at where it lies on the ground as good as dead, and that's how it was in that kitchen when out of the blue Babe let me have it. I looked down and saw myself. I looked down at that familiar bald spot, that elongated, olive-skinned face, those caramel-colored eyes I got from my Italian mother, El Greco eyes as Miriam called them, rolled heavenward, glassy, brimming with whatever El Greco eyes brim with. Father, Son or Holy Smoke? fat Babe asks. His question smells of peppermint and rain. The only answer I have is that I know what I've looked at but not what I've seen.

I have looked at my sister in a hospital room with storm-tinted windows and both legs in casts with a bar between them so she is a white A on a white bed. She smokes a cigarette, her hair tied back with a florist's ribbon. She asks if I think dying is going someplace or just going out, like a match.

I have looked at Stephen Kulak who sits in my ninth grade class as I explain what irony is. It is saying one thing and meaning another thing, I say—two things. I explain that life can be ironic too—double-barreled and double-dealing—and I watch his face fall like Rome to the barbarians as he understands about irony.

And I have looked at Lucille. Like an extinct species, half smashed on Tropicanas, she teeters up the aisle of Open Heart in her Aimee Semple MacPherson gauze because in the pulpit Bebb is opening his heart so wide she is terrified that he may at any moment pull out of it like a rabbit from a hat Bertha Stredwig in her young beauty on Shaw Hill, the brawl in Knoxville with his twin pounding him till one eye's never been right since.

It was Gertrude Conover who came to my rescue finally. She reached out her hand and pointed it at Babe. It was an old, bony hand with liver spots on it and a glittering diamond. If it had been a gun and she'd fired it, it would have gotten him right on his left nipple. She said, "You always have to get back at your brother, Babe. You always have to go him one better. It is your main trouble. He believes in the Mystery—well, more than believes, he keeps riding it back into the world like Pegasus—and so you believe in saucers, hardware. If he believed in hardware, you would believe in the Mystery, or let on you did. Anything to spite him. You were well named. You are a babe. The Mystery is deep and holy, and you have baby eyes that see only the nasty surfaces of things and the shiny toys in the sky."

Babe said, "Gertrude Conover, my brother had the gift of gab and a zipper he couldn't keep zipped. He made good business out of Jesus, but deep down he believed the same as me."

Gertrude Conover said, "I'm afraid you would have a hard time convincing me you know what Leo Bebb believed."

Babe said, "Then how's if I let him convince you his ownself?"

I thought for a moment that it was Callaway who spoke next but then found it was Brownie doing the best he could with only gums to do it with. He said, "Babe's going to give us a hearing, dear." And he was right.

Babe opened his mouth as wide as if Bildabian was about to work on a back molar and aimed it at us like a mortar. I was ready for anything. I was ready for the voice of Bebb himself speaking of how it would be when the Lone Ranger came riding into the world with justice on one hip and mercy on the other. I was ready for some Martian message to the effect that Bebb like Babe believed in nothing more hopeful than hardware or anything more mysterious than Mars, that the Gospel was just what he hid the dark truth behind, the one shamefulness he could not bear to bare. I was ready for anything except what happened, which was for a few moments nothing.

The tea kettle was whistling softly like a man through his teeth. It was still raining outside. Babe raised his hands to his gaping jaws as if to knead sound out of them. His face flushed dark, his eyes watered. He was giving it all he had, every muscle straining. But there was no message from Mars, no credo from Bebb, only the silence of a radio turned on between stations, dead air. And only then the unmistakable sound of a dry, weightlifter's fart.

Somebody might have laughed, God knows. Babe might have carried the day if he had, if he'd let the fart be his final word to us, the innermost, outermost word of outerspace. But he didn't, only closed his mouth far enough to say, "Sometimes it don't work worth a damn," then closed it the rest of the way.

I suppose somebody might have wept. Possibly Jesus. Instead nobody did much of anything for a while till finally Sharon did. She reached down into her jeans and pulled out Bebb's letter. She said, "Read it and weep, Babe," and handed it to him—"Dear One, I went and picked her up today . . . Luce has fixed on giving her the name of Sharon . . . Farewell, my own dear heart . . . Remember me."

Babe took it and tipped it toward the light. His lips moved as he read it. When he had finished, he said, "This here don't prove a thing I didn't know. It proves your daddy was a fornicator and a four-flusher. It proves you were got in shame and born to grief."

Sharon said, "It proves this is my kitchen you're letting them in."

He said, "Honey, it don't prove shit," and tore the letter in two.

What happened then is this. As Babe tore the letter, Brownie jumped up to grab it from him and Babe tried to keep it out of his reach by holding it up as high as he could above his head. Dancing around on his toes, Brownie made a number of unsuccessful snatches at it as if Babe was the school bully who'd run off with his hat. Or they could have been dancing together, because Babe was dancing around too a little, trying to keep away from Brownie. Then Babe brought his hand down hard with the letter in it, and hand, letter, arm, something, must have caught Brownie on the side of the head en route because he staggered backwards a few steps and his glasses went spinning off across the linoleum. Then, still on his toes, Brownie himself went spinning across the linoleum. Only he did it in slow motion.

An MGM stunt man couldn't have done it better, shot through the chest by Brian Donlevy on the edge of a cliff. In his short pants with his hairy, pale legs and bobby socks, Brownie revolved as slow as a dream, his bare arms crooked out to either side. His sunset shirt was all purples and reds. His face was colorless. He was trying to say something but all that came out were syllables of air. His legs buckled and he went down on his knees near the stove. He grabbed on to the stove with one hand, but one by one his fingers lost hold. He lay on the kitchen floor with his mouth open and his glance fixed on the ceiling. There was a coil of flypaper hanging down from the ceiling, but whatever he was looking at, if he was looking at anything, it wasn't the flypaper.

Finally he got a word out. Sharon and I were both down there with him by then and we both heard it, but the only dictionary to look up what it meant in would be a rhyming dictionary because without his choppers he couldn't handle the initial consonant and only the vowel sound came through.

Hear? He wanted to hear something, or for us to hear something he was hearing, or to hear with him that there wasn't anything to hear?

Or *here*, for all we could tell—not anywhere else in time or space or outerspace but just here, this place, this time, this intersection and meeting of many ways. If there was any answer to find that was worth a damn, the only place to find it finally was your own place, not there, or there, or there, but only here, stretched out in a kitchen in Poinsett, South Carolina, if it came to that, with your glasses shattered on the linoleum and your smile in a bureau drawer. *Here.*

Or even *beer* maybe. It's possible that all poor Brownie was trying to get across was that he wanted to take a little something once more while he still could, something to wet his lips with and keep his courage up.

But we came up with something else finally, Sharon and I. Nobody can live comfortably for long with uncertainty, and for comfort's sake if not accuracy's we decided to end Brownie's story with a period instead of a colon or a question mark or a little trailing row of dots. . . . So, discarding all the other possibilities, we finally put our money on the one that seemed to have the most of Brownie in it, and later on that day, when the dust settled a little and things quieted down and people started asking about the particulars, we told everybody that the last word we heard him speak there on the floor by Bert's stove was *dear*.

14

I FOUND I HAD to phone somebody what had happened if only to help get it through to myself, and since there was no next of kin, Mother presumably having long since passed, to use Bert's term, I phoned John Turtle at the Red Path Ranch. He arrived the next day with his friends.

He arrived at Spartanburg by chartered plane and brought his friends out from there in a pair of sky-blue Granadas complete with air-conditioning, tape decks, and whitewall tires. He brought Harry Hocktaw, Harry Hocktaw who could have passed for Jack Oakie any day, more Eskimo than Indian with his swelling cheeks and sparse, pussycat whiskers. He also brought the newlyweds, Buck Badger and Rose Trionka Badger and Rose's mother Bea. Herman Redpath's cousin Seahorn Redpath also came. Instead of returning to Laguna Beach after the wedding, he had apparently lingered on at the ranch, and having him come was almost like having Herman Redpath come himself. He was a good head shorter and as silent a man as his cousin had been a non-stop talker, but otherwise the resemblance was striking—the same narrow arrowhead of a face, the same high-bridged tomahawk of a nose. And last but not least, Maudie Redpath was there in her hundred and twelfth year looking as though the dance that was supposed to turn her into a blackbird had worked at last. She wore a black dress with feathery black wings for sleeves, and all you could see of her face through the wrinkles was a pair of glittering eyes and a hooked, seed-cracking beak. The Joking Cousin himself lifted her out of one of the Granadas into her collapsible wheelchair and wheeled her through Bert's chickens with the red, white and blue streamers a little the worse for wear but still laced through the spokes.

They came to escort Brownie's body back to Holy Love, but there were preliminaries to attend to first. The Spartanburg undertaker raised all kinds of objections, but John Turtle prevailed, and they were finally allowed in to wherever it was they had Brownie laid out. John Turtle, Buck Badger, and Harry Hocktaw were the ones who worked on him, and though I made a point of not asking about it, they told Sharon he was an honorary member of the tribe and they had done the same kind of thing for him that they had done for Herman Redpath and others before him. She said, "I suppose they put butter on his legs and salt on his tongue and up his nose and ears and up his rear end to keep the evil spirits out. Jesus. I wonder did John Turtle take a leak on him like he did on old Herman. I was going to ask him, but I didn't. I didn't want to know about it either way." So I asked him.

I said, "When Herman Redpath was in his box, you took a leak on him, John Turtle, and Bebb told me afterwards that it was what kept him from getting lost on his way to the Happy Hunting Ground. Don't ask me how he knew. Did you do the same for Brownie?"

I never saw John Turtle laugh harder, his gold-framed front teeth flashing at me like fire. His black hair was plastered down like the water-soak in the old ads, and he had on a checked sports jacket with padded shoulders and saddle shoes with the white parts so freshly whitened that you could smell the banana oil. He said, "You kill me, Cousin. Brownie get lost with all that after-shave on him? He don't need Joking Cousin to find his way. He need just one thing, and I give it to him. No sweat."

I said, "You want me to guess?" It is impossible to talk with a Joking Cousin very long without becoming his stooge.

He said, "Carraway found it."

"Callaway," I said.

He said, "Halloway found it in Brownie's bag. My, the pretty things old Brownie have in there. I took and give it to him before they shut the box anyhow." He cocked his head to one side and stared at me with a glazed smile. He said, "How you been, Cousin? Getting much lately?"

I said, "You wouldn't mean his teeth, would you?"

He said, "Once we get his mouth open, they slip in like nobody's business." He placed his right hand on my left shoulder. He said, "We shine them up real nice first. They look like a million dollars."

I said, "You didn't happen to notice if he had any real teeth coming in, did you?"

He said, "You crazy?"

I said, "Well, he'll rest easier now, John Turtle. It was a nice thing you did."

He said, "Nobody's going to slam the door on a nice smile like that."

I said, "Maybe you should have taken a leak on him too just to make sure."

He placed his left hand on my right shoulder so his arms were crossed between us and closed his eyes. He said, "Just a little one for the road maybe," and bent his head forward until his brow touched the place where his arms crossed. His hair smelled of nutmeg and olive oil. He dug his fingers into my shoulders so hard that it brought tears to my eyes.

I suppose that as with Herman Redpath they painted designs on him too, a red one for the earth and a blue one for the sky, and hung a deerskin pouch around his neck with things in it he'd need for the journey like an extra supply of after-shave maybe and a fresh Harry Truman shirt. Possibly they even put in what was left of his glasses although, as Saint Paul said in another of Bebb's favorite passages, "Now we see through a glass darkly, but then face to face, Antonio," so maybe glasses would have been to load him down unnecessarily. But the important thing, of course, was the teeth. Maybe they weren't his own—I was as relieved by the knowledge that the life-ray hadn't worked as I suppose poor Brownie was demolished by it—but they were his by adoption, his by grace, and if he ever made it to where he was going, I feel sure that if for no other reason they let him in for the sake of his million dollar smile.

It was a heart attack that killed him, not Babe, but it was Babe, of course, who brought it on by loading more on him than his heart could handle. He'd had Bebb shot out from under him and then Jesus. He'd given up Holy Love because he couldn't make the rough places of Scripture smooth any more even for himself and then took to taking a little something to help fill the empty places Jesus and the Scriptures and Bebb had left behind them. Then he'd latched on to Babe only to discover the terrible truth about him at Lola's Trailer Court. I suppose it was because of his teeth as much as anything that he stuck with Babe after that. New every morning was the love that Brownie's dream of a complete new set did ,prove, to take liberties with the old hymn. He would search around with his tongue until he convinced himself that he could feel them starting to poke through somewhere and then he would know that even if Jesus was only a spaceman, at least Mother was home and maybe Babe had his weaknesses but who hadn't. But then Babe tore the letter up. "Honey, it don't prove shit," he said, and tore it in two and Brownie's last hope with it.

It was the end of him, and yet it was also in a way the beginning— two things, as I might have explained it to Stephen Kulak. It killed him, but it also brought him to life for a few wild minutes and in a way that I think would have made Bebb take back all his remarks about how he let his life slip out sideways. Dancing around on his toes trying to snatch the letter back may not have looked like much, but for Brownie it was Little Big Horn and San Juan Hill. And only then did his heart attack him, flattening him out on the linoleum to be sure but only after he'd made that one last, first, and only stand. And routed Babe in the bargain.

An elderly doctor with a white face and pink, rabbity eyes drove out from Poinsett to pronounce him dead, and while he was checking him over where Callaway and I had placed him on the horsehair sofa, Sharon went upstairs and found Babe. It was her house and he was her uncle, and she went alone to find him although I had offered to go with her. She found him just inside the door of the little varnished room where Bert kept her treasure. She said he was standing there like a statue staring into space with his mouth open and a flap of his raincoat hanging down where it had gotten torn in the scuffle. The remains of the letter were still in his hand, and she said he hardly seemed to notice it when she took them out of his hand as you would out of a child's. She said she didn't make a big scene of it but just stepped into his line of vision so she was sure he noticed her and in a quiet, grim tone said, "Babe, if you don't start packing your things, I'm going to phone the troopers and say you killed him same as if you did it with a gun. I'm going to press manslaughter charges and get you jailed quicker than you can say moonflops." She said to me, "The crazy thing is I think he was almost grateful to me, Bopper. I think the poor slob was so shook up he was glad when somebody told him what the hell to do."

As Stephen Kulak is bound to discover someday, the effect of death on ,a household is not unlike the effect of a wedding—the same comings and goings, the same suspension of routine, the sense of holiday almost and of history, the gathering of the clan. The doctor came. The undertaker came with his two assistants in dark leisure suits and carried Brownie out through the Uforium on a stretcher with aluminum poles. I phoned John Turtle in Houston, and when he said he'd be flying in with his friends, Sharon in one of her rare flights of domesticity started worrying about feeding them and got Callaway to drive into town with her to help bring back provisions. Bert said, "Life's got to go on?" and went on herself about her usual chores, walking out through the drizzle with a raincoat over her head to feed her heekies, cleaning up after our unfinished breakfast, mopping up the red mud the undertakers had tracked in. I don't think any of us shed a tear for Brownie that day, not that there weren't tears to shed but simply that there were so many other things to get out of the way first.

What Gertrude Conover did was go sit in the front parlor with the door shut. She said, "The first few hours when you die are always the hardest. The gods, the bodhisattvas, the what-have-yous positively swarm about you. They are all trying to sell you the new birth that will suit you best. They are trying to be helpful, most of them, but it is like Nassau Street on Reunion weekend. I will sit in here and try to send a little good karma Brownie's way for the voyage. If you can get it through, it sometimes makes the difference between going tourist or first class for them."

And then with her hand on the doorknob, she said, "They shouldn't let death happen around people my age. It is like doing a *pas de chat* in front of a cripple." Then she shut the door between us.

All the time these things were going on, Babe was getting ready to leave, almost, as Sharon said, as though he was grateful for something to do, as though it had been his own idea in the first place. He made a number of phone calls from his office. He ran up and down stairs. He dragged suitcases out of the varnished room. He packed them, and you could hear him moving things around in the Uforium. He had destroyed his marriage and he had been accused of murder and he was being driven out of his own house, but if indeed it had been the day of a wedding instead of a death, it was as if Babe was the bride getting ready to set out on a new life. Sometime around the middle of the afternoon he called out to Sharon and me that he was leaving and we went into the Uforium to see him go. It was both the least and the most that we could do.

He had on his best clothes—a skimpy-looking dark suit that grabbed him under the arms with the collar of his shirt spread out over the suit collar and on his head a shiny little straw fedora with a feather in the band. He could have been bald for all you could see with the hat on, and that plus the tightness of the suit made him look so much like his brother in the dim, extraterrestrial light that I would have gasped if I'd had a gasp left in me by then.

He said, "I'm leaving most of this stuff behind, I won't need it. I'm taking the space suit and a couple of moonrocks and this." It was the colander with the wires threaded through it. He said, "You can have the rest. Maybe Jesus can use it if he moves in."

Sharon said, "Nobody here's got a use for it, Babe."

"Don't you bother yourself about it anyhow," he said.

He said, "There's no manslaughter charge would stick worth a damn because there was no man here got slaughtered. I'm leaving because I got

the biggest hearing I ever heard yet. I got it in the store room up there
when you busted in."

He said, "Antonio, spacelift's coming only not to Shaw Hill it isn't.
Once it was Shaw Hill but it's not Shaw Hill any more. There's things
they've found about Shaw Hill they wouldn't soil their feet with it.
They've picked them a new place, and that's where I'm heading out for.
I've been on the phone, and there's a few of them that's coming with me.
SOS, that's Save Our Skins. Antonio, looks like if you want your skin
saved, you better jump aboard. There's always room for one more."

For something around twenty or thirty seconds, I actually considered
it. Then I said, "Send us a postcard when you get there, Babe."

He said, "There's bats in the attic, and the sump backs up. The clapboard's all dozey under the shingles. Old Leo, he didn't leave you the
Ritz Hotel when he left it to you." He pulled one of the shades back
and glanced out at the house as if to confirm what he'd said about it.
The rainlight turned his face silver. He said, "What are you fixing to do
with it anyway?"

"Fumigate first," Sharon said.

He took it in silence except for some little noise at the back of his
throat, let the shade fall back in place so his face wasn't silver anymore.
He said, "Promise me one thing, hear?" He said, "Long as she wants to,
let Bert stay. I don't know where else in the world she'd find to go."

Sharon said, "Jesus, Babe. You think I'd turn her out?"

He said, "She turned you out once."

Sharon said, "Because you wouldn't let her keep me. She had her one
pitiful little fling, and you set out to ruin her life from then on."

Babe said, "Your daddy was the one that ruined her life. He ruined
both our lives."

Sharon said, "I don't think he ever got over it. I think every crazy,
half-ass thing he ever did was on account of it. Like in Miami, flashing it
like that. He was trying to get it out where somebody could tell him it
wouldn't count against him forever."

"Why shouldn't it count against him forever?" Babe said. There were
a couple of Sunshine Frisbees on the windowsill, and he picked them up
absently and dropped them in the carton where he had the charred
shoulder pads and the colander. He said, "Take a man that cheats on his
own brother like that, he deserves what he gets."

Sharon said, "It must give you a sour stomach, all that spite you've
got."

Babe said, "We slept in the same bed till we were twelve. We told
each other the secrets of our heart. We held onto each other in the dark
for comfort. There was a time it was him and me against the world." He
half picked up the charred shoulder pad by one shoulder and let it drop
again. He said, "I loved the sonofabitch."

Sharon sad, "Well, it's over and done with." Between where she was standing and Babe, the table with the relief map stood, the different colored pins, the question mark. She glanced down and with one finger traced the course of a blue stream. She said, "Bip was a lonesome man his whole life. He could have used somebody to hold onto in the dark for comfort."

Babe was staring straight ahead, his mouth snapped shut on its hinges, his nostrils slightly distended as if he was humming something under his breath. He said, "I used to figure he'd come back someday. I took to watching for him nights. I'd sit out under a tree. Talk about your lonesome, I'd sit there half the night sometimes. It's when I commenced seeing UFOs. You stare into the dark long enough, there's no telling what you'll start seeing."

He said, "The first time one of them landed, I thought it was him that got out. I saw a creature standing there looking up at the window for all the world like him the way his bald head shone in the moonlight like a silver hat. I whispered out, 'It's me. Babe. I won't shoot.' Hell, it wasn't me he wanted. Night after night, every shadow moved I thought was him and every sound of the night, a owl or some little creature in the dry leaves."

Like Bebb he had a handkerchief in his breast pocket with the points carefully arranged. Only his mouth moved. He said, "It was Bert he wanted so I took to going around other places nights he might think it was Bert out looking for him in that pitiful wig of hers with her heart and spirit broken, both, from the time he broke them. I took to doing damnfool things. A man can't only wait but so long for something to happen that never happens before he starts acting like a damn fool. The things I did never hurt a living soul, but they'd have locked me up if they'd ever caught me."

Sharon said, "You're lucky they never locked you up, Babe."

There was nothing more to say then, and none of us tried to say anything to pretend there was. Babe picked up his carton and stood there holding it against his stomach with both hands.

He said, "Tell her goodby for me, hear? Tell her I never meant her any harm." As things turned out, we never had to deliver the message.

When we got out to where he had his car parked in front of the house, Bert was there beside it in the rain. She had a plastic bandanna tied under her chin and a raincoat that almost reached to the ground. She had two big bags with her that Callaway must have helped her out with, one of them with a piece of clothesline around it. I remained standing in the doorway, but Sharon ran out. Even at that distance, you could see the awkwardness between them. Bert took a step backward, almost tripping over her raincoat. Sharon seemed to be saying something. Bert put both her hands out toward her daughter's face. Then they reached out and clumsily embraced in the rain. It was coming down hard by then, dimpling

the puddles in the road and running off the wings and beaks of the flamingos.

When Sharon got back to the house, her face and hair dripping wet,
all of her, she said, "She says I have you, Bopper, but Babe doesn't have
anybody. She says she'll send me a card when they get where they're going.
It must be some kind of a record, Bopper. I finally find my own mother,
and a couple of days later she takes off for outerspace. Maybe I ought to
try the spray can instead of the roll-on." She was so cold and miserable I
don't think she could tell any better than I could whether rain was the
only thing her face was wet with.

It was the next morning that the Indians arrived in their sky-blue
Granadas, and though John Turtle, Harry Hocktaw and Buck Badger
soon took off again to open negotiations with the Spartanburg undertaker,
that still left the three women together with Seahorn Redpath hanging
around the house with us at a time when we were least equipped to deal
with them. We had to pull ourselves together for the trip back to Sutton
for one thing, and we had to decide what to do with the house now that
Sharon had successfully taken possession of it for another. The question
of what to do with it for Jesus had gotten lost in the question of what to
do with it at all—to rent it, sell it, lock it up and get somebody to keep
an eye on it for us till we thought of something else to do. Selling it and
giving the money to some cause that Jesus would find congenial was the
most tempting because it was simple and final, and yet, as always before, it
struck us as something less than what Bebb had had in mind. It was too
pallid, too un-Bebbsian, so we kept hashing the thing over while at the
same time packing up and trying to keep the Indians out of our hair.

Seahorn Redpath and old Maudie were no problem. Their function
seemed mainly ceremonial, and they spent their time in the parlor sitting
at opposite ends of the horsehair sofa under the oval photograph of Bebb's
grandparents with their Sunday suits and goiterish stares. We looked in
on them occasionally. Maudie was in her black plumage with her feet
hardly touching the floor, and Seahorn Redpath had his hands folded in
his lap and a broad-brimmed Panama on his head. Neither of them said a
word. Once we thought we heard signs of distress, a high-pitched, piping
sound that came in short bursts like a bosun's whistle, but it turned out
to be only Maudie Redpath singing a song. In any case she did not say
anything to us but just kept on singing and Seahorn Redpath didn't say
anything either. He had shifted from the sofa to a squatting position on
the floor. He kept moving his head slowly to the right and then back
again as if something slow and solemn was passing by in front of him.

Bea Trionka and Rose, on the other hand, seemed to be everywhere
at once and into everything. They went into rooms and peered into
closets. They made themselves countless cups of instant coffee and used
the one toilet constantly. In the Uforium they burned something that

smelled like hair, and when I asked them about it, Bea Trionka said, "Of course it smelled like hair," and Rose said, "What you expect it to smell like? After-shave?" hunching up her shoulders and putting her hand over her mouth. The way she had her hair arranged, a thick loop of it almost covered one eye, the other one brimming with whatever the expression was that she was using her hand to hide.

John Turtle called us from Spartanburg where the undertaker was giving him a hard time about letting them in to do what they'd come to do for Brownie. He said the undertaker wanted to speak to us, and I was the one he spoke to. In a voice like Lester Maddox he said they had no embalmer's license and no respect for the dead and that one of them had some kind of a rattle he kept shaking with beans inside. He had already upset one funeral with it, and there was another funeral coming up that he was going to upset too. I said they were Brownie's friends and parishioners and maybe it would be best all round if he would just let them get on with it and then be on their way. In the background, as he paused for thought, I could hear the sound of Harry Hocktaw's rattle—chick chicka, chunk-chunk-chicka—and then finally, the undertaker gave in. For the dozenth time at least I could hear one of the Trionkas flush the can upstairs. One of Bert's roosters crowed. Then almost as soon as I'd hung it up, the phone rang, and it was my nephew Tony calling from a world farther away than Mars.

He said some independent film producer had seen a couple of the ads he was in and they wanted to run a screen test on him. With Laura working at the dentist's every day, he couldn't set it up till we came back, so if we would make it back as soon as we could, it would be a big help. He said, "Jesus, Tono. I just hope it's not one of these porn deals," and I said I hoped it wasn't too and we'd try to get started the next day if everything worked out. Then he put my son Bill on for a few minutes. Bill said, "A mouse got drowned in the toilet during Archie Bunker," and I said, "Well, I guess there are worse ways." In Spartanburg by then they had probably already started to put the salt in Brownie's nose and ears.

It was Gertrude Conover who solved the problem of the house, and like all great solutions—the wheel, the ripple in a hairpin—it was simplicity itself. She said, "My dear, you can give it to the Lubys," and we did. *Give* is perhaps not the right word—it remained Sharon's house but was theirs to look after, live in, report to us on, exorcise, debrief, hallow. It was surprisingly easy to arrange, people who live in mobile homes being more mobile than other people. And *Lubys* is not the right word either, of course—Jimmy Bob would be more accurate.

We did not leave the next day, as I told Tony I hoped we would, because John Turtle insisted we be there for the send-off at the airport, and all in all I'm glad we didn't miss it. Harry Hocktaw and Buck Badger wheeled Brownie in his box, and the women walked behind with Seahorn

Redpath pushing Maudie in her collapsible chair. John Turtle sang a
song as the box went slowly up into the plane on a hoist. He stood behind
little Seahorn Redpath with his arms around his neck and sang,

> *"Seahorn Redpath,*
> *Redpath from the sea,*
> *Sail old Brownie on to he.*
> *Red sail in the sunset,*
> *Oh red path in the sky,*
> *We all coming by and by*
> *You don't got no cause to cry."*

It could have been a lot worse.

We did not leave the next day but we left the day after the next, and
the last thing I saw before we drove off was Jimmy Bob. Ruby and her
husband were standing in the doorway with the other children crowded
around them to wave goodbye, but Jimmy Bob had staggered out a few
steps in front of them. He stood by the white tractor tire with the nasturtiums in it. His rubber pants were full as usual. His flat little eyes were
still, but he was pumping his fat arms up and down in the air. "Bye bye
bye," he called out to us, only it came out "Ba ba ba ba" in short, flat
bleats. He started lurching forward as if to follow us, but Ruby caught
him up around the middle, and he hung there over her arms bleating as
we pulled out toward shantytown in the brutalized Continental with
Callaway at the wheel.

Gertrude Conover said, "Well, there is nothing nicer you could have
done for Jesus than that," and I said, "Maybe that's who that was out
there with his rubber pants filled," and Sharon said, "I guess if he had rubber pants he'd fill them like everybody else."

Gertrude Conover said, "No. These always-returners, they never do
anything like anybody else. They keep on returning until the last blade of
grass has achieved cosmic consciousness. They keep coming back until a'
the seas gang dry, my dear, till a' the seas gang dry." She craned around
to give one last wave through the back window. She had her white gloves
on for the first time since she had used them for protection against moongerms. She said, "And I will love thee still, my dear, till a' the seas gang
dry."

Then Callaway almost put us through the windshield braking for a
yellow shantytown dog that ran out into the red clay road to menace us.
Callaway turned around to look at us from under the visor of his green
Agway cap and spoke the second word I ever heard him speak that I was
sure I understood. The first was the number sixty-two when he was counting the freight cars the day we drove into Poinsett, and the second, after
just missing the dog, was "Life." He pronounced it "Laff," flashing his
teeth at us as if it was the best and oldest joke in the world. I don't

know what he meant by it, though I suppose it had to do with the dog's narrow escape.

The same dog turned up in a dream I had that night in the Monticello Hotel in Charlottesville where we broke our trip on the ride home. The scene was the same as the terrible picture in Brownie's motel room of the sunlit millpond with the mill reflected in it and the boy sitting on the grassy bank fishing with his dog beside him. The dog was the shantytown dog, and the boy was Brownie. I wasn't myself a participant in the dream, only an observer, so there wasn't any chance to speak to Brownie or even to wave at him across the water, but I noticed to my relief that his smile was firmly back in place where John Turtle had put it. The dream didn't leave me feeling sad and neglected the way dreams about the dead usually do because no matter how well you once knew them, they have very little time for you when they meet you in dreams and generally seem in a great rush to get on with whatever it is they've got to do next. It was essentially a comic dream, not accidentally comic like a moment in real life, but comic on purpose like a Laurel and Hardy two-reeler.

Instead of Laurel and Hardy, it was Bebb and Babe, and they were floating on the pond side by side in the rowboat, each with an oar in his hands. They were both wearing straw boaters like a pair of vaudeville hoofers, both in their shirtsleeves with the sleeves rolled up. They weren't rowing anyplace, just resting their oars, and beyond them, on the far bank, the trees faded away into the golden haze. Brownie wasn't paying any attention to them, and after a while one of the brothers picked up something and tossed it at him, possibly a moonrock. When it splashed into the water, Brownie glanced up, and that was the signal for Babe and Bebb to start their act.

One of them started pulling on his oar and the other one started pushing on his, and the result was that instead of moving forward, of course, the boat started going around in a circle. Harder and harder they rowed, and faster and faster the boat went round. Their fat faces were flushed with excitement and effort, and sweat was rolling down from under their straw hats. Brownie set down his pole and gathered the dog into his lap. His smile was never more radiant even without his glasses to give it intensity. The boat spun so fast you could no longer make out what it was or who was in it, and like the tigers running around the tree in *Little Black Sambo* until they turn to butter, the oars, the oarsmen, their yellow straw boaters, all of it melted together and became part of the sunlight on the pond and the haze in the woods. When I looked back for Brownie he had gone, and the dog stood alone on the bank barking. Brownie was in the pond. He was already up to his chest in it, and before long only his head was above the surface as he waded out farther. His head looked like a beachball floating along in the water, and I laughed so hard at the ridiculous sight of it that I woke myself up with tears in my eyes.

*   *   *

"Tie a yellow ribbon round the old oak tree" was the song that was going strong that summer, and when we finally pulled into Sutton around supper time the next day, having parted company with Gertrude Conover and Callaway in Princeton and made the rest of the journey in our own car, Bill and some friends of his with the song in mind had gone to town on the homemade wooden mobile I'd carpentered years before and hung up with Tony's help from a tripod in the back yard. When they had run out of yellow ribbon, they had used whatever else they could lay their hands on including enough yellow toilet paper to stretch to Poinsett and back, and there it was when they led us out to it, gotten up, as Sharon said, like a whorehouse Christmas tree.

The sign on it said WELCOME HONE, that last little leg of the last M missing because my son Bill either didn't remember about it or had run out of steam by then stringing all that toilet paper around. It seemed oddly fitting. It was good to get home, but it was home with something missing or out of whack about it. It wasn't much, to be sure, just some minor stroke or serif, but even a minor stroke can make a major difference, to which I can hear Brownie saying, "There is a sermon in that, dear," as he used to say in the days when he was still preaching sermons instead of resting in peace in the shadow of Holy Love in Houston or doing whatever else he may be doing, wherever else he may be doing it.

To this day I cannot see my niece and former student Laura Fleischman Blaine without J. Alfred Prufrock's pair of ragged claws scuttling across my heart at the thought of days that might have been, of days that used to be. My namesake Tony's screentest turned out to be a smasher, and he went into the making of films which, if not technically hard core, are apparently close enough to it so that there are times when even he, as he likes to put it, isn't sure whether he's coming or going. I've never seen one of them, and I have no immediate plans to, but Sharon has seen them all and has gone on record, as she likes to put it, that he's really got something. I don't know how my sister Miriam would have felt about it, but I suspect she might have gotten a kick out of it. "You stay awake" were the last words she ever spoke to him the day I took him and his brother Chris to the hospital to say goodbye to her, and there is no question about his having done that. Besides, as I remind myself, it is a living.

WELCOME HONE the sign said, and I can't help thinking again of Gideon and Barak, of Samson and David and all the rest of the crowd that I had mentioned to Brownie once, who, because some small but crucial thing was missing, kept looking for it come hell or high water wherever they went till their eyes were dim and their arches fallen. And to think of them is to think of Babe too wherever he went off to with his transistorized teeth and his faithful Bert, and of Gertrude Conover letting Beethoven wash back over her under the stars at Revonoc. In the long run

I suppose it would be to think of everybody if you knew enough about them to think straight: of Jimmy Bob Luby's father even, with the mean-looking, caved-in upper lip—who knows what far bank he wades toward in his dreams. And of Jimmy Bob too, doubled up over his mother's arm like a small, soiled pillow.

And of course I also think of myself, as every day I leave HONE to teach track and irony to the young only to come back again to make amends if I can, to make peace, make love when I can. I think of Antonio Parr with his glassy El Greco eyes rolled heavenward like a fish on cracked ice in a fishstore window.

"The weight of this sad time we must obey," says dull, dutiful Edgar at the end of Act Five, "Speak what we feel, not what we ought to say," and by and large I have tried to do that in this account of my life and times, my own search, I suppose, for whatever it is we search for in Poinsett, South Carolina, and Sutton, Connecticut, for whatever it is that is always missing. I am not sure I have ever seen it even from afar, God knows, and I know I don't have forever to see it in either. Already, if I make the mistake of listening, I can hear a dim humming in the tracks, Time's wingéd chariot hurrying near, as Andrew Marvell said to his coy mistress. But to be honest I must say that on occasion I can also hear something else too—not the thundering of distant hoofs, maybe, or *Hi-yo, Silver. Away!* echoing across the lonely sage, but the faint chunk-chunk of my own moccasin heart, of the Tonto afoot in the dusk of me somewhere who, not because he ought to but because he can't help himself, whispers *Kemo Sabe* every once in a while to what may or may not be only a silvery trick of the failing light.

Frederick Buechner

*Frederick Buechner was born in New York City. He
was educated at Lawrenceville School, Princeton University, and Union Theological Seminary. In 1958 he
was ordained to the Presbyterian ministry. He has
written eleven novels and a number of works of non-
fiction including two volumes of meditations* (The Magnificent Defeat *and* The Hungering Dark), The Alphabet of Grace *(delivered as the Noble Lectures at
Harvard),* Wishful Thinking: A Theological ABC,
Telling the Truth: The Gospel as Tragedy, Comedy
and Fairy Tale *(delivered as the Lyman Beecher lectures at Yale) and* Peculiar Treasures: A Biblical
Who's Who. *He lives in Vermont and Florida with his
wife and family.*